MICHAEL CONNELLY

The Harry Bosch Novels

A former police reporter for the *Los Angeles Times*, Michael Connelly is the author of twenty-one acclaimed and bestselling novels. His books have been translated into 31 languages and have won awards all over the world. He lives in Florida with his wife and daughter.

Visit his website at www.MichaelConnelly.com

Also by Michael Connelly

Fiction

The Black Echo

The Black Ice

The Concrete Blonde

The Last Coyote

The Poet

Trunk Music

Blood Work

Angels Flight

Void Moon

A Darkness More Than Night

City of Bones

Chasing the Dime

Lost Light

The Lincoln Lawyer

The Overlook

The Brass Verdict

The Scarecrow

Nine Dragons

Non-Fiction

Crime Beat

Michael Connelly

The Harry Bosch Novels

The Narrows

The Closers

Echo Park

First published in Great Britain in 2009 by Orion Books,
an imprint of The Orion Publishing Group Ltd
Orion House, 5 Upper Saint Martin's Lane
London WC2H 9EA

An Hachette UK Company

1 3 5 7 9 10 8 6 4 2

A CIP catalogue record for this book
is available from the British Library.

ISBN (Trade Paperback) 978 1 4091 1318 8

Typeset by Deltatype Ltd, Birkenhead, Merseyside

Printed in Great Britain by Clays Ltd, St Ives plc

www.orionbooks.co.uk

Contents

The Narrows

In memory of Mary McEvoy Connelly Lavelle,
who kept six of us out of the narrows

All they did was trade one monster for another. Instead of a dragon they now have a snake. A giant snake that sleeps in the narrows and bides its time until the moment is right and it can open its jaws and swallow someone down.

– John Kinsey, *father of a boy lost in the narrows,* Los Angeles Times, *July 21, 1956*

I think maybe I only know one thing in this world. One thing for sure. And that is that the truth does not set you free. Not like I have heard it said and not like I have said it myself the countless times I sat in small rooms and jail cells and urged ragged men to confess their sins to me. I lied to them, tricked them. The truth does not salvage you or make you whole again. It does not allow you to rise above the burden of lies and secrets and wounds to the heart. The truths I have learned hold me down like chains in a dark room, an underworld of ghosts and victims that slither around me like snakes. It is a place where the truth is not something to look at or behold. It is the place where evil waits. Where it blows its breath, every breath, into your mouth and nose until you cannot escape from it. This is what I know. The only thing.

I knew this going in on the day I took the case that would lead me into the narrows. I knew that my life's mission would always take me to the places where evil waits, to the places where the truth that I might find would be an ugly and horrible thing. And still I went without pause. And still I went, not being ready for the moment when evil would come from its waiting place. When it would grab at me like an animal and take me down into the black water.

1

She was in darkness, floating on a black sea, a starless sky above. She could hear nothing and see nothing. It was a perfect black moment but then Rachel Walling opened her eyes from the dream.

She stared up at the ceiling. She listened to the wind outside and heard the branches of the azaleas scratching against the window. She wondered if it was the scratching on glass or some other noise from within the house that had awakened her. Then her cell phone rang. She wasn't startled. She calmly reached to the bed table. She brought the phone to her ear and was fully alert when she answered, her voice showing no indication of sleep.

'Agent Walling,' she said.

'Rachel? It's Cherie Dei.'

Rachel knew right away that this would not be a Rez call. Cherie Dei meant Quantico. It had been four years since the last time. Rachel had been waiting.

'Where are you, Rachel?'

'I'm at home. Where do you think I'd be?'

'I know you cover a lot of territory now. I thought maybe you—'

'I'm in Rapid City, Cherie. What is it?'

She answered after a long moment of silence.

'He's resurfaced. He's back.'

Rachel felt an invisible fist punch into her chest and then hold there. Her mind conjured memories and images. Bad ones. She closed her eyes. Cherie Dei didn't have to use a name. Rachel knew it was Backus. The Poet had resurfaced. Just as they knew he would. Like a virulent infection that moves through the body, hidden from the outside for years, then breaking the skin as a reminder of its ugliness.

'Tell me.'

'Three days ago we got something in Quantico. A package in the mail. It contained—'

'Three days? You sat on it for three—'

'We didn't sit on anything. We took our time with it. It was addressed to you. At Behavioral Sciences. The mail room brought it down to us and we had it X-rayed and then we opened it. Carefully.'

'What was in it?'

'A GPS reader.'

A global positioning system reader. Longitude and latitude coordinates. Rachel had encountered one on a case the previous year. An abduction out in the Badlands where the missing camper had marked her trail with a handheld GPS. They found it in her pack and traced her steps back to a camp where she had encountered a man and he had followed her. They got there too late to save her but they would have never gotten there at all if it hadn't been for the GPS.

'What was on it?'

Rachel sat up and swung her legs over the side of the bed. She brought her free hand to her stomach and closed it like a dead flower. She waited and soon Cherie Dei continued. Rachel remembered her as once being so green, just an observer and learner on the go team, assigned to her under the bureau's mentoring program. Ten years later and the cases, all the cases, had etched deep grooves into her voice. Cherie Dei wasn't green anymore and she needed no mentor.

'It had one waypoint in its record. The Mojave. Just inside the California border at Nevada. We flew out yesterday and we went to the marker. We've been using thermal imaging and gas probes. Late yesterday we found the first body, Rachel.'

'Who is it?'

'We don't know yet. It's old. It had been there a long time. We're just starting with it. The excavation work is slow.'

'You said the *first* body. How many more are there?'

'As of when I left the scene last we were up to four. We think there's more.'

'Cause of death?'

'Too early.'

Rachel was silent as she thought about this. The first questions that ran through her filters were why there and why now.

'Rachel, I'm not calling just to tell you. The point is the Poet is back in play and we want you out here.'

Rachel nodded. It was a given that she would go there.

'Cherie?'

'What?'

'Why do you think he was the one who sent the package?'

'We don't think it. We know it. We got a match a little while ago on a fingerprint from the GPS. He replaced the batteries on it and we got a thumb off of one of them. Robert Backus. It's him. He's back.'

Rachel slowly opened her fist and studied her hand. It was as still as a statue's. The dread she had felt just a moment before was changing. She could admit it to herself but no one else. She could feel the juice begin moving in her blood again, turning it a darker red. Almost black. She had been waiting for this call. She slept every night with the cell phone near her ear. Yes, it was part of the job. The call outs. But this was the only call she had truly been waiting for.

'You can name the waypoints,' Dei said in the silence. 'On the GPS. Up to twelve characters and spaces. He named this point 'Hello Rachel.' An exact fit. I guess he still has something for you. It's like he's calling you out, has some sort of plan.'

Rachel's memory dredged up an image of a man falling backward through glass and into darkness. Disappearing into the dark void below.

'I'm on my way,' she said.

'We're running it out of the Vegas field office. It will be easier to keep a blanket on it from there. Just be careful, Rachel. We don't know what he has in mind with this, you know? Watch your back.'

'I will. I always do.'

'Call me with the details and I'll pick you up.'

'I will,' she repeated.

Then she pushed the button that disconnected the call. She reached to the bed table and turned on the light. For a moment she remembered the dream, the stillness of the black water and the sky above, like black mirrors facing each other. And her in the middle, just floating.

2

Graciela McCaleb was waiting by her car outside my house in Los Angeles when I got there. She had been on time for our appointment but I had not. I quickly parked in the carport and jumped out to greet her. She didn't seem upset with me. She seemed to take it in stride. 'Graciela, I am so sorry I'm late. I got backed up on the ten with all the morning traffic.'

'It's okay. I was kind of enjoying it. It's so quiet up here.'

I used my key to unlock the door. When I pushed it open it wedged against some of the mail that was on the floor inside. I had to bend down and reach around the door to pull the envelopes free and get the door open.

Standing and turning back to Graciela I extended my hand into the house. She passed by me and entered. I didn't smile under the circumstances. The last time I had seen her was at the funeral. She looked only marginally better this time, the grief still holding in her eyes and at the corners of her mouth.

As she moved past me in the tight entry hall I smelled a sweet orange fragrance. I remembered that from the funeral, from when I had clasped her hands with both of mine, said how sorry I was for her loss and offered my help if she needed it in any way. She was wearing black then. This day she was wearing a flowery summer dress that went better with the fragrance. I pointed her to the living room and told her to have a seat on the couch. I asked if she wanted something to drink, even though I knew I had nothing in the house to respond with but probably a couple bottles of beer in the box and water from the tap.

'I'm fine, Mr. Bosch. No thank you.'

'Please, call me Harry. Nobody calls me Mr. Bosch.'

Now I tried a smile but it didn't work on her. And I didn't know why I expected it would. She'd been through a lot in her life. I'd seen the movie. And now this latest tragedy. I sat down in the chair across from the couch and waited. She cleared her throat before speaking.

'I guess you must be wondering why I needed to talk to you. I was not very forthcoming on the phone.'

'That's all right,' I said. 'But it did make me curious. Is something wrong? What can I do for you?'

She nodded and looked down at her hands, which held a small black-beaded purse on her lap. It looked like something she might have bought for the funeral.

'Something is very wrong and I don't know who to turn to. I know enough about things from Terry – I mean how they work – to know I can't go to the police. Not yet. Besides, they'll be coming to me. Soon, I suppose. But until then, I need someone I can trust, who will help me. I can pay you.'

Leaning forward I put my elbows on my knees and my hands together. I had only met her that one other time – at the funeral. Her husband and I had once been close but not in the last few years and now it was too late. I didn't know where the trust she spoke of came from.

'What did Terry tell you about me that would make you want to trust me? To choose me. You and I don't really even know each other, Graciela.'

She nodded like that was a fair question and assessment. 'At one time in our marriage Terry told me everything about everything. He told me about the last case you two worked together. He told me what happened and how you saved each other's life. On the boat. So that makes me think I can trust you.'

I nodded.

'He one time told me something about you that I always remembered,' she added. 'He told me there were things about you he didn't like and that he didn't agree with. I think he meant the way you do things. But he said at the end of the day, after all the cops and agents he had known and worked with, if he had to pick somebody to work a murder case with, that it would be you. Hands down. He said he would pick you because you wouldn't give up.'

I felt a tightness around my eyes. It was almost like I could hear Terry McCaleb saying it. I asked a question, already knowing the answer.

'What is it you want me to do for you?'

'I want you to investigate his death.'

3

Even though I knew it was going to be what she would ask me, Graciela McCaleb's request gave me pause. Terry McCaleb had died on his boat a month earlier. I had read about it in the *Las Vegas Sun*. It had made the papers because of the movie. FBI agent gets heart transplant and then tracks down his donor's killer. It was a story that had Hollywood written all over it and Clint Eastwood played the part, even though he had a couple decades on Terry. The film was a modest success at best, but it still gave Terry the kind of notoriety that guaranteed an obituary notice in papers across the country. I had just gotten back to my apartment near the strip one morning and picked up the *Sun*. Terry's death was a short story in the back of the A section.

A deep tremor rolled through me when I read it. I was surprised but not that surprised. Terry had always seemed to be a man on borrowed time. But there was nothing suspicious in what I had read or what I had then heard when I went out to Catalina for the funeral service. It had been his heart – his new heart – that had failed. It had given him six good years, better than the national average for a heart transplant patient, but then it had succumbed to the same factors that destroyed the original.

'I don't understand,' I said to Graciela. 'He was on the boat, a charter, and he collapsed. They said … his heart.'

'Yes, it was his heart,' she said. 'But something new has come up. I want you to look into it. I know you're retired from the police, but Terry and I watched on the news last year what happened here.'

Her eyes moved around the room and she gestured with her hands. She was talking about what had happened in my house a year earlier when my first post-retirement investigation had ended so badly and with so much blood.

'I know you still look into things,' she said. 'You're like Terry was. He couldn't leave it behind. Some of you are like that. When we saw on the news what happened here, that's when Terry said he would want you if he had to pick someone. I think what he was telling me was that if anything ever happened to him, I should go to you.'

I nodded and looked at the floor.

'Tell me what has come up and I will tell you what I can do.'

'You have a bond with him, you know?'

I nodded again. 'Tell me.'

She cleared her throat. She moved to the edge of the couch and began to tell it.

'I'm a nurse. I don't know if you saw the movie but they made me a waitress in the movie. That's not right. I'm a nurse. I know about medicine. I know about hospitals, all of it.'

I nodded and didn't say anything to stop her.

'The coroner's office conducted an autopsy on Terry. There were no signs of anything unusual but they decided to go ahead with the autopsy at the request of Dr. Hansen – Terry's cardio doctor – because he wanted to see if they could find out what went wrong.'

'Okay,' I said. 'What did they find?'

'Nothing. I mean, nothing criminal. The heart simply stopped beating … and he died. It happens. The autopsy showed that the muscles of the heart's walls were thinning, getting narrow. Cardiomyopathy. The body was rejecting the heart. They took the normal blood samples and that was it. They released him to me. His body. Terry didn't want to be buried – he always told me that. So he was cremated at Griffin and Reeves and after the funeral service Buddy took the children and me out on the boat and we did what Terry asked. We let him go then. Into the water. It was very private. It was nice.'

'Who is Buddy?'

'Oh, he is the man Terry worked with on the charter business. His partner.'

'Right. I remember.'

I nodded and tried to retrack her story, looking for the opening, the reason she had come to see me.

'The blood scan from the autopsy,' I said. 'What did they find in it?'

She shook her head.

'No, it's what they didn't find.'

'What?'

'You have to remember that Terry took a ton of meds. Every day, pill after pill, liquid after liquid. It kept him alive – I mean, until the end. So the blood scan was like a page and a half long.'

'They sent it to you?'

'No, Dr. Hansen got it. He told me about it. And he was calling because there were things missing from the scan that should have been there but weren't. CellCept and Prograf. They weren't in his blood when he died.'

'And they're important.'

She nodded.

'Exactly. He took seven capsules of Prograf every day. CellCept twice a day. These were his key meds. They kept his heart safe.'

'And without them he would die?'

'Three or four days would be all it would take. Congestive heart failure would come up quickly. And that is exactly what happened.'

'Why did he stop taking them?'

'He didn't and that is why I need you. Someone tampered with his meds and killed him.'

I pushed all of her information through the grinder again.

'First, how do you know he was taking his medicine?'

'Because I saw him and Buddy saw him and even their charter, the man they were with on the last trip, said he saw him taking his meds. I asked them. Look, I told you, I'm a nurse. If he wasn't taking his meds I would've noticed.'

'Okay, so you are saying he was taking his pills but they weren't really his pills. Somebody tampered with them. What makes you say that?'

Her body language indicated frustration. I wasn't making the logic jumps she thought I should be making.

'Let me back up,' she said. 'A week after the funeral, before I knew anything about all of this, I started to try to get things back to normal and I cleared out the closet where Terry kept all his meds. You see, the meds are very, very expensive. I didn't want them to go to waste. There are people who can barely afford them. *We* could barely afford them. Terry's insurance had run out and we needed Medi-Cal and Medicaid just to pay for his medicine.'

'So you donated the meds?'

'Yes, it's a tradition with transplants. When somebody ...'

She looked down at her hands.

'I understand,' I said. 'You give everything back.'

'Yes. To help the others. Everything is so expensive. And Terry had at least a nine-week supply. It would be worth thousands to somebody.'

'Okay.'

'So, I took everything across on the ferry and up to the hospital. Everybody thanked me and I thought that was that. I have two children, Mr. Bosch. As hard as it was, I had to move on. For their sake.'

I thought about the daughter. I had never seen her but Terry had told me about her. He'd told me her name and why he had named her. I wondered if Graciela knew that story.

'Did you tell Dr. Hansen this?' I asked. 'If somebody tampered with them you have to warn them that—'

She shook her head.

'There's an integrity procedure. All the containers are examined. You know, the seals on bottles are checked, expiration dates checked, lot numbers checked against recall and so on. Nothing came up. Nothing had been tampered with. Nothing I had given them, at least.'

'Then what?'

She moved closer to the edge of the couch. Now she would get to it.

'On the boat. The open containers I didn't donate because they don't take them. Hospital protocol.'

'You found tampering.'

'There was one more day's dosage of Prograf and two more days of CellCept in the bottles. I put them in a plastic bag and took them to the Avalon clinic. I used to work there. I made up a story. I told them a friend of mine found the capsules in her son's pocket while doing the laundry. She wanted to know what he was using. They ran tests and the capsules – all of them – were dummies. They were filled with a white powder. Powdered shark cartilage, actually. They sell it in specialty shops and over the Internet. It's supposed to be some sort of homeopathic cancer treatment. It's easily digestible and gentle. Contained in a capsule, it would have tasted the same to Terry. He would not have known the difference.'

From her small purse she pulled out a folded envelope and handed it to me. It contained two capsules. Both white with small pink printing running along the side.

'Are these from the last dosage?'

'Yes. I saved those two and gave four to my friend at the clinic.'

Using the envelope to catch its contents I used my fingers to pull one of the capsules open. It came apart freely without damaging the two pieces of the casing. The white powder it had held poured into the envelope. I knew then that it would not be a difficult process to pour the intended content of the capsules out and to replace it with a useless powder.

'What you are telling me, Graciela, is that when Terry was on that last charter he was taking pills he thought were keeping him alive but they weren't doing a thing for him. In a way, they were actually killing him.'

'Exactly.'

'Where did those pills come from?'

'The bottles came from the hospital pharmacy. But they could have been tampered with anywhere.'

She stopped and allowed time for this to register with me.

'What is Dr. Hansen going to do?' I asked.

'He said he has no choice. If tampering took place in the hospital, then he has to know. Other patients could be in danger.'

'That's not likely. You said two different medicines had been tampered with. That means it likely happened out of the hospital. It happened after they were in Terry's possession.'

'I know. He said that. He told me he is going to refer it to the authorities. He has to. But I don't know who that will be or what they will do. The hospital is in L.A. and Terry died on his boat about twenty-five miles off the coast of San Diego. I don't know who would—'

'It would probably go to the Coast Guard first and then it will be referred to the FBI. Eventually. But that will take several days. You could move it along if you called the bureau right now. I don't understand why you are talking to me instead of them.'

'I can't. Not yet anyway.'

'Why not? Of course you can. You shouldn't be coming to me. Go to the bureau with this. Tell the people he worked with. They'll go right at this, Graciela. I know they will.'

She stood up and went to the sliding door and looked out across the pass. It was one of those days when the smog was so thick it looked like it could catch on fire.

'You were a detective. Think about it. Someone killed Terry. It could not have been random tampering – not with two different meds from two different bottles. It was intentional. So, the next question is, who had access to his meds? Who had motive? They are going to look at me first and they may not look any further. I have two children. I can't risk that.'

She turned and looked back at me.

'And I didn't do it.'

'What motive?'

'Money, for one thing. There's a life insurance policy from when he was with the bureau.'

'For one thing? Does that mean there is a second thing?'

She looked down at the floor.

'I loved my husband. But we were having trouble. He was sleeping on the boat those last few weeks. It's probably why he agreed to take that long charter. Most of the time he just did day trips.'

'What was the trouble, Graciela? If I'm going to do this, then I have to know.'

She shrugged as if she didn't know the answer but then answered it.

'We lived on an island and I no longer liked it. I don't think it was a big secret that I wanted us to move back to the mainland. The problem was, his job with the bureau had left him afraid for our children. Afraid of the world. He wanted to shelter the children from the world. I didn't. I wanted them to see the world and be ready for it.'

'And that was it?'

'There were other things. I wasn't happy that he was still working cases.'

I stood up and joined her next to the door. I slid it open to let some of the stuffiness out. I realized I should have opened it as soon as we got inside. The place smelled sour. I'd been gone two weeks.

'What cases?'

'He was like you. Haunted by the ones that got away. He had files, boxes of files, down on that boat.'

I had been in the boat a long time ago. There was a stateroom in the bow McCaleb had converted into an office. I remembered seeing the file boxes on the top bunk.

'For a long time he tried to keep it from me but it became obvious and we dropped the pretext. In the last few months he was going over to the mainland a lot. When he didn't have charters. We argued about it and he just said it was something he couldn't let go of.'

'Was it one case or more than one?'

'I don't know. He never told me what exactly he was working on and I never asked. I didn't care. I just wanted him to stop. I wanted him to spend time with his children. Not those people.'

'Those people?'

'The people he was so fascinated by, the killers and their victims. Their families. He was obsessed. Sometimes I think they were more important to him than we were.'

She stared out across the pass as she said this. Opening the door had let the traffic noise in. The freeway down below sounded like a distant ovation in some sort of arena where the games never ended. I opened the door all the way and stepped out onto the deck. I looked down into the brush and thought about the life-and-death struggle that had taken place there the year before. I had survived to find out that, like Terry McCaleb, I was a father. In the months since, I had learned to find in my daughter's eyes what Terry had once told me he had already found in his daughter's. I knew to look for it because he had told me. I owed him something for that.

Graciela came out behind me.

'Will you do this for me? I believe what my husband said about you. I believe you can help me and help him.'

And maybe help myself, I thought but didn't say. Instead I looked down at the freeway and saw the sun reflected on the windshields of the cars moving through the pass. It was like a thousand bright, silver eyes were watching me.

'Yes,' I said, 'I will do it.'

4

My first interview was on the docks at the Cabrillo Marina in San Pedro. I always liked coming down this way but rarely did. I didn't know why. It was one of those things you forget about until you do it again and then you remember that you like it. The first time I arrived I was a sixteen-year-old runaway. I made my way down to the Pedro docks and spent my days getting tattooed and watching the tuna boats come in. I spent my nights sleeping in an unlocked towboat called *Rosebud.* Until a harbormaster caught me and I was sent back to the foster home, the words *Hold Fast* tattooed across my knuckles.

Cabrillo Marina was newer than that memory. These weren't the working docks where I had ended up so many years before. Cabrillo Marina provided dockage for pleasure craft. The masts of a hundred sailboats poked up behind its locked gates like a forest after a wildfire. Beyond these were rows of power yachts, many in the millions of dollars in value.

Some not. Buddy Lockridge's boat was not a floating castle. Lockridge, who Graciela McCaleb told me was her husband's charter partner and closest friend at the end, lived on a thirty-two-foot sailboat that looked like it had the contents of a sixty-footer on its deck. It was a junker, not by virtue of the boat itself but by how it was cared for. If Lockridge had lived in a house it would've had cars on blocks in the yard and walls of stacked newspapers inside.

He had buzzed me in at the gate and emerged from the cabin wearing shorts, sandals and a T-shirt worn and washed so many times the inscription across the chest was unreadable. Graciela had called him ahead of time. He knew I wanted to talk to him but not the exact reason why.

'So,' he said as he stepped off the boat onto the dock. 'Graciela said you are looking into Terry's death. Is this like an insurance thing or something?'

'Yes, you could say that.'

'You like a private eye or something?'

'Something like that, yeah.'

He asked for identification and I showed him the laminated wallet copy of my license that had been sent to me from Sacramento. He raised a quizzical eyebrow at my formal first name.

'Hieronymus Bosch. Like that crazy painter, huh?'

It was rare that someone recognized the name. That told me something about Buddy Lockridge.

'Some say he was crazy. Some think he accurately foretold the future.'

The license seemed to appease him and he said we could talk in his boat or we could walk over to the chandlery to get a cup of coffee. I wanted to get a look inside his home and boat – it was basic investigative strategy – but didn't want to be obvious about it so I told him I could use some caffeine.

The chandlery was a ship's store that was a five-minute walk down the dock. We small-talked as we walked over and I mostly listened to Buddy complain about his portrayal in the movie that had been inspired by McCaleb's heart transplant and his search for his donor's killer.

'They paid you, didn't they?' I asked when he was finished.

'Yes, but that's not the point.'

'Yes it is. Put your money in the bank and forget about the rest. It's just a movie.'

There were some tables and benches outside the chandlery and we took our coffees there. Lockridge started asking questions before I got the chance. I let him run his line out a little bit. My view was that he was a very important piece of my investigation, since he knew Terry McCaleb and was one of two witnesses to his death. I wanted him to feel comfortable with me so I let him ask away.

'So what's your pedigree?' he asked. 'Were you a cop?'

'Almost thirty years. With the LAPD. Half of the time I worked homicides.'

'Murders, huh? Did you know Terror?'

'What?'

'I mean, Terry. I called him Terror.'

'How come?'

'I don't know. I just did. I give everyone nicknames. Terry had seen firsthand the terror of the world, you know what I mean? I called him Terror.'

'What about me? What's my nickname going to be?'

'You … '

He looked at me like a sculptor sizing up a block of granite.

'Um, you are Suitcase Harry.'

'How come?'

'Because you're sort of rumpled, like you live out of a suitcase.'

I nodded.

'Pretty good.'

'So, did you know Terry?'

'Yes, I knew him. We worked a few cases together when he was with the bureau. Then one more after he got the new heart.'

He snapped his fingers and pointed at me.

'Now I remember, you were the cop. You were the one who was here that night on his boat when those two goons showed up to do him in. You saved him and then he turned around and saved you.'

I nodded.

'That's right. Now can I ask some questions, Buddy?'

He spread his hands wide, indicating he was available and had nothing to hide.

'Oh, sure, man, I didn't mean to be hogging the microphone, you know?'

I took out my notebook and put it on the table.

'Thanks. Let's start with that last charter. Tell me about it.'

'Well, what do you want to know?'

'Everything.'

Lockridge expelled his breath.

'That's a tall order,' he said.

But he began to tell me the story. What he initially told me matched the minimal accounts I had read in the Las Vegas papers and what I had then heard when I attended McCaleb's funeral. McCaleb and Lockridge had been on a four-day, three-night charter, taking a party of one into waters off Baja California to fish for marlin. While returning to Avalon Harbor on Catalina on the fourth day McCaleb collapsed at the boat's topside helm station. They were 22 miles off the coast, midway between San Diego and Los Angeles. A help call was radioed to the U.S. Coast Guard and a rescue chopper was dispatched. McCaleb was airlifted to a hospital in Long Beach, where he was pronounced dead on arrival.

When he was finished telling it I nodded like it had matched everything I had already heard.

'Did you actually see him collapse?'

'No, not really. I felt it, though.'

'How do you mean?'

'Well, he was up on top at the wheel. I was in the pit with the charter party. We were headed north, going home. The party'd had enough fishing by then so we weren't even trolling. Terry had it flat out, probably doing twenty-five knots. So me and Otto – he's the party – we were in the cockpit and the boat suddenly made a ninety-degree turn to the west. Out to sea, man. I knew that wasn't in the plan so I climbed up the ladder to poke my head up there and I see Terry sort of hunched over the wheel. He'd collapsed. I got to him and he was alive but, man, he was out of it.'

'What did you do?'

'I was a lifeguard once. Venice Beach. I still know my CPR. I called Otto up on top and I went to work on Terry while Otto got control of the boat and got on the radio to call the Coast Guard. I was never able to bring Terry around but I kept putting air into him until that helicopter showed up. Took them long enough, too.'

I wrote a note in my notebook. Not because it was important but because I wanted Lockridge to know I took him seriously and that whatever he thought was important was also important to me.

'How long did they take?'

'Twenty, twenty-five minutes. I'm not sure how long but it seemed like an eternity when you're trying to keep somebody breathing.'

'Yeah. Everybody I talked to said you did your best. So you're saying he never said a word. He just collapsed at the wheel.'

'Exactly.'

'Then what was the last thing he said to you?'

Lockridge started chewing the nail on one of his thumbs as he tried to recall this.

'That's a good question. I guess it was when he came back to the railing that looks down into the cockpit and he yelled down that we'd be home by sunset.'

'And how long was this before he collapsed?'

'Maybe a half hour, maybe a little longer.'

'He seemed fine then?'

'Yeah, he seemed like the regular Terror, you know? Nobody could've guessed what was going to happen.'

'By now you men had been on the boat for four straight days, right?'

'That's right. Pretty close quarters because the party got the stateroom. Me and Terry bunked it in the forward cabin.'

'During that time did you see Terry take his meds every day? You know, all the pills he had to take.'

Lockridge nodded emphatically.

'Oh, yeah, he was popping his pills right and left. Every morning and every night. We'd been out on a lot of charters together. It was his ritual – he set his watch by it. He never missed. And he didn't on this trip either.'

I made a few more notes just to keep silent so that Lockridge might keep talking. But he didn't.

'Did he say anything about them tasting different, or him feeling different after taking them?'

'Is that what this is about? You people are trying to say Terry took the wrong pills and then not have to pay the insurance? If I had known that, I would've never agreed to talk to you.'

He started to get up from his bench. I reached over and gripped his arm.

'Sit down, Buddy. That's not what this is about. I don't work for the insurance company.'

He dropped heavily back onto the bench and looked at his arm where I had gripped it. 'Then what is it about?'

'You already know what it's about. I'm just making sure Terry's death was what it was supposed to be.'

'Supposed to be?'

I realized that I had used an unfortunate choice of words.

'What I'm trying to say is that I want to make sure he didn't have any help.'

Lockridge studied me for a long moment and slowly nodded.

'You mean like the pills were tainted or messed with?'

'Maybe.'

Lockridge set his jaw tightly with resolve. It looked genuine to me.

'You need any help?'

'I might need some, yeah. I'm going over to Catalina tomorrow morning. I'm going to look at the boat. Can you meet me there?'

'Absolutely.'

He seemed excited and I knew I would eventually drop a rock on that but for now I wanted his full cooperation.

'Good. Now let me ask a few more questions. Tell me about the charter party. Did you know this guy Otto beforehand?'

'Oh, yeah, we take Otto out a couple times a year. He lives over there on the island, that's the only reason why we got the multiday charter. See, that was the problem with the business but Terror never cared. He just was happy to sit there in that little harbor and wait on half days.'

'Slow down a second, Buddy. What are you talking about?'

'I'm talking about Terry keeping the boat over there on that island. What we got over there were people who are visiting Catalina and want to go fishing for a few hours. We didn't get the big charters. The three-, four-, five-day jobs where you make the good money. Otto was the exception because he lives over there and he wanted to go fishing off Mexico a couple times a year and get his ashes hauled in the process.'

Lockridge was giving me more information and avenues of questioning than I could handle at once. I stayed on McCaleb but would definitely come back to Otto, their charter client. 'You're saying that Terry was content to sort of be small-time.'

'Exactly. I kept telling him, "Move the charter over here to the mainland, put out some ads and get some serious work." But he didn't want to.'

'Did you ever ask him why?'

'Sure, he wanted to stay on the island. He didn't want to be away from the family all the time. And he wanted time to work on his files.'

'You mean his old cases?'

'Yeah, that and some new ones.'

'What new ones?'

'I don't know. He was always clipping articles out of the newspaper and sticking them in files, making phone calls, things like that.'

'On the boat?'

'Yeah, on the boat. Graciela wouldn't allow it in the house. He told me that, that she didn't like him doing it. Sometimes it got to the point he was sleeping on the boat at night. At the end. I think it was because of the files. He'd get obsessed with something and she'd end up telling him to stay on the boat until he got over it.'

'He told you that?'

'He didn't have to.'

'Any case or file you remember he was interested in lately?'

'No, he no longer included me in that stuff. I helped him work on his heart case and then he sort of shut me out of that stuff.'

'Did that bother you?'

'Not really. I mean, I was willing to help. Chasing bad guys is more interesting than chasing fish, but I knew that was his world and not mine.'

It sounded too much like a stock answer, like he was repeating an explanation McCaleb had once given to him. I decided to leave it at that but I knew this was a subject I would come back to with him.

'Okay, let's go back to Otto. You fished with him how many times?'

'This was our third – no, fourth – trip.'

'Always down to Mexico?'

'Pretty much.'

'What does he do for a living that he can afford to do this?'

'He's retired. Thinks he's Zane Grey and wants to go sportfishing, catch a black marlin and put it up on his wall. He can afford it. He told me he was a salesman, but I never asked what he sold.'

'Retired? How old is he?'

'I don't know, midsixties.'

'Retired from where?'

'Just across the water. Long Beach, I think.'

'What did you mean a minute ago when you said he liked to go fishing and get his ashes hauled?'

'I meant exactly that. We took him fishing and when we'd stop off in Cabo, he always had something on the side.'

'So each night on this last trip, you guys brought the boat into port, always to Cabo.'

'The first two nights in Cabo and then the third night we made it to San Diego.'

'Who chose those places?'

'Well, Otto wanted to go to Cabo, and San Diego was just the halfway point on the trip back. We always take it slow going back.'

'What happened in Cabo with Otto?'

'I told you, he had a little something on the side down there. Both nights he got cleaned up and went into town. I think he was meeting a senorita there. He had made some calls on his cell phone.'

'Is he married?'

'Far as I know. I think that's why he liked the four-day charters. His wife thought he was out there fishing. She probably didn't know about stopping in Cabo for a Margarita – and I'm not talking about the drink.'

'What about Terry, did he go into town?'

He answered without hesitation.

'Nope, Terry had nothing going in that department and he would never leave the boat. He'd never even step on the dock.'

'How come?'

'I don't know. He just said he didn't need to. I think he was superstitious about it.'

'How so?'

'You know, the captain stays with the vessel, that sort of thing.'

'What about you?'

'Most of the time I hung with Terry and the boat. Every now and then I'd go to town to one of the bars or something.'

'What about on that last trip?'

'No, I stayed with the boat. I was a little short of bread.'

'So on that last trip, Terry never got off the boat?'

'That's right.'

'And nobody besides you, Otto and him were ever on the boat, right?'

'That's – well, not exactly.'

'What do you mean? Who was on the boat?'

'On the second night going into Cabo we got stopped by the *federales.* The Mexican Coast Guard. Two guys came on board and looked around for a few minutes.'

'Why?'

'It's sort of a routine. Every now and then they stop you, make you pay a little tariff, then they let you go.'

'A bribe?'

'A bribe, a payoff, a bite, whatever you want to call it.'

'And that happened this time.'

'Yeah, Terry gave them fifty bucks when they were in the salon and then they split. It was all pretty fast.'

'Did they search the boat? Did they look at Terry's medicine?'

'No, it didn't get to that. That's what the payoff is for, to avoid all of that.'

I realized I hadn't been taking notes. A lot of this information was new and worth exploring further but I sensed that I had enough for the moment. I would digest what I had and come back to it. I had a feeling that Buddy Lockridge would give me whatever time I needed, as long as I made him feel like a player in the investigation. I asked him for the exact names and locations of the marinas where they had docked overnight on the trip with Otto and I did write this information in my notebook. I then reconfirmed our appointment on McCaleb's boat for the next morning. I told him I was taking the first ferry across and he told me he'd be on it as well. I left him there because he said he wanted to go back into the chandlery to pick up some supplies.

As we dumped our coffee cups into the trash can, he wished me luck with the investigation.

'I don't know what you're going to find. I don't know if there is anything to find, but if Terry had help with this, I want you to get whoever it was who helped him. You know what I am saying?'

'Yes, Buddy, I think I know what you are saying. I'll see you tomorrow.'

'I'll be there.'

5

On the phone that night from Las Vegas my daughter asked me to tell her a story. Just five years old, she was always wanting me to sing to her or tell her stories. I had more stories than songs in me. She had a scruffy black cat she called No Name and Maddie liked me to make up stories involving great peril and bravery that ended with No Name winning the day by solving the mystery or finding the lost pet or the lost child or teaching a bad man a lesson.

I told her a quick story about No Name finding a lost cat named Cielo Azul. She liked it and asked me for another but I said it was late and I had to go. Then, out of the blue, she asked me if the Burger King and the Dairy Queen were married. I smiled and marveled at how her mind worked. I told her they were married and she asked me if they were happy.

You can become unhinged and cut loose from the world. You can believe you are a permanent outsider. But the innocence of a child will bring you back and give you the shield of joy with which to protect yourself. I have learned this late in life but not too late. It's never too late. It hurt me to think about the things she would learn about the world. All I knew was that I didn't want to teach her anything. I felt tainted by the paths I had taken in my life and the things I knew. I had nothing from it I wanted her to have. I just wanted her to teach me.

So I told her, yes, the Burger King and the Dairy Queen were happy and that they had a wonderful life together. I wanted her to have her stories and her fairy tales while she could still believe them. For soon enough, I knew, they would be taken away.

Saying good night to my daughter on the phone felt lonely and out of place. I had just come off of a two-week trip out there and Maddie had gotten used to seeing me and I had gotten used to seeing her. I picked her up at school, I watched her swim, I made dinner for her a few times in the small efficiency apartment I had rented near the airport. At night when her mother played poker in the casinos I took her home and put her to bed, leaving her under the watch of the live-in nanny.

I was a new thing in her life. For her first four years she had never heard of me and I had never heard of her. That was the beauty and difficulty of the relationship. I was struck with sudden fatherhood and reveled in it and did my best. Maddie suddenly had another protector who floated in and out of her life. An extra hug and kiss on the top of the head. But she also knew that this man who had suddenly entered her world was causing her mother a lot of pain and tears. Eleanor and I had tried to keep our discussions and sometimes harsh words away from our daughter but sometimes the walls are thin and kids, I was learning, are the best detectives. They are masterful interpreters of the human vibe.

Eleanor Wish had withheld the ultimate secret from me. A daughter. On the day she finally presented Maddie to me, I thought that everything was right in the world. My world, at least. I saw my salvation in my daughter's dark eyes, my own eyes. But what I didn't see that day were the fissures. The cracks below the surface. And they were deep. The happiest day of my life would lead to some of the ugliest days. Days in which I could not get past the secret and what had been kept from me for so many years. Whereas in one moment I thought I had everything I could possibly want from life, I soon learned I was too weak a man to hold it, to carry the betrayal hidden in it in exchange for what I had been given.

Other, better men could do it. I could not. I left the home of Eleanor and Maddie. My Las Vegas home is a one-room efficiency across the parking lot from the place where millionaire and billionaire gamblers park their private jets and head by whispery limos to the casinos. I have one foot in Las Vegas and one remains here in Los Angeles, a place I know I can never leave permanently, not without dying.

After saying good night my daughter handed the phone to her mother, who was on a rare night at home. Our relationship was more strained than it had ever been. We were at odds over our daughter. I didn't want her to grow up with a mother who worked nights in the casinos. I didn't want her eating at Burger King for dinner. And I didn't want her to learn about life in a city that wore its sins on its sleeve.

But I was in no position to change things. I know that I run the risk of seeming ridiculous because I live in a place where the randomness of crime and chaos is always near and poison literally hangs in the air, but I don't like the idea of my daughter growing up where she is. I see it as the subtle difference between hope and desire. Los Angeles is a place that operates on hope and there is still something pure about that. It helps one see through the dirty air. Vegas is different. To me it operates on desire and on that road is ultimate heartbreak. I don't want that for my daughter. I don't even want it for her mother. I am willing to wait, but not that long. As I spend time with my daughter and know her better and love her more, my willingness frays at the middle like a rope bridge crossing a deep chasm.

When Maddie handed the phone back to her mother neither of us had much to say, so we didn't. I just said I would check in with Maddie the next time I could and we hung up. I put the phone down, feeling an ache inside

I was not used to. It wasn't the ache of loneliness or emptiness. I knew those pains and had learned how to live with them. It was the pain that came with a fear for what the future holds for someone so precious, someone you would lay your own life down for without hesitation.

6

The first ferry got me to Catalina at 9:30 the next morning. I had called Graciela McCaleb on my cell while I was crossing, so she was waiting for me at the pier. The day was sunny and crisp and I could taste the difference in the smogless air. Graciela smiled at me as I approached the gate where people waited for travelers from the boats.

'Good morning. Thanks for coming.'

'No problem. Thanks for meeting me.'

I had half expected Buddy Lockridge to be with her. I had not seen him on the ferry and figured that maybe he had gone across the night before.

'No Buddy yet?'

'No. Is he coming?'

'I wanted to go over things on the boat with him. He said he would be on the first boat but he didn't show.'

'Well, they're running two ferries. The next will be here in forty-five minutes. He's probably on that. What would you like to do first?'

'I want to go to the boat, start there.'

We walked over to the tenders dock and took a Zodiac with a little one-horsepower engine on it out into the basin where the yachts were lined in rows, tied up to floating mooring balls and moving with the current in a synchronized fashion. Terry's boat, *The Following Sea,* was second from the end of the second row. An ominous feeling came over me as we approached and then bumped up against the fantail. On this vessel Terry had died. My friend and Graciela's husband. It used to be one of the tricks of the trade for me to find or manufacture an emotional connection to a case. It helped stoke the fire and gave me that needed edge to go where I had to go, do what I had to do. I knew I would not need to look for that in this case. No manufacturing necessary. It was already part of the deal. The largest part.

I looked at the boat's name, painted in black letters across the stern, and remembered how Terry had explained it to me once. He had told me that the following sea was the wave you had to watch out for. It came up in your blind spot, hit you from behind. A good philosophy. I had to wonder now why Terry hadn't seen what and who had come up behind him.

Unsteadily I stepped off the inflatable and onto the boat's fantail. I reached back for the rope to tie it up. But Graciela stopped me.

'I'm not going on board,' she said. She shook her head as if to ward off any coercing from me and handed a set of keys toward me. I took them and nodded my head.

'I just don't want to be on there,' she said. 'The one time I went to collect his meds was enough.'

'I understand.'

'This way the Zodiac will be back at the dock for Buddy to use if he shows up.'

'If?'

'He isn't always that reliable. At least that is what Terry said.'

'And if he doesn't show up, what do I do?'

'Oh, just flag down a water taxi. They come by about every fifteen minutes. You won't have a problem. You can just bill me. Which reminds me, we haven't talked about what I'll be paying you.'

It was something she had to bring up to make sure, but she knew and I knew that this wasn't a job for pay.

'That won't be necessary,' I said. 'If I do this, there is only one thing I'd like in return.'

'What's that?'

'Terry once told me about your daughter. He said you two named her Cielo Azul.'

'That's right. He picked the name.'

'Did he ever tell you why?'

'He just said he liked it. He said he knew a girl named Cielo Azul once.'

I nodded.

'What I would like for payment for doing this is to meet her someday – when this is all over, I mean.'

That gave Graciela a moment of pause. Then she nodded her agreement.

'She's a sweetheart. You'll like meeting her.'

'I'm sure I will.'

'Harry, did you know her? The girl Terry named our daughter after?'

I looked at her a moment and nodded.

'Yes, you could say I knew her. Someday if you'd like I'll tell you about her.'

She nodded and started to push the Zodiac off the fantail. I helped with my foot.

'The little key opens the salon door,' she said. 'The rest you should be able to figure out. I hope you find something that helps.'

I nodded and held up the keys as if they would open every door I would ever encounter. I watched her head back to the dock and then I climbed over the stern and into the cockpit.

Some sort of sense of duty made me climb the ladder to the upper helm before I went inside the boat. I pulled the canvas cover off the control station and stood for a moment next to the wheel and the seat and envisioned the story Buddy Lockridge had told me of Terry collapsing here. It somehow seemed appropriate for him to collapse at the wheel, yet with what I now knew, it also seemed so wrong. I put my hand on the top of the chair as if resting it on someone's shoulder. I decided that I would find the answers to all of the questions before I finished here.

The small chrome key on the ring Graciela had given me opened the mirrored sliding door that led inside the boat. I left it open to air out the interior. There was a briny, funky smell inside. I traced it to the rods and reels stored on ceiling racks, artificial baits still in place. I guessed that they had not been washed off and properly cared for after the last charter. There had not been time. There had not been a reason.

I wanted to go down the steps to the stateroom in the bow where I knew Terry kept all his investigative files. But I decided to leave that place for last. I decided to begin in the salon and work my way down.

The salon had a functional layout with a couch, chair and coffee table on the right side leading to a chart desk built behind the seat of the interior helm. On the opposite side was a restaurant-style booth with red leather padding. A television was locked down in a partition that separated the booth from the galley and then there was a short stairway I knew led down to the forward staterooms and a bathroom.

The salon was neat and clean. I stood in the middle of the space and just observed it for a half minute before going to the chart station and opening drawers. McCaleb had kept the charter business files here. I found listings of customers and a calendar for charter reservations. There were also records dealing with his collection from Visa and MasterCard, which he evidently accepted from customers as payment. The charter business had a bank account and there was a checkbook in the drawer, too. I checked the register and saw that just about everything that came in went back out again to cover fuel and mooring charges as well as fishing and other charter supplies. There was no record of cash deposits so I concluded that if the business was profitable it was in the unrecorded cash payments from customers, depending on how many of these there were.

In the bottom drawer there was a bad-check file. There were only a few and they were spread out over time, none so large that they could seriously damage the business.

I noticed that in the checkbook and with most of the business records either Buddy Lockridge's or Graciela's name was listed as the operator of the charter business. I knew this was because, as Graciela had told me, Terry was seriously limited in what he could earn as official income. If he made over a certain level – which was shockingly low – he was not eligible to receive state and federal medical assistance. If he lost that, he would then end up paying medical expenses himself – a quick route to personal bankruptcy for a transplant recipient.

In the bad-check file I also found a copy of a sheriff's report unrelated to bad paper. It was a two-month-old incident report stemming from an apparent burglary of *The Following Sea.* The complainant was Buddy Lockridge and the summary indicated that only one thing was taken from the boat, a handheld global positioning system reader. Its value was placed at $300 and the model was listed as a Gulliver 100. An added note said that the complainant could not provide the serial number of the missing device because he had won it in a poker game from a person he could not identify and he had never bothered to write the tracking number down.

Once I had made a quick check through all of the drawers in the chart station I went back to the client files and started going through them more thoroughly, looking carefully at each customer McCaleb and Lockridge had taken on board in the six weeks before Terry's death. None of the names struck me as curious or suspicious and there were no notations by Terry or Buddy in the file that raised any of those feelings either. Nevertheless, I took a notebook from the back pocket of my blue jeans and wrote a list that showed the name of each client, the number in the party and the date of the charter. Once I had this I was able to see that the charters were by no means regular. A good week for the business was three or four half-day charters. There was one week in which there were no charters at all and another in which there was only one. I was beginning to see Buddy's point about the need to move the business to the mainland in order to increase the frequency and length of charter bookings. McCaleb was running the charter business as a hobby and that wasn't the way to make it thrive.

Of course, I knew why he was running it that way. He had another hobby – if you want to call it that – and he needed time to devote to that as well. I was putting the records back into the chart station drawer, with the intention of heading down to the bow to explore Terry's other hobby, when I heard the salon door roll open behind me.

It was Buddy Lockridge. He had come up on the boat without my hearing the Zodiac's little engine or feeling its nudge against the fantail. I also hadn't felt Buddy's considerable weight as he climbed onto the boat.

'Morning,' he said. 'Sorry I'm late.'

'That's okay. I've got a lot to look through here.'

'Find anything interesting yet?'

'Not really. I'm about to go below, check out his files.'

'Cool. I'll help.'

'Actually, Buddy, where you can help is if maybe you called the man who was the last charter.'

I looked at the last name written on the page in my notebook.

'Otto Woodall. Could you call him and vouch for me and see if I could come by this afternoon to see him?'

'That's it? You wanted me to come all the way over to make a phone call?'

'No, I have questions for you. I need you here. I just don't think you should be going through the files down there. Not yet, at least.'

I had a feeling that Buddy Lockridge had probably already perused every file in the bow. But I was playing him this way on purpose. I had to keep him close but distant at the same time. Until I had cleared him to my satisfaction. Yes, he was McCaleb's partner and had received credit for his efforts to save his fallen friend, but I had seen stranger things in my time. At the moment I had no suspects and that meant I had to suspect everybody.

'Make the call and then come downstairs to see me.'

I left him there and headed down the short set of steps to the lower part of the boat. I had been here before and knew the layout. The two doors on the left side of the hallway led to the head and a storage closet. Straight ahead was a door to the small stateroom in the bow. The door on the right led to the master stateroom, the place where I would have been killed four years before if Terry McCaleb had not leveled a gun and fired on a man about to ambush me. This had occurred moments after I had saved McCaleb from a similar end.

I checked the paneling in the hallway where I remembered two of McCaleb's shots had splintered the wood. The surface was heavily varnished but I could tell it was newer wood.

The shelves in the storage closet were empty and the bathroom was clean, the overhead vent popped open on the forward deck above. I opened the master stateroom door and looked in but decided to leave it for later. I went to the forward room and had to use a key from the ring Graciela had given me to open the door.

The room was as I had remembered it. Two sets of V-bunks on each side, following the line of the bow. The bunks on the left still functioned as sleeping compartments, their thin mattresses rolled up and held by bungee cords. But on the right the lower bunk had no mattress and had been converted into a desk. The bunk above was where four long cardboard file boxes sat side by side.

McCaleb's cases. I looked at them for a long and solemn moment. If someone had murdered him, I believed I would find the suspect in there.

'Anytime today.'

I almost jumped. It was Lockridge standing behind me. Once again I had not heard or felt his approach. He was smiling because he liked sneaking up on me.

'Good,' I said. 'Maybe after lunch we can head over there. I'll need a break from this by then anyway.'

I looked down at the desk and saw the white laptop with the recognizable symbol of an apple with a bite out of it in silhouette. I reached down and opened it, unsure of how to proceed.

'Last time I was here, he had a different one.'

'Yeah,' Lockridge said. 'He got that one on account of the graphics. He was getting into digital photography and stuff.'

Without my bidding or approval Lockridge reached over and depressed a white button on the computer. It started to hum and then the black screen filled with light.

'What kind of photography?' I asked.

'Oh, you know, amateur stuff mostly. His kids and sunsets and shit. It started with the clients. We started taking their pictures with their trophy fish, you know? And Terry could just come down here and print out eight-by-ten glossies on the spot. There's a box of cheap-ass frames in here someplace. The client catches a fish, he gets a framed photo. Part of the deal. It worked pretty good. Our gratuities went way up with that.'

The computer finished booting up. The screen was a sky of light blue that made me think of McCaleb's daughter. Several icons were spread across the field. Right away I noticed one that was a miniature file folder. Underneath it the word PROFILES was printed. I knew that was a folder I wanted to open. Scanning across the bottom of the screen I saw an icon that looked like a camera set in front of a photo of a palm tree. Since the subject had just been photography I pointed to it.

'Is that where the photos are?'

'Yup,' Lockridge said.

Again he moved without my request. He moved his finger on a small square in front of the keyboard, which in turn moved the arrow on the screen to the camera icon. He used his thumb to depress a button below the square and the screen quickly took on a new image. Lockridge seemed at ease with the computer and it begged the questions why and how. Did Terry McCaleb allow him access to the computer – after all, they were in business together – or was this something Lockridge became efficient at without his partner's knowledge?

On the screen a frame opened under the heading iPhoto. There were several folders listed. Most were listed by dates, usually a few weeks or a month. There was one folder simply titled MAIL CALL.

'Here we go,' Lockridge said. 'You want to see some of this stuff? It's clients and fish.'

'Yeah, show me the most recent photos.'

Lockridge clicked on a folder that was labeled with dates ending just a week before McCaleb's death. The folder opened and there were several dozen photos listed by individual date. Lockridge clicked on the most recent date. A few seconds went by and a photo opened on the screen. It showed a man and woman, both badly sunburned and smiling as they held up a horribly ugly brown fish.

'Santa Monica Bay halibut,' Buddy said. 'That was a good one.'

'Who are they?'

'Um, they were from … Minnesota, I think. Yeah, St. Paul. And I don't think they were married. I mean, they were married but just not to each other. They were staying on the island. Shacking up. They were the last charter before the trip down to Baja. Pictures from that trip are probably still on the camera.'

'Where is the camera?'

'It should be here. If not, then Graciela probably has it.'

He clicked on a left arrow above the photo. Soon another photo appeared, the same couple and same fish. Lockridge kept clicking and eventually he came to a new customer and his trophy fish, a pinkish white creature about fourteen inches long.

'White sea bass,' Lockridge said. 'Nice fish.'

He kept clicking, showing me a procession of fishermen and their catches. Everybody seemed happy, some even had the obvious glaze of alcohol in their eyes. Lockridge named all the fish but not all the clients. He didn't remember them all by name. Some of them he simply classified as good or bad tippers and that was it.

Eventually, he came to a man with a delighted smile on his face as he held up a small white sea bass. Lockridge cursed.

'What's wrong?' I asked.

'He's the prick who walked off with my goddamn fish box.'

'What fish box?'

'My GPS. He's the guy who took it.'

7

Backus stayed at least a hundred feet behind her. Even in the crowded Chicago airport he knew she would be on what they always called 'Six Alert' when he had been with the bureau. Watching her back – her six – and always checking for a trailer. It had been tricky enough traveling with her so far. The plane from South Dakota had been small and fewer than forty people had been on board. The random assignment of seats had put him only two rows from her. So close he thought he could actually smell her scent – the one beneath the perfume and the makeup. The one the dogs could pick up.

It was intoxicating to be so close and still such a long distance apart. He wanted the whole time to turn and look back at her, maybe catch a glimpse of her face between the seats, see what she was doing. But he didn't dare. He had to bide his time. He knew that good things come to those who plan carefully and then wait. That was the thing, the secret. Darkness waits. All things come to the dark.

He followed her through half of the American Airlines terminal until she took a seat at gate K9. It was empty. No travelers were waiting here. No American employees were behind the gate counter waiting and ready to work the computers and check tickets. But Backus knew that this was only because she was early. They both were early. The flight to Las Vegas would not leave from gate K9 for another two hours. He knew this because he was on the Vegas flight as well. In a way he was Rachel Walling's guardian angel, a silent escort who would be with her until she reached her final destination.

He walked on by the gate, careful not to be obvious about glancing at her but curious to see how she was going to pass the time waiting for the next flight. He hooked the strap of his large cowhide carry-on bag over his right shoulder so that if she happened to look up, her eyes might be drawn to it instead of his face. He wasn't worried about her recognizing him for who he was. All the pain and the surgeries had taken care of that. But she might recognize him from the flight from Rapid City. And he didn't want that. He didn't want her to get suspicious.

His heart jumped in his chest like a baby kicking under a blanket as he made the one furtive glance while passing by. She had her head down and was reading a book. It was old and worn from many readings. There was a profusion of yellow Post-its poking out from its pages. But he recognized the cover design and the title. *The Poet.* She was reading about him!

He hurried on by before she could sense she had a watcher and look up. He went down two more gates and into the restroom. He went into a stall and carefully locked the door. He hung his bag on the door hook and quickly went to work. Off came the cowboy hat and the vest. He sat down on the toilet and took off the boots, too.

In five minutes Backus transformed himself from a South Dakota cowboy to a Las Vegas gambler. He put on the silk clothes. He put on the gold. He put on the earring and the shades. He clipped the gaudy chrome cell phone to his belt, even though there was no one who would call him and no one he would call. From the bag he took out another bag, much smaller and with the figure of the MGM lion emblazoned on it.

The components of his first skin were pushed into the new bag and he stepped out of the stall, the strap of the MGM bag over his shoulder.

Backus went to the sink to wash his hands. He admired himself for the preparation he had taken. It was the planning and attention to the small details like that that made him who he was, that made him a success at his craft.

For a moment he thought about what was waiting. He was going to take Rachel Walling on a tour. By the end of it she would know the depths of darkness. His darkness. She would pay for what she had done to him.

He felt himself getting an erection. He left the sink and stepped back into one of the stalls. He tried to change his thoughts. He listened to the fellow travelers coming and going in the restroom, relieving themselves, washing themselves. One man spoke on a cell phone while defecating in the next stall. The whole place smelled horrible. But that was okay. It smelled like the tunnel where he was reborn in blood and darkness so long ago. If they only knew who was in their presence here.

He momentarily caught a vision of a dark, starless sky. He was falling backward, his arms flailing, the featherless and useless wings of a baby bird pushed out of the nest.

But he had survived and had learned to fly.

He started to laugh and used his foot to flush the toilet and cover his sound.

'Fuck you all,' he whispered.

He waited for his erection to subside, pondering its cause and smiling. He knew his own profile so well. In the end it was always about the same thing. There was only a nanometer of difference between power and sex and fulfillment when it came to the narrow spaces between the synapses in the gray folds of the mind. In those narrows it all came down to the same thing.

When he was ready he flushed the toilet again, careful to use his shoe, and stepped out of the stall. He washed his hands again and checked his look in the mirror. He smiled. He was a new man. Rachel would not recognize him. Nobody would. Feeling confident, he unzipped the MGM bag and checked on his digital camera. It was there and ready to go. He decided he would take the risk and shoot some photos of Rachel. Just some keepsakes, a few secret shots he could admire and enjoy after everything was all over.

8

The fish box. Buddy's mention of it reminded me of the sheriff's report up in the chart station drawer.

'I meant to ask you about that. You say this guy took the GPS?'

'Phony bastard, I'm sure it was him. He went out with us, the next thing we know my GPS is gone and he starts a charter over on the isthmus. Put two and two together and you get asshole. I've been meaning to go over there and pay him a little visit.'

I was having trouble following the line of his story. I asked him to explain it to me in English, as if I didn't know a fish charter from a fish chowder.

'This is the deal,' he said. 'That little black box had all our best spots on it. Our fishing holes, man. Not only that, it had the points marked by the guy I won it from. I won it in a poker game from another fish guide. The value assigned was not for the box but what was on it. The guy was putting his best twelve spots on the table and I won 'em with a full fucking house.'

'All right,' I said. 'I get it now. Its value was in the coordinates of the fishing spots recorded on it, not the device itself.'

'Exactly. Those things cost a couple hundred bucks. But the fishing spots, those come from years of work and skill, fishing experience.'

I pointed at the photo on the computer screen.

'And this guy comes along and takes it and then he starts out his charter business ahead of the game. Using your experience as well as the guide's you won it from.'

'Way ahead. Like I said, I'm going to go pay him a visit one of these days.'

'Where is the isthmus?'

'On the other side, where the island pinches together like a figure eight.'

'Did you tell the sheriff's department you thought he stole it?'

'Not at first because we didn't know, you know? The thing turned up missing and we thought maybe some kids came onto the boat or something at night and grabbed whatever they saw. It gets pretty fucking boring growing up on the island, from what I hear. Just ask Graciela about Raymond – the kid's going stir crazy. So anyway we made a report and that was that. Then a couple weeks later I see this ad in *Fish Tales* and it's announcing this new charter out of the isthmus and there's a picture of the guy and I say, "Hey, I know that guy" and I put it together. He *stole* my fish box.'

'Did you call the sheriff then?'

'Yeah, I called and told them he was the guy. They didn't act too excited. I called back the next week and they said they talked to the guy – by phone. They didn't even bother to go out there for a face-to-face. He denied it like of course he would and that was that as far as they were concerned.'

'What's this guy's name?'

'Robert Finder. His operation is called Isthmus Charters. In the ad he calls himself Robert "Fish" Finder. My ass. More like "Fish Stealer."'

I looked down at the photo on the screen and wondered if this meant anything at all to my investigation. Could the missing GPS box be at the center of Terry McCaleb's death? It seemed unlikely. The idea that someone would steal a competitor's fishing spots was understandable. But then to engage in a complicated plot to also kill the competitor seemed on the far limit of belief. It would require a hell of a plan and execution on Finder's part, that was for sure. It would require a hell of a plan on anyone's part.

Lockridge seemed to read my thoughts.

'Hey, you think this bastard could've had something to do with Terror going down?'

I looked up at him for a long moment, realizing that the idea of Lockridge being involved in McCaleb's death as a means of gaining control and location of the charter business and *The Following Sea* was a more believable theory.

'I don't know,' I said. 'But I'll probably be checking it out.'

'Let me know if you want somebody to go with you.'

'Sure. But listen, I noticed on the sheriff's report that the GPS was the only thing reported stolen. Did that hold up? Nothing else ever turned up missing?'

'That was it. That's why me and Terry thought it was so strange at first. Until we figured out it was Finder.'

'Terry thought that, too, that it was him?'

'He was coming around to it. I mean, come on, who else could it have been?'

It was a worthy question, but not one I thought I needed to put front and center at the moment. I pointed at the laptop screen and told Lockridge to keep moving back through the photos. He did so and the procession of happy anglers continued.

We came across one more curiosity in the photo series. Lockridge backed up to a set of six photos that depicted a man whose face was not shown clearly at first. In the three initial shots he was posed holding a brilliantly colored fish up to the camera. But in each shot he held the fish up too high, obscuring most of his face. In each of these shots his dark glasses peeked over the ridge of the fish's dorsal fin. The fish appeared to be the same in each of these three shots, which led me to assume that the photographer was repeatedly trying to get a photo that included the fisherman's face. But to no avail.

'Who took these?'

'Terror. I wasn't there on that one.'

Something about the man or maybe the way he had avoided the camera in the trophy photo had made McCaleb suspicious. That seemed obvious. The next three photos in the series were shots of the man taken without his knowledge. The first two were taken from inside the salon, shooting out into the cockpit where the fisherman leaned against the right gunwale. Because the glass on the salon door had reflective film on it, the man would not have seen or known that McCaleb had taken photos of him.

The first of these two photos was in profile. The next a full-on face shot. Take away the setting and McCaleb had instinctively gotten mug shot poses, another confirmation of his suspicion. Even with these photos the man was still obscured. He had a full beard of brownish gray hair and wore dark sunglasses with large lenses and a blue L.A. Dodgers hat. What little could be seen of the man's hair appeared to be close cropped and matching the colorations of his beard. He had a gold hoop earring in his right ear.

In the profile shot his eyes were crinkled and hooded, naturally hidden even with the dark sunglasses. He wore blue jeans and a plain white T-shirt beneath a Levi's jacket.

The sixth photo, the last in the sequence, was taken after the charter had ended. It was a long shot of the man walking on the Avalon pier, apparently after leaving *The Following Sea*. His face was turned slightly toward the camera, though it still wasn't much more than a profile. But I wondered if the man had continued to turn after the shot and perhaps had then seen McCaleb and his camera.

'So what about this guy?' I asked. 'Tell me about him.'

'Can't,' Lockridge said. 'I told you, I wasn't there. That was one Terry picked up on the fly. No reservation. The guy just showed up on the water taxi while Terry was on the boat and asked to go out. He paid for a half a day, the minimum charter. He wanted to go out right away and I was over on the mainland. Terry couldn't wait on me, so he took him out without me. Alone, which is a pain in the ass. But they got a nice Spanish mack out there. Not bad.'

'Did he talk about the guy after?'

'No, not really. He only said that the guy didn't take the full half. He wanted to pack it in after just a couple hours. So they did.'

'Terry had an alert on. He took six photos, three while the guy wasn't looking. You sure he didn't say anything about that?'

'Like I said, not to me. But Terry kept a lot of stuff to himself.'

'Do you know this guy's name?'

'No, but I'm sure Terry put something in the charter book. You want me to go get it?'

'Yes. And I'd also like to know the exact date and how he paid. But first, can you print out these photos?'

'All six of them? It will take a while.'

'Actually, all six and give me one of Finder while we're at it. I have the time.'

'I don't suppose you want them framed, too.'

'No, Buddy, that won't be necessary. Just the photos.'

I stepped back while Buddy sat down on the cushioned stool in front of the computer. He turned on a nearby printer, loaded in photo-quality paper, and expertly went through the commands that sent the seven pictures to the printer. Again I noted his ease with the equipment. I had the feeling that there wasn't any content on the laptop that he was not familiar with. Probably nothing in the file boxes on the bunk above us either.

'Okay,' he said as he got up. 'Takes about a minute for each one. They come out a bit sticky, too. Might want to spread 'em out till they dry all the way. I'll go up and see what the charter book says about your mystery man.'

After he was gone I sat down on the stool. I had watched how Lockridge worked the photo files and was a quick learner. I went back to the main listing and double-clicked on the photo folder labeled MAIL CALL. A frame opened containing 36 small photos in a grid. I clicked on the first one and the photo enlarged. It showed Graciela pushing a stroller with a little girl sleeping in it. Cielo Azul. Terry's daughter. The setting appeared to be a shopping mall. The photo was similar to Terry's photos of the mystery man in that it appeared that Graciela did not know she was being photographed.

I turned around and looked back through the doorway toward the steps to the salon. There was no sign of Lockridge. I got up and moved quietly into the hallway. I slipped through the open door of the bathroom. I pressed myself against the wall and waited. Soon enough Lockridge moved across the opening in the hall, carrying the logbook. He was moving very quietly so as to make no noise. I let him pass and then moved into the hallway behind him. I watched as he went through the door of the forward stateroom, ready to startle me with his sudden appearance again.

But it was Lockridge who was startled when he realized I wasn't in the room. When he turned I was right behind him.

'You like sneaking up on people, don't you, Buddy?'

'Uh, no, not really. I was just—'

'Don't do it with me, okay? What's it say in the book?'

His face took on a pink hue beneath the permanent fisherman's tan. But I had given him an out and he quickly took it.

'Terry put his name down in the book but nothing else. It says "Jordan Shandy, half day." That's it.'

He opened the book and turned it to show me the entry.

'What about his method of payment? How much is half a day anyway?'

'Three bills for a half, five for a full. I checked the credit-card log and there was nothing there. Also the checking deposits. Nothing. That means he paid cash.'

'When was this? I assume it is logged by date.'

'Yeah. They went out on February thirteenth – hey, that was Friday the thirteenth. Think that was intentional?'

'Who knows? Was that before or after the charter with Finder?'

Lockridge put the logbook down on the desk so we could both look at it. He ran his finger down the list of clients and stopped it at Finder.

'He came a week after. He went out February nineteenth.'

'And what's the date on the sheriff's report on the boat burglary?'

'Shit, I have to go back up.'

He left and I heard him bound up the stairs. I took the first photo out of the printer and put it on the desk. It was the shot of Jordan Shandy hiding his face with sunglasses and the Spanish mackerel. I stared at it until Lockridge came back into the room. He didn't try to sneak up on me this time.

'We made the burglary report February twenty-second.'

I nodded. Five weeks before McCaleb's death. I wrote all the dates we had been talking about down in my notebook. I wasn't sure if there was significance to any of it.

'Okay,' I said. 'You want to do one more thing for me now, Buddy?'

'Sure. What?'

'Go on up and take those rods down off the ceiling and go out and wash them down. I don't think anybody did it after that last trip. They're making this place smell sour and I think I'm going to be hanging out here for a couple days. It would help me a lot.'

'You want me to go up and wash off the rods.'

He said it like a statement, a treatise of insult and disappointment. I looked from the photo to his face.

'Yes, that's right. It would help me a lot. I'll finish up with the photos and then we can go visit Otto Woodall.'

'Whatever.'

He left the room dejected and I heard him trudge up the steps, equally as loud as he had been silent before. I took the second photo out of the printer and placed it down next to the first. I took a black marker out of a coffee mug on the desk and wrote in the white border beneath the photo the name Jordan Shandy.

Back on the stool I turned my attention once again to the computer and the photo of Graciela and her daughter. I clicked on the forward arrow and the next photo came up. Again it was a photo from inside a mall. This one was taken from a further distance and there was a grainy quality to it. Also in this picture was a boy trailing behind Graciela. The son, I concluded. The adopted son.

Everyone in the family was in the photo but Terry. Was he the photographer? If so, why at such a distance? I clicked the arrow again and then continued through the photos. Almost all of them were from inside the mall and all were taken from a distance. In not one photo was any family member looking at or acknowledging the camera. After twenty-eight similar shots the venue changed and the family was now on the ferry to Catalina. They were heading home and the photographer was there along with them.

There were only four photos in this sequence. In each of these Graciela sat in the middle rear of the ferry's main cabin, the boy and girl on either side of her. The photographer had been positioned near the front of the cabin, shooting across several rows of seats. If Graciela had noticed, she probably would not have realized that she was the center of the camera's focus and would have dismissed the photographer as just another tourist going to Catalina.

The last two photos of the thirty-six seemed out of place with the others, as if they were part of a completely different project. The first was of a green highway sign. I enlarged it and saw that it had been shot through the windshield of a car. I could see the frame of the windshield, part of the dashboard and some sort of sticker in the corner of the glass. Part of the photographer's hand, resting on the steering wheel at eleven o'clock, was also in the picture.

The highway sign stood against a barren desert landscape. It said

ZZYZX ROAD
1 MILE

I knew the road. Or, more accurately, I knew the sign. Anybody from L.A. who made the road trip to and from Las Vegas as often as I had in the last year would have known it. At just about the halfway point on the 15 freeway was the Zzyzx Road exit, recognizable by its unique name if nothing else. It was in the Mojave and it appeared to be a road to nowhere. No gas station, no rest stop. At the end of the alphabet at the end of the world.

The last photo was equally puzzling. I enlarged it and saw that it was a strange still life. At center in the frame was an old boat – the rivets of its wooden planks sprung and its yellowed paint peeling back under the blistering sun. It sat on the rocky terrain of the desert, seemingly miles from any water on which to float. A boat adrift on a sea of sand. If there was any specific meaning at all to it, I did not readily see it.

Following the procedure I had watched Lockridge use, I printed the two desert photos and then went back to review the other photos to choose a sampling of shots to print. I sent two photos from the ferry and two photos from the mall to the printer. While I waited I enlarged several of the mall shots on the screen in hopes of seeing something in the background that would identify what mall Graciela and the children were in. I knew I could simply ask her. But I wasn't sure I wanted to.

In the photos I was able to identify bags carried by various shoppers as coming from Nordstrom, Saks Fifth Avenue and Barnes & Noble. In one of the photos the family walked through a food court that included the concessions Cinnabon and Hot Dog on a Stick. I wrote all of these down in my notebook and knew that with these five locations I would probably be able to determine in which mall the photos had been taken, if I decided it was necessary to know this information and I did not want to ask Graciela about it. That was still an open question. I did not want to alarm her if it was not necessary. Telling her she may have been stalked while with her family – and possibly by someone with a strange connection to her husband – might not be the best avenue to take. At least at first.

That connection turned stranger and more alarming when the printer finally spit out one of the photos I had chosen from the mall sequence. In the picture the family was walking in front of the Barnes & Noble bookstore. The shot had been taken from the other side of the mall but the angle was almost perpendicular to the storefront. The front display window of the bookstore caught a dim reflection of the photographer. I had not seen it on the computer screen but there it was in the print.

The image of the photographer was too small and too whispery against the display behind the window – a full-size stand-up photo of a man in a kilt that was surrounded by stacks of books and a sign that said IAN RANKIN HERE TONIGHT! I realized then that I could use the display to place the exact day that the photos of Graciela and her children were taken. All I had to do was call the store and find out when Ian Rankin had been there. But the display also helped hide the photographer from me.

I went back to the computer and found the photo among the miniatures and enlarged it. I stared at it, realizing I didn't know what to do.

Buddy was in the cockpit using a hose attached to a gunwale faucet to spray the eight rods and reels leaning against the stern. I told him to turn the water off and to come back down to the office. He did so without a word. When we were back in the office I signaled him to the stool and then leaned over him and outlined the area of the photographer's reflection on the screen.

'Can this be enlarged here? I want to see this area better.'

'It can be enlarged but you lose a lot of definition. It's digital, you know? You get what you get.'

I didn't know what he was talking about. I just told him to do it. He played with some of the square buttons that ran along the top of the frame and started enlarging the photograph and then repositioning it so the area of the reflection stayed on the screen. Soon he said that he had maximized the enlargement. I leaned in close. The image was even murkier. Not even the lines on the author's kilt were crisp.

'You can't tighten it up any?'

'You mean make it smaller again. Sure, I—'

'No, I mean like bring it more into focus.'

'No, man, that is it. What you see is what you get.'

'Okay, print it. It came out better before when I printed it. Maybe this will, too.'

Lockridge put in the commands and I spent an uneasy minute waiting.

'What is this, anyway?' Buddy asked.

'A reflection of the photographer.'

'Oh. You mean it wasn't Terry?'

'No, I don't think so. I think somebody took pictures of his family and sent them to him. It was some sort of message. Did he ever mention this?'

'No.'

I took a shot at seeing if Buddy might let something slip.

'When did you first notice this file on the computer?'

'I don't know. It must've been ... actually, I just saw them for the first time with you here.'

'Buddy, don't bullshit me. This could be important. I've watched you work this thing like it was yours since high school. I know you went into that machine when Terry wasn't around. He probably knew, too. He didn't care and neither do I. Just tell me, when did you first see this file?'

He let a few moments pass while he thought about it.

'I first saw them about a month before he died. But if your real question is when did Terry see them, then all you have to do is look at the file archive and see when it was created.'

'Then do it, Buddy.'

Lockridge took over the keyboard again and went into the photo file's history. In a few seconds he had the answer.

'February twenty-seventh,' he said. 'That was when that file was created.'

'Okay, good,' I said. 'Now, assuming that Terry didn't take these, how would they end up on his computer?'

'Well, there's a few ways. One is that he got them in an e-mail and downloaded them. Another is that somebody borrowed his camera and shot them. He then found them and downloaded them. The third way is maybe somebody just sent him a photo chip right out of the camera or a CD with the pictures already on it. That would probably be the most untraceable way.'

'Could Terry do e-mail from here?'

'No, up at the house. There is no hard line on the boat. I told him he ought to get one of those cellular modems, go wireless like that commercial where the guy's sitting at his desk in the middle of a field. But he never got around to it.'

The printer kicked out the photo and I grabbed it ahead of Buddy's reach. But then I placed it down on the desk so we could both view it. The reflection was blurred and dim but still more recognizable on the print than it was on the computer screen. I could now see that the photographer was holding the camera in front of his face, obscuring it completely. But then I was able to identify the overlapping L and A configuration of the Los Angeles Dodgers logo. The photographer was wearing a baseball cap.

On any given day there might be fifty thousand people wearing Dodgers caps in this city. I don't know for sure. But what I do know is that I don't believe in coincidences. I never have and I never will. I looked at the murky reflection of the photographer and my sudden guess was that it was the mystery man. Jordan Shandy.

Lockridge saw it, too.

'Goddamn,' he said. 'That's the guy, right? I think that's the charter. Shandy.'

'Yeah,' I said. 'Me, too.'

I put the print of Shandy holding up the Spanish mackerel next to the enlargement. There was no way to make a match but there was nothing that made me think the other way. There was no way to be sure but I was sure. I knew that the same man who had showed up unannounced for a private charter with Terry McCaleb had also stalked and photographed his family.

What I didn't know was where McCaleb had gotten these photos and whether he had made the same jump as I had just made.

I started stacking all of the photos I had printed. All the time I was trying to put something together, some connection of logic. But it wasn't there. I didn't have enough of the picture. Only a few pieces. My instincts told me that McCaleb had been baited in some way. Photos of his family came to him in the form of an e-mail or a photo chip or a CD. And the last two photos were the key. The first thirty-four were the bait. The last two were the hook hidden inside that bait.

I believed the message was obvious. The photographer wanted to draw McCaleb out to the desert. Out to Zzyzx Road.

9

Rachel Walling rode the escalator down into the cavernous baggage pickup area at McCarran International. She had carried her luggage during the journey from South Dakota but the airport was designed so that every passenger had to go this way. The escalator landing area was crowded with people waiting. Limo drivers held signs with the names of their clients, others just held up signs that announced the names of hotels or casinos or tour companies. The cacophony rising from the room assaulted her as she descended. It was nothing like the airport where she had started her travels that morning.

Cherie Dei was going to meet her. Rachel had not seen the fellow FBI agent in four years and that was only a brief interaction in Amsterdam. It had been eight years since she had really spent any kind of time with her and she wasn't sure she would recognize her or that she would be recognized herself.

It didn't matter. As she searched the sea of faces and signs it was a sign that caught her eye.

BOB BACKUS

The woman holding it was smiling at her. Her idea of a joke. Rachel approached, without returning the smile.

Cherie Dei had reddish brown hair pulled back into a ponytail. She was attractive and trim with a good smile, her eyes still with a lot of light in them. Rachel thought she looked more like the mother of a couple of Catholic school kids than a serial killer hunter.

Dei extended her hand. They shook and Dei proffered the sign.

'I know, bad joke, but I knew it would get your attention.'

'Yes, it did.'

'Did you have a long layover in Chicago?'

'A few hours. Not much choice flying out of Rapid City. Denver or Chicago. I like the food better at O'Hare.'

'Do you have bags?'

'No, just this. We can go.'

Rachel was carrying one bag – a midsize duffel. She had packed only a few changes of clothing. Dei pointed toward one of the banks of glass doors and they headed that way.

'We got you in at the Embassy Suites where the rest of us are staying. We almost didn't but they had a cancellation. The town is crowded because of the fight.'

'What fight?'

'I don't know. Some super heavyweight or junior middle-weight boxing match at one of the casinos. I didn't pay attention. I just know it's the reason this place gets so crowded.'

Rachel knew that Cherie was talking because she was nervous. She didn't know the reason for this, whether anything had happened or it was simply because Rachel had to be handled carefully in this situation.

'If you want we can go to the hotel, get you settled in there. You could even take some time to rest if you want. There's a meeting later at the FO. You could start there if—'

'No. I'd like to go to the scene.'

They stepped through the automatic glass doors and Rachel felt the dry Nevada air. It wasn't at all as hot as she'd expected and packed for. It was cool and crisp, even in the direct sun. She took out her sunglasses and decided the jacket she had worn to the airport in South Dakota would be needed here. It was stuffed into her bag.

'Rachel, the scene is two hours from here. Are you sure you—'

'Yes. Take me there. I'd like to start there.'

'Start what?'

'I don't know. Whatever it is that he wants me to start.'

This seemed to give Dei pause. She didn't respond. They walked into the parking garage and found her car – a government Crown Vic so dirty that it looked like it was in desert camouflage.

Once they were driving, Dei took out a cell phone and made a call. Rachel heard her tell someone – probably her boss or partner or the scene supervisor – that she had picked up the package and would be taking it to the scene. There was a long pause as the person she'd called responded at length. Then she said good-bye and hung up.

'You are cleared to the scene, Rachel, but you have to step back. You're here as an observer, okay?'

'What are you talking about? I'm an FBI agent, same as you.'

'But you're not in Behavioral anymore. This is not your case.'

'You're saying I am here because Backus wants me here, not you people.'

'Rachel, let's try to get off to a better start than we did in Am—'

'Anything new come up so far today?'

'We're up to ten bodies now. They think that's going to be it. At least for this location.'

'IDs?'

'They're getting there. What they have is tentative but they're putting it all together.'

'Is Brass Doran at the scene?'

'No, she is in Quantico. She's work—'

'She should be here. Don't you people know what you've got here? She—'

'Whoa, Rachel, slow down, okay? Let's get something straight here. I'm the case agent on this, okay? You are not running this investigation. This is not going to work if you confuse that.'

'But Backus is talking to me. He called me out.'

'And that's why you are here. But you aren't calling the shots, Rachel. You have to stand to the side and watch. And I have to tell you I don't like how this is starting out. This isn't Driving Miss Rachel. You mentored me but that was ten years ago. I've now been in Behavioral longer than you ever were and I've booked more cases than you ever did. So don't talk down to me and don't act like my mentor or my mother.'

Rachel didn't respond at first and then she simply asked Dei to pull over so she could get her jacket out of her bag, which was in the trunk. Dei pulled into the Travel America on Blue Diamond Road and popped the trunk. When Rachel got back into the car she was wearing a baggy black all-weather coat that looked like it might have been designed for a man. Dei didn't say anything about it.

'Thanks,' Rachel said. 'And you're right. I apologize. I guess you get like me when it turns out your boss – your mentor – is the same evil thing you've been hunting all your life. And they punish *you* for it.'

'I understand that, Rachel. But it wasn't just Backus. It was a lot of things. The reporter, some of the choices you made. Some people say you were lucky you still had a job at the end of it.'

Rachel's face grew hot. She was being reminded that she was one of the bureau's embarrassments. Even within the ranks. Even with the agent she had mentored. She had slept with a reporter working on her case. That was the shorthand version. It didn't matter that it was a reporter who was actually a part of the case, who was working with Rachel side by side and hour by hour. The shorthand version would always be the story that agents heard and whispered about. A reporter. Was there a lower breach in agent behavior and etiquette? Maybe a mobster or a spy, but nothing else.

'Five years in North Dakota followed by a promotion to South Dakota,' she said weakly. 'Yeah, I was lucky all right.'

'Look, I know you paid the price. My point is that you have to know your place here. Use some finesse. A lot of people are watching this case. If you play it right it could be your ticket back in.'

'Got it.'

'Good.'

Rachel reached down to the side of her seat and adjusted it so she could lean back.

'How long did you say?' she asked.

'About two hours. We've been using choppers from Nellis mostly, saves a lot of time.'

'Hasn't drawn attention?'

She was asking about the media, whether news of the investigation in the desert had leaked yet.

'We've had a few fires to put out but so far it is holding up. The scene is in California and we're working it out of Nevada. I think that has somehow kept the lid on. To be honest, there are some people worried about you now.'

Rachel thought about Jack McEvoy, the reporter, for a moment. 'Nobody has to worry,' she said. 'I don't even know where he is.'

'Well, if this thing finally hits the radar, you can expect to see him. He wrote a bestselling book on the first go-round. I guarantee he'll be back for the sequel.'

Rachel thought about the book she had been reading on the plane and that was now in her bag. She wasn't sure whether it was the subject or the author that had drawn her to read it so many times.

'Probably.'

She left it at that and pulled her jacket around her shoulders and folded her arms. She was tired, not having slept since getting the call from Dei.

She leaned her head against the side window and pretty soon she was out. Her dream of darkness returned. But this time she was not alone. She could not see anyone because she could only see blackness. But she sensed another presence. Someone close but not necessarily someone with her. She moved and turned in the darkness, trying to see who it was. She reached out but her hands touched nothing.

She heard a moaning sound and then realized it was her own voice from deep in her throat. Then she was grabbed. Something had her and shook her very hard.

Rachel opened her eyes. She saw the freeway rushing at her through the windshield. Cherie Dei let go of her jacket.

'You all right? This is the exit.'

Rachel looked up at a passing green freeway sign.

ZZYZX ROAD
1 MILE

She straightened up in the seat. She checked her watch and realized she had slept for over ninety minutes. Her neck was stiff and painful on the right side from leaning so long against the window. She started working it with her fingers, digging deeply into the muscle.

'You all right?' Dei asked again. 'Sounded like you were having a bad one.'

'I'm fine. What did I say?'

'Nothing. You just sort of moaned. I think you were running from something or something had you.'

Dei hit the blinker and turned into the exit lane. Zzyzx Road appeared to be in the middle of nowhere. At the top of the exit there was nothing, not even a gas station or even an abandoned structure. There was no visible reason for the exit or the road.

'We're over here.'

Dei turned left and took the overpass across the freeway. Once off the overpass the road disintegrated into an unpaved trail that wound south and down into the flat basin of the Mojave. The landscape was stark. The white soda on the surface of the flats looked like snow in the distance. Joshua trees reached their bony fingers toward the sky and smaller plants wedged themselves between the rocks. It was a still life. Rachel had no idea what sort of animal might be able to subsist in such a barren place.

They passed a sign that said they were headed toward Soda Springs and then the road curved and Rachel could suddenly see the white tents and RVs and vans and other vehicles ahead. She could see a military green helicopter, its blades still, parked to the left of the encampment. Further past the encampment there was a complex of small buildings set at the base of the hills. It looked like a roadside motel but there were no signs and no road.

'What is this place?' Rachel asked.

'This is Zzyzx,' Dei said, pronouncing it *zie-zix*. 'As far as I can tell, it is the asshole of the universe. Some radio preacher named it and built it sixty years ago. He got control of the land by promising the government he would be prospecting. He paid winos from skid row in L.A. to do that while he went on the radio and called on the faithful to come here to bathe in the spring waters and guzzle the mineral waters he bottled. It took the Bureau of Land Management twenty-five years to get rid of him. The place was then turned over to the state university system for desert studies.'

'Why here? Why did Backus bury them here?'

'Far as we can guess is because it is federal land. He wanted to make sure we – meaning you, probably – worked the case. If that's what he wanted, he got it. It's a major excavation. We've had to bring in our own power, shelter, food, water, everything.'

Rachel said nothing. She was studying everything, from the crime scene to the distant horizon of gray mountain ridges that enclosed the basin. She didn't agree with Dei's take on the place. She had heard the coastline of

Ireland described as a terrible beauty. She thought that the desert with its barren lunar landscape was in its own way beautiful, too. There was a harsh beauty to it. A dangerous beauty. She had never spent much time in the desert, but her years in the Dakotas had given her an appreciation for harsh places, the empty landscapes where people were the intruders. That was her secret. She had what the bureau called a 'hardship posting.' It was designed to wear her down and make her quit. But she had beaten them at this game. She could last forever there. She would not quit.

Dei slowed as they approached a checkpoint set up about a hundred yards before the tents. A man in a blue jumpsuit with the white letters FBI on the breast pocket stood beneath a beach-type tent with open sides. The desert winds were threatening to tear it from its moorings, just as they had already played havoc with the agent's hair.

Dei lowered the window. She didn't bother to give her own name or identification. She was a given. She gave the man Rachel's name and identified her as a 'visiting agent,' whatever that meant.

'Is she cleared with Agent Alpert?' he asked, his voice as dry and flat as the desert basin behind him.

'Yes, she's cleared.'

'Okay, then. I just need her credentials.'

Rachel handed over her ID wallet. The agent wrote down her serial number and handed it back.

'From Quantico?'

'No, South Dakota.'

He gave her a look, the kind that said he knew she was a fuckup.

'Have fun,' he said as he turned to go back to his tent.

Dei moved the car forward, raising her window, leaving the agent in a cloud of dust.

'He's from the Vegas FO,' she said. 'They're not too happy about things, playing second string.'

'So what's new?'

'Exactly.'

'Is Alpert the SAC?'

'That's him.'

'What's he like?'

'Well, remember your theory about agents being either morphs or empaths?'

'Yes.'

'He's a morph.'

Rachel nodded.

They came to a little cardboard sign taped to a branch of a Joshua tree. It said VEHICLES and had an arrow pointing to the right. Dei turned and they parked last in a row of four equally dirty Crown Vics.

'What about you?' Rachel asked. 'Which did you turn out to be?'

Dei didn't answer.

'You ready for this?' she asked Rachel instead.

'Absolutely. I've been waiting four years for another shot at him. This is where it starts.'

She cracked the door and stepped out into the bright desert sun. She felt at home.

10

Backus followed them down the exit ramp. He was a safe distance behind. He crossed over the freeway and put on his blinker to get back on in the opposite direction. If they were watching him in the mirror he would simply look like someone turning around to head back to Vegas.

Before turning back onto the freeway he watched the FBI car go off the paved road and head across the desert to the site. His site. A white cloud of dust kicked up behind the car. He could see the white tents in the distance. He felt an overwhelming sense of accomplishment. The crime scene was a city he had built. A city of bones. The agents were like ants between pieces of glass. They lived and worked in the world of his creation, unknowingly doing his bidding.

He wished he could get closer to that glass, to take it all in and see the horror he etched on their faces, but he knew the risk was too great.

And he had other things to do. He pushed his foot down hard on the accelerator and headed back toward the city of sin. He had to make sure everything was ready and things were set.

As he drove he felt a slight sense of melancholy slide in beneath his ribs. He guessed that this came with the letdown of leaving Rachel behind in the desert. He took a deep breath and tried to exorcize the feeling. He knew it would not be long before he was close to her again.

After a moment he smiled at the memory of seeing his name on the sign held by the woman who had met Rachel at the airport. An inside joke between agents. Backus recognized the greeter. Agent Cherie Dei. Rachel had mentored her just as he had mentored Rachel. That meant some of his special insights had been passed on through Rachel to this new generation. He liked that. He wondered what Cherie Dei's reaction would have been if he had stepped up to her and her stupid sign at the bottom of the escalator and said, 'Thanks for meeting me.'

He looked out through the car's windows at the flat, barren plain of the desert floor. He believed it was truly beautiful, made even more so by the things he had planted in the sand and rock out there.

He thought about that and soon the pressure in his chest eased and he felt wonderful again. He checked the rearview for trailers and saw nothing that was suspicious. He checked himself then and admired the surgeon's work once more. He smiled at himself.

11

As they got close to the tents Rachel Walling began to smell the scene. The unmistakable odor of decaying flesh was carried on the wind as it worked through the encampment, billowed the tents and moved out again. She switched her breathing to her mouth, haunted by knowledge she wished she didn't have, that the sensation of smell occurred when tiny particles struck sensory receptors in the nasal passages. It meant if you smelled decaying flesh that was because you were breathing decaying flesh.

There were three small square tents in the approach to the site. These were not the kind for camping. They were field command tents with straight sides to eight feet. Behind these three was a larger rectangular tent. Rachel noticed that all of the tents had open vent flaps on top. She knew that there were body excavations taking place in each. The vents were to let some of the heat and stink escape.

Overlapping everything was the noise. There were at least two gasoline-powered generators providing electricity to the scene. There were also two full-size RVs parked to the left of the tents and their rooftop air handlers were rumbling.

'Let's go in here first,' Cherie Dei said, pointing to one of the RVs. 'Randal is usually in here.'

The RV looked like any supercamper Rachel had seen on the freeway. This one was called the 'Open Road' and it had an Arizona plate on the back. Dei knocked on the door and then pulled it open without waiting for a response. They stepped up and in. The vehicle wasn't set up on the inside for camping on the open road. Partitions and the comforts of home had been removed. It was one long room set up with four folding tables and many chairs. Along the rear wall was a counter with all the usual office machinery – computer, fax, copier and coffeemaker. Two of the tables were covered with paperwork. On the third, incongruous to the purpose and setting, was a large bowl of fruit. The lunch table, Rachel guessed. Even at a mass burial site you have to have lunch. At the fourth table was a man on a cell phone, an open laptop computer in front of him.

'Have a seat,' Dei said. 'I'll introduce you as soon as he is off.'

Rachel sat at the lunch table and took a precautionary sniff of the air.

The RV's air handler was on recycle. The odor from the excavation wasn't noticeable. No wonder the man in charge stayed in here. She looked at the bowl of fruit and thought about taking a handful of grapes, just to keep her energy up, but decided not to.

'You want some fruit, go ahead,' Dei said.

'No, thanks, I'm fine.'

'Suit yourself.'

Dei reached over and picked off some grapes and Rachel felt foolish because she had painted herself into a corner with the fruit. The man on the cell, who she assumed was Agent Alpert, was talking too low to be heard – probably by the person he was talking to as well. Rachel noticed that the long wall along the left side of the RV was covered with photographs of the excavations. She looked away. She didn't want to study the photographs until after she had been in the tents. She turned and looked out the window next to the table. This RV had the premiere view of the desert. She could see down into the basin and the entire ridge-line. She wondered for a moment if the view meant anything. If Backus had chosen the spot because of the view and if so, what was the significance of it.

When Dei turned her back Rachel grabbed some grapes and put three in her mouth at once. At the same moment, the man snapped his phone closed and got up from his table and approached her with his hand out.

'Randal Alpert, special agent in charge. We're glad you are here.'

Rachel shook his hand but had to wait to get the grapes down before speaking.

'Nice to meet you. Not such nice circumstances.'

'Yeah, but look at that view. Sure beats the brick wall I've got back in Quantico. And at least we're out here the end of April and not August. That would have been a killer.'

He was the new Bob Backus. Running the shop at Quantico, coming out on the big ones and of course this was a big one. Rachel decided she didn't like him and that Cherie Dei was right about him being a morph.

Rachel had always found that agents in Behavioral were of two kinds. The first type she called 'morphs.' These agents were much like the men and women they hunted. Able to keep it all from getting to them. They could move on like a serial killer from case to case without being dragged down by all the horror and guilt and knowledge of the true nature of evil. Rachel called them morphs because these agents could take that burden and somehow morph it into something else. The site of a multiple body excavation became a beautiful view better than anything at Quantico.

The second type Rachel called 'empaths' because they took all the horror in and kept it in. It became the campfire they warmed themselves by. They used it to connect and motivate, to get the job done. To Rachel, these were the better agents because they would go to the limit and beyond to catch the bad guy and solve the case.

It was certainly healthier to be a morph. To be able to move on without any baggage. The halls of Behavioral were haunted by the ghosts of the empaths, the agents who couldn't go the distance, for whom the burden became too much. Agents like Janet Newcomb, who put her gun in her mouth, and Jon Fenton, who drove into a bridge abutment, and Terry McCaleb, who literally gave his heart to the job. Rachel remembered them all and above all she remembered Bob Backus, the ultimate morph, the agent who was both hunter and prey.

'That was Brass Doran on the phone,' Alpert said. 'She said to say hello.'

'She's back at Quantico?'

'Yes, she's agoraphobic about that place. Never wants to leave. She's heading up things on that end for us. Now, Agent Walling, I know you know the score. We've got a delicate situation here. We're glad you are here but you are here strictly as an observer and possibly a witness.'

She didn't like him being so formal with her. It was a way of keeping her outside the circle.

'A witness?' she asked.

'You might be able to give us some ideas. You knew this guy. Most of us were on the street chasing bank robbers when the whole thing with Backus went down. I came into the unit right after your thing went down. After OPR went through the place. Cherie here is one of the few still around from then.'

'My thing?'

'You know what I mean. You and Backus going at it.'

'Can I go look at the excavation now? I'd like to see what you've got.'

'Well, Cherie will take you out in a second. We don't have a lot to look at but today's carcass.'

Spoken like a true morph, Rachel thought. She glanced at Dei and their eyes met in confirmation.

'But there is something I want to talk about first.'

Rachel knew what was coming but let Alpert have his say. He moved toward the front of the RV and pointed through the windshield out into the desert. Rachel followed his line but couldn't see anything but the mountain ridge.

'Well, you can't really see it from this angle,' Alpert said, 'but out there lying on the ground we've got a great big sign. It says in big letters, FILMING – NO FLYOVERS, NO NOISE. That's for anybody up there who might get curious about all these tents and vehicles. Pretty good idea, huh? They think it's a movie set. Helps keep them away from us.'

'And your point?'

'My point? My point is we have thrown a real thick blanket over all of this. Nobody knows and we want to keep it that way.'

'And you are suggesting I am a media leak?'

'No, I am not suggesting that. I am giving you the same talk I give everybody that comes out here. I don't want this in the media. I want to control it this time. Is that understood?'

More like bureau command or the Office of Professional Responsibility wants to control it this time, she thought. The Backus revelations almost decimated the ranks and reputation of the Behavioral Sciences unit last time, not to mention the colossal public relations fiasco it was for the bureau as a whole. Now with the failings of 9/11 and the bureau's competition with Homeland Security for budget dollars as well as headlines, media focus on a mad killer agent was not what bureau command or the OPR had in mind. Especially when the general public had been led to believe that the mad killer agent was long since dead.

'I understand,' Rachel said coolly. 'You won't have to worry about me. Can I go out now?'

'One other thing.'

He hesitated for a moment. Whatever it was, it was delicate.

'Not everyone involved in this investigation is aware of the connection to Robert Backus. It's "need to know" and I want to keep it that way.'

'What do you mean? The people working out there don't know it was Backus who did this? They should be—'

'Agent Walling, this is not your investigation. Don't try to make it yours. You were brought here to observe and help, leave it at that. We don't know for sure it was Backus and until we do—'

'Right. His fingerprints were only all over the GPS and his MO all over everything else.'

Alpert glanced at Dei, throwing her a look of annoyance.

'Cherie should not have told you about the prints and as far as the MO goes, there is nothing known about that for sure.'

'Just because she shouldn't have told me doesn't mean it isn't true. You're not going to be able to cover this up, Agent Alpert.'

Alpert laughed in frustration.

'Who said anything about a cover-up? Look, all we're doing right now is controlling information. There is a right time for revealing data. That is all I am telling you. Your presence alone here will be revealing enough, okay? I just don't want you deciding what to reveal and who to reveal it to. That's my job. Understood?'

Rachel nodded without conviction. She glanced at Dei as she did so.

'Perfectly.'

'Good. Then, Cherie, take her away. Take her sight-seeing.'

They left the RV and Dei led her toward the first small tent.

'You certainly ingratiated yourself with him,' she said to Rachel as they went.

'It's funny. Some things just never change. I think it might be impossible for a bureaucracy to evolve, to learn anything from its mistakes. Anyway, never mind. What do we have here?'

'So far we have eight bags and gas on another two. We just haven't gotten to them yet. Classic inverted pyramid.'

Rachel knew the shorthand. She had invented some of it. Dei was saying eight bodies had been recovered and readings from gas probes indicated there were another two bodies still interred and waiting for excavation. Tragic history created data from which models of similar behavior were formed. It had been seen before, a killer who returns with victims to the same burial spot follows a pattern, the newer burials radiating out from the original in an inverted pyramid or V pattern. So was the case here, with Backus either unintentionally or consciously following a pattern based on data he helped accumulate as an agent.

'Let me ask you one thing,' Rachel said. 'He was talking to Brass Doran on the phone in there. She's got to know about the Backus connection, right?'

'Yes, she knows. She found the prints on the package.'

Rachel nodded. At least she had one confederate she could trust and who was in the know.

They reached the tent and Dei pulled back the entry flap. Rachel went in first. Because the overhead venting flap was open it was not dark in the tent. It was only dim. Rachel's eyes adjusted immediately and she saw a large rectangular hole in the center of the tent. There was no fill pile. She assumed the dirt and rock and sand removed from the grave had been shipped to Quantico or the field office lab for sifting and analysis.

'This first site is where the anomalies are,' Dei said. 'The others are straight burials. Very clean.'

'What are the anomalies?'

'The reading on the GPS came back to this spot. Sitting here when they got here was a boat. It was—'

'A boat? Here in the desert?'

'You remember that preacher I told you started this place? He dug a canal for the spring water to fill. We figure the boat came from back then. It had been sitting here for decades. Anyway, we moved it, sank a probe and started digging. Anomaly number two is that the grave contained the first two victims. All the other graves are individual.'

'These first two, were they buried at the same time?'

'Yes. One on top of the other. But one was wrapped in plastic and he had been dead a lot longer than the other. Seven months longer, we think.'

'So he sat on one body for a while. Wrapped it for safekeeping. And when he had the second he realized he had to do something and so he came out to the desert to bury them. He used the boat as a marker. As a sort of gravestone and for himself because he knew he'd be back with more.'

'Maybe. But why'd he need the boat if he had the GPS?'

Rachel nodded and felt a little buzz of adrenaline start to tick in her blood. The brainstorming had always been the best part of the job.

'The GPS came later. Recently. That was just for us.'

'Us?'

'You. The bureau. Me.'

Rachel moved to the edge and looked down into the hole. It had not been deep, especially for two bodies. She stopped breathing through her mouth and took the fetid air in through her nose. She wanted to remember this.

'IDs yet?'

'Nothing official. No contact with kin yet. But we know who some of them were. Five of them at least. The first one was three years ago. The second seven months after that.'

'Have you built a cycle?'

'Yes, we have it. About an eight percent reduction. We think the last two will bring us up to November.'

Meaning that the intervals between the killings were decreasing by eight percent from the initial seven-month period between killings one and two. Again, it was familiar. The decreasing interval was common in case history, a symptom of the killer's diminishing control of his urges at the same time his belief in his invincibility grows. You get away with the first one and the second comes easier and sooner. And so on.

'I guess that makes him overdue,' Rachel said.

'Supposedly.'

'Supposedly?'

'Come on, Rachel, it's Backus. He knows what we know. He's just playing with us. It's like Amsterdam. He's gone before we even recognize it is him. Same here. He's moved on. I mean, why send us the GPS if he hasn't? He's split already. He's not overdue and he's not coming back here. He's somewhere laughing at us, watching us follow our models and routines, knowing that we won't get any closer to him than we did the last time.'

Rachel nodded. She knew Dei was right but decided to be optimistic.

'He's got to make a mistake somewhere. What about the GPS? Anything on that?'

'We're working it, obviously. Brass is on that.'

'What else is there?'

'There is you, Rachel.'

Rachel didn't say anything. Again Cherie Dei was right. Backus had something in play. His obscure but direct message to Rachel seemed to make this obvious. He wanted her here, wanted her to be part of the play. But what was it? What did the Poet want?

Like Rachel had mentored Dei, Backus had mentored Rachel. He was a good teacher. In retrospect, better than she or anyone could have imagined. She was mentored by both agent and killer, hunter and prey, a unique combination in the annals of crime and punishment. Rachel always remembered a throwaway line Backus had spoken one night when they were walking up the stairs from the basement at Quantico, leaving the unit behind for the day.

'In the long run I think it is all bullshit. We can't predict how these people act. We can only react. And at the end of the day, that means we're largely useless. We make good headlines and Hollywood makes good movies about us, but that's about it.'

Rachel was a rookie in the unit at the time. She was full of ideals and plans and faith. She spent the next thirty minutes trying to talk Backus out of such a belief. Now she was embarrassed by the memory of the effort and the things she had said to a man she would later realize was a killer.

'Can I go into the other tents now?' Rachel asked.

'Sure,' Dei said. 'Whatever you want.'

12

It was late and the batteries on the boat were beginning to run low. The lights in the forward berth were steadily dimming. Or at least it seemed so to me. Maybe it was my eyes that were dimming. I had spent seven hours reading through files pulled out of the boxes on the top bunk. I had filled my notebook to the last page and then flipped it over and started back to front.

The afternoon interview had been uneventful if not unhelpful. Terry McCaleb's last charter was a man named Otto Woodall who lived in a luxury condo behind the fabled Avalon Casino building. I talked to him for an hour, getting much the same story I had already gotten from Buddy Lockridge. Woodall, who was sixty-six years old, confirmed all aspects of the trip that were of interest to me. He said he did leave the boat during their dockage in Mexico and spent time with women he knew there. He was unembarrassed and unashamed. His wife was over on the mainland shopping for the day and he apparently didn't mind opening up. He told me he was retired from his job but not from life. He said he still had a man's needs. I let that line of questioning go at that point and focused on the last moments of McCaleb's life.

Woodall's observations and recollections mirrored Buddy's in all important details. Woodall also confirmed that on at least two specific instances during the trip he saw McCaleb take his meds, downing the pills and liquids with orange juice each time.

I took notes but knew they wouldn't be needed. After an hour I thanked Woodall for his time and left him to his view of the Santa Monica Bay and the bloom of smog that rose beyond it on the mainland.

Buddy Lockridge was waiting for me out front in a golf cart I had rented. He was still brooding over my last-minute decision to interview Woodall without him. He'd accused me of using him to get the interview with Woodall. He was right about that but his complaints and concerns weren't even on my radar.

We drove silently back to the pier and I turned in the cart. I told Buddy he could head home because I was going to be busy reading files the rest of the day and into the night. He meekly offered to help but I told him he already had helped enough. I watched him walk off toward the ferry docks with his head down. I still wasn't sure about Buddy Lockridge. I knew I had some thinking to do about him.

Not wanting to fool around with the Zodiac I took a water taxi back to *The Following Sea.* I conducted a quick search of the master stateroom – finding nothing of note – and moved into the forward cabin.

I noticed that Terry had a compact disc player in the converted office. His small collection of music was mostly blues and 1970s rock and roll. I plugged in a more recent Lucinda Williams CD called *World Without Tears* and liked it so much I ended up letting it play over and over during the next six hours. The woman had long journeys in her voice and I liked that. By the time the power started faltering on the boat and I turned the music off I had unconsciously memorized the lyrics to at least three songs I could sing to my daughter the next time I put her to bed.

Back in McCaleb's converted office, the first thing I did was go back to his computer and open the folder marked PROFILES.

It gave me a listing of six different files, all titled by dates in the previous two years. One by one I called them up in chronological order and found each to be a forensic suspect profile of a murder case. Written in the unadorned and clinical language of the professional, each profile drew conclusions about a killer based on specific crime scene details. It was clear from these details that McCaleb had done more than simply read newspaper articles. It was obvious he had full access to the crime scenes – either in person or more likely by photos and tapes and investigators' notes. It was very clear to me that these were not practice runs worked up by a profiler who missed the job and wanted to keep in tune. These were the work of an invited guest. The cases were all from the jurisdictions of small police departments in the west. My guess was that McCaleb had heard of each case through news reports or other means and simply volunteered his help to the police department struggling with the case. Offer accepted, he was probably sent the crime scene information and he then set to work analyzing and drawing up the profile. I wondered if his notoriety helped or hindered him when he offered his talents. How many times was he turned down to be accepted these six times?

When accepted, he probably worked each case from the desk where I was sitting, without ever leaving the boat. Or thinking his wife knew in detail what he was doing.

But I could tell each profile had taken a good amount of his time and attention. I was beginning to understand more and more what Graciela had said had become a problem in their marriage. Terry couldn't draw a line. He couldn't let it go. This profile work was a testament not only to his dedication to his mission as an investigator but also to his blind spot as a husband and father.

The six profiles came from cases in Scottsdale, Arizona; Henderson,

Nevada; and the four California cities of La Jolla, Laguna Beach, Salinas and San Mateo. Two were child murders and the other four were sex slayings involving three women and one male victim. McCaleb drew no links between them. It was clear they were simply separate cases that had drawn his attention in the last two years. There was no indication in any of the files that Terry's work had been helpful or if any of the cases had been cleared. I wrote down the basics from each in my notebook with the idea that I would follow up with the departments to check the status of each investigation. It was a long shot but it was still possible that one of these profiles could have triggered McCaleb's death. It wasn't a priority but I would need to check it out.

Finished with the computer for the time being, I directed my attention to the file boxes stored on the top bunk. One by one I pulled them down until there was no room on the floor of the forward room. I found that they contained a mix of files from both solved and unsolved cases. I spent the first hour just sorting them and pulling out the open-unsolveds, thinking that it was more likely than not that if Terry's death was related to a case, then it was one with a suspect still at large. There was no reason for him to be working or reworking a closed case.

The reading was fascinating. Many of the files were on cases I was familiar with or had even had a part in. They were not files that had gathered dust. I got the distinct impression that the open cases were in endless rotation. From time to time McCaleb pulled them out and rethought the investigations, the suspects, the crime scenes, the possibilities. He made calls to investigators and lab people and even witnesses. All of this was clear because McCaleb's practice was to use the inside front flap of the file to write notes on the moves he made, meticulously dating these entries as well.

From these dates I could tell that McCaleb had been working many cases at once. And it was clear he still had a pipeline into the FBI and the Behavioral Sciences squad at Quantico. I spent a whole hour reading the fat file he had accumulated on the Poet, one of the more notorious if not embarrassing serial killer cases in the FBI annals. The Poet was a killer later revealed to be the FBI agent who had been heading the squad essentially hunting for himself. It was a scandal that had rocked the bureau and its vaunted Behavioral Sciences Section eight years before. The agent, Robert Backus, chose homicide detectives as his victims. He staged the killing scenes as suicides, leaving behind suicide notes containing verses from the poems of Edgar Allan Poe. He killed eight men across the country in a period of three years before a reporter discovered the false suicides and the manhunt began. Backus was revealed and shot by another agent in Los Angeles. At the time he was supposedly targeting a detective from the homicide table in the LAPD's Hollywood Division. That was my table. The target, Ed Thomas, was my colleague and that was my connection. I remember taking a very high personal interest in the Poet.

Now I was reading the inside story. Officially the case was closed by the bureau. But the unofficial word had always been that Backus had gotten away. After being shot Backus initially escaped into the storm-water tunnel system that ranged beneath Los Angeles. Six weeks later a body was found with a bullet hole in the right place but decomposition made a physical identification and fingerprint comparison impossible. Foraging animals – it was reported – had made off with parts of the body, including the lower mandible and the only teeth that could have been used for identification through dental records. Backus had also conveniently disappeared without leaving DNA exemplars behind. So they had the body with the bullet hole but nothing to compare it to. Or so they said. The bureau quickly announced that Backus was presumed dead and the file was closed, if only to bring a speedy end to the agency's humiliation at the hands of one of its own.

But the records McCaleb had accumulated since then confirmed that the folklore was true. Backus was still alive and out there. Somewhere. Four years earlier he had surfaced in Holland. According to confidential FBI bulletins provided by bureau sources to McCaleb, a killer took the lives of five men over a two-year period in Amsterdam. All the victims were foreign visitors who had disappeared after venturing into the city's red-light district. Each man was found strangled and floating in the Amstel River. What connected the killings to Backus were notes sent to local authorities in which the writer took credit for the killings and asked that the FBI be called into the case. The writer, according to the confidential reports, asked specifically for Agent Rachel Walling, the agent who had shot Robert Backus four years earlier. The police in Holland invited the FBI to take an unofficial look at the case. The sender had signed each letter as simply 'The Poet.' FBI handwriting analysis of the letter indicated – not conclusively – that the writer was not a killer trying to ride the notorious coattails of Robert Backus, but Backus himself.

Of course, by the time the bureau, local authorities and even Rachel Walling mobilized in Amsterdam, the killer was long gone. And Robert Backus had not been heard from again – at least as far as Terry McCaleb's sources knew.

I replaced the thick file in one of the boxes and moved on. I soon learned that McCaleb was not just working old cases. In fact, anything that caught his attention was subject to his focus and skills. There were dozens of files that contained only a single newspaper story and some notes jotted on the file flap. Some cases were high profile, others obscure. He put together a file of newspaper clips on the Laci Peterson case, the disappearance of a pregnant woman from Central California on Christmas Eve two years before. The case had garnered long-term media and public attention, particularly after her dismembered body was found in the bay where her husband had earlier told investigators he had been fishing when she disappeared. An entry on the file flap dated before the woman's body was found said, 'Definitely

Dead – in the water.' Another note dated before her husband's arrest said, 'There's another woman.'

There was also a file with seemingly prescient notes on Elizabeth Smart, a child kidnapped in Utah who was found and returned after nearly a year. He correctly wrote 'alive' under one of the newspaper photos of the young girl.

McCaleb also made an unofficial study of the Robert Blake case. The former film and television star was accused of murdering his wife in another headlining case. The notes in the file were intuitive and on point, ultimately borne out as correct as the case entered the courts.

I had to ask myself if it was possible that McCaleb had entered the notes in his files and predated them, using information from media accounts and making it appear that he was predicting case aspects or suspect traits from his own work when he wasn't. While anything was possible, it seemed entirely unrealistic to me to think McCaleb had done this. I could see no reason for him to commit such a quiet and self-defeating crime. I believed the work was real and was his.

One file that I found contained newspaper stories on the LAPD's new cold case squad. Noted on the flap were the names and cell numbers of four detectives assigned to the unit. Terry had obviously been able to cross the gulf between the LAPD and the FBI if he had their cell numbers. I knew detectives' cell numbers were not handed out to just anyone.

One of the four detectives I knew. Tim Marcia had spent time in Hollywood Division, including the homicide table. I knew it was late but cops expect to get late calls. I knew Marcia wouldn't mind. I took out my cell and called the number McCaleb had written next to his name on the file. Marcia answered immediately. I identified myself, got through the long-time-no-see pleasantries and explained that I was calling about Terry McCaleb. I didn't lie but I didn't say I was working a murder investigation. I said I was sorting through his files for his wife and came across Marcia's name and number. I was simply curious about what their relationship had been.

'Harry, you worked some cold cases in your time, right? That thing up at your house last year came out of a cold case, didn't it?'

'Right.'

'Then you know how it goes. Sometimes you grasp at straws, you take any help you can get. Terry called me up one day and offered his services. Not on a specific case. I think he had seen a story in the *Times* about the unit and he basically said if I ever needed him to work a profile he was there for me. He was one of the good ones. I was really sorry to hear what happened. I wanted to get over to Catalina for the service but things sort of came up.'

'Like they always do. Did you ever take him up on the offer to do a profile?'

'Yeah, sort of. I know I did and a couple other of the guys here did, too. You know how it is. The department has no profiling to speak of and sometimes waiting on the bureau and Quantico can take months. Here was this guy who knew what he was doing and he didn't want anything back. He just wanted to work. So we used him. We bounced a few things off him.'

'And how did he do?'

'He did good. We're working this one case now that's interesting. When the new chief put the squad together we started going back through the open-unsolveds. We linked six cases – body dumps up in the Valley. They had some similar aspects but were never connected before. We copied the files to Terry and he confirmed. He connected them through what he called "psychological commonalities." We're still working it but at least we know what we have now. We're on the track is what I mean. I'm not sure we would be where we are if Terry hadn't helped us out.'

'Good, I'm glad to hear he helped with it. I'll tell his wife and I'm sure it will help her to know that.'

'Good. So, Harry, you coming back in?'

I was expecting him to ask what I was really doing with McCaleb's files, not whether I was coming back to the department.

'What are you talking about?'

'You heard about the three-year ticket the chief instituted?'

'No, what's that?'

'He knows we lost a lot of talent in recent years. All the scandals and whatnot, good people saying, what the hell, I'm out of here. So he's opening the door for people to come back. If you reapply within three years of retirement and are accepted you can get back in without having to go to the academy. That's perfect for old guys like you.'

I heard the smile in his voice.

'Three years, huh?'

'Yeah. What's it been for you, two and a half?'

'Just about.'

'Well, there you go. Think about it. We could use you here in cold cases. We've got seven thousand open-unsolveds. Take your pick, man.'

I didn't say anything. Out of the blue, I was struck with the idea of going back. In that moment I was blind to the negatives. I only thought about what it would be like to carry the badge again.

'Then again, maybe you're having too much fun being retired. You need anything else, Harry?'

'Uh, no, that was it. Thanks, man, I appreciate it.'

'Anytime. And think about the three-year plan. We could sure use you, whether it's here or back in Hollywood or wherever.'

'Yeah, thanks. Maybe I will. I'm going to think about it.'

I closed the phone and sat there surrounded by another man's obsessions but thinking about my own. I thought about going back. I thought about seven thousand unanswered voices from the grave. That was more than the number of stars you see when you look up into the sky at night.

My phone buzzed while it was still in my hand. It pulled me out of the reverie and I opened it, expecting it to be Tim Marcia calling back and saying that three-year thing had just been a gag. But it was Graciela calling.
'I can see lights on in the boat,' she said. 'Are you still there?'

'Yeah, I'm here.'

'Why so late, Harry? You missed the last ferry.'

'I wasn't going to go back tonight. I was going to stay over and finish up here. Maybe head back tomorrow. I might want to come up and talk to you, too.'

'That's fine. I'm not working tomorrow. I'll be here packing.'

'Packing?'

'We're going to move back to the mainland. We'll live in Northridge. I got my old job back in the ER at Holy Cross.'

'Is Raymond one of the reasons you're moving back?'

'Raymond? What do you mean?'

'I was wondering if there were any troubles with the boy. I heard he didn't like living on the island.'

'Raymond doesn't have a lot of friends. He doesn't fit in so well. But the move is not just because of Raymond. I want to go back. I wanted to before Terry was gone. I told you that.'

'Yes, I know.'

She changed the subject.

'Is there anything you need? Did you get something to eat?'

'I found some stuff in the boat's kitchen. I'm fine.'

She groaned in disgust.

'That all must be old. Check the expiration dates before you eat anything else.'

'I will.'

She hesitated and then asked the question she had called to ask.

'Have you found anything yet?'

'Well, I've found some things I am curious about. But nothing that particularly stands out yet.'

I thought about the man in the Dodgers cap. He certainly stood out for me but I didn't want to bring him up yet with Graciela. I wanted to know more before talking to her about him.

'Okay,' she said. 'But keep me informed about things, okay?'

'That's the deal.'

'Okay, Harry, I'll talk to you tomorrow. Are you staying in a hotel or on the boat?'

'The boat, I think. If that's all right with you.'

'It's fine with me. Do what you want to.'

'Okay. Can I ask you something?'

'Sure, what?'

'You were talking about packing and I'm just curious about something. How often do you go over to the mainland? You know, to go to the mall or restaurants or see family.'

'Usually about once a month. Unless something specific comes up and I need to go.'

'You take the kids?'

'Usually. I want them to be used to it. You grow up on an island where they have golf carts instead of cars and everybody knows everybody ... it can be strange to suddenly move to the mainland. I'm trying to get them ready for it.'

'I guess that's smart. What mall is closest to the ferry docks?'

'I don't know what one is closest, but I always go up to the Promenade on Pico. I just shoot up the four-oh-five from the harbor. I know there are closer malls – Fox Hills, for example – but I like the Promenade. I like the stores there and it's easy. Sometimes I meet friends from the Valley and it is a good halfway point for all of us.'

And easy to be followed to, I thought but didn't say.

'Good,' I said, not sure what I was saying was good. 'One other thing. I'm running out of light here. The batteries, I guess. Is there a switch or something I should hit to recharge or how do you do that?'

'You didn't ask Buddy?'

'No, I didn't know I was going to run out of light when I was with Buddy.'

'Oh, Harry, I'm not sure. There's a generator that has to run. I'm not sure even where it is.'

'Okay, well, don't worry about it. I can call Buddy. I'll let you go, Graciela. I ought to get back to work while I still have some light.'

I hung up and wrote the name of the mall down in my notebook, then left the room and went around the boat turning off all the lights but the one on the desk in the forward berth in an effort to conserve power. I called Buddy on the cell after that and he answered in a groggy voice.

'Hey, Buddy, wake up. It's Harry Bosch.'

'Who? Oh. What do you want?'

'I need your help. Is there like a generator or something on this boat that will give me some light? The batteries are dying on me.'

'Man, don't let those things drain all the way down. You'll kill them.'

'Then what do I do?'

'You've got to crank the Volvos, man, and then turn on the generator. The thing is it's near midnight. Those folks sleeping on their boats in line with you aren't going to take so kindly to hearing that.'

'All right, forget it. But in the morning I should do it, so what do I do, use a key?'

'Yeah, just like a car. Go to the helm in the salon, put in the keys and turn them to the ON position. Then above each key is the ignition toggle. Flip it up and she should start right up – unless you've used all the juice up and there's no charge.'

'Okay, I'll do it. You got any flashlights on this thing?'

'Yeah, there's one in the galley, one over the chart table and one in the master in the built-in drawer to the left of the bed. There's also a lantern in the lower cabinet of the galley. But you don't want to use that down in the front room. The kerosene smell will build up in there and you might croak yourself. Then there'd be another mystery to solve.'

He said the last line with a note of contempt in his voice. I let it go.

'Thanks, Buddy. I'll talk to you.'

'Yeah. Good night.'

I hung up and went looking for the flashlights, coming back to the forward berth with a small one from the master stateroom and a large table light from the galley. I put the large light on the desk and turned it on. I then killed the berth's lights. The table light's glow hit the small room's low ceiling and spread. It wasn't bad. Between that and the handheld light I would still be able to get some work done.

I was down to less than half a box of files to go and wanted to finish before figuring out where I was going to sleep. These were all thin files, the most recent additions to McCaleb's collection, and I could tell most of them contained little more than a newspaper clip and maybe a few notes on the flap.

I reached in and picked one out at random. I should have been in Vegas throwing dice. Because the file I picked turned out to be a long-shot winner. It was the file that gave my investigation focus. It put me on the road.

13

The file tab simply said 6 MISSING. It contained a single clipping from the *Los Angeles Times* and several dated notes and names and phone numbers handwritten on the inside flap, as was McCaleb's routine. I sensed that the file was important before I even read the story or understood the meaning of some of the notes. It was the dating on the flap that triggered this response. McCaleb had jotted his thoughts down on the file four different times, beginning on January 7 and ending on February 28 of this year. He would be dead a month later on March 31. Those notes and those dates were the most recent found in any of the files I had reviewed. I knew I was looking at what might have been Terry's last work. His last case and obsession. There were still files to look at but this one gave me the vibe and I went with it.

A reporter I knew wrote the story. Keisha Russell had been working the cop beat at the *Times* at least ten years and was good at it. She was also accurate and fair. She had lived up to every deal I had ever made with her in the years I was on the job, and she had gone out of her way to play fair with me the year before, when I was no longer on the job and things turned bad on my first private case. The bottom line was that I felt comfortable taking anything she wrote as fact. I started to read.

SEARCH FOR A MISSING LINK
ARE NEVADA DISAPPEARANCES OF
2 L.A. MEN, 4 OTHERS CONNECTED?

by Keisha Russell
Times Staff Writer

The mysterious disappearances of at least six men, including two from Los Angeles, from gambling centers in Nevada have got investigators searching for a missing link among the men.

Detectives with the Las Vegas Metro Police said Tuesday that while the men did not know each other and came from widely disparate hometowns and backgrounds, there still may be a commonality among them that could be the key to the mystery.

The men, ranging in age from 29 to 61, were reported missing by their families during the past three years. Four were last known to be in Las Vegas, where police are heading the investigation, and two disappeared while on trips to Laughlin and Primm. None of the men left any indication in their hotel rooms or vehicles or homes as to where they were going or what became of them.

'At this point it is a stone-cold mystery,' said Detective Todd Ritz of Vegas Metro's Missing Persons unit. 'People disappear from here or anywhere all the time. But they usually show up later, dead or alive. And there's usually an explanation. With these guys there's nothing. It's a thin air case.'

But Ritz and other detectives are sure there is an explanation and they are enlisting the public's help in finding it. Last week detectives from Las Vegas, Laughlin and Primm gathered at the Vegas Metro offices to compare notes and set an investigative strategy. They also went public with the case, hoping photographs of the men and their stories would spark new information from the public. On Tuesday, a week later, Ritz reported that not much in the way of usable information had come in.

'There has got to be someone who knows something or saw something or heard something,' said Ritz in a telephone interview. 'Six guys just don't get up and disappear without somebody knowing something. We need that somebody to come forward.'

As Ritz said, missing persons cases are numerous. The fact that these six men came to Nevada for business or pleasure and never went home is what makes this case different. The publicity comes at a time Las Vegas is once again redefining its image. Gone is the marketing strategy that billed the neon city as a family destination. Sin is back in. In the past three years numerous clubs featuring nude or partially nude dancers have been licensed, and many of the casinos on the fabled strip have produced shows featuring nudity and strictly adult subject matter. Billboards featuring nudity in their advertisements have been erected and drawn the ire of some community activists. It has all helped change the complexion of the city. Once again it is being marketed as a leave-the-kids-at-home adult playground.

As the recent billboard skirmishes suggest, the change hasn't played well with everyone and many speculate that the disappearances of these six travelers may in some indirect way be linked to the region's return to an anything-goes atmosphere.

'Let's face it,' said Ernie Gelson, a columnist for the *Las Vegas Sun*, 'they tried the family fun thing and it didn't play. The town is going back to what plays. And what plays is what pays. Now, is that the missing link that connects these six guys? I don't know. Maybe we never will.'

Still, Gelson is uneasy about jumping to any conclusions that would link the missing men to the changing image of Las Vegas.

'First of all, remember, they didn't all disappear from Las Vegas,' he said. 'And second to that, there are not enough facts to substantiate any theory at the moment. I think we have to sit back and let the mystery resolve itself before we jump on any bandwagons.'

The missing men are:

– Gordon Stansley, 41, of Los Angeles, missing since May 17, 2001. He checked into the Mandalay Bay Resort and Casino in Las Vegas but his bed was never slept in and his suitcase never unpacked. He is married and has two children.

– John Edward Dunn, 39, of Ottawa, Canada, who was driving from his home to Los Angeles on a vacation. He never made it to his intended destination, his brother's home in Granada Hills. Dunn's 30-foot recreational vehicle was found Dec. 29, 2001, at an RV park in Laughlin. That was 20 days after his expected arrival in Granada Hills.

– Lloyd Rockland, 61, disappeared from Las Vegas on June 17, 2002. His plane from Atlanta arrived at 11 a.m. at McCarran International Airport. He picked up a Hertz rental car, but he never checked in to the MGM Grand, where he had a reservation. His car was returned to the Hertz rental car center at the airport at 2 p.m. the next day but nobody seems to remember the father of four and grandfather of three being the one who returned it.

– Fenton Weeks, 29, of Dallas, TX, was reported missing Jan. 25, 2003, after he did not return from a business trip to Las Vegas. Police determined he had checked in to the Golden Nugget in downtown Las Vegas and attended the first day of an electronics exposition held at the Las Vegas Convention Center but was not in attendance on the second and third days. His wife reported him missing. He has no children.

– Joseph O'Leary, 55, of Berwyn, PA, disappeared May 15 of last year from the Bellagio where he was staying with his wife. Alice O'Leary left her husband in the casino playing blackjack while she went to spend the day at the resort's spa. Several hours later her husband failed to return to their suite. O'Leary, a stockbroker, was reported missing the next day.

– Rogers Eberle, 40, of Los Angeles, disappeared Nov. 1 while on a day off from his work as a graphic designer at the Disney Studios in Burbank. His car was found parked in the lot outside the Buffalo Bill's Casino in Primm, NV, just across the California border on the Interstate 15 freeway.

Investigators say there are few leads in the investigation. They point to Rockland's rental car as possibly being the best clue they have. The car was returned 27 hours after it was picked up by Rockland. It had been driven 328 miles during that period, according to Hertz records. Whoever returned it to the Hertz airport center dropped it off without waiting for a receipt or to speak to a Hertz clerk.

'They just pulled in, got out of the car and walked away,' Ritz said. 'Nobody remembers anything. They process about a thousand cars a day in that center. There are no cameras and there is no record but the rental record.'

And it is those 328 miles that Ritz and the other detectives wonder about. 'That is a lot of miles,' said Detective Peter Echerd, Ritz's partner. 'That car could have gone a lot of places. You figure a hundred and sixty-four out and a hundred and sixty-four back in and you've got a hell of a big circle to cover.'

Nevertheless, the investigators are trying to do just that, hoping their efforts will uncover a clue that makes the circle smaller and possibly leads to the answers to the six missing family men.

'It's tough,' said Ritz. 'These guys all have families and we're doing our best for them. But at the moment we have lots of questions and not any answers.'

The article was nicely drawn with the *Times*'s signature method of finding larger significance to a story than the story itself. In this case it was the theorizing that the disappearance of these men was symptomatic of the newest permutation of Las Vegas as an adult playground. It reminded me of a time I was working a case in which a man who owned an auto garage cut the hydraulic lines on a lift and a seven-thousand-pound Cadillac came down and crushed his longtime partner beneath it. A *Times* reporter called me up for the details for a story and then asked if the killing was symptomatic of the tightening economy in which money woes turned partners against partners. I said, no, I thought it was symptomatic of one guy not liking his partner screwing his wife.

Larger implications aside, the story was a plant. I could tell that. I had done the same thing with the same reporter in my time. Ritz was trolling for information. Since half the missing men were either from or going to Los Angeles, why not call the *Times,* plant a story with the cop reporter and see who and what pops up?

One person who popped up was Terry McCaleb. He obviously read the story on January 7, the day it was published, because his first set of notes on the file flap was dated as such. The notes were short and cryptic. At the top of the flap the name Ritz and a phone number with a 702 area code had been jotted down. Beneath this, McCaleb had written:

1/7 –

44 avg.
41 – 39 – 40

find intersection
cycle disruption – there are more
car – 328
triangle theory?
1 point gives 3
DD – check desert

1/9 –
call back – png

2/2
Hinton – 702 259-4050
n/c story?

2/28
Zzyzx – possible? how?
miles

Written along the side border of the file were two more phone numbers with 702 area codes. These were followed with the name William Bing.

I reread the notes and looked at the clipping again. I noticed for the first time that McCaleb had circled two things on the newspaper article, the mention of the 328 miles found to have been put on the rental car and the word *circle* in Echerd's comment about the circle of the investigation being 164 miles in any direction. I didn't know why he had circled these two things but I did know what most of the notes on the flap meant. I had spent more than seven hours reading through McCaleb's files. I had seen notation after notation in file after file. The ex-agent used a shorthand of his own invention but one that was decipherable because in some files he spelled out what he chose to abbreviate in others.

Immediately recognizable to me was what he meant by the use of 'DD.' It meant 'definitely dead,' a classification and conclusion McCaleb made on the wide majority of the missing cases he reviewed. Also easy to decipher was 'png,' which meant *persona non grata,* meaning McCaleb's offer to help with the investigation was not received well or not received at all.

McCaleb had also found some significance in the age of the missing men. He wrote down an average age and then pulled out three of the victims' ages because they were within two years of each other and very close to the average. This appeared to me to be notes relating to a victim profile but there wasn't one in the file and I didn't know if McCaleb ever proceeded past the notes stage.

The 'find intersection' reference seemed to also be part of this profile. McCaleb was referring to a geographic or lifestyle intersection of the six missing men. Just as the Metro detective had put forth in the *Times* article, McCaleb was operating under the belief that there had to be a connection between these men. Yes, they were from as far apart as Ottawa and Los Angeles and did not know one another, but there had to be a point where they came together in some way.

'Cycle disruption – there are more' I suspected was a reference to the frequency of the disappearances. If someone was abducting and killing these men, as McCaleb believed, there would usually be a recognizable time cycle. Serial killers operate this way in most cases, with violent psychosexual urges building and then subsiding after a kill. McCaleb had apparently worked out the cycle and found holes in it – missing victims. He believed there were more than six men missing.

What puzzled me most about the notes was the reference to 'triangle theory' and the phrase '1 point gives 3' below it. This was something I had not seen come up in the previous files and I did not know what was meant by it. It was noted in conjunction with references to the car and the 328 miles that had been put on it. But the more I played with it, the more puzzled I became by it. It was code or shorthand for something I didn't know. It bothered me but there was nothing I could do about it with what I currently knew.

The January 9 reference was to a call back from Ritz. McCaleb had probably called and left a message and the Vegas detective had called back, listened to his pitch and maybe his profile, and had said not interested. This was not surprising. The FBI was often unwanted by the locals. The clash of egos between feds and locals was a routine part of the job. A retired bureau man would likely be treated no differently. Terry McCaleb was persona non grata.

That might have been it for this file and this case but then came the February 2 notation. A name and a number. I opened my cell phone and called the number, not caring about how late it was. Or early, depending on how you looked at it. I got a recording of a female voice.

'This is Cindy Hinton at the *Las Vegas Sun*. I can't take your call right now but it is important to me. Please leave your name and number and I will call you back as soon as I can. Thank you.'

There was a beep and I hesitated, not sure I wanted to make contact yet. But I went ahead anyway.

'Uh, yes, hello, my name is Harry Bosch. I'm an investigator from Los Angeles and would like to talk to you about Terry McCaleb.'

I left my cell phone number and closed the phone, still not sure I had made the right move but thinking that leaving it short and cryptic was the best way to go. It might get her to call me back.

The last reference in the notes was the most intriguing of all. McCaleb had written 'Zzyzx' and then asked if it was possible and if so, how. This had to be a reference to Zzyzx Road. This was a leap. A giant leap. McCaleb had received photos from someone who had watched and photographed his family. That same person had taken photographs at Zzyzx Road near the California-Nevada border. Somehow McCaleb saw a possible link and was asking himself if one mystery could be related to the other. Could he have set something in motion by calling Vegas Metro and offering to help with the missing men case? To be able to make the leap to such questions was impossible. It meant I was missing something. I was missing the bridge, the piece of information that made the jump possible. McCaleb had to have known something that wasn't noted in the file but that made the possibility of a link seem real to him.

The last notations to check were the two Las Vegas phone numbers written on the border of the file along with the name William Bing. I opened my cell again and called the first number. The call was picked up by a recorded voice announcing that I had reached the Mandalay Bay Resort and Casino. I hung up as the voice began to list a number of options I could choose from.

The second number was followed by the name. I punched it into the phone, prepared to awaken William Bing and ask him what his connection to Terry McCaleb was. But the call was answered after several rings by a woman who said, 'Las Vegas Memorial Medical Center, how would you like me to direct your call?'

I wasn't expecting that. To gain some time while I thought about what to do I asked her for the hospital's location. By the time she was finished giving me the address on Blue Diamond Road I had come up with a valid question.

'Do you have a doctor on staff named William Bing?'

After a moment the answer came back negative.

'Do you have any employee named William Bing?'

'No, we don't, sir.'

'How about a patient?'

There was another pause as she consulted a computer.

'Not currently, no.'

'Did you formerly have a patient there named William Bing?'

'I don't have access to that kind of information, sir.'

I thanked her and closed the phone.

I thought about the last two numbers in McCaleb's notes for a long moment. My conclusions were simple. Terry McCaleb was a heart transplant recipient. If he were to travel to another city he would need to know where to go and who to ask for if there was an emergency or any medical problem. My guess was that McCaleb had called information to get the two numbers noted on the file. He then made a reservation at the Mandalay Bay and checked in with a local hospital as a precaution. The fact that there was no William Bing on staff at Las Vegas Memorial Medical Center did not preclude that he might be a cardio specialist who handled patients there.

I opened the phone, checked the time on the display screen and called

Graciela anyway. She answered quickly, her voice alert, though I could tell she had been sleeping.

'Graciela, sorry to call so late. I have a few more questions.'

'Can I answer them tomorrow?'

'Just tell me, did Terry go to Las Vegas within the month before he died?'

'Las Vegas? I don't know. Why?'

'What do you mean you don't know? He was your husband.'

'I told you, we had … separated. He was staying on the boat. I know he went over to the mainland a few times but if he went to Vegas from there I wouldn't have any way of knowing unless he told me, and he didn't tell me.'

'What about credit-card bills and cell phone records, ATM withdrawals, things like that?'

'I paid them but I don't remember anything like that, like a hotel or anything.'

'Do you have those records still?'

'Of course. I have them here at the house somewhere. They're probably packed already.'

'Find them and I'll come for them in the morning.'

'I'm already in bed.'

'Then find them in the morning. First thing. It's important, Graciela.'

'Okay, I will. And look, the one thing I can tell you is that usually if Terry was going to the mainland, he took the boat across so he had a place to stay while he was there. If he was going across but wasn't going to be in L.A. or was going to be staying at Cedars for tests or something, he would take a ferry because otherwise it would cost too much in boat fuel.'

'Okay.'

'Well, there was one trip in that last month. I think he was gone for like three days. Yes, three days, two nights. He took the ferry. So that meant he was either going across and then somewhere else or to the hospital. And I'm pretty sure it wasn't the hospital. I think he would have told me and I know everybody in cardio at Cedars anyway. They would have let me know he was there and what was going on. I had that place wired.'

'Okay, Graciela, that's good. That helps. Do you remember exactly when that was?'

'Not exactly. It was the end of February, I think. Maybe the first couple days of March. I remember it was bill time. I called him on his cell to talk about money and he said he was on the mainland. He didn't say where. He just said he was over there and he'd be back in a couple days. I could tell he was driving when we talked. And I knew he hadn't taken the boat because I was on the balcony looking at it in the harbor when we talked.'

'Why were you calling him, do you remember?'

'Yes, we had bills to pay and I didn't know what if anything he had taken in on the boat in February. The credit-card payouts were sent directly here but Terry had a bad habit of walking around with personal checks and cash from customers in his wallet. When he died and I got his wallet back, there were three checks in there for nine hundred dollars that he'd had in there for two weeks. He wasn't very good at business.'

She said it as though it was one of her husband's endearing and humorous qualities, though I was pretty sure that during his life she didn't smile at these oversights.

'A couple more things,' I said. 'Do you know if it would be his routine to check in with a hospital in a city he was going to? In other words, if he was going to Las Vegas would he set things up at a local hospital in case he needed anything?'

There was a pause before she answered.

'No, that doesn't sound like anything he would do. Are you saying he did that?'

'I don't know. I found a phone number in one of the files. And a name. The number was for Vegas Memorial and I'm trying to figure out why he would call there.'

'Vegas Memorial has a transplant program, I know that. But I don't know why he would call there.'

'What about the name William Bing, does that mean anything? Could it be a doctor he was recommended to?'

'I don't know that … something about that name is familiar but I can't place it. It could be a doctor. Maybe that's where I heard it.'

I waited a moment to see if it came to her but it didn't. I pressed on.

'Okay, one last thing, where is Terry's car?'

'It should be over there at Cabrillo, at the marina. It's an old Jeep Cherokee. There's a key on the ring I gave you. Buddy also has a key because he uses it sometimes. He basically takes care of it for us. I mean, me now.'

'Okay, I'm going to check that out in the morning, so I'll need to keep the key. Do you know when the first ferry goes back across?'

'Not till nine-fifteen.'

'Then can we meet at seven-thirty or eight at your house? I want to get those records and also show you a few things. It won't take too long and then I'll grab the first ferry.'

'Um, can we make it eight? I should be back by then. I usually walk Raymond to school and take CiCi to day care.'

'No problem. I'll see you at eight.'

We ended the conversation and I immediately called Buddy Lockridge again, one more time rousing him from sleep.

'Buddy, it's me again.'

He groaned.

'Did Terry go to Las Vegas the month before he died? Like maybe around March first?'

'I don't know, man,' he said in a tired, annoyed voice. 'How would I know that? I can't remember what *I* did March first.'

'Think, Buddy. He made a road trip around then. He didn't bring the boat across. Where did he go? Did he tell you anything about it?'

'He didn't tell me jack. But I remember that trip now because the Jeep came back dirtier than shit. Had salt or some shit all over it. And I was the one who was left to wash it.'

'Did you ask him about it?'

'Yeah, I said, "Where have you been, out off-roading?" and he said, "Yeah, something like that."'

'And that was it?'

'That's all he said. I washed the car.'

'What about the inside? Did you clean that out?'

'No, I'm just talking about the outside. I took it over to the drive-through in Pedro and power-sprayed the thing. That's all I did.'

I nodded as I concluded I had gotten everything I needed from Lockridge. For the time being.

'You going to be around tomorrow?'

'Yup, I'm always around these days. Got nowhere to go.'

'All right. I'll see you then.'

After ending the conversation I made one more call, punching in the number McCaleb had written at the top of the file flap after the name of Ritz, the detective quoted in the *Times* article.

The call was picked up by a tape announcing that the Vegas Metro's Missing Persons unit was open from 8 a.m. to 4 p.m. Monday through Friday. The message advised anyone with an emergency to hang up and dial 911.

I closed the phone. It was late and I had an early start in the morning but I knew I wasn't going to sleep any time soon. I had the wire in the blood now and knew from long experience that sleep was not an option. Not yet.

I was marooned on a boat with two flashlights to see by, but there was still work to be done. I opened my notebook and started constructing a chronological record of the dates and times of events in the weeks and months before Terry McCaleb's death. I put everything on the page, the important and not important, the real connections and imagined connections. Just as experience had taught me about sleep and the ability to go long stretches without it, I knew the details were important. The answer is always in the details. What is seemingly not important now is all-important later. What is cryptic and unconnected now becomes the magnifying glass through which things become clear later.

14

You can always tell who the locals are. They're the ones who sit inside and work crossword puzzles while the ferry makes the ninety-minute crossing. The tourists are usually up top or lining the bow or stern with their cameras and last glimpses of the island as it shrinks in the mist behind them. On the first boat out the next morning I was inside with the locals. But I was working a puzzle of a different kind. I sat with the file in which Terry McCaleb had made his case notations open on my lap. I also had the chronology I had worked up the night before. I studied it, hoping to commit as much of it as I could to memory. An instant command of case details is required for the successful completion of an investigation.

Jan. 7 – McC reads about missing men in Nevada, calls Vegas Metro
Jan. 9 – Vegas Metro not interested
Feb. 2 – Hinton, Vegas Sun. Who called who?
Feb. 13 – Half-day charter with Jordan Shandy
Feb. 19 – Charter with Finder
Feb. 22 – GPS stolen/sheriff's report
Feb. 27 – McC creates photo file
March 1? – McC on mainland for three-day period
March 28 – Last charter. McC on *The Following Sea* with meds
March 31 – McC dies

I now added what I had learned an hour earlier from Graciela. The same credit-card records I had asked her to gather in regard to her husband's movements contained her purchases as well. There was a Visa charge attributed to a Nordstrom department store on February 21. When I asked about it she said she had made the purchase at the Promenade. I asked if she had been back since then and she said no.

As I added the date into the chronology I noted that it was the day before the GPS device was reported stolen from *The Following Sea*. This meant it was likely the same day it was stolen. The photo stalker had been on the ferry with Graciela on the way back to the island. Could he have been the one who snuck onboard *The Following Sea* that night and took the GPS device? If so, why? And if so, could this also have been the night that Terry McCaleb's medicine was tampered with, real capsules exchanged for dummies?

I circled the letters GPS on the chronology. What was the significance of this device and this theft? I wondered if I was putting too much emphasis on this. Perhaps Buddy Lockridge's theory was the correct one, the device had simply been stolen by Finder, a competitor. Perhaps that was all it was, but the proximity to the mall stalking of Graciela made me think otherwise. My instincts told me there was a connection. I just didn't have it yet.

Despite that, I felt as though I was getting close to something. The chronology was very helpful in allowing me to see connections and the timeliness of things. There was more still to add and I remembered I had intended to follow up with phone calls to Las Vegas this morning. I opened my cell phone and checked the battery. I had been unable to recharge it on *The Following Sea*. Now I was running out of juice. I had maybe one last call on it before it died. I punched in the number for the Missing Persons unit at Vegas Metro. The call went through and I asked for Detective Ritz. I was put on hold for nearly three minutes, during which time the phone started to beep every minute, warning me it was running low on power.

'This is Detective Ritz, how can I help you?'

'Detective, my name is Bosch. I'm LAPD retired. Homicide mostly. I'm doing a favor for a friend. Her husband passed away last month and I'm sort of putting his things in order. I came across a file of his that had your name and number in it and a newspaper article about one of your cases.'

'What case?'

'The six missing men.'

'And what was your friend's husband's name?'

'Terry McCaleb. He was FBI retired. He worked—'

'Oh, him.'

'You knew him?'

'I talked to him on the phone once. That doesn't qualify as knowing him.'

'You talked about the missing men?'

'Look, what did you say your name is?'

'Harry Bosch.'

'Well, listen, Harry Bosch, I don't know you and I don't know what you are doing, but it's usually not my practice to talk about open cases over the phone with strangers.'

'I could come see you.'

'That wouldn't change things.'

'You know he's dead, don't you?'

'McCaleb? I heard he had a heart attack and he was out on his boat and nobody could get to him in time. It sounded stupid. What's a guy with a heart transplant doing twenty-five miles out in the middle of nowhere?'

'Making a living, I guess. Look, some things have come up about that and I'm checking into what Terry was into at the time. To sort of see if he might've drawn somebody's eye, if you know what I mean. All I want—'

'Actually, I don't know what you mean. You talking voodoo? Somebody put the hex on him and gave him a heart attack? I'm kind of busy here, Bosch. Too busy for that bullshit. You retired guys think us working stiffs have all the time in the world for you and your long-shot voodoo theories. Well, guess what, we don't.'

'Is that what you said to him when he called? You didn't want to listen to his theory or his profile of the case? You called it voodoo?'

'Look, man, what good is a profile? Those things don't narrow down shit. They're bullshit and that's what I told him and that was—'

His last word was cut off by my phone's warning beep.

'What was that?' he asked. 'Are you recording this?'

'No, it's my phone's low-battery warning. Terry didn't come over there to talk to you about this?'

'Nope. I think he ran to the newspaper with it instead. Typical fed move.'

'There was a story about his take on this in the *Sun*?'

'I wouldn't call it that. I think they pretty much thought he was full of shit, too.'

That line revealed an untruth. If Ritz thought McCaleb and his theory were full of shit, he had to have listened to it in order to make such a determination. I believed that it revealed that Ritz had discussed the case with McCaleb, possibly at length.

'Let me ask you one last thing and then I'll leave you alone. Did Terry mention something about a triangle theory? Something about one point giving three? Does any of that make sense?'

The laugh I heard over the phone wasn't pleasant. It wasn't even good-natured.

'That was three questions, Bosch. Three questions, three sides of a triangle and three strikes and you're—'

The phone went dead, its battery drained.

'Out,' I said, completing Ritz's line. I knew it meant he was not going to answer my question. I closed the phone and dropped it back into my pocket. I had a charger in my car. I'd have the phone back up and running as soon as we got across the Santa Monica Bay. There was still the reporter at the *Sun* to talk to but I doubted I'd be having further conversations with Ritz.

I got up and walked out onto the stern to have the cool morning air refresh me. Catalina was far in the distance, just a jagged gray rock sticking up in the mist. We were more than halfway across. I heard a little girl exclaim, 'There!' very loudly to her mother and I followed her pointed finger out to the water where a school of porpoises were breaking the surface in the boat's wake. There must have been twenty of them and soon the stern became crowded with people and their cameras. I think maybe some of the locals even came out to look. The porpoises were beautiful, their gray skin shining like plastic in the morning light. I wondered if they were just having fun or had mistaken the ferry for a fishing boat and were hoping to feed on the debris of the day's catch.

Soon the show wasn't enough to hold everyone's attention and the passengers returned to their former positions. The little girl who first sounded the alert stayed at the gunwale and watched, and so did I, until the porpoises finally dropped off the wake and disappeared in the blue-black sea.

I went inside and took up McCaleb's file again. I reread everything he and I had written. No new ideas came up. I then looked at all the photos I had printed out the night before. I had shown the photos of the man named Jordan Shandy to Graciela but she didn't recognize him and hit me with more questions than answers about him, questions I didn't want to try to answer just yet.

Next in the review were the credit-card and phone records. I had already looked at these in Graciela's presence but wanted to check them more thoroughly. I paid closest attention to the end of February and the beginning of March, when Graciela was sure her husband had been on the mainland. But there was no purchase with a credit card nor phone call made on his cell that gave any indication of where he was, let alone in Los Angeles or maybe Las Vegas. It was almost as if he wanted to leave no trail.

A half hour later the boat pulled into the Los Angeles harbor and docked next to the *Queen Mary,* a permanently moored cruise ship that had been turned into a hotel and convention center. As I was walking through the parking lot to my car I heard a shriek and turned around to see a woman bouncing and swaying upside down from the end of a bungee cord extending down from a jumping platform at the stern of the *Queen Mary.* She had her arms clamped to the sides of her torso and I realized that the reason she had screamed was not because of the fear and adrenaline rush of the free fall, but because her T-shirt had apparently threatened to fall down over her shoulders and head, exposing her to the crowd that lined the railing of the cruise ship.

I turned away and headed on to my car. I drive a Mercedes-Benz sport utility vehicle, the kind some people think helps keep terrorists in business. I don't get involved in such debates but I do know that the people who go on talk shows to argue such things usually pull up in stretch limos. As soon as I got into the car and cranked it, I plugged my phone into the charger and waited for it to come back to life. When it did I saw I had gotten two messages in the forty-five minutes the phone had been out of commission.

The first was from my old partner Kizmin Rider, who now handled administrative and planning duties in the chief of police's office. She left no message other than a request for me to call her. This was curious because we hadn't talked in nearly a year and that conversation had not been the most pleasant. Her usual Christmas card to me had carried her signature only and not the usual cordial note and promise to get together soon. I wrote her direct number down – at least I still rated that – and saved the message.

The next message was from Cindy Hinton, the *Sun* reporter. She was simply returning my call. I started the Benz and headed toward the freeway so I could loop over to San Pedro and the Cabrillo Marina, where Terry McCaleb's Jeep was waiting for me. I called Hinton back on the way and she answered immediately.

'Yes, I was calling about Terry McCaleb,' I said. 'I'm sort of re-creating his movements in the last couple months of his life. I assume you had heard he passed away. I remember that the *Sun* carried an obituary.'

'Yes, I knew. You said on your message last night that you are an investigator. An investigator for what agency?'

'Actually, I'm a state-licensed private detective. But I was a cop for almost thirty years.'

'Is this related to the missing persons case?'

'In what way?'

'I don't know. You called me. I don't understand what it is you want.'

'Well, let me ask you a question. First of all, I know from Detective Ritz over at Metro that Terry had taken an interest in the missing persons case. He studied the facts that were available to him and called on Detective Ritz, offering his time and expertise to work on the case or provide investigative theories. You with me so far?'

'Yes. I know all of this.'

'Okay, good. Terry's offer to Ritz and Vegas Metro was rejected. What my question is is what happened next? Did he call you? Did you call him? Did you write a story that said he was investigating this case?'

'And why is it that you want to know these things?'

'Sorry, hold on a second.'

I had realized I should not have made the call while driving. I should have expected Hinton to be cagey with me and should have known the call would need my undivided attention. I glanced at the mirrors and cut across two lanes to go down an exit. I didn't even see the sign and didn't know where I was going. I found myself in an industrial area where trucking depots and warehouses lined the street. I pulled to a stop behind a tractor-trailer parked in front of the open garage doors of a warehouse.

'Okay, sorry, I'm back. You asked why I wanted to know the answers to these questions. Well, Terry McCaleb was my friend. And I'm picking up some of the things he was working on. I want to finish his work.'

'It sounds like there is something else, something you're not telling me.'

I thought for a moment of how to handle this. Giving a reporter information, especially a reporter you didn't know, was risky business. It could snap back on you in bad ways. I had to figure out a way to give her what she needed in order to help me, but then I needed to take it all back.

'Hello? Are you still there?'

'Uh, yeah. Tell you what, can we go off the record here?'

'Off the record? We're not even talking about anything here.'

'I know. I am going to tell you something if I can tell it to you off the record. Meaning, you can't use it.'

'Sure, fine, whatever, we're off the record. Could you please get to the point or whatever this important information is because I need to write a story this morning?'

'Terry McCaleb was murdered.'

'Uh, no, actually he wasn't. I read the story. He had a heart attack. He had a heart transplant like six years before. He—'

'I know what was put out in the press and I'm telling you it is wrong. And it will come out that it is wrong. And I'm trying to find out who killed him. Now can you tell me whether or not you put out a story that had his name in it?'

She seemed exasperated when she answered.

'Yes, I wrote one story that he was in. For like a paragraph or two. Okay?'

'Just a paragraph? What did it say?'

'It was a follow-up to my story on the missing men. I did a follow-up to see what had come in. You know, what new leads, if any. McCaleb was mentioned, that's all. I said he came forward and offered his help and a theory but Metro said no thanks. It was worth throwing in because the story was dry as a bone and he was sort of famous because of the movie and Clint Eastwood and all of that. Does that answer your question?'

'So he didn't call you?'

'Technically, yes, he did. I got his number from Ritz and called him. I left a message and he called me back. So technically he called me, if that's how you want it. What is it you think happened to him anyway?'

'Did he tell you what his theory was? The one Ritz wasn't interested in?'

'No, he said he didn't want to comment at all and he asked me to keep his name out of the paper. I talked to my editor and we decided to keep it in. Like I said, he was famous.'

'Did Terry know you put his name in the story?'

'I don't know. I never spoke to him again.'

'In that one conversation you had, did he say anything about the triangle theory?'

'Triangle theory? No, he didn't. Now I answered your questions, you answer mine. Who says he was murdered? Is that official?'

Now it was time to back out. I needed to stop her in her tracks, make sure she wouldn't hang up and immediately start making calls to check me or my story out.

'Well, not really.'

'Not really? Are you – well, what exactly makes you say this?'

'Well, because he was in perfect shape and he had a young person's heart in him.'

'So, what about organ rejection and infection? A thousand different things could have – do you have any official finding about this or confirmation? Is there an official investigation?'

'No. That would be like asking the CIA to investigate the Kennedy assassination. The third one. It would just be a cover-up.'

'What are you talking about? The third what?'

'The third Kennedy. The son. John-John. You think his plane just dove into the water like they said? There were three witnesses in New Jersey who saw men carrying their bodies onto that plane *before* it took off. The witnesses have disappeared, too. It was part of the triangle theory and then—'

'Okay, mister, thanks a lot for your call. But I'm on deadline right now and need to—'

She hung up before finishing her own sentence. I smiled. I thought I was safe and was particularly proud of my creativity. I reached over to the passenger seat and lifted the file. I opened it and looked at the chronology. Terry had noted the conversation with Hinton on February 2. The story probably ran in the next day or two. As soon as I got to a library with a computer I would be able to look the story up and get the exact date and read what had been written in the one reference to McCaleb.

For the time being I listed it on the chronology on February 3. I studied what I had for a few moments and started putting my own case theory into form:

McCaleb sees the January 7 *Los Angeles Times* story on the missing men. He gets interested. He sees something in the story that the cops may have missed or misinterpreted. He works up a theory and his thoughts and calls Ritz at Metro two days later. Ritz gives him the cold shoulder but happens to mention the call to Hinton when she does a follow-up. After all, it serves Ritz to keep the story circulating in the press and dropping a 'celebrity' investigator's name might help do so.

Hinton's follow-up story with the mention of McCaleb runs in the *Sun* the first week of February. Less than two weeks later – February 13 – McCaleb is alone on his boat when Jordan Shandy shows up on a water taxi and asks for a half-day charter. McCaleb grows suspicious of the man while they are fishing and surreptitiously takes photos of him. A week later Shandy is at the Promenade mall stalking McCaleb's family and surreptitiously taking photographs – the same thing McCaleb had done to him. That same night someone takes the GPS device from *The Following Sea* and possibly tampers with McCaleb's medicine.

By February 27 McCaleb has received the photos of his family at the mall. The origin or method of delivery of the photos is unknown but this date is documented by the creation record of the photo file on his computer. Just two days after putting the photos into his computer he leaves Catalina for the mainland. His destination is unknown but his car is returned in dirty condition, as if he had been off-road with it. There is also a record of him having phone numbers for a hospital in Las Vegas and the Mandalay Bay Resort, one of the last known locations of one of the missing men.

Possibilities and interpretations abounded. My guess was that everything turned on the photos. I believed that it was seeing those photos that drew McCaleb across to the mainland. I believed that his car came back dirty after three days because he had gone into the desert at Zzyzx Road. He had taken the bait, whether knowingly or not, and gone to the desert.

I looked at my chronology again and concluded that the mention of McCaleb in the follow-up story in the *Sun* had drawn a response. Shandy was somehow involved in the disappearances. If so, he would probably keep an eye on the media for any updates on the investigation. When he saw McCaleb's name in the follow-up, he came to Catalina to check him out. On the boat that morning during the four-hour charter he could have seen McCaleb taking his medicine, seen the capsules, and hatched a plan to eliminate the threat.

That left the question of the GPS device and why it was taken during the February 21 boat break-in. I now believed it was simply taken as cover. Shandy could not be sure his entry to the boat to change Terry's meds would go unnoticed. So he took the device so McCaleb wouldn't wonder further about the intentions of the intruder if he discovered there had been a break-in.

The larger question was why McCaleb was seen as a threat if his triangle theory was not revealed in the *Sun* story. I didn't know. I thought there was a possibility that he wasn't seen as a threat at all, that he was just a celebrity whom Shandy liked outwitting by killing. It was one of the unknowns.

It was also one of the contradictions. My theory certainly had contradictions. If the first six men disappeared without a trace, why was McCaleb killed in such a way that there were witnesses and a body that could possibly reveal the truth? This was incongruous. My only answer was that if McCaleb simply disappeared, then it would spark an investigation and perhaps a second look at his view and theory of the missing men case. This could not be allowed by Shandy, so McCaleb was eliminated in a way that would hopefully seem natural or accidental and below the radar of suspicion.

My theory was built on speculation and this made me uncomfortable. When I carried a badge, relying on speculation was like putting sand in your gas tank. It was the road to ruin. I felt ill at ease at how easily I had slipped into building theories upon interpretation and speculation instead of the bedrock of fact. I decided then to put theories aside and go back to concentrating on facts. I knew that Zzyzx Road and the desert were real and part of the chain of facts. I had the pictures to prove it. I didn't know if Terry McCaleb had actually gone there or what he might have found if he had. But I now knew I was going there. And that, too, was a fact.

15

Buddy Lockridge was waiting in the parking lot at Cabrillo Marina when I got there. I had called him and told him I was on the move and in a hurry. My plan to hook up with him for further discussion would be delayed. I told him I just wanted to quickly go through McCaleb's Cherokee and then move on. I knew what my destination was, whether or not I found anything in the car that pointed me toward the desert and Las Vegas.

'What's all the hurry?' he asked as I pulled up and got out.

'Velocity,' I told him. 'Main thing about an investigation is to keep your velocity up. You slow down ... and you slow down. I don't want that.'

Before returning the boat keys to Graciela I had taken the Cherokee's key off the ring. I now used it to unlock the driver's door. I leaned in and began a general observation of the car before getting in.

'Where are you headed?' Lockridge said from behind me.

'San Francisco,' I lied, just to see if I'd get a reaction.

'San Francisco? What's up there?'

'I don't know. But I think that's where he went on that last trip.'

'Must've taken the dirt road way.'

'Maybe.'

There was nothing readily apparent in the Cherokee that gave me a second thought. The car was in clean condition. There was a faintly sour odor. It smelled like the windows had been left open during a rainstorm at some point. I opened the compartment between the two front seats and found two pairs of sunglasses, a pack of breath-freshening gum and a small, plastic action figure toy. I handed it out the door behind me to Lockridge.

'You left your superhero in here, Buddy.'

He didn't take it.

'Funny. That's from McDonald's. There ain't one over there on the island, so the first thing they do when they get over here is take the kids to Mickey D's. It's like crack, man. They get the kids hooked on those French fries and shit early and then they're hooked for life.'

'There are worse things.'

I put the plastic hero back into the compartment and closed it. I leaned further in so I could reach across to open the glove box.

'Hey, you want me to come with you? Maybe I could help.'

'No, that's okay, Buddy. I'm leaving right from here.'

'Hell, I could be ready in five minutes. I mean, I'll just put some clothes in a bag.'

The glove box contained another plastic figure and operating manuals for the car. There was also a box containing a book on tape called *The Tin Collectors.* There was nothing else. This stop was turning into a bust. All I was getting out of it was Buddy pushing to be my partner. I pulled back out of the car and straightened up. I looked at Lockridge.

'No, thanks, Buddy. I'm working this alone.'

'Hey, I helped Terry, man. It wasn't like in the movie where I was made out to be the creep who—'

'Yeah, yeah, I know, Buddy. You told me all of that. This has got nothing to do with that. I just work alone. Even with the cops. That's the way I was, that's the way I am.'

I thought of something and leaned back into the car, checking the windshield on the passenger side for a sticker like the one seen in the photo of the Zzyzx Road sign on McCaleb's computer. There was no sticker or anything else in the lower corner of the windshield. It was another confirmation that McCaleb had not taken the photo.

I backed out of the car, walked around and opened the rear hatch. The storage compartment was empty except for a pillow shaped like a cartoon character named SpongeBob SquarePants. I recognized it because my daughter was a SpongeBob fan and I, too, enjoyed watching the show with her. I guessed he was a favorite in the McCaleb home, too.

I then went to one of the rear doors and looked into the passenger compartment. Clean again, but I noticed in the pocket behind the front passenger seat there was a map book that could be reached from the driver's seat. I pulled it out and paged through it, careful not to let Buddy see what I was looking at.

On the page for southern Nevada I noticed that the map included parts of contiguous states. In California, near the southwest corner of Nevada, someone had drawn a circle around the Mojave Preservation Area. And on the right border of the map someone had jotted down several numbers in ink, one above the other, and then added them together. The sum was 86. Below this was written 'Actual – 92.'

'What is it?' Lockridge asked, looking through the car at me from the other passenger door.

I closed the map book and dropped it on the car seat.

'Nothing. It looks like he wrote down some directions for one of his trips or something.'

I leaned into the car and then down so that I could look under the front passenger seat. I saw more McDonald's toys and some old food wrappers and other debris. Nothing that looked worthwhile. I got out and came around the other side, asking Buddy to step back so I could do the same thing with the driver's seat. Beneath the driver's seat there was more debris but I noticed several small crumpled balls of paper. I reached under and swept these out so I could see them. I opened one up and smoothed it out and saw that it was a credit-card receipt for a purchase of gas in Long Beach. It was dated almost a year earlier. 'You don't check under the seats when you clean the car, do you, Buddy?'

'They never asked me to,' he said defensively. 'Besides, I really just take care of the outside.'

'Oh, I see.'

I started unraveling the rest of the paper balls. I didn't expect anything that would help me. I had already reviewed the credit-card receipts and knew there were no purchases I could use to pinpoint McCaleb's location on his three-day trip. But the rule was always to be thorough.

There were a variety of receipts for local purchases. This included food items from Safeway and fishing equipment from a San Pedro tackle store. There was a receipt for ginseng extract from a health food store called BetterFit, and a receipt from a Westwood bookstore for a book on tape called *Looking for Chet Baker.* I never heard of the book but knew who Chet Baker was. I decided I would check into it later when I had time to read or listen to a book.

The rule paid off on the fifth paper ball. I unraveled a cash receipt from a Travel America truck stop in Las Vegas. It was located on Blue Diamond Road, the same street as Vegas Memorial. The date of the purchase was March 2. The purchase was for sixteen gallons of gasoline, a half-liter of Gatorade and the book on tape edition of *The Tin Collectors.*

The receipt placed McCaleb in Las Vegas during his three-day trip. It was another confirmation of what I thought I already knew. Nevertheless my adrenaline kicked in another notch. I wanted to get moving again, keep that case velocity going. 'You find something?' Lockridge asked.

I crumpled the receipt and threw it down onto the floor of the car with the others. 'Not really,' I said. 'Turns out Terry was a big books-on-tape guy. Didn't know that.'

'Yeah, he listened to a lot of them. Out on the boat when he was up on the helm. He usually had the earphones on.'

I reached back into the car and took the map book off the seat.

'I'm going to borrow this,' I said. 'I don't think Graciela's going anywhere where she'll need it.'

I didn't wait for Buddy's approval. I closed the passenger door, hoping that he was buying my act. I then closed the driver's door and locked the vehicle.

'That's it, Buddy. I'm out of here. You going to be near your phone if anything comes up and I need you?'

''Course, man, I'm around. It's a mobile, anyway.'

'All right then, you take care.'

I shook his hand and headed to my black Benz, half expecting to find him following me. But he let me go. As I drove out of the lot, I checked the mirror and saw him still standing next to the Cherokee, watching me go.

I took the 710 up to the 10 and rode that out to the 15 freeway. After that it would be a straight shot out of the smog and into the Mojave and then on to Las Vegas. I had been making this trip two or three times a month for the past year. I always enjoyed the drive. I liked the starkness of the desert. Maybe I drew from it what Terry McCaleb drew from living on an island. A sense of distance from all the nastiness. As I drove it I felt the constrictions lift, as if the molecules of my body expanded and got a little more space between each other. Maybe it was no more than a nanometer but that little narrow space was enough to make a difference.

But this time I felt different. I felt as though this time the nastiness was ahead of me, that it was waiting for me in the desert.

I was settling into the drive, letting the case facts rotate in my mind, when my cell buzzed. My guess was that it would be Buddy Lockridge making a final plea to be included but it was Kiz Rider. I had forgotten to call her back.

'So, Harry, I guess I don't even rate a call back from you?'

'Sorry, Kiz, I was going to call you. I had a busy morning and sort of forgot.'

'Busy morning? You're supposed to be retired. You're not running around on another case, are you?'

'Actually, I'm driving to Vegas. And I'm probably about to lose my signal in the dead zone. What's going on?'

'Well, I saw Tim Marcia this morning when I was getting my coffee. He told me you two had talked recently.'

'Yeah, yesterday. Is this about that three-year deal he told me about?'

'It certainly is, Harry. Have you thought about it?'

'I just heard about it yesterday. I haven't had time to think about it.'

'I think you should, Harry. We need you back here.'

'That's nice to hear, especially from you, Kiz. I thought I was PNG with you.'

'What does that mean?'

'Persona non grata.'

'Come on now. It was nothing a cooling-off period couldn't cure. Seriously, though, we could use you back here. You could probably work with Tim's unit if you wanted.'

'If I wanted? Kiz, you make it sound like all I have to do is waltz in there and sign on the dotted line. What do you think, everybody in that building is going to be there to welcome me back? Are they going to be lined up in the hallway on the sixth floor, throwing rice or something while I walk to the chief's office?'

'You talking about Irving? Irving got downsized. He's running the department of future planning. I'm calling to tell you, Harry, that if you want to come back, then you are back. It's that simple. After I talked to Tim I went up to six and had my usual nine a.m. with the chief. He knows of you. He knows your work.'

'I wonder how that could be, since I was gone before he was brought over from New York or Boston or wherever it was they got him from.'

'He knows because I told him, Harry. Look, let's not get into an argument over this. Okay? Everything is cool. All I'm saying is that you should think about it. The clock is ticking on it and you ought to think about it. You could help us and the city and maybe even help yourself, depending on where you're at in the world.'

That last part raised a good question. Where was I in the world? I thought about it for a long moment before speaking.

'Yeah, okay. Kiz, I appreciate it. And thanks for putting in the word with the man. Tell me something, when did Irving get dumped? I hadn't heard about that.'

'That happened a few months ago. I think the chief thought he had his finger in too many pies. He put him to the side.'

I couldn't help but smile. Not because Deputy Chief Irvin Irving had always had me under his heel, but because I knew a man like Irving wouldn't let anyone put him to the side, as Kiz had said.

'The man carries all the secrets,' I said.

'I know. We're waiting for his move. We'll be ready.'

'Then good luck to you.'

'Thanks. So what's it going to be, Harry?'

'What, you want my answer now? I thought you just told me to think about it.'

'A guy like you, I already think you know the answer.'

I smiled again but didn't answer. She was wasting her time in administration. She should be back in homicide. She knew how to read people better than anyone I had ever worked with.

'Harry, you remember the thing you told me when I first got assigned as your partner?'

'Um, chew your food, brush after every meal?'

'I'm serious.'

'I don't know, what?'

'Everybody counts or nobody counts.'

I nodded and was quiet for a moment.

'Do you remember?'

'Yeah. I remember.'

'Words to live by.'

'I guess so.'

'Well, think about that while you're thinking about coming back.'

'If I come back, I'm going to need a partner.'
'What, Harry? You're breaking up.'
'I'm going to need a partner.'
There was a pause and I think now she was smiling, too.
'That's a possibility. You—'
She cut out on me. I think I knew what she was going to say.
'I bet you miss it as much as me.'
'Harry, you're going into the dead zone. Call me back when … don't take too long.'
'Okay, Kiz, I'll let you know.'
I was still smiling after closing the phone. There is nothing like being wanted or being welcomed. Being valued.
But also the idea of having a badge again in order to do what I had to do. I thought about Ritz at Metro and how he had treated me. How I had to fight just to get the attention and help of some people. I knew a lot of that would go away with the badge again. In the last two years I had learned that the badge didn't necessarily make the man, but it sure as hell made the man's job easier. And for me it was more than a job. I knew that badge or no badge, there was one thing on this earth I could and should be doing. I had a mission in this life, just as Terry McCaleb had. Spending the day before in his floating shop of horrors, studying his cases and his dedication to his mission, made me realize what was important and what I had to do. In his dying my silent partner may have saved me.
After forty minutes of mulling over my future and considering my choices, I came to the sign I had seen in the photo on Terry's computer.

ZZYZX ROAD
1 MILE

It was not the exact sign. I could tell by the horizon behind it. The photo had been taken from the other side, by someone heading to L.A. from Vegas. Nevertheless, I felt a deep tug of anticipation. Everything I had seen or read or heard since Graciela McCaleb had called me led to this place. I put on the blinker and took the exit off the freeway.

16

Midmorning on the day after Rachel Walling's arrival the agents assigned to what had been labeled the 'Zzyzx Road case' gathered in person and by phone in the squad room on the third floor of the John Lawrence Bailey Building in Las Vegas. The room was windowless and poorly ventilated. A photograph of Bailey, an agent killed during a bank robbery twenty years earlier, looked upon the proceedings.

The agents in attendance sat at tables lined in rows, facing the front of the room. At the front was Randal Alpert and a two-way television that was connected by phone and camera to a squad room in Quantico, Virginia. On the screen was Agent Brasilia Doran, waiting to provide her report. Rachel was at the second row of tables, sitting off by herself. She knew her place here and outwardly tried to show it.

Alpert convened the meeting by graciously introducing those present. Rachel thought that this was a nicety allowed for her but soon realized that not everyone in attendance in person or by audiovisual hookup knew everyone else.

Alpert first identified Doran, also known as Brass, on the line from Quantico, where she was handling the collating of information and acting as liaison to the national lab. He then asked each person seated in the room to identify themselves and their specialty or position. First was Cherie Dei, who said she was the case agent. Next to her was her partner, Tom Zigo. Next was John Cates, a representative agent from the local FO and the only nonwhite person in attendance.

The next four people were from the science side and Rachel had seen and met two of them at the site the day before. They included a forensic anthropologist named Greta Coxe, who was in charge of the excavations, two medical examiners named Harvey Richards and Douglas Sundeen, and a crime scene specialist named Mary Pond. Ed Gunning, another agent from Behavioral Sciences in Quantico, brought the introductions around to Rachel, who was last.

'Agent Rachel Walling,' she said. 'Rapid City field office. Formerly with Behavioral. I have some … familiarity with a case like this.'

'Okay, thanks, Rachel,' Alpert said quickly, as though he thought Rachel was going to mention Robert Backus by name.

This told Rachel that there were people in the room who had not been informed of the major fact of the case. She guessed that would be Cates, the token agent from the FO. She wondered if some of the science team, or all of it, was in the dark as well.

'Let's start with the science side,' Alpert continued. 'First of all, Brass? Anything from out there?'

'Not on science. I think your crime scene people have all of that. Hello, Rachel. Long time.'

'Hello, Brass,' Rachel said quietly. 'Too long.'

She looked at the screen and their eyes met. Rachel realized that it had probably been eight years since she had actually seen Doran. She looked weary, her mouth and eyes drawn down, her hair short in a cut that suggested she didn't spend much time with it. She was an empath, Rachel knew, and the years were taking their toll.

'You look good,' Doran said. 'I guess all that fresh air and open country agrees with you.'

Alpert stepped in and saved Rachel from delivering a false compliment in return.

'Greta, Harvey, who wants to go first?' he asked, stepping all over the electronic reunion.

'I guess I will since everything starts with the dig,' Greta Coxe said. 'As of seven p.m. yesterday we have fully excavated eight bodies and they are at Nellis. This afternoon when we get back there, we will begin with number nine. What we saw with the first excavations is holding true with the latter. The plastic bags in each incidence and the—'

'Greta, we have a tape going here,' Alpert interrupted. 'Let's be fully descriptive. As if speaking to an uninformed audience. Don't hold back.'

Except when it comes to mentioning Robert Backus, Rachel thought.

'Okay, sure,' Coxe said. 'Um, all eight bodies excavated and exhumed so far have been fully clothed. Decomposition is extensive. Hands and feet bound by tape. All have plastic bags over the head, which in turn have been taped around the neck. There is no variation on this methodology, even between victims one and two. Which is unusual.'

Late the day before Rachel had seen the photos. She had gone back into the command RV and looked at the wall of photos. It seemed clear to her that the men had all been suffocated. The plastic bags had not been clear plastic but even in their opaqueness she could see the features of the faces and the mouths wide open and searching for air that wasn't going to come. They reminded her of photos of wartime atrocities, disinterred bodies from mass graves in Yugoslavia or Iraq.

'Why is that unusual?' Alpert asked.

'Because what we most often see is that the killing plan evolves. For lack of a better way of describing it, the killing gets better. The unsub learns from victim to victim how to do it better. That is usually seen in the data we have.'

Rachel noted that Coxe had used the word *unsub.* Short for unknown subject. It most likely meant she was out of the loop and didn't know that the subject was very much known to the FBI. 'Okay, so the methodology was set from day one,' Alpert said. 'Anything else, Greta?'

'Just that we will probably be finished with the excavations the day after tomorrow. Unless we get another hit with the probes.'

'Are we still probing?'

'Yes, when we have the time. But we've gone sixty feet past the last hit with the probes and haven't gotten anything. We also got another flyover from Nellis last night. There was nothing new from thermal imaging. So we feel pretty comfortable at this time that we've got them all.'

'And thank God for that. Harvey? What have you got for us?'

Richards cleared his throat and leaned forward so that his voice would be heard by the electronic pickups, wherever they were.

'Greta's right, we have all eight excavated so far in the morgue at Nellis. So far the veil of secrecy is holding up. I think people there think we're bringing in aliens off a crashed saucer in the desert. This is how urban legends start, people.'

Only Alpert cracked a smile. Richards continued.

'We've conducted full autopsies on four so far and initial exams of the others. Similar to what Greta said, we're not finding a hell of a lot of difference from body to body. This guy is a robot. No variation on theme. It's almost like the killings themselves are of no import. Perhaps it is the hunt that juices this guy. Or perhaps the killings are just part of a larger plan we don't know about yet.'

Rachel stared pointedly at Alpert. She hated that people working so closely on the case were still working in the dark. But she knew if she said anything she would quickly be on the outside looking in. She didn't want that.

'You have a question, Rachel?'

He'd caught her off guard. She hesitated.

'Why are the bodies being taken to Nellis instead of here or L.A.?'

She knew the answer before asking the question but needed to say something to escape the moment.

'It's easier to keep a lid on things this way. The military knows how to keep a secret.'

His tone suggested an unspoken final line: *Do you?* He swung his view back to Richards.

'Doctor, go on.'

Rachel picked up on the subtle difference. Alpert had called Richards Doctor, whereas he had simply addressed Greta Coxe by her first name. It was a character trait. Alpert either had trouble with women in positions of power and knowledge or he didn't respect the science of anthropology. She guessed it was the former.

'Well, we're looking at suffocation as the cause on these,' Richards said. 'It's pretty obvious from what we've got. There is not a lot left to work with on most of them but with what we've got we're not seeing other injuries. The unsub overpowers in some way, tapes wrists and ankles and then puts the bag in place over the head. The taping around the neck we think is significant. That is indicative of a slow death. In other words the unsub was not holding the bag in place. He took his time, pulled it over the head, taped it and then could step back to watch.'

'Doctor?' Rachel asked. 'Was the tape applied from the front or back?'

'The ends are at the back of the neck, indicating to me that the bag may have been pulled over from behind, possibly when the victim was in a sitting position, and then taped in place.'

'So he – the, uh, unsub – may have been ashamed or afraid to face his victims when he did this.'

'Quite possibly.'

'How are we doing on identification?' Alpert asked.

Richards looked at Sundeen and he took over.

'Still just the five that were included in the Las Vegas investigation. We assume the sixth from their group will be one of the final two excavations. The others we have nothing on so far. We've got no useable prints. We've forwarded the clothing – what's left of it – to Quantico and perhaps Brass has an update on that. Meantime, we—'

'No, no update,' Doran said from the television screen.

'Okay,' Sundeen said. 'We have the dental data just going into the computer today. So maybe we'll get a hit there. Other than that we're just waiting for something to happen.'

He nodded at the completion of his report. Alpert took back the lead.

'I want to go to Brass last, so let's hear about the soil.'

Mary Pond took it from there.

'We've sifted all of the sites and it's all come up clean except for one piece we got yesterday that is exciting. In excavation seven we found a wad of gum in a wrapper. Juicy Fruit, according to the wrapper. It was between twenty-four and thirty inches down in a three-foot grave. So we really feel it is related and could be a good break for us.'

'Dental?' Alpert asked.

'Yes, we have dental. I can't tell you what yet but it looked like three good impressions. I boxed it and sent it to Brass.'

'Yes, it is here,' Doran said from the television. 'Came in this morning. I put it in motion but I don't have anything on it yet either. Maybe late today. I agree, though. From what I saw we'll get at least three teeth out of it. Maybe even DNA.'

'Could be all we need,' Alpert added excitedly.

Even though she distinctly remembered that Bob Backus had a habit of chewing Juicy Fruit gum, Rachel was not excited. The gum in the grave was too good to be true. She thought there was no way that Backus would allow himself to leave such important evidence behind. He was too good as both a killer and agent for that. She could not properly express this doubt in the meeting, however, because of her agreement with Alpert not to bring up Backus in front of other agents.

'It's got to be a plant,' she said.

Alpert looked at her a moment, weighing the risk of asking her why.

'A plant. Why do you say that, Rachel?'

'Because I can't see why this guy who is burying a body in the middle of nowhere, probably in the middle of the night, would take the time to put his shovel down, take the gum out of his mouth, wrap it in its foil, which he had to take out of his pocket, and then drop it. I think if he'd been chewing gum he would have just spit it out. But I don't think he was chewing gum. I think he picked that little wad up somewhere, brought it to the grave and dropped it in so we would spin our wheels with it when he decided to lead us to the bodies with his GPS trick.'

She glanced around the room. She had their eyes but she could tell she was more of a curiosity to them than a respected colleague. The silence was broken by the television.

'I think Rachel is probably right,' Doran said. 'We have been manipulated from day one on this. Why not with the gum? It does seem like an incredible mistake for such a well-planned action.'

Rachel noticed Doran wink at her.

'One piece of gum, one mistake, in eight graves?' said Gunning, one of the agents from Quantico. 'I don't think that is such a long shot. We all know nobody's ever committed the perfect crime. Yes, people get away but they all make mistakes.'

'Well,' Alpert said, 'let's wait and see what we get with this before we jump to any conclusions one way or the other. Mary, anything else?'

'Not at this time.'

'Then let's go to Agent Cates to see how the locals are doing with the IDs.'

Cates opened a leather-bound folder on the table in front of him. It contained a legal pad with notes on it. That he had such a nice and expensive holder for a basic legal pad told Rachel that he was very proud of his work and what he did. Either that or the person who gave him the folder had those feelings. Either way, it made Rachel like him right away. It also made her feel like she was missing something. She no longer carried that kind of pride in the bureau or what she did.

'Okay, we started sniffing around Vegas Metro on their missing persons case. We're handicapped by the need for secrecy. So we're not going in there like gangbusters. We've just made contact and said we're interested because of the state line thing – victims from multiple states and even one other country. That gives us an in but we don't want to show our hand by blasting in there. So we're supposed to have a sitdown with them later today. Once we reach the beach, so to speak, we'll start back tracing these individuals and looking for the common denominator. Keep in mind these guys have been on this for several weeks and as far as we know don't have shit.'

'Agent Cates,' Alpert said. 'The tape.'

'Oh, excuse my language there. They don't have anything is what I meant to say.'

'Very good, Agent Cates. Keep me informed.'

And only silence followed. Alpert continued to smile warmly at Cates until the local agent got the message.

'Oh, um, you want me to leave?'

'I want you out there working on those victims,' Alpert said. 'No sense wasting time in here listening to us hash things around to no end.'

'Okay, then.'

Cates got up. If he had been a white man the embarrassment would have been more recognizable on his face.

'Thank you, Agent Cates,' Alpert said to his back as he went through the door. Alpert then turned his attention back to the table.

'I think Mary, Greta, Harvey and Doug can all be excused as well. We need you guys back in the trenches, I'm afraid. No pun intended.'

There was that administrative smile again.

'Actually,' Mary Pond said, 'I'd like to stay and hear what Brass has to say. It might help me in the field.'

Alpert lost his smile at the challenge.

'No,' he said firmly, 'that won't be necessary.'

An uneasy silence engulfed the room until it was finally punctuated by the sounds of the science team's chairs being pushed back from their tables. The four of them got up and left the room without speaking. It was painful for Rachel to watch. The unchecked arrogance of command staff was endemic in the bureau. It was never going to change.

'Now, where were we?' Alpert said, easily morphing past what he had just done to five good people. 'Brass, your turn now. I have you down here for the boat, the tape and bags, the clothes, the GPS device, and now you have the gum, which we all know will lead nowhere, thank you very much, Agent Walling.'

He said the word *agent* like it was synonymous with *idiot.* Rachel raised her hands in surrender.

'Sorry, I didn't know half the field team is in the dark on the suspect. Funny, but when I was in Behavioral we never did it that way. We pooled information and knowledge. We didn't hide it from one another.'

'You mean when you were working for the man we are looking for right now?'

'Look, Agent Alpert, if you are trying to taint me with that brush, then you—'

'This is a classified case, Agent Walling. That is all I am trying to get across to you. As I told you before, it is "need to know."'

'Obviously.'

Alpert turned away from her as if dismissing her from memory and looked at the television screen.

'Brass, can you begin please?'

Alpert made sure he stood between Rachel and the screen, to further underline her position as outsider on the case.

'Okay,' Doran said, 'I have something significant and ... well, strange, to begin with. I told you about the boat yesterday. The initial fingerprint analysis of manageable surfaces came back negative. It had been out there in the elements for who knows how long. So we took it another step. Agent Alpert approved disassembly of the evidence and that was done in the hangar at Nellis last night. On the boat there are grip locations – handholds for moving the boat. This at one time was a Navy lifeboat, built in the late thirties and probably sold off as military surplus after World War Two.'

As Doran continued Dei opened a file and pulled out a photo of the boat. She held it for Rachel to see, since Rachel had never actually seen the boat. It was already at Nellis by the time she had gotten to the excavation site. She thought it was amazing and typical that the bureau could amass so much information about a boat set adrift in the desert but so little about the crime it was attached to.

'We could not get into the interior of the grip holes with our first analysis. When we disassembled the piece we were able to get in there. This is where we got lucky because this little hollow was protected from the elements for the most part.'

'And?' Alpert asked impatiently. He obviously wasn't interested in the journey. He just wanted the destination.

'And we got two prints out of the port side grip on the bow. This morning we ran them through the data banks and got a hit almost right away. This is going to sound strange but the prints came from Terry McCaleb.'

'How can that be?' asked Dei.

Alpert didn't say anything. His eyes stared down at the table in front of him. Rachel sat quiet as well, her mind racing to catch up with and understand this latest piece of information.

'At some point he put his hand into the grip hole on the boat, that's the only way it can be,' Doran said.

'But he's dead,' Alpert said.

'What?' Rachel exclaimed.

Everyone in the room turned and looked at her. Dei slowly nodded.

'He died about a month ago. Heart attack. I guess the news didn't get to South Dakota.'

Doran's voice came from the speaker.

'Rachel, I am so sorry. I should have gotten word to you. But I was too upset about it and went out to California right away. I'm sorry. I should have told you.'

Rachel looked down at her hands. Terry McCaleb had been her friend and colleague. He was one of the empaths. She felt a sudden and deep sense of loss, despite the fact that she had not spoken to him in years. Their shared experiences had left them bonded for life and now that life, for him, was gone.

'Okay, people, let's take a break here,' Alpert said. 'Fifteen minutes and then back in here. Brass, can you call back?'

'I will. I've got more to report.'

'Talk to you then.'

They all filed out to get coffee or use the restrooms. To leave Rachel alone.

'Are you all right, Agent Walling?' Alpert asked.

She looked up at him. The last thing she would take would be comfort from him.

'I'm fine,' she said, moving her eyes back to the blank TV screen.

17

Rachel remained in the conference room by herself. Her initial shock gave way to a wave of guilt coming up behind her like a following sea. Terry McCaleb had attempted to contact her over the years. She had gotten the messages but had never responded. She had sent him a card and a note when he was in the hospital recovering from the transplant. That had been five or six years ago. She couldn't remember. She did remember specifically deciding not to put a personal return address on the envelope. At the time she told herself it was because she wasn't going to be stuck in Minot for very long. But she knew then as she knew now that the real reason was she didn't want the connection. She didn't want the questions about the choices she had made. She didn't want that link to the past.

Now she didn't have to worry, the link was forever gone.

The door opened and Cherie Dei looked in.

'Rachel, do you want a bottle of water?'

'Sure, that would be nice. Thank you.'

'Tissues?'

'No, that's all right, I'm not crying.'

'Be right back.'

Dei closed the door.

'I don't cry,' Rachel said to no one.

She put her elbows on the table and held her hands over her face. In the darkness she saw a memory. She and Terry on a case. They weren't partners but Backus had put them together on this one. It was a crime scene analysis. A bad one. A mother and daughter tied up and thrown into the water, the girl squeezing so hard on a crucifix it left its full impression on her hand. The mark was still there when the bodies were found. Terry was working with the photos and Rachel went to the cafeteria to get coffee. When she came back she could tell he had been crying. That was when she knew he was an empath, that he was her kind.

Dei came back into the room and put a bottle of spring water and a plastic cup down in front her.

'You okay?'

'Yes, fine. Thanks for the water.'

'It was quite a shock. I didn't really know him and it bowled me over when the word spread.'

Rachel just nodded. She didn't want to talk about it. The speakerphone rang and Rachel reached for it ahead of Dei. She picked up the handset rather than push the teleconference button. This way she could speak privately at first to Doran – at least, Doran's side of it would not be overheard.

'Brass?'

'Rachel, hi, I am so sorry I didn't—'

'It's all right. It isn't your job to keep me informed of everything.'

'I know, but this I should have told you about.'

'It was probably in one of the bulletins and I just missed it. It's just strange finding out about it this way.'

'I know. I'm sorry.'

'So you went to the funeral?'

'The service, yes. It was out on the island where he lived. Catalina. It was really beautiful there and really sad.'

'Were there many agents?'

'No, not too many. It was kind of hard to get to. You have to take a ferry. But there were a few and there were some cops and family and friends. Clint Eastwood was there. I think he took his own helicopter out.'

The door opened and Alpert came in. He seemed renewed, as if he had been sucking on pure oxygen during the break. The other two agents, Zigo and Gunning, followed him in and sat down.

'We're ready to start,' Rachel said to Doran. 'I've got to put you on the screen now.'

'Okay, Rachel. We'll talk later.'

Rachel handed the phone to Alpert, who set up the teleconference. Doran appeared on the screen, looking more tired than before.

'Okay,' Alpert said. 'We ready to continue?'

After no one said a word he continued.

'All right then, what do these prints on the boat mean?'

'It means we've got to find out when and why McCaleb was out in the desert before he died,' Dei said.

'And it means we've got to go over to L.A. and take a look at his death,' Gunning said. 'Just to be sure a heart attack was a heart attack.'

'I agree with that but there is a problem,' Doran said. 'He was cremated.'

'That sucks,' said Gunning.

'Was there an autopsy?' Alpert asked. 'Blood and tissue taken?'

'I don't know about that,' Doran said. 'All I know is that he was cremated. I flew out for the service. The family let his ashes go over the side of his boat.'

Alpert looked at the faces around the room and stopped at Gunning's.

'Ed, you're on it. Go over there and see what you can come up with. Do it quick. I'll call the FO over there and tell them to give you the people you need. And for God's sake keep it out of the press. McCaleb was a minor celebrity because of the movie thing. If the press gets a whiff of this they'll be on us like the jacket on a book.'

'Got it.'

'Other ideas? Suggestions?'

Nobody said anything at first. Then Rachel cleared her throat and spoke quietly.

'You know, Backus was Terry's mentor, too.'

There was a pause of silence and then Doran said, 'That's right.'

'When they started the mentoring program Terry was the first one Backus picked. I was next after that.'

'And what is the significance of that to us now?' Alpert asked.

Rachel shrugged.

'Who knows? But Backus called me out with the GPS. Maybe he called Terry out before me.'

Everybody paused for a moment to think about that.

'I mean, why am I here? Why did he send the package to me when he knows I'm not in Behavioral anymore? There's a reason. Backus has some kind of plan. Maybe Terry was the first part of it.'

Alpert slowly nodded his head.

'I think it is an angle we need to be aware of.'

'He could be watching Rachel,' Doran said.

'Well, let's not jump ahead of ourselves here,' Alpert said. 'Let's stay with the facts. Agent Walling, I want you to exercise all caution of course. But let's check out the McCaleb situation and see what we've got before we start jumping. Meantime, Brass, what else have you got?' They waited as Doran looked down and off camera at some paperwork and apparently shifted gears from McCaleb back to the rest of the evidence.

'We've got something that might tie in with McCaleb. But let me go down my list and get this other stuff out of the way first. Uh, first, we're just starting now with the tape and the bags recovered with the bodies. Give us another day on that and I'll have a report. Let's see, on the clothes, they're probably going to be in the drying room another week before they're ready for analysis. So nothing there. The gum we already talked about. We'll put the dental profile into the bite mark database by the end of the day. Which leaves the GPS.'

Rachel noticed that everyone in the room was staring intently at the television screen. It was as if Doran was in the room with them.

'We're making some good progress here. We traced the serial number to a Big Five Sporting Goods store in Long Beach, California. Agents from the Los Angeles FO went to the store yesterday and obtained a store sales record showing the purchase of this Gulliver one hundred model by a man named Aubrey Snow. Turns out Mr. Snow is a fishing guide and was out on the water yesterday. Last night, when he finally returned to dock he was questioned at length about his Gulliver. He told us that he lost the device about eleven months ago in a poker game with several other guides. It was valuable because at the time it had several waypoints corresponding to his favorite or most productive fishing spots along the coast of Southern California and Mexico.'

'Did he give us the guy who won it?' Alpert asked quickly.

'Unfortunately, no. It was an impromptu game. There was bad weather at the time and business was slow. A lot of guides were stuck in dock and they were getting together to play poker almost every night. Different nights, different players. A lot of drinking. Mr. Snow could not remember a name or much else about the man who won the GPS. He didn't think he was from the marina where Mr. Snow keeps his boat because he hasn't seen the man since. The FO was supposed to get together with Snow and an artist today so they can try to come up with a picture of this guy. But even if they get a good drawing, that area has marinas and fishing charters all over the place. I was already told that the FO has only two agents to spare on this.'

'I'll make a call and change that,' Alpert said. 'When I call to get Ed set up on the McCaleb thing, I'll get more bodies on this. I'll go right to Rusty Havershaw.'

Rachel knew the name. Havershaw was the special agent in charge of the Los Angeles field office.

'That'll be a help,' Doran said.

'You said this connects to McCaleb. How so?'

'Well, did you see the movie?'

'Actually, no, I didn't get around to it.'

'Well, McCaleb was running a fishing charter out of Catalina. I don't know how plugged in he was to that community but there is a possibility that he knew some of the guides in those poker games.'

'I see. It's a stretch but it is there. Ed, keep that in mind.'

'Got it.'

There was a knock on the door but Alpert ignored it. Cherie Dei got up and answered it. Rachel could see it was Agent Cates. He whispered something to Dei.

'Anything else, Brass?' Alpert asked.

'Not at the moment. I think we need to shift emphasis to L.A. and find—'

'Excuse me,' Dei said, bringing Cates back into the room. 'Listen to this.'

Cates flicked his hands up like he was signaling that this was no big deal.

'Uh, I just got a call from the checkpoint out at the site. They're holding a man there who just drove up. He's a private detective from L.A. His name is Huhromibus Bosch. He—'

'You mean Hieronymus Bosch?' Rachel asked. 'Like the painter?'

'Yeah, that's it. I don't know about any painter but that is how my guy said it. Anyway, this is the deal. They put him in one of the RVs and took a look in his car without him knowing. He had a file on the front seat. There are notes and stuff but there also are photos. One of the photos is of the boat.'

'You mean the boat from out there?' Alpert asked.

'Yeah, the one that marked the first grave. There also was a news article on the six missing men.'

Alpert looked at the others in the room for a moment before speaking.

'Cherie and Tom, call Nellis and have them get ready with a chopper,' he finally said. 'Get out there and get going. And take Agent Walling with you.'

18

They put me in an RV and told me to make myself at home. There was a kitchen and a table and a sitting area. There was a window but the view was of the side of another RV. The air-conditioning was on and that kept the smell out for the most part. When I asked questions they hadn't answered them. They told me that other agents were coming soon to speak to me.

An hour went by and it gave me time to think about what I had stumbled into. There was no doubt that this was a body recovery site. The smell, that unmistakable smell, was in the air. Besides that, I had seen two unmarked vans with no windows on the sides or back. That told me something right there. Body movers. And there was more than one body to be moved.

At the ninety-minute mark I was sitting on the couch reading a month-old FBI *Bulletin* I had picked up off the coffee table. I heard a helicopter fly over the RV and then its turbines rev down and quit after it landed. Five minutes later the RV's door opened and the agents I had been waiting for came in. Two women and a man. One of the women I recognized right off but I couldn't place from where. She was late thirties, tall and pretty with dark hair. There was a deadness in her eyes that I had seen before, too. She was an agent and that meant there could have been a lot of places where our paths had crossed.

'Mr. Bosch?' said the other woman, the one in charge. 'I'm Special Agent Cherie Dei. This is my partner, Tom Zigo, and this is Agent Walling. Thank you for waiting for us.'

'Oh, I had a choice? I didn't realize that.'

'Of course. I hope they didn't tell you that you had to stay.'

She smiled disingenuously. I decided not to argue the point and get things off to a bad start.

'Do you mind if we move into the kitchen and sit at the table?' Dei asked. 'I think it will be best to talk there.'

I shrugged like it didn't matter but I knew it did. They were going to sit me down and then corner me, one sitting across from me and then one on either side. I got up and took the seat I knew they'd want me in, the one where my back would be to the wall.

'So,' Dei said after sitting down across the table from me. 'What brings you out to the desert, Mr. Bosch?'

I made the shrug again. I was getting good practice at it.

'I was just on my way to Vegas and pulled off to look for a place to take care of some business.'

'What kind of business?'

I smiled.

'I had to take a leak, Agent Dei.'

Now she smiled.

'Oh, and then you just happened to stumble onto our little outpost here.'

'Something like that.'

'Something like that.'

'It is hard to miss. How many bodies you got out there?'

'What makes you ask that? Who said anything about bodies?'

I smiled and shook my head. She was going to play it hard all the way.

'Do you mind if we take a look inside your car, Mr. Bosch?' she asked.

'I think you probably already have.'

'And what makes you think that?'

'I was a cop in L.A. I worked with the FBI before.'

'And so you know it all.'

'Put it this way, I know what a body dig smells like and I know you've looked in my car. You just want to get my permission now to cover your ass. I'm not giving it to you. Stay out of my car.'

I looked at Zigo and then over at Walling. It was then that I placed her and a whole profusion of questions came up out of the depths.

'I remember you now,' I said. 'It's Rachel, right?'

'Excuse me?' Walling asked.

'We actually met once. A long time ago in L.A. In Hollywood Division. You were out from Quantico. You were chasing the Poet and you thought one of the guys on the table was the next target. All the time you were right there with the Poet.'

'You worked homicides?'

'That's right.'

'How is Ed Thomas?'

'Like me, he retired. But Ed went and opened a bookstore down in Orange. Sells mystery novels, if you can believe it.'

'I can.'

'You're the one who shot Backus, right? In the house on the hill.'

She didn't answer. Her eyes went from mine to Agent Dei's. There was something I didn't get. Walling was playing the lesser role here, but she obviously should have had seniority on Dei and her partner, Zigo. Then I put it together. She had probably been knocked down a notch or two in the scandal that came in the aftermath of the Poet investigation.

That leap led to another. I took a shot in the dark.

'That was a long time ago,' I said. 'Even before Amsterdam.'

Walling's eyes flared for a split second and I knew I had hit something solid.

'How do you know about Amsterdam?' Dei asked quickly.

I looked back over at her. I pulled out the shrug again and gave it to her.

'I just know, I guess. Is that what this is about? Is that the Poet's work out there? He's back, isn't he?'

Dei looked at Zigo and signaled him to the door. He got up and left the RV. Dei then leaned forward so that I would not misunderstand the severity of the situation and her words.

'We want to know what you are doing here, Mr. Bosch. And you are not going anywhere until we get what we want.'

I mirrored her posture by leaning forward. Our faces were two feet apart.

'Your guy at the checkpoint took my license. I'm sure you took a look at it and know what I do. I'm working a case. And it's confidential.'

Zigo came back in. He was short and squat, must've just made it in over bureau regs. His hair was cut short like a military man's. He carried Terry McCaleb's file on the missing men in his hand. I knew inside it were the photos I had printed from Terry's computer. Zigo put the file down in front of Dei and she opened it. The photo of the old boat was on top. She lifted it and slid it across to me.

'Where did you get this?'

'That's confidential.'

'Who are you working for?'

'That's confidential.'

She flipped through the photos and came to the surreptitious shot Terry had taken of Shandy. She held it up to me.

'Who is this?'

'I don't know for sure but I'm thinking it's the long lost Robert Backus.'

'What?' Walling exclaimed.

She reached over and grabbed the photo out of Dei's hands. I watched her eyes flick back and forth as she studied it.

'Jesus Christ!' she whispered.

She got up and walked with the photo over to the kitchen counter. She put it down and studied it some more.

'Rachel?' Dei asked. 'Don't say anything else.'

Dei turned back to the file. She spread the other photos of Shandy out on the table. She then looked back up at me. There was fire in her eyes now.

'Where did you take these photos?'

'I didn't.'

'Who did? And don't say it's confidential again, Bosch, or you are going to find yourself in a deep dark hole until it becomes *un*-confidential. This is your last chance.'

I had been in one of the FBI's deep dark holes before. I knew if I had to I could take her best shot. But the truth was I wanted to help. I knew I should help. I had to balance that desire with what would be the best move for Graciela McCaleb. I had a client and I had to protect her.

'Tell you what,' I said. 'I want to help. And I want you to help me. Let me make a phone call and see if I can't get released from confidentiality. How does that sound?'

'You need a phone?'

'I have one. I just don't know if it works out here.'

'It will. We put up a repeater.'

'That's nice. You guys think of everything.'

'Make your call.'

'I need to do it in private.'

'Then we'll leave you here. Five minutes, Mr. Bosch.'

I was back to Mr. Bosch with her. That was an improvement.

'Actually, I would rather you wait here while I took a walk out in the desert. More private that way.'

'Suit yourself. Just do it.'

I left Rachel standing at the counter staring at the photo and Dei at the table looking at the file. I was escorted out of the RV and out to the open desert near the makeshift helicopter landing pad. Zigo stopped and let me walk on out by myself. He lit a smoke and kept his eyes on me. I pulled out my phone and checked the screen showing my last ten calls. I chose Buddy Lockridge's number and called it. I knew I had a good shot at reaching him because his phone was a cell.

'Yeah?'

It didn't sound like him.

'Buddy?'

'Yeah, who is this?'

'It's Bosch, where are you?'

'I'm in bed, man. You always call me in bed.'

I looked at my watch. It was past noon.

'Well, get up. I'm putting you to work.'

His voice immediately took on an alertness.

'I'm up. What do you want me to do?'

I tried to quickly put together a plan. On the one hand I was annoyed with myself for not bringing McCaleb's computer with me, but on the other hand I knew that if I had brought it, then it would be in the bureau's hands now and not much use to me.

'I need you to get to *The Following Sea* as fast as you can. In fact, take a helicopter and I'll pay you back. Just get over there and get on the boat.'

'Not a problem. Then what?'

'Go on Terry's computer and into the photos. Print out the front and side shots of Shandy. Can you do that?'

'Yeah, but I thought you already printed—'

'I know, Buddy, I need you to do it again. Print those out, then go up into the file boxes on top. I forget which box but one of them has a file on a guy named Robert Backus. It's a—'

'The Poet – yeah, I know which one.'

Of course you do, I almost said.

'Okay, good. Take the file and the photos and bring them to Las Vegas.'

'Vegas? I thought you were in San Francisco.'

For a moment that confused me but then I remembered how I had lied to him to throw him off my track.

'Changed my mind. Bring it all to Las Vegas, check into a hotel and wait for my call. Make sure your phone is charged. But don't call me, I'll call you.'

'How come I can't call you when I get in?'

'Because in another twenty minutes I may not have this phone. Get moving now, Buddy.'

'You're going to pay for all of this, right?'

'I'll pay. I'll also pay you for your time. You're on the clock, Buddy, so get moving.'

'All right, I'm on it. You know, there's a ferry in twenty minutes. I could take that and save you a bunch of money, you know.'

'Take a chopper. You'll beat the ferry by an hour. I need that hour.'

'Okay, man, I'm gone.'

'And Buddy? Don't tell anybody where you're going and what you're doing.'

'Right.'

He hung up and I checked Zigo before disconnecting. The agent had on dark glasses now but it appeared he was watching me. I faked like I had lost the signal and yelled *hello* a few times into the phone. I then closed it and reopened it and called Graciela's number. My luck was holding. She was home and answered.

'Graciela, it's Harry. Some things are happening and I need your permission to talk with the FBI about Terry's death and my investigation.'

'The FBI? Harry, I told you I couldn't go to them first. Not until I—'

'I didn't go to them. They came to me. I'm out in the middle of the desert, Graciela. Things I found in Terry's office led me out here and the FBI was already here. I think it is safe to talk. I think the person they are looking for here is the one who hurt Terry. I don't think this is going to come back on you now. I think I should talk to them, tell them what I've got. It might help catch this guy.'

'Who is it?'

'Robert Backus. Do you know the name? Did Terry mention it?'

There was silence while she thought about it.

'I don't think so. Who is it?'

'A guy he used to work with.'

'An agent?'

'Yes. He was the one they called the Poet. Did you ever hear Terry talk about the Poet?'

'Yes, a long time ago. I mean, three or four years. I remember he was upset because I think he was supposed to be dead but it looked like he wasn't. Something like that.'

It must have been around the time that Backus had supposedly resurfaced in Amsterdam. Terry had probably just gotten the internal files on the investigation.

'Nothing since then?'

'No, I can't remember anything.'

'Okay, Graciela. So what do you think? I cannot talk to them unless you allow it. I think it is okay.'

'Then go ahead if you think it will help.'

'It means they'll be coming out there soon. FBI agents. They'll probably take *The Following Sea* back to the mainland to go over it.'

'What for?'

'Evidence. This guy was on the boat. First as a charter and then he came back and snuck on. That was when he changed the meds.'

'Oh.'

'And they'll also come to the house. They'll want to talk to you. Just be honest, Graciela. Tell them everything. Don't hold anything back and it will be all right.'

'Are you sure, Harry?'

'Yes, I'm sure. So you're all right with this?'

'I'm all right.'

We said good-bye and disconnected. As I was walking back toward Zigo I opened my phone again and called my home number. I then disconnected and repeated the process nine more times, wiping out any record on my phone of the calls to Buddy Lockridge and Graciela McCaleb. If things went wrong in the RV and Dei wanted to know who I called, it wouldn't be easy for her. She'd get nothing off my phone. She'd have to go to the phone company with a warrant.

As I approached, Zigo saw what I was doing. He smiled and shook his head.

'You know, Bosch, if we wanted your phone numbers, we would've picked them out of the air.'

'Is that right?'

'That's right, if we wanted to.'

'Wow, you guys are really rather special, aren't you?'
Zigo looked at me over his sunglasses.
'Don't be an asshole, Bosch. It gets tiring after a while.'
'You should know.'

19

Zigo escorted me back in without another word. Agent Dei was waiting at the table. Rachel Walling still stood by the counter. I calmly sat down and looked at Dei.

'How'd it go?' she asked in a pleasant tone.

'It went fine. My client says I can talk to you. But it's not going to be a one-way street. We trade. I answer your questions, you answer mine.'

She shook her head.

'Uh-uh, that's not how it works. This is an FBI investigation. We don't trade information with amateurs.'

'You're saying I'm an amateur? I bring you a photo of the long-lost Robert Backus and I'm the amateur?'

I saw movement and looked over to Rachel. She had brought her hand up to her face to hide a smile. When she saw me looking at her she turned toward the counter and acted like she was studying the photo of Backus again.

'We don't even know if that *is* Backus,' Dei said. 'You've got a guy with a beard, a hat and dark glasses. It could be anybody.'

'And it could be the guy that is supposedly dead but somehow managed to kill five men in Amsterdam a few years ago and now, what, six men here. Or is it more than the six listed in that newspaper story?'

Dei gave me a tight, unpleasant smile.

'Look, you may be impressing yourself with all of this, but we're still not impressed. It still comes down to one thing: you want to get out of here, then start talking to us. Now you have your client's permission. I suggest you start by telling us who this client is.'

I leaned back. She was a fortress I didn't think I could break through. But if nothing else, I had gotten that smile from Rachel Walling. That told me I might have a shot at climbing over the FBI barricade with her later.

'My client is Graciela McCaleb. Terry McCaleb's wife. Widow, I mean.'

Dei blinked, then quickly recovered from the surprise. Or possibly it wasn't surprise. Possibly it was a confirmation of some sort.

'And why did she hire you?'

'Because somebody switched out her husband's medicine and killed him.'

That brought a momentary silence. Rachel slowly stepped away from the counter and came back to her chair. With few questions or any direction from Dei I told them the story of how I had come to be called by Graciela, the details of her husband's tainted medications, and my investigation up until the point I reached the desert. I began to believe I was not surprising them with anything. Rather, it seemed more like I was confirming something or at least telling a story they already knew parts of. When I was finished Dei hit me with a few clarifying questions related to my movements. Zigo and Walling asked nothing.

'So,' Dei said after the story was finished. 'That's an interesting story. A lot of information. Why don't you put it into context for us now. What does it all mean to you?'

'You're asking me that? I thought that's what Quantico does, puts it all into the blender and pours out a case profile and all of the answers.'

'Don't worry, we will. But I'd like your view of it.'

'Well,' I said, but then didn't continue. I was trying to put it all together and into my own blender, adding Robert Backus in as the newest ingredient.

'Well, what?'

'Sorry, I was just trying to put it together.'

'Just tell us what you are thinking.'

'Did anybody here know Terry McCaleb?'

'We all did. What does that have to do with—'

'I mean really know him.'

'I did once,' Rachel said. 'We worked cases. But I hadn't been in touch. I didn't even know he was dead until today.'

'Well, you should know, and will know once you go over there and check his house and his boat and everything else, that he was still working cases. He couldn't let it go. He worked some of his own old unsolveds and he worked new cases. He read the papers and watched TV. He made calls to cops on cases that interested him and offered to help out.'

'And this got him killed?' Dei asked.

I nodded.

'Eventually. I think so. In January the *L.A. Times* ran that story in the file you have there. Terry read it and got interested. He called over to Vegas Metro to offer his services. They shined him on, not interested. But they weren't above dropping his name in the local paper when it ran a follow-up story on the missing men.'

'When was that?'

'Beginning of February. I'm sure you can check. Anyway, that story, his name in that story, drew the Poet to him.'

'Look, we're not confirming anything about the Poet. Do you understand that?'

'Sure, whatever you want. You can take this whole thing as a hypothetical if you want.'

'Go on with it.'

'Somebody was abducting those men – and we now know burying them in the desert. Like all good serial killers he kept his eye on the media, to see if anybody was putting two and two together and getting close. He sees the follow-up story and he sees McCaleb's name. It's an old colleague. My guess is he knew McCaleb back in the day. At Quantico, before Terry came out to set up the Behavioral Sciences outpost in L.A. Before he went down with the bad heart.'

'Actually, Terry was the first agent Backus mentored in the unit,' Walling said.

Dei looked at her like she had betrayed some trust. Walling ignored her and I liked that about her.

'There you go,' I said. 'They had that connection. Backus sees the name in the paper and one of two things happened. He took it as a challenge or he knew McCaleb was relentless and was going to keep coming, despite the apparent lack of interest in him from Metro.'

'So he went after McCaleb,' Dei said.

'Right.'

'And he had to eliminate him in a way that would not raise questions,' Rachel added.

'Right.'

I looked at Zigo. It was time for him to chime in but he said nothing.

'So he went over there and checked him out,' I continued. 'He had the beard, the hat, the glasses, probably a little plastic surgery to go with it. He hired Terry to take him fishing.'

'And Terry didn't know it was him,' Rachel said.

'Terry got suspicious of something but I'm not sure of what. Those photos were part of a series. Terry knew something was up with the guy and took extra photos. But I think that if he knew then that the guy was Backus he would've done something about it. He didn't, and that makes me think he wasn't sure what he had or who the guy was.'

I looked at Rachel.

'You looked at the photo. Can you tell, is it him? I mean, in a hypothetical sort of way.'

'I can't say, hypothetically or not. I can't see his eyes or enough of his face. If it's him he was cut. His nose is different. So are his cheeks.'

'Easily changeable,' I said. 'Come to L.A. sometime. I'll take you to a guy I know in Hollywood who does work for the escort trade. He's got some before and after photos that will make you praise the wonders of medical science.'

'I'm sure,' Dei said, even though I was talking to Rachel. 'Then what? When's he switch McCaleb's meds?'

I wanted to consult my chronology but my notebook was in my coat pocket. They hadn't searched me yet, so I wanted to keep the notebook out of it, maybe get out of there with it.

'Um, about two weeks after the charter Terry's boat was broken into. Whoever it was took a GPS device but I think that was just as a cover in case Terry realized somebody had – what is it?'

I had watched their reactions. The GPS meant something.

'What kind of GPS was it?' Rachel asked.

'Rachel,' Dei cut in quickly. 'You're an observer, remember?'

'A Gulliver,' I said. 'I don't remember the exact model. The sheriff's report is on the boat. It actually wasn't Terry's. It was his partner's.'

'Do you know the partner's name?' Dei asked.

'Yeah, Buddy Lockridge. Don't you remember him from the movie?'

'I didn't see it. Do you know anything more about the history of this GPS device?'

'Buddy told me he won it in a poker game. It had a lot of good fishing spots marked on it. He was pissed off when it got stolen, thought it was another fishing guide who took it.'

I could tell by their reactions that I was hitting every pitch. The GPS was important. It had not been taken simply as a cover. I was wrong about that. It took me a minute but then I put it together.

'I get it,' I said. 'That's how you found this place, isn't it? Backus sent you people the GPS with this place marked. He led you here like he did with Terry.'

'This is not about us,' Dei said. 'It's about you.'

But I glanced at Rachel and saw the confirmation in her eyes. I took the next jump and figured it had been sent to her. That was why she was here as an observer. Backus called her out, just as he had called out Terry.

'You said Terry was the first agent Backus mentored in the unit. Who was the second?'

'Let's move on,' Dei said.

Rachel didn't answer but she gave me that slight smile that looked so sad with those dead eyes. She was telling me I had it right. She came after Terry McCaleb in the mentoring program.

'I hope you are taking appropriate precautions,' I said quietly.

Dei opened the file on the table.

'That's actually no business of yours,' she said. 'Now, there are some things in your notes here I want to ask you about. First of all, who is William Bing?'

I looked at Dei. She thought that it was my file and my notes.

'I don't know. Just a name I came across.'

'Where?'

'I think Terry had written it down. I haven't figured out who it is yet.'

'And this reference to the triangle theory, what does it mean?'

'What does it mean to you?'

'Mr. Bosch, don't annoy me. Don't play cute.'

'Cherie?' Rachel asked.

'What?'

'I think those are probably Terry's notes.'

Dei looked down at the file and realized Rachel was right. I looked at Rachel like I was hurt that she had ratted me out. Dei closed the file abruptly.

'Right. Of course.'

She looked up at me.

'You know what that means?'

'No, but I think you'll tell me.'

'It means we'll take it from here. You can head on back to L.A. now.'

'I'm not going to L.A. I'm going to Las Vegas. I have a place there.'

'You can go wherever you want but stay away from this investigation. We are officially taking it over.'

'You know I don't work for any police department, Agent Dei. You can't take anything over from me unless I want you to. I'm a private operator.'

She nodded like she was understanding of my situation.

'That's fine, Mr. Bosch, we'll be speaking to your employer later today and you'll be unemployed before sunset.'

'I'm just trying to make a living.'

'I'm just trying to catch a killer. So understand me, your services are no longer required. Stay away from it. You're out. You're finished. Can I be any clearer?'

'Think maybe you could put it in writing, too?'

'You know what, I think you should get out of here and go home while you still can. Tom, would you get Mr. Bosch his license and keys and escort him to his car?'

'Gladly,' Zigo said, his first word uttered in the motor home.

I reached for the file but she snatched it away from my grasp.

'And we'll be keeping this.'

'Sure. Happy hunting, Agent Dei.'

'Thank you.'

I followed Zigo toward the door. I glanced back and nodded to Rachel and she did the same to me. I think I saw a trace of light enter her eyes.

20

The three agents were still talking about Bosch when the helicopter lifted off the desert floor and they began the forty-minute journey back to Las Vegas. The three agents wore headphones so they could communicate with each other despite the noise of the rotor wash. Dei clearly remained annoyed with the private detective and Rachel thought that maybe Cherie felt that somehow Bosch had gotten something over on her. Rachel remained amused. She knew they hadn't seen the last of Bosch. He had seen-it-all-twice eyes, and that nod at the end told her he wasn't going to just fold up his tent and go home.

'What about the triangle theory?' Dei said.

Rachel waited for Zigo to go first but as usual he said nothing.

'I think Terry was probably onto something,' she said. 'Somebody should go to work on it.'

'At the moment I don't know if we have the bodies to chase all of this stuff. I'll ask Brass if she's got anybody. And this William Bing – that name hasn't come up before.'

'My guess is that he is a doctor. Terry was coming over here and probably wanted to have a name in case something went wrong.'

'Rachel, when we get back, can you just run that down? I know what Alpert said, you're an observer and all, but if that's just a loose end, then it will be good to nail it down.'

'No problem. I can do it from my hotel room if you don't want him seeing me working a phone.'

'No, stay in the FO. If Alpert doesn't see you he'll start wondering what you're up to.'

Dei, who was in the front passenger seat, turned and looked back at Rachel, who was behind the pilot's seat.

'What was with you two, anyway?'

'What do you mean?'

'You know what I mean. You and Bosch. All the looks, the smiles. "I hope you are taking appropriate precautions." What's going on with that, Rachel?'

'Look, he's outnumbered here, okay? It's natural that he'd pick one of us to play to. It's covered in the manual on interview techniques and tendencies. Check it out sometime.'

'And what about you? Are you playing to him? Is that in the manual, too?'

Rachel shook her head as if to dismiss the whole discussion.

'I just like his style. He acts like he still has the badge, you know? He didn't stand down to us and I think that's sort of cool.'

'You've been out in the boonies too long, Rachel, or you wouldn't say that. We don't like people who won't stand down to us.'

'Maybe I have.'

'So does that mean you think he's going to be a problem?'

'Definitely,' said Zigo.

'Probably,' added Rachel.

Dei shook her head.

'I don't have the people for all of this. I can't spend my time watching this guy.'

'You want me to keep tabs on him?' Rachel asked.

'You volunteering?'

'I'm looking for something to do. So, yeah, I'm volunteering.'

'You know, before nine-eleven and Homeland Security, we used to get whatever we needed. Bagging serials were the best headlines the bureau got. Now it's terrorists twenty-four-seven and we can't even get overtime.'

Rachel noted how Dei pointedly did not say whether she wanted her to check up on Bosch or not. A nice way to have deniability if something went wrong. She decided that once back at the field office she would get Dei alone and get her to run a check on whether Bosch really had a home in Las Vegas. She'd try to find out what he was up to and keep a loose watch on him.

She looked out her window and down at the black asphalt ribbon that cut through the desert. They were following it back to the city. At that same moment she saw a black Mercedes-Benz SUV heading in the same direction. It was dirty from off-roading in the desert. She knew it was Bosch making his way to Vegas. Then she noticed the drawing on the roof of the Mercedes. He had used a rag or something to draw a happy face in the white dust on the roof. The drawing made her smile, too.

Dei's voice came in through the earphones.

'What is it, Rachel? What are you smiling at?'

'Nothing. I'm just thinking about something.'

'Yeah, I wish I could smile knowing that there might be a psycho-agent out there waiting to put a plastic bag over my head.'

Rachel looked at Dei, annoyed by such a snide and brutal remark. Dei apparently saw something in her eyes.

'Sorry. I just think you better start taking this more seriously.'

Rachel looked at her until Dei had to look away.

'You really think I'm not serious about this?'

'I know you are. I shouldn't have said anything.'

Rachel looked back down at the I-15 freeway. They were long past the black Mercedes. Bosch was gone, far behind them.

She studied the terrain for a while. It was all so different yet all the same. A moonscape carpet of rock and sand. She knew it was full of life but all life was hidden. The predators were underground, waiting to come out at night.

'Ladies and gentlemen?' the pilot's voice said in her ear. 'Switch to channel three. You've got an incoming call.'

Rachel had to take her headset off to figure out how to change the frequency. She thought that the headset had a stupid design. When she put the set back on she heard Brass Doran's voice. She was talking rapid-fire the way Rachel remembered she always did whenever something big came up.

' – cent integrity. It definitely came from him.'

'What?' Rachel said. 'I didn't hear any of that.'

'Brass,' Dei said, 'start again.'

'I said we got a match from the bite mark database. With the gum. It's got ninety-five percent integrity, which is one of the highest matches I've ever seen.'

'Who?' Rachel asked.

'Rach, you are going to love this. Ted Bundy. That gum was chewed by Ted Bundy.'

'That's impossible,' Dei said. 'First of all, Bundy's been dead for years, long before any of these men went missing. And he was never known to have gotten to Nevada or California or to have targeted men. Something's wrong with the data, Brass. It's a bad read or—'

'We ran it twice. Both times it came up Bundy.'

'No,' Rachel said. 'It's right.'

Dei turned and looked back at her. Rachel was thinking about Bundy. The ultimate serial killer. Handsome, smart and vicious. He was a biter, too. He had been the only one to really give her the creeps. The others she just felt a loathing and disgust for.

'How do you know it's right, Rachel?'

'I just know. Twenty-five years ago Backus helped set up the VICAP database. Brass remembers. Over the next eight years the data was collected. Agents from the unit were sent out to interview every serial killer and rapist who was incarcerated in the country. That was before I was there but even later, when I was there, we kept doing interviews and adding to the base. Bundy was interviewed several times, mostly by Bob. Right before his execution he called Bob down to Raiford and Bob took me with him. We spent three days interviewing him. I remember that Ted kept borrowing gum from Bob. It was Juicy Fruit. That's what Bob chewed.'

'Then what, he'd spit it back into Bob's hand?' Zigo asked incredulously.

'No, he'd throw it in the trash can. We interviewed him in the death house captain's office. There was a trash can. When we were done each day, Bundy was led out. There were many points when Bob was alone in that office. He could have just taken the gum out of the can.'

'So you're saying Bob more or less went Dumpster diving for Ted Bundy's gum and then held on to it so he could put it in a grave all these years later?'

'I'm saying he took the gum out of that prison, knowing it had Bundy's teeth marks in it. Maybe it was just a souvenir then. But it became something else later. Something maybe to taunt us with.'

'And where'd he been keeping it, in the fridge?'

'Maybe. That's where I'd keep it.'

Dei turned back around in her seat.

'What do you think, Brass?' she asked.

'I think I should've thought of it myself. I think Rachel is onto something. I think Bob and Ted actually got along. He went down there several times to talk to him. Sometimes alone. He could have gotten the gum any one of those times.'

Rachel watched Dei nod her head in agreement.

Zigo cleared his throat and spoke.

'So this was just another way of him coming out and telling us he did this and how smart he was about it. To taunt us. First the GPS with the prints and now the gum.'

'That's what I would say,' Doran agreed.

It wasn't that simple, Rachel knew. She unconsciously shook her head and Zigo, sitting next to her, picked up on it.

'You disagree, Agent Walling?'

She noted that Zigo must have attended the Randal Alpert school of building relations among fellow colleagues.

'I just don't think it is as simple as that. You are looking at it from the wrong angle. Remember, the GPS and his prints came to us first but that gum was in that grave first. He might have intended for the gum to be found first. Before there was any direct connection to him.'

'If that was the case, what was he doing?' Dei asked.

'I don't know. I don't have the answer. I'm just saying, don't assume at this point we know what the plan or even the sequence was supposed to be.'

'Rachel, you know we always keep an open mind on things. We take things as they come and never stop looking from all angles.'

That sounded like a line taped to the wall in the public information office in Quantico, where agents always had pithy policy and procedure statements to deliver over the phone to reporters. Rachel decided to step back from tangling with Dei on this. She had to be careful not to outstay her welcome and she sensed she was nearing that point with her former student.

'Yes, I know,' she said.

'Okay, Brass, anything else new?' Dei asked.

'That was it. That was enough.'

'Okay. Then we'll talk to you at the next one.'

Meaning the next conference room case session. Doran said good-bye and broke off and then the onboard communication link remained silent as the helicopter crossed the dividing line between the harsh undeveloped landscape and the beginning of the sprawl of Las Vegas. As Rachel looked down she knew it was merely a trading of one form of a desert for another. Down there, beneath all the barrel tile and gravel roofs, predators still waited to come out at night. To find their victims.

21

The Executive Extended Stay motel was off the south end of the strip. It had no neon lights flashing in front of it. It had no casino and no floor show. In fact, no executives stayed there. It was a place populated by the fringe dwellers of Vegas society. The addicted gamblers, the take-off men, the sex trade workers, the kind of people who can't leave the place but at the same time can't put down permanent roots either.

People like me. Often when you meet a fellow tenant at the Double X, as the longtimers call the place, they'll ask you how long you've been there and how long you're staying, as if you're working off jail time. I believe that many of the tenants of the motel have had the real experience of jail time and I chose such a place for two reasons. One was that I still carried a mortgage in Los Angeles and could not afford to stay over time at a place like the Bellagio or the Mandalay Bay or even the Riviera. And two was that I didn't want to get comfortable in Las Vegas. I didn't want things to feel right there. Because I knew when it was time for me to go, I just wanted to turn in the key and leave.

I got to Vegas by three and knew my daughter would be home from day care and I could go to my ex-wife's home to see her. I wanted to but I also wanted to wait. I had Buddy Lockridge coming in and I had things to do. The FBI had let me out of the RV with my notebook still in my pocket and Terry McCaleb's map book still in my car. I wanted to put them to good use before Agent Dei maybe realized her mistake and came back to me. I wanted to see if I could make the next step in the case before she did.

I pulled into the Double X and parked in my usual spot near the fence that separated the motel from the private jet stalls on the McCarran tarmac. I noticed that a Gulfstream 9 that was parked there when I left Vegas three mornings earlier was still in place. There was also a smaller but sleeker-looking black jet parked next to it. I didn't know what kind of jet it was, only that it looked like money. I got out and walked up the steps to my one-bedroom efficiency on the second floor. It was neat and functional and I tried to spend as little time there as I had to. The best thing about it was the small balcony off the living room. In the brochures they offered in the rental office it was called a smoking balcony. It was too small a space to actually fit a chair. But I could stand out there and lean on the extra-high railing and watch the billionaires' jets come in. And I found myself doing that often. I found myself standing there and even wishing that I still smoked. Oftentimes one of the tenants from the apartment on either side of my unit would be standing on their balcony smoking when I was out there. On one side was a card counter – or an 'advantage player,' as he called it – and on the other a woman of indeterminate means of income. My conversations with them were perfunctory. Nobody wanted to ask or answer too many questions at this place.

The last two days' editions of the *Sun* were on the worn rubber mat outside my door. I hadn't canceled it because I knew the woman who lived next door liked to sneak over and read the paper, after which she would refold it and put it back in its plastic bag. She didn't know that I knew this.

Inside I dropped the newspapers on the floor and put McCaleb's map book down on the dinette table. I took the notebook out of my pocket and put that down, too. I went over to the sliding door and opened it to let some of the stuffiness out. Whoever had the place before me didn't use the smoking balcony and the place seemed to have a permanent nicotine funk.

After plugging my phone's charger into the wall below the dinette I called Buddy Lockridge's number but the call rang through to voice mail. I disconnected before leaving a message. I next called Graciela McCaleb's number and asked if the FBI had shown up yet.

'They just left,' she said. 'They went through a lot of stuff here and they just went down to the boat. You were right, they're going to take the boat with them. I don't know when I'll get it back.'

'Have you seen Buddy around today?'

'Buddy? No, was he supposed to come by?'

'No, I was just wondering.'

'Are you still with the FBI?'

'No, they let me go a couple hours ago. I'm at my place in Vegas. I'm going to keep working on the case, Graciela.'

'Why? It seems – the agents told me it was a priority investigation now. They think that agent changed his meds. Backus.'

What she was asking was what it was I could do that the august powers of the Federal Bureau of Investigation couldn't do. The answer of course was nothing. But I remembered what Terry had said to Graciela about me. That he would want me on the case if anything ever happened to him. It left me unable to walk away.

'Because it's what Terry wanted,' I said. 'But don't worry, if I come up with anything the bureau doesn't have, I'll give it to them. Just like today. I'm not trying to compete with them. I'm just working the case, Graciela.'

'Okay.'

'But you know you don't have to tell them that if they ask. They might not be happy about it.'

'I know.'

'Thank you, Graciela. I'll call if anything comes up.'

'Thank you, Harry. Good luck.'

'I'll probably need it.'

After disconnecting I tried Buddy Lockridge once more but got voice mail again. I guessed that maybe he was on a plane with his phone turned off. I hoped, anyway. I hoped he had gotten onto the boat and then off before the bureau agents saw him. I put the phone down and went to the refrigerator. I made a quick sandwich of processed cheese and white bread. I had both in the box in case my daughter should want a grilled cheese sandwich when she visited. It was one of her staples. I skipped the grilling and just stood at the counter and quickly ate the tasteless sandwich to fill the void in my stomach. I then sat at the table and opened my notebook to a new page. I used a couple of self-relaxation exercises I had learned years ago in hypnosis class. In my mind I saw a blank chalkboard. Pretty soon I picked up the chalk and started writing in white across the black surface of the board. As best as I could I re-created Terry McCaleb's notes from the missing men file – the notes the FBI had taken away. When I had as much as I could remember on the board, I started rewriting it all in my notebook. I thought that I got most of it, except for the phone numbers and I didn't care so much about them because I could recover them by simply dialing information.

Through the open balcony door I heard the high-pitched whine of jet engines. Another plane was parking out there. I heard the engines quit and it got peaceful again.

I opened McCaleb's map book. I checked every page and found no handwritten notations other than those on the page illustrating southern Nevada and the contiguous sections of California and Arizona. Again, I looked at what McCaleb had done. He had circled the Mojave Preservation Area, which I knew included the Zzyzx Road exit and the location of the FBI's body excavation scene. On the outside margin of the map, he had written a column of numbers and added them up to 86. Beneath this he had drawn a line and written 'Actual – 92.'

My guess was that these numbers corresponded to miles. I looked at the map and found that it noted mile counts between distances on all significant roadways. In a matter of seconds I found numbers that matched the column McCaleb had written on the side of the page. He had added up the mileage counts between Las Vegas and a point on I-15 in the middle of the Mojave. Zzyzx Road was too small and inconsequential to be listed on the map by name. But my guess was that it was the unnamed point on the 15 from which McCaleb had started to add up the mileage.

In my notebook I wrote and added the numbers myself. McCaleb got it right – 86 miles, according to the map. But then he had disagreed or charted a different route, coming up with 92 miles. My guess was that he had driven the route himself and gotten a different count from the map on his car's odometer. This conflict would have occurred because in Las Vegas he would have had a specific destination. The map's mileage counts would have used a different end point in the city.

McCaleb's destination was unknown to me. I had no idea when the markings on the map page had been made or whether they were in any way connected to the case. But I thought they were because he began his count at Zzyzx Road. That could not be a coincidence. There are no coincidences.

From the balcony I heard a cough. I knew it was the woman next door smoking on her balcony. I found her very curious and kept somewhat of a watch on her whenever I was staying at the Double X. She wasn't much of a smoker and she seemed to go out on the balcony only when a private jet was coming into a parking stall. Sure, some people like to watch planes. But I thought she was up to something and that made me all the more curious. I thought maybe she was spotting marks for the casinos or maybe other gamblers.

I got up and walked out through the door. As I stepped out I looked to my right and saw my neighbor throw something backward into her apartment. Something she didn't want me to see.

'Jane, how you doing?'

'Fine, Harry. Haven't seen you around lately.'

'I've been gone a couple days. What do we have out here?'

I looked across the parking lot to the tarmac. Another sleek black jet had parked next to its twin. A matching black limo was waiting near the jet's stairs. A man wearing a suit, sunglasses and a maroon turban was coming out of the plane. I realized I was ruining Jane's surveillance if that was a camera or set of binoculars she tossed back into her place when she saw me.

'The sultan of swing,' I said, just to be saying something.

'Probably,' she said.

She took a drag on her cigarette and coughed again. I knew she wasn't a smoker. She smoked so it would look plausible for her to be on the balcony watching rich men and their airplanes. She also didn't have brown eyes – I had seen her on the balcony one day when she'd forgotten to put in the tinted contacts – and her hennaed black hair was probably not the real color either.

I wanted to ask her what she was up to, what the game or the con or the scheme was. But I also liked our balcony-to-balcony conversations and I wasn't a cop anymore. And the truth was that if Jane – I didn't know her last name – was in the business of separating those rich men from some of their riches, then down deep I couldn't work up a good deal of outrage over it. The whole city was built on the same principle. You roll the dice in the city of desire and you get what you deserve.

I sensed something intrinsically good about her. Damaged but good.

One time when I brought my daughter to the apartment we ran into Jane on the steps and she stopped to talk to Maddie. The next morning I found a little stuffed panther on the doormat next to my paper.

'How's your daughter?' she asked, as if she knew my thoughts.

'She's good. The other night she asked me if the Burger King and the Dairy Queen were married.'

Jane smiled and I saw that sadness in her eyes again. I knew it had something to do with kids. I asked her something I had been thinking about for a long time.

'You got kids?'

'One. She's a little older than yours. I'm not with her anymore. She lives in France.'

That was all she said and I left it at that, feeling guilty because of what I had in my life and because I knew before I asked the question that I was tempting the grief in her. But my question prompted her to ask one she had probably been holding on to for a while, too.

'Are you a cop, Harry?'

I shook my head.

'Was. In L.A. How'd you know that?'

'Just a guess. I think it was the way I saw you walking with your daughter out to your car. Like you were ready to jump on anything that moved. Anything bad.'

I shrugged. She had pegged me.

'I thought that was kind of nice,' she added. 'What do you do now?'

'Nothing really. I'm thinking about it, you know.'

'Yes.'

We were suddenly becoming more than neighbors exchanging superficial conversation.

'What about you?' I asked.

'Me? I'm just waiting on something.'

So much for that. I knew that was the end of the line in that direction. I turned from her and watched another sultan or sheik start his way down the jet's steps. The limo driver was waiting with the door open. It looked to me like the driver had something under his jacket, something he could pull out if the going got tough. I looked back at Jane.

'I'll see you, Jane.'

'Okay, Harry. Say hi to her for me.'

'I will. You be careful.'

'You, too.'

Back at the dinette I tried Buddy Lockridge once more and got the same result. Nothing. I picked up the pen and drummed it impatiently on my notepad. He should've answered by now. I wasn't getting concerned. I was getting annoyed. The reports on Buddy were that he was unreliable. That was not something I had time for.

I got up and went to the kitchenette and took a beer out of the under-the-counter refrigerator. There was a bottle opener on the doorjamb. I cranked the bottle open and took a long draw. The beer cut through the desert dust and tasted good going down. I figured I deserved it. I went back to the balcony door but didn't step out. I didn't want to spook Jane again. Staying inside, I glanced out and saw that the limousine was gone and the new jet was buttoned up tight. I leaned out and checked Jane's balcony. She was gone. I noticed that in the ashtray perched on top of the railing she had butted out her smoke after only a quarter burn. Somebody ought to tell her that was a giveaway.

A few minutes later the beer was gone and I was back at the dinette looking at my notes and McCaleb's map book. I knew I was missing something, I just couldn't touch it. It was there, it was close. But I just couldn't reach out to it yet.

My cell phone rang. Finally, it was Buddy Lockridge.

'Did you just call me?'

'Yeah, I did. But I told you not to call me at this number.'

'I know but you just called me. I thought that meant it was safe.'

'What if it hadn't been me?'

'I've got caller ID. I knew it was you.'

'Yeah, but how did you know it was me? What if it was someone else with my phone?'

'Oh.'

'Yeah, "oh" is right, Buddy. Look, if you're going to work for me you gotta listen to what I tell you.'

'All right, all right, I understand.'

'Good. Where are you?'

'Vegas, man. Like you told me.'

'You get the stuff off the boat?'

'Got it.'

'No FBI?'

'Nah, man. Everything's cool.'

'Where are you right now?'

As I was speaking I noticed something on my notes and remembered something else about the *Times* story on the missing men. Rather, I remembered the circle Terry had drawn on the newspaper clip.

'I'm at the B,' Lockridge said.

'The B? Where's the B?'

'The big B, man.'

'Buddy, what are you talking about? Where are you?'

He whispered his reply.

'I thought everything was on the QT, man. Like they might be listening.'

'Buddy, I don't care if they're listening. Quit with the code. What is the big B?'

'The Bellagio. It's a simple code, dude.'

'A simple code for a simple mind. You're telling me you checked into the Bellagio on my tab?'

'That's right.'

'Well, check out.'

'What do you mean? I just got here.'

'I'm not paying for the Bellagio. Check out and come here and get a room where I'm at. If I could afford to put you in the Bellagio I'd be staying there myself.'

'No expense account, huh?'

'None.'

'All right. Where are you at?'

I gave him the name and address of the Double X and right away he knew I was in a fringe location.

'They got pay-per-view there?'

'They don't have shit. Just get over here.'

'Well, look, I already checked in here. They're not going to give me my money back. They already charged my card and besides, I already crapped in the toilet. That's like implied ownership of the room, you know. I'll stay one night here and then I'll come stay over there tomorrow.'

There's only going to be one night, I thought but didn't say.

'Then everything above what this dump costs is coming out of your pay, man. I didn't tell you to check into the most expensive place on the strip.'

'All right, all right, dock my pay if you want. Be that way. I don't care.'

'All right, I will. You got a car?'

'No, I took a cab.'

'Okay, go down the elevator and get another one and bring that stuff over here to me.'

'Can I get a massage first?'

'Buddy, Jesus Christ, if you don't—'

'I'm kidding, I'm kidding! Can't you take a joke, Harry? I'm on my way.'

'Good. I'm waiting.'

I disconnected without saying good-bye and immediately dropped the conversation from my radar screen. I was excited. I moved on. I thought I had inexplicably solved one of the mysteries. I looked at my re-creation of McCaleb's file notes and at one line in particular.

Triangle theory? – 1 point gives 3

On the newspaper story he had also circled the word *circle* in the Metro detective's quote about the mileage on the rental car of one of the missing men, giving the investigators a large circle in which to look for clues as to what happened to the missing man.

I now believed that McCaleb may have circled the word because he thought it was wrong. The search zone was not a circle. It was a triangle, meaning that the miles on the rental car formed the three sides of a triangle. Point one was the airport, the origin. The renter picked up the car and drove to point two. Point two was the place where he crossed paths with the abductor. And point three was the place where the abductor took his victim. Afterward, the car was returned to point one, completing the triangle.

When McCaleb had written his notes he didn't know about Zzyzx Road. He had one point – the airport car rental return. So he wrote, '1 point gives 3,' because he knew that if one more point on the triangle was identified, it would lead to the remaining point as well.

'One more point of the triangle means we can figure out all three,' I said out loud, translating McCaleb's note from shorthand.

I got up and started pacing. I was jazzed and thought I was getting close. It was true that the abductor could have made any number of stops with the rental car, thereby leaving the triangle theory worthless. But if he didn't, if he avoided distractions and single-mindedly took care of the business at hand, then the triangle theory would hold. His thoroughness might contain his weakness. That would make Zzyzx Road point three on the triangle because that would have been the last stop for the car before it was returned to the airport. And that would make point two the remaining unknown. It was the intersection. The place where predator and prey came together. Its location was not known at the moment but thanks to my silent partner I knew how to find it.

22

Backus saw Rachel pull out of the side lot of the FBI building in a dark blue Crown Victoria. She turned left onto Charleston and headed toward Las Vegas Boulevard. He hung back. He was sitting behind the wheel of a 1997 Ford Mustang with Utah plates. He had taken the car from a man named Elijah Willows, who no longer needed it. His eyes left Rachel's car and held on the street scene, watching for movement.

A Grand Am with two men in it pulled out into traffic from the office building next to the FBI building. It went in the same direction as Rachel's car.

'There's one,' Backus said to himself.

He waited and then he watched a dark blue SUV with triple antennas pull out of the FBI lot and turn right onto Charleston, going in the opposite direction as Rachel. Another Grand Am pulled out behind it and followed.

'There's two and three.'

Backus knew it was what was called a 'sky bird' surveillance. One car to maintain a loose visual surveillance while the subject was tracked by satellite. Rachel, whether she knew it or not, had been given a car with a GPS transponder on it.

All of this was okay with Backus. He knew he could still track her. All he needed to do was follow the follow car and he would get there just the same.

He started the Mustang. Before pulling out onto Charleston to catch up to the Grand Am following Rachel, he reached over and opened the glove compartment. He was wearing surgeon's rubber gloves, size small so they would stretch across his hands and be almost unnoticeable from a distance.

Backus smiled. Sitting in the glove box was a little two-shot vest gun that would nicely complement his own remaining weapon. He knew he had sized Elijah Willows up perfectly when he had first seen him leaving the Slots-o-Fun on the down side of the strip. Yes, he was what Backus had been looking for physically – same size and build – but he had also sensed a detachment about the man. He was someone who dwelled alone and on the edge. The gun in the glove box seemed to prove that. It gave Backus confidence in his choice.

He hit the gas and pulled loudly out onto Charleston. He did this purposely. He knew that on the off chance there was a fourth car, a trailer, the car they would find the least suspicious would be the one with the driver boldly drawing attention to himself.

23

It came down to basic high school geometry. I had two of the three points on a triangle and I needed the third. It was that simple and that difficult at the same time. To get that point I had the total distances of all three sides of the triangle to work with. I sat down, opened my notebook to a new page and went to work with McCaleb's map.

I recalled from the *Times* article that the mileage recorded on the rental car of one of the missing men was 328 miles. Under what I believed McCaleb's theory to be, that mileage count would equal the total of all three sides of the triangle. I knew, thanks to the notations on the map page, that one side of the triangle – Zzyzx to the airport in Vegas – was 92 miles. That left 236 miles for the remaining two sides. That number could be divided in a variety of ways, putting the missing point of the triangle in a myriad of possible positions on the map. What I needed was a charting compass to accurately plot the triangle but I made do with what I had.

According to the map's legend, one inch equaled 50 miles of terrain. I took out my wallet and removed my driver's license. Holding one of its short edges to the legend I was able to determine that the side of the license equaled 100 miles on the map. Working with that I composed a number of triangles that approximated the remaining 236 miles of roadway. I plotted points both north and south of the baseline I had drawn from Zzyzx Road to Las Vegas. I spent twenty minutes working the possibilities, my plotting taking the third possible point of the triangle down into Arizona and as far as the Grand Canyon and then north into the bombing and gunnery ranges under the command and restriction of Nellis Air Force Base. I soon grew frustrated, realizing the possibilities were endless and that I could have already identified the missing point of the triangle and not even know it.

I got up and went to the half-fridge for another beer. Still annoyed with myself I opened the cell and called Buddy Lockridge. The call went through to voice mail without being answered.

'Buddy, where the hell are you?'

I slammed the device closed. It wasn't like I needed Buddy there that moment. I just needed to yell at somebody and he was the easy target.

I stepped back out onto the balcony and checked for Jane. She wasn't there and I felt a glimmer of disappointment. She was a mystery and I liked talking to her. My eyes swept across the parking lot and the jets beyond the fence and caught on the figure of a man standing in the far corner of the lot. He had on a black baseball hat with gold lettering I couldn't read. He was clean-shaven and wore mirrored glasses and a white shirt. His lower half was hidden by the car he stood behind. He seemed to be looking right at me.

The man in the hat did not move for at least two minutes and neither did I. I was tempted to leave the apartment and go down into the lot but was afraid if I lost sight of the man for even a few seconds he would disappear.

We stood locked in our stares until the man suddenly broke from position and started walking across the lot. As he came out from behind the car I saw he wore black shorts and some sort of equipment belt. That was also when I could make out the word *Security* on his shirt and realized he apparently worked for the Double X. He walked into the passageway that separated the two buildings that made up the Double X and was gone from my sight.

I let it go. It was the first time I had seen a security man at the place in daylight but it still wasn't that suspicious. I checked the next-door balcony for Jane again – there was no sign of her – and went back inside to the dinette table.

This time I approached the geometry differently. I ignored the miles and just looked at the map. My prior exercise had given me a general idea of how far and wide the triangle could stretch on the map. I started studying the roadways and towns in this zone. Each time a location interested me I measured the distances to see if I could come up with a triangle of approximately 328 miles.

I had measured out nearly two dozen locations, failing to get even close on the approximation of mileage each time, when I came across a town on the north side of the baseline that was so small that it was denoted by only a black dot, the smallest demarcation of a population center in the map legend. It was a town called Clear. I knew of this place and I suddenly got excited. In a moment of flash thought, I knew that it fit the Poet's profile.

Using my driver's license I measured the distances. Clear was approximately 80 miles north of Las Vegas on the Blue Diamond Highway. It was then another 150 miles approximately on rural routes across the California border and down through the Sandy Valley to the 15 freeway and the third point of the triangle at Zzyzx. Adding in the baseline mileage between Zzyzx and the airport in Vegas, I had a triangle of approximately 322 miles, just 6 miles shy of the total put on the rental car belonging to one of the missing men.

My blood started to jump in my veins. Clear, Nevada. I had never been there but I knew it was a town of brothels and whatever community and outside services are spawned by such businesses. I knew of it because on more than one occasion in my career as a cop I had traced suspects through Clear, Nevada. On more than one occasion a suspect who voluntarily surrendered to me in Los Angeles reported that he had spent his last few nights of freedom with the ladies of Clear, Nevada.

It was a place where men would go privately, taking care to leave no trail that would reveal them as having dipped in such murky moral waters. Married men. Men of success or religious piety. In a strong way it was much like the red-light district in Amsterdam, a place where the Poet had previously found his victims.

So much of cop work is pursuing gut instinct and hunches. You live and die by the hard facts and evidence. There is no denying that. But it is your instinct that often brings those crucial things to you and then holds them together like glue. And I was following instinct now. I had a hunch about Clear. I knew I could sit at the dinette table and plot triangles and map points for hours if I wanted to. But the triangle I had drawn with the town of Clear at the top was the one that held me still at the same time the adrenaline was jangling in my blood. I believed I had drawn McCaleb's triangle. No, more than believed it. I *knew* it. My silent partner. Using his cryptic notes as direction, I now knew where I was going. Using my license as a straight edge I added two lines to the map, completing the triangle. I tapped each point on the map and stood up.

The clock on the wall in the kitchenette said it was almost five. I decided it was too late to go north tonight. I would arrive in near darkness and I didn't want that – that could be dangerous. I quickly put a plan in motion to leave at dawn and have almost an entire day to do what I needed to do in Clear.

I was thinking about what I would need for the trip when there was a knock on my door that startled me even though I was expecting it. I walked over to let Buddy Lockridge in.

24

Harry Bosch opened the door and Rachel could tell he was angry. He was about to say something when he saw it was her and checked himself. That told her he was waiting for somebody and that that somebody was late.

'Agent Walling.'

'Expecting someone?'

'Uh, no, not really.'

She saw his eyes flick past her and check the rear parking lot.

'Can I come in?'

'Sorry, sure, come on in.'

He stepped back and held the door. She entered a sad little efficiency apartment that was sparsely furnished in depressing colors. On the left was a dinette table circa 1960s and she saw on it a bottle of beer, a notebook and a road atlas open to a map of Nevada. Bosch moved quickly to the table and closed the atlas and his notebook and stacked them one on top of the other. She then noticed his driver's license was on the table as well.

'So what brings you over here to this swell place?' he asked.

'Just wanted to see what you were up to,' she said, leaving suspicion out of her voice. 'I hope our little welcome wagon wasn't too difficult for you today.'

'Nope. Comes with the territory.'

'I'm sure it does.'

'How did you find me?'

She stepped further into the room.

'You're paying for this place with a credit card.'

Bosch nodded but didn't seem surprised by the speed or questionable legality of her search for him. She moved on, nodding at the map book on the dinette table.

'Planning a little vacation there? I mean, now that you're not working the case anymore.'

'A road trip, yeah.'

'Where to?'

'Not sure yet.'

She smiled and turned toward the open balcony door. She could see an expensive-looking black jet on the tarmac beyond the motel's parking lot.

'According to your credit-card records you've been renting a place here for nearly nine months. On and off but mostly on.'

'Yeah, they give me the long-term discount. Comes out to like twenty bucks a day or something.'

'That's probably too much.'

He turned and surveyed the place, as if for the first time.

'Yeah.'

They were both still standing. Rachel knew he didn't want her to sit down or stay because of the visitor he was expecting. So she decided to push things. She sat down without being asked on the threadbare couch.

'Why have you had this place for nine months?' she asked.

He pulled a chair away from the dinette and brought it over and sat down.

'It's got nothing to do with this, if that's what you mean.'

'No, I didn't think it did. I'm just curious, that's all. You don't look like a gambler to me – I mean, not with money. And this looks like a place for hard-core types.'

He nodded.

'It is. That and people with other addictions. I'm here because my daughter lives out here. With her mother. I've been trying to get to know her. I guess she's my addiction.'

'How old is she?'

'She'll be six soon.'

'That's nice. Her mother being Eleanor Wish, the former FBI agent?'

'That's her. What can I do for you, Agent Walling?'

She smiled. She liked Bosch. He got to the point. He apparently didn't let anybody or anything intimidate him. She wondered where that came from. Was it from carrying a badge or carrying other baggage?

'You can call me Rachel for starters. But I think it's more like what can I do for you. You wanted me to contact you, didn't you?'

He laughed but not with any humor attached to it.

'What are you talking about?'

'The interview. The looks, the nods and smiles, all that. You chose me as sort of a pen pal in there. Tried to connect. Tried to even it up, turn it from three against one to a game of two on two.'

Bosch shrugged and looked out the balcony.

'That was just sort of a shot in the dark. I … I don't know, I just sort of thought you weren't getting a fair shake there, that's all. And I guess I know what that's like.'

'It's been eight years since I got a fair shake from the bureau.'

He looked back at her.

'All because of Backus?'

'That and other things. I made some mistakes and the bureau never forgets.'

'I know what that is like, too.'

He stood up.

'I'm having a beer,' he said. 'Do you want one, or is this a duty visit?'

'I could use one, duty or not.'

He got up and took the open beer off the dinette table and went to the small efficiency kitchen. He put the bottle in the sink and got two more out of the refrigerator. He cranked off the caps and brought them out to the seating arrangement. Rachel knew she had to be careful and alert. There was a thin line between who played whom in these situations.

'This place comes with glasses in the cabinet but I wouldn't trust them,' he said, handing her a bottle.

'Bottle's fine.'

She took hers and made sure she chinked it off his. She then took a short pull on the bottle. Sierra Nevada, it tasted good. She could tell he was watching to see if she was really drinking. She wiped her mouth with the back of her hand even though she didn't have to.

'That tastes right.'

'Sure does. So what part of this are they giving you? Or do you have to stand around and just keep quiet – like Agent Zigo?'

Rachel gave him a short laugh.

'Yeah, I don't think I've heard him utter a full sentence yet. But then again, I've only been here a couple days. Basically, they brought me in because they didn't have much of a choice. I've got my little back story with Bob Backus and the GPS was sent to me at Quantico, even though I haven't set foot there in eight years. As you picked up on in the RV, this could be about me. Maybe, maybe not, but it cuts me in.'

'And where did they bring you in from?'

'Rapid City.'

Bosch grimaced.

'No, that's good,' she said. 'Before that it was Minot, North Dakota. A one-agent office. I think in my second year there they actually had a spring.'

'Man, that hurts. In L.A. what they do if they want to get rid of you is give you what they call "freeway therapy," transfer you to the division furthest from where you live so you have to fight the traffic every day. Couple years of two-hour commutes and guys turn in their badges.'

'Is that what happened to you?'

'No, but you probably already know what happened to me.'

She didn't respond to that, moving quickly back the other way.

'In the bureau they have the whole country and then some. They don't call it freeway therapy, they call it "hardship posting." They send you where nobody wants to go. And there are a lot of places like that, places they can bury an agent if they want to. In Minot it was all reservation stuff and on the res they don't take so kindly to those of us of the FBI persuasion. Rapid City is only a small improvement. At least there are other agents in the office. My fellow outcasts. We actually have a good time because the pressure's off. Know what I mean?'

'Yeah. How long have you been up there?'

'Eight years altogether.'

'Jeez.'

She waved her free hand dismissively, as if it was all water under the bridge. She knew she was drawing him in. Revealing herself would make him trust her. She wanted his trust.

'Tell me,' he said. 'Was it because you were the messenger? Because you shot Backus? Or because he got away?'

'All that and other things. Consorting with the enemy, chewing gum in class, the usual stuff.'

He nodded.

'Why didn't you just walk away, Rachel?'

'Well, Harry, because I didn't want them to win.'

He nodded again and she could see a gleam in his eyes. She had connected on that answer. She knew it, could feel it, and it felt good.

'Can I tell you something off the record, Harry?'

'Sure.'

'My assignment right now is to keep an eye on you.'

'Me? Why? I don't know if you were listening in that rolling field office today but I was kind of kicked off the case.'

'Yes, and I'm sure you just packed it in and are quitting.'

She turned and looked toward the table, at the map book and his notebook. She then turned back to him and spoke in a stern but even tone.

'My assignment is to watch you and to shut you down hard if you come anywhere near this investigation.'

'Look, Agent Walling, I don't think—'

'Don't suddenly go formal on me here.'

'Okay, Rachel, then. If this is some kind of threat, then all right, message received. I get it. But I don't think you—'

'I'm not threatening you. I'm here to tell you I don't plan to carry out my assignment.'

He paused and studied her for a long moment.

'What do you mean?'

'I mean I've checked you out. You were right about that. I know about you and I know about what kind of cop you were. I know what has happened with you and the bureau in the past. I know all of that and I know you're more than meets the eye. And my guess is that you're onto something, that you told us just enough today to get out of that RV in one piece.'

She stopped and waited and finally he responded.

'Hey, look, if all of that is a compliment, then I'll take it. But what's your point?'

'My point is that I have a history, too. And I'm not going to sit on the sideline while they go after Backus and leave me back in the FO making coffee. Not on this one. I want to get there first, and since this is a betting town I'm betting on you.'

Bosch didn't move and he didn't say anything for a long moment. She watched his dark eyes as he churned through everything she'd said. She knew she was taking an incredible risk with him. But eight years in the Badlands had made her look at risks much differently than she had when she was in Quantico.

'Let me ask you something,' he finally said. 'Why is it they don't have you in a hotel room with two guards on the door? You know, in case Backus shows up. Like you said, this could be all about you. First Terry McCaleb, then you.'

She shook her head, dismissing the idea.

'Because maybe they're using me. Maybe I'm bait.'

'Are they?'

She shrugged.

'I don't know. I'm not privy to everything about this investigation. Either way, it doesn't matter. If he is coming at me let him come. I'm not going to hide out in a hotel room. Not when he's out there and not as long as I have my pals Sig and Glock with me.'

'Oh, a two-gun agent. That's interesting. Most of the two-gun cops I knew had a little too much testosterone to go with all the extra bullets. I didn't like working with those guys.'

He said it with sort of a smile in his voice. She knew he was close to being hooked.

'I don't carry them both at once. One's on the job, one's off. And you're trying to change the subject.'

'Which is?'

'Your next move. Look, you know how they say it in the movies? We can do this the hard way or we can—'

'Hit you in the face with a phone book.'

'Exactly. You're working alone, against the grain, but you obviously have good instincts and probably know things about this we don't know yet. Why not work together?'

'And what happens when Agent Dei and the rest of the FBI hear about this?'

'I take the risk, I take the fall. But it won't be too hard. What are they going to do to me? Send me back to Minot? Big deal.'

He nodded. She watched him, tried to look through those dark eyes to see how his mind worked. Her take on Bosch was that he put case sense ahead of vanity and petty things. He would churn through it and ultimately know this was the way to go.

He finally nodded again and spoke.

'What are you doing tomorrow morning?'

'Watching you. Why?'

'Where are you staying?'

'The Embassy Suites on Paradise near Harmon.'

'I'll pick you up at eight.'

'And where are we going?'

'To the top of the triangle.'

'What do you mean? Where?'

'I'll explain tomorrow. I'm thinking I can trust you, Rachel. But let's take it one step at a time. Are you going with me?'

'All right, Bosch, I'll go with you.'

'You getting formal with me now?'

'Just a slip. I don't want to get formal with you.'

She smiled and she watched him try to read it.

'All right, then I'll see you tomorrow,' he said. 'I have to get ready now to go see my kid.'

He stood up and so did she. She took one more drink from her beer and put it down half finished on the dinette table.

'Eight o'clock tomorrow,' she said. 'You pick me up?'

'Right.'

'You sure you don't want me to drive? Uncle Sugar pay for the gas?'

'That's all right. Can you get the photos of the missing men? I had them on the newspaper clip but Agent Dei took it from me.'

'I'll see what I can do. There's probably a six-pack that won't be missed at the FO.'

'And one other thing. Bring both your friends.'

'What friends?'

'Sig and Glock.'

She smiled and shook her head at him.

'You can't carry a weapon now, can you? Legally, anyway.'

'No, I can't. I don't.'

'Must feel naked.'

'Yeah, you could say that.'

She gave him another smile.

'Well, I'm not giving you a weapon, Harry. No way.'

He shrugged.

'Had to ask.'

He opened the door and she walked out. After he closed it she walked down the steps to the parking lot and looked back up at the door. She wondered if he was watching her through the peephole. She got into the Crown Vic she had signed out of the car pool. She knew she was close to the edge of trouble. What she had revealed to Bosch and agreed to do the next day with him guaranteed the final stage of the destruction of her career if things went sideways. But she didn't care. It was a gambling town. She trusted Bosch and she trusted herself. She would not let them win.

As she backed the Crown Vic out she noticed a cab pull to a stop in the parking lot. A chubby man with sun-bleached hair and a loud Hawaiian shirt got out and studied the numbers on the doors of the rooms. He was carrying a thick envelope or a file folder that looked yellowed and old. Rachel watched as he bounded up the steps and walked to number 22, Bosch's door. The door was opened before he had to knock.

Rachel backed out and drove out of the lot onto Koval. She drove around the block and parked in a spot that gave her a good view of both of the parking lot exits of Bosch's sorry motel. She was sure Bosch was up to something and she was going to find out what it was.

25

Backus had caught only a glimpse of the man who answered the motel room door when Rachel Walling knocked. But he thought he recognized him from a time many years before. He felt his pulse quicken. If he was right about the man she was meeting in room 22, then the stakes had grown considerably higher.

He studied the motel and his situation. He had located the three bureau surveillance cars. The agents were hanging back. One agent had deployed and was sitting across Koval on a bus bench. He looked out of place, wearing a gray suit and supposedly waiting for a bus, but that was the FBI's style.

That left the motel clear for Backus to move about. It was L-shaped with parking on all sides. He realized that if he was on the other side of the building, he might catch another glimpse of the man Rachel was with through a rear window or balcony.

He decided not to risk moving the car from the front parking lot to the rear. It might draw the attention of the bench warmer across the street. Instead he cracked the door and slipped out of his car. He had the interior light switched off so there was no threat of exposure. He crab-walked between two other cars and straightened up, pulling a baseball cap over his head and yanking the brim down as he emerged. The hat said UNLV on it.

Backus walked through the breezeway on the bottom floor of the two-story motel. He passed the soda and candy machines and came out on the other side and started walking through the rear parking lot as if looking for his car. He glanced up at the lighted balcony that he believed corresponded with the door to room 22, where he had seen Rachel enter. He could see the sliding door was open.

Glancing around as if looking for his lost car, Backus saw that the agent on the bench did not have a visual angle on the rear lot. No one was watching him here. He casually moved to a position directly below the balcony of room 22. He tried to listen for any verbal morsel that would spill through the open slider. He heard Rachel's voice but could not make out the words until he very clearly heard her say, 'Must feel naked.'

This confused and intrigued him. He was thinking about the possibility of climbing up to the second level so that he could hear the conversation in room 22. The sound of a door shutting ended that idea. He guessed Rachel had just left. Backus returned to the breezeway and hid behind a Coke machine when he heard a car's ignition fire. He waited and listened. He detected the sound of another car entering the lot. He moved from the Coke machine to the corner and glanced out. A man was getting out of a taxi and Backus recognized him, too. It was Terry McCaleb's charter partner. There was no doubt. Backus felt like he had just tripped across a treasure of intrigue and mystery. What was Rachel up to? How had she connected with the charter partner so quickly? And what was the LAPD doing here?

He looked past the taxi and saw Rachel's Crown Victoria pull out onto the street and drive away. He waited a moment and saw one of the Grand Ams stop and pick up the man on the bus bench and then take off. Backus yanked the brim of his hat down again and stepped out of the breezeway. He walked toward his car.

26

I was looking through the peephole, thinking about Agent Walling, and wondering how the brutal terrain of the FBI and the Dakotas had not robbed her of her fire and sense of humor. I liked her for that and sensed a connection. I was thinking that I might be able to trust her at the same time I was thinking I had just been played by a pro. I was sure she hadn't told me everything she was up to, nobody ever does, but she had told me enough. We wanted the same thing, maybe for different reasons. But I wasn't second-guessing my decision to take on the extra rider in the morning.

The view through the peephole was suddenly filled with the concave image of Buddy Lockridge. I opened the door before he could knock and quickly pulled him inside. I wondered if Walling had seen him on her way out.

'Perfect timing, Buddy. Did anybody talk to you or stop you out there?'

'Where, here?'

'Yeah, here.'

'No, I just got out of the cab.'

'Okay, then where have you been?'

He explained his lateness by saying there were no cabs at the Bellagio, a story I didn't believe. I saw one of the pockets of his jeans bulging when I took from him the two files he carried.

'That's bullshit, Buddy. Cabs can be hard to find in this town but not at the Bellagio. There are always cabs there.'

I reached over and slapped my hand against his full pocket.

'You stopped to play, didn't you? You've got a pocket full of chips there.'

'Look, I stopped to play a couple quick shots of blackjack before coming. But I got lucky, man. I couldn't lose. Look at this.'

He reached into the pocket and pulled out a handful of five-dollar chips.

'I was kicking ass! And you can't walk away from good luck.'

'Yeah, great. That will help you pay for that room you've got.'

Buddy looked around my place, taking it in. Through the open balcony there was traffic and jetliner noise.

'Gladly,' he said. 'I ain't going to stay here.'

I almost laughed, considering what I had seen of his boat.

'Well, you're welcome to stay wherever you want because I don't need you out here anymore. Thanks for bringing the files.'

His eyes widened.

'What?'

'I've got a new partner. The FBI. So you can go back to L.A. as soon as you want or you can play blackjack until you own the Bellagio. I'll pay the airfare, like I said, and for the chopper ride to the island and forty bucks toward the room. That's the daily rate at this place.'

I held up the files.

'I'll throw in a couple hundred for your time getting these and getting here.'

'No way, man. I came all the way out here, man. I can still help. I've worked with the agents before, when me and Terry worked a thing.'

'That was then, Buddy, this is now. Come on. I'll give you a ride back to your hotel. I hear cabs are scarce and I'm going that way anyway.'

After closing the balcony door I walked him out of the apartment and locked up. I brought the files with me for reading later. As we were walking down the steps to the parking lot I looked around for the security man but didn't see him. I looked around for Rachel Walling and didn't see her either. I did see my neighbor Jane putting a shoebox into the trunk of a car, a white Monte Carlo. From my angle on the steps I could see the trunk was crowded with other, larger boxes.

'You're better off with me,' Buddy said, protest still clinging to his voice. 'You can't trust the bureau, man. Terry was in it and he didn't even trust them.'

'I know, Buddy. I've been dealing with the bureau for thirty years.'

He just shook his head. I watched Jane get in her car and back out. I wondered if it was the last time I would see her. I wondered if my telling her I had been a cop had spooked her and made her split. Maybe she had heard some of my conversation with Agent Walling through the thin walls.

Buddy's comments about the bureau reminded me of something.

'You know, when you get back there they're going to want to talk to you.'

'About what?'

'About your GPS. They found it.'

'Wow, great! You mean it wasn't Finder? It was Shandy?'

'Think so. But the news isn't all that great, Buddy.'

'How come?'

I unlocked the Mercedes and we got in. I looked at Buddy as I was starting the engine.

'All your waypoints were wiped out. There's only one on it now and you won't catch any fish there.'

'Ah, goddamnit! I should've known.'

'Anyway, they're going to ask you all about it and all about Terry and that last charter. Just like I did.'

'So they're running behind you, huh? Playing catch-up. You're the man, Harry.'

'Not really.'

I knew what was coming. Buddy turned in his seat and leaned toward me.

'Take me with you, Harry. I'm telling you I can help. I'm smart. I can figure things out.'

'Put your seat belt on, Buddy.'

I jumped into reverse before he got a chance and he almost went into the dashboard.

We headed over to the strip and slowly made our way down to the Bellagio. It was early evening and the sidewalks were cooling off and getting crowded. I saw that the overhead trams and walkways were becoming full. The neon from every façade on the street was lighting dusk up like a brilliant sunset. Almost. Buddy continued to lobby me for a part in the investigation but I fended him off at every turn. After we pulled in around the huge front fountain and under the casino's giant entry portico I told the valet man that we were just picking somebody up and he directed me to a curb, telling me not to leave the car unattended.

'Who we picking up?' Buddy asked, new life in his voice.

'Nobody. I just said that. Tell you what, you want to work with me, Buddy? Then stay here in the car for a few minutes so they won't tow it away. I need to run in here real quick.'

'What for?'

'To see if somebody's here.'

'Who?'

I jumped out of the car and closed the door without answering his question because I knew with Buddy that every answer led to another question and then another and I didn't have time for that.

I knew the Bellagio like I knew the turns on Mulholland Drive. This was where Eleanor Wish, my ex-wife, made her living, and where I had watched her do so on more than one occasion. I quickly made my way through the plush casino, around the orchard of slot machines and to the poker room.

There were only two poker tables working. It was very early. I quickly scanned the thirteen players and did not see Eleanor. I checked the podium and saw the table manager was a man I knew from coming here with Eleanor and then hanging out and watching while she played. I went over.

'Freddy, what's shaking?'

'A lot of ass shaking around here tonight.'

'That's good. Gives you something to look at.'

'I'm not complaining.'

'Do you know, is Eleanor coming in?'

It was Eleanor's habit to let the table managers know if she intended to come in and play on a particular night. Sometimes they would save places at tables of high rollers or higher skilled players. Sometimes they would set up private games. In a way, my ex was a secret Vegas attraction. She was an attractive woman who was damn good at poker. That presented a challenge to men of a certain kind. The smart casinos knew this and played to it. Eleanor was always treated well at the Bellagio. If she needed anything – from a drink to a suite to a rude player removed from a table – she got it. No questions asked. And that was why she usually played here on the nights she played.

'Yeah, she's coming in,' Freddy told me. 'I don't have anything for her right now but she'll be coming along.'

I waited before hitting him with another question. I had to finesse this. I leaned on the railing and casually watched the dealer at the hold'em table put down the final deal of the hand, the cards scraping on the blue felt like quiet little whispers. Five people had stayed in for the whole ride. I watched a couple of their faces when they looked at the last card. I was watching for tells but didn't see any.

Eleanor had told me once that the real players call the last card in hold'em the 'river' because it gives you life or takes it away with it. If you've played the hand through to the seventh card, everything rides on it.

Three of the five players folded right away. The remaining two went back and forth to a call and one of the men I had watched took the pot with three sevens.

'What time did she say she was coming in?' I asked Freddy.

'Uh, she said the usual time. Around eight.'

Despite my attempt at being casual about it I could tell Freddy was getting hesitant, realizing his allegiance should be to Eleanor and not her ex-husband. I had what I needed so I thanked him and walked away. Eleanor was planning on putting our daughter to bed and then coming in to work. Maddie would be left with the live-in nanny watching over her.

When I got back to the casino entrance my car was empty. I looked around for Buddy and spotted him talking to one of the valet men. I called to him and waved good-bye. But he came running over and caught me at the door of the Mercedes.

'You taking off?'

'Yeah, I told you. I was just going in for a couple minutes. Thanks for staying with the car like I asked.'

He didn't get it.

'No problem,' he said. 'You find him?'

'Find who?'

'Whoever you were going in there to see.'

'Yeah, Buddy, I found him. I'll see you—'

'Come on, man, let's do this thing together. Terry was my friend, too.'

That gave me pause.

'Buddy, I understand. But the best thing you can do right now if you want to do something for Terry is go back home, wait for the agents to show up and then tell them every single thing you know. Don't hold back anything.'

'You mean including that you sent me over there to the boat to steal the file and get the photos?'

Now he was just trying to taunt me because he finally understood that he was out.

'I don't care if you tell them,' I said. 'I told you, I'm working with them. They'll know it before you even meet them. But just so you have it straight, I didn't tell you to steal anything. I'm working for Graciela. That boat and everything in it belongs to her. Including those files and those photographs.'

I poked him hard in the chest.

'Got it, Buddy?'

He physically backed off.

'Yeah, I got it. I was just—'

'Good.'

I then put my hand out. We shook hands but there wasn't anything very pleasant about it.

'I'll catch you later, Buddy.'

He let go of my hand and I got in and closed the door. I started it up and drove away. In the mirror I watched him go in through the revolving door and knew he would lose all his money back to the casino before the night was over. He had been right. He should never have walked away from luck.

The dashboard clock told me that Eleanor would not be leaving her house for the night's work at the casino for another ninety minutes. I could head over there now but knew it would be best to wait. I wanted to see my daughter but not my ex-wife. To her everlasting credit Eleanor had been kind enough to allow me full visiting privileges while she was working. So that would not be a problem. And I didn't care if Maddie was awake or not. I just wanted to see her, hear her breathing and touch her hair. But it seemed that every time Eleanor and I crossed paths we skidded sideways and anger from both of us ruled the moment. I knew it was best this way, to come to the house when she was not there.

I could've gone back to the Double X and spent an hour reading the Poet file but instead I drove. Paradise Road was much less congested than the strip. It always is. I took Harmon over and then turned north and almost immediately into the parking lot of the Embassy Suites. I thought maybe Rachel Walling might want a cup of coffee and a fuller explanation of the next day's excursion. I cruised through the lot looking for a bureau car that would be obvious to me because of its cheap hub caps and government plate. But I didn't see one. I pulled out my cell, called information and got the number for the Embassy Suites. I called and asked for Rachel Walling's room and was put through. The phone rang repeatedly but was not answered. I hung up and thought for a moment. I then reopened my phone and called the cell number she had given me. She answered right away.

'Hey, it's Bosch, what are you up to?' I said as casually as I could.

'Nothing, just hanging out.'

'You at the hotel?'

'Yeah, why, what's up?

'Nothing. I just thought you might want a cup of coffee or something. I'm out and about and have some time to kill. I could be at your hotel in a couple minutes.'

'Oh, well, thanks but I think I'm going to stay in tonight.'

Of course you can't come out, I thought. You're not even there.

'I'm kind of jet-lagged, to tell you the truth. It always hits me the second day. Plus, tomorrow we've got the early start.'

'I understand.'

'No, it's not that I don't want to. Maybe tomorrow, okay?'

'Okay. Are we still on for eight?'

'I'll be out front.'

We hung up and I felt the first weight of doubt in my stomach. She was up to something, playing me in some way. But then I tried to dismiss it. Her assignment was to keep tabs on me. She'd been upfront about that. Maybe I had this latest thing all wrong.

I made another circuit around the parking lot, looking for a Crown Vic or an LTD, but didn't see one. I quickly drove out of the lot then and back onto Paradise Road. At Flamingo I turned west and went back across the strip and over the freeway. I pulled into the lot of a steakhouse near the Palms, the casino favored by many of the locals because it was off the strip and it drew a lot of celebrities. The last time Eleanor and I had talked civilly she told me she was thinking of switching her allegiance from the Bellagio to the Palms. The Bellagio was still where the money went, but most of that went into baccarat and pai gow and craps. Poker was a different skill and it was the only game where you weren't playing against the house. She had heard through the local grapevine that all the celebrities and athletes that came over from L.A. to the Palms were playing poker and losing lots of cash while they learned. In the steakhouse bar I ordered a New York strip and a baked potato. The waitress tried to talk me out of ordering the steak medium-well but I remained firm. In the places I had grown up I never got any food that was pink in the middle and I couldn't start enjoying it now. After she took the order back to the kitchen I thought about an army kitchen I once wandered into at Fort Benning. There were complete sides of beef being boiled gray through and through in a dozen huge vats. A guy with a shovel was scooping oil off the surface of one of the vats and dumping it in a bucket. That kitchen was the worst thing I had ever smelled until I went into the tunnels a few months later and one time crawled into a place where the VC hid their dead from the army statistic takers.

I opened the Poet file and was settling into a thorough read when my phone buzzed. I answered without checking the ID screen.

'Hello?'

'Harry, it's Rachel. You still want to get that coffee? I changed my mind.'

My guess was that she had hurried to the Embassy Suites so she could be there and not be caught in a lie.

'Um, I just ordered dinner on the other side of town.'

'Shit, I'm sorry. Well, that'll teach me. You by yourself?'

'Yeah, I've got some stuff to work on here.'

'Well, I know what that's like. I pretty much eat by myself every night.'

'Yeah, me too. If I eat.'

'Really? What about your kid?'

I was no longer comfortable or trusting while talking to her. I didn't know what she was doing. And I didn't feel like going over my sad marital or parental history.

'Uh, listen, I'm getting a look from somebody here. I think cell phones are against the rules.'

'Well, we don't want to break the rules. I'll see you tomorrow at eight then.'

'Okay, Eleanor. Good-bye.'

I was about to close the phone when I heard her voice.

'Harry?'

'What?'

'I'm not Eleanor.'

'What?'

'You just called me Eleanor.'

'Oh. That was a mistake. Sorry.'

'Do I remind you of her?'

'Maybe. Sort of. Not now, but from a while back.'

'Oh, well, I hope not from too far back.'

She was referring to Eleanor's fall from grace in the bureau. A fall so bad that even a hardship posting in Minot was out of the question.

'I'll see you tomorrow, Rachel.'

'Good night, Harry.'

I closed the phone and thought about my mistake. It had shot up right out of the subconscious but now that it was out in the open it was obvious. I didn't want to think about that. I wanted to retreat into the file in front of me. I knew I would be more comfortable studying the blood and madness of some other person and time.

27

At 8:30 I knocked on the door of Eleanor Wish's house and the Salvadoran woman who lived there and took care of my daughter answered. Marisol had a kind but worn face. She was in her fifties but looked much older. Her story of surviving was devastating and whenever I thought about it I was left feeling lucky about my own story. Since day one, when I had unexpectedly shown up at this house and discovered I had a daughter, Marisol had treated me kindly. She had never viewed me as a threat and was always completely cordial and respectful of my position as both father and outsider. She stepped back and let me in.

'She sleeping,' she said.

I held up the file I was carrying.

'That's okay. I have work. I just want to go sit with her for a while. How are you doing, Marisol?'

'Oh, I am fine.'

'Eleanor went to the casino?'

'Yes, she go.'

'And how was Maddie tonight?'

'Maddie, she a good girl. She play.'

Marisol always kept her reports to a minimum. I had tried speaking to her in Spanish before, thinking the reason she spoke so little was because of her English skills. But she said little more to me in her native language, preferring to keep her reports on my daughter's life and activities to a few words in any language.

'Okay, well, thank you,' I said. 'If you want to go to bed I'll just let myself out later. I'll make sure the door is locked.'

I had no key to the house but the front door would lock after I closed it.

'Yes, is okay.'

I nodded and headed down the hallway to the left. I entered Maddie's room and closed the door. There was a night-light plugged into the far wall and it cast a blue glow across the room. I made my way to the side of her bed and turned on the bed table light. I knew from experience that Maddie would not be disturbed by the light. The five-year-old's dreams were so deep she could seemingly sleep through anything, even a Lakers playoff game on the television or a 5.0 earthquake.

The light revealed a nest of tangled dark hair on the pillow. Her face was turned away from my view. I used my hand to sweep the ringlets back off her face and I leaned down and kissed her cheek. I turned my head sideways so my ear was closer to her. I checked for the sound of breathing and was rewarded. One little moment of unfounded fear fell away from me.

I walked over to the bureau and turned off the baby monitor, the other half of which I knew was in the TV room or Marisol's bedroom. There was no need for it now. I was there.

Maddie slept in a queen-size bed with a cover spread that had all manner of cats printed on it. With her little body taking up so little space in the bed, there was plenty of room for me to prop the second pillow against the headboard and climb on next to her. I slipped my hand under the covers and placed it gently on her back. I waited without moving until I could feel the slight rise and fall of her breathing. With the other hand I opened the Poet file and started to read.

At dinner I had gotten through most of the file. This included the suspect profile authored in part by Agent Rachel Walling as well as the investigative reports and crime scene photos that accumulated while the investigation was current and the bureau was tracking the killer dubbed the Poet across the country. That was eight years earlier, when the Poet killed eight homicide detectives, traveling from east to west, before his run came to an end in Los Angeles.

Now as my daughter slept next to me I began with the reports that came after FBI Special Agent Robert Backus had been identified as the suspect. After he had been shot by Rachel Walling and then disappeared.

The summary from the autopsy of a body found by a Department of Water and Power inspector in a storm water tunnel in Laurel Canyon was included here. The body was found almost three months after Backus was shot and had fallen through a window of a cantilevered home near the canyon and disappeared into the darkness and brush below. FBI credentials and a badge belonging to Robert Backus were found on the body. The deteriorated clothing was also his – a suit hand-tailored for Backus in Italy when he'd been sent over to consult on an investigation of a serial killer in Milan.

However, scientific identification of the body was inconclusive. The remains were badly decomposed, leaving fingerprint analysis impossible. And parts of the body were even missing, initially presumed to have been taken by rats and other animals foraging in the tunnels. The entire lower mandible and upper bridge were missing, precluding a comparison to the dental records belonging to Robert Backus.

Cause of death could not be determined either, though a gunshot wound channel was found in the upper abdomen – the area Agent Walling reported seeing her bullet strike – and a rib was fractured, possibly by the force of a bullet. No bullet fragments were recovered, however, suggesting a through and through wound, and so no comparison to a bullet from Walling's weapon was possible.

No DNA comparison or identification was ever made. After the shooting – when it was thought that Backus might still be alive and on the run – agents descended on the fugitive's home and office. But they were in search of evidence to the crimes he had committed and clues as to why. They did not plan for the possibility that they might one day need to identify his putrefied remains. In a gaffe that would haunt the investigation and leave the bureau open later to charges of malfeasance and cover-up, no potential DNA receptors – hair and skin from the shower drain, saliva from the toothbrush, fingernail clippings from the waste cans, dandruff and hair from the back of the desk chair – were ever collected. And three months later, when the body was found in the storm water tunnel, it was too late. Those receptors were compromised or nonexistent. The building where Backus had owned a condo mysteriously burned to the ground three weeks after the bureau had finished with it. And Backus's office had been taken over and completely renovated and redecorated by an agent named Randal Alpert, who took his place in the Behavioral Sciences unit.

A search for a blood sample from Backus proved futile and once again embarrassing for the bureau. When Agent Walling shot Backus in the house in Los Angeles a small amount of blood had spattered the floor. A sample was collected but then inadvertently destroyed in the lab in Los Angeles when medical waste was disposed of.

A search for blood that Backus may have given during personal medical examinations or as donations to blood banks proved fruitless. Through his own cunning planning, luck, and bureaucratic malfeasance, Backus had disappeared without leaving anything of himself behind.

The search for Backus officially ended with the discovery of the body in the drainage tunnel. Even though scientific confirmation of identity was never made, the credentials, badge and Italian suit were enough for bureau command to act swiftly in announcing closure to a case that had held wide sway in the media and had severely undercut the bureau's already tarnished image.

But meantime a quiet investigation continued into the psychological backgrounding of the killer agent. These were the reports I now read. Led by the Behavioral Sciences section – the very unit in which Backus worked – this investigation seemed more concerned with the question of why he did what he did than with the question of how he was able to do it under the noses of the top experts in the killing field. This investigative direction was probably a protective measure. They looked at the suspect, not the system. The file was replete with reports of investigations into Agent Backus's early nurturing, adolescence and upbringing. Despite the number of crisply written observations, speculations and summaries, there was very little there. Just a few threads unraveled from the full fabric of personality. Backus remained an enigma, his pathology a secret. He was the case that the best and brightest ultimately couldn't crack.

I sorted through the threads. Backus was the son of a perfectionist father – a decorated FBI agent, no less – and a mother he never knew. The father was reported to have been physically brutal to the boy, possibly blaming him for the mother's abandonment of the family, and punished him severely for infractions that included bed-wetting and taunting of neighborhood pets. One report came from a seventh-grade classmate who reported that Robert Backus had once confided that when he was young his father punished him for bed-wetting by handcuffing him to a towel rack in the bathroom shower enclosure. Another former classmate reported that Backus once claimed that he slept each night with a pillow and a blanket in a bathtub because he feared the punishment that wetting the bed might bring. A childhood neighbor reported suspicions that it had been Backus who had killed a pet Dachshund by cutting the dog in half and leaving its parts in a vacant lot.

As an adult Backus exhibited obsessive-compulsive tendencies. He had fixations on cleanliness and order. Many testimonials in this regard came from fellow agents in Behavioral Sciences. Backus was well known in the unit for delaying scheduled meetings for many minutes while he was in the restroom washing his hands. No one ever saw him eat anything for lunch in the cafeteria at Quantico but a simple grilled cheese sandwich. Every day, a grilled cheese sandwich. He also compulsively chewed gum and would take great pains to make sure he was never out of the Juicy Fruit brand he liked. One agent described his chewing as measured, meaning he believed that Backus may have counted the number of times he chewed each stick of gum, and when a specific number was reached he would then remove the gum and start over with a fresh stick.

There was a report on an interview with a former fiancée. She told the reporting agent that Backus required her to shower often and extensively, particularly before and after they made love. She said that while house hunting before the nuptials he told her he would want to have his own bedroom and bathroom. She called off the marriage and ended the relationship when one time he called her a slob because she had kicked off her high heels in her own living room.

The reports were just glimpses of a damaged psyche. They weren't really clues to anything. Whatever Backus's strange habits were, they still didn't fully explain why he began killing people. Thousands of people suffer from mild to severe forms of obsessive-compulsive disorder. They don't add killing to their list of personal tics. Thousands were abused as children. They do not then all become abusers.

McCaleb had acquired far fewer reports on the reappearance four years later of the Poet – Backus – in Amsterdam. All that was in the file was a nine-page summary report in which the facts of the killings and the forensic findings were recounted. I had skimmed this report before but now read it closely and found aspects of it tying in with the theory I was formulating about the town of Clear.

In Amsterdam the five known victims were men who were tourists traveling alone. This put them in the same profile as the victims known to be buried in Zzyzx, with the exception of one man who was in Las Vegas with his wife but away from her when she spent the day in their hotel's spa. In Amsterdam the men were last seen in the city's Rosse Buurt zone, where legalized prostitution is carried out in small rooms behind the neon-framed windows where women in provocative clothing offer themselves to passersby. In two of the incidents the Dutch investigators located prostitutes who reported being with the victims the night before their bodies were found floating in the nearby Amstel River.

Though the bodies were found in different locations in the river, the reports indicated that the point of entry into the water for all five victims was believed to have been the area around the Six House. This location was a property owned by an important family in Amsterdam history. I found this of interest, partly because Six House and Zzyzx sounded a bit alike to me. But also because of the question of whether the killer had chosen the Six House randomly or in some attempt to flaunt his crimes at authority by choosing a structure that symbolized it.

The Dutch detectives never got much further with the investigation. They never found the mechanism by which the killer got to the men, controlled them and killed them. Backus would have never even made a blip on their suspect radar if he hadn't wanted to be noticed. He sent the police the notes that asked for Rachel Walling and led to his identity. The notes, according to the summary report, contained information about the victims and crimes that seemingly only the killer would know. One note contained the passport of the last victim.

To me the connection between Amsterdam's Rosse Buurt and Clear, Nevada, was obvious. Both were places where sex was legally exchanged for money. But more important, they were places where I assumed men might go without telling others, where they might even take measures to avoid leaving a trail. In some ways this made them perfect targets for a killer and perfect victims. It added an extra degree of safety to the killer.

I finished my survey of McCaleb's file on the Poet and started through it once more, hoping that I had missed something, maybe just one detail that would bring the whole picture into focus. Sometimes it happens that way. A missed or misunderstood detail becomes the key to the whole puzzle.

But I didn't find that detail on the second go-round and soon the reports just seemed repetitive and tedious. I grew tired and somehow I ended up thinking about that kid handcuffed in the shower. I kept picturing that scene and I felt bad for the kid and angry for the father who did it and the mother who never cared to know about it.

Did this mean I felt sympathy for a killer? I didn't think so. Backus had taken his own tortures and turned them into something else and then turned it on the world. I had an understanding of that process and I felt sympathy for the boy he had been. But I felt nothing for Backus the man but a cold resolve to hunt him down and make him pay for what he did.

28

The place smelled horrible but Backus knew he could live with it. It was the flies that repulsed him the most. They were everywhere, dead and alive. Carrying germs and disease and dirt. As he huddled under the blanket, his knees drawn up, he could hear them buzzing in the darkness, flying blind, hitting the screens and the walls, making little sounds. They were out there, everywhere. He realized he should have known that they would come, that they were part of the plan.

He tried to block out their sounds. He tried to think and concentrate on the plan. It was his last day here. Time to move. Time to show them. He wished he could stay to watch, to bear witness to the event. But he knew that there was much work to do.

He stopped breathing. He could feel them now. The flies had found him and were crawling on the blanket, looking for a way in, a way to get to him. He had given them life but now they wanted to get to him and eat him.

His laugh broke sharply from beneath the blanket and the flies that had alighted on it scattered. He realized he was no different from the flies. He, too, had turned against the giver of life. He laughed again and he felt something go down his throat.

'Aaaggh!'

He retched. He coughed. He tried to get it out. A fly. A fly had gone down his throat.

Backus jumped up and almost tripped as he climbed out. He ran to the door and out into the night. He shoved his finger down his throat until everything came up and came out. He dropped to his knees, gagged and spit it all out. He then pulled the flashlight from his pocket and studied his effluent with the beam. He saw the fly in the greenish yellow bile. It was still alive, its wings and legs mired in the swamp of human discharge.

Backus stood up. He stepped on the fly and then nodded to himself. He wiped the bottom of his shoe on the red dirt. He looked up at the silhouette of the rock outcropping that rose a hundred feet above him. It was blocking the moon at this hour. But that was all right. That just made the stars all the brighter.

29

I put the thick file aside and studied my daughter's face. I wondered what she could be dreaming about. She had experienced so little in her life, what inspired her dreams? I was sure there were only good things waiting for her in that secret world and I wished it would always stay that way.

I grew tired myself and soon closed my eyes to rest for a few minutes. And soon I, too, dreamed. But in my dream there were shadow figures and angry voices, there were sudden and sharp movements in the darkness. I didn't know where I was or where I was going. And then I was grabbed by unseen hands and pulled up out of it, back to the light.

'Harry, what are you doing?'

I opened my eyes and Eleanor was pulling the collar of my jacket.

'Hey … Eleanor … what is it?'

For some reason I tried to smile at her but I was still too disoriented to know why. 'What are you doing? Look at this all over the floor.'

I was beginning to register that she was angry. I pulled myself forward and looked over the edge of the bed. The Poet file had slid off the bed and spilled on the floor. The crime scene photos were spread everywhere. Prominently displayed were three photos of a Denver Police detective who had been shot by Backus in a car. The back of his head was obliterated, blood and brain matter all over the seat. There were other photos of bodies floating in canals, photos of another detective whose head was taken off with a shotgun.

'Oh, shit!'

'You can't do this!' Eleanor said loudly. 'What if she woke up and saw this? She'd have nightmares the rest of her life.'

'She's going to wake up if you don't keep your voice down, Eleanor. I'm sorry, okay? I didn't mean to fall asleep.'

I slid off the bed and knelt on the floor, quickly gathering the file together. As I did so I checked my watch and saw it was almost five a.m. I had slept for hours. No wonder I was so groggy.

Seeing the time also told me that Eleanor was home late. She usually didn't play this long. It probably meant she'd had a bad night and had tried to chase her losses, a bad gambling strategy. I quickly gathered the photos and reports and slid them back into the file, then I stood up.

‘Sorry,’ I said again.

‘Goddamnit, it’s not what I need to come home and find.’

I didn’t say anything. I knew it was a no-win situation for me. I turned and looked back at the bed. Maddie was still sleeping, with her brown ringlets across her face again. If she could sleep through anything, then I hoped she could sleep right through the roaring silence of her parents’ anger toward each other.

Eleanor walked quickly out of the room and in a few moments I followed her. I found her in the kitchen leaning against a counter with her arms folded tightly in front of her. ‘Bad night?’

‘Don’t blame my reaction to this on what kind of night I had.’

I raised my hands in surrender.

‘I’m not. I blame it on me. I messed up. I just wanted to sit with her for a little while and I fell asleep.’

‘Maybe you shouldn’t do that anymore.’

‘What, come visit her at night?’

‘I don’t know.’

She moved to the refrigerator and took out a bottle of spring water. She poured a glass and then held the bottle up for me. I told her I didn’t want any.

‘What is that file anyway?’ she asked. ‘Are you working a case here?’

‘Yes. A murder. It started in L.A. and came over this way. I have to go up into the desert today.’

‘What a nice convenience for you. Along the way you get to drop in here and scare your daughter.’

‘Come on, Eleanor, it was stupid and I’m an idiot but at least she didn’t see anything.’

‘She could have. Maybe she did. Maybe she woke up and saw those dreadful pictures and then went back to sleep. She’s probably having a horrible nightmare.’

‘Look, she hasn’t moved all night. I can tell. She’s been down for the count. It won’t happen again, so can we just leave it at that?’

‘Sure. Fine.’

‘Look, Eleanor, why don’t you tell me about your night?’

‘No, I don’t want to talk about it. I just want to go to bed.’

‘I’ll tell you something then.’

‘What?’

I hadn’t planned on bringing this up but it all sort of snowballed and I knew I needed to tell her.

‘I’m thinking about going back to my job.’

‘What do you mean, the case?’

‘No, the cops. The LAPD has a program. Old guys like me can come back in. They’re looking for experience. If I do it now I won’t even have to go back to the academy.’

She took a long drink of water and didn't respond.

'What do you think about that, Eleanor?'

She shrugged like she didn't care.

'Whatever you want to do, Harry. But you won't see your daughter as much. You'll get involved in cases and ... you know how that goes.'

I nodded.

'Maybe.'

'And maybe it won't matter. She hasn't had you around for most of her life.'

'And whose fault is that?'

'Look, let's not open that can of worms again.'

'If I had known about her I would have been here. I didn't know.'

'I know, I know. I'm the one. It's all my fault.'

'I'm not saying that. I'm—'

'I know what you're saying. You don't even have to say it.'

We were both quiet for a moment, letting the anger ebb. I looked down at the floor.

'Maybe she could come over there, too,' I said.

'What are you talking about?'

'What we talked about before. About this place. About her growing up here.'

She shook her head very deliberately.

'And I haven't changed my mind about that. What do you think, that you're going to raise her by yourself? You, with middle-of-the-night call outs, long hours, long investigations, guns in the house, crime scene photos spread all over the floor. Is that what you want for her? You think that's better than Vegas?'

'No. I was thinking maybe you could come over there, too.'

'Forget it, Harry. I'm not talking about this again. I'm staying here and so is Madeline. You make whatever decision is best for you but you don't make it for me and Maddie.'

Before I could respond Marisol stepped into the kitchen, her eyes creased with sleep. She was wearing a white bathrobe with *Bellagio* written in script on the pocket.

'Very loud,' she said.

'You're right, Marisol,' Eleanor said. 'I'm sorry.'

Marisol went to the refrigerator and got out the water bottle. She poured herself a glass and then put the bottle away. She left the kitchen without further word.

'I think you should go,' Eleanor said to me. 'I'm too tired to talk about this right now.'

'All right. I'm just going to check on her and say good-bye.'

'Don't wake her up.'

'No kidding.'

I went back into my daughter's bedroom. We had left the light on. I sat on the side of the bed closest to her and just watched her sleep for a few moments. Then I brushed back her hair and kissed her cheek. I smelled the scent of baby shampoo in her hair. I kissed her again and whispered good night. I turned off the light and then sat there for another couple minutes, watching and waiting. For what, I don't know. I guess maybe I was hoping Eleanor would come in and sit on the bed, too, that maybe we could watch our sleeping daughter together.

After a while I got up and turned the monitor on again. I left the room to head out. The house was quiet as I walked back through to the front. I didn't see Eleanor. She had gone off to bed, not needing to see me again. I pulled the front door closed and made sure it was locked as I went out.

The loud snap of steel on steel had a finality to it that ricocheted through me like a tumbling bullet.

30

At 8 that morning I was in my Mercedes in front of the lobby entrance of the Embassy Suites on Paradise Road. I had two large Starbucks coffees in the cup holders and a bag of doughnuts. I was freshly showered and shaved. I had changed the clothes I slept in. I had gassed up the car and maxed out my withdrawal limit at the station's ATM. I was ready for a day in the desert but Rachel Walling did not come out through the glass doors. After waiting five minutes I was about to call her when my phone rang first. It was her.

'Give me five minutes.'

'Where are you?'

'I had to go into the FO for a meeting. I'm driving back now.'

'What meeting?'

'I'll tell you when I see you. I'm on Paradise now.'

'All right.'

I closed the phone and waited, looking at the billboard on the back of a cab that was waiting in front of me. It was an advertisement for a floor show at the Riviera. It showed the beautifully proportioned rear ends of a dozen women standing side by side and naked. It made me think about the changing nature of Vegas and what had been mentioned in the *Times* article on the missing men. I thought about all the people who had moved here on the family ticket only to have that ticket punched with this and a thousand other billboards just like it after they got here.

A basic G-car – a Crown Victoria – pulled up next to me from the opposite direction and Rachel put down the window.

'You want me to drive?'

'I want to drive,' I said, thinking it would give me a little slice of control over things.

She made no argument. She pulled the Crown Vic into a parking space and got into my car.

I didn't move the Mercedes.

'Are you going to drink both of those coffees?' she asked me.

'No, one's for you. Sugar's in the bag. They didn't have cream to go.'

'I don't use it.'

She lifted one of the coffees and drank from it. I looked forward, out through the windshield, then I checked the rearview. And I waited.

'Well,' she finally said, 'are we going?'

'I don't know. I think we need to talk first.'

'About what?'

'About what is going on.'

'What do you mean?'

'What were you doing at the field office so early? What's going on, Agent Walling?'

She let out her breath in annoyance.

'Look, Harry, you are forgetting something here. This investigation is of high importance to the bureau. You could say the director is directly involved.'

'And?'

'And so when he wants a ten a.m. briefing, that means us agents in Quantico and out in the field get together at nine a.m. to make sure we know what we're telling him and that there's not going to be blowback on anybody.'

I nodded. Now I got it.

'And nine a.m. in Quantico is six a.m. in Vegas.'

'You got it.'

'So what happened at the ten? What did you all tell the director?'

'That's FBI business.'

I looked at her and she was waiting with a smile.

'But I will tell you because you are about to tell me all of your secrets, too. The director is going to go public. It's too risky not to. It will look like a cover-up if this comes out later in an uncontrolled fashion. It's all about managing the moment, Harry.'

I put the car in drive and headed toward the parking lot exit. I had already plotted my route. I'd take Flamingo to the 15 and then a quick jog over to the Blue Diamond Highway. Then it would be a straight shot north to Clear.

'What's he going to say?'

'He'll hold a press conference late this afternoon. He'll announce that Backus is apparently alive and we're out looking for him. He'll hold up the picture Terry McCaleb took of the man who called himself Shandy.'

'Did they check all of that out yet?'

'Yes. There's no trace line on Shandy yet – it was probably just a name he gave Terry. But photographic analysis and comparison of the photos Terry took and photos of Backus are under way as we speak. The initial report is they're going to come in as a match. It was Backus.'

'And Terry didn't recognize him.'

'Well, he obviously recognized something. He took the pictures, so there was some sort of suspicion. But the guy had a beard, hat and glasses. The analyst on it said he'd also changed his nose and teeth and maybe had cheek implants. There's a lot of things he could have done, even a surgery that would have changed his voice. Look, I looked at the photos and didn't see it for sure and I worked directly with Backus for five years, much longer than Terry. Terry got moved out to L.A. to man the Behavioral Sciences outpost.'

'Any idea where he got all of that done?'

'We're pretty sure we know. About six years ago the bodies of a surgeon and his wife were found in their burned-out home in Prague. The home had a surgical suite and the doctor was the subject of an Interpol intelligence file. The wife was his nurse. He was suspected of being a face man – a surgeon who would change your face for a certain price. The theory was that someone he changed murdered him and his wife to cover the trail. All records he might have kept on the faces he changed were lost in the fire. It was ruled an arson.'

'What connected Backus to him?'

'Nothing for sure. But as you can imagine, everything Backus did or touched as an agent was gone over once he was revealed. His entire case history was audited as much as possible. He did a lot of consulting on cases abroad. Part of the FBI image machine. He went to places like Poland, Yugoslavia, Italy, France, you name it.'

'He went to Prague?'

She nodded.

'He went to Prague on a case. To consult. Young women disappearing and ending up in the river. Prostitutes. The doctor – the face man – was questioned in the investigation because he did the breast augmentations on three of the victims. Backus was there. He helped question the doctor.'

'And he could have been told about the doctor's suspected sideline.'

'Exactly. We think he knew and we think he went there to change his face.'

'That wouldn't have been easy. His real face was on the front of every newspaper and magazine back then.'

'Look, Bob Backus is a psychopathic killer but he is a very smart psychopath. Outside of the made-up guys in books and movies, nobody's ever been smarter at this. Not even Bundy. We have to assume that he had an escape plan all along. From day one. When I put him out that window eight years ago, you better believe he already had a plan in place. I'm talking about money, IDs, whatever he would need to reinvent himself and get away. He probably carried it with him. We assume from L.A. he made his way back east first and then split to Europe.'

'He burned down his condo,' I said.

'Right, we give him credit for that, which puts him in Virginia three weeks after I shot him in L.A. That was a shrewd move. He torched the place and then got to Europe, where he could lie low for a while, change his face and then start again.'

'Amsterdam.'

She nodded.

'The first killing in Amsterdam occurred seven months after the face man burned in Prague.'

I nodded. It all seemed to fit together. Then I thought of something else.

'How is the director going to announce the surprise that Backus is alive when four years ago you had Amsterdam?'

'He's got all kinds of deniability on that. First and most important, that was another director's watch. So he can lay anything he needs to off on him. That's FBI tradition. But realistically, that was another country and it wasn't an investigation we were running. And it was never absolutely confirmed. We had handwriting analysis, but that was really it and that is not in the same league as fingerprinting or DNA when it comes to confirming. So the director can simply say nothing was for sure about Backus in Amsterdam. Either way he's safe. He just has to worry about the here and the now.'

'Manage the moment.'

'FBI one-oh-one.'

'And you people are going along with his going public?'

'No. We asked for a week. He gave us the day. The press conference is at six p.m. eastern time.'

'Like anything's going to happen today.'

'Yeah, we know. We're fucked.'

'Backus will probably go under, change his face again and not turn up for another four years.'

'Probably. But the director won't get hit with any blowback on it. He'll be safe.'

We were silent for a few moments thinking about that. I could understand the director's decision but it certainly helped him more than it helped the investigation. We were on the 15 and I was pulling into the exit lane for the Blue Diamond Highway.

'What happened at the nine a.m., before the director's meeting?'

'The usual round-robin. Updates from every agent.'

'And?'

'And there's not a lot that is new. A few things. We talked about you mostly. I'm counting on you, Harry.'

'For what?'

'For a new lead here. Where are we going?'

'Do they know we're riding together, or are you still supposed to be watching me as in *watching* me?'

'I think they would prefer the latter – in fact, I know they would. But that would be boring and besides, like I said, what are they going to do to me if they find out I'm riding with you, send me back to Minot? BFD, I got to like that place.'

'Minot might not be a big fucking deal, but maybe they'll send you someplace else. Don't they have bureau offices in Guam and places like that?'

'Yes, but it's all relative. I heard Guam isn't that bad – a lot of terrorism angles, which is all the rage. And after eight years in Minot and Rapid City, a change like that might not be bad no matter what the investigations are about.'

'What was said about me at the meeting?'

'It was mostly me, since you are my assignment. I told them I ran a check through the L.A. field office and got your pedigree. I gave them that and told them you went behind the wall last year.'

'What do you mean, that I retired?'

'No, Homeland Security. You ran afoul of them, went behind the wall and came back out again. That impressed Cherie Dei. Made her more willing to let you run a little.'

'I had been wondering about that.'

Actually, I had been wondering why Agent Dei had not simply put the clamps on me.

'What about Terry McCaleb's notes?' I asked.

'What about them?'

'Better minds than mine must have gone to work on them. What did they come up with? What was their take on the triangle theory?'

'It is an established pattern with serials that they commit what we call "triangle crimes." We see it often. That is, the victim can be traced through three points of a triangle. There is their point of origin or entry – their home or in this case the airport. Then there is what we call the point of prey – the place where killer and victim come into contact, where they crisscross. And then there is the point of disposal. With serials the three points are never the same because it is the best way for them to avoid detection. That is what Terry saw when he read that newspaper story. He circled it because the Metro guy was going the wrong way with it. He wasn't thinking triangle, he was thinking circle.'

'So is the bureau working on the triangle now?'

'Of course they are. But some things take time. Right now there is a higher emphasis on crime scene analysis. But we've got somebody in Quantico working the triangle. The FBI is effective but sometimes slow, Harry. I am sure you know this.'

'Sure.'

'It's a tortoise-and-hare race. We're the tortoise, you're the hare.'

'What are you talking about?'

'You're moving faster than us, Harry. Something tells me you figured out the triangle theory and are taking a shot at the missing point. The point of prey.'

I nodded. Whether I was being used or not didn't matter. They were allowing me to stay in the hunt and that was what was important to me.

'You start with the airport and you end with Zzyzx. That leaves one more point – the intersection of predator and prey – and I think I've got it. We're going there.'

'Then tell me.'

'First tell me one more thing about McCaleb's notes.'

'I think I already told you everything. They're still being analyzed.'

'William Bing, who is that?'

She hesitated but only for a moment.

'That's a no-go, a dead end.'

'How so?'

'William Bing is a heart transplant patient who was in Vegas Memorial getting a checkup and some tests. We think Terry knew him and when he was over here he visited him in the hospital.'

'Did you people talk to Bing yet?'

'Not yet. We're trying to track him.'

'Seems odd.'

'What, that he would visit a guy?'

'No, not that. I mean that he would write that on the file if it wasn't connected to the case.'

'Terry wrote stuff down. It's pretty obvious from all his files and notebooks that he wrote stuff down. If he was coming over here to work on this, then maybe he wrote Bing's name and the hospital number down on the file so he wouldn't forget to visit or call him. Could be a lot of reasons.'

I didn't respond. I still had trouble seeing it.

'How did he know the guy?'

'We don't know. Maybe the movie. Terry got hundreds of letters from transplant people after that movie came out. He was sort of a hero to a lot of people in the same boat as he was.'

As we headed north on Blue Diamond I saw a sign for the Travel America truck stop and remembered the receipt I had found in Terry McCaleb's car. I pulled in, even though I had gassed up the Mercedes after leaving Eleanor's house that morning. I stopped the car and just looked at the travel complex.

'What is it? You need gas?'

'No, we're fine. It's just that ... McCaleb was here.'

'What is this? You getting a psychic reading or something?'

'No, I found a receipt in his car. I wonder if this means he went up to Clear.'

'To clear what?'

'No, the town of Clear. That's where we're going.'

'Well, we might never know unless we get up there and ask some questions.'

I nodded and pulled the car back onto Blue Diamond and started north again. Along the way I told Rachel my theory of the theory. That is, my take on McCaleb's triangle and how Clear fit into it. I could tell that my telling it drew her interest. She may have even been excited about it. She agreed with my take on the victims and how and why they may have been chosen. She agreed that it appeared to mirror the victimology – her word – in Amsterdam.

We brainstormed for an hour on it and then grew quiet as we started to get close. The barren, rugged landscape was giving way to outposts of humanity and we began to see billboards advertising the brothels that waited just ahead.

'Have you ever been to one of these?' Rachel asked me.

'No.'

I thought about the steam-and-cream tents in Vietnam but didn't bring them up.

'I didn't mean like as a customer. But as a cop.'

'Still no. But I tracked a few people through them. And by that I mean by credit cards and other means. We're not going to find the people here overly cooperative. At least I never did by phone. And calling in a local sheriff is a joke. The state collects taxes from these joints. A big chunk of it goes back to the home county.'

'I get it. So how do we handle it?'

Almost smiling because she had used the word *we,* I threw the question back at her.

'I don't know,' she said. 'I guess we just go in through the front door.'

Meaning we play it straight and just go in and ask our questions. I wasn't sure it was the right way to go but she had a badge and I didn't.

We cleared the town of Pahrump and in another 10 miles came to an intersection where a sign with CLEAR on it and an arrow to the left was posted. I turned and the asphalt soon gave way to a crushed rock road that kicked up a flume of dust behind my car. The town of Clear could see us coming from a mile away.

That is, if it was looking for us. But the town of Clear, Nevada, turned out to be little more than a trailer park. The gravel road led us to another intersection and another sign with an arrow. We turned north again and soon came to a clearing where an old trailer sat with rust dripping from its rivets. A sign running along the top edge of the trailer said, WELCOME TO CLEAR. SPORTS BAR OPEN. ROOMS FOR RENT. There were no cars parked in the clearing in front of the bar.

I drove on past the welcome wagon, and the new road curved into a neighborhood of trailer homes baking like beer cans in the sun. Few were in better shape than the welcome wagon. Eventually, we came to a permanent structure that appeared to be a town hall as well as the location of the spring the town was named for. We kept going and were rewarded by another arrow on another sign, this one reading simply BROTHELS.

Nevada licenses over thirty brothels across the state. In these places prostitution is legal, controlled and monitored. We found three of those state-licensed businesses at the end of the road in Clear. The gravel road widened into a large turnaround where three similar looking and designed brothels sat waiting for customers. They were called Sheila's Front Porch, Tawny's High Five Ranch and Miss Delilah's House of Holies.

'Nice,' Rachel said as we surveyed the scene. 'Why are these places always named after women – as if women actually own them?'

'You got me. I guess Mister Dave's House of Holies wouldn't go over so well with the guys.'

Rachel smiled.

'You're right. I guess it's a shrewd move. Name a place of female degradation and slavery after a female and it doesn't sound so bad, does it? It's packaging.'

'Slavery? Last I heard these women were volunteers. Some of them are supposedly housewives who come up from Vegas.'

'If you believe that, then you are naïve, Bosch. Just because you can come and go doesn't mean you're not a slave.'

I nodded thoughtfully, not wanting to get into a debate with her about this subject because I knew it would bring me back to examining and questioning things in my own past.

Rachel apparently wanted to drop it there, too.

'So which one do you want to start with?' she asked.

I pulled the car to a stop in front of Tawny's High Five Ranch. It didn't look like much of a ranch. It was a conglomeration of three or four trailers that were connected by covered walkways. I looked to my left and saw that Sheila's Front Porch was of similar design and configuration and it had no front porch. Miss Delilah's to my right was the same and I got the distinct impression that the three seemingly separate brothels were not competitors but rather branches of the same tree.

'I don't know,' I said. 'Looks like eenie, meenie, minie, moe to me.'

Rachel cracked her door open.

'Wait a second,' I said. 'I've got this.'

I handed her the file of photos Buddy Lockridge had brought to Vegas the day before. Rachel opened it and saw the front and side shots of the man known as Shandy but presumed to be Robert Backus.

'I'm not going to even ask where you got these.'

'Fine. But you carry them. It will have more weight coming from you, since you've got the badge.'

'For the moment, at least.'

'Did you bring the photos of the missing men?'

'Yes, I've got them.'

'Good.'

She took the file and got out of the car. I did likewise. We both walked around to the front of the car, where we stopped for a moment and surveyed the three brothels again. There were a few cars parked in front of each. There were also four flat-head Harleys lined up like a row of mean chrome in front of Miss Delilah's House of Holies. Air-brushed on the gas tank of one of the bikes was a skull smoking a joint with a smoke ring forming a halo above it.

'Let's take Delilah's last,' I said. 'Maybe we'll get lucky before we need to go there.'

'The bikes?'

'Yeah, the bikes. They're Road Saints. I say let sleeping dogs lie.'

'Good enough for me.'

Leading the way, Rachel marched toward the front door of Sheila's. She didn't wait for me because she knew I would be following in her wake.

31

Inside Sheila's we were greeted by the sickly sweet smell of perfume mixed with too much incense. We were also greeted by a smiling woman in a purple kimono who did not seem the least bit surprised or put out by the idea of a couple coming into the brothel. Her mouth drew into an edge as straight and sharp as a guillotine's when she saw the FBI credentials Rachel flipped open.

'That's nice,' she said with a falsely pleasant note in her voice. 'Now let me see the warrant.'

'No warrant today,' Rachel replied evenly. 'We would just like to ask a few questions.'

'I don't have to speak with you unless you have a court order telling me to. I run a legal and fully licensed business here.'

I noticed two women dressed in a page from Victoria's Secret sitting on a couch nearby. They were watching a television soap opera and seemingly uninterested in the verbal skirmish brewing at the front door. They were both attractive in a certain way but worn down around the eyes and mouths. The scene suddenly reminded me of my mother and some of her friends. The way they looked to me when I was a boy and I watched them getting ready to go out at night and work. I suddenly felt completely ill at ease in this place and wanted to go. I even hoped the woman in the kimono would succeed in sending us out.

'No one is doubting the legality of your operation,' Rachel said. 'We simply need to ask a few questions of you and … your staff and then we'll be gone.'

'Get the court order and we'll be happy to oblige.'

'Are you Sheila?'

'You can call me that. You can call me anything you want as long as you're saying good-bye when you do it.'

Rachel raised the ante by going to her don't-fuck-with-me voice.

'If I go for that court order, I'm going to first call for a sheriff's unit and I will have that car sit out in front of this trailer until I get back. You might run a legal operation here, Sheila, but which one of these places are all the guys going to pick when they see the sheriff sitting on this one? I figure two hours back to Vegas, a few hours waiting to get in to see the judge and then two hours back. I'm off at five so I probably won't be back till tomorrow. That okay with you?'

Sheila came back hard and swift.

'If you call the sheriff, ask him to send out Dennis or Tommy. They know the place real well and they're also customers.'

She smirked at Rachel and held firm. She'd called her bluff and Rachel had nothing left. They just stared at each other as the moments went by. I was about to step in and say something when one of the women on the couch beat me to the punch.

'She?' the one closest to us offered. 'Let's just get it over with.'

Sheila broke her stare from Rachel and looked at the woman on the couch. She then backed down but her anger remained barely below the surface. I'm not sure there was any other way to handle it once Sheila jumped on us like that, but it was clear to me that all the posturing and threatening was going to end up getting us nothing.

We set up in Sheila's small office and interviewed the women one by one, starting with Sheila and ending with two women who were working when we first entered the establishment. Rachel never introduced me to anyone, so the problem of my standing in the investigation never came up. Uniformly the women could not or would not identify any of the missing men who ended up in the ground in Zzyzx and the same went for the photographs of Shandy on McCaleb's boat.

At the end of a half hour we were out of there with nothing to show for it but an incense intoxication headache for me and stress fractures in Rachel's outlook.

'Disgusting,' she said as we walked down the pink sidewalk toward my car.

'What?'

'That place. I don't know how anyone could do that.'

'I thought you said they were slaves.'

'Look, it's not your job to throw things back at me.'

'Right.'

'What are you so upset about? I didn't see you in there saying anything to her. You were a big help.'

'That's because I wouldn't have done it that way. Two minutes into that place I knew we wouldn't get anything.'

'Oh, and you would have.'

'No, I'm not saying that. I told you, these places are like rocks. It's hard to get water. And bringing up the sheriff was definitely the wrong way to go. I told you, half his pay probably comes from the brothels in his territory.'

'So you just want to criticize and not offer any solution.'

'Look, Rachel, point your gun at somebody else. I'm not the one you're angry with, all right? If you want to try something different in this next place I'll give it a shot.'

'Go right ahead.'

'All right then, give me the photos and you wait in the car.'

'What are you talking about? I'm going in.'

'This is not the place for the pomp and circumstance, Rachel. I should've realized that when I invited you. But I didn't think you'd be shoving your badge down people's throats as soon as you walked in.'

'So you're going to go in there and finesse it.'

'I'm not sure I'd call it finesse. I'm just going to do it the old-fashioned way.'

'Does that mean taking off your clothes?'

'No, it means taking out my wallet.'

'The FBI doesn't buy information from potential witnesses.'

'That's right. I'm not the FBI. If I find a witness this way, the FBI won't have to pay a thing.'

I put my hand on her back and gently directed her to the Mercedes. I opened the door for her and ushered her in. I gave her the keys.

'Turn on the air-conditioner. Either way, this shouldn't take too long.'

I rolled the file up with the photos and put it into my back pocket under my jacket.

The sidewalk leading to the door of Tawny's High Five was also made of pink cement and I was beginning to see the appropriateness of that. The women we had encountered in Sheila's were hard cases with pink lining. And so was Rachel. I was beginning to feel like my feet were in buckets of pink cement.

I buzzed the door and was let in by a woman who was dressed in cutoff blue jeans and a halter top that barely contained her apparently surgically enhanced breasts.

'Come on in. I'm Tammy.'

'Thanks.'

I stepped into the front room of the trailer, where there were two couches facing each other on opposite walls. Three women sat on the couches and looked at me with practiced smiles.

'This is Georgette and Gloria and Mecca,' Tammy said. 'And I'm Tammy. You can choose one of us now or wait for Tawny. She's in the back with a customer.'

I looked at Tammy. She seemed the most eager. She was very small and top heavy and had short brown hair. She would be considered attractive to some men but not to me. I told her she would do just fine and she led me back through a hallway that turned to the right and into another trailer. There were three private rooms on the left and she went to the third one and used a key to open it. We went in and she closed the door but didn't lock it. There was barely enough room to stand because a king-size bed took up most of the space.

Tammy sat down on the bed and patted the spot next to her. I sat and she reached to a shelf full of well-thumbed mystery novels and pulled down what looked like a restaurant menu and gave it to me. It was a thin folder with a caricature drawing on the front. It showed a naked woman on her hands and knees and bent over, turning to look back at and wink at the man who was entering her from the rear. The man was naked, too, except for a cowboy hat and the holstered six-shooters on his hips. One hand was up in the air and holding a lasso. The rope rose above the couple and formed the words *Tawny's High Five.*

'You can get a T-shirt with that on it,' Tammy informed me. 'Twenty bucks.'

'Great,' I said, as I opened the folder.

It turned out that it was a menu of sorts. It was personalized to Tammy. It contained a single sheet of paper with two columns on it. One listed the sexual acts she was willing to perform and the lengths of individual sessions, and the other listed the prices these services would cost the customer. After two of the listed sexual acts were asterisks. At the bottom it was explained that an asterisk denoted a personal specialty.

'So,' I said, staring at the columns. 'I think I might need a translator for some of these.'

'I'll help you. Which ones?'

'How much is it just to talk?'

'What do you mean, like talk dirty to you? Or you talk dirty to me?'

'No, just talk. I want to ask you about a guy I'm looking for. He's from around here.'

Her posture changed. She sat up straighter and in doing so put a couple inches of space between us, which was fine because her perfume was searing my already incense-burned nasal plates.

'I think you better talk to Tawny when she's finished.'

'I want to talk to you, Tammy. I've got a hundred bucks for five minutes. I'll double it if you give me a line on this guy.'

She hesitated as she thought about it. Two hundred bucks wouldn't even cover an hour's work, according to the menu. But I had a feeling the menu prices were negotiable and, besides, there was nobody lined up on the pink cement to get in here.

'Somebody's going to take my money here,' I said. 'It might as well be you.'

'Okay, but it has to be quick. If Tawny finds out you ain't a paying customer she's going to kick you out and put me at the back of the line.'

Now I understood. She had answered the door because she was up. I could have picked from any of the women on the couches but Tammy got the first shot at me. I reached into my pocket for my money and gave her the hundred. I kept the rest in my hand as I pulled out the file and opened it. Rachel had made a mistake asking the women at Sheila's if they recognized any of the men in the photos. That was because she didn't have the confidence I had. I was more certain of my theory and I didn't make that mistake with Tammy.

The first photo I showed her was the front shot of Shandy on Terry McCaleb's boat.

'When was the last time you saw him around here?' I asked.

Tammy looked at the photo for a long moment. She didn't take it from me, though I would have given it to her to hold. After what seemed like an interminable moment, when I thought the door would swing open and the woman named Tawny would order me out, she finally spoke.

'I don't know … at least a month, maybe more. He hasn't been around.'

I felt like climbing on the bed and bouncing, but I kept my cool. I wanted her to believe I knew everything she was telling me. She would feel more comfortable that way and be more forthcoming.

'Do you remember where it was you saw him?'

'Just out front. I walked a customer out and Tom was there waiting.'

'Uh-huh. Did he say anything to you?'

'No, he never does. He doesn't even know me really.'

'Then what happened?'

'Nothing happened. My guy got in the car and they drove away.'

I was beginning to get a picture. Tom had a car. He was a driver.

'Who called him? Was it you or had the client already done that?'

'It was Tawny probably. I don't really remember.'

'Because it happened all the time.'

'Yeah.'

'But he hasn't been around in, what, a month?'

'Yeah. Maybe more. Is that enough of a lead? I mean, what do you want?'

She was looking at the second hundred in my hand.

'Two things. You know Tom's last name?'

'No.'

'Okay, how does somebody get a hold of him if they need a ride?'

'Call him, I guess.'

'Can you get me the number?'

'Just go over to the sports bar, that's where we call him. I don't know the number offhand. It's up there next to the phone in front.'

'The sports bar, okay.'

I didn't give her the money.

'One last thing.'

'You keep saying that.'

'I know but I mean it this time.'

I showed her the six-pack of photos Rachel had brought of the missing men. These were better and much clearer than the photos that had run with the newspaper article. These were full-color candids given to Vegas Metro by their families and then turned over as a courtesy to the FBI.

'Any of these guys your customers?'

'Look, mister, we don't talk about customers. We're very discreet and don't give out that kind of information.'

'They're dead, Tammy. It doesn't matter.'

Her eyes widened and then lowered to the photos in my hand. These she took and she looked through them like they made up a hand of cards. I could tell by the way her eyes flared that she'd been dealt an ace.

'What?'

'Well, this one guy looks like a guy that was here. He was with Mecca, I think. You could ask her.'

I heard a horn honk twice. I knew it was from my car. Rachel was getting impatient.

'Go get Mecca and bring her back here. I'll give you the rest of the money then. Tell her I've got some money for her, too. Don't tell her what I want. Tell her I just want two girls at once.'

'All right, but that's it. You pay me.'

'I will.'

She left the room and I sat on the bed looking around while I waited. The walls were paneled with fake cherry wood. There was one window with a frilly curtain. I leaned across the bed and pulled the curtain open. The view was of nothing but barren desert. The bed and the trailer might as well be sitting on the moon.

The door opened and I turned back, ready to give Tammy the rest of her money and to dive into my pocket for Mecca's share. But there weren't two women in the doorway. There were two men. They were big – one larger than the other – and their arms below their black T-shirts were completely carved up with jailhouse ink. On the bigger man's bulging biceps was a skull with a halo above it and that told me who they were.

'What's up, Doc?' said the bigger one.

'You must be Tawny,' I said.

Without a word he reached down and grabbed two fists full of my jacket. He pulled me up off the bed and tossed me out into the hallway to the waiting arms of his partner. The new one shoved me down the hallway in the opposite direction I had come into the trailer from. I realized that the horn honk from Rachel had been a warning, not a sign of impatience. I was wishing I had read that right when Big and Little Steroid shoved me through a back door and onto the rocky terrain of the desert.

I went down to my hands and knees and was gathering myself and getting up when one of them put his boot on my hip and shoved me down again. I tried to get up again and this time they let me.

'I said, what's up, Doc? You got business here?'

'I was just asking questions and I was willing to pay for the answers. I didn't think that was a problem.'

'Well, pal, that *is* a problem.'

They were advancing on me, the big man first. He was so big I couldn't even see his little brother behind him. I was taking a step backward for every one they took forward. And I had a bad feeling that that was what they wanted. They were backing me toward something, maybe a hole in the ground out there in the sand and rock.

'Who are you, boy?'

'I'm a private detective from L.A. I'm just looking for a missing man, that's all.'

'Yeah, well, people who come here don't want to be looked for.'

'I understand that now. I'll just clear out of here and you won't—'

'Excuse me.'

We all stopped. It was Rachel's voice. The bigger man turned back toward the trailer and his shoulder lowered a few inches. I could see Rachel coming out the back door of the trailer. Her hands were at her sides.

'What's this, you bring your mother?' Big Steroid said.

'Something like that.'

While he was looking at Rachel I clasped my hands together and swung a sledgehammer into the back of his neck. He went forward and into his partner. But the blow was nothing more than a surprise attack. He didn't go down. He wheeled on me and started coming at me, balling his fists into twin sledgehammers. I saw Rachel move her arm under her blazer and flip it back to get to her gun. But her hand caught momentarily in the material and she was late getting to her weapon.

'Hold it!' she yelled.

But the Steroid boys didn't stop. I ducked under the bigger man's first punch but when I came up behind him I was right in front of little brother. He grabbed me in a bear hug and lifted me off the ground. For some reason at this point I noticed that there were women watching from the three back windows of the rear trailer. I had drawn an audience to my own destruction.

My arms were trapped inside of my attacker's embrace and I was feeling severe pressure building on my spine at the same time the air was crushed out of my lungs. Just then Rachel finally freed her weapon and fired two shots into the air. I was dropped to the ground and I watched as Rachel crab-walked away from the trailer to make sure no one could get up behind her.

'FBI,' she shouted. 'On the ground. Both of you on the ground.'

The big men complied. As soon as I got some air back into my lungs I got back up. I tried to dust some of the dirt off my clothes but all that did was spread it around. I looked at Rachel and nodded. She kept her distance from the men on the ground and signaled me over with her finger.

'What happened?'

'I was interviewing one of the women and asked her to bring in another. But then these guys showed up and dragged me out here. Thanks for the warning.'

'I *did* try to warn you. I honked.'

'I know, Rachel. Take it easy. That's what I'm thanking you for. I just misread it.'

'So what do we do?'

'I don't care about these guys. Cut 'em loose. But there are two women inside, Tammy and Mecca, we need to take them. One knows Shandy and the other I think can ID one of the missing men as being a customer.'

Rachel computed this and slowly nodded.

'Good. Is Shandy a customer?'

'No, he's some sort of driver. We need to get over to the sports bar and ask around there.'

'Then we can't just cut these two loose. They might just come meet us again over there. Besides there were four bikes out front. Where are the other two?'

'I don't know.'

'Hey, come on!' Big Steroid yelled. 'We're breathing sand over here.'

Rachel approached the two men on the ground.

'Okay, get up.'

She waited until they were up and staring at her with malevolent eyes. She dropped her gun down to her side and spoke calmly to them, as if this was the way she normally got to know people.

'Where are you guys from?'

'Why?'

'Why? Because I'm trying to get to know you. I'm deciding whether to arrest you.'

'For what? He started it.'

'Not what I saw. I saw two big men assaulting a smaller man.'

'He was trespassing.'

'Last I checked, trespassing was not a valid defense of assault. If you want to see if I'm wrong then keep—'

'Pahrump.'

'What?'

'Pahrump.'

'And do you own these three operations?'

'No, we're just security.'

'I see. Well, I'll tell you what. If you two find the other two whose bikes are out front and go back to Pahrump, then we'll let bygones be bygones here.'

'That's not fair. He was in there asking—'

'I'm the FBI. I'm not interested in what's fair. Take it or leave it.'

After a moment the bigger man broke from his stance and started walking toward the trailer. The smaller big man followed.

'Where are you going?' Rachel barked.

'We're leaving. Like you told us.'

'Good. Make sure you put on your helmets, gentlemen.'

Without looking back the bigger man raised a brawny arm and shot us a bird as he walked. The smaller big man saw this and did the same.

Rachel looked at me and said, 'I hope this works.'

32

The women in the backseat were angry but Rachel didn't care. This was the closest she had been – the closest anybody had been – to Backus since that night in Los Angeles. The night she had watched him crash backward through the glass and into the void that seemed to swallow any trace of him.

Until now. And the last thing she was going to let bother her were the protests of the two prostitutes in the backseat of Bosch's car. The only thing that bothered her was her decision to let Bosch drive. They now had two custodies and were transporting them in a private car. It was a security issue and she wasn't sure yet how they were going to handle the stop at the sports bar.

'I know what we'll do,' Bosch said as he drove away from the three brothels at the end of the road.

'So do I,' Rachel said. 'You'll stay with them while I go in.'

'No, that won't work. You'll need backup. We just proved that we shouldn't split up.'

'Then what?'

'I turn on the child locks on the back doors. They won't be able to open them.'

'And what's to stop them from climbing over to the front seat and getting out?'

'Look, where are they going to go? They have no choice, right, ladies?'

He looked up into the rearview mirror.

'Fuck you,' answered the one named Mecca. 'You can't just do this. We're not the ones who committed any crimes.'

'Actually, as I explained before, we can,' Rachel said in a bored tone. 'You have been taken into federal custody as material witnesses in a criminal investigation. You will be formally interviewed and then released.'

'Well, just do it now and get it over with.'

Rachel had been surprised to learn when she looked at the woman's driver's license that her name really was Mecca. Mecca McIntyre. What a name.

'Well, Mecca, we can't. I already explained that, too.'

Bosch pulled into the gravel lot in front of the sports bar. There were no other cars. He lowered all the windows a couple of inches and turned off the car.

'I'm going to put the alarm on,' he said. 'If you climb over and open the door it will set off the alarm. We'll then come out and chase you down. So don't bother, okay? We won't be gone long.'

Rachel got out and closed the door. She checked her cell phone again and was still not getting service. She saw Bosch check his and shake his head. She decided she would commandeer the phone in the sports bar, if there was one, and call the Vegas FO to report what she had. She expected Cherie Dei to be very angry and pleased.

'By the way,' Bosch said as they came to the ramp leading up to the door of the trailer, 'do you carry an extra magazine for your Sig?'

'Of course.'

'Where, on your belt?'

'That's right, why?'

'Nothing, I just saw back there behind the trailer that your hand sort of got caught in your jacket.'

'It didn't get caught. I just – what's your point?'

'Nothing. I was just going to say that I always carried my extra in my jacket pocket. It gave it some weight, you know. So when you had to flip it back the extra weight carried it all the way back and out of the way.'

'Thanks for the tip,' she said evenly. 'Can we concentrate on this now?'

'Sure, Rachel. You going to take the lead here?'

'If you don't mind.'

'Not at all.'

He followed her up the ramp. She thought she saw a smile on his face in the reflection on the glass of the trailer's door. She opened it, engaging an overhead bell that announced their arrival.

They stepped into a small and empty barroom. To their right was a pool table, its green felt faded by time and stained by drink spills. It was a small table but still did not have enough clearance in the small space. Even breaking a rack would probably require holding a cue at a forty-degree angle.

To the left of the door was a six-stool bar with three shelves of glasses and take-your-pick poison behind it. There was no one in the bar but before Rachel or Bosch could call out a hello, a set of black curtains to the left of the bar split and a man stepped out, his eyes creased with sleep even though it was almost noon.

'Can I he'p you? Kind a' early, idn't it?'

Rachel hit him with the credentials and that seemed to crack his eyes open a little wider. He was in his early sixties, she guessed, though his unkempt bed hair and the unshaven white stubble on his cheeks may have skewed her estimate.

He nodded as though he had just solved some sort of internal mystery.

'So you're the sister, right?' he asked.
'Excuse me?'
'You're Tom's sister, right? He said you might come.'
'Tom who?'
'Tom Walling. Who do you think?'
'We're looking for a man named Tom who drives customers from the brothels. Is that Tom Walling?'
'That's what I'm telling you. Tom Walling was my driver. He told me that one day his sister might come here looking for him. He never said she was no FBI agent.' Rachel nodded, trying to cover the jolt. It wasn't necessarily the surprise that buzzed her. It was the audacity and the deeper meaning, the magnitude of Backus's plan.
'What is your name, sir?'
'Billings Rett. I own this place and I'm also the mayor around here.'
'The mayor of Clear.'
'That's right.'
Rachel felt something tap her arm and looked down to see the file containing the photos. Bosch was giving it to her but staying back. He seemed to know things had suddenly swung. This was now more about her than Terry McCaleb, or even Bosch. She took the file and removed one of the photographs McCaleb had taken of the fishing client known to him as Jordan Shandy. She showed it to Billings Rett.
'Is that the man you knew of as Tom Walling?'
Rett spent only a few seconds looking at the photo.
'That's it. Right down to that Dodgers hat. We get all the games here on the dish and Tom was Dodger blue through and through.'
'He drove a car for you?'
'The only car. I'm not that big of an operation.'
'And he told you his sister would come here?'
'No, he said she might. And he gave me something.'
He turned and looked at the shelves behind the bar. He saw what he was looking for and reached up to the top shelf. He pulled down an envelope and handed it to Rachel. The envelope left a rectangle in the dust on the glass shelf. It had been up there awhile.
The envelope had her full name on it. She turned her body slightly as if to shield it from Bosch and started to open it.
'Rachel,' Bosch said. 'Should you process it first?'
'It doesn't matter. I know it's from him.'
She tore the envelope open and pulled out a three-by-five card. She started to read the handwritten note on it.

Dear Rachel,
If as I hope you are the first to read this, then I have taught you well. I hope this finds you in good health and spirits. Most of all, I hope this

means you have survived your interment within the bureau and are back on top. I hope he who taketh away can also giveth back. It was never my intention, Rachel, to doom you. It is my intention now, with my last act, to save you. Good-bye, Rachel.

R

She reread it quickly and then handed it over her shoulder to Bosch. As he read she continued with Billings Rett.

'When did he give you that and what exactly did he say?'

'It was about a month ago, give or take a few days, and it was when he told me he was leaving. He paid me the rent, said he wanted to keep the place, and he gives me the card and says that it's for his sister and that she might come by looking for him. And here you are.'

'I'm *not* his sister,' she snapped at him. 'When did he first come to Clear?'

'Hard to remember, three or four years ago.'

'Why did he come here?'

Rett shook his head.

'Beats me. Why do people go to New York City? Everybody's got their reasons. He didn't share his particular reason with me.'

'How did he end up driving for you?'

'He was in here shootin' balls one day and I asked him if he needed some work. He said he wouldn't mind and it went from there. It's not a full-time gig. Just when we get a call for somebody looking for a ride. Most people drive themselves up here.'

'And back then, three or four years ago, he told you his name was Tom Walling?'

'No, he told me that when he rented the trailer from me. That was when he first got here.'

'What about a month ago? Did you say he paid rent and then left?'

'Yeah, he said he'd be back and wanted to keep the place. He rented it up through August. But he went traveling and I haven't heard from him.'

From outside the trailer an alarm sounded. The Mercedes. Rachel turned to Bosch but he was already heading to the door.

'I got it,' he said.

He went through the door, leaving Rachel alone with Rett. She turned back to him.

'Did Tom Walling ever tell you where he came from?'

'No, he never mentioned it. He didn't talk much.'

'And you never asked.'

'Honey, you don't ask questions in a place like this. People that come here, they don't like answering questions. Tom, he liked to do the driving and pick up a few bucks and every now and then he'd come in and shoot a game by hisself. He didn't drink, he just chewed gum. He never messed with the whores and he was never late on a pickup. All that was fine by me. The guy I got driving now, he's always—'

'I don't care about the guy you've got now.'

The bell rang behind her and she turned to see Bosch coming through. He nodded to her, telling her everything was all right.

'They tried the door. I guess the child lock doesn't work.'

She nodded and turned her attention back to Rett, proud mayor of a brothel town.

'Mr. Rett?' she asked. 'Where is Tom Walling's place?'

'He's got the single-wide on the ridge west of town.'

Rett smiled, revealing a rotten tooth on the front lower row, and continued.

'He liked being outside of town. He told me he didn't like being so close to all the excitement around here. So I set him up out there behind Titanic Rock.'

'Titanic Rock?'

'You'll know when you get there – if you saw the movie. One of these smart-ass rock climbers that comes out here marked it, too. You'll see it. Just take the road behind this place west and you'll be all right. Just look for the ship going down.'

33

I was outside with the two women in the Mercedes, running the air-conditioning and cooling them down. Rachel was still inside on the bar's phone talking to Cherie Dei and coordinating the arrival of backup. My guess was that agents would soon drop out of the sky in helicopters and descend on Clear, Nevada, in force. The trail was fresh. They were close.

I tried to talk to the two girls – it was hard to think of them as women despite what they did for a living and even though they were old enough. They probably knew everything there was to know about men but they didn't seem to know anything about the world. In my mind they were just girls who had taken wrong turns or been kidnapped and taken away from womanhood. I was beginning to understand what Rachel had said earlier.

'Did Tom Walling ever come into the trailer and hire any of the girls?' I asked.

'Not that I seen,' Tammy said.

'Somebody said he was probably queer or something,' Mecca added.

'Why did they say that?'

''Cause he lived like a hermit or something,' Mecca replied. 'An' he never wanted no pussy even though Tawny would've thrown him some on the house like with the other drivers.'

'Are there a lot of drivers?'

'He was the only one from around here,' Tammy said quickly, apparently not liking Mecca in the lead. 'The others come up from Vegas. Some of 'em work for the casinos.'

'If there are drivers down there, how come somebody would hire Tom to go all the way down and get them?'

'They didn't,' Mecca said.

'Sometimes they did,' Tammy corrected.

'Well, sometimes. The dummies. But mostly we called for Tom if somebody got dropped off and stayed awhile or rented one of Old Billings's trailers and then needed a ride back 'cause his ride was long gone. The casino rides don't wait around too long. Unless you're one of those high rollers and then probably ... '

'And then what?'

'Then you wouldn't come to Clear in the first place.'

'They got prettier girls in Pahrump,' Tammy said matter-of-factly, as if it was strictly a business disadvantage and not something that bothered her personally.

'An' it's a bit closer an' the pussy costs more,' Mecca said. 'So what we get up in Clear is your cost-conscious consumer.'

Spoken like a true marketing expert. I tried to get the conversation back on track.

'So, for the most part, Tom Walling came over and drove customers back to Las Vegas or wherever they came from.'

'Right.'

'Right.'

'And these guys – these customers – could have been totally anonymous. You don't check IDs, right? The customers could use whatever name they wanted when they came in there.'

'Uh-huh. Unless they look like maybe they ain't twenty-one yet.'

'Right. We check the ID of the young ones.'

I could see how it could be done, how Backus could have sized up brothel customers as his victims. If it appeared they had taken measures to guard their identities and hide that they had made the trip to Clear, then they had inadvertently made themselves perfect victims. It also played into what was known about the demons that drove his killing spree. The profile work in the Poet file indicated that Backus's pathology was wrapped up in his relationship with his father, a man who on the outside held the vaunted image of FBI agent, hero and good man, but on the inside was a man who abused his wife and son to the extent that one fled the home because she could, while the one who couldn't get away was left to retreat into a world of fantasies involving the killing of his abuser.

I realized there was something missing. Lloyd Rockland, the victim who had rented a car. How did he fit in if he didn't need a driver?

I opened the file Rachel had left in the car and pulled out the photo of Rockland. I showed it to the women. 'This guy, do either of you recognize him? His name was Lloyd.'

'Was?' Mecca asked.

'Yeah, that's right, was. Lloyd Rockland. He's dead. Do you recognize him?'

Neither of them did. I knew it was a long shot. Rockland disappeared in 2002. I tried to think of an explanation that would allow Rockland to fit into the theory.

'You serve alcohol in there, right?'

'If the customer wants it we can provide it,' Mecca said. 'We got a license.'

'Okay, what happens when a guy drives all the way up from Vegas and gets too drunk to drive home?'

'He can sleep it off,' she responded. 'He can take a room if he pays for it.'

'What if he wants to get back? What if he needs to get back?'

'He can call over here and the mayor will take care of it. The driver will take him back in his car and then the driver just catches a ride back like with one of the casino cars or something. It works out.'

I nodded. It worked out for my theory as well. Rockland could have gotten drunk and had to be driven back by the driver, Backus. Only he wasn't driven back to Vegas. I knew I would have to ask Rachel to check the remains identified as Rockland's for a high alcohol level. It would be another confirmation.

'Mister, are we gonna have to stay here all day?' Mecca asked.

'I don't know,' I said as I looked up at the trailer door.

Rachel tried to keep her voice low because Billings Rett was at the other end of the bar acting like he was doing a crossword puzzle, when she knew he was trying to listen to and understand everything she was saying and that could be heard from the phone.

'What's the ETA?' she asked.

'We'll be in the air within twenty and then another twenty to you,' Cherie Dei said. 'So sit tight, Rachel.'

'Got it.'

'And Rachel, I know you. I know what you will want to do. Stay out of the suspect's trailer until we can go in there with an ERT. Let them do their job.'

Rachel almost told Dei that the fact was that she didn't know her, that she couldn't begin to understand the first thing about her. But she didn't.

'Got it,' she said instead.

'What about Bosch?' Dei asked next.

'What about him?'

'I want him kept away from this.'

'That will be sort of hard since he found the place. This is all because of him.'

'I understand that but we would have gotten there eventually. We always do. We'll thank him but we have to brush him aside after that.'

'Well, you get to tell him that.'

'I will. So are we set? I've got to get over to Nellis.'

'All set. See you inside the hour.'

'Rachel, one last thing, why didn't you drive up there?'

'It was Bosch's hunch, he wanted to drive. What's the difference?'

'You were giving him control of the situation, that's all.'

'That's second-guessing after the fact. We thought we might get a line on the missing men, not be led right to—'

'That's fine, Rachel. I shouldn't have brought it up. I have to go.'

Dei hung up on her end. Rachel couldn't hang up because the phone was stretched from the back wall and over the bar. She held it up to Rett and he put down his pencil and came over. He took the phone and hung it up.

'Thank you, Mr. Rett. In about an hour a couple helicopters are going to land here. Probably right in front of this trailer. Agents will want to talk to you. More formally than I did. They will probably talk to a lot of people in your town.'

'Not good for business.'

'Probably not, but the faster people cooperate, the faster they'll take off and be out of here.'

She didn't mention anything about the horde of media that would also probably descend on the place once it was revealed publicly that the little brothel town in the desert was where the Poet had holed up unnoticed for all of these years and had chosen his latest victims.

'If the agents ask where I am, tell them I went up to Tom Walling's trailer, okay?'

'Sounded like you were getting told *not* to go up there.'

'Mr. Rett, just tell them what I asked you to tell them.'

'Will do.'

'By the way, have you been up there since he came in here and told you he was leaving for a while?'

'No, I haven't managed to get up there. He paid the rent on the place so I didn't think it was my business to snoop around his things. That's not the way we are here in Clear.'

Rachel nodded.

'Okay, Mr. Rett, thanks for your cooperation.'

He shrugged as if to say he either had no choice or his cooperation was minimal. Rachel turned from the bar and headed for the door. But just as she got there she hesitated. She reached inside her blazer and pulled the extra magazine for her Sig Sauer off her belt. She hefted its weight once in her hand and then slipped it into the pocket of her blazer. She then went out the door and got into the Mercedes next to Bosch.

'So,' he said, 'is Agent Dei mad?'

'Nope. We just brought in the case break, how could she be mad?'

'I don't know. Some people have the ability to be mad no matter what you bring them.'

'Are we just going to sit here all day?' Mecca asked from the backseat.

Rachel turned around to look back at the two women.

'We're going over to the western ridge to check out a trailer. You can go with us and stay in the car or you can go into the bar and wait. More agents are on the way. You'll probably be able to get your interviews over with here and not have to go into Vegas.'

'Thank God,' Mecca said. 'I'll wait here.'

'Me, too,' said Tammy.

Bosch let them out of the car.

'Just wait here,' Rachel called to them. 'If you go back to your trailer or go anywhere else you won't get far and it will just make them mad.'

They didn't acknowledge this cautioning. Rachel watched them walk up the ramp and into the bar. Bosch got back in and put the car into reverse.

'You sure about this?' he asked. 'My guess is that Agent Dei told you to sit still until the reinforcements got here.'

'She also said one of the first things she was going to do was send you on your way. You want to wait for that or do you want to go see this trailer?'

'Don't worry, I'll go. I'm not the one with the career to worry about.'

'Such as it is.'

We followed the dirt road Billings Rett had directed us to, and it ranged west from the settlement of Clear and up a sloping landscape for a mile. The road then leveled off and curved behind a reddish-orange outcropping of rock that was exactly as Rett had described it. It looked like the tail-end of the great passenger ship as it drew upward out of the water at a sixty-degree angle and then plunged downward into the sea. According to the movie, anyway. The rock climber Rett mentioned had climbed to the appropriate spot at the top and had used white paint to scrawl 'Titanic' across the rock surface.

We didn't stop to appraise the rock or the paintwork. I drove the Mercedes around it and we soon came to a clearing where there was a small trailer sitting on concrete blocks. There was a junked car on four flats next to it and an oil drum used to burn trash nearby. On the other side was a large fuel tank and a power generator.

To preserve possible crime scene evidence I stopped just outside the clearing and killed the engine. I noticed that the generator was silent. There was a stillness about the whole scene that seemed ominous in some way. I had a real sense that I had come to the end of the world, a place of darkness. I wondered if this was where Backus had taken his victims, if this was the end of the world for them. Probably, I concluded. It was a place of waiting evil.

Rachel broke the silence.

'Well, are we just going to look at it or are we going to check it out?'

'Just waiting on you to make the move.'

She opened her door and then I opened mine. We met at the front of the car. That was when I noticed that the trailer's windows were all open, not what I would expect someone would do if they were leaving their home for a long period of time. After that recognition came the odor.

'You smell that?'

She nodded. Death was in the air. It was much worse, much stronger than at Zzyzx. I instinctively knew that what we would find here would not be the buried secrets of the killer. Not this time. There was a body in that trailer – at least one – that was open to the air and decomposing.

'With my last act,' Rachel said.

'What?'

'The card. What he wrote on the card.'

I nodded. She was thinking suicide.

'You think?'

'I don't know. Let's check.'

We walked slowly forward, neither saying a word after that. The smell grew stronger and we both knew that whatever and whoever was dead inside the trailer had been baking in there for a long time.

I broke from her side and walked to a set of windows to the left of the trailer's door. Cupping my hands to the screen I tried to look into the darkness within. My hands hitting the screen set off an alarm of buzzing flies within the trailer. They were bouncing against the screen, looking to get out as if maybe the scene and the smell inside were too much even for them.

There was no curtain across the window but I couldn't see much from the angle I had – at least not a body or an indication of one. It looked like a small sitting area with a couch and a chair. There was a table with two stacks of hardback books on it. Behind the chair was a bookcase with its shelves full of books.

'Nothing,' I said.

I stepped back from the window and looked up the length of the trailer. I saw Rachel's eyes focused on the door and then the doorknob. Something came to me then, something that didn't fit.

'Rachel, why did he leave the note for you at the bar?'

'What?'

'The note. He left it at the bar. Why there? Why not here?'

'I guess he wanted to make sure I got it.'

'If he hadn't left it there you would have still come up here. You would've still found it here.'

She shook her head.

'What are you saying? I don't get—'

'Don't try the door, Rachel. Let's wait.'

'What are you talking about?'

'I don't like this.'

'Why don't you look around the back, see if there is another window you can see in or something.'

'Okay, I will. You just wait.'

She didn't answer me. I walked around the left side of the trailer, stepped over the hitch and headed toward the other side. But then I stopped and walked out to the trash barrel.

The barrel was one-third full with the charred remains of burned refuse. There was a broom handle on the ground that was charred on one end. I picked it up and dug around in the ashes in the barrel, as I was sure Backus had done while the fire was burning. He had wanted to make sure everything got burned.

It appeared to be mostly paperwork and books that had been burned. There was nothing recognizable until I came across a blackened and melted credit card. There was nothing I recognized on it but I guessed that the forensics experts might be able to connect it to one of the victims. I dug around further and saw pieces of melted black plastic. Then I noticed one book that was burned beyond recognition on the outside but still had some partially intact pages on the inside. With my fingers I lifted it out and gingerly opened it. It looked like it was poetry, though it was hard to be sure, since all the pages were partially burned away. Between two of these pages I found a half-burned receipt for the book. At the top it said 'Book Car' but the rest was burned away.

'Bosch? Where are you?'

It was Rachel. I was out of her sight. I placed the book back into the barrel and stuck the broom handle in as well. I headed toward the back side of the trailer. I saw another open window.

'Hold on a second.'

Rachel waited. She was growing impatient. She was listening for the distant sound of helicopters crossing the desert. She knew as soon as she heard them that her chance would be over. She would be pushed back, possibly even punished for how she had handled Bosch.

She looked back down at the doorknob. She thought about Backus and whether this could be his last play. Was four years here in the desert enough? Did he kill Terry McCaleb and send her the GPS only to lead her eventually to this? She thought about the note he had left, his telling her he had taught her well. An anger welled up inside her, an anger that wanted her to throw open the door and—

'We've got a body!'

It was Bosch, calling from the other side of the trailer.

'What? Where?'

'Come around. I've got a view. There's a bed and I see one body. Two, three days old. I can't see the face.'

'Okay, anything else?'

She waited. He didn't say anything. She put her hand on the knob. It turned.

'The door's not locked.'

'Rachel, don't open it,' Bosch called. 'I think . . . I think there is gas. I smell something besides the body. Something besides the obvious. Something underneath.'

Rachel hesitated but then turned the knob fully and opened the door an inch. Nothing happened.

She slowly pulled the door all the way open. Nothing happened. Flies saw the opening and buzzed by her and into the light. She waved them away from her eyes.

'Bosch, I'm going in.'

She stepped up into the trailer. More flies. They were everywhere. The smell hit her fully then, invading her and tightening her stomach.

Her eyes adjusted to the dimness after the brightness outside and she saw the photos. They were stacked on tables and taped to the walls and refrigerator. Photos of the victims, alive and dead, tearful, pleading, pitiful. The table in the trailer's kitchen had been turned into a work station. There was a laptop connected to a printer on one side and three separate stacks of photos. She picked up the largest stack and started to flip through it, again recognizing some of the men in the photos as the missing men whose photos she had carried with them to Clear. But these weren't the sort of family photos she had carried. These were shots of a killer and his victims. Men whose eyes pleaded to the camera, asking forgiveness and mercy. Rachel noticed that all of the shots were at a downward angle, with the shooter – Backus – in the dominant position, focusing down on his victims as they hoped and pleaded for their lives.

When she could look no more at them she put the photos down and took up the second stack. There were fewer photos here and these were mostly focused on a woman and two children as they moved through a shopping mall. She put them down and was about to move the camera weighing down the third stack of photos when Bosch stepped into the trailer.

'Rachel, what are we doing?'

'Don't worry. We have five, maybe ten minutes. We'll back out as soon as we hear the choppers and let the evidence recovery team take over. I just want to see if— '

'I'm not talking about beating other agents to the punch. I don't like this – the door being left open. Something's not—'

He stopped when he caught his first glimpse of the photos.

She turned back to the table and lifted the camera that rested on the last stack of photos. She looked down at a photo of herself. It took her a moment to place it but then realized where she had been photographed.

'He was with me all the way,' she said.

'What are you talking about?' Bosch asked.

'This is O'Hare. My layover. Backus was there watching me.'

She quickly shuffled through the photos. There were six of them, all shots of her on the day she traveled. The last shot was of Rachel and Cherie Dei greeting each other in baggage claim, Cherie holding a sign down at her side that said BOB BACKUS on it.

'He's been watching me.'

'Like he watched Terry.'

Bosch reached to the printer's tray and used a finger from each hand to lift a photo by its edges and without leaving a print. It apparently was the last image Backus had printed here. It showed the front of a two-story house of no particular design. In the driveway was a station wagon. An old man stood next to the driver's door and was looking at a keychain as if searching for the key to unlock the car. Bosch proffered the photo to Rachel.

'Who is this?'

She looked at it for a long moment.

'I don't know.'

'The house?'

'Never seen it before.'

Bosch carefully put the photo back in the tray so that it would be found in its original position by the evidence team.

Rachel moved behind him and walked down the hallway toward a closed doorway. Before she reached it she stepped through the open door of a bathroom. It was neat except for the dead flies covering all surfaces. In the bathtub she saw two pillows and a blanket arranged as if for sleeping. She remembered the intelligence gathered on Backus and felt a physical repulsion building in her chest.

She stepped out of the bathroom and went to the closed door at the end of the hallway.

'Is this where you saw it?' she asked.

Bosch turned and watched her approach the door.

'Rachel … '

Rachel didn't stop. She turned the knob and pulled the door open. I heard a distinct metallic *ching* sound that my mind did not associate with any door lock. Rachel stopped her movement and her posture stiffened.

'Harry?'

I started moving toward her.

'What is it?'

'Harry!'

She turned toward me in the close confines of the wood-paneled hallway. I looked past her face and saw the body on the bed. A man on his back, a black cowboy hat canted down on his head to obscure his face. A pistol in his right hand. A bullet wound to the upper left chest.

Flies were buzzing all around us. I heard a louder, hissing sound and pushed further by her and saw the fuse on the floor. I recognized it as a chemical fuse, a braiding of wires treated with chemicals that would burn anywhere under any condition, even underwater.

The fuse was burning fast. We could not stop it. There were maybe four feet of it coiled on the floor and then it disappeared under the bed. Rachel bent down and reached for it to pull it.

'No, don't! That could set it off. There's nothing – we have to get out of here.'

'No! We can't lose this scene! We need—'

'Rachel, no time! Go! Run! Now!'

I pushed her back up the hallway and turned my body to block any attempt by her to return. I started moving backward, my eyes fixed on the figure on the bed. When I thought Rachel had given up I turned and she was waiting. She shoved by me.

'We need DNA!' she yelled.

I watched her move into the room and leap onto the bed. Her hand came up and grabbed the hat off the dead man's head, revealing a face that was distorted and gray with decomposition. She then backed off the bed and headed toward the doorway.

Even in the moment I admired her thinking and what she had just done. The hat brim would most definitely contain skin cells that would hold the body's DNA. She carried the hat past me and started running for the door. I looked down to see the burn point on the fuse line disappear under the bed. I started to run behind her.

'Was it him?' she yelled over her shoulder.

I knew what she meant. Was the cadaver on the bed the man who showed up on Terry McCaleb's boat? Was it Backus?

'I don't know. *Just go! Go! Go!*'

I hit the door two seconds behind Rachel. She was already on the ground heading directly away, in the direction of Titanic Rock. I followed her lead. I had taken maybe five strides when the explosion ripped through the air behind me. I was hit with the full force of the deafening concussion and knocked forward to the ground. I remembered the tuck-and-roll maneuver from basic training and it served to give me a few more yards' distance from the explosion.

Time became disjointed and slow. One moment I was running. The next I was on my hands and knees, my eyes open, trying to raise my head. Something momentarily eclipsed the sun and I managed to look up to see the shell of the trailer thirty feet in the air over me. Its walls and roof intact. It seemed to float and almost hang up there. Then it came crashing down ten yards in front of me, its splintered aluminum sides as sharp as razors. It made a sound like a five-car pile-up when it hit the ground.

I checked the sky for more incoming and saw I was clear. I turned to look back at the trailer's original location and saw intense fire and thick black smoke billowing into the sky. Nothing was recognizable on the trailer pad. Everything had been consumed by the blast and fire. The bed and the man in it were gone. Backus had planned this exit perfectly.

I got to my feet but was unsteady because my eardrums were still reacting and my equilibrium was off. It sounded as though I was walking through a tunnel with trains speeding by me on both sides. I wanted to put my hands over my ears but knew that it would do no good. The noise was reverberating from inside.

Rachel had been only a few feet from me before the blast but now I couldn't see her. I stumbled around in the smoke and started to think that maybe she was under the trailer's skin.

But finally I found her on the ground to the left of the trailer debris. She was lying still in the dirt and rocks. The black hat was on the ground next to her, like a sign of death. I moved as quickly as I could to her.

'Rachel?'

I got down on my hands and knees and first examined her without touching her. She was lying facedown and her hair had fallen forward to further hide her eyes from my view. I was suddenly reminded of my daughter as I used a hand to gently pull the hair back. As I did this I noticed blood on the back of my palm and for the first time realized I was wounded in some minor way. I decided I would worry about that later.

'Rachel?'

I couldn't tell if she was breathing or not. It seemed that my senses were working on the domino theory. With my hearing gone at least temporarily, the coordination of the other senses was gone as well. I patted her cheek lightly.

'Come on, Rachel, wake up.'

I didn't want to turn her over in case there were unseen injuries that I might aggravate. I patted her cheek again, this time harder. I put my hand on her back, hoping that I would feel the rise and fall of breath as I could with my daughter.

Nothing. I put my ear to her back but this was laughable considering my condition. It was just instinct moving ahead of logic. I was thinking that I had no choice and had to turn her over when I saw the fingers of her right hand twitch and then form a fist.

Rachel suddenly lifted her head off the ground and groaned. It was loud enough that I could hear it.

'Rachel, are you all right?'

'I – I'm … there's evidence in the trailer. We need it.'

'Rachel there is no trailer anymore. It's gone.'

She struggled to turn over and sit up. Her eyes opened wide at the sight of the burning debris of what had been the trailer. I could see that her pupils were dilated. She had a concussion.

'What did you do?' she asked in an accusatory tone.

'It wasn't me. The place was rigged to go up. When you opened the bedroom door …'

'Oh.'

She turned her head back and forth as if working a kink out of her neck. She saw the black cowboy hat on the ground next to her.

'What is this?'

'His hat. You grabbed it on the way out.'

'DNA?'

'Hopefully, though I'm not sure what good it will be.'

She looked back at the flaming trailer bed. We were too close. I could feel the heat of the fire. But I still wasn't sure she should be moving.

'Rachel, why don't you lie back down? I think you have a concussion. You might have other injuries.'

'Yeah, I think that's a good idea.'

She put her head down on the ground and just looked up at the sky. I decided that wasn't a bad position and did the same. It was like we were at the beach or something. If it had been night we could have counted the stars.

Before I could hear them coming, I felt the approach of the helicopters. A deep vibration in my chest made me look to the southern sky and I saw the two air force choppers coming over the top of Titanic Rock. I weakly raised an arm and waved them in.

34

'What the hell happened out there?'

Special Agent Randal Alpert's face was rigid and almost purple. He had been waiting for them in the hangar at Nellis when the helicopter landed. His political instincts had apparently told him not to go to the scene himself. At all costs he had to be able to distance himself from the blowback that would rise from the explosion in the desert and possibly reach all the way to Washington.

Rachel Walling and Cherie Dei stood in the huge hangar and braced for the onslaught. Rachel didn't answer his question because she thought it was only the opener on a tirade. She was reacting slowly, her head still a bit fuzzy from the blast.

'Agent Walling, I asked you a question!'

'He had rigged the trailer,' Cherie Dei said. 'He knew she—'

'I asked her, not you,' Alpert barked. 'I want Agent Walling to tell me exactly why she could not follow orders and how this whole thing has gotten completely fucked up beyond recognition.'

Rachel raised her hands palms out as if to signify there was not a damn thing she could have done about what happened out there in the desert.

'We were going to wait for the ERT,' she said. 'As Agent Dei instructed. We were on the periphery of the location and that's when we realized it smelled like there was a body in there and then we thought maybe there could be someone alive in there. Somebody hurt.'

'And how the hell did you get that idea simply because you smelled a dead body?'

'Bosch thought he heard something.'

'Oh, here we go, the old cry for help routine.'

'No, he did. But it was the wind, I guess. Out there it picks up. The windows were left open. It must have created a sound that he heard.'

'And what about you? Did you hear it?'

'No. I didn't.'

Alpert looked at Dei and then back at Rachel. She could feel his eyes burning through her. But she knew it was a good story and she wasn't going to blink. She and Bosch had worked it out. Bosch was beyond Alpert's reach.

If she was acting on Bosch's alarm she could not be faulted either. Alpert could rant and rave but could do nothing more than that.

'You know what the problem with your story is? It's with your first word. We. You said *we*. There was no we. You were given an assignment of maintaining a cover on Bosch. *Not* joining him in the investigation. Not joining him in his car and driving up there. Not questioning witnesses together and entering that trailer *together*.'

'I understand that, but given the circumstances I decided it was in the best interest of the investigation to pool our knowledge and resources. Quite frankly, Agent Alpert, Bosch was the one who found that place. We wouldn't have what we have right now if not for him.'

'Don't kid yourself, Agent Walling. We would have gotten there.'

'I know that. But velocity was a factor. You said so yourself after the morning briefing. The director was going before the cameras. I wanted to push the case so that he would have as much information as possible.'

'Well, forget about that now. Now we don't know what we have. He postponed the news conference and has given us until noon tomorrow to figure out what we have out there.'

Cherie Dei cleared her voice and risked intruding again.

'That's impossible,' she said. 'That's a well-done crispy critter out there. They're using multiple bags to get it out of there. ID and cause of death are going to take weeks, if an ID and cause of death are even possible. Luckily, it appears that Agent Walling was able to obtain a DNA sampling from the body and that would speed things but we have no comparative evidence. We—'

'Maybe you weren't listening ten seconds ago,' Alpert said, 'but we don't have weeks. We've got less than twenty-four hours.'

He turned away from them and put his hands on his hips, striking a pose that showed the burden that weighed upon him as the only intelligent and savvy agent left on the planet.

'Then let us go back up there,' Rachel said. 'Maybe in the debris we'll find something that—'

'No!' Alpert yelled.

He spun back around to them.

'That won't be necessary, Agent Walling. You have done enough.'

'I know Backus and I know the case. I should be out there.'

'I decide who should be and shouldn't be out there. I want you to get back to the field office and start the paperwork on this fiasco. I want it on my desk by eight a.m. tomorrow. I want a detailed listing of everything you saw inside that trailer.'

He waited to see if she would argue the order. Rachel remained silent and this seemed to please him.

'Now, I've got the media all over this. What do we put out that doesn't give away the store and won't upstage the director tomorrow?'

Dei shrugged.

'Nothing. Tell them the director will address it tomorrow, end of story.'

'That won't work. We have to give them something.'

'Don't give them Backus,' Rachel said. 'Tell them agents wanted to speak to a man named Thomas Walling about a missing persons case. But Walling had rigged his trailer and it exploded while agents were on the premises.'

Alpert nodded. It sounded good to him.

'What about Bosch?'

'I'd leave him out of it. We don't have any control over him. If a reporter got to him he might lay the whole thing out.'

'And the body. Do we say it was Walling?'

'We say we don't know because we don't. ID is forthcoming, so on and so forth. That should be enough.'

'If the reporters go to the brothels they'll get the whole story.'

'No, they won't. We never told anyone the whole story.'

'By the way, what happened to Bosch?'

Dei answered that one.

'I took his statement and released him. Last I saw he was driving back to Vegas.'

'He'll keep quiet about this?'

Dei looked at Rachel and then back at Alpert.

'Put it this way, he isn't going to be looking to talk to anybody about it. And as long as we keep his name out of it, there will be no reason for anyone to go looking for him.'

Alpert nodded. He dug a hand into one of his pockets and came out with a cell phone.

'When we are finished here I have to call Washington. Gut reaction time: Was that Backus in that trailer?'

Rachel hesitated, not wanting to respond first.

'At this point there is no way to tell,' Dei said. 'If you are asking if you should tell the director that we got him, my answer right now is no, don't tell the director that. That could've been anybody in that trailer. For all we know it was an eleventh victim and we may never know who it was. Just somebody who went to one of the brothels and was intercepted by Backus.'

Alpert looked at Rachel, expecting her take.

'The fuse,' she said.

'What about it?'

'It was long. It was like he wanted me to see the body but not get too close. But he also wanted me to get out of there.'

'And?'

'On the body there was a black cowboy hat. I remember there was a man on my plane from Rapid City in a black cowboy hat.'

'For chrissake, you were flying from South Dakota. Doesn't everybody wear cowboy hats there?'

'But he was there, with me. I think this whole thing was a setup. The note in the bar, the long fuse, the photos in the trailer and the black hat. He wanted me to get out of there in time to tell the world he was dead.'

Alpert didn't respond. He looked down at the phone in his hands.

'There's too much we don't know yet, Randal,' Dei offered.

He shoved the phone back into his pocket.

'Very well. Agent Dei, is your car here?'

'Yes.'

'Take Agent Walling to the field office now.'

They were dismissed, but not before Alpert looked at Rachel and threw one more grimace at her.

'Remember, Agent Walling, my desk by eight.'

'You got it,' Rachel said.

35

Eleanor Wish answered my knock and that surprised me. She stepped back to let me in.

'Don't look at me that way, Harry,' she said. 'You have this impression that I'm never here and that I work every night and leave her with Marisol. I don't. I work three or four nights a week and that's usually it.'

I raised my hands in surrender and she saw the bandage around my right palm.

'What happened to you?'

'Cut myself on a piece of metal.'

'What metal?'

'It's a long story.'

'That thing up in the desert today?'

I nodded.

'I should have known. Is that going to hurt you playing the saxophone?'

Bored with retirement, I had started taking lessons the year before from a retired jazzman I had come across on a case. One night, when things were good between Eleanor and me, I had brought the instrument with me and played her a tune called 'Lullaby.' She had liked it.

'Actually, I haven't been playing anyway.'

'How come?'

I didn't want to tell her that my teacher had died and music had dropped out of my life for a while.

'My teacher wanted me to switch from alto to tenor – as in *ten or* fifteen miles away from him.'

She smiled at the lame joke and we left it at that. I had followed her through the house and into the kitchen, where the table was actually a felt-covered poker table – with cereal milk stains on it thanks to Maddie. Eleanor had dealt six hands faceup for practice. She sat down and started gathering up the cards.

'Don't let me stop you,' I said. 'I just came by to see if I could put Maddie to bed. Where is she?'

'Marisol's giving her a bath. But I was counting on putting her to bed tonight. I've worked the last three nights.'

'Oh, well, that's fine. I'll just say hello then. And good-bye. I'm driving back tonight.'

'Then why don't you do it? I got a new book to read her. It's on the counter.'

'No, Eleanor, I want you to do it. I just want to see her because I don't know when I'll get back.'

'Are you still working a case?'

'No, that all sort of ended up there today.'

'The TV news didn't have much on it when I watched. What is it?'

'It's a long story.'

I didn't feel like telling it once again. I walked over to the counter to look at the book she had bought. It was called *Billy's Big Day* and its cover showed a monkey standing on the highest step at an Olympics-style award ceremony. The gold medal was being put around his neck. A lion had received the silver and an elephant the bronze.

'Are you going back to join the department again?'

I was about to open the book but I put it down and looked at Eleanor.

'I'm still thinking about it but it's looking that way.'

She nodded as though it was a done deal.

'Any further thoughts from you on it?'

'No, Harry, I want you to do what you want.'

I wondered why it was that when people tell you what you want them to tell you, it always comes with suspicion and second-guessing attached. Did Eleanor really want me to do what I wanted to do? Or was her saying that a way of undermining the whole thing?

Before I could say anything my daughter came into the kitchen and stood at attention. She wore blue-and-orange-striped pajamas and her dark hair was wet and slicked back on her head.

'Presenting a little girl,' she said.

Eleanor and I both broke out the smiles and simultaneously offered our opened arms for hugs. Maddie went to her mother first and that was all right with me. But it felt a little like when you hold out your hand to someone to shake and they don't see it or just plain ignore it. I lowered my arms and after a few moments Eleanor saved me.

'Go give Daddy a hug.'

Maddie came to me and I lifted her up into a hug. She was no more than forty pounds. It is an amazing thing to be able to hold everything that is important to you in one arm. She put her damp head against my chest and I didn't mind that she was getting my shirt wet. That was no problem at all.

'How are you, baby?'

'I'm fine. I drew your picture today.'

'You did? Can I see it?'

'Put me down.'

I did as instructed and she ran off, out of the kitchen, her bare feet slapping on the stone tiles as she headed to the playroom. I looked at Eleanor and smiled. We both knew the secret. No matter what we had or didn't have for each other, we would always have Madeline and that might be enough.

The running of tiny feet could be heard again and soon she was back in the kitchen, towing a piece of paper held high like a kite. I took it from her and studied it. It showed the figure of a man with a mustache and dark eyes. He had his hands out and in one hand was a gun. On the other side of the page was another figure. This one was drawn in reds and oranges and had eyebrows drawn in a severe black V to indicate he was a bad guy.

I crouched down to my daughter's height to look at the drawing with her.

'Is this me with the gun?'

'Yes, because you were a policeman.'

I nodded. She had said it like *pleaseman.*

'And who is this mean guy?'

She pointed a tiny finger at the other figure on the drawing.

'That is Mr. Demon.'

I smiled.

'Who is Mr. Demon?'

'He's a wrestler. Mommy says you wrestle with demons and he's the boss of all of them.'

'I see.'

I looked over her head at Eleanor and smiled. I wasn't mad about anything. I was simply in love with my daughter and how she viewed her world. The literal way in which she took it all in and took it on. I knew it wouldn't last long and so I treasured every moment I saw and heard of it.

'Can I keep this picture?'

'How come?'

'Because it is beautiful and I want to always have it. I have to go away for a while and I want to be able to look at it all the time. It will remind me of you.'

'Where are you going?'

'I'm going back to the place they call the City of Angels.'

She smiled.

'That's silly. You can't see angels.'

'I know. But look, Mommy has a new book to read to you about a monkey named Billy. So I'm going to say good night now and I'll get back to see you as soon as I can. Is that okay, baby?'

'Okay, Daddy.'

I kissed her on both cheeks and hugged her tight. Then I kissed the top of her head and let her go. I stood up with my picture and handed her the book Eleanor would read to her.

'Marisol?' Eleanor called.

Marisol appeared within a few seconds, as if she had been waiting in the nearby living room for her cue. I smiled and nodded to her as she received her instructions.

'Why don't you take Maddie in and get her set up and I'll be right in after saying good night to her father.'

I watched my daughter leave with her nanny.

'I'm sorry about that,' Eleanor said.

'What, the picture? Don't worry about it. I love it. It's going on my refrigerator.'

'I just don't know where she picked it up. I didn't directly say to her that you fight demons. She must have overheard me on the phone or something.'

Somehow I would have liked it better knowing she had said it directly to our daughter. The idea that Eleanor was talking about me in such a way to someone else – someone she didn't mention at the moment – bothered me. I tried not to show it.

'It's all right,' I said. 'Look at it this way, when she goes to school and kids say their dad is a lawyer or a fireman or a doctor or something, she's got the trump card. She'll tell them her daddy fights demons.'

Eleanor laughed but then cut it off when she thought of something.

'I wonder what she'll say her mother does.'

I couldn't answer that, so I changed the subject.

'I love how her view of the world is uncluttered by deeper meanings,' I said as I looked at the picture again. 'It is so innocent, you know?'

'I know. I love that, too. But I can understand if you don't want her thinking you're out there literally wrestling with demons. Why didn't you explain it to her?'

I shook my head and thought of a story.

'When I was a kid and I was still with my mother, there was this time that she had a car. A two-tone Plymouth Belvedere with push-button automatic transmission. I think her lawyer gave it to her to use or something. For a couple years. Anyway, she suddenly decided she wanted to go cross-country on a vacation. So we packed the car and just took off, her and me.

'Anyway, somewhere in the south – I don't remember where – we stopped for gas and there were two water fountains on the side of this service station. There were signs, you know. One said WHITE and the other said COLORED. And I just sort of went up to the one marked COLORED because I wanted to see what color the water was. Before I got to it my mom yanked me back and sort of explained things to me.

'I remember that and sort of wish she'd just let me see the water and didn't explain anything.'

Eleanor smiled at the story.

'How old were you?'

'I don't know. About eight.'

She stood up then and came over to me. She kissed me on the cheek and

I let her. I put my arm loosely around her waist.

'Good luck with your demons, Harry.'

'Yeah.'

'If you ever change your mind about things, I'm here. We're here.'

I nodded.

'She's going to change *your* mind, Eleanor. You wait and see.'

She smiled but in a sad way and gently caressed my chin with her hand.

'Will you make sure the door is locked when you leave?'

'Always.'

I let go of her and watched her walk out of the kitchen. I then looked down at the drawing of the man fighting his demon. In the picture my daughter had put a smile on my face.

36

Before going up to my efficiency at the Double X, I stopped by the office and told Mr. Gupta, the night man, that I would be checking out. He told me that because I had been keeping the place on a weekly basis, my credit card had already been dinged for the entire week and I told him that was fine, I was still leaving. I told him I would leave the key on the dinette table after I gathered up my belongings. I was about to leave the office when I hesitated and then asked him about my neighbor Jane.

'Yes, she is gone, too. Same thing.'

'What do you mean, same thing?'

'We charge her for a week but she not stay a week.'

'Hey, do you mind me asking, what was her full name? I never got it.'

'She is Jane Davis. You like?'

'Yeah, she was nice. We talked on the balconies. I didn't get to say good-bye. She didn't leave a forwarding address or anything like that, did she?'

Gupta smiled at the prospect of this. He had very pink gums for someone with such dark skin.

'No address,' he said. 'Not that one.'

I nodded my thanks for the information he had given me. I left the office and went up the stairs and then down the walkway to my room.

It took me less than five minutes to gather my things. I had some shirts and pants on hangers. I then took out of the closet the same box in which I had brought everything and filled it with the rest of my belongings and a couple of toys I kept in the place for Maddie. Buddy Lockridge had been close, calling me Suitcase Harry. But Beer Box Harry would have been better.

Before leaving I checked the refrigerator and saw I had one bottle of beer left. I took it out and cranked it open. I figured one beer for the road wouldn't hurt me. I had done worse in the past before a drive. I thought about making another cheese sandwich but skipped it when the thought reminded me of Backus's routine of eating grilled cheese sandwiches each day at Quantico. I went out onto the balcony with the beer for one last look at the rich men's jets. It was a cool and crisp evening. The blue lights on the far runway twinkled like sapphires.

The two black jets were gone, their owners either quick winners or losers. The big Gulfstream remained in place, red dust caps over the intakes on its jet engines. It was settled in. I wondered what the jets might have had to do with Jane Davis and her stay at the Double X.

I looked over at Jane's empty balcony, just four feet from my own. The ashtray was sitting on the railing and I could see it was still filled with half-smoked butts. Her unit had not been cleaned yet.

And that gave me an idea. I looked around and down at the parking lot. I saw no human movement except for out on Koval, where the traffic was stalled at a traffic light. I saw no sign of the night security man or anyone else in the parking lot. I quickly hoisted myself up onto the railing and was about to climb across to the next balcony when I heard a knock on my door. I quickly dropped back down and went in and answered the door.

It was Rachel Walling.

'Rachel? Hello. Is something wrong?'

'No, nothing that catching Backus couldn't cure. Can I come in?'

'Sure.'

I stepped back to let her enter. She saw the box with my belongings piled into it. I spoke first.

'How did it go today when you got back into town?'

'Well, I got the usual tongue-lashing from the SAC.'

'Did you lay it all on me?'

'As planned. He fumed and fussed but what's he going to do? I don't want to talk about him right now.'

'Then what?'

'Well, for starters, do you have another one of those?'

She meant the beer.

'Actually, no. I was just finishing this one and was going to take off.'

'Then I'm glad I caught you.'

'You want to split it? I'll get you a glass.'

'You said you wouldn't trust the glasses here.'

'Well, I could wash—'

She reached over for the bottle and took a sip from it. She handed it back, her eyes staying on mine. She then turned and pointed to the box.

'So you're leaving.'

'Yeah, back to L.A. for a while.'

'You'll miss your daughter, I guess.'

'A lot.'

'You'll come back to see her?'

'As often as I can.'

'That's nice. Anything else?'

'What do you mean?' I asked, though I thought I knew what she meant.

'Will you be coming back for anything else?'

'No, just my daughter.'

We stood there looking at each other for a long moment. I held the beer out to her but when she came forward it was for me. She kissed me on the lips and then quickly we put our arms around each other.

I know it had something to do with the trailer, our nearly dying together out there in the desert, that made us press so hard against each other and move toward the bed, that made me reach over and put the beer bottle on the table so I could use both my hands as we pulled at each other's clothes.

We fell onto the bed and made survivors' love. It was quick and maybe to some degree even brutal – on both our parts. But most of all it satisfied the primal urge in both of us to fight death with life.

When it was over we were entwined on top of the bed covers, she on top of me, my fists still tangled in her hair.

She leaned to her left and reached for the beer bottle, knocking it over first and spilling most of what was left on the bed table and floor.

'There goes my security deposit,' I said.

There was enough left in the bottle for her to take a draw and then pass it to me.

'That was for today,' she said as I drank.

I gave her the rest.

'What do you mean?'

'After what happened out there, we had to do this.'

'Yeah.'

'Gladiator love. That's why I came here. To catch you.'

I smiled, thinking of a gladiator joke from an old movie I liked. But I didn't tell her and she probably thought I was smiling at her words. She leaned down and put her head on my chest. I held up some of her hair, more gently this time, to look at the singed ends. I then moved my hands down and rubbed her back, thinking it was strange that we were being so gentle with each other now, just moments after being gladiators.

'I don't suppose you'd be interested in opening a branch of your private investigations office in South Dakota, would you?'

I smiled and stifled a laugh in my chest.

'How about North Dakota?' she asked. 'I could be going back there, too.'

'You have to have a tree to have a branch.'

She hit me with a gentle fist on the chest.

'I didn't think so.'

I shifted my body so that I came out of her. She groaned but stayed on top of me.

'Does that mean you want me to get up and get off and get out of here?'

'No, Rachel. Not at all.'

I looked over her shoulder and saw that the door was unlocked. I had a vision of Mr. Gupta coming up to see if I had left yet and finding the two-backed monster on the bed in the supposedly empty unit. I smiled. I didn't care.

She raised her face up to look at me.

'What?'

'Nothing. We left the door unlocked. Somebody could come in.'

'*You* left it unlocked. This is your place.'

I kissed her, realizing I had not kissed her lips during the entire time we had made love. Another strange thing.

'You know what, Bosch?'

'What?'

'You're good at this.'

I smiled and told her thanks. A woman can play that card anytime and every time and always get the same response.

'I mean it.'

She dug her nails into my chest to underline her point. With one arm I held her tightly to me and we rolled over. I figured I had at least ten years on her but I wasn't worried about it. I kissed her again and got up, gathering my clothes off the floor and walking over to the door to lock it.

'I think there's one last clean towel in there,' I said. 'You can use it.'

She insisted I take the first shower and I did. Then while she showered I left the unit and walked across Koval to a convenience store to pick up two more beers. I was going to limit it to that because I was driving that night and didn't want alcohol to slow me down getting to the road or while on it. I was sitting at the dinette when she came out of the bathroom fully dressed and smiling when she saw the two bottles.

'I knew you'd make yourself useful.'

She sat down and we clicked bottles.

'To gladiator love,' she said.

We drank and just were quiet for a few moments. I was trying to figure out what the last hour now meant to me and to us.

'What are you thinking about?' she asked.

'About how this could get complicated.'

'It doesn't have to. We can just see what happens.'

That didn't sound the same to me as being asked to move to the Dakotas.

'Okay.'

'I better get going.'

'Where to?'

'Back to the FO, I guess. See what's shaking.'

'Did you hear what happened to the fire barrel out there after the blast? I forgot to look.'

'No, why?'

'I looked in it when we were out there. For just a minute. It looked like he had been burning credit cards, maybe IDs.'

'The victims'?'

'Probably. He burned books in it, too.'

'Books? Why do you think he did that?'

'I don't know but it's strange. Inside the trailer he had books all over the place. So he burned some and some he didn't burn. Seems strange.'

'Well, if there is anything left of the barrel the ERT will get to it. Why didn't you mention it before, when you were interviewed out there?'

'Because my head was ringing and I sort of forgot, I guess.'

'Short-term memory loss associated with concussion.'

'I don't have a concussion.'

'I meant the blast. Could you tell what books they were?'

'Not really. I didn't have time. There was one I picked out. It was the least burned of what I could see. It looked like it was poetry. I think.'

She looked at me and nodded but didn't say anything.

'What I don't get is why he burned the books. He set the whole trailer to go up but he takes the time to go out to the barrel and burn some books. Almost like ... '

I stopped talking and tried to put the pieces together.

'Almost like what, Harry?'

'I don't know. Like he didn't want to leave the trailer thing to chance. He wanted to make sure those books were destroyed.'

'You are assuming that both things are together. Who knows, maybe he burned the books six months ago or something. You can't just connect the two things.'

I nodded. She was right about that but still the incongruity bothered me.

'The book I found was near the top of the barrel,' I said. 'It was burned the last time the barrel was used. There was also a receipt in it. Half burned. But maybe they can trace it.'

'When I get back I'll check it out. But I don't remember seeing that barrel after the blast.'

I shrugged.

'Neither do I.'

She stood up and so did I.

'There's one other thing,' I said as I reached into the inside pocket of my jacket. I pulled out the photo and handed it to her.

'I must've grabbed it while I was in the trailer and then sort of forgot about it. I found it in my pocket.'

It was the photo taken from the printer tray. The two-story house with the old man out front next to the station wagon.

'Great, Harry. How am I going to explain this?'

'I don't know but I figured you'd want to try to ID the place or the old man.'

'What's the difference now?'

'Come on, Rachel, you know it's not over.'

'No, I don't know that.'

It bothered me that she could not talk to me after we had been so intimate just a few minutes before.

'Okay.'

I picked up my box and the clothing I had on hangers.

'Wait a minute, Harry. You're just going to leave it like that? What do you mean it's not over?'

'I mean we both know that wasn't Backus in there. If you and the bureau aren't interested in it, that's fine. But don't bullshit me, Rachel. Not after what we went through today, and not after what we just did.'

She relented.

'Look, Harry, it's out of my hands, okay? Right now we are waiting on forensics to make a call on it. The bureau's official position probably won't be formulated until tomorrow when the director holds a press conference.'

'I'm not interested in the official position of the bureau. I was talking to you.'

'Harry, what do you want me to say?'

'I want you to say you are going to get this guy, no matter what the director says tomorrow.'

I headed to the door and she followed. We left the efficiency and she pulled the door closed for me.

'Where's your car?' I asked. 'I'll walk you over.'

She pointed the way and we went down the steps and to her car, parked near the office. After she opened the door we turned and faced each other.

'I want to get this guy,' she said. 'More than you could know.'

'Okay, good. I'll be in touch.'

'Well, what are you going to do?'

'I don't know. When I do, I'll let you know.'

'Okay. See you, Bosch.'

'Good-bye, Rachel.'

She kissed me and then she got in the car. I walked to my car, ducking between the two buildings that made up the Double X to get to the other parking lot. I was pretty sure it was not the last time I would see Rachel Walling.

37

On the way out of town I could have avoided the traffic of the strip but I decided not to. I thought all the lights might cheer me up. I knew I was leaving my daughter behind. I was going to Los Angeles to rejoin the department. I would see my daughter again but I wouldn't be able to spend the kind of time with her I needed and wanted to. I was leaving to join the depressing legions of weekend fathers, the men who have to compress their love and duty into twenty-four-hour stands with their children. The thought of it raised a dark dread in my chest that a billion kilowatts of light could not cut through. There was no doubt I was leaving Las Vegas as a loser.

Once I cleared the lights and the city limits the traffic grew sparse and the skies dark. I tried to ignore the depression my choice had put upon me. Instead, I worked the case as I drove, following the logic of the moves from the perspective of Backus, grinding it down until the story was smooth powder and I had only unanswered questions left. I saw it the same way the bureau did. Backus, having adopted the name Tom Walling, was living in Clear and preying on the customers he drove from the brothels. He operated with impunity for years because he chose the perfect victims. That is until the numbers went against him and investigators from Vegas started to see a pattern and put together their list of six missing men. Backus probably knew that it was only a matter of time before the connection might be made to Clear. He probably knew that that time would be even shorter once he saw Terry McCaleb's name in the newspaper. Maybe he even got wind that McCaleb had gone to Vegas. Maybe McCaleb had even gone up to Clear. Who knows? Most of the answers died with McCaleb and then in that trailer in the desert.

There were so many unknowns in this story. But what did seem obvious from this point was that Backus had closed up shop. He made plans to end his desert run in a blaze of glory – to take out his two protégés, McCaleb and Rachel, in a pathological display of mastery, and to leave behind in his trailer a burned and destroyed body that would beg the question of whether he was alive or dead. In recent years Saddam Hussein and Osama bin Laden had gotten good mileage by leaving behind the same question. Maybe Backus saw himself on the same stage.

The books in the fire barrel bothered me the most. Despite Rachel's dismissing them because the circumstances of their burning were unknown, it still seemed like an important piece of the investigation to me. I wished I had spent more time studying the book I had pulled out, maybe even identifying it. The burned book gave an indication of a part of the Poet's plan nobody knew about yet.

Remembering the partial receipt I had seen in the book, I opened my cell phone, checked to make sure I had service and called information for Las Vegas. I asked if there was a listing for a business called Book Car and the operator told me there was not. I was about to hang up when she told me there was, however, a listing for a store called Book Caravan on Industry Road. I told her I would try it and she connected me.

I guessed that the store would be closed because it was late. I was hoping for a message machine on which I could ask the owner to call me in the morning. But the call was answered after two rings by a gruff voice.

'You're open?'

'Twenty-four hours. How can I help you?'

I got an idea what kind of store it was by the hours. I took a shot anyway. 'You don't sell any books of poetry there, do you?'

The gruff man laughed.

'Very funny,' he said. 'There once was a man from Timbuktu. As far as poetry goes, fuck you.'

He laughed again and hung up on me. I closed the phone and had to smile at his on-the-spot rhyming skill.

Book Caravan seemed like a dead end but I would call Rachel in the morning and tell her it might be worth checking for connections to Backus.

A green highway sign came out of the darkness and into the spray of my headlights.

ZZYZX ROAD
1 MILE

I thought about pulling off and driving down the bouncing desert road into the darkness. I wondered if there was still a forensic crew on duty at the burial site. But what would the point of going down that road be other than to engage with the ghosts of the dead? The mile came and went and I drove on by the exit, leaving the ghosts alone.

The beer and a half I'd had with Rachel proved to be a mistake. By Victorville I was growing fatigued. Too much thinking with the added mix of alcohol. I pulled off for coffee in a McDonald's that was open late and designed to look like a train depot. I bought two coffees and two sugar cookies and sat in a booth in an old train car reading through Terry McCaleb's file on the Poet investigation. I was getting to know the order of reports and their summaries just about by heart.

After one cup of coffee I had nothing going and closed the file. I needed something new. I needed to either let it go and hope and believe the bureau would get the job done or find a new angle to pursue.

I'm not against the bureau. My take is that it's the most thorough, well-equipped and relentless law enforcement agency in the world. Its problems lie in its size and the many cracks in communication between offices, squads and so on down the line to the agents themselves. It only takes a debacle like 9/11 to make clear to the world what most people in the law enforcement world, including the FBI agents, already know.

As an institution it cares too much about its reputation and it carries too much weight in politics, going all the way back to J. Edgar Hoover himself. Eleanor Wish once knew an agent who had been assigned to Washington headquarters back during the time J. Edgar ruled the place. He said the unspoken law was that if an agent was in an elevator and the director got on, the agent was not allowed to address him, even to say hello, and was required to immediately step off so the big man could ride alone and ponder his great responsibilities. That story always stuck with me for some reason. I think because it carries the perfect arrogance of the FBI.

The bottom line was I didn't want to call Graciela McCaleb and tell her that her husband's killer was still out there and that the FBI would handle it. I still wanted to handle it. I owed that to her and to Terry and I always paid what I owed.

Back on the road the coffee and sugar got me going again and I pressed on toward the City of Angels. When I hit the 10 freeway I also hit the rain and traffic slowed to a crawl. I flipped on the radio to KFWB and learned it had rained all day and wasn't expected to stop until the end of the week. There was a live report from Topanga Canyon where residents were sandbagging their doors and garages, expecting the worst. Mud slides and flooding were the dangers. The catastrophic fires that swept through the hills the year before had left little ground cover to hold the rain or soil. It was all coming down.

I knew the weather would cost me an extra hour getting home. I checked my watch. It was just past midnight. I had planned to wait until getting home to call Kiz Rider but decided it might be too late to call by then. I opened my phone and called her at home. She picked up right away.

'Kiz, it's Harry. You up?'

'Sure, Harry. I can't sleep when it rains.'

'I know what you mean.'

'So what's the good word?'

'Everybody counts or nobody counts.'

'Which means?'

'I'm in if you're in.'

'Come on, Harry, don't put that on me.'

'I'm in if you're in.'

'Come on, man, I'm already in.'

'You know what I mean. This is your salvation, Kiz. We got sidetracked. We both did. You and I know what we should be doing. It's time we both went back to it.'

I waited. There was a long period of silence from her, then finally she spoke.

'This is going to upset the man. He's got me on a lot of things.'

'If he's the man you say he is he'll understand. He'll get it. You'll be able to make him get it.'

More silence.

'Okay, Harry, okay. I'm in.'

'All right then, I'll come down tomorrow and sign up.'

'All right, Harry. I'll see you then.'

'You knew I'd call, didn't you?'

'Put it this way, I have the papers you have to fill out sitting on my desk.'

'You were always too smart for me.'

'I meant what I said about us needing you. That's the bottom line. But I also didn't think you'd last long out there on your own. I know guys who have pulled the pin and gone the PI route, sold real estate, cars, appliances, even books. It worked fine for most of them, but not you, Harry. I figured you knew that, too.'

I didn't say anything. I was staring into the darkness beyond the reach of my lights. Something Kiz had just said triggered the avalanche.

'Harry, you still there?'

'Yeah, listen, Kiz, you just said *books.* You knew a guy who retired and sold books. Is that Ed Thomas?'

'Yeah, I came to Hollywood about six months before he put in his papers. He left and opened a bookstore down in Orange.'

'I know. You ever been there?'

'Yeah, one time he had Dean Koontz signing one of his books there. I saw it in the paper. He's my favorite and he doesn't sign books too many places. So I went down. There was a line out the door and down the sidewalk but as soon as Ed saw me he ushered me right on up to the front and he introduced me and I got my book signed. It was embarrassing, actually.'

'What's the name of it?'

'Um ... I think it was *Strange Highways.*'

That deflated me. I thought I was about to make a leap in logic and a connection.

'No, actually, it was after that,' Kiz said. 'It was *Sole Survivor* – the plane crash story.'

I realized what she was saying and how we'd gotten confused.

'No, Kiz, what's the name of Ed's bookstore?'

'Oh, it's called Book Carnival. I think that was what it was called when he bought the business. Otherwise I think he'd have called it something else, something mysterious, since he sells mostly mystery books there.'

Book Car as in Book Carnival. I involuntarily pressed the accelerator down harder.

'Kiz, I gotta go. I'll talk to you later.'

I closed the phone without waiting for a good-bye from her. Glancing between the road and the phone's display I scrolled through my recent calls list and pressed the connect button after highlighting Rachel Walling's cell number. She answered before I even heard it ring.

'Rachel, it's Harry. Sorry to call so late but it's important.'

'I'm in the middle of something,' she whispered.

'You're at the field office still?'

'That's right.'

I tried to think of what would keep her there after midnight on a day that had started so early.

'Is it the trash barrel? The burned book?'

'No, we haven't gotten there yet. It's something else. I have to go.'

Her voice was somber and because she had not used my name I got the idea there were other agents present and that whatever she was in the middle of was not good.

'Rachel, listen, I have something. You have to come to L.A.'

Her tone changed. I think she could tell by the urgency in my voice that this was serious.

'What is it?'

'I know the Poet's next move.'

38

'I'll have to call you back.'

Rachel closed her phone and slid it into the pocket of her blazer. Bosch's last words echoed in her heart.

'Agent Walling, I'd appreciate it if you could stay in our conversation.'

She looked up at Alpert.

'Sorry.'

She looked past him at the telecommunication screen where Brass Doran's face was larger than life. She was smiling.

'Agent Doran, continue,' Alpert said.

'Actually, I'm finished. That's all we have at this time. We can confirm through the latents that Robert Backus was at that trailer. We cannot confirm that he was in it when it exploded.'

'What about the DNA?'

'The DNA evidence gathered by Agent Walling, at great danger, I might add, and later by the ERT will only be useful if we have something to compare it with. That is, if we somehow find a source of Robert Backus's DNA. Or we use it to identify the body that was in the trailer as someone else.'

'What about Backus's parents? Can't we extract his DNA from—'

'We went that route before. His father was dead and cremated before we thought of it – the science wasn't really there back then – and his mother has never been located. There is some thought that she might have been his first victim. She disappeared some years ago without the proverbial trace.'

'This guy thought of everything.'

'In the case of the mother it was more likely a revenge thing for her abandonment. It is hard to believe that he did something back then in order to prevent later DNA extraction.'

'All I meant was that we are genuinely fucked.'

'I am sorry, Randal, but the science can only go so far.'

'I know that, Agent Doran. Can you tell me anything else? Anything new?'

'I guess not.'

'Terrific. Okay, so then I will tell the director just that. That we know Backus was in that trailer – we have forensics and witness accounts to that effect. But as of this time we cannot take the next step and say he is dead and good riddance.'

'Is there no way we can convince the director to sit tight and give us more time to sew it all up? For the good of the investigation.'

Rachel almost laughed. She knew the good of the investigation would always take second place to political considerations in the Hoover Building in D.C.

'I have already tried,' Alpert said. 'The answer is no. There is too much at stake. The cat is out of the bag on this – thanks to the explosion in the desert. If that was Backus blown to bits out there, then fine, we'll eventually confirm it and everything will be fine. If that was not Backus and he has some other play in mind, the director has to get on record with this now or the consequences of the blowback could be fatal. So he is going on record with what we know now: Backus was there, Backus is the suspect in the killings in the desert, Backus may or may not be dead. There is no dissuading him at this point.'

Alpert had thrown Rachel a look when he said the cat was out of the bag, as if he held her responsible for everything. She thought about revealing what Bosch had just told her but in that instant decided against it. Not yet. Not until she knew more.

'Okay, people, that's it,' Alpert announced abruptly. 'Brass, we'll see you on the big screen tomorrow morning. Agent Walling, can you stay behind for a moment?'

Rachel watched Brass leave the screen and then it went black, the transmission ended. Alpert then walked up close to the table where Rachel sat.

'Agent Walling?'

'Yes?'

'Your work is done here.'

'Excuse me?'

'You're finished. Go back to your hotel and pack your bags.'

'There's still a lot to do here. I want to—'

'I don't care what you want. I want you out of here. You have undermined this investigation since you arrived. Tomorrow morning I want you on the first plane back to wherever it is you come from. Understand?'

'You are making a mistake. I should be a part of—'

'You are making a mistake arguing with me about it. I can't make it any clearer for you. I want you out of here. Turn in your paperwork and get on a plane.'

She stared at him, trying to communicate all the anger that was behind her eyes. He held a hand up as if to ward something off.

'Be careful what you say. It could come back to bite you on the ass.'

Rachel swallowed back her anger. She spoke in a controlled and calm voice.

'I'm not going anywhere.'

Alpert looked like his eyes might pop out of his head. He turned and waved Dei out of the room. He then turned back to Rachel and waited for the sound of the door closing.

'Excuse me? What did you just say?'

'I said I am not going anywhere. I am staying on this case. Because if you put me on a plane, I won't go back to South Dakota. I'll go to D.C. headquarters and right into the Office of Professional Responsibility to file on you.'

'For what? What are you going to file?'

'You've used me as bait since the beginning. Without my knowledge or consent.'

'You don't know what you are talking about. Go ahead. Go to the OPR. They'll laugh you back to the Badlands and put you down for another ten years out there.'

'Cherie made a mistake and then you did, too. When I called in from Clear she asked me why we took Bosch's car. Then in the hangar you did the same thing. You knew I had gone up there in Bosch's car. I started thinking about that and then I figured out why. You put a GPS tag on my car. I went underneath it tonight and found it. Standard bureau issue, even has the code label still on it. There will be a record of who checked it out.'

'I have no idea what you are talking about.'

'Well, I'm sure the OPR will be able to figure it out. My guess is Cherie will help them. I mean if I were her I wouldn't tie my career to you. I'd tell the truth. That you brought me out here as bait, that you thought I would draw Backus out. I bet you had a shadow team on me the whole time. There will be a record of that, too. What about my phone and my hotel room? Did you bug them?'

Rachel saw Alpert's eyes change. He went inward, his mind no longer consumed by her accusations but by the future consequences of an ethics complaint and investigation. She saw him recognize his own doom. One agent bugging and following another agent, using her as unwitting bait in a high-stakes gamble. Under the current climate of media scrutiny and bureau-wide avoidance of any controversy, his actions wouldn't hold up. It would be he who would go down, not her. Quickly and quietly he would be dealt with. Maybe, if he was lucky, he'd end up working side by side with Rachel in the Rapid City office.

'The Badlands are really quite beautiful in the summer,' she said.

She stood up and headed to the door.

'Agent Walling?' Alpert said to her back. 'Hold on a second.'

39

Rachel's plane landed a half hour late at Burbank because of the rain and wind. It had not let up through the night and the city was cast in a shroud of gray. It was the kind of rain that paralyzed the city. Traffic moved at a crawl on every street and every freeway. The roads weren't built for it. The city wasn't either. By dawn the storm water culverts were overflowing, the tunnels were at capacity and the runoff to the Los Angeles River had turned the concrete-lined canal that snaked through the city to the sea into a roaring rapids. It was black water, carrying with it the ash of the fires that had blackened the hills the year before. There was an end-of-the-world gloom about it all. The city had been tested by fire first and now rain. Living in L.A. sometimes felt like you were riding shotgun with the devil to the apocalypse. People I saw that morning carried a what's-next look in their eyes. Earthquake? Tsunami? Or maybe a disaster of our own making? A dozen years earlier fire and rain had been the harbingers of both tectonic and social upheaval in the City of Angels. I didn't think there was anybody here who doubted it could happen again. If we are doomed to repeat ourselves in our follies and mistakes, then it is easy to see nature and balance operating on the same cycle.

I thought about this as I waited for Rachel at the curb outside the terminal. The rain pounded the windshield, turning it translucent and murky. The wind rocked the car on its springs. I thought about rejoining the cops, already second-guessing my decision and wondering if I would be repeating myself in folly or if I had a chance this time at grace.

I didn't see Rachel in the rain until she knocked on the passenger-side window. She then opened the back hatch and threw in her bag. She was wearing a green parka with the hood up. It must have done her well facing the elements in the Dakotas but it looked too large and bulky on her in L.A.

'This better be good, Bosch,' she said as she climbed in and dropped wetly onto the passenger seat. She showed no outward sign of affection and neither did I. It was one of the agreements we'd made on the phone. We were to act as professionals until we played my hunch out.

'Why, you got alternatives?'

'No, it's just that I put everything on the line last night with Alpert. I'm one fuckup short of a permanent posting in South Dakota, where, by the way, the weather might actually be nicer than this.'

'Well, welcome to L.A.'

'I thought this was Burbank.'

'Technically.'

After we cleared the airport I dropped down to the 134 and took that east to the 5. Between the rain and the morning rush hour our progress was slow as we skirted around Griffith Park and pointed south. I wasn't ready to begin worrying about time yet but I was getting close.

For a long time we rode silently because the mix of rain and traffic made the drive intense, probably more so for Rachel who had to sit and do nothing while I had control of the wheel. Finally she spoke, if only to siphon off some of the tension in the car.

'So are you going to tell me this grand plan of yours?'

'No plan, just a hunch.'

'No, you said you *knew* his next move, Bosch.'

I noticed that since we had made love on the bed of my efficiency unit she had started calling me by my last name. I wondered if this was part of the agreement to act as professionals or some form of reverse endearment, calling someone you had been most intimate with by his least intimate name.

'I had to get you here, Rachel.'

'Well, all right then, I'm here. Tell it to me.'

'It's the Poet who has the grand plan. Backus.'

'What's he going to do?'

'Remember the books I told you about yesterday, the books in the barrel and the one I pulled out?'

'Yes.'

'I think I figured out what it all means.'

I told her about the partially burned receipt I had seen and how I thought Book Car was actually Book Carnival, the bookstore operated by retired police detective Ed Thomas, the last intended target of the Poet eight years before.

'You think because of this book in the fire barrel that he's here and is going to make good on the killing we took away from him eight years ago.'

'Exactly.'

'That's a stretch, Bosch. I wish you had told me all of this before I risked my ass flying over here.'

'There's no such thing as coincidence, especially like this.'

'Okay, run the story out for me, then. Give me the profile. Tell me the Poet's grand plan.'

'Well, that's the bureau's job, to profile crimes. I'm not going to do that.

But this is what I think he's doing. I think the trailer and the explosion were all set up to look like the grand finale. And then, as soon as the director steps in front of the television cameras and says I think we've got him, he's going to take out Ed Thomas. The symbolism would be perfect. It's the grand gesture, the ultimate fuck-you. It's checkmate, Rachel. While the bureau is bragging about itself he moves in right under their noses and takes out the guy the bureau was all puffed up about saving the last time.'

'And why the books in the barrel? How does all of that fit in?'

'I think they were books he bought from Ed Thomas. From Book Carnival by mail order or maybe even in person. Maybe they were marked in some way and could be traced back to the store. He didn't want that so he burned them. He couldn't risk that they might survive the trailer blast.

'But then on the other end, after Ed Thomas is gone and Backus has split, the agents would find his connection to the store and would begin to see how long and how hard Backus was planning this. It would help show his genius. That's what he wants, right? I mean, you are the profiler. Tell me if I'm wrong.'

'I *was* the profiler. Right now I handle reservation crimes in the Dakotas.'

The traffic was starting to open up as we passed by downtown, the spires of the financial district disappearing in the upper mist of the storm. The city always looked haunting in the rain to me. There was a foreboding sense about it that always depressed me, that always made me feel like something had broken loose in the world and was wrong.

'There is only one thing wrong with all of that, Bosch.'

'What?'

'The director is holding a press conference today but he isn't going to say we caught the Poet. Just like you, we don't think that was Backus in that trailer.'

'So, Backus doesn't know that. He'll watch it on CNN like everybody else. But it won't change his plan. Either way, I say he hits Ed Thomas today. Either way, he makes his point. "*I am better and smarter than you.*"'

She nodded and thought about that for a long moment.

'Okay,' she finally said. 'What if I'm buying it? What is our play? Have you called Ed Thomas?'

'I don't know what our play is yet and I haven't called Ed Thomas. We're heading toward his store now. It's down in Orange and he opens up at eleven. I called and got his hours off the answering machine.'

'Why his store? All the other cops Backus killed were in their homes, one in his car.'

'Because at the moment I don't know where Ed Thomas lives and because of the book. My guess is Backus will make his move at the bookstore. If I'm wrong and Ed doesn't show up at the store, then we find out where he lives and go there.'

Rachel nodded in agreement with the plan.

'There were three different books written on the Poet case. I read them all and they all had postscripts on the players. They said Thomas retired and opened a bookstore. I think one even named the store.'

'There you go.'

She looked at her watch.

'Are we going to make it there before he opens?'

'We'll make it. Did they set a time for the director's press conference?'

'Three o'clock D.C. time.'

I checked the dash clock. It was 10 a.m. We had an hour before Ed Thomas opened for business and two hours before the press conference. If my theory and hunch were correct we would be in the presence of the Poet very soon. I was ready and I was juiced. I felt the high octane moving in my blood. By old habit I dropped my hand off the wheel and checked my hip. I had a Glock 27 holstered there. It was illegal for me to be carrying a weapon and if I ended up using it, there could be trouble – the kind that could prevent me from rejoining the police department.

But sometimes the risks you face dictate the other risks you must take. And my guess was that this was going to be one of those times.

40

The rain made it hard to watch the store. If we had left the windshield wipers on, it would have been a dead giveaway. So we watched at first through the murk of water on glass.

We were parked in the lot of a strip shopping center on Tustin Boulevard in the city of Orange. Book Carnival was a small business between a rock shop and what looked like a vacant slot. Three doors down was a gun store.

There was a single public entrance. Before taking our position in the front lot we had driven behind the shopping center and seen a rear door with the store's name on it. There was a doorbell and a sign that said RING BELL FOR DELIVERIES.

In a perfect world we'd have been on the front and back of the store with a minimum of four sets of eyes. Backus could come in either way, posing as a customer through the front or as a deliveryman through the back. But nothing was perfect about the world on this day. It was raining and it was just the two of us. We parked the Mercedes at a distance from the front of the store but still close enough to see and act if necessary.

The front counter and cash register were just behind the front window of Book Carnival. This worked in our favor. Shortly after we watched him open the store for business, we watched Ed Thomas take a position behind the counter. He put a cash drawer into the register and made some phone calls. Even with the rain and the blurring of the windshield we could keep him in view as long as he stayed at the register. It was the recesses of the store behind him that disappeared in the gloom. On the occasions that he left his post and walked back toward the shelves and displays in the rear, we lost sight of him and the tingling sense of panic took hold.

On the way down Rachel had told me about the discovery of the GPS tag on her car and the confirmation that she had been used by fellow agents as bait for Backus. And now here we sat watching a former colleague of mine, in a way using him as the new bait. It didn't sit well with me. I wanted to go in and tell Ed the crosshairs were on him, that he should take a vacation, get out of town. But I didn't because I knew if Backus was watching Thomas and saw any deviation in the norm, then we might lose our only chance at him. So Rachel and I got selfish with Ed Thomas's life and I knew in the days ahead I would deal with the guilt from that. The only question was, depending on how things turned out, how much guilt there would be.

The first two customers of the day were women. They arrived shortly after Thomas had unlocked the front door. And while they were browsing in the store a man pulled up, parked in front and went in as well. He was too young to be Backus so we didn't go to full alert. He left in a hurry and without purchasing a book. Then, when the two women left, clutching their bags of books, I got out of the Mercedes and ran across the lot to the overhang in front of the gun shop.

Rachel and I had decided not to bring Thomas into our investigation, but that wasn't going to stop me from going into the store on a reconnaissance mission. We decided that I would go into the store with a cover story, nonchalantly reacquaint myself with Thomas and see if he might already be alert to the idea that he was being watched. So once the first customers of the day had come and gone, I made the move.

I first ducked into the gun store since it was the store closest to where we had parked and it would have looked odd to anyone watching the shopping plaza for me to park on one end and go directly to the bookstore at the other end. I took a cursory look at the gleaming firearms displayed in the glass counter and then up at the paper shooting targets on the back wall. They had the usual silhouettes but they also had versions featuring the faces of Osama bin Laden and Saddam Hussein. I guessed that these were the big sellers.

When a man behind the counter asked if I needed help I told him I was just browsing and then walked out of the store. I walked down toward Book Carnival, stopping first to check out the empty storefront next door. Through the soaped glass I could see boxes marked with what I guessed were the titles of books. I realized Thomas was using the slot for storing books. There was a FOR LEASE sign and a phone number, which I committed to memory in case it played into an angle we would work later.

I entered Book Carnival and Ed Thomas was behind the counter. I smiled and he smiled in recognition but I could tell that it took a few seconds for him to place the face he recognized.

'Harry Bosch,' he said once he had it.

'Hey, Ed, how are you doing?'

We shook hands and his eyes behind the glasses had a warmth to them I liked. I was pretty sure I hadn't seen him since his retirement dinner at the Sportsman's Lodge up in the Valley six or seven years before. There was more white than not in his hair. But he was still tall and thin like I remembered him from the job. He had a tendency at crime scenes to hold his notebook up high and close to his face when he was writing. This was because his glasses were always a prescription or two behind his eyes. The arms-high pose got him the nickname of the Praying Mantis around the homicide table. I suddenly remembered that now. I remembered the flyer for his retirement party showed a caricature of Ed as a superhero with a cape and a mask and a large P on his chest.

'How's the book business doing?'

'It's doing good, Harry. What brings you down here from the big bad city? I heard you retired a couple years ago.'

'Yeah, I did. But I'm thinking about going back.'

'You miss it?'

'Yeah, I sort of do. We'll see what happens.'

He seemed surprised and I knew then that he didn't miss a thing about the job. He'd always been a reader, always had a box of paperbacks in the trunk for surveillances and while sitting on wiretaps. Now he had his pension and his bookstore. He was doing well without all of the nastiness of the job.

'You just passing by?'

'No, actually, I came here for a real reason. You remember my old partner, Kiz Rider?'

'Yeah, sure, she's been in here before.'

'That's what I mean. She's been helping me with something and I want to get her a little gift. I remember she told me once that your store was like the only place around where you could get a book signed by a writer named Dean Koontz. So I was wondering if you got any of those around. I'd like to get her one.'

'I think I might have something left in the back. Let me go check. Those things go fast but I usually keep a stash.'

He left me at the counter and walked through the store to a door at the back that appeared to lead to a stockroom. I assumed the rear delivery door was back there. When he was out of sight I leaned over the counter and looked at the shelves beneath. I saw a small video display tube with its screen cut into four segments. There were four interior camera angles showing the cash register area, with me leaning over the counter; a long view of the entire store; a tighter view of a group of shelves; and the rear stockroom, where I could see Thomas looking at a similar VDT tube on a shelf.

I realized he was looking at me leaning over his counter. I straightened up, my mind quickly trying to come up with an explanation. A few moments later Thomas came back to the counter carrying a book.

'Find what you were looking for, Harry?'

'What? Oh, you mean me looking over the counter? I was just sort of wondering if you, you know, had any protection back there. You being a former cop and all. You ever worry about somebody coming in here who you knew from back when?'

'I take precautions, Harry. Don't worry about that.'

I nodded.

'Good to hear. Is that the book?'

'Yeah, does she have this one? It came out last year.'

He showed me a book called *The Face.* I didn't know if Kiz had it or not but I was going to buy it.

'I don't know. Did he sign it?'

'Yeah, signed and dated.'

'Okay, I'll take it.'

While he rang up the sale I tried some small talk which really wasn't small talk.

'I saw you have the camera set up underneath there. Seems like a little much for a bookstore.'

'You'd be surprised. People like to steal books. I got a collectibles section back there – expensive stuff from the collections I buy and sell. I keep a camera right on it and I caught a kid in there just this morning trying to shove a copy of *Nick's Trip* down his pants. Early Pelecanos is tough to find. That would've been about a seven-hundred-dollar loss for me.'

That seemed like an inordinate amount of money for a single book. I had never heard of the book but guessed that it must have been fifty or a hundred years old.

'You call the cops?'

'No, I just kicked him in the pants and told him if he came back again I would call the law.'

'You're a nice guy, Ed. You must have mellowed out since you left. I don't think the Praying Mantis would've just let the kid slide.'

I handed him two twenties and he gave me the change.

'The Praying Mantis was a long time ago. And my wife doesn't think I'm so mellow. Thanks, Harry. And tell Kiz I said hello.'

'Yeah, I will. You ever run into anybody else from the table?'

I didn't want to leave yet. I wanted more information so I continued the banter. I looked up over his head and spotted a small two-camera dome. It was mounted up near the ceiling, one lens angled down on the register and one taking in the long view of the store. There was a small red light glowing and I could see a small black cable snaking from the camera housing and up into the drop ceiling. While Thomas answered my question I was thinking about the possibility that Backus had been in the store and was captured on a surveillance tape.

'Not really,' Thomas said. 'I sort of left all of that behind. You say you miss it, Harry, but I don't miss a thing about it. Not really.'

I nodded like I understood but I didn't. Thomas had been a good cop and a good detective. He took the work to heart. That was one reason why the Poet had put him in the sights. He was paying lip service to something I didn't think he really believed.

'That's good,' I said. 'Hey, do you have that kid you kicked out of here on tape from this morning? I'd like to see how he tried to rip you off.'

'Nah, I just have live feeds. I got the cameras out in the open and a sticker on the door. It's supposed to be a deterrent but some people are dumb. A setup with a recorder would be too expensive and a pain in the ass in maintenance. I just have the live setup.'

'I see.'

'Listen, if Kiz already has that book I'll take it back. I can sell it.'

'No, that's cool. If she already has it I'll keep it and read it myself.'

'Harry, when's the last time you read a book?'

'I read a book about Art Pepper a couple months ago,' I said indignantly. 'He and his wife wrote it before he died.'

'Nonfiction?'

'Yeah, it was real stuff.'

'I'm talking about a novel. When was the last time you read one?'

I shrugged. I didn't remember.

'That's what I thought,' Thomas said. 'If she doesn't want the book bring it back and I'll get it to somebody who'll read it.'

'Okay, Ed. Thanks.'

'Be careful out there, Harry.'

'I will be. You, too.'

I was heading to the door when things came together – what Thomas had told me and what I knew about the case. I snapped my fingers and acted like I just remembered something. I turned back to Thomas.

'Hey, I got a friend lives all the way in Nevada but he says he's a customer of yours. Mail order probably. You do mail order?'

'Sure. What's his name?'

'Tom Walling. Lives all the way up in Clear.'

Thomas nodded but not in any happy sort of way.

'He's your friend?'

I realized I might have stepped in it.

'Well, an acquaintance, you could say.'

'Well, he owes me some money.'

'Really? What happened?'

'It's a long story. But I sold him some books out of a collection I was handling and he paid very promptly. Paid with a money order and everything was fine. So when he wanted more books I sent them before I got his money order. Big mistake. That was three months ago and I haven't gotten a dime from him. If you see this acquaintance of yours again, tell him I want my money.'

'I will, Ed. That's too bad. I didn't know the guy was a rip-off artist. What books did he buy?'

'He's into Poe, so I sold him some books out of the Rodway collection. Some old ones. Pretty nice books. Then he ordered more when I got another collection in. He didn't pay for them.'

My heart rate was kicking into an upper gear. What Thomas was telling me was confirmation that Backus was somehow in play here. I wanted to stop the charade at that moment and tell Thomas what was happening and that he was in danger. But I held back. I needed to talk to Rachel first and form the right plan.

'I think I saw those books in his place,' I said. 'Was it poetry?'

'Mostly, yeah. He didn't really care for the short stories.'

'Did these books have the original collector's name in them? Rodman?'

'No, Rodway. And yes, they had his library seal embossed in them. That hurt the price but your friend wanted the books.'

I nodded. I saw my theory coming together. It was more than theory now.

'Harry, what are you really up to?'

I looked at Thomas.

'What do you mean?'

'I don't know. You're asking a lot of—'

A loud ring sounded from the back of the store, cutting Thomas off.

'Never mind, Harry,' he said. 'It's more books. I need to go take a delivery.'

'Oh.'

'I'll see you later.'

'Yeah.'

I watched him leave the counter area and head to the back. I checked my watch. It was noon. The director was stepping before the cameras to talk about the explosion in the desert and say that it was the work of the killer known as the Poet. Could this be the moment Backus chose to strike Thomas? My throat and chest tightened as though the air had been sucked out of the room. As soon as Thomas slipped through the doorway to the stockroom, I moved back to the counter and leaned over to look at the security monitor. I knew if Thomas checked the backroom monitor he would see that I hadn't left the store, but I was counting on him going right to the door.

On the corner of the screen showing the stockroom I saw Thomas lean his face up to the rear door and look through a peephole. Apparently unalarmed by what he saw, he proceeded to turn the dead bolt and open the door. I stared intently at the screen, even though the image was small and I was viewing it upside down.

Thomas stepped back from the door and a man entered. He was wearing a dark shirt and matching shorts. He was carrying two boxes, one stacked on top of the other, and Thomas directed him to a nearby worktable. The deliveryman put the boxes down and then took an electronic clipboard off the top box and turned back to Thomas for a delivery confirmation signature.

Everything seemed all right. It was a routine delivery. I quickly got off the counter and went to the door. As I opened it I heard an electronic chime sound but I didn't worry about that. I headed back to the Mercedes, running through the rain after putting the autographed book under my raincoat.

'What was all of that, with you leaning over the counter like that?' Rachel asked once I was behind the wheel again.

'He's got a security box. There was a delivery and I wanted to make sure it was legit before I left. It's after three o'clock in D.C.'

'I know. So what did you learn from him or were you just in there buying a book?'

'I learned a lot. Tom Walling is a customer. Or was, until he stiffed him for an order of Edgar Allan Poe books. It was mail order like we thought. He never saw him, just sent the books out to Nevada.'

Rachel sat up straight.

'Are you kidding me?'

'No. The books were out of some guy's collection that Ed was selling. So they were marked and therefore traceable. That was why Backus burned them all in the fire barrel. He couldn't risk that they'd survive the blast intact and be traced back to Thomas.'

'Why?'

'Because he is definitely in play here. He's got to be setting up on Thomas.'

I started the car.

'Where are you going?'

'Around back to make sure about the delivery. Besides, it's good to change locations every now and then.'

'Oh, you're giving me surveillance one-oh-one lessons now.'

Without responding I drove around to the back of the plaza and saw the brown UPS van parked by the open rear door of Book Carnival. We drove on by and during the brief glimpse I had of the back of the truck and the open door of the stockroom, I saw the deliveryman struggling to carry several boxes up a ramp to the back of his truck. The returns, I guessed. I kept driving without hesitation.

'He's legit,' Rachel said.

'Yeah.'

'You didn't give yourself away with Thomas, did you?'

'No. He was suspicious but then I was sort of saved by the bell. I wanted to talk to you first. I think we need to bring him in on it.'

'Harry, we talked about this. If we bring him into it he may change his routine and demeanor. It might be a giveaway. If Backus has been watching him, any little change could be a tell.'

'And if we don't warn him and this thing goes wrong, then we ... '

I didn't finish. We had been over this argument twice before, each of us alternately taking the other side. It was a classic contradiction of intentions. Do we ensure Thomas's safety at the risk of losing Backus? Or do we risk Thomas's safety to ensure getting close to Backus? It was all about the means to an end and neither of us would be happy no matter which way we went.

'I guess that means we can't let anything go wrong,' she said.

'Right. What about backup?'

'I also think it's too risky. The more people we bring into this, the greater the chance of tipping our hand.'

I nodded. She was right. I found a spot on the opposite end of the parking lot from where we had parked and watched before. I wasn't kidding myself, though. There were only so many cars in the lot in the middle of a rainy weekday and we were noticeable. I started to think that maybe we were like Ed Thomas's cameras. Strictly a deterrent. Maybe Backus had seen us and it had stopped him from moving forward with his plan. For now.

'Customer,' Rachel said.

I looked across the lot and saw a woman heading toward the store. She looked familiar to me and then I remembered her from the Sportsman's Lodge.

'That's his wife. I met her once. I think her name is Pat.'

'She bringing him lunch, you think?'

'Maybe. Or maybe she works there.'

We watched for a while but there was no sign of Thomas or his wife in the front of the store. I grew concerned and took out my cell phone and called the store, hoping the call would bring them to the front counter, where the phone was.

But a woman answered right away and there was still no one at the counter. I quickly hung up.

'There must be a phone in the stockroom.'

'Who answered?'

'The wife.'

'Should I take a walk and go in?'

'No. If Backus is watching he'll recognize you. You can't be seen.'

'All right, then what?'

'Then nothing. They're probably at the table I saw in the back room having lunch. Be patient.'

'I don't want to be patient. I don't like just sitting—'

She stopped when we saw Ed Thomas walk out the front of the store. He was wearing a raincoat and carrying an umbrella and a briefcase. He got into the car we had seen him arrive at the store in that morning, a green Ford Explorer. Through the store's front window I saw his wife take a seat on a stool behind the front counter.

'Here we go,' I said.

'Where's he going?'

'Maybe he's going to get lunch.'

'Not with a briefcase. We stay on him, right?'

I restarted the car.

'Right.'

We watched as Thomas pulled out of a parking space in his Ford SUV. He headed toward the exit and turned right on Tustin Boulevard. After his car was absorbed into the passing traffic I pulled up to the exit and followed him into the rain. I pulled out my phone and called the store. Ed Thomas's wife answered.

'Hi, is Ed there?'

'No, he's not. Can I help you?'

'Is this Pat?'

'Yes, it is. Who's this?'

'It's Bill Gilbert. I think we met at the Sportsman's Lodge a while back. I used to work with Ed in the department. I was going to be in the area and thought I'd drop by the store today to say hello. Will he be back later?'

'That's hard to say. He went to do an appraisal and who knows, it might take the rest of the day. With this rain and the distance he had to go.'

'An appraisal? What do you mean?'

'A book collection. Someone wants to sell his collection and Ed just left to go see what it is worth. It's all the way up in the San Fernando Valley and from what I understand it's a big collection. He told me I'd probably be closing the store tonight.'

'Is it more of the Rodway collection? He told me about that the last time we talked.'

'No, that's just about all been sold. This is a man named Charles Turrentine and he has over six thousand books.'

'Wow, that's a lot.'

'He's a well-known collector but I guess he needs the money because he told Ed he wants to sell everything.'

'Strange. A guy spends all that time collecting and then he sells it all.'

'We see it happen.'

'Well, Pat, I'll let you go. And I'll catch Ed next time. Tell him I said hello.'

'What was your name again?'

'Tom Gilbert. Bye now.'

I closed the phone.

'You were Bill Gilbert at the start of the conversation.'

'Whoops.'

I recounted the conversation for Rachel. I then called information in the 818 area code but there was no listing for a Charles Turrentine. I asked Rachel if she had a connection in the bureau's Los Angeles field office who could get an address for Turrentine and maybe an unlisted number.

'Don't you have somebody in the LAPD you can use?'

'At the moment I think I've used up all the favors owed me. Besides, I'm an outsider. You're not.'

'I don't know about that.'

She pulled out her phone and went to work on it and I concentrated on the taillights of Thomas's SUV, just fifty yards ahead of me on the 22 freeway. I knew Thomas had a choice up ahead. He could turn north on the 5 and go through downtown L.A., or he could keep on going and take the 405 north. Both routes would lead him to the Valley.

Rachel got a call back in five minutes with the information she had asked for.

'He lives on Valerio Street in Canoga Park. Do you know where that is?'

'I know where Canoga Park is. Valerio runs east-west across the whole Valley. Did you get a phone number?'

She answered by punching in a number on her cell phone. She then held it to her ear and waited. After thirty seconds she closed the phone.

'There was no answer. I got the tape.'

We drove in silence as we thought about that.

Thomas passed by the exit to the 5 north and proceeded on toward the 405. I knew he would turn north there and take the Sepulveda Pass into the Valley. Canoga Park was on the west side. With the weather we were talking about at least an hour's drive. If we were lucky.

'Don't lose him, Bosch,' Rachel said quietly.

I knew what she meant. She was telling me she had the vibe, that she thought this was it. That she believed Ed Thomas might be leading us to the Poet. I nodded because I had it, too, almost like a humming coming from the center of my chest. I knew without really knowing that we were there.

'Don't worry,' I said. 'I won't.'

41

The rain was getting to Rachel. The relentlessness of it. It never let up, never paused. It just came down and hit the windshield in a nonstop torrent that overpowered the wipers. Everything was a blur. There were cars pulled off on the shoulders of the freeway. Lightning cracked the sky to the west, somewhere out over the ocean. They passed accident after accident and these just made Rachel all the more nervous. If they got into an accident and lost Thomas, they would carry an awful burden of responsibility for what happened to him.

She was afraid that if she looked away from the red glow of the tail-lights on Thomas's car, they would lose him in the sea of blurred red. Bosch seemed to know what she was thinking.

'Relax,' he said. 'I'm not going to lose him. And even if I do, we know where he is going now.'

'No, we don't. We only know where Turrentine lives. That doesn't mean his books are there. Six thousand books? Who keeps six thousand books in their house? He probably has them in a warehouse somewhere.'

Rachel watched Bosch adjust his grip on the steering wheel and add a few more miles to his speed, drawing them closer to Thomas.

'Didn't think about that, did you?'

'No, not really.'

'So don't lose him.'

'I told you, I won't.'

'I know. It just helps me to say it.'

She gestured toward the windshield.

'How often does it get like this?'

'Almost never,' Bosch said. 'They said on the news that it's a hundred-year storm. It's like something's wrong, something's broken. The canyons are probably washing out in Malibu. Landslides in the Palisades. And the river's probably over its sides. Last year we had the fires. This year maybe it's going to be rain. One way or another it's always something. It's like you always have to pass a test or something.'

He turned on the radio to pick up a weather report. But Rachel immediately reached over and turned it off and pointed ahead through the windshield.

'Concentrate on this,' she ordered. 'I don't care about the weather report.'

'Right.'

'Get closer. I don't care if you're right behind him. He won't be able to see you in this mess.'

'I get behind him I might hit him, then what do we say?'

'Just don't—'

'Lose him. Yeah, I know.'

They drove for the next half hour without a word. The freeway rose and crossed over the mountains. Rachel saw a large stone structure on the top of the mountain. It looked like some sort of postmodern castle in the gray and gloom and Bosch told her it was the Getty Museum.

As they descended into the Valley she saw the turn signal flare from the back of Thomas's car. Bosch moved into the turning lane three cars back.

'He's taking the one-oh-one. We're almost there.'

'You mean to Canoga Park?'

'That's right. He'll take this out west and then go north again on surface streets.'

Bosch grew quiet again as he concentrated on the driving and following. In another fifteen minutes the turn signal on the Explorer flared again and Thomas exited on DeSoto Avenue and headed north. Bosch and Walling trailed behind on the exit ramp, but this time without the cover of other traffic.

On DeSoto, Thomas almost immediately pulled to the curb in a no parking area and Bosch had to drive by him or the surveillance would have been obvious.

'I think he's looking at a map or directions,' Rachel said. 'He had the light on and his head was down.'

'Okay.'

Bosch pulled into a service station, circled around the pumps and then drove back out to the street. He paused before pulling out, looking left down the street at Thomas's Explorer. He waited and after a half minute Thomas pulled his Explorer back into traffic. Bosch waited for him to go by, holding his cell phone up to his left ear to block any view of his face in case Thomas was looking and could see in the rain. He let another car go by and then pulled out.

'He must be close,' Rachel said.

'Yeah.'

But Thomas drove several more blocks before turning right. Bosch slowed before doing the same.

'Valerio,' Rachel said, seeing the street sign in the murk. 'This is it.'

When Bosch made the turn she saw the brake lights on Thomas's car. He was stopped in the middle of the road three blocks ahead. He was at a dead end.

Bosch quickly pulled to the curb behind a parked car.

'The dome light's on,' Rachel said. 'I think he's looking at his map again.'

'The river,' Bosch said.

'What?'

'I told you, Valerio cuts across the whole Valley. But so does the river. So he's probably figuring out a way to get around it. The river cuts off all these streets in here. He probably has to get to Valerio on the other side.'

'I don't see any river up there. I see a fence and concrete.'

'It's not what you would consider a river. In fact, technically that isn't the river. It's probably either the Aliso or Brown's Canyon wash. It goes to the river.'

They waited. Thomas didn't move.

'The river used to flood in storms like this. It would wipe out a third of the city. So they tried to control it. Contain it. Somebody had the idea to capture it in stone, put it in concrete. So that's what they did and everybody's house and home was supposedly safe after that.'

'I guess that's called progress.'

Bosch nodded and then re-gripped his hands on the wheel.

'He's moving.'

Thomas turned left and once his car was out of sight Bosch pulled away from the curb and followed. Thomas drove north to Saticoy and then took a right. He went over a bridge crossing the wash below. As they followed, Rachel looked down and saw the torrent of water in the concrete channel.

'Wow. I thought I lived in Rapid City.'

Bosch didn't answer. Thomas turned south on Mason and came back down to Valerio. But now he was on the other side of the concrete channel. He turned right again on Valerio.

'That'll be another dead end,' Bosch said.

He stayed on Mason and drove on by Valerio. Rachel looked through the rain and saw that Thomas had pulled into a driveway in front of a large two-story home that was one of five homes on the dead-end street.

'He pulled into a driveway,' she said. 'He's there. Jesus, it's the house!'

'What house?'

'The one from the photo in the trailer. Backus was so sure of himself he left us a goddamn picture.'

Bosch pulled to the curb. They were out of sight of the homes on Valerio. Rachel turned and looked out all of the windows. Every home around them was dark.

'There must be a power outage around here.'

'Under your seat there's a flashlight. Take it.'

Rachel reached down and got it.

'What about you?'

'I'll be all right. Let's go.'

Rachel started to open her door but then looked back at Bosch. She wanted to say something but hesitated.

'What?' he asked. 'Be careful? Don't worry, I will.'

'Actually, yes, be careful. But what I was going to say is that I have my second gun in my bag. Do you—'

'Thanks, Rachel, but this time I brought my own.'

She nodded.

'I should have figured that. And what are your views on backup now?'

'Call it in if you want. But I'm not waiting. I'm going down there.'

The rain felt cold on my face and neck as I got out of the Mercedes. I pulled the collar on my jacket up and started heading back toward Valerio. Rachel came over and walked next to me without saying a word. When we got to the corner we used the wall surrounding the corner property as cover and looked down into the cul-de-sac and the dark house where Ed Thomas had parked his car. There was no sign of Thomas or anyone else. Every window at the front of the house was dark. But even in the grayness I could tell that Rachel was right. It was the house from the photo Backus had left for us.

I could hear the river but not see it. It was hidden behind the homes. But its furious power was almost palpable, even from this distance. In storms like this the whole city washed itself out over its smoothed concrete surfaces. It snaked through the Valley and around the mountains to downtown. And from there west to the ocean.

It was a mere trickle most of the year. A municipal joke even. But a rainstorm would awaken the snake and give it power. It became the city's gutter, millions and millions of gallons banging against its thick stone walls, tons of water raging to get out, moving with a terrible force and momentum. I remembered a boy who was taken when I was a kid. I didn't know him. I knew of him. Four decades later I even remembered his name. Billy Kinsey was playing on the river's shoulder. He slipped in and in a moment he was gone. They found his body hung up in a viaduct 12 miles away.

My mother had taught me early and often, when it rains …

'Stay out of the narrows.'

'What?' Rachel whispered.

'I was thinking about the river. Trapped between those walls. When I was a kid we called it "the narrows." When it rains like this the water moves fast. It's deadly. When it rains you stay away from the narrows.'

'But we're going to the house.'

'Same thing, Rachel. Be careful. Stay out of the narrows.'

She looked at me. She seemed to understand what I meant.

'Okay, Bosch.'

'How about you take the front and I take the back?'

'Fine.'

'Be ready for anything.'

'You, too.'

The target house was three properties away. We walked quickly along the wall surrounding the first property and then cut up the driveway of the next. We skirted the fronts of two houses until we came to the home where Thomas's car was parked. Rachel gave me a last nod and we separated then, both of us pulling our weapons in unison. Rachel moved to the front while I started down the driveway toward the rear. The gloom and the sound of the rain and the river channel gave me visual and sound cover. The driveway was also lined with squat bougainvillea trees that had been let go for some time without training or trimming. But the house behind the windows was dark. Someone could be behind any glass watching me and I wouldn't know it.

The rear yard was flooded. In the middle of the big puddle stood the rusted twin A-frames of a swing set with no swings left on it. Behind it was a six-foot fence that separated the property from the river channel. I could see the water was near the top of its concrete siding and was rushing by in a mad torrent. It would flood by day's end. Further upstream, where the channels were shallower, it probably already had stemmed its sides.

I turned my attention back to the house. There was a full porch off the rear. There were no gutters on the roof here and the rain was coming off in sheets, so heavy that it obscured everything within. Backus could've been sitting in a rocker on the porch and I wouldn't have seen him. The line of bougainvilleas carried along the porch railing. I ducked below the sight line and moved quickly to the steps. I took the three steps up in one stride and was in out of the rain. My eyes and ears took a moment to adjust and that was when I saw it. There was a white rattan couch on the right side of the porch. On it a blanket covered the unmistakable shape of a human form sitting upright but slumped against the left arm. Dropping to a crouch I moved closer and reached for a corner of the blanket on the floor. I slowly pulled it off the form.

It was an old man. He looked like he had been dead at least a day. The odor was just starting. His eyes were open and bugged, his skin was the color of white paint in a smoker's bedroom. A snap-cuff had been pulled tight – too tight – around his neck. Charles Turrentine, I presumed. I also presumed he was the old man in the photo Backus had taken. He had been killed and then left there on the porch like a stack of old newspapers. He'd had no business with the Poet. He'd just been a means to an end.

I raised my Glock and went to the house's back door. I wanted to get a warning to Rachel but there was no way to do it without revealing my own position and possibly compromising hers. I just had to keep moving, going further into the darkness of this place until I came across her or Backus.

The door was locked. I decided I would go around, catch up to Rachel from the front. But as I turned, my eyes fell back on the body and I was struck with a possibility. I moved to the couch and patted down the old man's pants. And I was rewarded. I heard the jingle of keys.

*

Rachel was surrounded. Stacks and stacks of books lined every wall in the front hallway. She stood there, gun in one hand and flashlight in the other, and looked into the living room to her right. More books. Shelves lined every wall and every shelf was filled to capacity. Books stacked on the coffee table and the end tables and every horizontal surface. Somehow it made the place seem haunted. It was not a place of life but a place of doom and gloom where bookworms ate through the words of all the authors.

She tried to keep moving without dwelling on her rising fears. She wavered and thought about turning back to the door and leaving before she was discovered. But then she heard the voices and knew she must press on.

'Where is Charles?'

'I said *sit down.*'

The words came to her from an unknown direction. The pounding of the rain outside, the rage of the nearby river, and the books stacked everywhere combined to obliquely camouflage the origin of sounds. She heard the voices but could not tell where they came from.

More sounds and voices came to her. Murmurs mostly and every few moments a recognizable word, sculpted in anger or fear.

'You thought . . . '

She bent down and left the flashlight on the floor. She had not used it yet and couldn't risk it now. She moved into the deeper gloom of the hallway. She had already checked the front rooms and knew the voices were coming from somewhere further into the house.

The hallway led to a foyer from which doors opened in three different directions. As she got there she heard the voices of two men and thought for sure that they came from somewhere to the right.

'Write it!'

'I can't see!'

Then a popping sound. A ripping sound. Curtains being pulled off a window.

'There, you see now? Write it or I'll end it right now!'

'All right! All right!'

'Exactly as I say it. Once upon a midnight dreary . . .'

She knew what it was. She recognized the words of Edgar Allan Poe. And she knew it was Backus, though the voice was different. He was using the poetry again, re-creating the crime taken from him so long ago. Bosch had been right.

She moved into the room to the right and found it empty. A billiard table stood in the middle of the room, every inch of its surface taken up by stacks of more books. She understood what Backus had done. He had lured Ed Thomas here because the man who lived here – Charles Turrentine – was a collector. He knew Thomas would come for this collection.

She started to turn in order to retreat, to check the next room off the foyer. But before she had moved more than a few inches she felt the cold muzzle of a gun pressed against her neck.

'Hello, Rachel,' Robert Backus said with his surgically changed voice. 'What a surprise to see you here.'

She froze and in that moment knew that he could not be played in any way, that he knew all the plays and all the angles. She knew she only had one chance. That was Bosch.

'Hello, Bob. It's been a long time.'

'Yes, it has. Would you like to leave your weapon here and join me in the library?'

Rachel put her Sig down on one of the stacks on the billiard table.

'I sort of thought the whole place was a library, Bob.'

Backus didn't respond. She felt him grab the back of her collar, press his gun against her spine and then push her in the direction he wanted her to go. They left the room and went into the next, which was a small room with two high-backed wooden chairs arranged to face a large stone fireplace. There was no fire and Rachel could hear rain dripping down the chimney into the hearth. She saw that it was creating a puddle there. Windows on either side of the fireplace had rain washing down them, turning them translucent.

'We happen to have just enough chairs,' Backus said. 'Have a seat, won't you?'

He roughly brought her around one of the chairs and pushed her down into it. He made a quick check of her body for other weapons and then stepped back and dropped something onto her lap. Rachel looked into the other chair and saw Ed Thomas. He was still alive. His wrists were held to the arms of the chair by plastic snap-cuffs. Two more cuffs had been joined and then used to hold him by his neck to the back of the chair. He had been gagged with a cloth napkin and his face was overly red with exertion and lack of oxygen.

'Bob, you can stop this,' Rachel said. 'You've made your point. You don't—'

'Put the cuff around your right wrist and lock it to the chair's arm.'

'Bob, please. Let—'

'Do it!'

She wrapped the plastic cuff around the arm of the chair and her wrist. She then pulled the tab through the slide lock.

'Tight, but not too tight. I don't want to leave a mark.'

When she was done he told her to put her free arm on the other arm of the chair. He then moved in and grabbed the arm to keep it in place while he looped another snap-cuff around it and locked it. He stepped back to admire his work.

'There.'

'Bob, we did a lot of good work together. Why are you doing this?'

He looked down at her and smiled.

'I don't know. But let's talk about it later. I have to finish with Detective Thomas. It's been a long time coming for him and me. And just think, Rachel, you get to watch. What a rare opportunity for you.'

Backus turned to Thomas. He stepped over and yanked the gag out of his mouth. He then reached into his pocket and pulled out a folding knife. He opened it and in one swift movement sliced through the cuff holding Thomas's right arm to the chair.

'Now, where were we, Detective Thomas? Line three, I believe.'

'More like the end of the line.'

Rachel recognized Bosch's voice from behind her. But when she turned to look for him the chair back was too high.

I held the gun steady, trying to figure out the best way to handle him.

'Harry,' Rachel called out calmly. 'He's got a gun in his left and a knife in his right. He's right-handed.'

I steadied my aim and told him to put the weapons down. He complied without hesitation. This gave me pause, as if he was moving too quickly to plan B. Was there another weapon? Another killer in the house?

'Rachel, Ed, you all right?'

'We're fine,' Rachel said. 'Put him on the ground, Harry. He's got snap-cuffs in his pocket.'

'Rachel, where's your gun?'

'In the other room. Put him down on the ground, Harry.'

I took a step further into the room but then paused to study Backus. He had changed again. He no longer looked like the man who had called himself Shandy. No beard, no hat over gray hair. His face and head were shaved. He looked completely different.

I took another step but stopped again. I suddenly thought about Terry McCaleb and his wife and his daughter and his stepson. I thought about the shared mission and what had been lost. How many bad men would roam the world free because Terry was taken away? A rage as strong as the river built inside me. I didn't want to put Backus on the ground, cuff him and watch him driven away in a patrol car to a life behind bars of celebrity attention and fascination. I wanted to take from him everything he had taken from my friend and all of the others.

'You killed my friend,' I said. 'For that you—'

'Harry, don't,' Rachel said.

'I'm sorry,' Backus said. 'But I've been kind of busy. Who might your friend be?'

'Terry McCaleb. He was your friend, too, and you—'

'Actually, I wanted to take care of Terry. Yes, he had the potential of becoming a stone in my shoe. But I—'

'Shut up, Bob!' Rachel yelled. 'You couldn't carry Terry's lunch. Harry, this is too dangerous. Put him down! Do it now!'

I broke off my rage and focused on the moment at hand. Terry McCaleb retreated in the gloom. I stepped toward Backus, wondering what Rachel was telling me. Put him down? Did she want me to shoot him?

I took two more steps.

'Get on the ground,' I ordered. 'Away from the weapons.'

'Whatever you say.'

He turned as if to move away from where he had dropped his weapons and to choose a spot to get down.

'Do you mind, there's a puddle here. Leaky fireplace.'

Without waiting for an answer from me he took a step toward the window. And I suddenly saw it. I knew what he was going to do.

'Backus, no!'

But my words did not stop him. He planted his foot and dove headfirst into the window. Its framework softened by years of sunlight and rains like this day's, the window gave way as easily as a Hollywood prop. Wood splintered and glass shattered as his body went through. I quickly ran to the opening and saw the immediate muzzle flash from Backus's second gun. Plan B.

Two quick pops and I heard the bullets zing by and hit the ceiling above and behind me. I ducked back behind the wall and fired off two quick returns without looking. I then dropped to the floor, crawled beneath the window and came up on the other side. I looked out and Backus was gone. On the ground I saw a little two-shot derringer. His second had been a little vest gun and he was now unarmed, unless there was a plan C.

'Harry, the knife,' Rachel called from behind me. 'Cut me loose!'

I grabbed the knife from the floor and quickly sliced through her bonds. The plastic cut easily. I then turned to Thomas and put the knife in his right hand so he could free himself.

'I'm sorry, Ed,' I said.

I could give him the rest of the apology later. I turned back to Rachel, who was at the window, looking through the gloom. She had picked up Backus's gun.

'See him?'

I joined her there. Thirty yards to the left was the river wash. Just as I looked I saw the overflowing torrent carrying a whole oak tree on its surface. Then there was movement. We saw Backus jump from the cover of a bougainvillea and start to scale the fence that kept people away from the river. Just as he was going over the top Rachel raised a gun and fired two quick shots. Backus dropped down onto the gravel shoulder next to the channel. But he then jumped up and started running. Rachel had missed.

'He can't get across the river,' I said. 'He's hemmed in. He's heading up to the bridge at Saticoy.'

I knew if Backus made it to the bridge we would lose him. He could cross and disappear in the neighborhood on the west side of the channel or the business district near DeSoto.

'I'll go from here,' Rachel said. 'You get the car and get there faster. We'll trap him at the bridge.'

'Got it.'

I headed for the door, getting ready to run through the rain. I pulled my cell phone from my pocket and threw it to Thomas as I went.

'Ed,' I called over my shoulder. 'Call the cops. Get us some backup.'

42

Rachel ejected the magazine from Backus's gun and found it had been fully loaded until she took the two shots at him. She slapped it back into place and went to the window.

'You want me to go with you?' Ed Thomas asked from behind.

She turned. He had cut himself free. He was standing, holding the knife up and ready.

'Do what Harry said. Get us backup.'

She stepped onto the sill and jumped out into the rain. She quickly moved along the bougainvillea until she found an opening and pushed through to the river fence. She put Backus's gun in her holster and climbed up and over, snagging her jacket sleeve on the top and tearing it. She dropped onto the gravel shoulder two feet from the edge. She looked over the side and saw the water was only three feet from the overflow. It was cascading against the concrete, creating the roaring sound of death. She looked away and then further down the track. She saw Backus running. He was halfway to the bridge at Saticoy. Rachel got up and started running. She fired a shot into the air so he would think about what was coming behind him, not what might be waiting for him at the bridge.

The Mercedes skidded into the curb on the top of the bridge. I jumped out, not bothering to kill the engine, and ran to the railing. I saw Rachel running toward me, gun up, on the shoulder of the canal. But I didn't see Backus.

I stepped back and looked in all directions but still didn't see him. I thought that it would have been impossible for him to have reached the bridge ahead of me. I ran down to the gate that sided the bridge and offered entrance to the channel's shoulder. It was locked but I could see that the shoulder continued under the bridge. It was the only alternative. I knew Backus had to be hiding under there.

Quickly I climbed over the gate and dropped down to the gravel. I came up, gun pointed in both hands at the dark opening beneath the bridge. I ducked and moved into the darkness. The noise of the rushing water echoed loudly beneath the bridge. The underside of the bridge was segmented by four large concrete supports. Backus could easily be hidden behind any one of them.

'Backus!' I called out. 'You want to live, come out! Now!'

Nothing. Only the sound of the water. Then I heard the far-off sound of a voice and I turned back to see Rachel. She was still a hundred yards away. She was yelling but her words were lost in the water noise.

Backus huddled in the darkness. He tried to stave off all the emotions and concentrate on the moment. He had been here before. Cornered in the dark. He had survived before and he would survive now. What was important now was to concentrate on the moment, draw his strength from the darkness.

He heard his pursuer call out to him. He was close now. He had the weapon but Backus had the darkness. Darkness had always been on his side. He pressed back against the concrete and willed himself to disappear in the shadows. He would be patient and make his move when the time was right.

I turned away from the distant figure of Rachel and focused back on clearing the bridge. I moved forward, staying as far back from the concrete shelters as I could without falling into the channel. I cleared the first two and glanced back at Rachel again. She was fifty yards away now. She started signaling with her left arm but I didn't understand the hooked movement she was repeating.

I suddenly realized my mistake. I had left the keys in the car. Backus could come up on the other side of the bridge and get to the car.

I started to run, hoping to get there in time to take a shot at the tires. But I was wrong about the car. As I passed the third concrete support Backus suddenly leaped out at me, hitting me solidly with his shoulder. I went sprawling backward with him on top of me, sliding on the gravel to the edge of the concrete channel.

He was going for my gun, using both hands to tear it from my grip. I knew in an instant that if he got the gun everything was over, that he'd kill me and then Rachel. He couldn't get the gun.

He slammed his left elbow into my jaw and I felt my grip weaken. I fired the gun twice, hoping I might catch a finger or a palm. He yelped in pain but then I felt the pressure even more as he redoubled his effort, now fueled by pain and red anger.

His blood worked its way into my grip and helped loosen it. I was going to lose the gun. I could tell. He had position on me and an animal strength. My grip was slipping. I could try to hang on a few more seconds until Rachel got there but by then she could also be running into a death trap.

Instead I took the only alternative I had left. I dug my heels into the gravel and flexed my whole body upward. My shoulders slid over the concrete edge. I replanted my heels and did it again. This time it was enough.

Backus seemed to suddenly realize his situation. He let go of the gun and reached back to the edge. But it was too late for him, too.

Together we went over the edge and into the black water.

Rachel saw them fall from just a few yards away. She yelled '*No!*' as if that might stop them. She got to the spot and looked down and saw nothing. She then ran along the edge and out from beneath the bridge. She saw nothing. She looked downriver for any sign of them in the cascading current.

Then she saw Bosch come up and whip his head around as if to check his position. He was struggling with something under the water and then she realized it was his raincoat. He was trying to take it off.

She scanned the river but didn't see the bald head of Backus anywhere. She looked back at Bosch as he was carried away from her. She saw him looking back at her. He raised an arm out of the water and pointed. She followed and saw the Mercedes parked on top of the bridge. She saw its windshield wipers moving back and forth and she knew the keys were still there.

She started running.

The water was cold, more so than I would have imagined. And I was already weak from the struggle with Backus. I felt heavy in the water and found it difficult to keep my face up and clear. The water seemed to be alive, as if it was gripping me and pulling me down.

My gun was gone and there was no sign of Backus. I spread my arms and tried to maneuver my body so that I could simply ride the rapids until I had some strength back and could make a move or Rachel got help.

I remembered the boy who had gone into the river so many years before. Firemen, cops, even passersby tried to save him, hanging down hoses and ladders and ropes. But they all missed and he went down. Eventually, they all go down in the narrows.

I tried not to think about that. I tried not to panic. I turned my palms down and I seemed to be able to keep my face up out of the water better. It increased my speed in the current but it kept my head up out of the water. It gave me confidence. I started to think that I could make it. For a while. It all depended on when help got to me. I looked up into the sky. No helicopters. No fire department. No help yet. Just the gray void of emptiness up there and rain coming down.

The 911 operator told Rachel to stay on the line but she couldn't drive fast and well and safely with the phone to her ear. She dropped it on the passenger seat without disconnecting. When she came to the next stop sign she stopped so short that the phone was hurled into the foot well and out of her reach. She didn't care. She was speeding down the street checking to her left at every intersection for the next bridge crossing the channel. When she finally saw one she sped to it and stopped the Mercedes right on top of it in a traffic lane. She jumped out and went to the railing.

Neither Bosch nor Backus was in sight. She thought she might have gotten ahead of them. She ran across the street, drawing a horn blast from a motorist but not caring, and went to the opposite rail.

She studied the roiling surface for a long moment and then saw Bosch. His head was above the surface and canted back, his face to the sky. She panicked. Was he still alive? Or was he drowned and his body just moving in the current? Then almost as quickly as the fear had grabbed her she saw movement as Bosch whipped his head, as swimmers often do to get hair and water out of their eyes. He was alive and maybe a hundred yards from the bridge. She could see him struggling to move his position in the stream. She leaned forward and looked down. She knew what he was doing. He was going to try to catch one of the bridge's support beams. If he could grab it and hold on, he could be extracted and saved right here.

Rachel ran back to the car and threw open the rear hatch. She looked in the back for anything that might help. Her bag was there and almost nothing else. She yanked it out to the ground without caring and lifted the carpeted floor panel. Someone stuck behind the Mercedes on the street started honking. She didn't even turn to look.

I hit the middle pier of the bridge so hard that I lost all of my breath and thought I'd broken four or five ribs. But I held on. I knew this was my shot. I held on with everything I had left.

The water had claws. I could feel them as it rushed by me. Thousands of claws pulling at me, grabbing me, trying to take me back into the dark torrent. The water backed up on me and rose into my face. Arms on either side of the pier, I tried to shimmy up the slippery concrete but every time I gained a few inches, the claws would grab me and pull me back down. I quickly learned that the best I could do was hold on. And wait.

As I hugged the concrete I thought of my daughter. I thought of her urging me to hold on, telling me I had to make it for her. She told me no matter where I was or what I did, she still needed me. Even in the moment, I knew it was illusion but I found comfort in it. I found the strength to hold on.

There were tools and a spare tire in the compartment, nothing that would work. Then, beneath the tire, through the design holes in the wheel, she saw black and red cables. Jumper cables.

She put her fingers through the holes in the wheel and yanked it upward. It was large, heavy and awkward but she was not deterred. She pulled the wheel up and out and just dropped it on the road. She grabbed the cables and ran back across the road, causing a car to slide sideways as its driver hit the brakes.

At the railing she looked into the river but didn't see Bosch at first. Then she looked down and saw him clinging to the support beam, the water backing up against him as it grabbed and pulled at him. His hands and fingers were scratched and bloody. He was looking up at her and had what she thought might have been a small smile on his face, almost like he was telling her that he was going to be all right.

Not sure how she was going to complete the rescue, she dropped one end of the cables over the side. They were far too short.

'Shit!'

She knew she had to go over. There was a utility pipe running along the side of the bridge. She knew if she could get down to that she could lower the cables another five feet down. It might be enough.

'Lady, are you all right?'

She turned. There was a man standing there. He was under an umbrella. He had been crossing the bridge.

'There's a man down there in the river. Call nine-one-one. Do you have a cell? Call nine-one-one.'

The man began pulling a cell phone from his jacket pocket. Rachel turned back to the railing and started to climb up on it.

That was the easy part. Going over the railing and climbing down to the pipe was the risky maneuver. She put the cables around her neck and slowly reached one foot down to the pipe, then the other. She slid down with one leg on either side of the pipe like she was riding a horse. This time she knew the cable would reach Bosch. She started lowering it to him and he reached for it. But just as his hand grabbed it, there was a blur of color in the water and Bosch was struck by something and knocked loose from the support beam. In that moment Rachel realized it was Backus, either alive or dead, that had knocked him loose.

She hadn't been ready. When Bosch was knocked loose he kept his grip on the cable line. But his weight and Backus's weight and the current were too much for Rachel. The other end of the cable was jerked out of her grasp and it went down into the water and under the bridge.

'They're coming! They're coming!'

She looked up at the man under the umbrella at the top of the railing.

'It's too late,' she said. 'He's gone.'

I was weak but Backus was weaker. I could tell he didn't have the same strength he'd brought to the confrontation on the river's edge. He had pulled me loose from the bridge because I hadn't seen him coming and he'd hit me with all his weight. But now he was grabbing at me like a drowning man, just trying to hold on.

We tumbled through the water, drawing down to the bottom. I tried to open my eyes but the water was too dark to see through. I drove him down hard into the concrete floor and then shifted behind him. I wrapped the cable I still gripped around his neck. I did it again and again until his hands let go of me and went to his own neck. My lungs were burning. I needed air. I pushed off him to move toward the surface. As we separated he made a last grab for my ankles but I was able to kick away and break his grasp.

In the last moments Backus saw his father. Long dead and burned, he appeared alive. He had the stern set of eyes that Backus always remembered. He had one hand behind his back, as if he was hiding something. His other hand beckoned his son to come forward. To come home.

Backus smiled and then he laughed. Water rushed into his mouth and lungs. He didn't panic. He welcomed it. He knew he would be reborn. He would return. He knew evil could never be vanquished. It just moved from one place to another and waited.

I surfaced and gulped down air. I spun in the water to look for Backus but he was gone. I was safe from him but not from the water. I was exhausted. My arms felt so heavy in the water that I could barely bring them to the surface. I thought about the boy again, about how scared he must have been, all alone and the claws grabbing at him.

Up ahead I could see where the wash emptied into the main river channel. I was fifty yards away and I knew the river would be wider and shallower and more violent there. But the concrete walls were sloped in the main channel and I knew I might have a shot at pulling myself out if I could somehow slow my speed and find purchase.

I lowered my eyes and decided to move as close to the wall as I could without getting pushed hard into it. Then I saw a more immediate salvation. The tree I had seen in the channel from the window of Turrentine's house was a hundred yards ahead of me in the river. It must have gotten hung up at the bridge or in the shallows and I had caught up to it.

Using my last reserve of strength I started swimming with the current, picking up speed and heading to the tree. I knew it would be my boat. I'd be able to ride it all the way to the Pacific if I needed to.

Rachel lost the river. The streets took her further away from it and soon she had lost it. She couldn't get back to it. There was a GPS screen in the car but she didn't know how to work it and doubted she'd be able to get a satellite fix in this weather anyway. She pulled over and banged the wheel angrily with the heel of her palm. She felt like she was deserting Harry, that it was going to be her fault if he drowned.

Then she heard the helicopter. It was low flying and moving fast. She leaned forward to see up through the windshield. She didn't see anything. She got out in the rain and turned circles on the street looking. She could still hear it but she couldn't see it.

It had to be the rescue, she thought. In this weather, who else would be flying? She got a bead on the sound and jumped back into the Mercedes.

She took the first right she came to and started heading to the sound. She drove with the window down, with the rain coming in but her not caring. She listened to the sound of the helicopter in the distance.

Soon she saw it. It was circling ahead and to the right. She kept going and when she came to Reseda Boulevard she turned right again and could see there were actually two helicopters, one low and the other above it. Both were red with white lettering on the side. Not television or radio call letters. The helicopters were marked LAFD.

There was a bridge ahead and Rachel could see cars stopped and people getting out in the rain to rush to the railing. They were looking down into the river.

She pulled up, stopped in a traffic lane and did the same. She rushed to the railing in time to see the rescue. Bosch was in a yellow safety harness being lifted on a wire out of a fallen tree that was stalled in the shallows where the river widened to fifty yards across.

As he was raised to the helicopter Bosch looked down into the raging current below him. Soon the tree broke free of its catch and tumbled over and over in the cascades. It picked up speed and washed beneath the bridge, its branches crashing into the support pylons and shearing off.

Rachel watched the rescuers bring Bosch into the helicopter. Not until he was inside and safe and the helicopter started to bank away did she look away. And that was only when some of the others on the bridge had started to yell and point down into the river. She looked down and saw what it was. Another man in the water. But for this man there would be no rescue. He floated face-down, his arms loose and his body limp. Red and black jumper cables were tangled around his body and neck. His shaven skull looked like a child's lost ball bobbing in the current.

The second helicopter followed the body from above, waiting for it to get hung up like the tree had before any extraction was risked. There was no hurry this time.

As the current thickened to move between the pylons of the bridge, the body's fluid travel was disturbed and it turned over in the water. Just before it went under the bridge Rachel caught a glimpse of Backus's face. His eyes were open beneath the glaze of water. But it seemed to her that he was looking right at her before he disappeared under the bridge.

Many years ago, when I served in the army in Vietnam, I was wounded in a tunnel. I was extracted by my comrades and put on a helicopter back to base camp. I remember that as the chopper rose and took me from harm's way, I felt an elation that far obscured the pain of my wound and the exhaustion I had felt.

I felt the same way that day on the river. Déjà vu all over again, as they say. I had made it. I had survived. I was out of harm's way. I was smiling as a fireman in a safety helmet wrapped a blanket around me.

'We're taking you to USC to get checked out,' he yelled over the roar of the rotor and the rain. 'ETA in ten minutes.'

He gave me the okay sign and I gave it back to him, noticing that my fingers were a bluish white and that I was shaking with something more than cold.

'I'm sorry about your friend,' the fireman yelled.

I saw he was looking down through a glass panel on the lower part of the door he had just slid closed. I leaned over and looked and I could see Backus in the water below. He was faceup and moving languidly in the current.

'I'm not sorry,' I said, but not loud enough to be heard.

I leaned back on the jump seat they had put me on. I closed my eyes and nodded to the conjured image of my silent partner, Terry McCaleb, smiling and standing in the stern of his boat.

43

The skies cleared a couple days later and the city started to dry out and dig out. There had been landslides in Malibu and Topanga. The coast highway was down to two lanes for the foreseeable future. In the Hollywood Hills there had been flooding in the lower streets. One house on Fareholm Drive had broken free and was washed into the street, leaving an aging movie star homeless. Two deaths were attributed to the storm – a golfer who had inexplicably decided to get in a few holes between bands of the storm and was hit on a backswing by a bolt of lightning, and Robert Backus, the fugitive serial killer. The Poet was dead, the headlines and news anchors said. Backus's body was fished out of the river at the Sepulveda Dam. Cause of death: drowning.

The seas calmed, too, and I took a morning ferry out to Catalina to see Graciela McCaleb. I rented a golf cart and drove up to the house, where she answered the door and received me with her family. I met Raymond, the adopted son, and Cielo, the girl Terry had told me about. Meeting her made me miss my own daughter and reminded me of the new vulnerability I would soon have in my life.

The house was filled with boxes and Graciela explained that the storm had delayed their move back to the mainland. In another day their belongings would be shuttled down to a barge and then taken across to the port, where a moving truck would be waiting. It was complicated and expensive but she had no regrets. She wanted to leave the island and the memories it held.

We went out to the table on the porch so we could talk without the children hearing. It was a nice spot with a view of all of Avalon Harbor. It made it hard to believe she wanted to leave. I could see *The Following Sea* down there and I noticed there was someone in the stern and that one of the deck hatches was open.

'Is that Buddy down there?'

'Yes, he's getting ready to move the boat. The FBI brought it back yesterday without calling ahead. I would have told them to take it to Cabrillo. Now Buddy has to do it.'

'What's he going to do with it?'

'He's going to continue the business. He'll run the charters from over there and pay me rent on the boat.'

I nodded. It sounded like a decent plan.

'Selling the boat wouldn't bring that much in. And, I don't know, Terry worked so hard on that boat. It feels wrong to just sell it to a stranger.'

'I understand.'

'You know, you could probably get a ride back with Buddy instead of waiting for the ferry. If you want. If you're not sick of Buddy.'

'No, Buddy's fine. I like Buddy.'

We sat in silence for a long moment. I didn't feel I needed to explain anything about the case to her. We had talked on the phone – because I wanted to explain things before it hit the media – and the story had been all over the papers and television. She knew the details, large and small. There was little left to say but I thought I needed to visit with her in person one last time. It had all started with her. I figured it should end with her as well.

'Thank you for what you did,' Graciela said. 'Are you all right?'

'I'm fine. Just a few scratches and bruises from the river. It was a wild ride.'

I smiled. The only visible injuries I had were scrapes on my hands and one above my left eyebrow.

'But thank you for calling me. I'm glad I got the chance. That's why I came, just to say thanks and to say good luck with everything.'

The sliding door opened and the little girl came out carrying a book. 'Mommy, will you read this to me now?'

'I'm visiting with Mr. Bosch right now. In a little while, okay?'

'No, I want you to read it now.'

The girl looked like it was a life-or-death request and her face knotted up, ready for a cry.

'It's okay,' I said. 'Mine's like that, too. You can read it.'

'It's her favorite book. Terry used to read it to her just about every night.'

She pulled the girl up onto her lap and brought the book up to read. I saw that it was the same book Eleanor had just gotten for my daughter. *Billy's Big Day,* with the monkey receiving the gold medal on the cover. Cielo's copy was worn around the edges from reading and rereading. The cover had been ripped in two places and then taped.

Graciela opened it and started to read.

'One bright summer day the circus animal Olympics were held under the big top in Ringlingville. All the animals had the day off from all of the circuses and were allowed to compete in the many different events.'

I noticed that Graciela had changed her voice and was reading the story with an inflection of excitement and anticipation.

'All the animals lined up at the bulletin board outside Mr. Farnsworth's office. The list of events was posted on the board. There were races and relays and many other contests. The big animals got closest to the board and were crowding it, so the others couldn't see. A little monkey squeezed between the legs of an elephant and then climbed the pachyderm's trunk so that he could see the list. Billy Bing smiled when he finally saw it. There was one race called the hundred-yard dash and he knew he was very good at dashing.'

I didn't hear the rest of the story after that. I got up and went to the railing and looked down into the harbor. But I didn't see anything down there either. My mind was too busy for the external world. I was flooded with ideas and emotions. I suddenly knew that the name William Bing, the name Terry McCaleb had scrawled on the flap of his file, belonged to a monkey. And I suddenly knew that the story wasn't finished, not by a long shot.

44

Rachel came to see me at my house later that day. I had just gotten in after filing my paperwork with Kiz Rider at Parker Center and was listening to a phone message from Ed Thomas. He was thanking me for saving his life when all along it was I who owed him an apology for not warning him in the first place. I was feeling guilty about that and thinking about calling the bookstore when Rachel knocked. I invited her in and we went out to the back deck.

'Wow, nice view.'

'Yeah, I like it.'

I pointed down to the left, where a small cut of the river was in the view behind the soundstages on the Warner Brothers lot.

'There it is, the mighty Los Angeles River.'

She squinted and looked and then found it.

'The narrows. Looks pretty weak right now.'

'It's resting. Next storm, it will be back.'

'How are you feeling, Harry?'

'Good. Better. I've been sleeping a lot. I'm surprised you're still in town.'

'Well, I took a few days. I'm actually looking at apartments.'

'Really?'

I turned with my back to the railing so I could just look at her.

'I'm pretty sure this whole thing will be my ticket out of South Dakota. I don't know what squad they'll put me on but I'm going to ask for L.A. Or I was, until I saw what some of these apartments go for. In Rapid City I pay five-fifty a month for a really nice and secure place.'

'I could find you five-fifty here but you probably won't like the location. You'd probably have to learn another language, too.'

'No, thanks. I'm working on it. So what have you been doing?'

'I just came back from Parker Center. I put in my papers. I'm going back on the job.'

'Then I guess this is it for us. I heard the FBI and the LAPD don't talk.'

'Yeah, there is a wall there. But it's been known to come down from time to time. I have some friends with the bureau. Believe it or not.'

'I believe it, Harry.'

I noticed that she was back to calling me by my first name. I wondered if that meant the relationship was over.

'So,' I said, 'when did you know about McCaleb?'

'What do you mean? Know what?'

'I mean when did you know that Backus didn't kill him? That he killed himself.'

She put both hands on the railing and looked down into the arroyo. But she wasn't really looking at anything down there.

'Harry, what are you talking about?'

'I found out who William Bing is. He's a monkey from the pages of his daughter's favorite book.'

'So? What's that mean?'

'It means he checked himself into the hospital in Vegas under a phony name. He had something wrong with him, Rachel. Something inside.'

I touched the center of my chest.

'Maybe he was chasing the case, maybe not. But he knew something was wrong and he went over there to that hospital to have it checked and to keep it quiet. He didn't want his wife and his family to know. And so they checked him out and gave him the bad news. His second heart was going the way his first one went. Cardio … myo … whatever it's called. Bottom line was he was dying. He needed another heart or he was going to die.'

Rachel shook her head like I was a fool.

'I don't know how you think you know all of this but you can't possib—'

'Look, I know what I know. And I know he had already burned through his medical insurance and if he was going to get in line for another heart, they would lose everything, the house, the boat, everything. Everything for another heart.'

I paused and then continued in a quiet and calm voice.

'He didn't want that. He also didn't want his family to see him waste away and die, on the public dole. And he didn't like the idea of another person dying so he could live. He had already been through that, too.'

I stopped there to see if she would protest again and try to dissuade me. She remained silent this time.

'The only things he had left were his life insurance and his pension. He wanted them to have that. So he was the one who changed out his pills. There's a receipt for a health food store under the seat of his car. I called there this morning to see if they sell powdered shark cartilage. They do.

'He changed out his pills and just kept on taking them. He figured as long as he made a show of taking them there'd be no autopsy and everything would work out fine.'

'But it didn't, did it?'

'No, but he had a backup plan for that, too. That's why he waited for the long charter. He wanted to die out there on the boat. He wanted it to be in waters that would come under federal jurisdiction. His hope was that if anything came of it, his friends in the bureau would take care of everything for him.

'The only problem with his whole big plan was that he had no idea about the Poet. He had no idea his wife would come to me or that a few lines scribbled in a file would lead to all that happened.'

I shook my head.

'I should have seen it. The med switch wasn't Backus's style. Too complicated. The complicated ones are usually inside jobs.'

'What about the threat to his family? Whether or not he knew it was Backus, he knew somebody had threatened his family. He got those photographs – somebody stalking his family. You are saying he checked out and left his family at risk? That's not the Terry McCaleb I knew.'

'Maybe he thought he was ending the risk. The threat to his family was aimed at him. If he was gone, then so, too, was the threat.'

Rachel nodded, but it wasn't in any sort of confirmation.

'If nothing else, your fact chain is interesting, Harry. I'll give you that. But what makes you think we know about this, that I know about it?'

'Oh, you know. The way you dismissed my questions about William Bing for one thing. But the other is what you did in that house the other day. When I had the gun on Backus, he was about to say something about Terry and you cut him off. You jumped all over what he was about to say. I think he was about to say he didn't kill Terry.'

'Oh, yeah, a killer denying one of his victims. Isn't that unusual.'

Her sarcasm sounded defensive to me.

'This time it would have been. He was no longer hiding. He was out in the open and he would have taken credit if credit was due him. You knew that and that's why you cut him off. You knew he was going to deny it.'

She came away from the railing and stood in front of me.

'Okay, Harry, you think you've got it all figured out. You found a sad little suicide hidden in all the murders. What are you going to do with it? You going to go out there and announce it to the world? The only thing that might do is take the money away from the family. Is that what you want? Maybe you can get a piece of it as the whistleblower reward.'

Now I turned away from her and leaned down on the railing.

'No, I don't want that. I just don't like being lied to.'

'Oh, I get it. This really isn't about Terry. It's about you and me, isn't it?'

'I don't know what it's about, Rachel.'

'Well, when you do, when you figure it all out, let me know, okay?'

She suddenly came up next to me and kissed me hard on the cheek.

'Good-bye, Bosch. Maybe I'll see you around once the transfer comes through.'

I didn't turn around to watch her go. I listened as her angry footsteps crossed the deck and then the maple floor inside. I heard the front door slam with a finality that reverberated right through me. It was that tumbling bullet again.

45

I stood on the porch, elbows on the railing, for a long time after Rachel left. My guess was that I would never see her again, whether or not she took a transfer to Los Angeles. I felt a loss. I felt like something good had been taken from me before I really knew how good it could be.

I tried to put her out of my mind for a little while. Terry McCaleb, too. I looked out at the city and thought it was beautiful. The rain had cleaned the sky out and I could see all the way to the San Gabriels and the snow-covered peaks beyond. The air seemed to be as clean and as pure as the air breathed by the Gabrieleños and the padres so many years before. I saw what they had seen in the place. It was the kind of day you felt you could build a future on.

Acknowledgments

The author would like to thank many individuals who helped with the writing of this book. They include Michael Pietsch, Jane Wood, Pamela Marshall, Perdita Burlingame, Jane Davis, Terry Hansen, Terrill Lee Lankford, Ed Thomas, Frederike Leffelaar, Jerry Hooten, and researcher Carolyn Chriss. Also of great help to the author were Philip Spitzer, Joel Gotler, Shannon Byrne, Sophie Cottrell, John Houghton, Mario Pulice, Mary Capps, Ken Delavigne, Patricia and George Companioni, and the entire staff at Little, Brown and Company as well as the Time Warner Book Group.

Two books that were very helpful to the author were *Zzyzx: History of an Oasis,* by Anne Q. Duffield-Stoll, and *Rio L.A.: Tales from the Los Angeles River,* by Patt Morrison with photographs by Mark Lamonica.

Special thanks go to Chief William Bratton and Detective Tim Marcia of the Los Angeles Police Department and special agents Gayle Jacobs and Nina Roesberry of the FBI's Las Vegas field office.

The Closers

To the detectives
who have to look into the abyss

Part One
Blue Religion

1

Within the practice and protocol of the Los Angeles Police Department a two-six call is the one that draws the most immediate response while striking the most fear behind the bulletproof vest. For it is a call that often has a career riding on it. The designation is derived from the combination of the Code 2 radio call out, meaning 'respond as soon as possible,' and the sixth floor of Parker Center, from which the chief of police commands the department. A two-six is a forthwith from the chief's office, and any officer who knows and enjoys his position in the department will not delay.

Detective Harry Bosch spent over twenty-five years with the department in his first tour and never once received a forthwith from the chief of police. In fact, other than receiving his badge at the academy in 1972, he never shook hands or spoke personally with a chief again. He had outlasted several of them – and, of course, seen them at police functions and funerals – but simply never met them along the way. On the morning of his return to duty after a three-year retirement he received his first two-six while knotting his tie in the bathroom mirror. It was an adjutant to the chief calling Bosch's private cell phone. Bosch didn't bother asking how they had come up with the number. It was simply understood that the chief's office had the power to reach out in such a way. Bosch just said he would be there within the hour, to which the adjutant replied that he would be expected sooner. Harry finished knotting his tie in his car while driving as fast as traffic allowed on the 101 Freeway toward downtown.

It took Bosch exactly twenty-four minutes from the moment he closed the phone on the adjutant until he walked through the double doors of the chief's suite on the sixth floor at Parker Center. He thought it had to have been some kind of record, notwithstanding the fact that he had illegally parked on Los Angeles Street in front of the police headquarters. If they knew his private cell number, then surely they knew what a feat it had been to make it from the Hollywood Hills to the chief's office in under a half hour.

But the adjutant, a lieutenant named Hohman, stared him down with disinterested eyes and pointed to a plastic-sealed couch that already had two other people waiting on it.

'You're late,' he said. 'Take a seat.'

Bosch decided not to protest, not to make matters possibly worse. He stepped over to the couch and sat between the two men in uniform, who had staked out the armrests. They sat bolt upright and did not small-talk. He figured they had been two-sixed as well.

Ten minutes went by. The men on either side of him were called in ahead of Bosch, each dispensed with by the chief in five minutes flat. While the second man was in with the chief, Bosch thought he heard loud voices from the inner sanctum, and when the officer came out his face was ashen. He had somehow fucked up in the eyes of the chief and the word – which had even filtered to Bosch in retirement – was that this new man did not suffer fuckups lightly. Bosch had read a story in the *Times* about a command staffer who was demoted for failing to inform the chief that the son of a city councilman usually allied against the department had been picked up on a deuce. The chief only found out about it when the councilman called to complain about harassment, as if the department had forced his son to drink six vodka martinis at Bar Marmont and drive home via the trunk of a tree on Mulholland.

Finally Hohman put down the phone and pointed his finger at Bosch. He was up. He was quickly shuttled into a corner office with a view of Union Station and the surrounding train yards. It was a decent view but not a great one. It didn't matter because the place was coming down soon. The department would move into temporary offices while a new and modern police headquarters was rebuilt on the same spot. The current headquarters was known as the Glass House by the rank and file, supposedly because there were no secrets kept inside. Bosch wondered what the next place would become known as.

The chief of police was behind a large desk signing papers. Without looking up from this work he told Bosch to have a seat in front of the desk. Within thirty seconds the chief signed his last document and looked up at Bosch. He smiled.

'I wanted to meet you and welcome you back to the department.'

His voice was marked by an eastern accent. *De-paht-ment.* This was fine with Bosch. In L.A. everybody was from somewhere else. Or so it seemed. It was both the strength and the weakness of the city.

'It is good to be back,' Bosch said.

'You understand that you are here at my pleasure.'

It wasn't a question.

'Yes sir, I do.'

'Obviously, I checked you out extensively before approving your return. I had concerns about your . . . shall we say *style,* but ultimately your talent won the day. You can also thank your partner, Kizmin Rider, for her lobbying effort. She's a good officer and I trust her. She trusts you.'

'I have already thanked her but I will do it again.'

'I know it has been less than three years since you retired but let me assure you, Detective Bosch, that the department you have rejoined is not the department you left.'

'I understand that.'

'I hope so. You know about the consent decree?'

Just after Bosch had left the department the previous chief had been forced to agree to a series of reforms in order to head off a federal takeover of the LAPD following an FBI investigation into wholesale corruption, violence and civil rights violations within the ranks. The current chief had to carry out the agreement or he would end up taking orders from the FBI. From the chief down to the lowliest boot, nobody wanted that.

'Yes,' Bosch said. 'I've read about it.'

'Good. I'm glad you have kept yourself informed. And I am happy to report that despite what you may read in the *Times*, we are making great strides and we want to keep that momentum. We are also trying to update the department in terms of technology. We are pushing forward in community policing. We are doing a lot of good things, Detective Bosch, much of which can be undone in the eyes of the community if we resort to old ways. Do you understand what I am telling you?'

'I think so.'

'Your return here is not guaranteed. You are on probation for a year. So consider yourself a rookie again. A boot – the oldest living boot at that. I approved your return – I can also wash you out without so much as a reason anytime in the course of the year. Don't give me a reason.'

Bosch didn't answer. He didn't think he was supposed to.

'On Friday we graduate a new class of cadets at the academy. I would like you to be there.'

'Sir?'

'I want you to be there. I want you to see the dedication in our young people's faces. I want to reacquaint you with the traditions of this department. I think it could help you, help you rededicate yourself.'

'If you want me to be there I will be there.'

'Good. I will see you there. You will sit under the VIP tent as my guest.'

He made a note about the invite on a pad of paper next to the blotter. He then put the pen down and raised his hand to point a finger at Bosch. His eyes took on a fierceness.

'Listen to me, Bosch. Don't ever break the law to enforce the law. At all times you do your job constitutionally and compassionately. I will accept it no other way. This *city* will accept it no other way. Are we okay on that?'

'We are okay.'

'Then we are good to go.'

Bosch took his cue and stood up. The chief surprised him by also standing and extending his hand. Bosch thought he wanted to shake hands and extended his own. The chief put something in his hand and Bosch looked down to see the gold detective's shield. He had his old number back. It had not been given away. He almost smiled.

'Wear it well,' the police chief said. 'And proudly.'

'I will.'

Now they shook hands, but as they did so the chief didn't smile.

'The chorus of forgotten voices,' he said.

'Excuse me, Chief?'

'That's what I think about when I think of the cases down there in Open-Unsolved. It's a house of horrors. Our greatest shame. All those cases. All those voices. Every one of them is like a stone thrown into a lake. The ripples move out through time and people. Families, friends, neighbors. How can we call ourselves a city when there are so many ripples, when so many voices have been forgotten by this department?'

Bosch let go of his hand and didn't say anything. There was no answer for the chief's question.

'I changed the name of the unit when I came into the department. Those aren't cold cases, Detective. They never go cold. Not for some people.'

'I understand that.'

'Then go down there and clear cases. That's what your art is. That's why we need you and why you are here. That's why I am taking a chance with you. Show them we do not forget. Show them that in Los Angeles cases don't go cold.'

'I will.'

Bosch left him there, still standing and maybe a little haunted by the voices. Like himself. Bosch thought that maybe for the first time he had actually connected on some level with the man at the top. In the military it is said that you go into battle and fight and are willing to die for the men who sent you. Bosch never felt that when he was moving through the darkness of the tunnels in Vietnam. He had felt alone and that he was fighting for himself, fighting to stay alive. That had carried with him into the department and he had at times adopted the view that he was fighting *in spite* of the men at the top. Now maybe things would be different.

In the hallway he punched the elevator button harder than he needed to. He had too much excitement and energy and he understood this. The chorus of forgotten voices. The chief seemed to know the song they were singing. And Bosch certainly did, too. Most of his life had been spent listening to that song.

2

Bosch rode the elevator just one flight down to five. This, too, was new territory for him. Five had always been a civilian floor. It primarily housed many of the department's mid- and low-level administrative offices, most of them filled with nonsworn employees, budgeters, analysts, pencil pushers. Civilians. Before now there had been no reason to come to the fifth.

There were no placards in the elevator lobby that pointed the way to specific offices. It was the kind of floor where you knew where you were going before you stepped off the elevator. But not Bosch. The hallways on the floor formed the letter H and he went the wrong way twice before finally finding the door marked 503. There was nothing else on the door. He paused before opening it and thought about what he was doing and what he was starting. He knew it was the right thing. It was almost as if he could hear the voices coming through the door. All eight thousand of them.

Kiz Rider was sitting on a desk just inside, sipping a cup of steaming coffee. The desk looked like a place for a receptionist but Bosch knew from his frequent calls in the prior weeks that there was no receptionist in this squad. There was no money for such a luxury. Rider raised her wrist and shook her head as she checked her watch.

'I thought we agreed on eight o'clock,' she said. 'Is that how it's going to be, partner? You waltzing in every morning whenever you feel like it?'

Bosch looked at his watch. It was five minutes after eight. He looked back at her and smiled. Rider smiled and said, 'We're over here.'

Rider was a short woman who carried a few extra pounds. Her hair was short and now had some gray in it. She was very dark complected, which made her smile all the more brilliant. She slipped off the desk, and from behind where she had perched she raised a second cup of coffee to him.

'See if I remembered that right.'

He checked and nodded.

'Black, just like I like my partners.'

'Funny. I'll have to write you up for that.'

She led the way. The office seemed to be empty. It was large, even for a squad room serving nine investigators – four teams and an OIC. The walls were painted a light shade of blue, like Bosch often saw on the screens of computers. It was carpeted in gray. There were no windows. At the positions on the walls where there should have been windows there were bulletin boards or nicely framed crime scene photos from many years back. Bosch could tell that in these black and whites the photographers had often put their artistic skills ahead of their clinical duties. The shots were heavy on mood and shadows. Not many of the crime scene details were apparent.

Rider must have known he was looking at the photos.

'They told me that writer James Ellroy picked these out and had them framed for the office,' she said.

She led him around a partial wall that broke the room in two and into an alcove where two gray steel desks were pushed together so the detectives who sat at them would face each other. Rider put her coffee down on one. There were already files stacked on it and personal things like a coffee mug full of pens and a picture frame at an angle that hid the photo it held. A laptop computer was open and humming on the desk. She had moved into the squad the week before while Bosch was still clearing customs – customs being the medical exam and final paperwork that brought him back onto the job.

The other desk was clean, empty and waiting for him. He moved behind it and put his coffee down. He suppressed a smile as well as he could.

'Welcome back, Roy,' Rider said.

That made the smile break through. It made Bosch feel good to be called Roy again. It was a tradition carried by many of the city's homicide detectives. There was a legendary homicide man named Russell Kuster who had worked out of Hollywood Division many years back. He was the ultimate professional, and many of the detectives working murders in the city today had come under his tutelage at one point or another. He was killed in an off-duty shootout in 1990. But his habit of calling people Roy – no matter their real name – was carried on. Its origin had become obscure. Some said it was because Kuster once had a partner who loved Roy Acuff and it had started with him. Others said it was because Kuster liked the idea of the homicide cop being the Roy Rogers type, wearing the white hat and riding to the rescue, making things right. It didn't matter anymore. Bosch knew it was an honor just to be called Roy again.

He sat down. The chair was old and lumpy, guaranteed to give him a backache if he spent too much time in it. But he hoped that would not be the case. In his first run as a homicide detective he had lived by the adage *Get off your ass and knock on doors.* He didn't see any reason that should change this time around.

'Where is everybody?' he asked.

'Having breakfast. I forgot. They told me last week that the routine is that on Monday mornings everybody meets early for breakfast. They usually go over to the Pacific. I didn't remember until I got in here this morning and found the place dead, but they should be back here soon.'

Bosch knew the Pacific Dining Car was a longtime favorite with LAPD brass and the Robbery-Homicide Division. He also knew something else.

'Twelve bucks for a plate of eggs. I guess that means this is an overtime-approved squad.'

Rider smiled in confirmation.

'You got that right. But you wouldn't have been able to finish your fancy eggs anyway, once you got the forthwith from the chief.'

'You heard about that, huh?'

'I still have an ear out on six. Did you get your badge?'

'Yeah, he gave it to me.'

'I told him what number you'd want. Did you get it?'

'Yeah, Kiz, thanks. Thanks for everything.'

'You already told me that, partner. You don't need to keep saying that.'

He nodded and looked around their space. He noticed that on the wall behind Rider was a photo of two detectives huddled beside a body lying in the dry concrete bed of the Los Angeles River. It looked like a shot from the early fifties, judging by the hats the detectives wore.

'So, where do we start?' he asked.

'The squad breaks the cases up in three-year increments. It provides some continuity. They say you get to know the era and some of the players in the department. It overlaps. It also helps with identifying serials. In two years they've already come up with four serials nobody ever knew about.'

Bosch nodded. He was impressed.

'What years did we get?' he asked.

'Each team has four or five blocks. Since we're the new team we got four.'

She opened the middle drawer of her desk, took out a piece of paper and handed it across to him.

Bosch/Rider – Case Assignments

1966	1972	1987	1996
1967	1973	1988	1997
1968	1974	1989	1998

Bosch studied the listing of years for which they would be responsible. He had been out of the city and in Vietnam for most of the first block.

'The summer of love,' he said. 'I missed it. Maybe that's what's wrong with me.'

He said it just to be saying something. He noticed that the second block included 1972, the year he had come onto the force. He remembered a call out to a house off of Vermont on his second day on the job in patrol. A woman back east asked police to check on her mother, who was not answering the phone. Bosch found her drowned in a bathtub, her hands and feet bound with dog leashes. Her dead dog was in the tub with her. Bosch wondered if the old woman's murder was one of the open cases he would now be charged with solving.

'How was this arrived at? I mean, why did we get these years?'

'They came from the other teams. We lightened their caseload. In fact, they already started the ball rolling on cases from a lot of those years. And I heard on Friday that a cold hit came in from 'eighty-eight. We're supposed to run with it starting today. I guess you could say it's your welcome-back present.'

'What's a cold hit?'

'When a DNA stamp or a latent we send through the computers or the DOJ makes a blind match.'

'What's ours?'

'I think it's a DNA match. We'll find out this morning.'

'They didn't tell you anything last week? I could have come in over the weekend, you know.'

'I know that, Harry. But this is an old case. There was no need to start running the minute a piece of paper came in the mail. Working Open-Unsolved is different.'

'Yeah? How come?'

Rider looked exasperated, but before she could answer they heard the door open and the squad room started filling with voices. Rider stepped out of the alcove and Bosch followed. She introduced Bosch to the other members of the squad. Two of the detectives, Tim Marcia and Rick Jackson, Bosch knew well from previous cases. The other two pairs of partners were Robert Renner and Victor Robleto, and Kevin Robinson and Jean Nord. Bosch knew them, as well as Abel Pratt, the officer in charge of the unit, by reputation. Every one of them was a top-notch homicide investigator.

The greeting was cordial and subdued, a bit overly formal. Bosch knew that his posting in the unit was probably viewed with suspicion. An assignment on the squad would have been highly coveted by detectives throughout the department. The fact that he had gotten the posting after nearly three years in retirement raised questions. Bosch knew, as the chief of police had reminded him, that he had Rider to thank for the job. Her last posting had been in the chief's office as a policy analyst. She had cashed in whatever markers she had accrued with the chief in order to get Bosch back inside the department and working open-unsolved cases with her.

After all the handshakes, Pratt invited Bosch and Rider back into his office for a private welcome-aboard speech. He sat behind his desk and they took the side-by-side chairs in front of it. There was no room in the closet-sized space for other furnishings.

Pratt was a few years younger than Bosch, on the south side of fifty. He kept himself in shape and carried the esprit de corps of the vaunted Robbery-Homicide Division, of which the Open-Unsolved Unit was just one branch. Pratt appeared confident in his skills and his command of the unit. He had to be. The RHD took on the city's most difficult cases. Bosch knew that if you did not believe you were smarter, tougher and more cunning than the people you were after then you didn't belong.

'What I really should do is split you two up,' he began. 'Make you work with guys already established here in the unit because this is different from what you've done in the past. But I got the word from six and I don't mess with that. Besides, I understand you two have a prior chemistry that worked. So forget what I should do and let me tell you a little bit about working open-unsolveds. Kiz, I know you already got this speech last week but you'll just have to suffer along, okay?'

'Of course,' Rider said.

'First of all, forget closure. Closure is bullshit. Closure is a media term, something they put in newspaper articles about cold cases. Closure is a joke. It's a fucking lie. All we do here is provide answers. Answers have to be enough. So don't mislead yourself about what you are doing here. Don't mislead the family members you deal with on these cases and don't be misled by them.'

He paused for reaction, got none and moved on. Bosch noticed that the crime scene photo framed on the wall was of a man collapsed in a bullet-riddled phone booth. It was the kind of phone booth you only saw in old movies and at the Farmers Market or over at Phillippe's.

'Without a doubt,' Pratt said, 'this squad is the most noble place in the building. A city that forgets its murder victims is a city lost. This is where we don't forget. We're like the guys they bring in in the bottom of the ninth inning to win or lose the game. The closers. If we can't do it, nobody can. If we blow it, the game is over because we're the last resort. Yes, we're outnumbered. We've got eight thousand open-unsolveds since nineteen sixty. But we are undaunted. Even if this whole unit clears only one case a month – just twelve a year – we are doing something. We're the closers, baby. If you're in homicide, this is the place to be.'

Bosch was impressed by his fervor. He could see sincerity and even pain in his eyes. He nodded. He immediately knew that he wanted to work for this man, a rarity in his experience in the department.

'Just don't forget that closure isn't the same as being a closer,' Pratt added.

'Got it,' Bosch said.

'Now, I know you both have long experience working homicides. What you are going to find different here is your relationship with the cases.'

'Relationship?' Bosch asked.

'Yes, relationship. What I mean is that working fresh kills is a completely different animal. You have the body, you have the autopsy, you carry the news to the family. Here you are dealing with victims long dead. There are no autopsies, no physical crime scenes. You deal with the murder books – if you can find them – and the records. When you go to the family – and believe me you don't go until you are good and ready – you find people who have already suffered the shock and found or not found ways to get past it. It wears on you. I hope you are prepared for that.'

'Thanks for the warning,' Bosch said.

'With fresh kills it is clinical because things move fast. With old cases it is emotional. You are going to see the toll of violence over time. Be prepared for it.'

Pratt pulled a thick blue binder from the side of his desk to the center of his calendar blotter. He started to push it across to them then stopped.

'Another thing to be prepared for is the department. Count on files being incomplete or even missing. Count on physical evidence being destroyed or disappeared. Count on starting from scratch with some of these. This unit was put together two years ago. We spent the first eight months just going through the case logs and pulling out open-unsolveds. We fed what we could into the forensics pipelines, but even when we've gotten a hit we have been handicapped by the lack of case integrity. It has been abysmal. It has been frustrating. Even though there is no statute of limitations on murder we are finding that evidence and even files were routinely disposed of during at least one administration.

'What I am saying is that you are going to find that your biggest obstacle on some of these cases may very well be the department itself.'

'Somebody said we have a cold hit that came out of one of our time blocks,' Bosch said.

He'd heard enough. He just wanted to get moving on something.

'Yes, you do,' Pratt said. 'We'll get to that in a second. Let me just finish up with my little speech. After all, I don't get to make it that often. In a nutshell, what we try to do here is apply new technology and techniques to old cases. The technology is essentially threefold. You have DNA, fingerprints, and ballistics. In all three areas the advancements in comparative analysis have been phenomenal in the last ten years. The problem with this department is that it never took any of these advances and looked backward at old cases. Consequently, we have an estimated two thousand cases in which there is DNA evidence that has never been typed and compared. Since nineteen sixty we have four thousand cases with fingerprints that have never been run through a computer. Ours, the FBI's, DOJ's, anybody's computer. It's almost laughable but it's too fucking sad to laugh about. Same with ballistics. We are finding the evidence is still there in most of these cases but it has been ignored.'

Bosch shook his head, already feeling the frustration of all the families of the victims, the cases swept away by time, indifference and incompetence.

'You will also find that techniques are different. Today's homicide copper is just plain better than one from, say, nineteen sixty or seventy. Even nineteen eighty. So even before you get to the physical evidence and you review these cases you are going to see things that seem obvious to you now, but that weren't obvious to anyone back at the time of the kill.'

Pratt nodded. His speech was finished.

'Now, the cold hit,' he said, pushing the faded blue murder book across the desk. 'Run with that baby. It's all yours. Close it down and put somebody in jail.'

3

After leaving Pratt's office they decided that Bosch would go get the next round of coffee while Rider started in on the murder book. They knew from prior experience that she was the faster reader and it didn't make sense to split the book up. They both needed to read it front to back, to have the investigation presented to them in the linear fashion in which it occurred and was documented.

Bosch said he would give her a good head start. He told her he might drink a cup in the cafeteria just because he missed the place. The place, not the coffee.

'Then I guess that gives me a few minutes to go down the hall,' she said.

After she left the office for the restroom Bosch took the page listing the years that were assigned to them and put it into the inside pocket of his jacket. He left 503 and took the elevator down to the third floor. He then walked through the main RHD squad room to the captain's office.

The captain's office suite was broken into two rooms. One room was his actual office and the other was called the murder room. It was furnished with a long meeting table where murder investigations were discussed, and its walls on two sides were lined with shelves containing legal books and the city's murder logs. Every homicide that had occurred in Los Angeles, going back more than one hundred years, had a listing in these leather-bound journals. The routine over the decades was to update the journals every time one of the murders was cleared. It was the easy reference in the department for determining what cases were still open or had been closed.

Bosch ran his finger along the cracked spines of the books. Each one simply said HOMICIDES followed by the listing of the years the book recorded. Several years fit into each of the early books. But by the 1980s there were so many murders committed in the city that each book contained the accounts of only one year. He then noted that the year 1988 was reported in two books, and he suddenly had a very good idea why that year had been assigned to him and Rider as the new members of the Open-Unsolved Unit. The high point for murders in the city would certainly also mean the high point for unsolved cases.

When his finger found the book containing cases from 1972 he pulled the tome out and sat down with it at the table. He leafed through it, skimming the stories, hearing the voices. He found the old lady who was drowned in her bathtub. It was never solved. He moved on, through 1973 and 1974, then he went through the book containing 1966, '67 and '68. He read about Charles Manson and Robert Kennedy. He read about people whose names he had never heard or known. Names that were taken away from them along with everything else they'd had or would ever have.

As he read through the catalogs of the city's horrors, Bosch felt a familiar power begin to take hold of him and move in his veins again. Only an hour back on the job and he was already chasing a killer. It didn't matter how long ago the blood had fallen. There was a killer in the wind and Bosch was coming. Like the prodigal son returning, he knew he was back in his place now. He was baptized again in the waters of the one true church. The church of the blue religion. And he knew that he would find his salvation in those who were long lost, that he would find it in these musty bibles where the dead lined up in columns and there were ghosts on every page.

'Harry Bosch!'

Jarred by the intrusion, Bosch slammed the book closed and looked up. Captain Gabe Norona was standing in the doorway of the inner office.

'Captain.'

'Welcome back!'

He came forward and vigorously shook Bosch's hand.

'Good to be back.'

'I see they already have you doin' your homework.'

Bosch nodded.

'Just sort of getting acquainted with it.'

'New hope for the dead. Harry Bosch is on the case again.'

Bosch didn't say anything. He didn't know if the captain was being sarcastic or not.

'It's the name of a book I read once,' Norona said.

'Oh.'

'Well, good luck to you. Get out there and lock 'em up.'

'That's the plan.'

The captain shook his hand again and then disappeared back into his office and closed the door.

His sacred moment ruined by the intrusion, Bosch stood up. He started returning the heavy murder catalogs to their places on the shelves. When he was finished, he left the office for the cafeteria.

4

Kiz Rider was almost halfway through the murder book when Bosch got back with the fresh round of coffees. She took her cup directly out of his hand.

'Thanks. I need something to keep me awake.'

'What, you're going to sit there and tell me that this is boring compared to pushing paper in the chief's office?'

'No, it's not that. It's just all the catching up, the reading. We've got to know this book inside and out. We've got to be alert for the possibilities.'

Bosch noticed she had a legal tablet next to the murder book and the top page was almost full of notes. He couldn't read the notes but could see that most of the lines were followed by question marks.

'Besides,' she added, 'I'm using different muscles now. Muscles I didn't use on the sixth floor.'

'I get it,' he said. 'All right if I start in behind you now?'

'Be my guest.'

She popped open the rings of the binder and pulled out the two-inch-thick sheaf of documents she had already read through. She handed them across to Bosch, who had sat down at his desk.

'You got an extra pad like that?' he asked. 'I just have a little notebook.'

She sighed in an exaggerated way. Bosch knew it was all an act and that she was happy they were working together again. She had spent most of the last two years evaluating policy and troubleshooting for the new chief. It wasn't the real cop work that she was best at. This was.

She slid a pad across the desk to him.

'You need a pen, too?'

'No, I think I can handle that.'

He put the documents down in front of him and started reading. He was ready to go and he didn't need the coffee to stay charged.

The first page of the murder book was a color photograph in a plastic three-hole sleeve. The photo was a yearbook portrait of an exotically attractive young girl with almond-shaped eyes that were startling green against her mocha skin. She had tightly curled brown hair with what looked like natural blonde highlights that caught the flash of the camera. Her eyes were bright and her smile genuine. It was a grin that said she knew things nobody else did. Bosch didn't think she was beautiful. Not yet. Her features seemed to compete with one another in an uncoordinated way. But he knew that teenage awkwardness often smoothed over and became beauty later.

But for sixteen-year-old Rebecca Verloren there would be no later. Nineteen eighty-eight would be her last year. The cold hit had come from her murder.

Becky, as she was known by family and friends, was the only child of Robert and Muriel Verloren. Muriel was a homemaker. Robert was the chef and owner of a popular Malibu restaurant called the Island House Grill. They lived on Red Mesa Way off of Santa Susana Pass Road in Chatsworth, at the northwest corner of the sprawl that made up Los Angeles. The backyard of their house was the wooded incline of Oat Mountain, which rose above Chatsworth and served as the northwest border of the city. That summer Becky was between her sophomore and junior years at Hillside Preparatory School. It was a private school in nearby Porter Ranch, where she was on the honor roll and her mother volunteered in the cafeteria and often brought jerk chicken and other specialties from her husband's restaurant for the faculty lunchroom.

On the morning of July 6, 1988, the Verlorens discovered their daughter missing from their home. They found the back door unlocked, though they were sure it had been secured the night before. Thinking the girl might have gone for a walk they waited worriedly for two hours but she did not return. That day she was scheduled to go to the restaurant with her father to work the lunch shift as an assistant hostess and it was well past the time to leave for Malibu. While her mother called her friends hoping to locate her, her father went up the hillside behind the house looking for her. When he came back down the hill without finding a sign of her they decided it was time to call the police.

Patrol officers from the Devonshire Division were called to the home. They found no evidence of a break-in at the house. Citing this and the fact that the girl was in an age group with one of the highest runaway rates, the disappearance was viewed as a possible runaway situation and handled as a routine missing-persons case. This was against the protests of the missing girl's parents, who did not believe she had run away or left their home of her own volition.

The parents were proved horribly correct two days later when the decomposing body of Becky Verloren was found hidden beside the fallen trunk of an oak tree about ten yards off an equestrian trail on Oat Mountain. A woman riding her Appaloosa had gone off the path to investigate a bad smell and came across the body. The rider might have ignored the odor but had earlier seen signs posted on telephone poles about the missing girl from the area.

Becky Verloren had died less than a quarter mile from her house. It was likely that her father had passed within yards or even feet of her body when he was hiking the hillside and calling out her name. But on that morning there had been no odor yet to draw his attention.

Bosch was the father of a young girl. Though she lived far away from him with her mother, she was never far from his thoughts. He thought now of a father climbing a steep hillside, calling for a daughter who would never come home.

He tried to concentrate on the murder book.

The victim had been shot once in the chest by a high-powered pistol. The weapon, a .45 caliber Colt semi-automatic, was lying in the leaves by her left ankle. As Bosch studied the crime scene photos he saw what appeared to be a burn from a contact shot on the fabric of her light blue nightgown. The bullet hole was located directly above the heart, and Bosch knew by the size of the gun and the entry wound that death was likely immediate. Her heart would have been shattered by the round as it blasted through her body.

For a long time Bosch studied the photographs of the body as it had been found. The victim's hands were not bound. She was not gagged. Her face was turned in toward the trunk of the fallen tree. There were no indications of defensive wounds of any nature. There was no indication of sexual molestation or any other assault.

The police misinterpretation of the girl's disappearance was initially compounded by the misinterpretation of the death scene. The assessment at the scene resulted in the death being viewed as a probable suicide. As such the case was kept by the local division's homicide squad and the two detectives who rolled on the body call, Ron Green and Arturo Garcia. Devonshire Division was at that time and still is the LAPD's quietest station. Representing a large bedroom community with high property values and mostly upper-middle-class residents, Devonshire always had crime tables that were among the lowest in the city. Inside the department the station was known as Club Dev. It was a highly sought-after posting by officers and detectives who had put in many years and were tired or had simply seen enough action. Devonshire Division also represented the part of the city closest to Simi Valley, a quiet, relatively crime-free community in Ventura County where hundreds of LAPD officers chose to live. A posting at Devonshire made the commute a breeze and the workload the lightest in the department.

The Club Dev pedigree played in the back of Bosch's mind as he read the reports. He knew part of his task here was to make a judgment on Green and Garcia's work, to determine if they had been up to the task. He did not know them and had no experience with them. He had no idea what level of skills and dedication they had brought to the case. There was the initial misinterpretation of the death as a suicide. But by the appearance of the records, the two investigators seemed to recover quickly and move on with the case. Their reports seemed to be well written, thorough and complete. They seemed to have taken the extra step wherever possible.

Still, Bosch knew that a murder book could be manipulated to give this impression. The truth would be revealed as he delved deeper and continued his own investigation. He knew there could be a vast difference between what was recorded and what was not.

According to the murder book, Green and Garcia quickly reversed investigative directions when suicide was dismissed after the autopsy was completed and the gun found with the body was analyzed. The case was reclassified as a homicide that had been disguised as a suicide.

Bosch first came to the autopsy findings in the murder book. He had read a thousand autopsy protocols and had attended several hundred of the procedures as well. He knew to skip all the weights and measurements and descriptions of the actual procedure and go right to the summary section and the attendant photographs. Unsurprisingly, he found the cause of death listed as a gunshot wound to the chest. The estimated time of death was between midnight and 2 a.m. on July 6. The summary noted that no witness reported hearing the shot, so the time of death estimate was based solely on measuring loss of body temperature.

The surprises were in the other findings. Rebecca Verloren had long, thick hair. At the right side of the base of her neck, beneath the fall of her hair, the medical examiner found a small circular burn mark that was about the size of a button off an oxford shirt. Two inches from this mark was another burn mark, much smaller than the first. High white cell counts in the blood surrounding these wounds indicated that both had been sustained close to but not at the time of death.

The report concluded that the burns were caused by a stun gun, a handheld device that emits a powerful electric charge and renders its victims unconscious or incapacitated for several minutes or longer, depending on the charge. Normally, a charge from a stun gun would leave two small and almost unnoticeable marks on the skin indicating the location of the twin contacts. But if the contact points of the device were held unevenly against the skin, the electric charge would arc and often burn the skin in the manner seen on Becky Verloren's neck.

The autopsy summary also noted that an examination of the victim's bare feet found no soil deposits or cuts or bruises, which would be evident had the girl walked barefoot up the mountainside in the dark.

Bosch drummed his pen on the report and thought about this. He knew this was a mistake made by Green and Garcia. The victim's feet should have been examined at the scene and they should have made the jump right then to the idea that the suicide was a setup. Instead they missed it and they lost two days waiting for the autopsy on a weekend. Those days plus the two days lost when patrol wrote off the parents' call as a runaway case added up to a bad number in a murder investigation. There was no doubt that the case was slow out of the blocks. Bosch was beginning to see how badly the department had let Rebecca Verloren down.

The autopsy report also contained the results of a gunshot residue test conducted on the victim's hands. While GSR was found on Becky Verloren's right hand, there was no indication of it on her left. Even though Verloren was right-handed Bosch knew that the GSR test was an indicator that she had not actually fired the gun that killed her. Experience – no matter how limited – and common sense would have told the investigators that the girl would have needed to use both hands to properly hold the heavy gun pointed against her own chest and to pull the trigger. The result would have been GSR on both her hands.

There was one more notable point in the autopsy summary. The examination of the body determined that the victim had been sexually active, and scarring on the walls of the uterus was indicative of a recent gynecological dilation and curettage procedure to eliminate a pregnancy. The deputy coroner who conducted the autopsy estimated that this had occurred four to six weeks prior to her death.

Bosch read the first Investigator's Summary report, which was written and added to the book after the autopsy. Green and Garcia had now classified the death as a murder and established the theory that someone had entered the girl's bedroom while she was sleeping, incapacitated her with a stun gun and then carried her from the room and the house. She was carried up the mountainside to the location by the fallen oak tree, where the murder was committed and clumsily disguised as a suicide in what was possibly a spur-of-the-moment decision by her killer. The report was filed Monday, July 11 – five days after Rebecca Verloren had been left dead on the hillside.

Bosch moved on to the firearm analysis report. Though the autopsy had produced more than convincing evidence of staged suicide, the study of the gun and the attendant ballistics further confirmed the investigative theory.

The gun was found to be devoid of fingerprints except for those from Becky Verloren's right hand. The fact that there were no prints from her left hand or smudges of any kind on the pistol indicated to the investigators that the weapon had been carefully wiped clean of prints before being placed and held in Becky's hand, then turned toward her chest and fired. It was likely that the victim was unconscious – from the stun gun assault – at the time this manipulation occurred.

The bullet casing ejected from the pistol when the fatal shot was fired was recovered six feet from the body. There were no fingerprints or smudges on it, an indication that the weapon had been loaded with gloved hands.

The investigation's single most important piece of evidence was recovered during the analysis of the gun itself. It was actually found *inside* the gun. The weapon was the Mark IV Series 80 model manufactured by Colt in 1986, two years before the murder. It featured a long hammer spur, which was notable because the gun had a reputation for leaving a 'tattoo' injury on the shooter if the weapon was not handled properly while firing. This usually occurred when a two-handed grip on the weapon pushed the primary shooting hand up high on the grip and too close to the hammer spur. The primary hand could then receive a painful stamp when the trigger was pulled, the weapon fired and the slide automatically came backward to eject the bullet casing. As the slide returned to firing position, it would pinch the skin of the shooter's hand – usually the webbing between the thumb and forefinger, often taking a piece of skin back with it inside the gun. All of this occurred in a fraction of a second, the novice shooter often not even knowing what had 'bitten' him.

That was exactly what had happened with the gun used to kill Becky Verloren. When a firearms expert broke open the weapon he found a small piece of skin tissue and dried blood on the underside of the slide. It would not have been noticeable to someone examining the exterior of the gun or wiping it clean of blood and fingerprints.

Green and Garcia added this to their investigative theory. In the second Investigator's Summary report they wrote that evidence indicated that the killer wrapped Becky Verloren's hand around the gun and then pressed the muzzle to her chest. The killer used one or both of his own hands to steady the weapon and push or pull her finger over the trigger. The gun fired and the slide 'tattooed' the killer, taking a piece of his skin with it inside the gun.

Bosch noted to himself that Green and Garcia made no mention of another possibility in their investigative theory. That being that the tissue and the blood found inside the weapon was already there on the night of the murder, that the weapon had tattooed someone other than the killer when it was fired at some point before the killing.

Regardless of that potential oversight, the blood and tissue was collected from the weapon and, while it was already known from the autopsy that Becky Verloren had no wounds on her hands, a routine blood comparison test was conducted. The blood collected from the gun was type O. Becky Verloren's blood was type AB positive. The investigators concluded they had the killer's blood on the weapon. The killer was blood type O.

But in 1988 the use of DNA comparison in criminal investigation was still years away from common and, more important, court-accepted practice in California. Databases containing the DNA profiles of criminal offenders were only on the verge of being funded and created. During the course of the 1988 investigation the detectives were left to compare blood type only to potential suspects as they arose. And no one emerged as a primary suspect in the Verloren killing. The case was worked hard and long but ultimately without an arrest ever being made. And it went cold.

'Until now,' Bosch said out loud without realizing it.

'What?' Rider asked.

'Nothing. Just thinking out loud.'
'You want to start talking about it?'
'Not yet. I want to finish reading first. You're done?'
'Just about.'
'You know who we have to thank for this, don't you?' Bosch asked.
She looked at him quizzically.
'I give up.'
'Mel Gibson.'
'What are you talking about?'
'When did *Lethal Weapon* come out? Right around this time, right?'
'I guess. But what are you talking about? Those movies were so far-fetched.'
'That's my point. That's the movie that started all of this holding the gun sideways and with two hands, one over the other. We got blood on this gun because the shooter was a *Lethal Weapon* fan.'
Rider shook her head dismissively.
'You watch,' Bosch said. 'I'm going to ask the guy when we bring him in.'
'Okay, Harry, you ask him.'
'Mel Gibson saved a lot of lives. All those sideways shooters, they couldn't hit shit. We ought to make him like an honorary cop or something.'
'Okay, Harry, I'm going to go back to reading, okay? I want to get through this.'
'Yeah, okay. Me too.'

5

Shortly after the LAPD's Open-Unsolved Unit began operation the DNA evidence from the Verloren case was forwarded to the California Department of Justice. It was delivered to the DNA lab along with evidence from dozens of other cases drawn from the unit's initial survey of the department's unsolved murders. The DOJ operated the state's primary DNA database. The backlog of comparison requests to the underfunded and undermanned lab was running more than a year at the time. But thanks to the tide of requests from the new LAPD unit it took almost eighteen months before the Verloren evidence was re-typed by DOJ analysts and compared to thousands of DNA profiles in the state data bank. It produced a single match, a 'cold hit' in the parlance of DNA work.

Bosch looked at the single-page DOJ report unfolded in front of him. It stated that twelve of a possible fourteen markers matched the DNA from the weapon used to murder Rebecca Verloren to a now thirty-five-year-old man named Roland Mackey. He was a native of Los Angeles whose last known address was in Panorama City. Bosch felt his blood start moving a little faster as he read the cold hit report. Panorama City was in the San Fernando Valley, not more than fifteen minutes from Chatsworth, even in bad traffic. It added a level of credibility to the match. It was not that Bosch didn't believe the science. He did. But he also believed you needed more than the science to convince a jury beyond a doubt. You needed to bolster the scientific fact with connections of circumstantial evidence and common sense. This was one of those connections.

Bosch noticed the date on the cover letter of the DOJ report.

'You said we just got this?' he asked Rider.

'Yeah. I think it came in Friday. Why?'

'The date on it is from two Fridays ago. Ten days.'

Rider shrugged.

'Bureaucracy,' she said. 'I guess it took its time getting down here from Sacramento.'

'I know the case is old but you'd think they'd move a little faster than that.'

Rider didn't respond. Bosch dropped it and read on. Mackey's DNA was in the DOJ computer base because all offenders convicted of any sex--related crime in California were forced under state law to submit blood and oral swabs for typing and inclusion in the DNA data bank. The offense that resulted in Mackey's DNA going into the bank was on the far margin of the state mandate. Two years earlier Mackey was convicted of lewd behavior in Los Angeles. The DOJ report did not offer details of the crime but stated Mackey was placed on twelve months probation, an indication that his was a minor offense.

Bosch was about to write a note on his pad when he looked up and saw Rider closing the murder book on the second half of the documents.

'Done?'

'Done.'

'Now what?'

'I figured that while you were finishing the book I'd go over to the ESB and pick up the box.'

Bosch had no trouble remembering the meaning of what she said. He had slipped easily back into the world of acronyms and copspeak. The ESB was the Evidence Storage Building over at the Piper Tech compound. She would go there to pick up the physical evidence that would have been stored from the case. Items like the murder weapon, the victim's clothing and anything else accumulated while the case was initially worked. It was usually stored in a taped cardboard box and put on a shelf. The exception to this was storage of perishable and biological evidence – such as the blood and tissue recovered from the Verloren murder weapon – which was stored in lab vaults in the Scientific Investigation Division.

'Sounds like a good idea,' Bosch said. 'But first why don't you run this guy through DMV and NCIC and see if we can get a location?'

'Already did that.'

She turned her laptop around on her desk so Bosch could see the screen. He recognized the National Crime Index Computer template on the screen. He reached across and started scrolling down the screen, his eyes scanning the information.

Rider had run Roland Mackey through NCIC and gotten his criminal record. His conviction two years earlier for lewd behavior was only the latest in a string of recorded arrests dating back to when he was eighteen – the same year as Rebecca Verloren's murder. Anything prior would not be listed because juvenile protection laws shielded that part of his record. Most of the crimes listed were property and drug-related crimes, beginning with car theft and a burglary at eighteen and leading to two drug-possession raps, two driving under the influence arrests, another burglary charge and a receiving stolen property hit. There was also an early solicitation of prostitution arrest. Overall it was the pedigree of a small-time criminal and drug user. It appeared that Mackey never went to state prison for any of his crimes. He was often given second chances and then, through plea agreements, was sentenced to probation or to short stints in county jail. It appeared that the longest he ever stayed in stir was six months served after pleading guilty to receiving stolen property when he was twenty-eight years old. He served his time at the county-run Wayside Honor Rancho.

Bosch leaned back after he was finished scrolling through the computer records. He felt uneasy about what he had just read. Mackey had the kind of record that might be seen as a pathway to murder. But in this case the murder came first – when Mackey was only eighteen years old – and the petty crimes came after. It didn't seem to quite fit.

'What?' Rider asked, sensing his mood.

'I don't know. I thought there'd be more, I guess. It's backwards. This guy goes from murder to petty crime? Doesn't seem to hold.'

'Well, this is all he's ever gotten popped for. Doesn't mean it's all he ever did.'

He nodded.

'Juvenile?' he asked.

'Maybe. Probably. But we'll never get those records now. They're probably long gone.'

It was true. The state went out of its way to protect the privacy of juvenile offenders. Crimes rarely tailed offenders into the adult justice system. Nevertheless, Bosch thought that there had to be childhood crimes that would fit better with the seemingly cold-blooded murder of a sixteen-year-old girl who had been incapacitated with a stun gun and abducted from her home. Bosch began to have an uneasy feeling about the cold hit they were working. He was beginning to sense that Mackey was not the target. He was a means to the target.

'Did you run him through DMV for an address?' he asked.

'Harry, that's old-school. You only have to update your driver's license every four years. You want to find somebody you go to AutoTrack.'

She opened the murder book and slid a loose piece of paper across to him. It was a computer printout that said AutoTrack at the top. Rider said it was a private company the police department contracted with. It provided computer searches of all public records, including DMV, public utility and cable service databases, as well as private databases such as credit reporting services, to determine an individual's past and current addresses. Bosch saw that the printout contained a listing of Roland Mackey's various addresses dating back to when he was eighteen. His current listing on all current data, including driver's license and car registration, was the address in Panorama City. But on the page, Rider had circled the address ascribed to Mackey when he was eighteen through twenty years old – the years 1988 through 1990. It was an apartment on Topanga Canyon Boulevard in Chatsworth. This meant that at the time of the murder Mackey was living very close to Rebecca Verloren's home. This made Bosch feel a little better about things. Proximity was a key piece to the puzzle. Bosch's misgivings over Mackey's criminal pedigree aside, knowing that he was in the immediate vicinity in 1988 and therefore could have seen or even known Rebecca Verloren was a large check mark in the positive column.

'Make you feel any better, Harry?'

'A little bit.'

'Good. I'm going, then.'

'I'll be here.'

After Rider left, Bosch jumped back into his review of the murder book. The third Investigator's Summary focused on how the intruder got into the house. The door and window locks showed no signs of having been compromised and all known keys to the home were accounted for among family members and a housekeeper who was cleared of any suspicion. The investigators theorized that the killer came in through the garage, which had been left open, and then entered the house through the connecting door, which was usually not locked until after Robert Verloren came home from work at night.

According to Robert Verloren the garage was open when he came home from his restaurant about ten-thirty on the night of July fifth. The connecting door from the garage into the house was unlocked. He entered his home, closed the garage and locked the connecting door. The investigators theorized that by then the killer was already in the house.

The Verlorens' explanation for the open garage was that their daughter had recently received her driver's license and was on occasion allowed to use her mother's car. However, she had not yet acquired the habit of remembering to close the garage door upon leaving or coming home, and had been chastised by her parents on more than one occasion for this. Late in the afternoon before her abduction Rebecca was sent on an errand by her mother to pick up dry cleaning. She used her mother's car. The investigators confirmed that she picked up the clothing at 5:15 p.m. and then returned home. It was believed by the investigators that she once again forgot to close the garage or lock the connecting door after returning. Her mother said she never checked the garage that night, assuming wrongly that it was closed.

Two residents in the neighborhood canvassed after the murder reported seeing the garage door open that evening. This left the house easily accessible until Robert Verloren came home.

Bosch thought about how many times over the years he had seen someone's seemingly innocent mistake turn into one of the keys to their own doom. A routine chore to pick up clothes may have led to the opportunity for a killer to get inside the house. Becky Verloren may have unwittingly engineered her own death.

Bosch pushed his chair back and stood up. He had finished the review of the first half of the murder book. He decided to get another cup of coffee before taking on the second half. He asked around in the office if anybody needed anything from the cafeteria and got one order for coffee from Jean Nord. He took the stairs down to the cafeteria and filled two cups from the urn, then paid for them and went over to the condiments counter to get Nord's cream and sugar. While he was pouring a shot of cream into one of the cups he felt a presence next to him at the counter. He made room at the station but no one reached for any condiments. He turned toward the presence and found himself looking at the smiling face of Deputy Chief Irvin S. Irving.

There had never been any love lost between Bosch and Deputy Chief Irving. The chief had at various times been his adversary and unwitting savior in the department. But Bosch had heard from Rider that Irving was on the outs now. He had been unceremoniously pushed out of power by the new chief and given a virtually meaningless posting and assignment outside of Parker Center.

'I thought that was you, Detective Bosch. I'd buy you a cup of coffee but I see you already have more than enough. Would you like to sit down for a minute anyway?'

Bosch held up both cups of coffee.

'I'm kind of in the middle of something, Chief. And somebody's waiting for one of these.'

'One minute, Detective,' Irving said, a stern tone entering his voice. 'The coffee will still be hot when you get to where you have to go. I promise.'

Without waiting for an answer he turned and walked to a nearby table. Bosch followed. Irving still had a shaved and gleaming skull. His muscular jaw was his most prominent feature. He took a seat and held his posture ramrod straight. He didn't look comfortable. He didn't speak until Bosch sat down. The pleasant tone was back in his voice.

'All I wanted to do was welcome you back to the department,' he said.

He smiled like a shark. Bosch hesitated like a man stepping across a trapdoor before answering.

'It's good to be back, Chief.'

'The Open-Unsolved Unit. I think that is the appropriate place for someone of your skills.'

Bosch took a sip from his scalding cup of coffee. He didn't know if Irving had just complimented or insulted him. He wanted to leave.

'Well, we'll see,' he said. 'I hope so. I think I better—'

Irving held his hands out wide, as if to show he wasn't hiding anything.

'That's it,' he said. 'You can go. I just wanted to say welcome back. And to thank you.'

Bosch hesitated, but then bit.

'Thank me for what, Chief?'

'For resurrecting me in this department.'

Bosch shook his head and smiled as if he didn't understand.

'I don't get it, Chief,' he said. 'How am I supposed to do that? I mean, you're across the street in the City Hall Annex now, right? What is it, the Office of Strategic Planning or something? From what I hear, you get to leave your gun at home.'

Irving folded his arms on the table and leaned in close to Bosch. All pretense of humor, false or otherwise, evaporated. He spoke strongly but quietly.

'Yes, that is where I am. But I guarantee you that it will not be for long. Not with the likes of you being welcomed back into the department.'

He then leaned back and just as quickly adopted a casual manner for what he delivered as casual conversation.

'You know what you are, Bosch? You are a retread. This new chief likes putting retreads on the car. But you know what happens with a retread? It comes apart at the seams. The friction and the heat – they're too much for it. It comes apart and what happens? A blowout. And then the car goes off the road.'

He nodded silently as he let Bosch think about that.

'You see, Bosch, you are my ticket. You will fuck up – if you will excuse my language. It is in your history. It is in your nature. It is guaranteed. And when you fuck up, our illustrious new chief fucks up for being the one who put a cheap retread on our car.'

He smiled. Bosch thought that all he needed was a gold earring to complete the picture. Mr. Clean all the way.

'And when he goes down my stock goes right back up. I'm a patient man. I've waited for over forty years in this department. I can wait longer.'

Bosch expected more but that was it. Irving nodded once and stood up. He quickly turned and headed out of the cafeteria. Bosch felt the anger rise in his throat. He looked down at the two cups of coffee in his hands and felt like an idiot for having sat there like a defenseless errand boy while Irving had verbally punched him out. He got up and threw both cups into a trash can. He decided that when he got back to room 503 he would tell Jean Nord to get her own damn coffee.

6

With the unease of the Irving confrontation still lingering, Bosch took the second half of the murder book over to his desk and sat down. He thought the best way to forget about the threat that Irving posed was to immerse himself in the case again. What he found left in the file was a thick sheaf of ancillary reports and updates, the things investigators always lumped into the back of the book, the reports that Bosch called the tumblers because they often seemed disparate but nevertheless could unlock a case when seen from the right angle or put together in the right pattern.

First was a lab report stating that testing was unable to determine exactly how long the blood and tissue sample taken from the murder weapon could have been in the gun. The report said that while most of the sample was preserved for comparison purposes, an examination of selected blood cells indicated decomposition was not extensive. The criminalist who wrote the report could not say the blood was deposited on the gun at the time of the killing – no one could. But he would be prepared to testify that the blood was deposited on the gun 'close to or at the time of the killing.'

Bosch knew this was a key report in terms of mounting a prosecution of Roland Mackey. It might also give Mackey the opportunity to build a defense around having had possession of the gun before the murder but not at the time of the murder. It would be a risky move to admit being in possession of the murder weapon, but the DNA match dictated that it was a move he would likely have to make. With the science unable to pinpoint exactly when the deposit of blood and tissue on the gun occurred, Bosch saw a gaping hole in the prosecution's case. The defense could clearly jump through it. Again, he felt the certainty of the cold hit DNA match slipping away. Science gives and takes at the same time. They needed more.

Next in the murder book was a report from the Firearms Unit, which had been assigned the ownership trace of the murder weapon. The serial number on the Colt had been filed down, but the number was raised in the lab with the application of an acid which accentuated the compressions in the metal where the number had been stamped during manufacture. The number was traced to a gun purchased from the manufacturer in 1987 by a Northridge gun shop. It was then traced through its sale that year to a man who lived in Chatsworth on Winnetka Avenue. The gun had then been reported stolen by the owner when his home was burglarized on June 2, 1988, just a month before it was used in the murder of Rebecca Verloren.

This report helped their case somewhat because unless Mackey had a relationship with the gun's original owner, the burglary compressed the time period during which Mackey would have had possession of the gun. It made it more likely that he had the gun on the night Becky Verloren was taken from her home and murdered.

The original burglary report was contained in the file. The victim was named Sam Weiss. He lived alone and worked as a sound technician at Warner Bros. in Burbank. Bosch scanned the report and found only one other note of interest. In the investigating officer's comments section it was stated that the burglary victim had recently purchased the gun for protection after being harassed by anonymous phone calls in which the caller threatened him because he was Jewish. The victim reported that he did not know how his unlisted number fell into the hands of his harasser and he did not know what had brought on the threats.

Bosch quickly read through the next report from the Firearms Unit, which identified the stun gun used in the abduction. The report said the 214-inch span between contact points – as exhibited by the burn marks on the victim's flesh – was unique to the Professional 100 model manufactured by a company called SafetyCharge in Downey. The model was sold over the counter and through mail order and there were more than twelve thousand Professional 100 models distributed at the time of the murder. Bosch knew that without the actual device in hand there was no way to connect the marks on Becky Verloren's body with an ownership trail. That was a dead end.

He moved on, leafing through a series of 8 × 10 photos taken in the Verloren house after the body was found up on the hillside behind it. Bosch knew these were cover-your-ass photos. The case had been handled – or mishandled – as a runaway situation. The department did not go full field with it until after the body was found and an autopsy concluded the death was a homicide. Five days after the girl was reported missing, the police came back and turned the house into a crime scene. The question was what was lost in those five days.

The photos included interior and exterior shots of all three doors to the house – front, back, garage – and several close-ups of window locks. There was also a series of shots taken in Becky Verloren's bedroom. The first thing Bosch noticed was that the bed was made. He wondered if the abductor had made it, thereby further selling the suicide, or Becky's mother had simply made the bed at some point during the days she hoped and waited for her daughter to come home.

The bed was a four-poster with a white-and-pink spread with cats on it and a matching pink ruffle. The bedspread reminded Bosch of the one that had covered his own daughter's bed. It seemed to be something that a child much younger than sixteen would like and he wondered if Becky Verloren had kept it for nostalgic reasons or as some sort of psychological security blanket. The bed's ruffle did not uniformly skirt the floor. It was a couple inches too long, and so it bunched on the floor and alternately fluffed out or tucked under the bed too far.

There were photos of her bureau and bed tables. The room was festooned with stuffed animals from her younger years. There were posters on the walls from music groups that had come and gone. There was a poster of a John Travolta movie three comebacks old. The room was very neat and orderly, and again Bosch wondered if this was how it had been on the morning Rebecca Verloren was discovered missing or if her mother had straightened the room while awaiting her daughter's return.

Bosch knew the photos had to have been taken as the first step of the crime scene investigation. Nowhere did he see any fingerprint powder or any other indication of the upset that would come with the intrusion of the criminalists.

The photos were followed in the murder book by a packet of summaries from interviews the detectives conducted with numerous students at Hillside Prep. A checklist on the top page indicated that the investigators had talked to every student in Becky Verloren's class and every boy who attended the upper grades of the school. There were also summaries from interviews of several of the victim's teachers and school administrators.

Included in this section was a summary of a phone interview conducted with a former boyfriend of Becky Verloren's who had moved with his family to Hawaii the year before her murder. Attached to the summary was an alibi confirmation report stating that the teenager's supervisor had confirmed that the boy had worked in the car wash and detail facility at a Maui rent-a-car franchise on the days of and after the murder, making it unlikely that he could have been in Los Angeles to kill her.

There was a separate packet of summaries of interviews with employees of the Island House Grill, the restaurant owned by Robert Verloren. His daughter had just started a part-time summer job at the restaurant. She was an assistant hostess during lunch. Her job was to lead customers to their tables and to put down the menus. Though Bosch knew restaurants often drew a variety of drifters to the low-level kitchen jobs, Robert Verloren avoided hiring men with criminal records, instead drawing on the population of surfers and other free spirits who flocked to the beaches of Malibu. These people would have had limited contact with Rebecca, who worked in the dining room, but they were interviewed just the same and seemingly dismissed by the investigators.

There was also a victim's chronology in which the investigators outlined Rebecca Verloren's movements in the days leading up to her murder. In 1988 July Fourth fell on a Monday. Rebecca spent most of the holiday weekend at home, except for a Sunday-night sleepover with three girlfriends at one of their houses. The attached summaries of interviews with these three girls were long but contained no information of investigative value.

On Monday, the holiday, she stayed home until she and her parents went to Balboa Park to watch a fireworks display. It was a rare night off for Robert Verloren and he insisted that the family stay together, much to Becky's reported upset at missing out on a friend's party in the Porter Ranch area.

On Tuesday the summer routine began again with Rebecca going to the restaurant with her father to work the lunch shift as a hostess. At three o'clock her father drove her home. He stayed at home through the afternoon and then headed back to the restaurant for the dinner shift at about the same time Rebecca used her mother's car to run the errand of collecting the dry cleaning.

Bosch saw nothing in the schedule that raised suspicions, nothing that was missed by the original investigators.

He next came to a transcript of a formal interview with the parents. It was taken at Devonshire Division on July 14, more than a week after their daughter was discovered missing. By this point the detectives had accumulated a lot of case knowledge and were specific with their questions. Bosch carefully read this transcript, as much for the answers as for the insight it would give to the investigators' view of the case at that point.

Case No. 88-641, Verloren, Rebecca (DOD 7-6-88),
I/O A. Garcia, #993
7/14/88 – 2:15 p.m., Devonshire Homicide

GARCIA: Thank you for coming in. I hope you don't mind but we are recording this so we will have a record. How are you managing?

ROBT. VERLOREN: About as well as expected. We're devastated. We don't know what to do.

MURIEL VERLOREN: We keep thinking, what could we have done to prevent this from happening to our little girl?

GREEN: We're truly sorry, ma'am. But you can't blame yourself for this. As far as we can tell it was nothing you did or didn't do. It just happened. Don't blame yourself. Blame the person who did this.

GARCIA: And we are going to get him. You don't have to worry about that. Now, we have some questions we need to ask. Some of these might be painful but we need the answers if we are going to get this guy.

ROBT. VERLOREN: You keep saying 'guy.' Is there a suspect? Do you know it was a man?

GARCIA: We don't know anything for sure, sir. We're mostly going with the percentages there. But also you have that steep hill behind your house. Becky was definitely carried up that hill. She wasn't a big girl but we definitely think it would have to be a man.

MURIEL VERLOREN: But you said she wasn't . . . that there was no sexual assault.

GARCIA: That is true, ma'am. But that does not preclude this from being a sexually motivated or related crime.

ROBT. VERLOREN: How do you mean?

GARCIA: We will get to that, sir. If you don't mind, let us ask our questions and then we will get to your questions if you would like.

ROBT. VERLOREN: Go ahead, please. I'm sorry. It's just that we cannot understand what has happened. It's like we are underwater all the time.

GARCIA: That is completely understandable. As I said, you have our deepest sympathy. From the department, too. We have the upper echelon of this department watching over this case very closely.

GREEN: We would like to start by going back before her disappearance. Maybe a month before. Did your daughter go away at all during that time?

ROBT. VERLOREN: What do you mean, away?

GARCIA: Was she away from you at any time?

ROBT. VERLOREN: No. She was sixteen. She was in school. She didn't go away on her own.

GREEN: What about a sleepover with her friends?

MURIEL VERLOREN: No, I don't think so.

ROBT. VERLOREN: What are you looking for?

GREEN: Was she sick at all in the month or two prior to the disappearance?

MURIEL VERLOREN: Yes, she had the flu the first week after school ended. It delayed her going to work for Bob.

GREEN: Was she in bed sick?

MURIEL VERLOREN: A lot of the time. I don't see what this has to—

GARCIA: Mrs. Verloren, did your daughter go to see a doctor at this time?

MURIEL VERLOREN: No, she just said she had to rest. To tell you the truth, we thought she just didn't want to go to work in the restaurant. She didn't have a fever or a cold. We just thought she was being lazy.

GREEN: She didn't confide in you at this time that she had been pregnant?

MURIEL VERLOREN: What? No!

ROBT. VERLOREN: Look, Detective, what are you telling us?

GREEN: The autopsy revealed that Becky had had a procedure called a dilation and curettage about a month before her death. An abortion. Our guess is that she was resting and recovering from this procedure when she told you she had the flu.

GARCIA: Would you two like to take a break here?

GREEN: Why don't we take a break? We'll step out and get all of us some water.

[Break]

GARCIA: Okay, we're back. I hope you understand and forgive us. We do not ask questions or attempt to shock you to hurt you. We need to follow procedure and employ methods that allow us to collect information that is unfettered by preconceived perceptions.

ROBT. VERLOREN: We understand what you are doing. It's part of our life now. What's left of it.

MURIEL VERLOREN: You are saying our daughter was pregnant and chose to get an abortion?

GARCIA: Yes, that's right. And we think there is a possibility that it could have a bearing on what happened to her a month later. Do you have any idea where she would have gone for this procedure?

MURIEL VERLOREN: No. I had no idea about this. Neither of us.

GREEN: And as you said before, she did not go away overnight during that time?

MURIEL VERLOREN: No, she was home every night.

GARCIA: Any idea who the relationship could have been with? In our earlier talks you said she had no current boyfriend.

MURIEL VERLOREN: Well, obviously I guess we were wrong about that. But, no, we don't know who she was seeing or who could have . . . done this.

GREEN: Have either of you ever read the journal that your daughter kept?

ROBT. VERLOREN: No, we didn't even know there was a journal until you found it in her room.

MURIEL VERLOREN: I would like to get that back. Will I get that back?

GREEN: We will need to keep it through the investigation but you will eventually get it back.

GARCIA: There are several references in the journal to an individual referred to as MTL. This is a person we would like to identify and talk to.

MURIEL VERLOREN: I don't know anyone with those initials offhand.

GREEN: We looked at the school's yearbook. There is one boy named Michael Lewis. But we checked and his middle name is Charles. We think the initials were a code or an abbreviation. It could stand for My True Love.

MURIEL VERLOREN: So there was obviously someone we didn't

know about, that she kept from us.

ROBT. VERLOREN: I can't believe this. You two are telling us we didn't really know our little girl.

GARCIA: I'm sorry, Bob. Sometimes the damage from a case like this goes deep. But it's our job to follow it where it goes. This is the current we are in right now.

GREEN: Basically, we need to pursue this aspect of the investigation and find out who MTL is. Which means we need to ask questions of your daughter's friends and acquaintances. Word about this, it will get around, I'm afraid.

ROBT. VERLOREN: We understand this, Detective. We will deal with it. As we said on the day we met, do what you have to do. Find the person who did this.

GARCIA: Thank you, sir. We will.

[End of interview, 2:40 p.m.]

Bosch read the transcript a second time, this time writing down notes on his pad as he went. He then moved on to three more formal interview transcripts. These were conducted with Becky Verloren's three closest friends, Tara Wood, Bailey Koster and Grace Tanaka. But none of the girls – girls at the time – said they had knowledge of Becky's pregnancy or the secret relationship that produced it. All three said they did not see her the week after school got out because she was not answering her phone and when they called the house's main number Muriel Verloren told them her daughter was sick. Tara Wood, who was splitting a work schedule as a hostess at the Island House Grill with Becky, said that her friend was moody and incommunicative in the weeks prior to her murder, but the reason for this was unknown because she rebuffed Wood's efforts to find out what was wrong.

The last entry in the murder book was the media file. It was where Garcia and Green kept the newspaper stories that accumulated in the early stages of the case. The crime played bigger in the *Daily News* than in the *Times*. This was understandable because the *News* circulated primarily in the San Fernando Valley and the *Times* usually treated the Valley as an unwanted stepchild, relegating the news emanating from its environs to the inside pages.

There was no coverage of Becky Verloren's initial disappearance. The newspapers had obviously viewed it in the same way as the police had. But once the body was found there were several stories on the investigation, the funeral and the impact the young girl's death had at her school. There was even a mood piece set at the Island House Grill. This story had been in the *Times* and had apparently been a stab at making the case meaningful to the paper's Westside circulation base. A restaurant in Malibu was something the Westsiders could relate to.

Both newspapers linked the murder weapon to a burglary that occurred a month before the killing but neither had the anti-Semitic angle. Neither reported on the blood evidence recovered from the weapon either. Bosch guessed that the blood and tissue recovery was the investigators' ace in the hole, the one piece of evidence held close to the vest to give them the advantage if a prime suspect was ever identified.

Finally Bosch noticed that there were no media interviews with the grieving parents. The Verlorens apparently chose not to hold their loss out for public consumption. Bosch liked that about them. It seemed to him that increasingly the media forced the victims of tragedy to grieve in public, in front of cameras and in newspaper stories. Parents of murdered children became talking heads who appeared on the tube as experts the next time there was another child murdered and another set of parents grieving. It all didn't sit well with Bosch. It seemed to him that the best way to honor the dead was to keep them close to the heart, not to share them with the world across the electronic spectrum.

At the back of the murder book there was a pocket containing a manila envelope with the *Times*'s eagle insignia and address in the corner. Bosch pulled it out and opened it and found a series of 8 × 10 color photos taken at Rebecca Verloren's funeral one week after her murder. Apparently there had been a deal cut, the photos traded for access. Bosch remembered making such deals in the past when he was unable because of scheduling or budget to get a police photographer out to a funeral. He would promise the reporter working the story that he or she would be in line for an exclusive if the newspaper photographer wouldn't mind running off a complete set of crowd shots of the people attending the service. You never knew when the killer might show up to get a rise out of the anguish and grief he had caused. Reporters always went for the deal. Los Angeles was one of the most competitive media markets in the world and reporters lived and died by the access they had.

Bosch studied the photos but was handicapped in looking for Roland Mackey because he didn't know what he looked like in 1988. The photos Kiz Rider had pulled up on the computer were from his most recent arrest. They showed a balding man with a goatee and dark eyes. It was hard to trace that visage back to any of the teenaged faces that gathered to put one of their own in the ground.

For a while he studied Becky Verloren's parents in one of the photos. They were standing at the graveside, leaning against each other as if holding each other from falling. Tears lined their faces. Robert Verloren was black and Muriel Verloren was white. Bosch now understood where their daughter had gotten her growing beauty. The mix of races in a child often rose above the attendant social difficulties to achieve such grace.

Bosch put the photos down and thought for a moment. Nowhere in the murder book had there been mention of the possibility of race playing a part in the murder. But the murder weapon's coming from the burglary of a man being threatened because of his religion seemed to give rise to the possibility of at least a tenuous link to the murder of a girl of mixed races.

The fact that this was not mentioned in the murder book meant nothing. The aspect of race was always something held close to the vest in the LAPD. To commit something to the paperwork was to make it known within the department – investigative summaries were reviewed all the way up the line on hot cases. It could then be leaked and turned into something else, something political. So its absence was not seen by Bosch as a taint on the investigation. Not yet, at least.

He returned the photos to the envelope and closed the murder book. He guessed that there were more than three hundred pages of documents and photos in it, and nowhere on any of those pages had he seen the name Roland Mackey. Was it possible that he had escaped even peripheral notice in the investigation so many years before? If so, was it still possible he was indeed the killer?

These questions bothered Bosch. He always tried to keep faith in the murder book, meaning that he believed the answers usually lay within its plastic sides. But this time he was having difficulty believing the cold hit. Not the science. He had no doubt about Mackey being matched to the blood and tissue found inside the murder weapon. But he believed something was wrong. Something was missing.

He looked down at his pad. He had taken few notes. He had really only composed a list of people he wanted to talk to.

Green and Garcia
Mother/Father
school/friends/teachers
former boyfriend
probation agent
Mackey – school?

He knew that every note he had taken was obvious. He realized how little they had besides the DNA match, and once again he was uneasy about building a case without anything else.

Bosch was staring at his notes when Kiz Rider walked into the office. She was empty-handed and unsmiling.

'Well?' Bosch asked.

'Bad news. The murder weapon's gone. I don't know if you've read the whole book but there's mention of a journal in there. The girl kept a journal. That's gone, too. Everything's gone.'

7

They decided that the best way to deal with and discuss bad news was to eat. Besides that, nothing made Bosch hungrier than sitting in an office all morning and reading through a murder book. They went over to Chinese Friends, a small place on Broadway at the end of Chinatown where they knew they could still get a table this early. It was a place where you could eat well and to capacity and barely go over five bucks. The trouble was that it filled up fast, mostly with headquarters staff from the Fire Department, the gold badges from Parker Center and the bureaucrats from City Hall. If you didn't get there by noon you ordered takeout and you had to sit and eat on the bus benches out front in the sun.

They left the murder book in the car so as not to disturb other patrons in the restaurant, where the tables were jammed as close as the desks in a public school. They did bring their notes, and discussed the case in an improvised shorthand designed to keep their conversation private. Rider explained that when she had said the gun and the journal were missing from the ESB what she meant was that no evidence carton from the case could be found during an hour-long search by two evidence clerks. This was not much of a surprise to Bosch. As Pratt had warned earlier, the department had taken haphazard care of evidence for decades. Evidence cartons were booked and filed on shelves in chronological order and without any sort of separation according to crime classification. Consequently, evidence from a murder might sit on a shelf next to evidence from a burglary. And when clerks came through periodically to clear out evidence from cases where the statute of limitations had expired, sometimes the wrong box got tossed. The security of the ESB was also a low priority for many years. It was not difficult for anyone with an LAPD badge to gain access to any piece of evidence in the facility. So the evidence cartons were subject to pilfering. It was not unusual for weapons to be missing, or other kinds of evidence from famous cases like the Black Dahlia, Charles Manson, and the Dollmaker crimes.

There was no indication in the Verloren case of evidence theft. It was probably more a case of carelessness, of trying to find a box that had been stored seventeen years ago in an acre-sized room crowded with matching boxes.

'They'll find it,' Bosch said. 'Maybe you can even get your buddy up on six to put the fear of God into them. Then they'll find it for sure.'

'They better. The DNA is no good to us without that gun.'

'I don't know about that.'

'Harry, it's the chain of evidence. You can't go into trial with the DNA and not be able to show the jury the weapon it came from. We can't even go into the district attorney's office without it. They'll throw us right out on our asses.'

'Look, all I'm saying is, right now we're the only ones who know we don't have the gun. We can fake it.'

'What are you talking about?'

'Don't you think that this is all going to come down to Mackey and us in a little room? I mean, even if we had the gun in evidence we can't prove beyond a doubt that he left his blood in it during the shooting of Becky Verloren. All we can prove is that the blood is his. So if you ask me, it's going to come down to a confession. We're going to put him in the room, hit him with the DNA and see if he cops to it. That's it. So all I'm saying is, we put together a few props for the interview. We go to the armory and borrow a Colt forty-five and we pull that out of the box when we're in the room with him. We convince him we have the chain and he cops or he doesn't.'

'I don't like tricks.'

'Tricks are part of the trade. There's nothing illegal about that. The courts have even said so.'

'I think we're going to need more than the DNA to turn him anyway.'

'Me too. I was thinking we—'

Bosch stopped and waited while the waitress put down two steaming plates. Bosch had ordered shrimp fried rice. Rider ordered pork chops. Without a word he lifted his plate and pushed half of its contents onto her plate. He then used a fork to take three of her six pork chops. He almost smiled while he did this. He was back on the job with her less than a day and they had already dropped back into the easy rhythm of their prior partnership. He was happy.

'Hey, what's Jerry Edgar up to?' he asked.

'I don't know. I haven't talked to him in a while. We never really got over that thing.'

Bosch nodded. When Bosch had worked at Hollywood Division with Rider the homicide table had been divided into teams of three. Jerry Edgar had been the third partner. Then Bosch retired and soon after Rider was promoted downtown. It left Edgar still in Hollywood, feeling isolated and passed over. And now that Bosch and Rider were working again and assigned to RHD, there had been only silence from Edgar.

'What were you going to say, Harry, when the food came?'

'Just that you're right. We'll need more. One thing I was thinking was that I heard that since Nine-Eleven and the Patriot Act it's easier for us to get a wiretap.'

She ate a piece of shrimp before responding.

'Yes, that's true. It's one of the things I was monitoring for the chief. Our request filings have gone up about three thousand percent. The approvals are way up, too. The word's sort of gotten around that this is a tool we can use now. How is it going to work here?'

'I was thinking we put a tap on Mackey and then we plant a story in the paper. You know, it says we're working the case again, mention the gun, maybe mention the DNA – you know, something new. Not that we have a match but that we *could* get a match. Then we sit back and watch him and listen to him and see what happens. We could follow up by paying him a visit, see if that stirs things up any.'

Rider thought about this while eating a pork chop with her fingers. She seemed uneasy about something and it couldn't be the food.

'What?' Bosch asked.

'Who would he call?'

'I don't know. Whoever he did it with or did it for.'

Rider nodded thoughtfully while chewing.

'I don't know, Harry. You're back on the job less than a day after three years in the fun and sun and already you are reading things into a case I don't see. I guess you are still the teacher.'

'You're just rusty from sitting up there behind a big desk on six.'

'I'm serious.'

'So am I. Sort of. I think I've waited so long for this that I'm sort of on full alert, I guess.'

'Just tell me how you see this, Harry. You don't have to make up excuses for your instincts.'

'I actually don't see it yet and that's part of the problem. Roland Mackey's name is nowhere in that book and that's a problem starting out the door. We know he was in the vicinity but we have nothing connecting him to the victim.'

'What are you talking about? We have the gun with his DNA in it.'

'The blood connects him to the gun, not the girl. You read the book. We can't prove his DNA was deposited at the time of the killing. That single report could blow this whole case out of the water. It's a big hole, Kiz. So big a jury could drive through it. All Mackey has to do at trial is get up there on the stand and say, "Yeah, I stole the gun during a burglary on Winnetka. I then went up into the hills and shot it a few times, and I was making like Mel Gibson and the next thing I knew the damn thing bit me, took a chunk right out of my hand. I never saw that happen to Mel before. So I got so mad I threw that damn gun into the bushes and went home to get some Band-Aids." The SID report – our *own* damn report – backs him up and that is the end of it.'

Rider didn't smile during the story at all. He could tell she was seeing his point.

'That's all he has to say, Kiz, and he's got reasonable doubt and we can't prove otherwise. We've got no prints at the scene, we've got no hair, no fiber, we've got nothing. But added to this we do have his profile. And if you looked at his sheet before we were on this and knew about the DNA you would have never pegged this guy as a killer. Maybe spur-of-the-moment or heat of passion. But not something like this, something planned, and certainly not at age eighteen.'

Rider shook her head in an almost wistful manner.

'A few hours ago this was given to us as a welcome-aboard present. It was supposed to be a slam dunk . . . '

'The DNA made everybody jump to a conclusion. It's what's wrong with the world. People think technology is an easy ride. They're watching too much TV.'

'Is that your weird way of saying you don't think he did this?'

'I don't know what I'm thinking yet.'

'So we put a tail on him, tap his phone, spook him somehow and then see who he calls and how he acts.'

Bosch nodded.

'That's what I'm thinking,' he said.

'We'd need to clear it with Abel first.'

'We follow the rules. Just like the chief told me today.'

'Holy smoke – the new Harry Bosch.'

'You're looking at him.'

'Before we go for the tap we have to finish the due diligence. We have to make sure Roland Mackey was not known to any of the players. If that turns out to be the case then I say we go see Pratt about the tap.'

'Sounds right to me. What else did you get on the read?'

He wanted to see if she picked up on the undercurrent of race before suggesting it.

'Just what was there,' Rider responded. 'Was there something I missed?'

'I don't know – nothing obvious.'

'Then what?'

'I was thinking about the girl being biracial. Even in 'eighty-eight there would have been people that didn't like the idea of that. Then you add in the burglary the gun came from. The vic was Jewish. He said he was being harassed. That's why he bought the gun.'

Rider nodded thoughtfully while she finished a mouthful of rice.

'It's something to look for,' she said. 'But I don't see enough there to hang a lantern on at the moment.'

'There was nothing in the book . . .'

They ate in silence for a few minutes. Bosch always thought Chinese Friends had the softest and sweetest shrimp he had ever tasted in fried rice.

The pork chops, as thin as the plastic plates they ate off of, were also perfect. And Kiz was right, they were best eaten by hand.

'What about Green and Garcia?' Rider finally asked.

'What about them?'

'How would you grade them on this?'

'I don't know. Maybe a C if I was being charitable. They made mistakes, slowed things down. After that they seemed to cover the bases. You?'

'Same thing. They wrote a good murder book but it's got CYA written all through it. Like they knew they were never going to break it but wanted the book to look like they turned over every stone.'

Bosch nodded and looked down at his pad on the empty chair to the side. He looked at the list of people to interview.

'We've got to talk to the parents and Garcia and Green. We need to get a photo of Mackey, too. From when he was eighteen.'

'I think we hold back on the parents until we talk to everybody else. They might be most important but they should be last. I want to know as much as possible before we hit them with this after seventeen years.'

'Fine. Maybe we should start at probation. He only cleared a year ago. He probably was assigned to Van Nuys.'

'Right. We could go there and then walk over to talk to Art Garcia.'

'You found him? He's still around?'

'Didn't have to look. He's commander of Valley Bureau now.'

Bosch nodded. He was not surprised. Garcia had done well. The rank of commander put him just below deputy chief. It meant he was second in command over the Valley's five police divisions, including Devonshire, where years earlier he had worked the Verloren case.

Rider continued.

'In addition to our regular projects in the chief's office, each of the special assistants was assigned as sort of a liaison to one of the four bureaus. My assignment was the Valley. So Commander Garcia and I spoke from time to time. Most often I dealt with his staff, or Deputy Chief Vartan, that sort of thing.'

'I know what you're saying – I have a highly connected partner. You were probably telling Vartan and Garcia how to run the Valley.'

She shook her head in false annoyance.

'Don't give me shit about all of that. Working on six gave me a good view of the department and how it works.'

'Or doesn't. Speaking of which, there's something I should tell you.'

'What is it?'

'I ran into Irving when I went down to get coffee. Right after you left.'

Rider immediately looked concerned.

'What happened? What did he say?'

'Not a lot. He just called me a retread and mentioned that I was going to crash and burn and that when I did I would take the chief down with me for hiring me back. Then, of course, when the dust settles Mr. Clean would be there to step up.'

'Jesus, Harry. One day on the job and you already have Irving biting you on the ass?'

Bosch spread his hands wide, almost hitting the shoulder of a man sitting at the next table.

'I went to get coffee. He was there. He approached me, Kiz. I was just minding my own business. I swear.'

She bent her face down to look at her plate. She continued eating without talking to him. She dropped her last pork chop half eaten on the plate.

'I can't eat any more, Harry. Let's get out of here.'

'I'm ready.'

Bosch left more than enough money on the table and Rider said she would get the next one. Outside they got into Bosch's car, a black Mercedes SUV, and drove back through Chinatown to the entrance of the northbound 101. They made it all the way to the freeway before Rider spoke again about Irving.

'Harry, don't take him lightly,' she said. 'Be very careful.'

'I am always careful, Kiz, and I have never taken that man lightly.'

'All I'm saying is, he's been passed over twice for the top spot. He may be getting desperate.'

'Yeah, you know what I don't get? Why didn't your guy get rid of him when he came in here? I mean, just clean house. Pushing Irving across the street doesn't put an end to the threat. Anybody knows that.'

'He couldn't push him. Irving's got forty-plus years on the job. He has a lot of connections that go outside the department and into City Hall. And he knows where a lot of the bodies are buried. The chief couldn't make a move against him unless he was sure there wouldn't be any blowback from it.'

More silence followed. The early afternoon traffic out to the Valley was light. They had KFWB, the all news and traffic channel, on the radio and there were no reports of problems ahead. Bosch checked the gas and saw he had half a tank. That was plenty.

They had decided earlier to alternate use of their personal cars. A department car had been requisitioned and approved for them to share, but they both knew that getting the R&A was the easy part. It would most likely be months if not longer before they would actually get the wheels. The department had neither the spare car nor the money for a new one. Getting the R&A had simply been a paperwork approval needed before they could charge the department for gas and mileage on their personal cars. Bosch knew that over time he would probably put so many miles on his SUV that the expense payout would likely cost the department more than the approved car.

'Look,' he finally said, 'I know what you're thinking even if you're not saying it. It's not just me you're worried about. You stuck your neck out for me and you convinced the chief to take me back in. Believe me, Kiz, I know it's not just me riding on this – on this retread. You don't have to worry and you can tell the chief he doesn't have to worry. I get it. There won't be a blowout. There won't be any blowback from me.'

'Good, Harry. I'm glad to hear that.'

He tried to think of something that he could say to convince her further. He knew words were just words.

'You know, I don't know if I ever told you this, but after I quit I really sort of liked it at first. You know, being out of the squad and just sort of doing what I wanted. Then I started to miss it and then I started working cases again. On my own. Anyway, one thing that happened was I started walking with sort of a limp.'

'A limp?'

'Just a little thing. Like one of my heels was lower than the other. Like I was uneven.'

'Well, did you check your shoes?'

'I didn't need to check my shoes. It wasn't my shoes. It was my gun.'

He looked over at her. She was staring straight ahead, her eyebrows set in that deep V she used so much with him. He looked back at the road ahead.

'I carried a gun for so long that when I no longer had it on me it threw off my balance. I was uneven.'

'Harry, that's a strange story.'

They were going through the Cahuenga Pass. Bosch looked out his window and up the hillside, searching for his house nestled in among the others in the folds of the mountain. He thought he saw a glimpse of the back deck sticking out over the brown brush.

'You want to call Garcia and see if we can drop in and see him after we go by probation?' he asked.

'Yeah, I will – as soon as you get to the point of that story.'

He thought for a long moment before answering.

'The point is, I need the gun. I need the badge. Otherwise I'm out of balance. I need all of this. Okay?'

He looked over at Rider. She looked back at him but didn't answer.

'I know what I got with this chance. So fuck Irving and his calling me a retread. I won't fuck up.'

8

Twenty minutes later they stepped into one of Bosch's least favorite places in the city: the probation and parole office of the state's Department of Corrections in Van Nuys. It was a single-story brick building crowded with people waiting to see probation and parole agents, to give urine samples, to make their court-ordered check-ins, to turn themselves in for incarceration or to plead for one more chance of freedom. It was a place where desperation, humiliation and rage were palpable in the air. It was a place where Bosch tried not to make eye contact with anyone.

Bosch and Rider had something none of the others had: badges. It helped them cut through the lines and get an immediate audience with the agent Roland Mackey had been assigned to after his arrest two years earlier for lewd and lascivious behavior. Thelma Kibble was recessed in a standard government-issue cubicle in a room crowded with many identical cubicles. Her desk and the one government-issue shelf that came with the cubicle were crowded with the files of the convicts she was charged with shepherding through probation or parole. She was of medium size and build. Her eyes were brightly set off against her dark brown skin. Bosch and Rider introduced themselves as detectives from RHD. There was only one chair in front of Kibble's desk so they remained standing.

'Is it robbery or homicide we are talking about here?' Kibble asked.

'Homicide,' Rider said.

'Then why doesn't one of you grab the extra chair from that cubicle over there. She's still at lunch.'

Bosch took the chair she pointed at and brought it back. Rider and Bosch sat down and told Kibble they wanted a look at the file belonging to Roland Mackey. Bosch could tell that Kibble recognized the name but not the case.

'It was a lewd and lash probation you caught two years ago,' he said. 'He cleared after twelve months.'

'Oh, he's not current, then. Well, I need to go grab that one in archives. I don't remem – oh, yes I do, yes I do. Roland Mackey, yeah. I rather enjoyed that one.'

'How so?' Rider asked.

Kibble smiled.

'Let's just say he had some difficulty reporting to a woman of color. Tell you what, though, let me go grab the file so we get the details right.'

She double-checked the spelling of Mackey's name with them and left the cubicle.

'That might help,' Bosch said.

'What?' Rider asked.

'If he had a problem with her he'll probably have a problem with you. We might be able to use it.'

Rider nodded. Bosch saw she was looking at a newspaper article that was tacked to the fiberboard wall of the cubicle. It was yellowed with age. Bosch leaned closer to read it but he was too far away to read anything but the headline.

WOUNDED PAROLE OFFICER
GETS HERO'S WELCOME

'What is it?' he asked Rider.

'I know who this is,' Rider said. 'She got shot a few years ago. She went to some ex-con's house and somebody shot her. The convict called for help but then split. Something like that. We gave her an award at the BPO. God, she's lost a lot of weight.'

Something about the story rang a bell with Bosch, too. He noticed there were two photographs accompanying the story. One was of Thelma Kibble standing in front of the DOC building, a banner welcoming her back hanging from the roof. Rider was right. Kibble looked like she'd dropped eighty pounds since the photo. Bosch suddenly remembered seeing that banner across the front of the building a few years back while one of his cases was in trial at the courthouse across the street. He nodded. Now he remembered.

Then something about the second photo caught his eye and memory. It was a mug shot of a white woman – the ex-convict who lived in the house where Kibble had been shot.

'That's not the shooter, right?' he asked.

'No, she's the one who called it in, who saved her. She disappeared.'

Bosch suddenly stood up and leaned across the desk, putting his hands on stacks of files for support. He looked at the mug shot photo. It was a black-and-white shot that had darkened as the newspaper clipping had aged. But Bosch recognized the face in the photo. He was sure of it. The hair and eyes were different. The name underneath the photo was different, too. But he was sure he had encountered the woman in Las Vegas in the past year.

'Those are my files you're messing up.'

Bosch immediately pulled himself back across the desk as Kibble came around it.

'Sorry about that. I was just trying to read the story.'

'That's old news. Time I took that thing down. A lot of years and a lot of pounds ago.'

'I was at the Black Peace Officers meeting when you were honored,' Rider said.

'Oh, really?' Kibble said, her face breaking into a smile. 'That was a really nice night for me.'

'Whatever happened to the woman?' Bosch asked.

'Cassie Black? Oh, she's in the wind. Nobody's seen her since.'

'She has charges?'

'The funny thing is, no. I mean, we violated her because she ran, but that's all she's got on her. Hell, she didn't shoot me. All she did was save my life. I wasn't going to have 'em charge her for it. But the parole violation I couldn't do anything about. She split. Far as I know, the guy who shot me might've got her and buried her out in the desert somewhere. I hope not, though. She did me a good turn.'

Bosch was suddenly not so sure the woman he had temporarily lived next to in an airport motel while visiting his daughter in Las Vegas the year before had been Cassie Black. He sat down and didn't say anything.

'So you found the file?' Rider said.

'Right here,' Kibble said. 'You two can have at it. But if you want to ask me about the boy then do it now. My afternoon slate starts in five minutes. If I start late then I have a domino effect running through the whole damn day and I get outta here late. Can't do that tonight. I gotta date.'

She was beaming at the prospect of her date.

'Okay, well, what do you remember about Mackey? Did you look at the file?'

'Yeah, I looked when I was coming back with it. Mackey was just a pissant weenie wagger. Small-time drug user who got racial religion somewhere along the way. He was no big thing. I rather enjoyed having him under my thumb. But that was about it.'

Rider had opened the file and Bosch was leaning toward her to look into it.

'The lewd and lash was an exposure case?' he asked.

'Actually, I think you'll find in there that our boy got himself high on speed and alcohol – a lot of alcohol – and he decided to relieve himself in somebody's front yard. A thirteen-year-old girl happened to live there and she happened to be out front shooting baskets. Mr. Mackey decided upon seeing the girl that since he already had his little pud out and about in the wind that he might as well go ahead and ask the girl if she wanted to partake of it. Did I mention that the girl's father was LAPD Metro Division and happened to be off-duty and home at the time of this incident? He stepped outside and put Mr. Mackey on the ground. In fact, Mr. Mackey later complained that coincidentally or maybe not so coincidentally he had been put on the ground right on top of the puddle he had just made. He was rather unhappy about that.'

Kibble smiled at the story. Bosch nodded. Her version was more colorful than the case summary in the file.

'And he just pleaded out.'

'That's right. He got a probation deal and took it. He came to me.'

'Any problems during his twelve months?'

'Nothing other than his problem with me. He asked for another agent and it got turned down and he got stuck with me. He kept it in check but it was there. Underneath, you know? Couldn't ever tell which bugged his ass more, me being black or me being a woman.'

She looked at Rider as she said this last part and Rider nodded.

The file contained details of Mackey's past crimes and life. It had photos taken during earlier arrests. It would become the baseline resource on their target. There was too much in it to go through in front of Kibble.

'Can we get this copied?' Bosch asked. 'We'd also like to borrow one of these early photos if we could.'

Kibble's eyes narrowed for a moment.

'You two working an old case, huh?'

Rider nodded.

'From way back,' she said.

'Like a cold case, huh?'

'We call it open-unsolved,' Rider said.

Kibble nodded thoughtfully.

'Well, nothing surprises me in this place – I've seen people shoplift a frozen pizza and get popped two days before the end of a four-year tail. But from what I remember of this guy Mackey, he didn't seem to me to have the killer instinct. Not if you ask me. He's a follower, not a doer.'

'That's a good read,' Bosch said. 'We're not sure he is the one. We just know he was involved.'

He stood up, ready to go.

'What about the photo?' he asked. 'A photocopy won't be clear enough to show.'

'You can borrow that one as long as I get it back. I need to keep the file complete. People like Mackey have a tendency to come back to me, know what I mean?'

'Yes, and we'll get it back to you. Also, can I get a copy of your story there? I want to read it.'

Kibble looked at the newspaper clip tacked to the cubicle's wall.

'Just don't look at the picture. That's the old me.'

After clearing the DOC office Rider and Bosch crossed the street to the Van Nuys Civic Center and walked between the two courthouses to get to the plaza in the middle. They sat down on a bench by the library. Their next appointment was with Arturo Garcia in the LAPD's Van Nuys Division, which also was one of the buildings in the government center, but they were early and wanted to study the DOC file first.

The file contained detailed accounts of all the crimes Roland Mackey had been arrested for since his eighteenth birthday. It also contained biographical summaries used by probation and parole agents over the years in determining aspects of his supervision. Rider handed Bosch the arrest reports while she started going through the biographical details. She then immediately proceeded to interrupt his reading of a burglary case by calling out details of Mackey's bio that she thought might be pertinent to the Verloren case.

'He got a general education degree at Chatsworth High the summer of 'eighty-eight,' she said. 'So that puts him right in Chatsworth.'

'If he got a GED, then he dropped out first. Does it say from where?'

'Nothing here. Says he grew up in Chatsworth. Dysfunctional family. Poor student. He lived with his father, a welder at the General Motors plant in Van Nuys. Doesn't sound like Hillside Prep material.'

'We still need to check. Parents always want their kid to do better. If he went there and knew her and then dropped out, it would explain why he was never interviewed back in 'eighty-eight.'

Rider just nodded. She was reading on.

'This guy never left the Valley,' she said. 'Every address is in the Valley.'

'What's the last known?'

'Panorama City. Same as the AutoTrack hit. But if it's in here, then it's probably old.'

Bosch nodded. Anybody who had been through the system as many times as Mackey would know to move house the day after clearing a probation tail. Don't leave an address with the man. Bosch and Rider would go to the Panorama City address to check it out but Bosch knew that Mackey would be gone. Wherever he had moved, he had not used his name on public utility applications and he had not updated his driver's license or vehicle registration. He was flying below radar.

'Says he was in the Wayside Whities,' Rider said as she reviewed a report.

'No surprise.'

The Wayside Whities was the name of a jail gang that had existed for years in the Wayside Honor Rancho in the northern county. Gangs usually formed along racial lines in the county jails as a means of protection rather than out of racial enmity. It was not unusual to find members of the Nazi-leaning Wayside Whities to secretly be Jewish. Protection was protection. It was a way of belonging to a group and staving off assault from other groups. It was a measure of jail survival. Mackey's membership was only a tenuous connection to Bosch's theory that race possibly played a part in the Verloren case.

'Anything else on that?' he asked.

'Not that I see.'

'What about physical description? Any tattoos?'

Rider rifled through the paperwork and pulled out a jail intake form.

'Yeah, tattoos,' she said, reading. 'He's got his name on one bicep and I guess a girl's name on the other. RaHoWa.'

She spelled the name and Bosch started to get the first tingling sense that his theory was coming strongly into play.

'It's not a name,' he said. 'It's code. Means 'racial holy war.' First two letters of each word. The guy's one of the believers. I think Garcia and Green missed this and it was right there.'

He could feel the adrenaline picking up.

'Look at this,' Rider said urgently. 'He also has the number eighty-eight tattooed on his back. The guy's got a reminder of what he did in 'eighty-eight.'

'Sort of,' Bosch replied. 'It's more code. I worked one of these white power cases once and I remember all the codes. To these guys eighty-eight stands for double H because H is the eighth letter of the alphabet. Eighty-eight equals H-H equals Heil Hitler. They also use one ninety-eight for Sieg Heil. They're pretty clever, aren't they?'

'I still think the year 'eighty-eight might have something to do with this.'

'Maybe it does. You got anything in there about employment?'

'Looks like he drives a tow truck. He was driving a tow truck when he stopped to take the leak that got him the lewd and lash last time. This lists three different previous employers – all tow services.'

'That's good. That's a start.'

'We'll find him.'

Bosch looked back down at the arrest report in front of him. It was a burglary from 1990. Mackey had been caught by a police dog in the concessions shop of the Pacific Drive-in Theater. He had broken in after hours, setting off a silent alarm. He had pilfered the cash drawer and filled a plastic bag with two hundred candy bars. His exit was slowed because he decided to turn on the cheese warmer and make himself some nachos. He was still inside the building when a responding officer with a dog sent the animal inside the shop. The report said Mackey was treated for dog bite injuries to the left arm and upper left thigh at County-USC Medical Center before being booked.

The record indicated that Mackey pleaded guilty to breaking and entering, a lesser charge, and was sentenced to time served – sixty-seven days in the Van Nuys jail – and two years probation.

The next report was a violation of that probation for an assault arrest. Bosch was about to read the report when Rider took the sheaf of photocopies out of his hands.

'It's time to go see Garcia,' she said. 'His sergeant said if we're late we'll miss him.'

She stood up and Bosch followed. They headed toward the Van Nuys Division. The Valley Bureau Command offices were on the third floor.

'In nineteen ninety Mackey was popped for a burglary at the old Pacific Drive-in,' Bosch said as they walked.

'Okay.'

'It was at Winnetka and Prairie. There's a multiplex there now. That puts it about five or six blocks from where the Verloren weapon was stolen a couple years before. The burglary.'

'What do you think?'

'Two burglaries five blocks apart. I think maybe he liked working that area. I think he stole the gun. Or he was with the person who stole it.'

Rider nodded and they went up the stairs to the police station lobby and then took the elevator the rest of the way up to Valley Bureau Command. They were on time but still were made to wait. While sitting on a couch Bosch said, 'I remember that drive-in. I went there a couple times when I was a kid. The one in Van Nuys, too.'

'We had our own on the south side,' Rider said.

'They turn it into a multiplex, too?'

'No. It's just a parking lot. They don't put multiplex money down there.'

'What about Magic Johnson?'

Bosch knew the former Laker basketball star had invested heavily in the community, including opening movie theaters.

'He's only one man.'

'One man is a start, I guess.'

A woman with P2 stripes on her uniform's sleeves came up to them.

'The commander will see you now.'

9

Commander Arturo Garcia was standing behind his desk waiting as Bosch and Rider were led into his office by the uniformed assistant. Garcia was in uniform, too, and he wore it well and proudly. He had steel gray hair and a matching bottle-brush mustache. He exuded the confidence that the department used to carry and was fighting to recover.

'Detectives, come in, come in,' he said. 'Sit down here and tell an old homicide dick how it's hanging.'

They took the chairs in front of the desk.

'Thank you for seeing us so quickly,' Rider said.

Bosch and Rider had decided that she would take the lead with Garcia since she was more familiar with him through her liaison work in the chief's office. Bosch also wasn't sure he would be able to disguise his distaste for Garcia and the mistakes and missteps he and his partner had made on the Verloren investigation.

'Well, when Robbery-Homicide calls, you make the time, right?'

He smiled again.

'We actually work in the Open-Unsolved Unit,' Rider said.

Garcia lost his smile and for a moment Bosch thought he saw a flash of pain enter his eyes. Rider had made the appointment through an assistant in the commander's office and had not revealed what case they were working.

'Becky Verloren,' the commander said.

Rider nodded.

'How did you know?'

'How did I know? I was the one who called that guy down there, the OIC, and I told him there was DNA on that case and they ought to send it through.'

'Detective Pratt?'

'Yeah, Pratt. As soon as that unit was up and operational I called him and said check out Becky Verloren, nineteen eighty-eight. What have you got? You got a match, right?'

Rider nodded.

'We got a very good match.'

'Who? I've been waiting seventeen years for this. Somebody from the restaurant, right?'

This gave Bosch pause. In the murder book there were interview summaries from people who worked in Robert Verloren's restaurant but nothing that rose above the routine. Nothing that indicated suspicion or follow-up. Nothing in the investigative summaries that pointed the case toward the restaurant. To now hear one of the original investigators voice a long-held suspicion that the killer had come from that direction was incongruous with what they had spent the morning reading.

'Actually, no,' Rider said. 'The DNA matches a man named Roland Mackey. He was eighteen at the time of the murder. He was in Chatsworth at the time. We don't think he worked at the restaurant.'

Garcia frowned as though he was puzzled or maybe disappointed.

'Does that name mean anything to you?' Rider asked. 'We didn't come across it anywhere in the book.'

Garcia shook his head.

'I don't place it, but it's been a long time. Who is he?'

'We don't know who he is yet. We're circling him. We're just starting.'

'I'm sure I would have remembered the name. His blood was on the gun, right?'

'That's what we got. He's got a history. Burglaries, receiving, drugs. We're thinking he might be good for the burglary when the gun was taken.'

'Absolutely,' Garcia said, as if his excitement for the idea could make it so.

'We can connect him to the gun, no doubt,' Rider said. 'But we're looking for the connection to the girl. We thought maybe you'd remember something.'

'Have you talked to the mother and father yet?'

'Not yet. You're our first stop.'

'That poor family. That was it for them.'

'You stayed in touch with the parents?'

'Initially, yeah. As long as I had the case. But once I made lieutenant and went back to patrol I had to give up the case. I kind of lost contact with them after that. It was Muriel mostly – the mother – who I had talked to. The father . . . there was something going on with him. He didn't do well. He left home, they divorced, the whole thing. Lost the restaurant. Last I heard, he was living on the street. He would show up at the house from time to time and ask Muriel for money.'

'What made you guess it was somebody from the restaurant when we came in here?'

Garcia shook his head like he was frustrated by reaching for a memory he couldn't quite grasp.

'I don't know,' he said. 'I can't remember. It was more like a feeling. There was stuff wrong with the case. Something was hinky about it.'

'How so?'

'Well, you read the book, I'm sure. She wasn't raped. She was carried up that hill and it was made to look like a suicide. It was done badly. It was really an execution. So we weren't talking about the random intruder. Somebody she knew wanted her dead. And they either went in that house or sent somebody in that house.'

'You think it was related to the pregnancy?' Rider asked.

Garcia nodded.

'We thought that was tied in but we could never nail it down.'

'MTL – you never figured that one out.'

Garcia looked at her, confusion on his face.

'Empty L?'

'No, M-T-L. The initials Rebecca used in her journal. You mentioned it in the formal interview with the parents. 'My true love,' remember?'

'Oh, yeah, the initials. It was like a code. We never knew for sure. We never found out who that was. Are you looking for the journal?'

Bosch nodded and Rider spoke.

'We're looking for everything. The journal, the gun, the whole evidence carton is lost somewhere in the ESB.'

Garcia shook his head like a man who had spent a career dealing with the department's frustrations.

'That is not surprising. Par for the course, right?'

'Right.'

'Tell you one thing, though. If they find the carton there won't be any journal in it.'

'Why?'

'Because I gave it back.'

'To the parents?'

'To the mother. Like I said, I made lieutenant and was shipping out, going to South Bureau. Ron Green had already retired. I was passing the case off and I knew that was going to be the end of it. Nobody was going to pay attention to it like we did. So I told Muriel I was leaving and I gave her the journal . . .

'That poor woman. It was like time stood still for her on that day in July. She became frozen. Couldn't go forward, couldn't go back. I remember I went to see her before I left. This was a year or so after the murder. She had me look at Becky's bedroom. It was untouched. It was exactly the way it was on the night she was taken.'

Rider nodded somberly. Garcia said nothing else. Bosch finally cleared his throat, leaned forward and spoke, hitting Garcia with the same question again.

'When we first came in and said we got a DNA match, you guessed it was somebody from the restaurant. Why?'

Bosch looked at Rider to see if she was annoyed that he was entering the questioning. She didn't appear to be.

'I don't know why,' Garcia said. 'Like I said, I always sort of thought that it might have come from that side of things, because I never felt we nailed everything down over there.'

'You're talking about the father?'

Garcia nodded.

'The father was hinky. I don't know if you even say that anymore. But back then the word was hinky.'

'How so?' Rider asked. 'How was the father hinky?'

Before Garcia could answer the question one of the uniformed adjutants came into the office.

'Commander? They're all in the conference room and ready to start.'

'Okay, Sergeant. I'll be there shortly.'

After the sergeant left, Garcia looked back at Rider as if he had forgotten the question.

'There is nothing in the murder book that casts any suspicion on the father,' Rider said. 'Why did you think he was hinky?'

'Oh, I don't really know. Sort of a gut feeling. He never really acted like you would think a father would act, you know? He was too quiet. He never got mad, never yelled – I mean, somebody took his little girl. He never once took Ron or me aside and said, 'I want first shot at the guy when you find him.' I expected that.'

As far as Bosch was concerned, everybody was still a suspect, even with the cold hit tying Mackey to the murder weapon. This certainly included Robert Verloren. But he immediately dismissed Garcia's gut instinct based on the father's emotional responses to his daughter's murder. He knew from working hundreds of murders that there was absolutely no way to judge such responses or to build suspicion on them. Bosch had seen every permutation of it and it all meant nothing. One of the biggest criers and screamers he had ever encountered on a case ended up being the killer.

In dismissing Garcia's instinct and suspicion Bosch was also dismissing Garcia. He and Green had made early mistakes but recovered to conduct a by-the-numbers investigation of the murder. The murder book bore this out. But Bosch now guessed that whatever was done well was probably done by Green. He knew he should have suspected as much when he heard that Garcia had given up homicide for management.

'How long did you work homicide?' Bosch asked.

'Three years.'

'All in Devonshire Division?'

'That's right.'

Bosch quickly did the math. Devonshire would have had a light caseload. He figured that Garcia had worked no more than a couple dozen murders at the most. It wasn't enough experience to do it well. He decided to move on.

'What about your former partner?' he asked. 'Did he feel the same way about Robert Verloren?'

'He was willing to give the guy a little more slack than me.'

'Are you still in touch with him?'

'Who, the father?'

'No. Green.'

'No, he retired way back.'

'I know, but are you still in touch?'

Garcia shook his head.

'No, he's dead. He retired up to Humboldt County. He should've left his gun down here. All that time and nothing to do up there.'

'He killed himself?'

Garcia nodded.

Bosch looked down at the floor. It wasn't Ron Green's death that struck him. He didn't know Green. It was the loss of the connection to the case. He knew Garcia wasn't going to be much help.

'What about race?' Bosch asked, again stepping on Rider's lead.

'What about it?' Garcia asked. 'In this case? I don't see it.'

'Interracial couple, biracial kid, the gun came from a burglary where the victim was being harassed on religious lines.'

'That's a stretch. You got something with this Mackey character?'

'There might be something.'

'Well, we didn't have the luxury of a named suspect to work with. We didn't see any aspect of that with what we had back then.'

Garcia said it forcefully and Bosch knew he had touched a nerve. He didn't like to be second-guessed. No detective did. Even an inexperienced one.

'I know it's Monday-morning quarterbacking to start with the guy and go backwards,' Rider quickly said. 'It's just something we're looking at.'

Garcia seemed placated.

'I understand,' he said. 'Leave no stone unturned.'

He stood up.

'Well, Detectives, I hate to rush this. I wish we could kick this around all day. I used to put people in jail. Now I go into meetings about budget and deployment.'

That's what you deserve, Bosch thought. He glanced at Rider, wondering if she understood that he had saved her from a similar fate when he talked her into partnering with him in the Open-Unsolved Unit.

'Do me a favor,' Garcia said. 'When you hook up this guy Mackey, let me know. Maybe I'll come down and look through the window at him. I've been waiting for this one.'

'No problem, sir,' Rider said, breaking her stare away from Bosch. 'We'll do that. If you think of anything else that might help us with this, give me a call. All my numbers are on this.'

She stood up, placing a business card down on the table.

'I'll do it.'

Garcia started to go around his desk to head to his meeting.

'There's something we might need you to do,' Bosch said.

Garcia stopped in his tracks and looked at him.

'What is it, Detective? I need to get in that meeting.'

'We might try to flush the birds out of the bushes with a newspaper story. It might be good if it came from you. You know, former homicide guy, now a commander, haunted by the old case. He calls Open-Unsolved and gets them to run the DNA through the pipeline. What do you know, they get a cold hit.'

Garcia nodded. Bosch could tell it played to his ego perfectly.

'Yeah, it might work. Whatever you want to do. Just call me and we'll set it up. The *Daily News*? I've got connections there. It's the Valley paper.'

Bosch nodded.

'Yeah, that's what we were thinking,' he said.

'Good. Let me know. I've got to go.'

He quickly left the office. Rider and Bosch looked at each other and then followed. Out in the hallway, waiting for the elevator, Rider asked Bosch what he was doing when he asked him about planting the news story.

'He'd be perfect for the story because he doesn't know what he's talking about.'

'So, we don't want that. We want to be careful.'

'Don't worry. It'll work.'

The elevator opened and they got on. No one else was in it. As soon as the door closed Rider was on him.

'Harry, let's get something straight right now. We're either partners or we're not. You should have told me you were going to hit him with that. We should've talked about it first.'

Bosch nodded.

'You're right,' he said. 'We're partners. It won't happen again.'

'Good.'

The elevator door opened and she stepped out, leaving Bosch behind.

10

Hillside Preparatory School was a structure of Spanish design nestled against the hills of Porter Ranch. Its campus was marked by magnificent green lawns and the daunting rise of mountains behind it. The mountains almost seemed to cradle the school and protect it. Bosch thought it looked like a place that any parent would want their child to go. He thought about his own daughter, just a year away from starting school. He would want her to go to a school that looked like this – on the outside, at least.

He and Rider followed signs that led them to the administration offices. At a front counter Bosch showed his badge and explained that they wanted to see if a student named Roland Mackey had ever attended Hillside. The clerk disappeared into a back office and soon a man emerged. His most notable features were a basketball-sized paunch and thick glasses shaded by bushy eyebrows. Across his forehead his hair left the perfect line of a toupee.

'I'm Gordon Stoddard, principal here at Hillside. Mrs. Atkins told me you are detectives. I'm having her check that name for you. It didn't ring a bell with me and I've been here almost twenty-five years. Do you know exactly when he attended? It might help her with the search.'

Bosch was surprised. Stoddard looked like he was in his mid-forties. He must have come to Hillside fresh from his own schooling and never left. Bosch didn't know if that was a testament to what they paid teachers here or Stoddard's own dedication to the place. But from what he knew about teachers private and public, he doubted it was the pay.

'We'd be talking about the eighties, if he went here. That's a long time ago for you to remember.'

'Yes, but I have a memory for the students that have come through. Most of them. I haven't been principal for twenty-five years. I was a teacher first. I taught science and then I was dean of the science department.'

'Do you remember Rebecca Verloren?' Rider asked.

Stoddard blanched.

'Yes, as a matter of fact I do. I taught her science. Is that what this is about? Have you arrested this boy, Mackey? I mean, I guess he'd be a man now. Is he the one?'

'We don't know that, sir,' Bosch said quickly. 'We're reviewing the case and his name came up and we need to check on it. That's all.'

'Did you see the plaque?' Stoddard asked.

'Excuse me?'

'Outside on the wall in the main hallway. There is a plaque dedicated to Rebecca. The students in her class collected the funds for it and had it made. It is quite nice but of course it is also quite sad. But it does serve its purpose. People around here remember Rebecca Verloren.'

'We missed it. We'll look at it on our way out.'

'A lot of people still remember her. This school might not pay that well, and most of the faculty might have to work two jobs to make ends meet, but it has a very loyal faculty nonetheless. There are several teachers still here who taught Rebecca. We have one, Mrs. Sable, who was actually a student with her and then returned here to teach. In fact, Bailey was one of her good friends, I believe.'

Bosch glanced at Rider, who raised her eyebrows. They had a plan for approaching Becky Verloren's friends but here was an opportunity presenting itself. Bosch had recognized the name Bailey. One of the three friends Becky Verloren had spent the evening with two nights before her disappearance was named Bailey Koster.

Bosch knew that it was more than an opportunity to question a witness in the case. If they didn't get to Sable now she would likely hear about Roland Mackey from Stoddard. Bosch didn't want that. He wanted to control the flow of information on the case to the players involved in it.

'Is she here today?' Bosch asked. 'Could we talk to her?'

Stoddard looked up at the clock on the wall next to the counter.

'Well, she is in class now but school lets out for the day in about twenty minutes. If you don't mind waiting I am sure you could talk to her then.'

'That's no problem.'

'Good, I will send a message to her classroom and have her come to the office after school.'

Mrs. Atkins, the counter clerk, appeared behind Stoddard.

'Actually, if you don't mind,' Rider said, 'we'd rather go to her classroom to talk to her. We don't want to make her uncomfortable.'

Bosch nodded. Rider was on the same frequency. They didn't want a message of any kind going to Mrs. Sable. They didn't want her thinking about Becky Verloren until they were right there watching and listening.

'Either way,' Stoddard said. 'Whatever you want to do.'

He noticed Mrs. Atkins standing behind him and asked her to report her findings.

'We have no record of a Roland Mackey as a student here,' she said.

'Did you come across anyone with that last name?' Rider asked.

'Yes, one Mackey, first name Gregory, attended for two years in nineteen ninety-six and -seven.'

There was a long-shot possibility that it was a younger brother or a cousin. It might become necessary to check the name out.

'Can you see if there is a current address or contact number for him?' Rider asked.

Mrs. Atkins looked at Stoddard for approval and he nodded. She disappeared to go get the information. Bosch checked the wall clock. They had almost twenty minutes to kill.

'Mr. Stoddard, are there yearbooks from the late eighties that we could look at while we're waiting to see Mrs. Sable?' he asked.

'Yes, of course, I will take you to the library and get those for you.'

On the way to the library Stoddard took them by the plaque Rebecca Verloren's classmates had put on the wall of the main hallway. It was a simple dedication with her name, the years of her birth and death and the youthful promise of WE WILL ALWAYS REMEMBER.

'She was a sweet kid,' Stoddard said. 'Always involved. Her family, too. What a tragedy.'

Stoddard used the sleeve of his shirt to wipe the dust off the laminated photograph of the smiling Becky Verloren on the plaque.

The library was around the corner. There were few students at the tables or browsing the shelves as the end of the day drew near. In a whisper Stoddard told them to have a seat at a table and then he went off into the stacks. Less than a minute later he came back with three yearbooks and put them down on the table. Bosch saw that each book had the title *Veritas* and the year on the cover. Stoddard had brought yearbooks from 1986, 1987 and 1988.

'These are the last three years,' Stoddard whispered. 'I remember she went here from grade one, so if you want earlier books just let me know. They're on the shelf.'

Bosch shook his head.

'That's okay. This will be fine for now. We'll come back by the office before we leave. We need to get that information from Mrs. Atkins anyway.'

'Okay, then I will leave you to it.'

'Oh, can you tell us where Mrs. Sable's classroom is?'

Stoddard gave them the room number and told them how to get there from the library. He then excused himself, saying he was returning to the office. Before leaving he whispered a few words to a table of boys near the door. The boys then reached down to the backpacks they had dropped on the floor and pulled them underneath the table so as to not impede foot traffic. Something about the way they had haphazardly dropped their packs reminded Bosch of the way the boys of Vietnam had done it – where they stood, not caring about anything but getting the weight off their shoulders.

After Stoddard had left, the boys made faces at the door he had passed through.

Rider took the 1988 yearbook ahead of Bosch and he took the 1986 edition.

He wasn't expecting to find anything of value now that Mrs. Atkins had knocked down his theory that Roland Mackey had attended the school at one point but had dropped out before the murder. He was already resigned to the idea that the connection between Mackey and Becky Verloren – if it even existed – would be found somewhere else.

He did the math in his head and flipped through the book until he found the eighth grade photos. He quickly found Becky Verloren's picture. She wore pigtails and braces. She was smiling but looked like she was just beginning that period of prepubescent awkwardness. He doubted she had been happy with her appearance in the book. He checked the group photos showing the class's different clubs and organizations and was able to track her extracurricular activities. She played soccer and was seen in the photos for the science and art clubs and the homeroom representatives in student government. In all the photos she was always in the back row or off to the side. Bosch wondered if that was where she had been placed by a photographer or where she had felt comfortable.

Rider was taking her time with the 1988 edition. She was going through every page, at one point holding the book up to Bosch when she was going through the faculty section. She pointed to a photo of a young Gordon Stoddard, who had much longer hair back then and didn't wear glasses. He was leaner and looked stronger as well.

'Look at him,' she said. 'Nobody should grow old.'

'And everybody should get the chance.'

Bosch moved on to the 1987 yearbook and found that the photos of Becky Verloren showed a young girl who appeared to be blossoming. Her smile was fuller, more confident. If the braces were still there they were no longer noticeable. In the group photos she had moved to front and center. In the student government photos she was not a class officer yet, but she had her arms folded in a take-charge pose. Her posture and her unflinching stare at the camera told Bosch she was going places. Only somebody had stopped her.

Bosch flipped through a few more pages and then closed the book. He was waiting for the bell to ring so they could go interview Bailey Koster Sable.

'Nothing?' Rider asked.

'Of any value,' he said. 'It's good to look at her back then, though. In place. In her element.'

'Yes. Look at this.'

They were sitting across from each other. She turned the 1988 book around on the table so he could see it. She had finally gotten to the sophomore class photos. The top half of the page on the right showed a boy and four girls posing on a wall Bosch recognized as the entrance to the student parking lot. One of the girls was Becky Verloren. The caption above the photo said STUDENT LEADERS. Below the photo the students were identified and their positions listed. Becky Verloren was listed as student council representative. Bailey Koster was class president.

Rider tried to spin the book back toward herself but Bosch held it for a moment, studying the photograph. He could tell by her pose and her style that Becky Verloren had left her teen awkwardness behind. He would not describe the student in the photograph as a girl. She was on her way to becoming an attractive and confident young woman. He let the book go and Rider took it back.

'She was going to be a heartbreaker,' he said.

'Maybe she already was. Maybe she picked the wrong one to break.'

'Anything else in there?'

'Take a look.'

She flipped the open book around again. The two pages were spread with photos from the Art Club's trip to France the summer before. There were photos of about twenty students, boys and girls, and several parents or teachers in front of Notre Dame, in the courtyard of the Louvre and on a tourist boat on the Seine. Rider pointed out Rebecca Verloren in one of the photos.

'She went to France,' Bosch said. 'What about it?'

'She could have met someone over there. Could be an international link to this thing. We might have to go over there and check it out.'

She was trying to hold back a smile.

'Yeah,' Bosch said. 'You put the req in on that. Send it on up to six.'

'Boy, Harry, I guess your sense of humor stayed retired.'

'Yeah, I guess so.'

The school bell rang, ending the discussion as well as classes for the day. Bosch and Rider got up, leaving the yearbooks on the table, and left the library. They followed Stoddard's directions to Bailey Sable's classroom, along the way dodging students hurrying to leave the school. The girls wore plaid skirts and white blouses, the boys khakis and white polo shirts.

They looked into the open door of room B-6 and saw a woman sitting at a desk at the front center of the classroom. She did not look up from the papers she was apparently grading. Bailey Sable bore almost no resemblance to the sophomore class president whose photo Bosch and Rider had just studied in the yearbook. The hair was darker and shorter now, the body wider and heavier. Like Stoddard, she wore glasses. Bosch knew she was only thirty-two or thirty-three but she looked older.

There was one last student in the room. She was a pretty blonde girl who was shoving books into a backpack. When she was finished she zipped the pack closed and headed to the door.

'See you tomorrow, Mrs. Sable.'

'Good-bye, Kaitlyn.'

The student gave Bosch and Rider a curious look as she went by them.

The detectives stepped into the classroom and Bosch pulled the door closed. That made Bailey Sable look up from her papers.

'Can I help you?' she asked.

Bosch took the lead.

'You might be able to,' he said. 'Mr. Stoddard said it would be all right if we came to your classroom.'

He approached the desk. The teacher looked up at him warily.

'Are you parents?'

'No, we're detectives, Mrs. Sable. My name is Harry Bosch and this is Kizmin Rider. We wanted to ask you a few questions about Becky Verloren.'

She reacted as if she had just been punched in the gut. All these years and it was still that close to the surface.

'Oh my God, oh my God,' she said.

'We're sorry to hit you with this out of the blue,' Bosch said.

'Is something happening? Did you find who . . .?'

She didn't finish.

'Well, we're working on it again,' Bosch said. 'And you might be able to help us.'

'How?'

Bosch reached into his pocket and pulled out the mug shot taken from Roland Mackey's DOC probation file. It was a portrait of Mackey as an eighteen-year-old car thief. Bosch put it down on top of the paper she had been grading. She looked down at it.

'Do you recognize the person in that photo?' Bosch asked.

'It was taken seventeen years ago,' Rider added. 'About the time of Becky's death.'

The teacher looked down at Mackey's defiant glare into the police camera. She didn't say anything for a long time. Bosch looked at Rider and nodded, a signal that maybe she should take over.

'Does it look like anyone you or Becky or any of your friends may have encountered back then?' Rider asked.

'Did he go to school here?' Sable asked.

'No, we don't think so. But we know he lived in this area.'

'Is he the killer?'

'We don't know. We're just trying to see if there is a connection between Becky and him.'

'What is his name?'

Rider looked at Bosch and he nodded again.

'His name is Roland Mackey. Does he look familiar?'

'Not really. It is hard for me to remember back then. Remember the faces of strangers, I mean.'

'So he definitely is not someone you knew, right?'

'Definitely.'

'Do you think Becky could have known him without you being aware of it?'

She thought for a long moment before answering.

'Well, it's possible. You know, it came out that she'd gotten pregnant. I didn't know about that, so I guess I might not have known about him. Was he the father?'

'We don't know.'

Unbidden, she had jumped the interview forward to Bosch's next line of questioning.

'Mrs. Sable, you know, it's been a lot of years since then,' he said. 'If you were sort of sticking up for a friend back then, we understand that. But if there is more you know, you can tell us now. This is probably the last shot that anybody is going to take at solving this thing.'

'You mean about her being pregnant? I really didn't know about it. I'm sorry. I was just as shocked as everybody else when the police started asking about that.'

'If Becky were going to confide in someone about that, would it have been you?'

Again, she didn't answer right away. She gave it some thought.

'I don't know,' she said. 'We were very close but she was that way with a few other girls, too. There were four of us who had been together since first grade here. In first grade we called ourselves the Kitty Cat Club because we all had pet cats. At different times and different years one of us would be closer to one of the others. It changed all the time. But as a group we always stuck together.'

Bosch nodded.

'That summer when Becky was taken, who would you say was closest to her?'

'It was probably Tara. She took it the hardest.'

Bosch looked at Rider, trying to remember the names of the girls Becky had been with two nights before her death.

'Tara Wood?' Rider asked.

'Yes, that's Tara. They hung out together a lot that summer because Becky's dad owned a restaurant in Malibu and they were both working there. They were splitting a schedule there. It seemed that summer that all they did was talk about it.'

'What would they say about it?' Rider asked.

'Oh, you know, like what stars came in there. People like Sean Penn and Charlie Sheen. And sometimes they talked about what guys worked there and who was cute. Nothing too interesting to me since I didn't work there.'

'Was there any one guy in particular they talked about?'

She thought a moment before answering.

'Not really. Not that I remember. They just liked to talk about them because they were so different. They were surfers and would-be actors. Tara and Becky were Valley girls. It was like a culture clash for them.'

'Was she dating anybody from the restaurant?' Bosch asked.

'Not that I knew of. But it's like I said, I didn't know about the pregnancy, so there was obviously somebody in her life I didn't know about. She kept it a secret.'

'Were you jealous of them because they worked there?' Rider asked.

'Not at all. I didn't have to work and I was pretty happy about that.'

Rider was going somewhere so Bosch let her continue.

'What did you guys do for fun when you got together?' she asked.

'I don't know, the usual,' Sable said. 'We went shopping and to movies, stuff like that.'

'Who had cars?'

'Tara did and so did I. Tara had a convertible. We used to go up …'

She cut it off when she came to a memory.

'What?' Rider asked.

'I just remember driving up into Limekiln Canyon a lot after school. Tara had a cooler in the trunk and her dad never noticed if she'd taken some of his beers out of the refrigerator. One time we got pulled over up there by a police car. We hid the beers under our uniform skirts. They worked perfect for that. The policeman didn't notice.'

She smiled at the memory.

'Of course, now that I teach here I'm on the watch for that sort of thing. We still have the same uniforms.'

'What about before she started working at the restaurant?' Bosch said, drawing the interview back to Rebecca Verloren. 'She was sick for a week, right after school let out. Did you visit her or talk to her then?'

'I'm sure I did. That is when they said she probably, you know, ended the pregnancy. So she wasn't really sick. She was just recovering. But I didn't know. I must have just thought she was sick, that's all. I can't really remember if we talked that week or not.'

'Did the detectives back then ask you all of these questions?'

'Yes, I'm pretty sure they did.'

'Where would a girl from Hillside Prep go if she got pregnant?' Rider asked. 'Back then, I mean.'

'You mean like a clinic or a doctor?'

'Yes.'

Bailey Sable's neck flushed. She was embarrassed by the question. She shook her head.

'I don't know. That was as shocking really as Becky being, you know, killed. It made us all think we didn't really know our friend. It was really sad because I realized she hadn't trusted me enough to tell me these things. You know, I still think about that when I remember things back then.'

'Did she have any boyfriends that you did know about?' Bosch asked.

'Not then. I mean, at the time. She had a boyfriend freshman year but he had moved away to Hawaii with his family. That was like the summer before. Then the whole school year I thought she was alone. You know, she didn't go to any of the dances or the games with anybody. But I was wrong, I guess.'

'Because of the pregnancy,' Rider said.

'Well, yeah. That's sort of obvious, isn't it?'

'Who was the father?' Bosch asked, hoping the direct question might elicit a response with something to pursue.

But Sable shrugged.

'I have no idea, and don't think I've ever stopped wondering.'

Bosch nodded. He had gotten nothing.

'The breakup with the boy who moved to Hawaii – how was that with her?' he asked.

'Well, I thought it broke her heart. She took it really hard. It was like Romeo and Juliet.'

'How so?'

'They were broken up by the parents.'

'You mean they didn't want them going together?'

'No, his dad took a job or something in Hawaii. They had to move and it broke them up.'

Bosch nodded again. He didn't know if any of the information they were getting was useful but he knew it was important to cast as wide a net as possible.

'Do you know where Tara Wood is these days?' he asked.

Sable shook her head.

'We had a ten-year reunion and she didn't come. I lost touch with her. I still talk to Grace Tanaka from time to time. But she lives up in the Bay Area so I don't see her too much.'

'Can you give us her number?'

'Sure, I have it here.'

She reached down and opened a desk drawer and pulled out her purse. While she was getting out an address book Bosch took the photo of Mackey off the desk and put it back into his pocket. When Sable read off a phone number Rider wrote it down in a small notebook.

'Five ten,' Rider said. 'What is that, Oakland?'

'She lives in Hayward. She wants to live in San Francisco but it costs too much for what she makes.'

'What does she do?'

'She's a metal sculptor.'

'Her last name is still Tanaka?'

'Yes. She never married. She ...'

'What?'

'She turned out to be gay.'

'Turned out?'

'Well, what I mean is, we never knew. She never told us. She moved up there and once about eight years ago I went up to visit and then I knew.'

'It was obvious?'

'Obvious.'

'Did she come to the ten-year high school reunion?'

'Yes, she was there. We had fun, but it was sort of sad, too, because people talked about Becky and how it was never solved. I think that's probably why Tara didn't come. She didn't want to be reminded of what happened to Becky.'

'Well, maybe we'll change that by the twentieth reunion,' Bosch said, immediately regretting the flippant remark. 'Sorry, that wasn't a nice thing to say.'

'Well, I hope you do change it. I think about her all the time. Always wondering who did it and why they have never been found. I look at her picture every day on the plaque when I come into school. It's weird. I helped raise the money for that plaque when I was class president.'

'They?' Bosch asked.

'What?'

'You said they have never been found. Why did you say *they*?'

'I don't know. He, she, whatever.'

Bosch nodded.

'Mrs. Sable, thanks for your time,' he said. 'Would you do us a favor and not talk about this with anyone? We don't want people being prepared for us, you know what I mean?'

'Like with me?'

'Exactly. And if you think of anything else, anything at all you want to talk about, my partner will give you a card with our numbers on it.'

'Okay.'

She seemed to be in a far-off reverie. The detectives said good-bye and left her there with the stack of papers to grade. Bosch thought she was probably remembering a time when four girls were the best of friends and the future sparkled in front of them like an ocean.

Before leaving the school they stopped by the office to see if the school had any current contact information for former student Tara Wood. Gordon Stoddard had Mrs. Atkins check but the answer was no. Bosch asked if they could borrow the 1988 yearbook to make copies of some of the photos and Stoddard gave his approval.

'I'm on my way out,' he said. 'I'll walk with you.'

They small-talked on the way back to the library and Stoddard gave them the yearbook, which had already been returned to the shelves. On the way out to the parking lot Stoddard stopped with them once more in front of the memorial plaque. Bosch ran his fingers over the raised letters of Becky Verloren's name. He noticed that the edges had been worn smooth over the years by many students doing the same thing.

11

Rider worked the file and the phone while Bosch drove toward Panorama City, which was just on the east side of the 405 and across the Devonshire Division line.

Panorama City was a district carved off the north side of Van Nuys many years before when residents there decided they needed to distance themselves from negative connotations ascribed to Van Nuys. Nothing about the place was changed but the name and a few street signs. Still, Panorama City sounded clean and beautiful and crime free, and the residents felt better about themselves. But many years had passed and resident groups had petitioned to rename their neighborhoods again and to distance themselves, if not physically then image-wise, from negative connotations associated with Panorama City. Bosch guessed it was one of the ways Los Angeles kept reinventing itself. Like a writer or actor who keeps changing his name to leave past failings behind and start fresh, even with the same pen or face.

As expected, Roland Mackey was no longer at the auto towing company he had worked for while on his most recent stint of probation. But also as expected, the ex-con was not particularly smart when it came to covering his trail. The probation file contained his entire work history through a life that had largely been spent on probation or parole. He drove a tow truck for two other concerns during past periods of state monitoring. Posing as an acquaintance, Rider called each of them and easily located his current employer: Tampa Towing. She then called the tow service and asked if Mackey was working today. After a moment she closed the phone and looked at Bosch.

'Tampa Towing. He comes on at four.'

Bosch checked his watch. Mackey reported for work in ten minutes.

'Let's go by and get a look at him. We'll check his address after. Tampa and what?'

'Tampa and Roscoe. Must be across from the hospital.'

'The hospital is Roscoe and Reseda. I wonder why they didn't call it Roscoe Towing.'

'Funny. Then what do we do after we get a look at him?'

'Well, we go up to him and ask him if he killed Becky Verloren seventeen years ago and then he says yes and we take him downtown.'

'Come on, Bosch.'

'I don't know. What do you want to do next?'

'We check his address like you said, and then I think we're ready for the parents. I'm thinking that we need to talk to them about this guy before we set up on him and make a play – especially in the newspaper. I say we go by the house and see the mother. We're already up here. Might as well.'

'You mean if she's still there,' he said. 'Did you run an AutoTrack on her, too?'

'Didn't have to. She'll be there. You heard how Garcia was talking. Her baby's ghost is in that house. I doubt she'll ever leave it.'

Bosch guessed that she was right about that but didn't respond. He drove east on Devonshire Boulevard to Tampa Avenue and then dropped down to Roscoe Boulevard. They got to the intersection a few minutes before four. Tampa Towing was actually a Chevron service station with two mechanics' bays. Bosch parked in the lot of a small strip shopping plaza across the street and killed the engine.

Bosch wasn't surprised when four o'clock came and went without any sign of Roland Mackey. He didn't strike Bosch as somebody who would be excited to come to work to tow cars.

At four-fifteen Rider said, 'What do you think? You think my call could have—'

'There he is.'

A thirty-year-old Camaro with gray primer on all four fenders pulled into the service station and parked near the air pump. Bosch had caught only a glimpse of the driver but it was enough for him to know. He reached over to the glove compartment and took out a pair of field glasses he had bought through an airline catalog he had read while on a flight to Las Vegas.

He slouched down in his seat and watched through the glasses. Mackey got out of the Camaro and walked toward the service station's open garage. He was wearing a uniform of dark blue pants and a lighter blue shirt. There was an oval-shaped patch over the left breast pocket that said *Ro.* He had work gloves sticking out of one of his back pockets.

There was an old Ford Taurus up on a hydraulic lift in the garage and a man working beneath it with an air wrench. When Mackey entered, the man with the wrench nonchalantly reached out and gave him a high five. Mackey stopped while the man told him something.

'I think he's telling him about the phone call,' Bosch said. 'Mackey doesn't look too concerned about it. He just pulled a cell out of his pocket. He's calling the person he probably thinks called him.'

Reading Mackey's lips, Bosch said, 'Hey, did you call me?'

Mackey quickly ended the conversation.

'I guess not,' Bosch said.

Mackey put his phone back into his pocket.

'He tried one person,' Rider said. 'Must not have much of a social life.'

'The name on the patch on his shirt is Ro,' Bosch said. 'If his buddy told him that the caller asked for Roland, then he may have narrowed it down to the one person who calls him that. Maybe it was dear old dad, the welder.'

'So what's he doing?'

'Can't see him. He went into the back.'

'Maybe we should get out of here before he starts looking around.'

'Come on. One call and you think he's going to think somebody's onto him after seventeen years?'

'No, not for Becky. I'm worried about whatever else he's into now. We might be stumbling right into the middle of something and not even know it.'

Bosch put down the binoculars. She was right about that. He started the car.

'Okay, we got our look,' he said. 'Let's get out of here. Let's go see Muriel Verloren.'

'What about Panorama City?'

'PC can wait. We both know he doesn't live at that address anymore. Checking it is just a formality.'

He started backing out of the space.

'Do you think we should call Muriel first?' Rider asked.

'No. Let's just go knock on the door.'

'We're good at that.'

12

In ten minutes they were in front of the Verloren house. The neighborhood where Becky Verloren had lived still seemed pleasant and safe. Red Mesa Way was wide, with sidewalks on both sides and no shortage of shade trees. Most of the homes were ranch houses that sprawled across the extra-large lots. In the sixties, the larger properties were what drew people to settle the northwest corner of the city. Forty years later the trees were mature and the neighborhood had a cohesive feel to it.

The Verlorens' house was one of the few that had a second floor. It was still the classic ranch-style home but the roof popped up over the double-slot garage. Bosch knew from the murder book that Becky's bedroom had been upstairs over the garage and in the back.

The garage door was closed. There was no apparent sign that anyone was home. They parked in the driveway and went to the front door. When Bosch pushed a doorbell button he could hear a chime echo inside, a single tone that seemed very distant and lonely to him.

The door was answered by a woman who wore a shapeless blue pullover dress that helped hide her own shapeless body. She wore flat sandals. Her hair was dyed a color red that had too much orange in it. It looked like a home job that didn't go as planned, but she either didn't notice or didn't care. As soon as she opened the door a gray cat shot out of the opening and into the front yard.

'Smoke, don't get hit!' she yelled first. Then she said, 'Can I help you?'

'Mrs. Verloren?' Rider asked.

'Yes, what is it?'

'We're with the police. We'd like to talk to you about your daughter.'

As soon as Rider said the word 'police' and before she got to 'daughter,' Muriel Verloren brought both hands up to her mouth and reacted as though it was the moment she had learned her daughter was dead.

'Oh my God! Oh my God! Tell me you caught him. Tell me you caught the bastard who took my baby away from me.'

Rider reached a comforting hand to the woman's shoulder.

'It's not quite that simple, ma'am,' Rider said. 'Can we come in and talk?'

She stepped back and let them in. She seemed to be whispering something and Bosch thought it might be a prayer. Once they were in she closed the door after yelling a warning one more time into the front yard to the escaped cat.

The home smelled as though the cat had not escaped often enough. The living room to which they were led was neatly kept but with furniture that was old and worn. There was the distinct odor of cat urine in the place.

Bosch suddenly wished they had invited Muriel Verloren down to Parker Center for the interview, but knew that would have been a mistake. They needed to see this place.

They sat side by side on the couch and Muriel rushed to one of the chairs across the glass-topped coffee table from them. Bosch noticed paw prints on the glass.

'What is it?' she asked desperately. 'Is there news?'

'Well, I guess the news is that we are looking into the case again,' Rider said. 'I am Detective Rider and this is Detective Bosch. We work for the Open-Unsolved Unit out of Parker Center.'

By agreement while driving to the house Bosch and Rider decided to be cautious with the information they gave members of the Verloren family. Until they knew the family situation it would be better to take rather than to give.

'Is there anything new?' Muriel asked urgently.

'Well, we are just starting out,' Rider replied. 'We're covering a lot of the old ground right now. Trying to get up to speed. We just wanted to come by and tell you we were working the case again.'

She seemed a bit crestfallen. She had apparently thought that for the police to show up after so many years there would have to be something new. Bosch felt a twinge of guilt over withholding the fact that they had a rock-solid DNA lead – a cold hit – to work with, but at the moment he felt that it was for the best.

'There are a couple things,' he said, speaking for the first time. 'First, in looking through the files on the case, we came across this photo.'

He took the photo of Roland Mackey as an eighteen-year-old out of his pocket and put it down on the coffee table in front of Muriel. She immediately leaned down to look at it.

'We're not sure what the connection is,' he continued. 'We thought maybe you might recognize this man and tell us if you knew him back then.'

She continued to look without responding.

'This is a photo from nineteen eighty-eight,' Bosch said as a means of prompting her.

'Who is he?' she finally asked.

'We're not sure. His name is Roland Mackey. He's got a small-time record for crimes committed after your daughter's death. We're not sure why his photo was in the file. Do you recognize him?'

'Did you ask Art or Ron about it?'

Bosch started to ask who Art and Ron were when he realized.

'Actually, Detective Green retired and passed away a long time ago. Detective Garcia is Commander Garcia now. We talked to him but he wasn't able to help us with Mackey. How about you? Could he have been one of your daughter's acquaintances? Do you recognize him?'

'He could have been. There is something about him that I recognize.'

Bosch nodded.

'Do you know how you recognize him or from where?'

'No, I don't remember. Why don't you tell me and maybe that will help jog my memory.'

Bosch made a quick side glance at Rider. This was not totally unexpected, but it always complicated things when the parent of a victim was so eager to help that he or she simply asked what it was the police wanted them to say. Muriel Verloren had waited seventeen years for her daughter's killer to be brought forward into the light of the justice system. It was very clear that she was going to carefully choose answers that would in no way hinder the possibility of that happening. At this point it might not even matter if it was a false light. The past years had been cruel to her and the memory of her daughter. Someone still needed to pay.

'We can't tell you that because we don't know, Mrs. Verloren,' Bosch said. 'Think about it and let us know if you remember him.'

She nodded sadly, as if she thought it was yet another missed opportunity.

'Mrs. Verloren, what do you do for a living?' Rider asked.

It seemed to bring the woman in front of them back from her memories and desires.

'I sell things,' she said matter-of-factly. 'Online.'

They waited for further explanation and didn't get any.

'Really?' Rider asked. 'What things do you sell?'

'Whatever I can find. I go to yard sales. I find things. Books, toys, clothes. People will buy anything. And they'll pay anything. This morning I sold two napkin rings for fifty dollars. They were very old.'

'We want to ask your husband about the photo,' Bosch said then. 'Do you know where we could find him?'

She shook her head.

'Somewhere down there in toyland. I haven't heard from him in a long, long time.'

A somber moment of silence passed by. Most of the homeless missions in downtown Los Angeles were clustered at the edge of the Toy District, several blocks of toy manufacturers and wholesalers, even a few retailers. It wasn't unusual to find homeless people sleeping in the doorways of toy stores.

What Muriel Verloren was telling them was that her husband was lost in the world of floating human debris. He had descended from restaurateur to the stars to a homeless existence on the streets. But there was a contradiction there. He still had a home here. He just couldn't stay because of what had happened. Yet his wife would never leave.

'When were you divorced?' Rider asked.

'We never did get a divorce. I guess I always thought Robert would wake up and realize that no matter how far you run you can't get away from what happened to us. I thought he would realize that and come home. It hasn't happened yet.'

'Do you think you knew all of your daughter's friends?' Bosch asked.

Muriel thought about this one for a long moment.

'Until the morning she disappeared I did. But then we learned things. She kept secrets. I think that is one of the things that bothers me most. Not that she kept secrets from us, but that she thought she had to. I think that maybe if she had come to us things would have been different.'

'You mean the pregnancy?'

Muriel nodded.

'What makes you think that played into what happened to her?'

'Just a mother's instinct. I have no proof. I just think it started with that.'

Bosch nodded. But he couldn't blame the daughter for her secrets. By the time he had been her age Bosch had been on his own, without real parents. He had no idea what that relationship would have been like.

'We spoke to Commander Garcia,' Rider said. 'He told us that several years ago he returned your daughter's journal to you. Do you still have that?'

Muriel looked alarmed.

'I read part of it every night. You're not going to take that away from me, are you? It's my bible!'

'We need to borrow it and make a copy of it. Commander Garcia should have made a copy back then but he didn't.'

'I don't want to lose it.'

'You won't, Mrs. Verloren. I promise. We'll copy it and get it right back to you.'

'Do you want it now? It's by my bed.'

'Yes, if you could get it.'

Muriel Verloren left them and disappeared down a hallway that led toward the left side of the house. Bosch looked at Rider and raised his eyebrows in a what-do-you-think sort of way. Rider shrugged, meaning that they would talk about it later.

'Once my daughter wanted to get another cat,' Bosch whispered. 'My ex said no, one was enough. Now I know why.'

Rider was smiling inappropriately when Muriel came back in, carrying a small book with a flowery cover and the words *My Journal* embossed in gold on it. The gold was flaking off. The book had been handled a lot. She gave it to Rider, who went out of her way to handle it reverently.

'If you don't mind, Mrs. Verloren, we'd like to look around,' Bosch said. 'To sort of connect what we've seen and read in the book with the actual layout of the house.'

'What book?'

'Oh, I'm sorry. That's copspeak. All the investigative records from the case are kept in a large binder. We call it a book.'

'A murder book?'

'Yes, that's right. Is it all right if we look around? I would like to look at the back door and look around out back, too.'

She signaled with a raised arm which way they should go. Bosch and Rider got up.

'It's changed,' Muriel said. 'It used to be there were no houses up there. You'd go out our door and walk straight up the mountain. But they terraced it. Now there are houses. Millions of dollars. They built a mansion on the spot where my baby was found. I hate it.'

There was nothing to say to that. Bosch just nodded and followed her down a short hallway and into the kitchen. There was a door with a glass window in it. It led to the backyard. Muriel unlocked the door and they all stepped out. The yard was on a steep incline that led to a grove of eucalyptus trees. Through the trees Bosch could see the Spanish-tiled roofline of a large house.

'It used to be all open up there,' Muriel said. 'Just trees. Now there are houses. It's got a gate. They don't let me walk up there like I used to. They think I'm a bag lady or something because I liked to go up there sometimes and have a picnic at Becky's spot.'

Bosch nodded and thought for a moment about a mother having a picnic at the spot where her daughter was murdered. He tried to drop the idea and instead study the terrain of the hillside. The autopsy had said Becky Verloren weighed ninety-six pounds. Even as light as that, it would have been a struggle taking her up that incline. He wondered about the possibility that there had been more than one killer. He thought of Bailey Sable saying *they*.

He looked at Muriel Verloren, who was standing still and silent, her eyes closed. She had canted her head so that the late afternoon sun warmed her face. Bosch wondered if this was some form of communion with her lost daughter. As if sensing that they were looking at her, she spoke, keeping her eyes closed.

'I love this place. I'll never leave.'

'Can we look at your daughter's bedroom?' Bosch asked.

She opened her eyes.

'Just wipe your feet when we go back inside.'

She led them back through the kitchen and into the hallway. The stairway up began next to the door that led to the garage. The door was open and Bosch caught a glimpse of a battered minivan surrounded by stacks of boxes and things Muriel Verloren had apparently collected on her rounds. He also noted how close the door to the garage was to the stairs. He didn't know whether this meant anything. But he recalled the summary report in the murder book that suggested the killer had hidden somewhere in the house and waited for the family to go to sleep. The garage was the likely place.

The stairway was narrow because there were boxes of yard sale purchases lining one side all the way up. Rider went first. Muriel signaled for Bosch to go next and when he passed by her she whispered to him.

'Do you have children?'

He nodded, knowing his answer would hurt.

'A daughter.'

She nodded back.

'Never let her out of your sight.'

Bosch didn't tell her that she lived with her mother far out of his sight. He just nodded and started up the stairs.

On the second floor there was a landing and two bedrooms with a bathroom in between them. Becky Verloren's bedroom was to the rear, with windows that looked up the hillside.

The door was closed and Muriel opened it. When they stepped inside they stepped into a time warp. The room was unchanged from the seventeen-year-old photos Bosch had studied in the murder book. The rest of the house was crowded with junk and the detritus from a disintegrated life, but the room where Becky Verloren had slept and talked on the phone and written in her secret journal was unchanged. It had now been preserved longer than the girl had actually lived.

Bosch stepped further into the room and looked around silently. Even the cat didn't intrude here. The air smelled clean and fresh.

'This is just how it was on the morning she was gone,' Muriel said. 'Except I made the bed.'

Bosch looked at the quilt with the cats on it. It flowed over the edges and draped down to the bed skirt, which flowed neatly to the floor.

'You and your husband were sleeping on the other side of the house, right?' Bosch asked.

'Yes. Rebecca was at that age where she wanted her privacy. There are two bedrooms downstairs, on the other side of the house. Her first bedroom was down there. But when she was fourteen she moved up here.'

Bosch nodded and looked around before asking anything else.

'How often do you come up here, Mrs. Verloren?' Rider asked.

'Every single day. Sometimes when I can't sleep – which is a lot of the time – I come in here and lie down. I don't get under the covers, though. I want it to be her bed.'

Bosch realized he was nodding again, as if what she had said made some sort of sense to him. He stepped over to the vanity. There were photos slid into the frame of the mirror. Bosch recognized a young Bailey Sable in one of them. There was also a photo of Becky by herself in front of the Eiffel Tower. She was wearing a black beret. None of the other kids from the Art Club trip were present.

Also on the mirror was a photo of a boy with Becky. It looked like they were on a ride at Disneyland, or maybe just down at the Santa Monica pier.

'Who is this?' he asked.

Muriel came over and looked.

'The boy? That's Danny Kotchof. Her first boyfriend.'

Bosch nodded. The boy who had moved to Hawaii.

'When he moved away it just broke her heart,' Muriel added.

'When exactly was that?'

'The summer before, in June. Right after her freshman year and his sophomore. He was a year older.'

'Why did the family move, do you know?'

'Danny's dad worked for a rent-a-car company and he got transferred to a new franchise in Maui. It was a promotion.'

Bosch glanced at Rider to see if she picked up on the significance of the information Muriel had just given them. Rider subtly shook her head once. She didn't get it. But Bosch wanted to pursue it.

'Did Danny go to Hillside Prep?' he asked.

'Yes, that's where they met,' Muriel said.

Bosch looked down at the vanity and noticed a cheap souvenir snow globe with the Eiffel Tower in it. Some of the water had evaporated, leaving a bubble in the top of the globe and the tip of the tower poking from the water into the air pocket.

'Was Danny in the Art Club?' he asked. 'Did he make the trip to Paris with her?'

'No, they moved away before,' Muriel said. 'He left in June and the club went to Paris the last week of August.'

'Did she ever see or hear from Danny again?' he asked.

'Oh, yes, they sent letters back and forth and there were phone calls. At first they phoned back and forth, but it got too expensive. And then Danny did all the calling. Every night before bedtime. That lasted almost right up until . . . until she was gone.'

Bosch reached up and removed the photo from the mirror's border. He looked closely at Danny Kotchof.

'What happened when your daughter was taken? How did Danny find out? How did he react?'

'Well . . . we called there and told his father so that he could sit Danny down and tell him the bad news. We were told he did not take it well. Who would?'

'The father told Danny. Did either you or your husband talk directly to Danny?'

'No, but Danny wrote me a long letter about Becky and how much she meant to him. It was very sad and very sweet. Everything was.'

'I'm sure it was. Did he come to the funeral?'

'No, no he didn't. His, uh, his parents thought it best for him if he stayed there in the islands. The trauma, you know? Mr. Kotchof called and said he wouldn't be coming.'

Bosch nodded. He turned from the mirror, sliding the photo into his pocket. Muriel didn't notice.

'What about after?' he asked. 'After the letter, I mean. Did he ever contact you? Maybe call and talk to you?'

'No, I don't think we ever heard from him. Not since the letter.'

'Do you still have that letter?' Rider asked.

'Of course. I kept everything. I have a drawer full of letters we got about Rebecca. She was a well-loved girl.'

'We need to borrow that letter from you, Mrs. Verloren,' Bosch said. 'We also might need to look through the whole drawer at some point.'

'Why?'

'Because you never know,' Bosch said.

'Because we want to leave no stone unturned,' Rider added. 'We know this is disruptive but please remember what we are doing. We want to find the person who did this to your daughter. It has been a long time but that doesn't mean anybody should get away with it.'

Muriel Verloren nodded. She had absentmindedly picked up a small decorative pillow off the bed and was clutching it with both hands in front of her chest. It looked like it might have been made by her daughter many years ago. It was a small blue square with a red felt heart sewn across its middle. Holding it made Muriel Verloren look like a target.

13

While Bosch drove, Rider read the letter Danny Kotchof had sent to the Verlorens after Becky's murder. It was a single page, filled mostly with his fond memories of their lost daughter.

"All I can tell you is that I am so sorry this had to happen. I will miss her always. Love, Danny.' And that's it.'

'What's the postmark on it?'

She flipped over the envelope and looked at it.

'Maui, July twenty-ninth, nineteen eighty-eight.'

'Sure took his time writing it.'

'Maybe it was hard for him. Why are you keying on him, Harry?'

'I'm not. It's just that Garcia and Green relied on a phone call to clear him. You remember what it said in the book? It said the kid's supervisor said he was washing cars at the rent-a-car agency the day of and the day after. No time to fly to L.A., kill Becky, and get back home in time for work.'

'Yeah, so?'

'Well, now we find out from Muriel that his old man ran a rent-a-car. There was nothing about that in the murder book. Did Garcia and Green know that? How much you want to bet that dad was running the place where the son washed cars? How much you want to bet that the supervisor who alibied the son was working for the father?'

'Man, I was kidding about going to Paris. Sounds like you're jonesing for a trip to Maui.'

'I just don't like sloppy work. It leaves loose ends. We have to talk to Danny Kotchof and clear him ourselves. If that's even possible after so many years.'

'AutoTrack, baby.'

"That might find him for us. It won't clear him.'

'Even if we knock down his alibi, what are you saying, that this sixteen-year-old kid snuck over here from Hawaii, knocked off his old girlfriend and then went back without anybody seeing him?'

'Maybe it wasn't planned like that. And he was seventeen – Muriel said he was a year older.'

'Oh, seventeen,' she said sarcastically, as if that made all the difference in the world.

'When I was eighteen I got a leave from Vietnam to Hawaii. You were not allowed to go stateside from there. Once I got there I changed clothes, bought a civilian-looking suitcase and walked right by the MPs to get on a plane to L.A. I think a seventeen-year-old could have done it.'

'Okay, Harry.'

'Look, all I'm saying is that it was sloppy work. According to the murder book, Green and Garcia cleared this guy with a phone call. There's nothing in there about checking airlines and now it's too late. It bugs me.'

'I understand. But just remember. We have a logic triangle we have to complete. We can connect Danny to Becky easy enough, and the gun connects Becky to Mackey. But what connects Danny to Mackey?'

Bosch nodded. It was a good point. But it didn't make him feel any better about Danny Kotchof.

'Another thing is what he wrote in that letter,' he said. 'He said he was sorry that it had to happen. *Had* to happen – what does that mean?'

'It's just a figure of speech, Harry. You can't build a case on it.'

'I'm not talking about building a case on it. I just wonder why he chose to say it that way.'

'If he's still alive, we'll find him and you'll get to ask him.'

They had crossed under the 405 and were in Panorama City. Bosch dropped the discussion of Danny Kotchof and Rider brought up Muriel Verloren.

'She's frozen solid,' Rider said.

'Yeah.'

'It's pitiful. There was no reason for them to take the daughter up the hill. They might as well have killed everybody in the house. They did anyway.'

Bosch thought that was a harsh way of looking at it but didn't say anything.

'Them?' he asked instead.

'What?'

'You said there was no reason for *them* to take the daughter up the hill. You sound like Bailey Sable.'

'I don't know. Looking at that hill. It would have been tough for one person. It's steep back there.'

'Yeah. I was thinking the same thing. Two people.'

'Your idea about spooking Mackey is getting better. If he was there, he could lead us to the other – whether it's Kotchof or somebody else.'

Bosch turned south on Van Nuys Boulevard and stopped in front of an aging apartment complex that covered half the block. It was called the Panorama View Suites. There was a sign that said RENTAL OFFICE to the left of the glass doors of the lobby. It also announced that units were available on a monthly and weekly basis. Bosch put the transmission into park.

'Besides Kotchof, what else were you thinking, Harry?'

'I was thinking that I want to track down and talk to the other two friends. Maybe you can take the lesbian. But the father is my priority – if we can find him.'

'Okay, you take the father and I'll take the lesbian. Maybe I'll get to go up to San Francisco.'

'It's Hayward. And if you need help I know an inspector up there who will track her down and save L.A. the cost of the trip.'

'You are really no fun, Harry. I'd like to hang out with the northern sisters.'

'Did the chief know about you?'

'Not at first. When he found out he didn't care.'

Bosch nodded. He liked the chief for that.

'What else?' Rider asked.

'Sam Weiss.'

'Who is that?'

'The burglary victim. The one whose gun was used to kill the girl.'

'Why him?'

'They didn't have Roland Mackey back then. Might be worth running the name by him.'

'Check.'

'After that I think we'll be ready to make the play with Mackey, see how he reacts.'

'Then let's get this over with and then go talk to Pratt.'

They cracked the doors at the same time and got out. As Bosch came around the SUV he could feel her looking at him, studying him.

'What?' he asked.

'There's something else.'

'What do you mean?'

'With you. When you get that little crease on your left eyebrow I know something's going on.'

'My ex-wife always told me I'd make a bad poker player. Too many tells.'

'Well, what is it?'

'I don't know yet. Something about that room.'

'Back at the house? Her bedroom? You mean like it was creepy her keeping it like that?'

'No, actually, her keeping it was okay with me. I think I get that. It's something else. Something wrong, something different. I'll grind it out and let you know when I know.'

'Okay, Harry, that's what you're good at.'

They went through the glass doors into the Panorama View Suites. In ten minutes they confirmed what they knew going in; that Mackey had moved out soon after he had completed his probation.

As expected, he'd left no forwarding address.

14

Abel Pratt was behind his desk eating a concoction of yogurt and cornflakes out of a plastic tub. He made both a sucking and crackling sound as he ate and it was getting on Bosch's nerves. They had been sitting with him for twenty minutes, updating him on the day's progress on the cold hit.

'Shit, I'm still hungry,' he said after finishing the last spoonful.

'What is that, the South Beach diet?' Rider asked.

'No, just my own thing. What I need, though, is the South Bureau diet.'

'Really? And what is the South Bureau diet?'

Bosch could feel Rider tense. The South Bureau encompassed the majority of the city's black community. She had to wonder if what Pratt had just said was some sort of backhanded racial comment. Bosch had often seen in the department the elevation of the us versus them ethic to the point that white cops would make racially tinged comments in front of black or Latino cops simply because they believed that within the rank and file, the color blue superseded skin color. Rider was about to find out if Pratt was one of these cops.

'Put down your antenna,' Pratt said. 'All I'm saying is that I worked in South for ten years and I never had to worry about my weight. You're always on the run down there. Then I got to RHD and gained fifteen pounds in two years. It's sad.'

Rider relaxed and so did Bosch.

'Get off your ass and knock on doors,' Bosch said. 'That was the rule in Hollywood.'

'Good rule,' Pratt said. 'Except it's hard when they put you in charge. I have to sit in here and hear about how you guys get to knock on doors.'

'But you get the big bucks,' Rider said.

'Oh, yeah.'

This was a joke because as a supervisor Pratt could not pull overtime. But those on his squad could, thereby setting up the possibility that some of his detectives would make more than him, even though he was the unit boss.

Pratt turned in his chair and opened a cooler on the floor beside him. He took out another tub of yogurt.

'Fuck it,' he said as he straightened up and opened it.

He didn't add cornflakes this time. Bosch only had to put up with the slurping as he started spooning the white gunk into his mouth.

'Okay, back to this,' Pratt said, his mouth full of it. 'What you are telling me is that at the end of the day you can tie the gun to this mope Mackey. He fired this weapon. But you've got nobody who ties him to the victim yet and therefore you cannot tie him to the fatal shot.'

'That and other things,' Rider said.

'So if I was a defense lawyer,' Pratt continued, 'I would have Mackey cop to the burglary because the statute of limitations has long expired. He would say the gun bit him when he tried it out so he got rid of the damn thing – long before any murder. He'd say, "No sir I didn't kill that little girl with it and you can't prove I did. You can't prove I ever laid eyes on her."'

Rider and Bosch nodded.

'So you got nothing.'

They nodded again.

'Not bad for a day's work. What do you want to do about it?'

'We want a wiretap,' Bosch said. 'Two, maybe three locations. One on his cell, one on the phone at the gas station. And then one on his home once we find it and if he's got a line there. We plant a story in the paper that says we're working the case again and make sure he sees it. Then we see if he talks about it with anybody.'

'And what makes you think he would talk to someone else about a murder he may or may not have committed seventeen years ago?'

'Because, like we said, so far we can't connect this guy to the girl in any way. So we're thinking there is somebody in the middle in this thing. Mackey either did this for somebody or he got the gun for that somebody to do it himself.'

'There is a third possibility,' Rider added. 'That he helped. That girl was carried up a steep hillside. It was either somebody big or somebody with help.'

Pratt took two spoonfuls of yogurt, frowning as he looked down into the tub, before responding.

'Okay, what about the newspaper? You going to be able to make a plant?'

'We think so,' Rider said. 'We're going to use Commander Garcia of Valley Bureau. He was on the case originally. Haunted by the one that got away, that sort of pitch. He says he's got a connection at the *Daily News.*'

'Okay, sounds like a plan. Write up the warrants and give them to me. The captain has to approve them and then they go to the DA's office for approval before going to the judge. It's going to take some time. Once we get a judge to okay it we'll take the other teams off what they're doing and put them on the wire while you watch our guy.'

Bosch and Rider stood up at the same time. Bosch felt a little charge of adrenaline drop into his blood.

'There's no chance this guy Mackey is into something right now, is there?' Pratt asked.

'What do you mean?' Bosch asked.

'It's just that if we could make a case that he was about to commit a crime we could probably expedite the warrants.'

Bosch thought about this.

'We don't have that now,' he said. 'But we could work on it.'

'Good. That would help.'

15

Rider was the writer. She had an ease with the computer as well as the language of law. Bosch had seen her put these skills to use on several previous investigations. So their decision was unspoken. She would write the warrants seeking court authorization to trace and listen to calls made by or to Roland Mackey on his cell phone, the office phone at the service station where he worked, and his home if an additional phone existed there. It would be painstaking work; she had to lay out the case against Mackey, making sure the chain of logic and probable cause had no weak links. Her paper case had to first convince Pratt, then Captain Norona, then a deputy district attorney charged with making sure local law enforcement did not run roughshod over civil liberties, and finally a judge who had the same responsibilities but also answered to the electorate should he make a mistake that blew up in his face. They had one shot at this and they had to do it right. Rather, Rider had to do it right.

But all of that came after the initial hurdle of getting Mackey's various phone numbers without tipping the suspect to the investigation taking form around him.

They started with Tampa Towing, which ran a half-page ad in the yellow pages that carried two 24-hour phone numbers. Next, a call to directory assistance established that Mackey had no hardwired phone listing private or otherwise in his name. It meant he either had no phone at his home or he was living in a place where the phone was registered to someone else. That could be dealt with later once they established Mackey's residence.

Last and most difficult was Mackey's cell phone number. Directory assistance did not carry cell listings. To check every cellular service provider for a listing could take days if not weeks because most required a court-ordered search warrant before revealing a customer's private number. Instead, law enforcement investigators routinely planned ruses in order to get the numbers they needed. This often entailed leaving innocuous messages at workplaces so that the cell phone number could be captured upon callback. The most popular of these was the standard call-back-for-your-prize message, promising a television or DVD player to the first one hundred people who returned the call. However, this involved setting up a non-police line and could also result in long waiting periods with no guarantee of success if the target had masked his or her cell number. Rider and Bosch did not feel they had the luxury of time. They had put Mackey's name out into the public. They had to move quickly toward their goal.

'Don't worry,' Bosch told Rider. 'I've got a plan.'

'Then I'll just sit back and watch the master.'

Since he knew Mackey was on duty at the service station Bosch simply called the station and said he needed a tow. He was told to hold on and then a voice he believed belonged to Roland Mackey came onto the line.

'You need a tow?'

'Either a tow or a jump. I can't get it started.'

'Where?'

'The Albertson's parking lot on Topanga near Devonshire.'

'We're all the way over on Tampa. You can get somebody closer.'

'I know but I live by you guys. Right off Roscoe and behind the hospital.'

'Okay, then. What are you driving?'

Bosch thought of the car they had seen Mackey in earlier. He decided to use it to pull Mackey off the fence.

''Seventy-two Camaro.'

'Restored?'

'I'm working on it.'

'It should be about fifteen minutes before I'm there.'

'Okay, great. What's your name?'

'Ro.'

'Ro? Like row a boat?'

'Like in Roland, man. I'm on my way.'

He hung up. Bosch and Rider waited five minutes, during which Bosch told her the rest of the plan and what part she would play in it. Her goal was to get two things: Mackey's cell number and his service provider so that a search warrant authorizing the wiretap could be delivered to the proper company.

Following Bosch's instructions, Rider called the Chevron station and started making a service appointment, going into great detail in describing the screeching her car's brakes made. While she was in the middle of it, Bosch called the station on the second line listed in the phone book. As expected Rider was put on hold. Bosch's call was answered and he said, 'Do you have a number I can reach Ro on? He's coming here to give me a jump and I got it started already.'

Mackey's harried co-worker said, 'Try him on his cell.'

He gave Bosch the number and Bosch flashed the thumbs-up across the desk to Rider. She finished her call without breaking the act and hung up.

'One down, one to go,' Bosch said.

'You got the easy one,' Rider said.

With Mackey's number in hand, Rider took over while Bosch listened on an extension. Putting a disinterested bureaucratic glaze over her voice she called the number and when Mackey answered – presumably while looking for a stalled '72 Camaro in a shopping center parking lot – she announced that she was his AT&T Wireless provider and that she had some exciting news for savings over his current long-distance minutes plan.

'Bullshit,' Mackey said, interrupting her in the middle of her spiel.

'Excuse me, sir?' Rider replied.

'I said bullshit. This is some sort of scam to make me switch.'

'I don't understand, sir. I have you listed as an AT&T Wireless customer. Is that not the case?'

'Yeah, that's not the fucking case. I'm with Sprint and I like it and I don't even have or want long-distance service. So fuck off. Can you hear me now?'

He hung up and Rider started laughing.

'This is an angry guy we're dealing with,' she said.

'Well, he just drove all the way across Chatsworth for nothing,' Bosch said. 'I'd be angry too.'

'He's with Sprint,' she said. 'I'm ready to rock and roll on the paper. But maybe you should call him, so he won't be suspicious about you not calling when the guy in the shop tells him he gave out his number.'

Bosch nodded and called Mackey's number. Thankfully it went to a message; Mackey was probably on the phone angrily telling the guy in the shop he could not find the car he was supposed to tow. Bosch left a message saying he was sorry but he was able to get his car started and was trying to get it home. He closed his phone and looked at Rider.

They talked some more about scheduling and decided that she would work exclusively on the warrant that night and the next day and then babysit it through the approval stages. She said she wanted Bosch with her when it got to the final approval. Having both members of the team in the judge's chambers would help cement the deal. Until then, Bosch would continue to work the field, tracking the remaining names on their list of people to be interviewed and putting the newspaper story in motion. Timing was going to be the issue. They didn't want a story about the case in the newspaper until they had taps in place on the phones Mackey used. Finessing all of this would be the key maneuver.

'I'm going home, Harry,' Rider said. 'I can get this started on my laptop.'

'Have a good one.'

'What will you do?'

'I've got a few things I want to get done tonight. Maybe go down to the Toy District, I think.'

'By yourself?'

'They're only homeless people.'

'Yeah, and eighty percent of them are homeless because they've got faulty wiring, faulty plumbing, the whole bit. You be careful. Maybe you ought to call Central Division and see if they'll send a car with you. Maybe they can spare the U-boat tonight.'

The U-boat was a single-officer car primarily used as a gopher for the watch commander. But Bosch didn't think he needed a chaperone. He told Rider he would be all right and that she could go as soon as she showed him how to use the AutoTrack computer.

'Well, Harry, first you have to have a computer. I did it right from my laptop.'

He came around to her side and watched as she went to the AutoTrack website, entered password information and arrived at a template for a name search.

'Who do you want to start with?' she asked.

'How about Robert Verloren?'

She typed in the name and set parameters for the search.

'How fast does this work?' Bosch asked.

'Fast.'

In a few minutes she had located an address trail for Rebecca Verloren's father. But it stopped short at the house in Chatsworth. Robert Verloren had not updated his driver's license, bought property, registered to vote, applied for a credit card or had a utilities account in over ten years. He was a blank. He had disappeared – at least from the electronic grid.

'He must still be on the street,' Rider said.

'If he's even still alive.'

Rider put the names Tara Wood and Daniel Kotchof through the AutoTrack moves and came up with multiple name hits for both of them. But by using their approximate ages and focusing on Hawaii and California they narrowed the searches to two address trails they believed belonged to the correct Tara Wood and Daniel Kotchof. Wood may not have gone to her high school reunion but it wasn't because she had moved far away. She had only moved from the Valley over the hills to Santa Monica. Meanwhile, it appeared that Daniel Kotchof had returned from Hawaii many years earlier, lived in Venice for a few years and then returned to Maui, where his current address was located.

The last name Bosch gave Rider to run through the computer was Sam Weiss, the burglary victim whose gun was used to murder Rebecca Verloren. Though there were hundreds of hits on the name, it was easy to find the right Sam Weiss. He had never left the home where the burglary had taken place. He even had the same phone number. He had stood his ground.

Rider printed everything out for Bosch and also gave him the number for Grace Tanaka, which they had gotten earlier from Bailey Sable. She then gathered what she would need to work on the search warrant at home.

'If you need me give me a page,' she said as she put her computer into a padded case.

After she was gone Bosch checked the clock over Pratt's door and saw it was just past six. He decided he would spend an hour or so chasing names before heading down to the Toy District to look for Robert Verloren. He knew he was just procrastinating over a search through the human throw-away zone that would be certain to leave him depressed. So he checked the clock again and promised himself he would spend no more than an hour working the phone.

He decided to go with the locals first but quickly struck out. Calls to both Tara Wood and Sam Weiss went unanswered and connected him with automated message systems. He left a message for Wood identifying himself, giving his cell phone number and mentioning that the call was in regard to Becky Verloren. He hoped that mentioning her friend's name would be enough to intrigue and draw a response from her. With Weiss he only left his name and number, not wanting to forewarn him that the call was about what might be a source of guilt for the man who had indirectly provided the weapon that killed a sixteen-year-old girl.

Next he called Grace Tanaka's number in Hayward and she answered after six rings. From the start she seemed put out by the call, as if it had interrupted something important, but her gruff manner and voice softened as soon as Bosch said he was calling about Rebecca Verloren.

'Oh my God, is something happening?' she asked.

'The department has taken an avid interest in reinvestigating the case,' Bosch said. 'A name has come up. This is an individual who may have been involved in the case in nineteen eighty-eight and we are trying to figure out if he fit in with Becky or her friends in any way.'

'What's his name?' she asked quickly.

'Roland Mackey. He was a couple years older than Becky. Didn't go to Hillside but he lived right there in Chatsworth. Does the name mean anything to you?'

'Not really. I don't remember it. How was he connected? Was he the father?'

'The father?'

'The police said she was pregnant. I mean, that she had been pregnant.'

'No, we don't know if he was connected that way or not. So you don't recognize the name?'

'No.'

'He goes by Ro for short.'

'Still don't.'

'And you're saying you didn't know about the pregnancy, is that right?'

'I didn't. None of us did. I mean, her friends.'

Bosch nodded even though he knew she couldn't see this. He didn't say anything, hoping that she might get uncomfortable with the silence and say something that might be of value.

'Um, do you have a picture of this man?' she finally asked.

It wasn't what Bosch was looking for.

'Yes,' he said. 'I'll have to figure out a way to get it up there for you to look at, see if it jogs anything loose.'

'Can you just scan it and e-mail it?'

Bosch knew what she was asking him to do, and while he could not do it himself he guessed that Kiz Rider probably could.

'I think we could do that. My partner's the computer person and she's not here at the moment, though.'

'I'll give you my e-mail address and she can send me the picture when she comes back.'

Bosch wrote the address she recited in his small notebook. He told her she'd get the e-mail the following morning.

'Is there anything else, Detective?'

Bosch knew he could end the call and have Rider take a shot at bonding with Grace Tanaka after the photo was sent to her. But he decided not to miss the opportunity to start stirring emotions and memories. Maybe something would break loose.

'I have just a few more questions. Uh, that summer, how would you characterize your relationship with Becky?'

'What do you mean? We were friends. I'd known her since first grade.'

'Right, well, were you the closest to her, do you think?'

'No, I think that would have been Tara.'

Another confirmation that Tara Wood had been tightest with Becky at the end.

'So she didn't confide in you when she found out she was pregnant.'

'No, I already told you, I didn't know about it until after she was dead.'

'What about you? Did you confide in her?'

'Of course I did.'

'Everything?'

'Detective, what are you getting at?'

'Did she know you were gay?'

'What did that have to do with anything?'

'I'm just trying to get a picture of the group. The Kitty Kat Club, I think the four of you called—'

'No,' she said abruptly. 'She didn't know. None of them knew. I don't think I even knew back then. Okay, Detective? Is that enough?'

'I'm sorry, Ms. Tanaka. I'm just trying to get as full a picture as I can. I appreciate your candor. One last question. If Becky was at a clinic after going through the procedure and she needed a ride home because she didn't think she could drive, who would she have called?'

There was a long silence before Grace Tanaka answered.

'I don't know, Detective. I would have hoped that it would have been me. That I was that kind of friend. But obviously it was somebody else.'

'Tara Wood?'

'You'll have to ask her. Good night, Detective Bosch.'

She hung up and Bosch pulled open the yearbook so he could look at her photo. She was a petite Asian and the photo – so many years old – didn't match the gruff demeanor of the voice he had just heard on the phone.

Bosch wrote a note for Rider that contained the e-mail address and instructions to scan and send the photo of Mackey. He also wrote a short warning about his encountering resistance from Tanaka when he brought up her sexuality. He slid the note over to her desk so she would see it first thing in the morning.

That left one last call, this one to Daniel Kotchof, who lived, according to AutoTrack, in Maui, where it was two hours earlier.

He called the number he had gotten from the Auto-Track search and a woman answered the line. She said she was Daniel Kotchof's wife and told Bosch that her husband was at work at the Four Seasons Hotel, where he was employed as the hospitality manager. Bosch called the work number she gave him and was put through to Daniel Kotchof. He said he could only talk for a few minutes and put Bosch on hold for five of them while he went to a more private spot in the hotel to talk. When he finally came back on the line the call started out unproductively. Like Grace Tanaka, he did not recognize the name Roland Mackey. He also seemed to treat the call as a nuisance or an intrusion. He explained that he was married and had three children and that he rarely thought about Becky Verloren anymore. He reminded Bosch that he and his family had moved from the mainland a year before her death.

'But I was led to believe that after you moved to Hawaii, you two continued to call each other quite often,' Bosch said.

'I don't know who told you that,' Kotchof said. 'I mean, we talked. Especially at first. I would have to call her 'cause she said her parents told her it was too much money for her to call me. I thought that was kind of bogus. They just wanted me out of the picture is all. So I had to call, but it was like, what's the use? I was in Hawaii and she was in L.A. It was over, man. And pretty soon I got a girlfriend here – in fact, she's my wife now – and I stopped calling Beck. That was it until, you know, later, when I heard about what happened and the detective called me.'

'Did you know about it before the detective called?'

'Yeah, I'd heard. Mrs. Verloren called my dad and he broke the news to me. I also got some calls on it from some of my friends out there. They knew I'd want to know about it. It was weird, man, this girl that I knew gets wiped out like that.'

'Yeah.'

Bosch thought about what else he could ask. Kotchof's story conflicted in small ways with Muriel Verloren's account. He knew he would need to square the stories at some point. Kotchof's alibi also continued to bother him.

'Hey, look, Detective, I should get going,' Kotchof said. 'I'm at work. Is there anything else?'

'Just a few more questions. Do you remember how long before Rebecca's death it was that you stopped calling her?'

'Um, I don't know. Somewhere around the end of that first summer. Something like that. It had been a while, almost a year.'

Bosch decided to try to rattle Kotchof and see what came out. It was something he would rather have attempted in person but there was no time or money for a trip to Hawaii.

'So your relationship was definitely over by the time of her death?'

'Yes, definitely.'

Bosch thought the chances of recovering phone records from back then were not very high.

'When you were still calling was it always at a certain time? You know, like an appointment.'

'Sort of. I was two hours behind so I couldn't call too late. I usually called right after dinner and that was right before she was going to go to bed. But like I said, it didn't last too long.'

'Okay. Now I have to ask you something pretty personal. Did you have sex with Rebecca Verloren?'

There was a pause.

'What's that got to do with this?'

'I can't explain that, Dan. But it is part of the investigation and it could have a bearing on the case. Do you mind answering?'

'No.'

Bosch waited but Kotchof said nothing else.

'Is that your answer?' Bosch finally asked. 'You two never had sex?'

'We never did. She said she wasn't ready and I didn't push it. Look, I have to go.'

'Okay, Dan, just a few more. I'm sure you would like for us to catch the guy who did this, right?'

'Yes, right, it's just that I'm at work.'

'Yes, you said that. Let me ask you, when was the last time you saw Rebecca?'

'I don't remember the exact date but it was like the day we left. When we said good-bye. That morning.'

'So you never came back from Hawaii once your family moved?'

'No, not at first. I mean, I've been back since. I lived in Venice for a couple years after I finished school, but then I came back here.'

'But not between the time your family moved and the time of Rebecca's murder. Is that what you are saying?'

'Yes, right.'

'So if another witness I have spoken to said she saw you in town that weekend of July Fourth, right before Rebecca disappeared, then she would be wrong about that?'

'Yeah, she'd be wrong. Look, what is this? I told you. I never went back. I had a new girlfriend. I mean, I didn't even go back for the funeral. Who told you they saw me? Was it Grace? She never liked me – that dyke. She was always trying to get me in trouble with Beck.'

'I can't tell you who it is, Dan. Just like if you want to tell me something in confidence then I will respect that.'

'Whoever it is, she's a fucking liar,' Kotchof said, his voice turning shrill. 'That is a goddamn lie! Check your records, man! I had an alibi. I was working on the day she was taken, and I was working the next day, too. How could I have gotten there and back? Whoever told you that is totally fucking bogus!'

'It's your alibi that is bogus, Dan. Your old man could have put your supervisor up to it. That was easy.'

A moment of silence passed before there was a response.

'I don't know what you are talking about. My father didn't put anybody up to anything and that's a goddamn fact. We had the time cards and my boss talked to the cops and that was it. Now you come along seventeen years later with this shit? Are you fucking kidding me?'

'Okay, Dan, take it easy. Sometimes people make mistakes. Especially when you are going back all those years.'

'This is all I need, to be dragged into this. Man, I've got a family over here.'

'I said take it easy. You aren't being dragged into anything. This is just a phone call. Just a conversation, okay? Now, is there anything else you can tell me or want to tell me to help with this thing?'

'No. I told you all I know, which is nothing. And I have to go. I mean it this time.'

'So were you upset when Rebecca told you she was pregnant and it was obvious to you that it was with another guy?'

There was no answer at first so Bosch tried to turn the screw a bit.

'Especially since she would never have relations with you when you two were together.'

Bosch realized he had gone too far and tipped his hand. Kotchof realized that Bosch was playing good cop and bad cop with him all at once. When he responded, his voice was calm and modulated.

'She never told me that,' he said. 'I never knew until it came out after.'

'Really? Who told you?'

'I can't remember. One of my friends, I guess.'

'Really? Because Rebecca kept a journal. And you're all over it, man. And she says she told you and you weren't too happy about it.'

Now Kotchof laughed and Bosch knew he had really blown it.

'Detective, you are full of shit. You're the one who's lying. This is really weak, man. I mean, I watch *Law and Order*, you know.'

'Do you watch *CSI*?'

'Yeah, so?'

'Well, we got the killer's DNA. If we match it to somebody they're going to take a fall. DNA is the ultimate closer.'

'Good. Check mine and maybe this can all be over for me.'

Bosch knew he was the one backpedaling now. He had to end the call.

'Okay then, Dan, we'll let you know about that. Meantime, thank you for your help. One last question. What's a hospitality manager?'

'You mean here at the hotel? I take care of large parties and conferences and weddings and things like that. I make sure it all runs smoothly when these big groups come in here.'

'Okay, well, I'll let you get back to it. Have a good day.'

Bosch hung up and sat at the desk thinking about the call. He was embarrassed by how he had let the upper hand slip across the line to Kotchof. He knew his interviewing skills had largely been dormant for three years but that did not salve the burn. He knew he had to get better and it had to be soon.

Aside from that, there was a lot of content from the call to consider. He didn't read much into Kotchof's angry reaction to supposedly being seen in L.A. right before the murder. After all, Bosch had fabricated the witness and Kotchof's angry response would certainly be justified. But what was notable was how Kotchof's anger zeroed in on Grace Tanaka. Their relationship might be worth exploring further, maybe through Kiz Rider.

He also considered Kotchof's statement about not knowing about Rebecca Verloren's pregnancy. Bosch instinctively believed him. All in all it didn't drop Kotchof from the suspect list, but it at least pushed him to a back burner. He would discuss all of Kotchof's answers with Rider and see if she agreed.

The most interesting information gleaned from the call was in the conflicts between Kotchof's memories and those of Muriel Verloren, the victim's mother. Muriel Verloren had said Kotchof had called her daughter religiously, right up until the time of her death. Kotchof said he had done no such thing. Bosch didn't see any reason for Kotchof to lie about it. If he hadn't, then Muriel Verloren's memory was wrong. Or it was her daughter who had lied about who called her every night before bed. Since the girl was hiding a relationship and the pregnancy that came from it, it seemed likely that the phone calls did come in every night but they were not from Kotchof. They were from someone else, someone Bosch started thinking of as Mr. X.

After looking up Muriel Verloren's number in the murder book Bosch called the house. He apologized for intruding and said he had a few follow-up questions. Muriel said she was not bothered by the call.

'What are your questions?'

'I saw the phone on the table next to your daughter's bed. Was that an extension of the house phone or did she have her own phone number?'

'She had her own number. A private line.'

'So when Daniel Kotchof called her at night she would be the one who answered the phone, right?'

'Yes, in her room. It was the only extension.'

'So the only way you know that Danny was calling was because she told you.'

'No, I heard the phone ring sometimes. He called.'

'What I mean, Mrs. Verloren, is that you never answered those calls and you never talked to Danny Kotchof, right?'

'That's right. It was her private line.'

'So when that phone rang and she talked to somebody, the only way you would know who it was on the line was if she told you. Is that correct?'

'Uh, yes, I guess that is right. Are you saying it wasn't Danny who called all of those times?'

'I'm not sure yet. But I talked to Danny in Hawaii and he said he stopped calling your daughter long before she was taken. He had a new girlfriend, you see. In Hawaii.'

This information was treated with a long pause. Finally, Bosch spoke into the void.

'Do you have any idea who it could have been that she was talking to, Mrs. Verloren?'

After another pause Muriel Verloren weakly offered an answer.

'Maybe one of her girlfriends.'

'It's possible,' Bosch said. 'Anybody else you can think of?'

'I don't like this,' she responded quickly. 'It's like I'm learning things all over again.'

'I'm sorry, Mrs. Verloren. I will try not to hit you with these sorts of things unless it is necessary. But I am afraid this is necessary. Did you and your husband ever come to any conclusion about the pregnancy?'

'What do you mean? We didn't know about it until after.'

'I understand that. What I mean is, did you think it came out of a hidden relationship or was it simply a mistake she made one day with, you know, someone she was not really in a relationship with?'

'You mean like a one-night stand? Is that what you are saying about my daughter?'

'No, ma'am, I am not saying anything about your daughter. I am simply asking questions. I do not want to upset you but I want to find the person who killed Rebecca. And I need to know all there is to know.'

'We could never explain it, Detective,' she responded coldly. 'She was gone and we decided not to delve into it. We left everything to the police and we just tried to remember the daughter we knew and loved. You said you have a daughter. I hope you understand.'

'I think I do. Thank you for your answers. One last question – and there is no pressure on this – but would you be willing to talk to a newspaper reporter about your daughter and the case?'

'Why would I do that? I didn't before. I don't believe in putting it out there for the public.'

'I admire that. But this time I want you to do it because it might help us flush out the bird.'

'You mean it might make the person who did this come out from cover?'

'Exactly.'

'Then I'd do it in a heartbeat.'

'Thank you, Mrs. Verloren. I will let you know.'

16

Abel Pratt came out of his office with his suit jacket on. He noticed Bosch sitting at his desk in the alcove, using two fingers to type up a report on his telephone conversation with Muriel Verloren. The finished reports on the phone interviews with Grace Tanaka and Daniel Kotchof were on the desk.

'Where's Kiz?' Pratt asked.

'She's working on the warrant at home. She can think better there.'

'I can't think when I get home. I can only react. I have twin boys.'

'Good luck.'

'Yeah, I need it. I'm going that way now. I'll see you tomorrow, Harry.'

'Okay.'

But Pratt didn't walk away. Bosch looked up from the typewriter at him. He thought maybe something was wrong. Maybe it was the typewriter.

'I found this on a desk on the other side,' Bosch said. 'It didn't look like it was being used by anybody.'

'It wasn't. Most people use their computers now. You are definitely an old-school kind of guy, Harry.'

'I guess. Kiz usually does the reports, but I have some time to kill.'

'Working late?'

'I've got to go over to the Nickel.'

'Fifth Street? What do you want over there?'

'Looking for our victim's father.'

Pratt shook his head somberly.

'Another one of those. We've seen it before.'

Bosch nodded.

'Ripples,' he said.

'Yeah, ripples,' Pratt agreed.

Bosch was thinking about offering to walk out with Pratt, maybe have a conversation and get to know him better, but his cell phone started to chirp. He pulled it off his belt and saw the name Sam Weiss in the caller ID screen.

'I better take this.'

'All right, Harry. Be careful over there.'

'Thanks, Boss.'

He flipped open the phone.

'Detective Bosch,' he said.

'Detective?'

Bosch remembered he had left no information on his message to Weiss.

'Mr. Weiss, my name is Harry Bosch. I am a detective with the LAPD. I'd like to ask you a few questions about an investigation I am conducting.'

'I have all the time you need, Detective. Is this about my gun?'

The question caught Bosch off guard.

'Why would you ask that, sir?'

'Well, because I know it was used in a murder that was never solved. And that's the only thing I can think of that the LAPD would want to ask me about.'

'Well, yes, sir, it's about the gun. Can I talk to you about it?'

'If it means you are trying to find who killed that girl, then you can ask me anything you want.'

'Thank you. I guess the first thing I'd like is for you to tell me how and when you knew or were told that the weapon stolen from you was used in a homicide.'

'It was in the papers – the murder was – and I put two and two together. I called the detective assigned to my burglary and asked and got the answer I wish I hadn't.'

'Why is that, Mr. Weiss?'

'Because I've had to live with it.'

'But you didn't do anything wrong, sir.'

'I know that, but it doesn't make a person feel any better. I bought that gun because I was having trouble with a bunch of punks. I wanted protection. Then the gun I bought ended up being the instrument of death for that young girl. Don't think I haven't thought about changing history. I mean, what if I wasn't so stubborn? What if I just pulled up stakes and moved instead of going and buying that damn thing? You see what I mean?'

'Yes, I see.'

'Now, that said, what else can I tell you, Detective?'

'I have just a few questions. Calling you was sort of a shot in the dark. I thought it might be easier than trying to find my way back through seventeen years of paperwork and department history. I have the initial report on the burglary and the investigator is listed as John McClellan. Do you remember him?'

'Sure, I remember him.'

'Did he ever clear the case?'

'Not as far as I know. At first John thought it might have been connected to the punks who had threatened me.'

'And was it?'

'John told me no. But I was never sure. The burglars really tore the place apart. It wasn't like they were really looking for stuff to steal. They were just destroying things – my belongings. I walked in this place and, man, I could feel a lot of anger.'

'Why do you say burglars? Did the police think it was more than one?'

'John figured it had to be at least two or three. I was only gone an hour – went to the store. One guy couldn't have done all that damage in that time.'

'The report lists the gun, a coin collection and some cash that was taken. Anything else come up missing after?'

'No, that was it. That was enough. At least I got the coins back, and that was the most valuable thing. It was my father's collection from when he was a boy.'

'How did you get it back?'

'John McClellan. He brought them back to me a couple weeks later.'

'Did he say where he recovered them from?'

'He said a pawnshop in West Hollywood. And then, of course, we know what became of the gun. But that was not given back to me. I wouldn't have taken it anyway.'

'I understand, sir. Did Detective McClellan ever tell you who he thought burglarized your home? Did he have any theories?'

'He thought it was just another set of punks, you know. Not the Chatsworth Eights.'

The mention of the Chatsworth Eights stirred something in Bosch, but he couldn't place it.

'Mr. Weiss, act like I don't know anything. Who were the Chatsworth Eights?'

'It was a gang out here in the Valley. They were all white kids. Skinheads. And back in nineteen eighty-eight they committed a number of crimes out here. They were hate crimes. That's what they called them in the papers. Back then it was the new term for crimes motivated by race or religion.'

'And you were the target of this gang?'

'Yeah, I started getting calls. The typical kill-the-Jew stuff.'

'But then the police told you the Eights did not commit the burglary.'

'That's right.'

'Strange, isn't it? They didn't see any connection.'

'That's what I thought at the time but he was the detective, not me.'

'What made the Eights target you, Mr. Weiss? I know you are Jewish but what made them pick you out?'

'Simple. One of the little shits was a kid who lived in my neighborhood. Billy Burkhart was four houses away. I put a menorah in my window during Chanukah and that's when it all started.'

'What happened to Burkhart?'

'He went to jail. Not for what he did to me, but to others. They got him and the others on other crimes. They burned a cross a few blocks from me.

In the front lawn of a black family. And they did other things. Mean things, vandalism. They tried to burn a temple, too.'

'But not the burglary at your house.'

'That's right. That's what the police told me. You see, there was no graffiti or indication of religious motivation. The place was just torn apart. So they didn't classify the burglary as a hate crime.'

Bosch hesitated, wondering if there was anything else to ask. He decided he didn't know enough to ask smart questions.

'Okay, Mr. Weiss, I appreciate your time. And I am sorry to reawaken bad memories.'

'Don't worry about it, Detective. Believe me, they weren't asleep.'

Bosch closed the phone. He tried to think of whom he could call about all of this. He didn't know John McClellan and the chances of his still being in Devonshire Division seventeen years later were slim. Then it hit him: Jerry Edgar. His old partner at Hollywood Division had previously been assigned to Devonshire detectives. He would have been there in 1988.

Bosch called the Hollywood homicide table but got the machine. Everybody had cut out early. He called the main detective bureau number and asked if Edgar was around. Bosch knew that there was a sign-out chart at the front counter. The clerk who answered the phone said Edgar had signed out for the day.

The third call was to Edgar's cell phone. His old partner answered it promptly.

'You guys go home early in Hollywood,' Bosch said.

'Who the hell is – Harry, that you?'

'That me. How's it hanging, Jerry?'

'I was wondering when I'd hear from you. You start again today?'

'The world's oldest boot. And I already got a hot shot. Kiz and I are working a breaking case.'

Edgar didn't respond and Bosch knew mentioning Rider had been a mistake. The gulf between them not only still existed but was apparently frozen over.

'Anyway, I need to tap into that big brain of yours. This is going back to Club Dev days.'

'Yeah, which day?'

'Nineteen eighty-eight. The Chatsworth Eights. You remember them?'

There was silence while Edgar thought for a moment.

'Yeah, I remember the Eights. They were a bunch of peckerwoods that thought shaved heads and tattoos made them men. They did a lot of shit, then they got stepped on. They didn't last long.'

'You remember a guy named Roland Mackey? Would've been about eighteen back then.'

After a pause Edgar said he didn't remember the name.

'Who was working the Eights?' Bosch asked.

'Not Club Dev, man. Everything with them went straight down the rabbit hole.'

'PDU?'

'You got it.'

The Public Disorder Unit. A shadowy downtown squad that gathered data and intelligence on conspiracies but made few cases. Back in 1988 the PDU would have been under the aegis of then commander Irvin Irving. The unit was not in existence anymore. When Irving rose to the level of deputy chief he promptly disbanded the PDU, with many in the department believing it was a measure taken to cover up and distance himself from its activities.

'That's not going to help,' Bosch said.

'Sorry about that. What are you working?'

'The murder of a girl up on Oat Mountain.'

'The one taken out of her house?'

'Yeah.'

'I remember that one, too. I didn't work it – I had just gotten to the homicide table. But I remember that one. You're saying the Eights were in on that one?'

'No. Just that a name came up that might have a connection to the Eights. Might. So does Eights mean what I think?'

'Yeah, man, eight for H. Eighty-eight for H-H. And H-H for Heil—'

'—Hitler. Yeah, I thought so.'

Then it struck Bosch that Kiz Rider had been right when she thought the year of the crime might be significant. The murder and the rest of the crimes committed by the Chatsworth Eights had occurred in 1988. It was all part of a confluence of seemingly small things coming together. And now Irvin Irving and the PDU were mixed into the soup as well. A cold hit match of DNA to a loser who drove a tow truck for a living was blossoming into something bigger.

'Jerry, you remember a guy who worked at Devonshire named John McClellan?'

'John McClellan? No, I don't remember. What did he work?'

'I got his name here on a burglary report.'

'No, definitely not the burglary table. I worked burglary before going over to homicide. There was no John McClellan on burglary. Who is he?'

'Like I said, just a name on a report. I'll figure it out.'

Bosch knew that this meant McClellan was likely in the PDU at the time and the investigation of the burglary of Sam Weiss's home was folded into the investigation of the Chatsworth Eights. He didn't care to discuss all of this with Edgar.

'Jerry, so you were new on the homicide table back then?'

'That's right.'

'Did you know Green and Garcia very well?'

'Not really. I just got to the table and they weren't there that long after. Green pulled the pin and about a year after that Garcia made lieutenant.'

'From what you saw, what was your take on them?'

'How so?'

'As homicide men.'

'Well, Harry, I was pretty fresh back then. I mean, what did I know? I was still learning. But the take on them was that Green was the power. Garcia was just the housekeeper. What some people said about Garcia was that he couldn't find shit in his own mustache with a mirror and comb.'

Bosch didn't respond. By labeling Garcia a housekeeper Edgar was saying that Garcia rode his partner's coattails. Green was the real homicide cop and Garcia was the guy who backed him up and kept the murder books tidy and up to date. A lot of partnerships got sanded down into such relationships. An alpha dog and his assistant.

'I guess he didn't need to,' Edgar said.

'Didn't need to what?'

'Find shit in his mustache. He was going places, man. He made lieutenant and was out of there. You know he's currently second in command in the Valley, right?'

'Yeah, I know. In fact, if you see him you might not want to mention that mustache bit.'

'Yeah, probably not.'

Bosch thought some more about what this might have meant to the Verloren investigation. A small crack was moving under the surface of things.

'That it, Harry?'

'I heard Green ate his gun not too long after pulling the pin.'

'Yeah, I heard that. I don't remember being surprised. He always looked like a guy carrying a full load of somethin'. You going to take a run at PDU, Harry? You know that was Irving's squad, don't you?'

'Yeah, Jerry, I know. I doubt I'm going that way.'

'Be careful if you do, my man.'

Bosch wanted to change the subject before hanging up. Edgar had always been a department gossip. Harry didn't want his old partner's loose lips to spread the word that Bosch was taking a run at Irving now that he was back with a badge.

'So how's things in Hollywood?' he asked.

'We just got back into the bureau after the earthquake retrofit. You missed all of that. We were stuck upstairs in roll call for like a year.'

'How is it?'

'It's like an insurance office now. We have pods and sound filters between the desks. All done up in government gray. Nice but not the same.'

'I know what you mean.'

'Then they gave the D-threes double-wides – desks with two sides of drawers. The rest of us get one side.'

Bosch smiled. Little slights like that got magnified in the department and the administrators who made such decisions never learned. Like when most of Internal Affairs moved out of Parker Center and into the old Bradbury Building and the word spread through the ranks that the captain over there had a fireplace in his office.

'So what are you gonna do, Jerry?'

'Same old same old, that's what I'm gonna do. Get off my ass and knock on doors.'

'I hear you, man.'

'Watch your six, Harry.'

'Always.'

After hanging up, Bosch sat motionless at his desk for a few moments as he thought through the conversation and the new meanings it brought to the case. If there was a connection between the case and PDU then they had a whole new ball game.

He looked down at the murder book, still open to the burglary report, and stared at the scrawled signature of John McClellan. He picked up the phone and called the Department of Operations in Parker Center and asked the duty officer for an assignment location for a detective named John McClellan. He read McClellan's badge number off the burglary report. He was put on hold and expected that he would be told that McClellan was long retired. It had been seventeen years.

But when the duty officer came back on the line he reported that an officer named John McClellan with the badge number Bosch provided was now a lieutenant assigned to the Office of Strategic Planning. The synapse connections in Bosch's brain started tripping. Seventeen years ago McClellan worked for Irving in the PDU. Now the assignment and rank were different but he was still working for him. And Irving just happened to run into Bosch in the Parker Center cafeteria on the day Bosch caught a case with ties to the PDU.

'High jingo,' Bosch whispered to himself as he hung up.

Like a battleship going into a turn, the case was slowly, surely and unstoppably moving in a new direction. Bosch could feel something building inside his chest. He thought about the coincidence of Irving crossing his path. If it was a coincidence. Bosch wondered if the deputy chief already knew at that moment what case they had pulled the cold hit on and where it was going to lead.

The department buried secrets every day. It was a given. But who would have thought seventeen years ago that a chemical test run one day in a DOJ lab in Sacramento might put a shovel into the greasy dirt and turn over the past, bringing this secret to light.

17

Driving home Bosch thought about the many different tendrils of the investigation that were wrapping around the body of Rebecca Verloren. He knew he had to keep his eyes on the prize. The evidence was the key. The elements of departmental politics and possible corruption and cover-up all amounted to what was known as high jingo. It could be threatening and distracting from the intended goal. He had to avoid this at the same time that he had to be wary of it.

Eventually he was able to push thoughts of Irving's shadow over the investigation aside and concentrate on the case. His thoughts somehow led him to Rebecca's bedroom and how her mother had left it unchanged by time. He wondered if it was the loss of the daughter that did it or was it the circumstances of the loss? What if you lost a child by natural causes or accident or circumstances like divorce? Bosch had a daughter he rarely saw. It weighed on him. He knew that near or far his daughter left him completely vulnerable, that he could end up like the mother who preserved a daughter's bedroom like a museum, or the father who was long lost to the world.

More so than this question, something about the bedroom bothered him. He couldn't quite reach what it was but he knew it was there and it nagged at him. He looked from the elevated freeway out across Hollywood to his left. There was still some light in the sky but the evening was starting. Darkness had waited long enough. Searchlights that he knew could be traced down to the corner of Hollywood and Vine were crisscrossing the horizon. To him it looked nice. To him it looked like home.

When he got to his house on the hill he checked the mail and the phone for messages and then changed out of the suit he had bought for his return to the job. He carefully hung it in the closet, thinking he could wear it at least once more before having to take it in to the cleaners. He put on blue jeans, black sneakers and a black pullover shirt. He put on a sport coat that was fraying on the right shoulder from his cutting corners too close. He transferred his gun and badge and wallet. Then he got back into his car and headed downtown to the Toy District.

He decided to park in Japantown in the museum lot so he wouldn't have to worry about the car being broken into or vandalized. From there he walked over to Fifth Street, encountering an increasing density of homeless people as he progressed. The city's primary homeless encampments and the missions that catered to them lined a five-block stretch of Fifth Street south of Los Angeles Street. The sidewalks outside the missions and cheap residence hotels were lined with cardboard boxes and shopping carts filled with the dirty and meager belongings of lost people. It was as if some sort of social disintegration bomb had gone off and the shrapnel of damaged, disenfranchised lives had been hurled everywhere. Up and down the street there were men and women yelling, their shouts unintelligible or simply eerie non sequiturs in the night. It felt like a city with its own rule and reason, a hurt city with a wound so deep that the bandages the missions applied could not stop the bleeding.

As he walked, Bosch noted that he was not asked once for money or cigarettes or any kind of handout. The irony was not lost on him. It appeared that the place with the highest concentration of homeless people in the city was also the place where a citizen was safest from their entreaties, if nothing else.

The Los Angeles Mission and the Salvation Army had major help centers here. Bosch decided to start with them. He had a twelve-year-old driver's license photo of Robert Verloren and an even older photograph of him at his daughter's funeral. He showed these to the people operating the help centers and the kitchen workers who put free food on hundreds of plates every day. He got little response until a kitchen worker remembered Verloren as a 'client' who came through the chow line pretty regularly a few years before.

'It's been a while,' the man said. 'Haven't seen him.'

After spending an hour in each center Bosch started working his way down the street, stepping into the smaller missions and flop hotels and showing the photos. He got a few recognitions of Verloren but nothing fresh, nothing to lead him to the man who had completely dropped off the human radar screen so many years before. He worked it until ten-thirty and decided he would return the next day to finish canvassing the street. As he walked back toward Japantown he was depressed by what he had just immersed himself in and by the dwindling hopes of finding Robert Verloren. He walked with his head down, hands in his pockets, and therefore didn't see the two men until they had already seen him. They stepped out of the alcoves of two side-by-side toy stores as Bosch passed. One blocked his path. The other stepped out behind him. Bosch stopped.

'Hey, missionary man,' said the one in front of him.

In the dim glow from a streetlight half a block away Bosch saw the glint of a blade down at the man's side. He turned slightly to check the man behind him. He was smaller. Bosch wasn't sure but it looked like he was simply holding a chunk of concrete in his hand. A piece of broken curb.

Both men were dressed in layers, a common sight in this part of the city. One was black and one was white.

'The kitchens are all closed up and we're still hungry,' said the one with the knife. 'You got a few bucks for us? You know, like we could borrow.'

Bosch shook his head.

'No, not really.'

'Not really? You sure 'bout that, boy? You look like you got a nice fat wallet on you now. Don't be holding back on us.'

A black rage grew in Bosch. In a moment of sharp focus he knew what he could and would do. He would draw his weapon and put bullets into both of these men. In that same instant he knew he would walk away from it after a cursory departmental investigation. The glint of the blade was Bosch's ticket and he knew it. The men on either side of him didn't know what they had just walked into. It was like being in the tunnels so many years before. Everything closed down to a tight space. Nothing but kill or be killed. There was something absolutely pure about it, no gray areas and no room for anything else.

Then suddenly the moment changed. Bosch saw the one with the knife staring intently at him, reading something in his eyes, one predator taking the measure of another. The knife man seemed to grow smaller by an almost imperceptible measure. He backed off without physically backing off.

Bosch knew there were people considered to be mind readers. The truth was they were face readers. Their skill was interpreting the myriad muscle constructions of the eyes, the mouth, the eyebrows. From this they decoded intent. Bosch had a level of skill in this. His ex-wife made a living playing poker because she had an even higher skill. The man with the knife had a measure of this skill as well. It had surely saved his life this time.

'Nah, never mind,' said the man.

He took a step back toward the store's alcove.

'Have a good night, missionary man,' he said as he retreated into the darkness.

Bosch turned fully and looked at the other man. Without a word, he too stepped back into his crack to hide and wait for the next victim.

Bosch looked up and down the street. It seemed deserted now. He turned and headed on toward his ride. As he walked he took out his cell phone and called the Central Division patrol office. He told the watch sergeant about the two men he encountered and asked him to send a patrol car.

'That kind of stuff happens on every block down there in that hellhole,' the sergeant said. 'What do you want me to do about it?'

'I want you to send a car and roust them. They'll think twice about doing anything to anybody.'

'Well, why didn't you do anything about it yourself?'

'Because I'm working a case, Sergeant, and I can't get off it to do your job or your paperwork.'

‘Look, buddy, don’t be telling me how to do my job. You suits are all the same. You think—’

‘Look, Sergeant, I’m going to check the crime reports in the morning. If I read that somebody got hurt down here and the suspects were a black and white team, then you’re going to have more suits around you than at the Men’s Warehouse. I guarantee it.’

Bosch closed his phone, cutting off a last protest from the watch sergeant. He picked up his pace, got to his car and started back over to the 101 Freeway. He then headed back up to the Valley.

18

Finding cover with a visual line on Tampa Towing was difficult. Both strip shopping plazas located on the other corners were closed and their parking lots empty. Bosch would be obvious if he parked in either one. The competing service station on the third corner was still open and thus, unusable for surveillance. After considering the situation Bosch parked on Roscoe a block away and walked back to the intersection. Borrowing an idea from the would-be robbers of less than an hour before, he found a darkened alcove in one of the strip plazas from which he could watch the service station. He knew the problem with his choice of surveillance was getting back to his car fast enough to avoid losing Mackey when he went off shift.

The ad he had checked earlier in the phone book said Tampa Towing offered twenty-four-hour service. But it was coming up on midnight and Bosch was betting that Mackey, who had come on duty at 4 p.m., would be getting off soon. He would either be replaced by a midnight man or would be on call through the night.

It was at times like this that Bosch thought about smoking again. It always seemed to make the time go faster and it took the edge off the anxiety that always built through a surveillance. But it had been more than four years now and he didn't want to break stride. Learning two years earlier that he was a father had helped him get past the occasional weaknesses. He thought that if not for his daughter he'd probably be smoking again. At best he had controlled the addiction. By no means had he broken it.

He took out his cell phone and angled the light from its screen away from view of the service station while he punched in Kiz Rider's home number. She didn't answer. He tried her cell and got no answer again. He assumed she had shut down the phones so she could concentrate on writing the warrant. She had worked it that way in the past. He knew she would leave her pager on for emergencies but he didn't think the news he had gathered during the evening's phone calls rose to the level of emergency. He decided to wait until he saw her in the morning to tell her what he had learned.

He put his phone in his pocket and raised the binoculars to his eyes. Through the glass windows of the service station office he could see Mackey sitting behind a weathered gray desk. There was another man in a similar blue on blue uniform in the office. It must have been a slow night. Both of the men had their feet propped up on the desk and were looking up at something high on the wall over the front window. Bosch could not see what they were focused on but the changing light in the room told him it was a television.

Bosch's phone chirped and he pulled it from his pocket and answered without lowering the binoculars. He didn't check the display because he assumed it was Kiz Rider calling after noticing that she had missed his call.

'Hey.'

'Detective Bosch?'

It wasn't Rider. Bosch lowered the field glasses.

'Yes, this is Bosch. How can I help you?'

'This is Tara Wood. I got your message.'

'Oh, yeah, thanks for calling back.'

'It sounds like this is your cell. I'm sorry to call so late. I just got in. I thought I was just going to leave a message on your office line.'

'No problem. I'm still working.'

Bosch went through the same interview process he had employed with the others. As he mentioned the name Roland Mackey to her he checked on Mackey through the glasses. He was still at the desk, watching the tube. Like Rebecca Verloren's other friends, Tara Wood didn't recognize the tow truck driver's name. Bosch added a new question, asking if she remembered the Chatsworth Eights, and her memory was vague about that as well. Lastly he asked if the next day he could continue the interview and show her a photograph of Mackey.

She agreed but told him he would have to come to the CBS television studios, where she worked as a publicist. Bosch knew that CBS was next to the Farmers Market, one of his favorite places in the city. He decided he could go to the market, maybe eat a bowl of gumbo for lunch, and then go see Tara Wood to show the photo of Mackey and ask about Rebecca Verloren's pregnancy. He made the appointment for 1 p.m. and she agreed to be in her office.

'This is such an old case,' Wood said. 'Are you like on a cold case squad?'

'We actually call it the Open-Unsolved Unit.'

'You know, we have a show called *Cold Case*. It's on Sunday nights. It's one of the shows I work on. I'm thinking ... maybe you could visit the set and meet some of your television counterparts. I am sure they would love to meet you.'

Bosch realized she might be working up some sort of publicity angle. He looked through the glasses at Mackey staring up at the television and thought for a moment of trying to use her interest in the wiretap play they were going to put into motion. He then quickly shelved it, concluding that it would be easier to start the play with a newspaper plant.

'Yeah, maybe, but I think that would have to wait awhile. We're working this case pretty hard right now and I just need to talk to you tomorrow.'

'No problem. I really hope you find who you are looking for. Ever since I was assigned to this show I've been thinking about Rebecca. You know, wondering if there was anything happening. Then out of the blue you called. It's weird, but in a good way. I'll see you tomorrow, Detective.'

Bosch said good night and hung up.

A few minutes later, at midnight, the lights at the service station went out. Bosch knew that offering twenty-four-hour tow service didn't necessarily translate into being open twenty-four hours a day. Mackey or another driver was probably on call through the night.

Bosch slipped from his hiding spot and hustled down Roscoe to the SUV. Just as he got to it he heard the deep thrumming sound of Mackey's Camaro coming to life. He started his engine, pulled away from the curb, and headed back toward the intersection. As he got there and was stopping for the red light he saw the Camaro with the gray-painted fenders cross the intersection, heading south on Tampa. Bosch waited a few moments, checked all lanes of the intersection for other cars, and blew through the red light to follow.

Mackey's first stop was a bar called the Side Pocket. It was on Sepulveda Boulevard in Van Nuys near the railroad tracks. It was a small place with a blue neon sign and the barred windows painted black. Bosch had an idea what it would be like inside and what kind of men would be in there. Before leaving his car he took off his sport coat, wrapped his gun, handcuffs and extra clip in it and put it on the floor in front of the passenger seat. He got out and locked the door and headed toward the bar, pulling his shirt out of his jeans as he went.

The inside of the bar was as he expected. A couple of pool tables, a stand-up bar and a row of scarred wood booths. Even though smoking inside the place was illegal, blue smoke was heavy in the air and hanging like a ghost beneath each table light. Nobody was complaining.

Most of the men took their medicine straight up, meaning they were standing. Most had chains on their wallets and tattoos ringing their lower arms. Even with the changes to his appearance Bosch knew he would stand out, possibly even be advertising that he didn't belong. He saw an opening in the shadows where the bar curved under the television mounted in the corner. He slipped into the spot and leaned over the bar, hoping it helped hide his appearance.

The bartender, a worn woman wearing a black leather vest over a T-shirt, ignored Bosch for a while but that was all right. He wasn't there to drink. He watched Mackey put quarters on one of the tables and wait for his turn to play. He hadn't ordered a drink either.

Mackey spent ten minutes going through the assortment of pool cues on the wall racks until he found one he liked the feel of. He then stood by waiting and talking to some of the men standing around the pool table. It didn't appear to be anything more than casual conversation, as though he knew them but only from playing pool on previous nights.

While he waited and watched, nursing the beer and whisky shot the bartender had finally delivered to him, Bosch at first thought people were watching him as well, but then realized they were only staring at the television screen less than a foot above his head.

Finally Mackey got his game and he turned out to be good at it. He quickly won control of the table and defeated seven challengers, collecting money or beers from all of them. After a half hour he seemed to tire from the lack of competition and got sloppy. The eighth challenger beat him after Mackey missed a clean shot at the eight ball. Mackey took the loss well and slapped a five-dollar bill down on the green felt before stepping away. By Bosch's count he was at least twenty-five dollars and three beers ahead for the night.

Mackey took his Rolling Rock to a space at the bar and that was Bosch's cue to withdraw. He put a ten under his empty shot glass and turned away, never giving Mackey his face. He left the bar and went back to his car. The first thing he did was put the gun back on his right hip, grip forward. He started the engine and drove out onto Sepulveda and then a block south. He turned around and pulled to the curb in front of a hydrant. He had a good angle on the front door of the Side Pocket and was in position to follow Mackey's car north on Sepulveda toward Panorama City. Mackey may have changed apartments after completing probation but Bosch expected that he had not moved far.

The wait this time was not long. Mackey apparently only drank free beer. He left the bar ten minutes after Bosch had, got in the Camaro and headed south on Sepulveda.

Bosch had guessed wrong. Mackey was driving away from Panorama City and the north Valley. This meant Bosch had to pull a U-turn on a largely deserted Sepulveda Boulevard in order to follow him. The move would be highly noticeable in Mackey's rearview mirror. So he waited, watching the Camaro get smaller in his side-view mirror.

When he saw the turn signal on the Camaro start to blink he pinned the accelerator and took the SUV into a hard one-eighty. He almost lost it by overcompensating on the wheel but then righted the car and took off down Sepulveda. He turned right on Victory and caught up with the Camaro at the traffic signal at the 405 overpass. Mackey stayed off the freeway, however, and continued west on Victory.

With Bosch employing a variety of driving maneuvers to avoid detection, Mackey drove all the way into Woodland Hills. On Mariano Street, a wide street near the 101 Freeway, he finally pulled down a long driveway and parked beside a small house. Bosch drove by and parked further down, then got out and doubled back on foot. He heard the front door of the house closing and then saw the light over the porch go out.

Bosch looked around and realized it was a neighborhood of flag lots. When the neighborhood was first gridded decades before, the properties were cut into large pieces because they were meant to be horse ranches and small vegetable farms. Then the city grew out to the neighborhood and the horses and vegetables were crowded out. The lots were cut up, one property up front on the street and a narrow driveway running down the side of it to the property in the back – the flag-shaped lot.

It made observation difficult. Bosch crept down the long driveway, watching both the house on the front property and Mackey's house on the back piece. Mackey had parked his Camaro next to a beat-up Ford 150 pickup. It meant Mackey might have a roommate.

When he got closer Bosch stopped to write down the tag number on the F150. He noticed an old bumper sticker on the pickup that said WOULD THE LAST AMERICAN TO LEAVE L.A. PLEASE BRING THE FLAG. It was just one more small brushstroke on what Bosch felt was an emerging picture.

As quietly as he could, Bosch walked down a stone pathway that ran alongside the house. The house was built on knee-high footings which put the windows too far up for him to see in. When he got to the back of the house he heard voices and then realized it was television when he saw the undulating blue glow on the shades of the back room. He started to cross the backyard when suddenly his phone started to chirp. He quickly reached for it and cut off the sound. At the same time he moved quickly back down the pathway and to the driveway. He then ran up the driveway toward the street. He listened for any sound behind him but heard none. When he made it to the street he looked back at the house but saw nothing that gave him reason to believe the chirping from his phone had been heard inside the house above the sounds of the television.

Bosch knew it had been a close call. He was out of breath. He walked back to his car, trying to gather himself and recover from the near disaster. As with the badly handled interview with Daniel Kotchof, he knew he was showing signs of rust. He had forgotten to mute his phone before creeping the house. It was a mistake that could have blown everything and maybe put him into a confrontation with an investigative target. Three years ago, before he had left the job, it would never have happened. He started thinking about what Irving had said about his being a retread that would come apart at the seams, that would blow out.

Inside the car he checked the caller ID list on his phone and saw that the call had come from Kiz Rider. He called her back.

'Harry, I checked my call list and saw you had called me a little while ago. I had my phones off. What's up?'

'Nothing much. I was checking in to see how it was going.'

'Well, it's going. I've got it all structured and most of the writing done. I'll finish tomorrow morning, then I'll start it through the channels.'

'Good.'

'Yeah, I'm about to call it a night. What about you? Did you find Robert Verloren?'

'Not yet. But I've got an address for you. I followed Mackey after he left work. He's got a little house by the freeway in Woodland Hills. There might be a phone line in there that you'll want to add to the tap.'

'Good. Give me the address. That should be easy enough to check. But I'm not sure I want you following the suspect alone. That's not smart, Harry.'

'We had to find his address.'

He wasn't going to tell her about the near miss. He gave her the address and waited a moment while she wrote it down.

'I've got some other stuff, too,' he said. 'I made some calls.'

'You've been busy for just a day back on the job. What've you got?'

He recounted the phone calls he made and received after she had left the office. Rider asked no questions and then was silent after he finished.

'That brings you up to date,' Bosch said. 'What do you think, Kiz?'

'I think there might be a picture coming together, Harry.'

'Yeah, I was thinking the same thing. Plus, the year, nineteen eighty-eight. I think you were onto something about that. Maybe these assholes were trying to prove a point in 'eighty-eight. The problem is, it all went under the door at PDU. Who knows where all of that stuff ended up. Irving probably dumped it in the evidence incinerator at the ESB.'

'Not all of it. When the new chief came in he wanted a full assessment of everything. He wanted to know where the bodies were buried. Anyway, I wasn't involved in that but I knew about it and I heard that a lot of the PDU files were kept after the unit was disbanded. A lot of it Irving put in Special Archives.'

'Special Archives? What the hell is that?'

'It just means limited access. You need command approval. It's all in the basement at Parker Center. It's mostly in-house investigations. Political stuff. Dangerous stuff. This Chatsworth business doesn't really seem to qualify, unless it was connected to something else.'

'Like what?'

'Like somebody in the department or somebody in the city.'

The latter meant someone powerful in city politics.

'Can you get in there and see if any files on this still exist? What about your pal on six? Maybe he'd—'

'I can try.'

'Then try.'

'First thing. What about you? I thought you were going out to find Robert Verloren tonight, and now I hear you were following our suspect.'

'I went down there. I didn't find him.'

He proceeded to update her on his earlier swing through the Toy District, leaving out his encounter with the would-be robbers. That incident and the phone fiasco behind Mackey's house were not things he cared to share with her.

'I'll go back out there tomorrow morning,' he said in conclusion.

'Okay, Harry. Sounds like a plan. I should have the warrant together by the time you get in. And I'll check on the PDU files.'

Bosch hesitated but then decided not to hold back any warnings or concerns with his partner. He looked out the windshield at the dark street. He could hear the hiss from the nearby freeway.

'Kiz, be careful.'

'How do you mean, Harry?'

'You know what it means when a case has high jingo?'

'Yeah, it means it's got command staff's fingers in the pie.'

'That's right.'

'And so?'

'So be careful. This thing has Irving all over it. It's not that obvious but it's there.'

'You think his little visit with you at the coffee counter wasn't coincidence?'

'I don't believe in coincidences. Not like that.'

There was silence for a bit before Rider answered.

'Okay, Harry, I'll watch myself. No holding back, though, right? We take it where it goes and let the chips fall. Everybody counts or nobody counts, remember?'

'Right. I remember. I'll see you tomorrow.'

'Good night, Harry.'

She hung up and Bosch sat in the car for a long time before turning the key.

19

Bosch started the engine, pulled a slow U-turn on Mariano and drove by the driveway that led to Mackey's house. It appeared to be all quiet down there. He saw no lights behind the windows.

He cut over to the freeway and took it east across the Valley and then down into the Cahuenga Pass. On the way he used his cell phone to call central dispatch and run the plate off the Ford pickup that Mackey had parked next to. It came back registered to a William Burkhart, who was thirty-seven years old and had a criminal record dating back to the late 1980s but nothing else in fifteen years. The dispatcher gave Bosch the California penal code numbers for his arrests because that's how they were listed on the computer.

Bosch immediately recognized aggravated assault and receiving stolen property charges. But there was one charge in 1988 with a code that he didn't recognize.

'Anybody there with a code book who can tell me what that is?' he asked, hoping things were quiet enough that the dispatcher would just do it herself. He knew that copies of the penal code were always in the dispatch center because officers often called in to get the proper citations when they were in the field.

'Hold on.'

He waited. Meantime, he exited on Barham and took Wood-row Wilson up into the hills toward his home.

'Detective?'

'Still here.'

'That was a hate crime violation.'

'Okay. Thanks for looking it up.'

'No problem.'

Bosch pulled into his carport and killed the engine. Mackey's roommate or landlord was charged with a hate crime in 1988 – the same year as the murder of Rebecca Verloren. William Burkhart was likely the same Billy Burkhart whom Sam Weiss had identified as a neighbor and one of his tormentors. Bosch didn't know how all of this fit together but he knew it was part of the same picture. He now wished he had taken home the

Department of Corrections file on Mackey. He was feeling too tired to go all the way back downtown to get it. He decided he would leave it be for the night and read it cover to cover when he got back to the office the next day. He would also get the file on William Burkhart's hate crime arrest.

The house was quiet when he got inside. He grabbed the phone and a beer out of the box and headed out onto the deck to check on the city. On the way he turned on the CD player. There was already a disc in the machine and he soon heard the voice of Boz Scaggs on the outside speakers. He was singing 'For All We Know.'

The song competed with the muted sound of the freeway down below. Bosch looked out and saw there were no searchlights cutting across the sky from Universal Studios. It was too late for that. Still, the view was captivating in the way it could only be at night. The city shimmered out there like a million dreams, not all of them good.

Bosch thought about calling Kiz Rider back and telling her about the William Burkhart connection but decided to let it wait until the morning. He looked out at the city and felt satisfied with the day's moves and accomplishments, but he was also out of sorts. High jingo did that to you.

The man with the knife had not been too far off in calling him a missionary man. He almost had it right. Bosch knew he had a mission in life and now, after three years, he was back on the beat. But he could not bring himself to believe it was all good. He felt that there was something out there beyond the shimmering lights and dreams, something he could not see. It was waiting for him.

He clicked on the phone and listened to an uninterrupted dial tone. It meant he had no messages. He called the retrieval number anyway and replayed a message he had saved from the week before. It was his daughter's tiny voice, left the night she and her mother went traveling far away from him.

'Hello, Daddy,' she said. 'Good night, Daddy.'

That was all she had said but that was enough. Bosch saved the message for the next time he needed it and then killed the line.

Part Two
High Jingo

20

At 7:50 a.m. the next day Bosch was back on the Nickel.

He was watching the food line at the Metro Shelter and he had his eye on Robert Verloren back in the kitchen behind the steam tables. Bosch had gotten lucky. In the early morning, it was almost as if there had been a shift change among the homeless. The people who patrolled the street in darkness were sleeping off the night's failures. They were replaced by the first shift of homeless, the people who were smart enough to hide from the street at night. Bosch's intention had been to start at the big centers again and go from there. But as he had made his way into the homeless zone after parking again in Japantown, he started showing the photo of Verloren to the most lucid of the street people he encountered and almost immediately started getting responses. The day people recognized Verloren. Some said they had seen the man in the photo around but that he was much older now. Eventually Bosch came across one man who matter-of-factly said, 'Yeah, that's Chef,' and he pointed Bosch toward the Metro Shelter.

The Metro was one of the smaller satellite shelters that were clustered around the Salvation Army and the Los Angeles Mission and designed to handle the overflow of street people, particularly in the winter months when warmer weather in L.A. drew a migration from colder points north. These smaller centers didn't have the means to provide three squares a day and by agreement specialized in one service. At the Metro Shelter the service was a breakfast that started at 7 a.m. daily. By the time Bosch got there the line of wobbling, disheveled men and women was extending out the door of the chow center and the long rows of picnic-style tables inside were maxed out. The word on the street was that the Metro had the best breakfast on the Nickel.

Bosch had badged his way through the door and very quickly spotted Verloren in the kitchen beyond the serving tables. It didn't appear that Verloren was doing one particular job. Instead, he seemed to be checking on the preparation of several things. It appeared that he was in charge. He was neatly dressed in a white, double-breasted kitchen shirt over dark pants, a spotless white apron that went down past his knees and a tall white chef's hat.

The breakfast consisted of scrambled eggs with red and green peppers, hash browns, grits and disc sausages. It looked and smelled good to Bosch, who had left home without eating anything because he wanted to get moving. To the right of the serving line was a coffee station with two large serve-yourself urns. There were racks containing cups made of thick porcelain that had chipped and yellowed over time. Bosch took a cup and filled it with scalding black coffee and he sipped it and waited. When Verloren strode to the serving table, using the skirt of his apron to hold a hot and heavy replacement pan of eggs, Bosch made his move.

'Hey, Chef,' he called above the clatter of serving spoons and voices.

Verloren looked over and Bosch saw him immediately determine that Bosch was not a 'client.' As with the night before, Bosch was dressed informally, but he thought Verloren might have even been able to guess he was a cop. He stepped away from the serving table and approached. But he didn't come all the way. There seemed to be an invisible line on the floor that was the demarcation between kitchen and eating space. Verloren didn't cross it. He stood there using his apron to hold the near-empty serving pan he had taken from the steam table.

'Can I help you?' he asked.

'Yes, do you have a minute? I would like to talk to you.'

'No, I don't have a minute. I'm in the middle of breakfast.'

'It's about your daughter.'

Bosch saw the slight waver in Verloren's eyes. They dropped for a second and then came back up.

'You're the police?'

Bosch nodded.

'Can I just get through this rush? We're putting out the last trays now.'

'No problem.'

'You want to eat? You look like you're hungry.'

'Uh . . . '

Bosch looked around the room at the crowded tables. He didn't know where he would sit. He knew that these sorts of chow halls had the same unspoken protocols as prisons. Add in the high degree of mental illness in the homeless population and you could be crossing some sort of line just by the seat you chose.

'Come back with me,' Verloren said. 'We have a table in the back.'

Bosch turned back to Verloren but the breakfast chef was already heading back to the kitchen. Bosch followed and was led through the cooking and prep areas to a rear room where there was an empty stainless steel table with a full ashtray on it.

'Have a seat.'

Verloren removed the ashtray and held it behind his back. It was not like he was hiding it. It was like he was a waiter or a maître d' and he wanted his table perfect for the customer. Bosch thanked him and sat down.

'I'll be right back.'

It seemed that in less than a minute Verloren brought a plate back loaded with all the things Bosch had seen on the serving table. When he put down the silverware Bosch saw the shake in his hand.

'Thank you, but I was just thinking, will there be enough? You know, for the people coming through?'

'We're not turning anybody away today. Not as long as they're on time. How's your coffee?'

'It's fine, thanks. You know, it wasn't like I didn't want to sit out there with them. I just didn't know where to sit.'

'I understand. You don't have to explain. Let me get those trays out and then we can talk. Is there an arrest?'

Bosch looked at him. There was a hopeful, maybe even pleading look in Verloren's eyes.

'Not yet,' Bosch said. 'But we're getting close to something.'

'I'll be back as soon as I can. Eat. I call that Malibu scrambled.'

Bosch looked down at his plate. Verloren went back to the kitchen.

The eggs were good. So was the whole breakfast. No toast, but that would have been asking too much. The break area where he sat was between the cooking area of the kitchen and the large room where two men loaded an industrial dishwasher. It was loud, the noise from both directions ricocheting off the gray tiled walls. There was a set of double doors leading to the back alley.

One door was open and cool air came in and kept the steam from the dishwasher and the heat from the kitchen at bay.

After Bosch cleaned his plate and washed it down with the rest of his coffee he got up and stepped into the alley to make a phone call away from all the noise. He immediately saw the alley was an encampment. The rear walls of the missions on one side and the toy warehouses on the other were lined almost end to end with cardboard and canvas shanties. It was quiet. These were probably the self-made shelters of the night people. It wasn't that there was no room for them in the mission dormitories. It was that those beds came with basic rules attached and the people in the alley did not want to abide by such rules.

He called Kiz Rider's cell phone number and she answered right away. She was already in room 503 and had just finished distributing the wiretap application. Bosch spoke in a low voice.

'I found the father.'

'Great work, Harry. You still got it. What did he say? Did he recognize Mackey?'

'I haven't talked to him yet.'

He explained the situation and asked if there was anything new on her end.

'The warrant's on the captain's desk. Abel's going to push him on it if we don't hear back by ten, and then it goes up the chain.'

'How early did you come in?'

'Early. I wanted to get this done.'

'Did you ever get a chance to read the girl's journal last night?'

'Yeah, I read it in bed. It's not much help. It's high school confidential stuff. Unrequited love, weekly crushes, stuff like that. MTL is mentioned but no clue to identity. He might even be a fantasy figure, the way she writes about how special he is. I think Garcia was right to give it back to the mom. It's not going to help us.'

'Is MTL referred to in the book as a *he*?'

'Hmm, Harry, that's clever. I didn't notice. I have it here and I'll check. You know something I don't know?'

'No, just covering all the bases. What about Danny Kotchof? Is he in there?'

'In the beginning. He's mentioned by name. Then he drops off and mysterious MTL takes his place.'

'Mr. X . . .'

'Listen, I'm going up to six in a few minutes. I'm going to see about getting access to those old files we were talking about.'

Bosch noticed that she hadn't mentioned that they were PDU files. He wondered if Pratt or someone else was nearby and she was taking precautions against being overheard.

'Is somebody there, Kiz?'

'That's right.'

'Take all precautions, right?'

'You got it.'

'Good. Good luck. By the way, did you find a phone on Mariano?'

'Yes,' she said. 'There's one phone and it's under the name William Burkhart. Must be a roommate. This guy is just a few years older than Mackey and has a record that includes a hate crime. Nothing in recent years but the hate crime was in 'eighty-eight.'

'And guess what,' Bosch said, 'he was also Sam Weiss's neighbor. I must've left that out last night when we talked.'

'Too much information coming in.'

'Yeah. You know I was wondering about something. How come Mackey's cell didn't come up on the Auto-Track?'

'I'm ahead of you on that. I ran a check on the number and it's not his. It's held in the name of Belinda Messier. Her address is over on Melba, also in Woodland Hills. Her record's clean except for some traffic stuff. Maybe she's his girlfriend.'

'Maybe.'

'When I get time I will try to track her down. I'm sensing something here, Harry. It's all coming together. All of this eighty-eight stuff. I tried to pull the file on the hate crime but—'

'Public Disorder?'

'Exactly. And that's why I'm going up to six.'

'Okay, anything else?'

'I checked with the ESB first thing. They still haven't found the evidence box. We still don't have the gun. I'm now wondering if it got misplaced or if it was taken.'

'Yeah,' Bosch said, thinking the same thing. If this case went inside the department, the evidence could have been purposely and permanently lost.

'All right,' Bosch said. 'Before I do this interview let's go back to the journal for a minute. Is there anything in it about the pregnancy?'

'No, she didn't write about it. The entries are dated and she stopped writing in the book in late April. Maybe it was when she found out. I think maybe she stopped writing in it in case her parents were secretly reading it.'

'Does she mention any hangouts? You know, places she would go?'

'She does mention a lot of movies,' Rider said. 'Not who she went with but just that she saw specific movies and what she thought of them. What are you thinking, target acquisition?'

They needed to know where Mackey and Rebecca Verloren could have crossed paths. It was a hole in the case no matter what the motivation was. Where did Mackey come into contact with Verloren in order to target her?

'Movie theaters,' he said. 'It could have been where they intersected.'

'Exactly. And I think all the theaters up there in the Valley are in malls. That makes the crossing zone even wider.'

'It's something to think about.'

Bosch said he would come into the office after talking with Robert Verloren, and they hung up. Bosch went back into the break room and the noise from the dishwashing room seemed louder. The meal service was almost over and the dishwashers were getting slammed. Bosch sat down at the table again and noticed that someone had cleared his empty plate. He tried to think about the conversation with Rider. He knew that a shopping mall would be a huge crossroads, a place where it would be easy to see someone like Mackey crossing paths with someone like Rebecca Verloren. He wondered if the crime could have all come down to a chance encounter – Mackey seeing a girl with the obvious mix of races in her face and hair and eyes. Could this have incensed him to the point that he followed her home and later came back alone or with others to abduct and kill her?

It seemed like a long shot but most theories began as long shots. He thought about the original investigation and the possibility of it having been tainted from within the department. There had been nothing in the murder book that played to the racial angle. But in 1988 the department would have gone out of its way not to play to it. The department and the city had a blind spot. An infection of racial animosities was festering beneath the surface in 1988 but the department and the city looked away. The skin over the seething wound finally broke a few years later and the city was torn apart by three days of rioting, the worst in the country in a quarter-century. Bosch had to consider that the investigation of Rebecca Verloren's murder might have been stunted in deference to keeping the sickness beneath the surface.

'You ready?'

Bosch looked up and saw Robert Verloren standing over him. His face was sweating from exertion. He now held the chef's hat in his hand. There was still a slight tremor in his arm.

'Yeah, sure. Do you want to sit down?'

Verloren took the seat across from Bosch.

'Is it always like this?' Bosch asked. 'This crowded?'

'Every morning. Today we served a hundred sixty-two plates. A lot of people count on us. No, wait, make that a hundred sixty-three plates. I forgot about you. How was it?'

'It was damn good. Thank you, I needed the fuel.'

'My specialty.'

'A little different than cooking for Johnny Carson and the Malibu set, huh?'

'Yeah, but I don't miss that. Not at all. Just a stop-off on the road to finding the place where I belong. But I'm here now, thanks to the Lord Jesus, and this is where I want to be.'

Bosch nodded. Whether intentionally or not, Verloren was communicating to Bosch that his new life had been achieved through the intervention of faith. Bosch had often found that those who talked about it the most had the weakest hold on it.

'How did you find me?' Verloren asked.

'My partner and I talked to your wife yesterday and she told us that the last time she had heard anything about you, you were down here. I started looking last night.'

'I wouldn't go on these streets at night, if I were you.'

There was a slight Caribbean lilt in his voice. But it was something that seemed to have receded over time.

'I thought I was going to find you standing in a line, not feeding the line.'

'Well, not too long ago I was in the line. I had to stand there to stand where I am today.'

Bosch nodded again. He had heard these one-day-at-a-time mantras before.

'How long have you been sober?'

Verloren smiled.

'This time? A little over three years.'

'Look, I don't want to force you to relive the trauma of seventeen years ago, but we've reopened the case.'

'It's okay, Detective. I reopen the case every night when I shut my eyes and every morning when I say my prayers to Jesus.'

Bosch nodded again.

'Do you want to do this here or take a walk or go over to Parker Center where we can sit in a quiet room?'

'Here is good. I am comfortable here.'

'Okay, then let me tell you a little bit about what is going on. I work for the Open-Unsolved Unit. We are currently looking into your daughter's murder again because we have some new information.'

'What information?'

Bosch decided to take a different approach with him. Where he had held information back from the mother, he decided to give it all to the father.

'We have a match between blood found on the weapon used in the crime and an individual who we are pretty sure was living up there in Chatsworth at the time of the killing. It's a DNA match. Do you know what that is?'

Verloren nodded.

'I know. Like in O.J.'

'This one's solid. It doesn't mean he is the one who killed Rebecca, but it means he was close to the crime, and that makes us closer.'

'Who is it?'

'I'll get to that in a minute. But first, Mr. Verloren, I want to ask you some questions relating to yourself and the case.'

'What about me?'

Bosch felt the tension rise. The skin around Verloren's eyes grew tighter. He realized that he could have been careless with this man, mistaking his position in the kitchen as a sign of health and forgetting the warning Rider had issued about the homeless population.

'Well,' he said, 'I'd like to know a little bit about what has happened to you in the years since Rebecca was taken.'

'What's that got to do with anything?'

'Maybe nothing, but I want to know.'

'What happened to me is that I tripped and fell into a black hole. Took me a long time to see the light and my way out. You got kids?'

'One. A girl.'

'Then you know what I mean. You lose a kid the way I lost my girl and that's it, my friend. It's all over. You are like an empty bottle tossed out the window. The car keeps going but you are on the side of the road, broken.'

Bosch nodded. He did know this. He lived a life of screaming vulnerability, knowing that what might happen in a city far away could cause him to live or die, or fall into the same black hole as Verloren.

'After your daughter's death you lost the restaurant?'

'That's right. It was the best thing that could have happened. I needed that to happen for me to find out who I really was. And to make my way here.'

Bosch knew that such emotional defenses were fragile. Following Verloren's logic it could be said that his daughter's death was the best thing that could have happened because it led to the loss of the restaurant, which triggered all the wonderful personal discoveries he had made. It was bullshit and both men at the table knew it; one just couldn't admit it.

'Mr. Verloren, talk to me,' Bosch said. 'Leave all the self-help lessons for your meetings and the ragged people in line. Tell me how you tripped. Tell me how you fell into that black hole.'

'I just did.'

'Not everybody who loses a child falls so far into the hole. You're not the only one this has happened to, Mr. Verloren. Some people end up on TV, some run for Congress. What happened to you? Why are you different? And don't tell me it is because you loved your kid more. We all love our kids.'

Verloren was quiet a moment. He pressed his lips tightly together as he composed. Bosch could tell he had made him angry. But that was okay. He needed to push things.

'All right,' Verloren finally said. 'All right.'

But that was all. Bosch could see the muscles of his jaw working. The pain of the last seventeen years had set in his face. Bosch could read it like a menu. Appetizers, entrees, desserts. Frustration, anger, irredeemable loss.

'All right what, Mr. Verloren?'

Verloren nodded. He removed the final barricade.

'I could blame you people but I must blame myself. I abandoned my daughter in death, Detective. And then the only place I could hide from the betrayal was in the bottle. The bottle opens up the black hole. Do you understand?'

Bosch nodded.

'I am trying to. Tell me what you mean about blaming *you people.* Do you mean cops? Do you mean white people?'

'I mean all of it.'

Verloren turned in his seat so that his back was against the tile wall next to the table. He looked toward the door to the alley. He wasn't looking at Bosch. Bosch wanted the eye contact, but he was willing to let things ride as long as Verloren kept talking.

'Let's start with the cops, then,' Bosch said. 'Why do you blame the cops? What did the cops do?'

'You expect me to talk to you about what *you* people did?'

Bosch thought carefully before responding. He felt this was the make-or-break point of the interview and he sensed that this man had something important to give up.

'We start with the fact that you loved your daughter, right?' Bosch said.

'Of course.'

'Well, Mr. Verloren, what happened to her should never have happened. I can't do anything about it. But I can try to speak for her. That's why I am here. What the cops did seventeen years ago is not what I am going to do. Most of them are dead now anyway. If you still love your daughter, if you love the memory of her, then you will tell me the story. You will help me speak for her. It's your only way of making up for what you did back then.'

Verloren started nodding halfway through Bosch's plea. Bosch knew he had him, that he would open up. It was about redemption. It didn't matter how many years had gone by. Redemption was always the brass ring.

A single tear rolled down Verloren's left cheek, almost imperceptible against the dark skin. A man in dirty kitchen whites came into the break area with a clipboard in hand but Bosch quickly waved him away from Verloren. Bosch waited and finally Verloren spoke.

'I chose myself over her and in the end I lost myself anyway,' he said.

'How did that happen?'

Verloren covered his mouth with his hand, as if to try to keep the secrets from being dispelled. Finally he dropped it and spoke.

'I read one day in the newspaper that my daughter had been killed with a gun that came from a burglary. Green and Garcia, they hadn't told me that. So I asked Detective Green about it and he told me the man with the gun had it because he was afraid. He was a Jewish man and there had been threats against him. I thought . . . '

He stopped there and Bosch had to prompt him.

'You thought that maybe Rebecca had been targeted because of her mixed races? Because her father was black?'

Verloren nodded.

'I thought, yes, because from time to time there would be a comment or something. Not everybody saw the beauty in her. Not like we did. I wanted to live on the Westside, but Muriel, she was from up there. It was home to her.'

'What did Green tell you?'

'He told me, no, that it wasn't there. They had looked at that and it wasn't a possibility. It wasn't . . . it didn't seem right to me. They were ignoring this, it seemed to me. I kept calling and asking. I was pushing it. Finally I went to a customer I had at the restaurant who was a member of the police commission. I told him about this thing and he said he would check into it for me.'

Verloren nodded, more to himself than to Bosch. He was fortifying his faith in his actions as a father seeking justice for his daughter.

'And then what happened?' Bosch prompted.

'Then I got a visit from two police.'

'Not Green and Garcia?'

'No, not them. Different police. They came to my restaurant.'

'What were their names?'

Verloren shook his head.

'They never gave me their names. They just showed me their badges. They were detectives, I think. They told me I was wrong about what I was pushing Green about. They told me to back off it because I was just stirring the pot. That is what they called it, stirring the pot. Like it was about me and not my daughter.'

He shook his head tightly, that anger still sharp after all the years. Bosch asked an obvious question, obvious because he knew so well how the LAPD worked back then.

'Did they threaten you?'

Verloren snorted.

'Yes, they threatened me,' he said quietly. 'They told me that they knew my daughter had been pregnant but they couldn't find the clinic she had gone to to get it taken care of. So there was no tissue they could use to identify the father. No way to tell who it was or wasn't. They said that all it would take was for them to ask a few questions about me and her, like with my customer on the police commission, and the rumors would start to run. They said just a few questions in the right places and pretty soon people would think it was me.'

Bosch didn't interrupt. He felt his own anger tightening his throat.

'They said it would be hard for me to keep my business if everybody thought I had . . . I had done that to my daughter . . .'

Now more tears came down his dark face. He did nothing to stop their flow.

'And so I did what they wanted. I backed off and dropped it. Stopped stirring the pot. I told myself it didn't matter; it wouldn't bring Becky back to us. So I never called Detective Green again . . . and they never solved the case. After a while I started drinking to forget what I had lost and what I had done, that I had put myself and my pride and my reputation and my business ahead of my daughter. And pretty soon, before you knew it, I came to that black hole I was telling you about. I fell in and I'm still climbing out.'

After a moment he turned and looked at Bosch.

'How's that for a story, Detective?'

'I'm sorry, Mr. Verloren. I'm sorry that happened. All of it.'

'Is that the story you wanted to hear, Detective?'

'I just wanted to know the truth. Believe it or not, it is going to help me. It will help me speak for her. Can you describe these two men who came to you?'

Verloren shook his head.

'It's been a long time. I probably wouldn't recognize them if they stood in front of me. I just remember they were both white men. One of them I always thought of as Mr. Clean because his head was shaved and he stood with his arms folded like the guy on the bottle.'

Bosch nodded and he felt his anger working into the muscles of his shoulders. He knew who Mr. Clean was.

'How much of all this did your wife know?' he asked in a calm tone.

Verloren shook his head.

'Muriel didn't know anything about this. I kept it from her. It was my water to carry.'

Verloren wiped his cheeks and seemed to have earned some relief from finally telling the story.

Bosch reached into his back pocket and came up with the old photograph of Roland Mackey. He put it down on the table in front of Verloren.

'Do you recognize this kid?'

Verloren looked for a long moment before shaking his head in the negative.

'Should I? Who is he?'

'His name is Roland Mackey. He was a couple years older than your daughter in 'eighty-eight. He didn't go to school at Hillside but he lived in Chatsworth.'

Bosch waited for a response but didn't get any. Verloren just stared at the photo on the table.

'That's a mug shot. What did he do?'

'Stole a car. But he has a record of associating with white power extremists. In and outside of jail. Does the name mean anything to you?'

'No. Should it?'

'I don't know. I'm just asking. Can you remember if your daughter ever mentioned his name or maybe somebody named Ro?'

Verloren shook his head.

'What we are trying to do is figure out if they could have intersected anywhere. The Valley's a big place. They could've—'

'What school did he go to?'

'He went to Chatsworth High but never finished. He got a GED.'

'Rebecca went to Chatsworth High for driver's ed the summer before she was taken.'

'You mean 'eighty-seven?'

Verloren nodded.

'I'll check it out.'

But Bosch didn't think it was a good lead. Mackey had dropped out before the summer of 1987 and didn't come back for his general education degree until 1988. Still, it was worth a thorough look.

'What about the movies? Did she like to go to movies and the mall?'

Verloren shrugged.

'She was a sixteen-year-old girl. Of course she liked movies. Most of her friends had cars. Once they hit sixteen and got mobile they were all over the place. My wife called it the three Ms – movies, malls, and Madonna.'

'Which malls? Which theaters?'

'They went to the Northridge Mall because it was close, you know. They also liked to go to the drive-in over on Winnetka. That way they could sit in the car and talk during the movie. One of the girls had a convertible and they liked going in that.'

Bosch zeroed in on the drive-in. He had forgotten about it when he had spoken about movie theaters with Rider earlier. But Roland Mackey had once been arrested burglarizing the same drive-in on Winnetka. That made it a key possibility as the point of intersection.

'How often did Rebecca and her friends go to the drive-in?'

'I think they liked to go on Friday nights, when the new movies were just out.'

'Did they meet boys there?'

'I would assume so. You see, this is all just second-guessing. There was nothing wrong or unnatural about our daughter going to the movies with her friends and meeting up with boys and whatnot. It is only after the worst-case scenario happens that people ask, "Why don't you know who she was with?" We thought everything was fine. We sent her to the best school we could find. Her friends were from nice families. We couldn't watch her every minute of the day. Friday nights – hell, most nights – I worked late at the restaurant.'

'I understand. I am not judging you as a parent, Mr. Verloren. I see nothing wrong with that, okay? I am just dragging a net. I'm collecting as much information as I can because you never know what might become important.'

'Yeah, well, that net got snagged and ripped on the rocks a long time ago.'

'Maybe not.'

'You think this Mackey fellow is the one, then?'

'He's connected somehow, that's all we know for sure. We'll know more soon enough. I promise you that.'

Verloren turned and looked directly into Bosch's eyes for the first time during the interview.

'When you get to that point, you will speak for her, won't you, Detective?'

Bosch nodded slowly. He thought he knew what Verloren was asking.

'Yes sir, I will.'

21

Kiz Rider sat at her desk with her arms folded, as if she had been waiting for Bosch all morning. She had a somber look on her face and Bosch knew something was up.

'You get the PDU file?' he asked.

'I got to look at it. I wasn't allowed to take it.'

Bosch nodded. He slid into his seat across from her.

'Good stuff?' he asked.

'Depends on how you look at it.'

'Well, I got some stuff, too.'

He looked around. Abel Pratt's door was open and Bosch could see him in there, bending over to the little cooler he kept next to his desk. Pratt was in earshot. It wasn't that Bosch didn't trust Pratt. He did. But he didn't want to put him in a position of hearing something he didn't want to or was not ready to hear. Same as Rider when they had spoken on the phone earlier.

He looked back at his partner.

'You want to take a walk?'

'Yes, I do.'

They got up and headed out. When Bosch went past the OIC's door he leaned in. Pratt was now on the phone. Bosch caught his attention and pantomimed drinking from a cup and then pointed to Pratt. Shaking his head no to the offer of coffee, Pratt held up a tub of yogurt as if to say he had what he needed. Bosch saw little chunks of green in the gunk. He tried to think of a green fruit and only came up with kiwi. He walked away thinking that the only possible way to make yogurt taste worse was to put kiwi into it.

They took the elevator down to the lobby and walked out front to where the memorial fountain was.

'So where do you want to go?' Kiz asked.

'Depends on how much there is to talk about.'

'Probably a lot.'

'Last time I worked in Parker Center I was a smoker. When I needed to walk and think I'd go over to Union Station and buy smokes in the shop over there. I liked that place. It's got those comfortable chairs in the main hall. Or it used to, at least.'

'Sounds good to me.'

They headed that way, taking Los Angeles Street to the north. The first building they passed was the federal office building, and Bosch noticed that the concrete barriers erected in 2001 to keep potential vehicle bombs away from the building were still in place. The threat of danger didn't seem to bother the people in the line stretching across the front of the building. They were waiting to get into the immigration offices, each clutching paperwork and ready to make a case for citizenship. They waited beneath the tile mosaics on the front façade that depicted people dressed like angels, their eyes skyward, waiting on heaven.

'Why don't you start, Harry,' Rider said. 'Tell me about Robert Verloren.'

Bosch walked a little further before beginning.

'I liked the guy,' he said. 'He's digging himself out of the hole. He cooks a hundred or so breakfasts a day over there. I had a plate and it was pretty good stuff.'

'And I'm sure it beats the hell out of the prices at Pacific Dining Car. What did he give you that's made you so angry?'

'What are you talking about?'

'You read me, I read you. I know he told you something that's got you going.'

Bosch nodded. It sure didn't seem like three years since they had worked together.

'Irving. Or at least I think he gave me Irving.'

'Tell it.'

Bosch took her through the story Verloren had told him less than an hour before. He finished with Verloren's description, limited as it was, of the two men with badges who came to his restaurant and threatened him in order to make him back off the racial angle.

'Sounds like Irving to me, too,' Rider said.

'And one of his poodles. Maybe it was McClellan.'

'Maybe. So you think Verloren was straight? He's been on the Nickel a long time.'

'I think so. He claims to have been sober for three years this time. But you know, grinding over something for seventeen years, pretty soon perceptions become facts. Still, everything he said just seems to fit into the underpinnings of this. I think they pushed this case, Kiz. It was going in one direction and they pushed it the other way. Maybe they knew what was coming, that the city was going to burn. Rodney King wasn't the gasoline. He was only the match. Things had been building and maybe the powers that be looked at this case and said for the public good, we have to go the other way. They sacrificed justice for Rebecca Verloren.'

They were crossing over the 101 Freeway on the Los Angeles Street overpass. Eight lanes of crawling traffic smoked beneath them. The sun was bright, reflecting off windshields and buildings and concrete. Bosch put on his Ray-Bans.

The traffic was loud, too, and Rider had to raise her voice.

'That's not like you, Harry.'

'What isn't?'

'Looking for a good reason for them to have done something so wrong. You usually look for the sinister angle.'

'Are you telling me you found the sinister angle in that PDU file?'

She nodded glumly.

'I think so,' she said.

'And they just let you waltz in there and get it?'

'I got in to see the man first thing this morning. I brought him a cup of coffee from Starbucks – he hates the cafeteria crap. That got me in. Then I told him what we had and what I wanted to do, and the bottom line is he trusts me. So he more or less let me have a look around in Special Archives.'

'The Public Disorder Unit came and went long before he was here. Did he know about it?'

'I'm sure after he took the job he was briefed. Maybe even before he took it.'

'Did you tell him specifically about Mackey and the Chatsworth Eights?'

'Not specifically. I just told him the case we caught was connected to an old PDU investigation and I needed to get into Special Archives to look for a file. He sent Lieutenant Hohman with me. We went in, found the file and I had to look through it while Hohman sat across a table from me. You know what, Harry? There are a hell of a lot of files in Special Archives.'

'Where all the bodies are buried . . . '

Bosch wanted to say something more but wasn't sure how to say it. Rider looked at him and read him.

'What, Harry?'

He didn't say anything at first but she waited him out.

'Kiz, you said the man on six trusts you. Do you trust him?'

She looked him in the eye when she answered.

'Like I trust you, Harry. Okay?'

Bosch looked at her.

'That's good enough for me.'

Rider made a move to turn down Arcadia but Bosch pointed toward the old pueblo, the place where the City of Angels was founded. He wanted to take the long way and walk through.

'I haven't been down here in a while. Let's check this out.'

They cut through the circular courtyard where the padres blessed the animals every Easter and then past the Instituto Cultural Mexicano. They followed the curving arcade of cheap souvenir booths and churro stands. Recorded mariachi music came from unseen speakers, but in counterpoint was the sound of a live guitar.

They found the musician sitting on a bench in front of the Avila Adobe. They stopped and listened as the old man played a Mexican ballad Bosch thought he had heard before but could not identify.

Bosch studied the mud-walled structure behind the musician and wondered if Don Francisco Avila had any idea what he was helping to set in motion when he staked his claim to the spot in 1818. A city would grow tall and wide from this place. A city as great as any other. And just as mean. A destination city, a city of invention and reinvention. A place where the dream seemed as easy to reach as the sign they put up on the hill, but a place where the reality was always something different. The road to that sign on the hill had a locked gate across it.

It was a city full of haves and have-nots, movie stars and extras, drivers and the driven, predators and prey. The fat and the hungry and little room in between. A city that despite all of that still had them lining up and waiting every day behind the bomb barriers to get in and stay in.

Bosch pulled the fold of money from his pocket and dropped a five in the old musician's basket. He and Rider then cut through the old Cucamonga Winery, its cask rooms converted into galleries and artists' stalls, and out to Alameda. They crossed the street to the train station, its clock tower rising in front of them. In the front walkway they passed a sundial with an inscription cut into its granite pedestal.

Vision to See
Faith to Believe
Courage to Do

Union Station was designed to mirror the city it served and the way in which it was supposed to work. It was a melting pot of architectural styles – Spanish Colonial, Mission, Streamline Moderne, Art Deco, Southwestern and Moorish design flourishes among them. But unlike the rest of the city, where the pot more often than not boiled over, the styles at the train station blended smoothly into something unique, something beautiful. Bosch loved it for that.

Through the glass doors they came into the cavernous entry hall, and an archway three stories tall led to the immense waiting room beyond. As Bosch took it in he remembered that he used to walk over here not only for cigarettes, but also to renew himself a little bit. Going to Union Station was like paying a visit to church, a cathedral where the graceful lines of design and function and civic pride all intersected. In the central waiting room the voices of travelers rose into its high empty spaces and were transformed into a choir of languid whispers.

'I love this place,' Rider said. 'Did you ever see the movie *Blade Runner*?'

Bosch nodded. He had seen it.

'This was the police station, right?' he asked.

'Yeah.'

'Did you ever see *True Confessions*?' he asked.

'No, was it good?'

'Yeah, you should see it. Another take on the Black Dahlia and LAPD conspiracy.'

She groaned.

'Thanks, but I don't think that's what I need right now.'

They got cups of coffee at Union Bagel and then walked into the waiting room, where rows of brown leather seats were lined up like luxurious pews. Bosch looked up as he was always drawn to do. Six huge chandeliers hung forty feet above them in two rows. Rider looked up, too.

Bosch then pointed to two side-by-side seats open near the newsstand. They sat down on the soft padded leather and put their cups on the wide wooden armrests.

'You ready to talk about this now?' Rider asked.

'If you are,' he answered. 'What was in the file you saw in Special Archives? What was so sinister?'

'For one thing, Mackey is in there.'

'As a suspect in Verloren?'

'No, the file has nothing to do with Verloren. Verloren was not even a blip on the screen as far as the file goes. It's all about an investigation that went down and was buttoned up before Rebecca Verloren was even pregnant, let alone snatched from her bed in the night.'

'All right, then what's it got to do with us?'

'Maybe nothing and maybe everything. You know the guy Mackey lives with, William Burkhart?'

'Yeah.'

'He's in there, too. Only back then he was better known as Billy Blitzkrieg. That was his moniker in this gang, the Eights.'

'Okay.'

'In March of 'eighty-eight Billy Blitzkrieg went away for a year for vandalizing a synagogue in North Hollywood. Property damage, graffiti, defecation, the whole thing.'

'The hate crime. He was the only one they bagged?'

She nodded.

'They got a latent off a spray can they found in a gutter trap about a block from the synagogue. So he went down for it. Took a plea or they would have made an example of him and he knew it.'

Bosch nodded. He didn't want to say anything that would interrupt her flow.

'In the reports and in the press Burkhart – or Blitzkrieg or whatever you want to call him – was portrayed as the leader of the Eights. They said he called for nineteen eighty-eight to be a year of racial and ethnic upheaval to honor their beloved Adolf Hitler. You know the crap. RaHoWa, revenge of the white trash and all that. They all ran around in Minnesota Vikings jerseys – the Vikings apparently were a pure race. They all wore number eighty-eight.'

'I'm getting the picture.'

'Anyway, they had a lot on Burkhart. They had him cold on the synagogue and they had the feds chomping at the bit to do a civil rights dance on his pointy little head. There were a lot of crimes, beginning right at the start of the year, when they toasted New Year's by burning a cross on a black family's lawn in Chatsworth. After that there were more cross burnings, threatening phone calls, bomb scares. The synagogue break-in. They even trashed a Jewish daycare center in Encino. This was all in early January. They also started going to street corners, picking up Mexican laborers and taking them out into the desert, where they assaulted or abandoned them or both, usually both. To use their terminology, they were fomenting disharmony, which they believed would help lead to a separation of the races.'

'Yeah, I've heard the song.'

'Okay, well, like I said, they were ready to make Burkhart the poster boy for all of this and, if they went with it to Justice, he could have ended up going away for a ten-year minimum in a federal pen.'

'So it was a no-brainer. He took a deal.'

Rider nodded.

'He took a year in Wayside and a five-year tail, and the rest of it went away. And the Eights went away with it. They were broken up and that was the end of the threat. All of this went down by the end of March, long before Verloren.'

As he thought about all of this Bosch watched a woman in a hurry as she pulled a young girl by the hand toward the gateway to the Metroline tracks. The woman was also lugging a heavy suitcase and her focus was only on the gate ahead. The child was pulled along with her face turned upward as she looked at the ceiling. She was smiling at something. Bosch looked up and saw a child's balloon trapped in one of the ceiling's vaulted squares. One child's disaster was another's secret smile. The balloon was orange and white and shaped like a fish, and Bosch knew because of his daughter that it was an animated character named Nemo. He had a flash of his daughter but just as quickly pushed it away so he could concentrate. He looked at Rider.

'So where was Mackey in all of this?' he asked.

'He was sort of the runt of the litter,' Rider answered. 'One of the minions. He was thought to be the perfect recruit. High school dropout with no life and no prospects. He was on probation for burglary and his juvie jacket was full of pops for car theft, burglary and drugs. So he was just the kind of guy they were looking for. A loser they could mold into a white warrior. But once they jumped him in they found out he was – to use a quote from Burkhart – dumber than a nigger off the boat. He apparently was so stupid that they had to take him off the graffiti runs because he couldn't even spell their basic racist vocabulary. In fact, his homey name in the group became Wej. Not like you wedge your way into a door. Wej like Jew spelled backwards because that was how he sprayed it once on a synagogue wall.'

'Dyslexic?'

'I'd say.'

Bosch shook his head.

'Even with the giveaways in the Verloren scene, I'm not seeing this guy.'

'I agree. I think he had a part but not the main part. He doesn't have it between the ears.'

Bosch decided to drop Mackey and double back to the beginning of her report.

'So if they had all of this intel on these guys, how come only Burkhart went down?'

'I'm getting to that.'

'This is where the high jingo comes in?'

'You got it. You see, Burkhart was a leader of the Eights but he wasn't *the* leader.'

'Ah.'

'The leader was identified as a guy named Richard Ross. He was older than the others. A true believer. He was twenty-one and was the smooth talker who recruited Burkhart and then most of the other Eights and got the whole thing going.'

Bosch nodded. Richard Ross was a common name but he thought he knew where this was going.

'This Richard Ross, was that as in Richard Ross Junior?'

'Exactly. The good Captain Ross's progeny.'

Captain Richard Ross had been the longtime head of Internal Affairs Division during the early part of Bosch's career in the department. He was now retired.

For Bosch the rest of the story tumbled into place.

'So they kept Junior out of it and saved Senior and the department all the embarrassment,' he said. 'They laid it all on Burkhart, Ross's second in command. He went away to Wayside and the group was broken up. Chalk it all up to youthful misadventure.'

'You got it.'

'And let me guess: all the intel came from Richard Ross Junior.'

'You're good. It was part of the deal. Richard Junior gave up everybody and it was all PDU needed to quietly splinter the group. Junior then got to walk away from it.'

'All in a day's work for Irving.'

'And you know what's funny? I think Irving is a Jewish name.'

Bosch shook his head.

'Whether it is or isn't, it's not very funny,' he said.

'Yeah, I know.'

'Not if Irving saw an angle.'

'Reading between the lines of the report, I would say he saw all the angles.'

'This deal gave him control of IAD. I mean real, absolute control over who was investigated and how investigations were conducted. It put Ross deep in his pocket. It explains a lot about what was going on back then.'

'It was mostly before my time.'

'So they take care of the Eights and Irving gets a nice big prize in having Richard Ross Senior wearing a collar on the poodle squad,' Bosch said, thinking out loud. 'But then Rebecca Verloren ends up dead by a gun stolen from a guy the Eights had been harassing, a gun likely stolen by one of the little runts they let run free. Their whole deal could fall apart if the murder came back on the Eights and then on them.'

'That's right. So they step in and push the investigation. They steer it away and nobody ever goes down for it.'

'Motherfuckers,' Bosch whispered.

'Poor Harry. You still must have a lot of rust from your lay-off. You thought maybe they pushed the case because they were trying to save the city from burning. It was nothing so heroic.'

'No, they were just trying to save their own asses and the position the deal with Ross had given them. Given Irving.'

'This is all supposition,' Rider cautioned.

'Yeah, just reading between the fucking lines.'

Bosch felt the strongest craving for a cigarette he'd had in at least a year. He looked over at the newsstand and saw all of the packages in the racks behind the counter. He looked away. He looked up at the balloon trapped at the ceiling. He thought he knew how Nemo felt being stuck up there.

'When did Ross retire?' he asked.

''Ninety-one. He rode it out until he hit twenty-five years – they allowed him that – and then he retired. I checked – he moved up to Idaho. I ran Junior on the box, too, and he'd already moved up there ahead of him. Probably one of those gated white enclaves where he felt right at home.'

'And he was probably up there laughing his ass off when this place came apart after Rodney King in 'ninety-two.'

'Probably, but not for long. He was killed in a DUI in 'ninety-three. He was coming back from an antigovernment rally out in the boonies. What goes around comes around, I guess.'

A dull thud hit Bosch in the stomach. He had started liking Richard Ross Jr. for the Verloren killing. He could have used Mackey to procure the weapon and maybe help carry the victim up the hill. But now he was dead. Could their investigation be leading them to such a dead end? Would they end up going back to Rebecca Verloren's parents and telling them their long-dead daughter had been taken from them by someone who also was long dead? What kind of justice would that be?

'I know what you're thinking,' Rider said. 'He could have been our guy. But I don't think so. According to the box, he got his Idaho driver's license in May of 'eighty-eight. He was supposedly already up there when Verloren went down.'

'Yeah, supposedly.'

Bosch wasn't convinced by a simple DMV computer check. He pushed all of the information through the filters again to see if anything else jumped out at him.

'Okay, let's review for a minute, make sure I have it all straight. Back in 'eighty-eight we have a bunch of these Valley boys calling themselves the Eights and running around in their football jerseys trying to kick-start a racial holy war. The department takes a look and pretty soon finds out that the brains behind this group is the son of our own Captain Ross of IAD. Commander Irving puts his finger into the wind and thinks, "Hmmm, I think I can use this to my advantage." So he puts the kibosh on going after Richard Junior and they sacrifice William "Billy Blitz" Burkhart to the Justice Gods instead. The Eights are splintered, score one for the good guys. And Richard Junior skates away, score one for Irving because now he has Richard Senior in his pocket. Everybody lives happily ever after. Am I missing anything?'

'Actually, it's Billy *Blitzkrieg*.'

'Blitzkrieg, then. So all of this gets wrapped up by early spring, right?'

'By the end of March. And by early May Richard Ross Junior has moved to Idaho.'

'Okay, so then in June somebody breaks into Sam Weiss's house and steals his gun. Then in July – the day after our nation's birthday, no less – a girl of mixed race is taken out of her house and murdered. Not raped, but murdered – which is important to remember. The murder is made to look like a suicide. But it is done badly, by all appearances by someone who was new at this. Garcia and Green catch the case, eventually see through it and conduct an investigation that leads them nowhere because, whether knowingly or not, they are pushed in that direction. Now, seventeen years later, the murder weapon is incontrovertibly tied to someone who just a few months before the killing was running around with the Eights. What am I missing here?'

'I think you've got it all.'

'So the question is, could it be that the Eights were not finished? That they continued to foment, only they tried to disguise their signature now? And that they raised the ante to include murder?'

Rider slowly shook her head.

'Anything is possible, but it doesn't make much sense. The Eights were about statements – public statements. Burning crosses and painting synagogues. But it's not much of a statement if you murder somebody and then try to disguise it as a suicide.'

Bosch nodded. She was right. There was not a smooth flow to any of the logic.

'Then again, they knew they had the LAPD on their backs,' he said. 'Maybe some of them continued to operate but as sort of an underground movement.'

'Like I said, anything is possible.'

'Okay, so we have Ross Junior supposedly up in Idaho and we have Burkhart in Wayside. The two leaders. Who was left besides Mackey?'

'There are five other names in the file. None of the names jumped out at me.'

'That's our suspect list for now. We need to run them and see where they went from – wait a minute, wait a minute. *Was* Burkhart still in Wayside? You said he got a year, right? That meant he'd be out in five or six months unless he got into trouble up there. When exactly did he go in?'

Rider shook her head.

'No, it would have been late March or early April when he checked into Wayside. He couldn't have—'

'Doesn't matter when he checked into Wayside. When was he popped? When was the synagogue thing?'

'It was January. Early January. I have the exact date back in the file.'

'All right, early January. You said prints on a paint can tripped them to Burkhart. What did that take back in 'eighty-eight, when they were probably still doing it by hand – a week if it was a hot case like this? If they popped Burkhart by the end of January and he didn't make bail …'

He held his hands wide, allowing Rider to finish.

'February, March, April, May, June,' she said excitedly. 'Five months. With gain time he could easily have been out by July!'

Bosch nodded. The county jail system housed inmates awaiting trial or serving sentences of a year or less. For decades the system had been overcrowded and under court-ordered maximum population counts. This resulted in the routine early release of inmates through gain-time ratios that fluctuated according to individual jail population but sometimes were as high as three days earned for every one day served.

'This looks good, Harry.'

'Maybe too good. We have to nail it down.'

'When we get back I'll go on the computer and find out when he left Wayside. What's this do to the wiretap?'

Bosch thought for a moment about whether they should slow things down.

'I think we go ahead with the wiretap. If the Wayside date fits, then we watch Mackey *and* Burkhart. We still spook Mackey because he's the weak one. We do it when he's at work and away from Burkhart. If we're right, he'll call him.'

He stood up.

'But we still have to run down the other names, the other members of the Eights,' he added.

Rider didn't get up. She looked up at him.

'You think this is going to work?'

Bosch shrugged.

'It has to.'

He looked around the cavernous train station. He checked faces and eyes, looking for any that might quickly turn away from his own. He half expected to see Irving in the crowd of travelers. Mr. Clean on the scene. That's what Bosch used to think when Irving would show up at a crime scene.

Rider stood up. They dropped their empty cups into a nearby trash can and walked toward the front doors of the station. When he got there Bosch looked behind them, again searching for a follower. He knew they now had to consider such possibilities. The place that had been so warm and inviting to him twenty minutes before was now suspicious and forbidding. The voices inside were no longer graceful whispers. There was a sharp edge to them. They sounded angry.

When they got outside he noticed that the sun had moved behind the clouds. He wouldn't need his sunglasses for the walk back.

'I'm sorry, Harry,' Rider said.

'For what?'

'I just thought that it would be different, you coming back. Now here we are, your first case back and what do you get, a case with high jingo all over it.'

Bosch nodded as they crossed to the front walkway. He saw the sundial and the words etched in granite beneath it. His eyes held on the last line.

Courage to Do

'I'm not worried,' he said. 'But they should be.'

22

'Good to go,' Commander Garcia replied when Bosch asked if he was ready.

Bosch nodded and went to the door to usher in the two women from the *Daily News.*

'Hi, I'm McKenzie Ward,' said the one leading the way. She was obviously the reporter. The other woman was carrying a camera bag and a tripod.

'I'm Emmy Ward,' said the photographer.

'Sisters?' Garcia asked, though the answer was obvious because of how much the two women, both in their twenties, looked alike: both attractive blondes with big smiles.

'I'm older,' said McKenzie. 'But not by much.'

They all shook hands.

'How did two sisters get on the same paper together, then the same story together?' Garcia said.

'I was here a few years and then Emmy just applied. It's no big deal. We've worked together a lot. It's just a blind draw on who gets the photo assignments. Today we work together. Tomorrow maybe not.'

'Do you mind if we take some photos first?' Emmy asked. 'I have another assignment I need to get to right after this.'

'Of course,' Garcia said, ever accommodating. 'Where do you want me?'

Emmy Ward set up a shot with Garcia seated at the meeting table with the murder book open in front of him. Bosch had brought it with him to use as a prop. As the photo session proceeded, Bosch and McKenzie Ward stood off to the side and talked casually. Earlier, they had spoken at length on the phone. She had agreed to the deal. If she got the story into the paper the following day, she would be first in line for the exclusive when they took down the killer. She had not agreed easily. Garcia had initially been clumsy in his approach to her before turning the negotiation over to Bosch. Bosch was wise enough to know that no reporter would allow the police department to dictate when a story would be published and how it would be written. So Bosch concentrated on the when, not the how. He went with the assumption that McKenzie Ward would and could write a story that would serve his purposes. He just needed it in the paper sooner rather than later. Kiz Rider had an appointment with a judge that afternoon. If the wiretap application was approved, they would be in business by the next morning.

'Did you talk to Muriel Verloren?' the reporter asked Bosch.

'Yeah, she's there all afternoon and she's ready to talk.'

'I pulled the clips and read everything from back then – like I was eight years old at the time – and there were several mentions of the father and his restaurant. Will he be there, too?'

'I don't think so. He's gone. It's more of a mother's story, anyway. She's the one who has kept her daughter's bedroom untouched for seventeen years. She said you could photograph in there, too, if you want.'

'Really?'

'Really.'

Bosch watched her looking at the shot being set up with Garcia. He knew what she was thinking. The mother in the bedroom frozen in time would be a lot better shot than an old cop at a table with a binder. She looked at Bosch while she started digging in her purse.

'Then I have to make a call to see if I can keep Emmy.'

'Go ahead.'

She left the office, probably because she didn't want Garcia to overhear her telling an editor that she needed Emmy to stay on the assignment because she had a better shot with the mother.

She was back in three minutes and nodded to Bosch, which he took to mean that Emmy was going to stay with her on the story.

'So this thing is a go for tomorrow?' he asked, just to make sure once again.

'It's slotted for the window – depending on the art. My editor wanted to hold it for Sunday, make a nice long feature, but I told him we were competitive on it. Anytime we can beat the *Times* on a story we do.'

'Yeah, but what will he say when the *Times* doesn't run anything? He'll know you tricked him.'

'No, he'll think that the *Times* killed their story because we beat them to the punch. Happens all the time.'

Bosch nodded thoughtfully, then asked, 'What did you mean about it being slotted for the window?'

'We run a news feature every day with a photo on the front page. We call it the window because it's in the center of the page. Also because you can see the art in the window of the newspaper boxes on the street. It's a prime spot.'

'Good.'

Bosch was excited by the play the story was going to get.

'If you guys screw me on this, I won't forget it,' McKenzie said quietly.

There was a threat in her tone, the tough reporter coming to the surface. Bosch held his hands wide, as if he had nothing to hide.

‘That’s not going to happen. You’ve got the exclusive. As soon as we wrap somebody up, I’m calling you and you only.’

‘Thank you. Now, just to go over the rules again, I can quote you by name in the story but you don’t want to be in any photos, right?’

‘Right. I may have to do some undercover work on this. I don’t want my face in the paper.’

‘Got it. What undercover?’

‘You never know. I just want to keep the option open. Besides, the commander is better for the photo. He’s lived with the case longer than I have.’

‘Well, I think I already have most of what I need from the clips and our call earlier but I still want to sit down with you two for a few minutes.’

‘Whatever you need.’

‘Done,’ Emmy said, a few minutes later. She started breaking down her equipment.

‘Call the photo desk,’ her sister said. ‘I think there’s been a change and you are staying with me.’

‘Oh,’ Emmy said, not seeming to mind.

‘Why don’t you make the call outside while we get going with the interview?’ McKenzie said. ‘I want to get back to writing this as soon as we can.’

The reporter and Bosch took seats at the table with Garcia while the photographer went out to check on her new assignment. McKenzie started by asking Garcia what stuck with him about the case for so long and what made him push it forward through the Open-Unsolved Unit. While Garcia gave a rambling response about the ones that haunt you, Bosch felt the waters of contempt rise in him. He knew what the reporter didn’t know, that Garcia had knowingly or unknowingly allowed the investigation to be shunted aside seventeen years earlier. The fact that it appeared Garcia did not know that his investigation had been tampered with somehow seemed like the lesser sin to Bosch. Still, if it didn’t show personal corruption or a giving way to pressure from the upper reaches of the department, at the very least it showed incompetence.

After a few more questions of Garcia the reporter turned her attention to Bosch and asked what was new in the case seventeen years later.

‘The main thing is we have the DNA of the shooter,’ he said. ‘Tissue and blood from the murder weapon was preserved by our Scientific Investigation Division. We are hoping that analysis of it will allow us either to match it to a suspect whose DNA is already in the Department of Justice data bank, or to use it in comparisons to eliminate or identify suspects. We are in the process of going back to everybody in the case. Anybody who looks like a suspect will have their DNA checked against what we’ve got. That is something Commander Garcia couldn’t do in ’eighty-eight. We’re hoping it will change things this time.’

Bosch further explained how the weapon extracted a DNA sample from the person who shot it. The reporter seemed very interested in the happenstance of this and took detailed notes.

Bosch was pleased. The gun and DNA story was what he wanted to get into the paper. He wanted Mackey to read the story and know that his DNA was in the pipeline. It was being analyzed and compared. He would know that a sample from him was already in the DOJ database. The hope was that this would make him panic. Maybe he would try to run, maybe he would make a mistake and make a call in which he discussed the crime. One mistake would be all it would take.

'How long before you get results from the DOJ?' McKenzie asked.

Bosch fidgeted. He was trying not to lie directly to the reporter.

'Uh, that's hard to say,' he answered. 'The DOJ prioritizes comparison requests and there is always a backup. We should have something any day now.'

Bosch was pleased with his response but then the reporter threw another grenade into his foxhole.

'What about race?' she said. 'I read all the clips and it seemed like nothing was ever brought up one way or the other about this girl being biracial. Do you think that played at all into the motivation of this murder?'

Bosch flicked a look at Garcia and hoped he would answer first.

'The case was fully explored in that regard in nineteen eighty-eight,' Garcia said. 'We found nothing to support the racial angle. That's probably why it wasn't in the clips.'

The reporter turned her focus to Bosch, wanting the present take on the question as well.

'We've thoroughly reviewed the murder book and there is nothing there that would support a racial motivation in the case,' Bosch said. 'We obviously are in the process of reworking the case, front to back, and we'll be looking for anything that might have played a part in the motivation behind the crime.'

He looked at her and braced himself for her not accepting his answer and pressing it further. He thought about floating the racial angle into the story. It might improve the chances of some kind of response from Mackey. But it might also tip Mackey to how close they were to him. He decided to leave his answer as is.

Instead of pursuing the question further, the reporter flipped her notebook closed.

'I think I have what I need for right now,' she said. 'I am going to go talk to Mrs. Verloren and then I have to hurry back and write this up to get it in tomorrow. Is there a number I can reach you at, Detective Bosch? Quickly, if I need to.'

Bosch knew she had him. He reluctantly gave her his cell number, knowing it meant that in the future she would have a direct line to him and would use it in regard to any case or story. It was the last payment on the deal they had made.

Everyone got up from the table and Bosch noticed that Emmy Ward had quietly come back into the office and had been sitting by the door during the interview. He and Garcia thanked them both for coming in and said good-bye. Bosch remained in the office with Garcia.

'I think that went well,' Garcia said after the door had closed.

'I hope so,' Bosch said. 'It cost me a cell phone number. I've had that number for three years. Now I'll have to change it and notify everybody about the new number. A big pain in the ass is what it's going to be.'

Garcia ignored the complaint.

'How sure are you that this guy Mackey will even see the story?'

'We're not. In fact, we believe he's dyslexic. He might not read at all.'

Garcia's jaw dropped.

'Then what are we doing?'

'Well, we have a plan for making sure he's aware of the story. Don't worry about that. We've got it covered. There's also another name that's come up since yesterday. An associate of Mackey then and now. His name is William Burkhart. Back when you were on the case he was known as Billy Blitzkrieg. That ring a bell?'

Garcia put on his best deep thinking look, like the one he had used for the camera, and moved around behind his desk. He then shook his head.

'Don't think it came up,' he said.

'Yeah, you probably would have remembered.'

Garcia remained standing but leaned over the desk to look at his schedule.

'Let's see. What have I got next?'

'You've got me, Commander,' Bosch said.

Garcia looked at him.

'Excuse me?'

'I need a few more minutes to clear up some of this stuff that's come up.'

'What stuff? You mean this new guy, Blitzkrieg?'

'Yes, and the stuff the reporter asked about and we lied about. The racial angle.'

Bosch watched Garcia's face set sternly into stone.

'I didn't lie to her and I didn't lie to you yesterday. We didn't find it. We didn't see a racial angle to this.'

'We?'

'My partner and I.'

'Are you sure about that?'

The phone on his desk buzzed. Garcia grabbed it up angrily and said, "No calls, no intrusions," into it before dropping it back into its cradle.

'Detective, I want to remind you whom you are talking to,' Garcia said evenly. 'Now what the fuck do you mean, "Are you sure?" What are you saying?'

'With all due respect to the rank, sir, the case was pushed away from the racial angle in 'eighty-eight. I believe you when you say you didn't see it. Otherwise, I can't see you calling Pratt down at Open-Unsolved and reminding him there was DNA in the case. But if you didn't know what was happening, then your partner certainly did. Did he ever talk about the pressure brought to bear on him from the command side on this case?'

'Ron Green was the finest detective I ever knew or worked with. I'm not going to let you besmirch his reputation.'

They stood just a few feet apart, the desk between them, their eyes locked in battle.

'I'm not interested in reputations. I'm interested in the truth. You said yesterday he ate his own gun a few years after this case. Why? Was there a note?'

'The burden, Detective. He couldn't carry it anymore. He was haunted by the ones who got away.'

'What about the ones he *let* get away?'

Garcia pointed an angry finger at Bosch.

'How fucking dare you? You are on thin ice here, Bosch. I could make one call to the sixth floor and you'd be out on the street before sundown. You understand me? I know about you. You're just back from retirement and that makes you expendable with one phone call. You understand me?'

'Sure. I understand you.'

Bosch sat down in one of the chairs in front of the desk, hoping it might defuse the tension in the room a little bit. Garcia hesitated and then he sat down as well.

'I find what you have just said to me completely insulting,' he said, his voice juiced with anger.

'I'm sorry, Commander. I was trying to see what you knew.'

'I don't understand.'

'I am sorry, sir, but the case was definitely stonewalled by chain of command. I don't want to get into names with you at this point. Some of them are still active. But I think this case revolved on race – the connection to Mackey and now Burkhart proves it. And you didn't have Mackey or Burkhart back then, but you had the gun and there were other things. I needed to find out if you were part of it. I would say by your reaction that you weren't.'

'But you are telling me my partner was, and that he kept it from me.'

Bosch nodded.

'Impossible,' Garcia protested. 'Ron and I were close.'

'All partners are close, Commander. But not that close. From what I understand, you took care of the book and Green pressed the case forward. If he encountered resistance from within the department, he might have chosen to keep it from you. I think he did. Maybe he was protecting you, maybe he was humiliated about being vulnerable to the push. '

Garcia dropped his eyes from Bosch and looked down at his desk. Bosch could tell he was looking at a memory. Something in the stone wall of his face broke and gave way.

'I think maybe I knew something was wrong,' he said quietly. 'About halfway through.'

'How so?'

'Early on we decided to split up the parents. Ron took the father and I took the mother. You know, to establish relationships. Ron was having trouble with the father. He was volatile. He had been passive and then all of a sudden he's on Ron's ass wanting results. But there was something more there and Ron kept it from me.'

'Did you ask about it?'

'Yeah. I asked. He just told me the father was a handful. He said he was paranoid about race, that he thought his daughter was killed because of the race thing. And then he said something that I still remember. He said, "We can't go there." That's all he said, but it stuck with me because that didn't sound like the Ron Green I knew. We can't go there. The Ron Green I knew would go wherever it led. There were no can't-go-theres with him. Not until that case.'

Garcia raised his eyes to Bosch and Bosch nodded, his way of thanking him for opening up.

'You think it had something to do with what happened later?' Bosch asked.

'You mean the suicide?'

'Yeah.'

'Maybe. I don't know. Anything's possible. After this case we sort of went in different directions. The thing about partners is that once the work stops, there isn't a whole lot to talk about.'

'True,' Bosch said.

'I was in a command staff meeting at Seventy-seventh – I was assigned there after making lieutenant. That was when I found out he was dead. It came across in a staff notice. I guess that shows how far apart we had gotten. I found out he had killed himself a week after he did it.'

Bosch just nodded. There was nothing he could say to that.

'I think I have a staff meeting now, Detective,' Garcia said. 'It's time for you to go.'

'Yes, sir. But you know, I was thinking, in order for them to push Ron Green so hard, they must have already had something to push him with. You remember anything like that? Did he have an IAD beef running at the time?'

Garcia shook his head. He wasn't saying no to Bosch's question. He was saying something else.

'You know, this department has always had more cops assigned to investigating cops than it has to investigating murders. I always thought that if I reached the top, I would change that.'

'Are you saying there was an investigation?'

'I'm saying it was rare in the department not to have something on your record. There was a file on Ron, sure. He had been accused of assaulting a suspect. It was bullshit. The kid bumped his head and needed stitches when Ron was putting him in the back of the car. Big deal, right? Turned out the kid had connections and the IAD wasn't letting it go away.'

'So they could have used that to push this case.'

'Could have, depending on how much a believer in conspiracy theories you are.'

When it comes to the LAPD I am a believer, Bosch thought but didn't say.

'Okay, sir, I think I have the picture,' he said instead. 'I'll get out of here now.'

Bosch stood up to leave.

'I understand your need to know all of this,' Garcia said. 'I just don't appreciate how you sandbagged me.'

'I'm sorry, sir.'

'No you're not, Detective Bosch. Not really.'

Bosch said nothing. He moved to the door and opened it. He looked back at Garcia and tried to think of something to say. He came up blank. He turned and left, closing the door behind him.

23

Kiz Rider was still sitting in the waiting area outside Judge Anne Demchak's chambers when Bosch got there. He had been caught in mid-afternoon traffic coming back to downtown from Van Nuys and thought he might have missed the conference with the judge. Rider was reading a magazine, but Bosch's first thought was that at this point in the case he would be unable to leisurely start flipping through a magazine. At this point his focus could not be split. He was all about one thing. In a strange way, he likened it to surfing, a pursuit he had not followed since the summer of 1964, when he ran away from a foster home and lived on the beach. Many years had passed since then but he still remembered the water tunnel. The goal was to tuck yourself into the tube, the place where water swirled completely around you, where there was nothing but the water and the ride. Bosch was in the tube now. There was nothing but the case.

'How long you been here?' he asked.

Rider checked her watch.

'About forty minutes.'

'Has she been in there with it the whole time?'

'Yup.'

'You worried?'

'No. I've gone to her before. Once on a Hollywood case after you left. She's just thorough. She reads every page. It takes a while but she's one of the good ones.'

'The story's running tomorrow. We need her to sign this today.'

'I know, Harry. Relax. Sit down.'

Bosch stayed standing. The judges rotated warrant duty. Getting Demchak was luck of the draw.

'I've never dealt with her before,' he said. 'Was she a DA?'

'No. Other side. Public defender.'

Bosch groaned. His experience had been that criminal defense attorneys who became judges always brought at least the shadow of their allegiance to the defendant with them to the bench.

'We're in trouble,' he said.

'No we're not. We'll be okay. Please sit down. You're making me nervous.'

'Is Judy Champagne still on the bench? Maybe we can take it in to her.'

Judy Champagne was a former prosecutor married to a former cop. They used to say he hooked them and she cooked them. Once she became a judge she was Bosch's favorite for taking warrants to. Not because she leaned toward the cops. She didn't. She was down-the-line fair, and that's what Bosch could count on.

'She's still a judge but we can't shop search warrants around the building. You know that, Harry. Now would you please sit down? I've got something to show you.'

Bosch sat down in a chair next to her.

'What?'

'I've got Burkhart's probation jacket.'

She pulled a file from her bag, opened it and slid it in front of Bosch on the coffee table. She tapped a fingernail on a line on a release form. Bosch leaned down to read it.

'Released from Wayside July first, nineteen eighty-eight. Reported to probation and parole in Van Nuys on July fifth.'

He straightened up and looked at her.

'So he's in play.'

'Absolutely. They took him in on the synagogue vandalism on January twenty-sixth. Never made bail and, with time served credits, got out of Wayside five months later. He's totally in play on this, Harry.'

Bosch felt a charge of excitement as things seemed to fall closer together.

'Okay, good. Did you amend the warrant to include him?'

'I put him in but not in too big a way. Mackey's still the direct link because of the gun.'

Bosch nodded and looked across the room at the empty desk where the judge's clerk would normally sit. The name plate on the desk said KATHY CHRZANOWSKI and Bosch wondered how the name would be pronounced and where she was. He then decided to try not to think about what was happening inside the judge's chambers.

'You want to hear the latest from Commander Garcia?' he asked.

Rider was putting the probation file back in her bag.

'Sure.'

Bosch spent the next ten minutes recounting his visit to Garcia's office, the newspaper interview, and the commander's revelations at the end.

'You think he told you everything?' she asked.

'You mean about how much he knew of what happened back then? No, but he told me as much as he was willing to.'

'I think he had to have been part of the deal. I can't see one partner making a deal the other one doesn't know about. Not a deal like that.'

'Then if he was in on it, why would he call up Pratt and tell him to send the DNA through the DOJ? Wouldn't he have just sat on it like he had been doing for seventeen years?'

'Not necessarily. A guilty conscience works in strange ways, Harry. Maybe this has been working on Garcia all these years and he decided to call Pratt to make himself feel better about it. Plus, say he was in on the deal back then with Irving. He might have felt safe to make that call once Irving was pushed to the side by the new chief.'

Bosch thought about Garcia's reaction to his saying Green might have been haunted by the ones he let get away. Maybe Garcia got heated because it was he who was haunted.

'I don't know,' Bosch said. 'Maybe—'

Bosch's cell phone chirped. As he pulled it out of his pocket, Rider said, 'You better turn that off before we go in. That's one thing Judge Demchak doesn't like going off in chambers. I heard about a DA whose phone she confiscated.'

Bosch nodded and opened his phone and said hello.

'Detective Bosch?'

'Yes.'

'It's Tara Wood. I thought we had an appointment.'

It struck Bosch before she finished the sentence that he had forgotten the meeting at CBS and the bowl of gumbo he was planning for lunch beforehand. He hadn't even had time for lunch.

'Tara, I am really sorry. Something came up and we had to sort of run with it. I should have called you but it slipped my mind. I'm going to need to reschedule the interview, if you will still talk to me after this.'

'Um, sure, no problem. I just had a couple of the writers from the show hanging around. They were going to try to talk to you.'

'What show?'

'*Cold Case*. Remember, I told you we have a—'

'Oh, right, the show. Well, I'm sorry about that.'

Now Bosch didn't feel so bad. She had been trying to use his interview appointment to work up a publicity angle of some kind. He wondered if there was any feeling left in her for Rebecca Verloren. As if knowing his thoughts, she asked about the case.

'Is something happening on the case? Is that why you weren't here?'

'Sort of. We're making progress but there is nothing I can tell you right – actually, there is something. Did you think at all about that name I mentioned last night? Roland Mackey? Ringing any bells?'

'No, still no.'

'I've got another one. What about William Burkhart? Maybe Bill Burkhart?'

There was a long silence while Wood did a memory scan.

'No, I'm sorry. I don't think I know him.'

'What about the name Billy Blitzkrieg?'

'Billy Blitzkrieg? You're kidding, right?'

'No, why, you recognize it?'

'No, not at all. It sounds like a heavy metal rock star or something.'

'No, he's not. But you're sure none of the names do anything for you?'

'I'm sorry, Detective.'

Bosch looked up and saw a woman beckoning to them from the open door of the chambers. Rider looked at him and drew a finger across her throat.

'Look, Tara, I need to go now. I will call you to set up the interview as soon as I can. I apologize again and I will call you soon. Thank you.'

He closed the phone before she could respond and then he turned it off. He followed Rider through the door being held open by a woman Bosch assumed was Kathy Chrzanowski.

The shades were drawn over the floor-to-ceiling windows at the far end of the room. A single desk lamp lit the chambers. Behind the desk Bosch saw a woman who appeared to be in her late sixties. She looked small behind the large dark wood desk. She had a kind face, which gave Bosch hope that they would get out of the office with her approval for the phone taps.

'Detectives, come in and sit down,' she said. 'I am sorry to have held you out there waiting.'

'No problem, Your Honor,' Rider said. 'We appreciate your taking a thorough look at this.'

Bosch and Rider sat in chairs in front of the desk. The judge was not wearing her black robe. Bosch noticed it hanging on a hat rack in the corner. Next to it on the wall was a framed photograph of Demchak with a notoriously liberal state supreme court justice. Bosch felt his stomach tighten. Then on the desk he saw two framed photographs. One was of an older man and a young boy holding golf clubs. Her husband and a grandson maybe. The other photo showed a young girl of maybe nine or ten riding on a swing. But the colors were fading. It was an old photo. Maybe it was her daughter. Bosch started to think that the connection to children might make the difference.

'You seem to be in quite a hurry with this,' the judge said. 'Is there a reason for that?'

Bosch looked at Rider and she leaned forward to answer. This was her show. He was just there as a backup and to send the message to the judge that this one was important. Cops had to be lobbyists on occasion.

'Yes, Your Honor, a couple reasons,' Rider began. 'The main one is that we believe there is a newspaper article that will be in the *Daily News* tomorrow. It may cause our primary suspect, Roland Mackey, to contact other suspects – one of whom is listed in the warrant – and talk about the murder. As you can see from the warrant, we believe more than one individual was involved in this crime but we have only directly linked Mackey to it. If we are up and running our taps when the newspaper story hits, we might be able to identify the others involved through his calls and conversations.'

The judge nodded but she wasn't looking at them. Her eyes were cast down on the application and authorization forms. She had a serious look on her face and Bosch began to get a bad feeling. After a few moments of silence, she said, 'And the other reason for your hurry?'

'Oh, yes,' Rider said, having apparently forgotten. 'The other reason is we believe Roland Mackey still may be engaged in criminal activities. We don't know exactly what they are at this time, but we believe that the quicker we can start listening in on his conversations the sooner we will ascertain that and be able to stop someone from becoming a victim. As you can see from the application, we know he has been involved in at least one murder before. We didn't think we should waste time.'

Bosch admired Rider's response. It was a carefully designed answer that would put a lot of pressure on the judge to sign the authorization. After all, she was an elected official. She had to consider the ramifications of her turning down the application. If Mackey committed a crime that could have been stopped had the police been listening to his phone calls, the judge could be held responsible by an electorate that wouldn't care much about whether she had been trying to safeguard Mackey's personal rights.

'I see,' Demchak said coldly in response to Rider. 'And what is your probable cause to believe he is engaged in current criminal activities since you cannot cite a specific crime.'

'A variety of things, Judge. Mr. Mackey cleared probation for a sex crime twelve months ago and immediately moved to a new address where his name is not listed on a deed or rental agreement. He left no forwarding address with his former landlord or the post office. He is living on the same property as an ex-convict with whom he has previously engaged in documented criminal activity. That is William Burkhart, also listed in the application. And, as you can see from the application, he is using a phone not registered in his name. He is clearly flying below radar, Your Honor. All of these things together paint a picture of someone taking precautions to hide involvement in criminal activity.'

'Or maybe he just wants to avoid government intrusion,' the judge said. 'It is still very thin, Detective. Do you have anything else? I could use something else.'

Rider glanced sideways at Bosch, her eyes wide. Her confidence in the waiting room was leaving her. Bosch knew she had put everything into the application and her comments in chambers. What was left? Bosch cleared his throat and leaned forward to speak for the first time.

'The previous criminal activity he took part in with the man he now lives with were hate crimes, Judge. These guys hurt and threatened a lot of people. A lot of people.'

He settled back in his seat, hoping he had just ratcheted the pressure up at least another notch.

‘And how long ago were these crimes?’ the judge asked.

‘They were prosecuted in the late eighties,’ Bosch said. ‘But who knows how long they have continued? The association of these two men has obviously continued.’

The judge said nothing for another minute as she seemed to be reading and rereading the summation section of Rider’s application. A small red light at the side of the desk went on. Bosch knew it meant that whatever was scheduled in her courtroom was ready to begin. All attorneys and parties were present.

Finally, Judge Demchak shook her head.

‘I just don’t think you have it here, Detectives. You have him with the gun but not at the murder scene. He could have handled the gun days or weeks before the killing.’

She waved dismissively at the papers spread in front of her.

‘This bit about him burglarizing a drive-in movie theater where the victim and her friends liked to go is tenuous at best. You really put me on the spot here by asking me to sign off on something that just isn’t there.’

‘It is there,’ Bosch said. ‘We know it is there.’

Rider put a hand on his arm, a warning not to lose it.

‘I’m not seeing it, Detective,’ Demchak said. ‘You are asking me to bail you out here. You don’t have enough probable cause and you are asking me to make up the difference. I can’t do it. Not as it is.’

‘Your Honor,’ Rider said. ‘If we don’t get this signed we will lose the opportunity with the newspaper story.’

The judge smiled at her.

‘That has nothing to do with me and what I must do here, Detective. You know that. I am not an arm of the police department. I am independent and I have to deal with the facts of the case as presented.’

‘The victim was biracial,’ Bosch said. ‘This guy is a documented hater. He stole that gun and it was used to kill a girl of mixed race. The connection is right there.’

‘Not a connection of evidence, Detective. A circumstantial connection of inference.’

Bosch stared at the judge for a moment and the judge stared right back.

‘Do you have children, Judge?’ he asked.

The color immediately rose in the judge’s cheeks.

‘What does that have to do with this?’

‘Your Honor,’ Rider broke in. ‘We’ll come back to you with this.’

‘No,’ Bosch said. ‘No, we’re not coming back. We need this now, Judge. This guy has been out there free for seventeen years. What if it had been your daughter? Could you look away then? Rebecca Verloren was an only child.’

Judge Demchak’s eyes grew darker. When she spoke it was with measures of both calm and anger.

'I am not looking away from anything, Detective. I happen to be the only one in this room that is looking closely at this. And I might add that if you continue to insult and question the court, then I will remand you to the lockup for contempt. I could have a bailiff in here in five seconds. Perhaps you could use the downtime to contemplate the deficiencies of your presentation.'

Bosch pressed on undaunted.

'Her mother still lives in the house,' Bosch said. 'The bedroom she was taken from is still the same as the day she was killed. Same bedspread, same pillows, same everything. The room – and the mother – are frozen in time.'

'But those facts are not germane to this.'

'Her father became a drunk. He lost his business, then his wife and home. I visited with him on Fifth Street this morning. That's where he lives now. I know that's not germane either, but I thought you might want to know. I guess we don't have enough facts for you but we have a lot of the ripples, Your Honor.'

The judge held his eyes and Bosch knew he was either about to go to jail or walk out with a signed warrant. No in-between. After a moment he saw the glimmer of pain in her eyes. Anybody who spends time in the trenches of the criminal justice system – either side – gets that look after a while.

'Very well, Detective,' she finally said.

She looked down and scribbled a signature at the bottom of the last page and started to fill in the spaces that dictated the length of the wiretaps.

'But I am still not convinced,' she said sternly. 'So I am giving you seventy-two hours.'

'Your Honor,' Bosch said.

But Rider put her hand on Bosch's arm again, trying to stop him from turning a yes into a no. Then she spoke.

'Your Honor, seventy-two hours is a very short time period for this. We were hoping that we would have at least a week.'

'You said the newspaper article is coming out tomorrow,' the judge responded.

'Yes, Judge, it is supposed to, but—'

'You will know something pretty quick then. If you feel you need to extend it then come back and see me on Friday and try to convince me. Seventy-two hours, and I want daily summaries delivered each morning. If I don't get them I am going to hold you both in contempt. I am not going to allow you to go fishing. If what is on the summaries is not on point then I will shut you down early. Is all of that clear?'

'Yes, Your Honor,' Bosch and Rider said in unison.

'Good. Now, I have a status conference in my courtroom. It is time for you to go and for me to go back to work.'

Rider collected the paperwork and they said their thanks. As they headed to the door, Judge Demchak called out to their backs.

'Detective Bosch?'

Bosch turned around and looked at her.

'Yes, Judge?'

'You saw the picture, didn't you?' she said. 'Of my daughter. You guessed I have only one child.'

Bosch looked at her for a moment and then nodded.

'I only have one myself,' he said. 'I know what it's like.'

She held his eyes for a moment before speaking.

'You can go now,' she said.

Bosch nodded and followed Rider through the door.

24

They didn't speak to each other as they left the courthouse. It was as if they wanted to get out of there without putting the jinx on it, as if their saying one word about what had happened might echo back through the building and make the judge change her mind and recall them. Now that they had the judge's signature on the authorization forms, all they cared about was getting out.

Once on the sidewalk in front of the monolithic courthouse Bosch looked at Rider and smiled.

'That was close,' he said.

She smiled and nodded her approval.

'Ripples, huh? You took it right up to the red line with her. I thought I was going to have to go downstairs and post a bond for you.'

They started walking toward Parker Center. Bosch pulled his phone out and turned it back on.

'Yeah, it was close,' he said. 'But we got it. You want to tell Abel to set up the meeting with the others?'

'Yeah, I'll tell him. I was just going to wait until we got over there.'

Bosch checked his phone and saw he had missed a call and had a message. He didn't recognize the number but it had an 818 area code – the Valley. He checked the message and heard a voice he didn't want to hear.

'Detective Bosch, it's McKenzie Ward at the *News*. I need to talk to you about Roland Mackey as soon as possible. I need to hear from you or I may have to hold the story. Call me.'

'Shit,' Bosch said as he deleted the message.

'What?' Rider asked.

'It's the reporter. I told Muriel Verloren not to mention Mackey to her. But it sounds like she let it slip. Either that or the reporter is talking to somebody else.'

'Shit.'

'That's what I said.'

They walked a little further without speaking. Bosch was thinking of a way to deal with the reporter. They had to keep Mackey out of the story or else he'd probably just cut and run without bothering to call anyone else.

'What are you going to do?' Rider finally asked.

'I don't know. Try to talk her out of it. Lie to her if I have to. She can't put his name in the story.'

'But she has to run the story, Harry. We only have seventy-two hours.'

'I know. Let me think.'

He opened his phone and called Muriel Verloren. She answered and he asked her how the interview went. She said it was fine and she was glad it was over.

'Did they take photos?'

'Yes, they wanted pictures of the bedroom. I didn't feel good, opening it up like that to them. But I did.'

'I understand. Thank you for doing that. Just remember, the story is going to help us. We're getting close, Muriel, and the newspaper story will push things. We appreciate your doing it.'

'If it helps, then I am glad to do it.'

'Good. Let me ask you something else. Did you mention the name Roland Mackey to the reporter?'

'No, you told me not to. So I didn't.'

'Are you sure?'

'I'm more than sure. She asked me what you people were telling me but I didn't say anything about him. Why?'

'No reason. I just wanted to make sure, that's all. Thank you, Muriel. I'll call you as soon as I have some news.'

He closed the phone. He didn't think Muriel Verloren would lie to him. The reporter had to have another source.

'What?' Rider asked.

'She didn't tell her.'

'Then who did?'

'Good question.'

The phone started to vibrate and chirp while he was still holding it. He looked at the screen and recognized the number.

'It's her – the reporter. I have to take this.'

He answered the call.

'Detective Bosch, it's McKenzie Ward. I'm on deadline and we need to talk.'

'Right. I just got your message. My phone was off because I was in court.'

'Why didn't you tell me about Roland Mackey?'

'What are you talking about?'

'Roland Mackey. I was told you already have a suspect named Roland Mackey.'

'Who told you that?'

'That doesn't matter. What matters is that you withheld a key piece of information from me. Is Roland Mackey your prime suspect? Let me guess. You are playing both sides and giving that to the *Times*.'

Bosch had to think quickly. The reporter was sounding pressed and upset. A reporter who goes off angry could be a problem. He had to calm the situation and at the same time take Mackey out of the mix. The one thing he had going for him was that she had not mentioned a DNA link between Mackey and the gun. This made Bosch think that her source of information was outside the department. Someone with limited information.

'First of all, I'm not talking to the *Times* on this. As long as it runs tomorrow, you are the only one with this story. Secondly, it does matter where you got that name from because your information is wrong. I am trying to help you here, McKenzie. You would be making a big mistake if you put that name in the article. You might even get sued.'

'Then who is he?'

'Who is your source?'

'You know I can't give you that.'

'Why not?'

Bosch was stalling for time while he thought it out. While the reporter rattled off a standard response about shield laws and protecting sources, Bosch was ticking off the names of people outside the department whom he and Rider had talked to about Mackey. They included Rebecca Verloren's three friends – Tara Wood, Bailey Sable and Grace Tanaka. There was also Robert Verloren, Danny Kotchof, Thelma Kibble, the parole agent, and Gordon Stoddard, the school principal, as well as Mrs. Atkins, the secretary who looked for Mackey's name in the school's rolls.

There was also Judge Demchak but Bosch dismissed that as a long shot. Ward's message had been left on his line while he and Rider were with the judge. The idea that the judge would have picked up the phone and called the reporter while she had been alone in chambers studying the search warrant application seemed out of the question. She hadn't even known of the pending newspaper story let alone the reporter assigned to it.

Bosch guessed that because of time constraints, the reporter had simply gone back to the office and made a few phone calls to round out the story. She had gotten the name Roland Mackey from someone she had called. Bosch doubted that she could have located or even contacted Robert Verloren in the few hours since the interview. He also scratched Grace Tanaka and Danny Kotchof because they weren't local. Without Mackey's name, there was no link to Kibble. That left Tara Wood and the school – either Stoddard, Sable or the secretary. The most obvious answer was the school because it would have been the easiest link for the reporter to make. He now felt better and thought he could contain the threat.

'Detective, are you still there?'

'Yes, sorry, I'm trying to dodge some traffic here.'

'Then what is your answer? Who is Roland Mackey?'

'He's nobody. He's a loose end. Or was, actually. We've tied that up now.'

'Explain that.'

'Look, we inherited this case, right? Well, over the years the murder book got shelved, reshelved, moved around a bit. Things got mixed up. So part of what we had to do was some basic housekeeping. We had to put things in order. We found a picture of this Roland Mackey guy loose in the book and we weren't sure who he was and what his connection was. When we were out doing interviews, getting acquainted with the players in the case, we showed his picture to a few people to see if they knew who he was and where he fit. At no time, McKenzie, did we tell anyone he was a prime suspect. That is the truth. So either you are exaggerating or whoever mentioned this guy to you was exaggerating.'

There was a silence and Bosch guessed she was revisiting the interview that gave her the name Mackey.

'Then who is he?' she finally asked.

'Just some guy with a juvie record who was living in Chatsworth back then. He hung out at the old drive-in on Winnetka, and that was apparently a hangout for Rebecca and her friends as well. But it turns out that back in 1988 he was cleared of any involvement. We didn't find out until after we showed the photo to a few people.'

It was a mixture of truth and shadings of the truth. Again the reporter was silent while she considered his answer.

'Who told you about him, Gordon Stoddard or Bailey Sable?' Bosch asked. 'We took the photo to the school to see if he fit in there, and it turns out he didn't even go to school there. We dropped it after that.'

'You sure about this?'

'Look, do what you want but if you put that guy's name in the paper simply because we asked about him, you could be getting calls from him and his lawyer. We ask about a lot of people, McKenzie. That's our job.'

More silence slipped by. Bosch thought the silence meant he had successfully defused the bomb.

'We went over to the school to look at the yearbook and copy photos,' Ward finally said. 'We found out you took the only one they had in the library from 'eighty-eight.'

It was her way of confirming that Bosch had it right, but without giving up her source.

'Sorry about that,' he said. 'I have the yearbook on my desk. I don't know what kind of time you have but you can send somebody over to pick it up if you want.'

'No, there's no time. We took a picture of the plaque that's on the wall at the school. That will work. Besides, I found a shot of the vic in our archives. We'll use that.'

'I saw the plaque. It's nice.'

'They're very proud of it.'

'So we're all right on this, McKenzie?'

'Yes, we're fine. I just got a little excited there when I thought you were holding back something big.'

'Don't have anything big to report. Yet.'

'All right, then I better get back to finishing the story.'

'It's still running in the window tomorrow?'

'If I get it finished. Call me tomorrow and tell me what you think.'

'I will.'

Bosch closed the phone and looked at Rider.

'I think we're okay,' he said.

'Boy, Harry, you've really got it going today. The artful dodger. I think you could probably talk a zebra out of his white stripes if you had to.'

Bosch smiled. He then looked up at the City Hall Annex on Spring Street. Banished from Parker Center, Irvin Irving now operated from the Annex. Bosch wondered if Mr. Clean was looking down on them right now from behind one of the mirrored windows of the Office of Strategic Planning. He thought of something.

'Kiz?'

'What?'

'Do you know McClellan?'

'No, not really.'

'But you know what he looks like?'

'Sure. I saw him at command staff meetings. Irving stopped going once he was moved out to the Annex. He sent McClellan most of the time as his representative.'

'So you could pick him out, then?'

'Sure. But what are you talking about, Harry?'

'Maybe we should go talk to him, maybe spook him and send a message back down the pipe to Irving.'

'You mean right now?'

'Why not? We're here.'

He gestured toward the Annex building.

'We don't have the time, Harry. Besides, why pick a fight you can avoid? Let's not deal with Irving until we have to.'

'All right, Kiz. But we will have to deal with him. I know we will.'

They didn't speak again, each focused on thoughts on the case, until they reached the Glass House and went inside.

25

Abel Pratt convened all members of the Open-Unsolved Unit in the squad room as well as four other RHD detectives loaned to the unit for the surveillance. The meeting was turned over to Bosch and Rider, who took a verbal walk through the case that lasted a half hour. On a bulletin board behind them they pinned blowups of the most recent driver's license photos of Roland Mackey and William Burkhart. The other detectives asked few questions. Bosch and Rider then turned the show back over to Pratt.

'All right, we're going to need all hands on deck with this,' he said. 'We'll be working the sixes. Two pairs working the sound room, two pairs working Mackey and two pairs working Burkhart. I want the OU teams on Mackey and the surveillance room. The four loaners from RHD will watch Burkhart. Kiz and Harry have dibs and they want the second shift on Mackey. The rest of you can work out how you want to cover the remaining shifts. We start tomorrow morning at six, just about the time the paper will be hitting the streets.'

The plan translated into six pairs of detectives working twelve-hour shifts. The shifts changed at 6 a.m. and 6 p.m. Since it was their case, Bosch and Rider got first choice of shifts and had elected to cover Mackey beginning each day at 6 p.m. This meant working through the night, but it was Bosch's hunch that if Mackey made a move or a call it would occur in the evening. And Bosch wanted to be there when it happened.

They would alternate with one of the other teams. The remaining two OU teams would alternate their time in the City of Industry, where a private contractor called Listen-Tech had what amounted to a wiretap center which was used by all law enforcement agencies in Los Angeles County. Sitting in a van next to the telephone pole carrying the line you were listening to was a thing of the past. ListenTech provided a quiet, air-conditioned center where electronic consoles were set up for monitoring and recording conversations placed or received on any phone numbers in the county, including cell phones. There was even a cafeteria with fresh coffee and vending machines. Pizza could be delivered if needed.

ListenTech could service as many as ninety taps at a time. Rider had told Bosch that the company was spawned in 2001 when law enforcement agencies began taking increasing advantage of the widening laws governing wire-taps. A private company that saw the growing need stepped in with regional wiretap centers, also known as sound rooms. They made the work easier. But there were still rules to follow.

'We're going to hit a bit of a snag in the sound room,' Pratt said. 'The law still requires that each line be monitored by a single individual – no listening to two lines at once. But we need to monitor three lines with two cops because that's all we got. So how do we do this and still stay within the law? We alternate. One line is Roland Mackey's cell. We monitor that full-time. But the other two lines are secondary. That's where we alternate. They come from the property where he lives and the place where he works. So what we do is we stay with the first line when he is home and then from four to midnight, when he is at work, we switch to the work line. No matter what lines we are actually listening to, we will still get twenty-four-hour pen registers on all three.'

'Can't we get one more loaner from RHD to cover the third line?' Rider asked.

Pratt shook his head.

'Captain Norona gave us four bodies and that's it,' Pratt said. 'We won't miss much. Like I said, we have the pen registers.'

Pen registers were part of the telephone monitoring process. While the investigators were allowed to listen in on phone calls on the monitored lines, the equipment also registered all incoming and outgoing calls on all the lines listed in the warrant, even if they were not being monitored. This would provide the investigators with a listing by time and length of call, as well as the numbers dialed on outgoing calls and the originating numbers for incoming calls.

'Any questions?' Pratt asked.

Bosch didn't think there would be any questions. The plan was simple enough. But then an OU detective named Renner raised his hand and Pratt nodded at him.

'Is this thing OT authorized?'

'Yes, it is,' Pratt replied. 'But as was said before, as of now we only have seventy-two hours on the warrant.'

'Well, let's hope it goes the whole seventy-two,' Renner said. 'I gotta pay for my kid's summer camp in Malibu.'

The others laughed.

Tim Marcia and Rick Jackson volunteered to be the other street team working with Bosch and Rider. The other four got the sound-room detail, with Renner and Robleto taking the day shift and Robinson and Nord taking the same shift as Bosch and Rider. The ListenTech center was nice and comfortable, but some cops didn't want to be cooped up no matter what the circumstances. Some would always choose the street and, like Marcia and Jackson, Bosch knew he was one of them.

Pratt ended the meeting by handing out copies of a piece of paper with everyone's cell phone number on it as well as the radio channel they would use during the surveillance.

'For you teams in the field, I've got rovers on hold down in the equipment shed,' Pratt said. 'Make sure you have the radio on. Harry, Kiz, did I miss anything?'

'I think you got it covered,' Rider said.

'Since our time is short on this one,' Bosch said, 'Kiz and I are working something up to sort of push the action if we don't see any signs by tomorrow night. We have the newspaper article and we have to make sure he sees it.'

'How's he going to read it if he's dyslexic?' Renner asked.

'He got a GED,' Bosch said. 'He should be able to read it. We just have to make sure it somehow gets in front of him.'

Everybody nodded their agreement and then Pratt wrapped things up.

'Okay, gang, that's it,' Pratt said. 'I will be checking with everybody through the days and nights. Stay loose and be careful with these guys. We don't want anything turning back on us. You people taking the first shift might want to head home now and get a good night. Just remember, the clock's ticking on the warrant. We have till Friday night and then it's pumpkins. So let's get out there and get what's to be got. We're the closers. So let's close this one out.'

Bosch and Rider stood and small-talked about the case with the others for a few minutes and then Bosch made his way back to their alcove. He pulled the copy of the probation file out of the stack of accumulated case files. He had not gotten a chance to read through it thoroughly and now was the time.

The file was an add-on file, meaning that as Mackey repeatedly was arrested and continued a lifelong trek through the criminal justice system the reports and court transcripts were merely added to the front of the file. Therefore the reports ran in reverse chronological order. Bosch was most interested in Mackey's earlier years. He went to the back of the file with the idea of moving forward in time.

Mackey's first arrest as an adult came only a month after he turned eighteen. In August 1987 he was picked up for car theft in what the follow-up reports classified as a joyriding incident. Mackey had been living at home at the time and stole a neighbor's Corvette. He had jumped in the car and taken off after the neighbor had left it running in the driveway and gone back inside his house for a forgotten pair of sunglasses.

Mackey pleaded guilty and the presentencing report contained in the file cited his juvenile record but made no mention of the Chatsworth Eights. In September 1987 the young car thief was placed on one year probation by a superior court judge, who tried to talk Mackey out of a life of crime.

The transcript of the sentencing hearing was in the file. Bosch read the judge's two-page lecture, in which he told Mackey he had seen young men like him a hundred times before. He told Mackey he was standing at the same precipice as the others. One simple crime could be a life lesson, or it could be the first step down a spiral. He urged Mackey not to go down the wrong path. He told him to think hard and make the right decision on which way to go.

The words of warning had obviously fallen on deaf ears. Six weeks later Mackey was arrested for burglarizing a neighborhood home while the husband and wife who lived there were at work. Mackey had cut an alarm, but the break in current had registered with the alarm company and a patrol car was dispatched. When Mackey came out the back door carrying a video camera and assorted other electronics and jewelry, two officers were waiting with guns drawn.

Because Mackey had been on probation for the car theft he was held in the county jail while awaiting disposition of the case. After thirty-six days in stir he stood before the same judge again and, according to the transcript, begged forgiveness and for one more chance. This time the presentencing report noted that drug testing indicated that Mackey was a marijuana user and that he had begun hanging around an unsavory group of young men from the Chatsworth area.

Bosch knew that these men were likely the Chatsworth Eights. It was early December and their plan of terror and symbolic homage to Adolf Hitler was just a few weeks away. But none of this was in the PSR. The report simply stated that Mackey was hanging with the wrong crowd. As he sentenced Mackey, the judge would not have known how wrong that crowd was.

Mackey was sentenced to three years of prison reduced to time served. He was also placed on two years probation. The judge, knowing that prison would be just a finishing school for a young criminal like Mackey, was giving him a break and attempting to break him at the same time. Mackey walked out of court free, but the judge had placed a series of heavy restrictions on his probation. They included weekly drug tests, maintaining gainful employment and a requirement that the high school dropout get his general education degree within nine months. The judge told Mackey that if he failed in any part of the probation order he would be sent to a state prison to complete his three-year sentence.

'You may consider this harsh, Mr. Mackey,' the judge said in the transcript. 'But I consider it quite kind. I am giving you a last chance here. If you fail me on this, you will without a doubt be going to prison. Society will be through with trying to help you at that point. It will simply throw you away. Do you understand this?'

'Yes, Your Honor,' Mackey said.

The file came with copies of the court-requested completion reports from

Chatsworth High. Mackey got his GED in August 1988, a little more than a month after Rebecca Verloren was taken from her bed and murdered.

Despite the judge's admirable efforts to steer Mackey from a life of crime, Bosch had to wonder if those efforts had cost Rebecca Verloren her life. Whether Mackey was the actual triggerman or not, he'd had possession of the gun that killed her. Was it reasonable to think that the chain of events leading to the murder would have been broken if Mackey had been behind bars? Bosch wasn't sure. It was possible that Mackey simply filled a role as weapon delivery man. If it wasn't him it could have been someone else. Bosch knew there was no sense in breaking down the chain into what could or could not have happened.

'Anything?'

Bosch looked up from his thoughts. Rider was standing at her desk. He flipped the file closed.

'Nah, not really. I was reading the probation file. The early stuff. A judge took an interest at first but then sort of let him go. The best he could do was make him get the GED.'

'And that served him so well, didn't it?'

'Yeah.'

Bosch said nothing else. He only had a GED himself. He'd also stood before a judge once as a car thief. The car he had gone joyriding in had also been a Corvette. Except it had not been a neighbor's. It had been his foster father's. Bosch had taken it as a way to say fuck you. But it was the foster father who sent the ultimate fuck you. Bosch was sent back to the youth hall to fend for himself.

'My mother died when I was eleven,' Bosch suddenly said.

Rider looked at him, doing her eyebrow thing.

'I know. Why'd you bring that up?'

'I don't know. I spent a lot of time in the youth hall after that. I mean, I had some stays with foster families but it never lasted long. I always went back.'

Rider waited but Bosch didn't continue.

'And?' she prompted.

'Well, we didn't have gangs in the hall,' he said. 'But there was sort of a natural segregation. You know, the whites stuck together. The blacks. The Hispanics. There weren't any Asians back then.'

'What are you saying, that you feel sorry for this asshole Mackey?'

'No.'

'He killed a girl or at least helped kill her, Harry.'

'I know that, Kiz. That's not my point.'

'What is your point?'

'I don't know. I'm just sort of wondering, you know, what makes people go down different paths. How come this guy became a hater? How come I didn't?'

'Harry, you're overthinking. Go home tonight and get a good night's sleep. You'll need it because there won't be any tomorrow night.'

Bosch nodded but didn't move.

'You going to take off?' Rider asked.

'Yeah, in a few. You heading out?'

'Yeah, unless you want me to go with you over to Hollywood Vice.'

'Nah, I'll be all right. Let's talk in the morning after we get the paper.'

'Yeah, I'm not sure where I can get the *Daily News* in the south end. I might have to call you up and let you read it to me.'

The *Daily News* was circulated widely in the Valley but sometimes hard to locate elsewhere in the city. Rider lived down near Inglewood, in the same neighborhood where she had grown up.

'That's cool. Give me a call and I'll have it. There's a box down at the bottom of the hill from my place.'

Rider opened one of her desk drawers and pulled out her purse. She looked at Bosch and did her eyebrow thing once again.

'You sure about doing this, marking yourself like that?'

She was talking about their plan for pushing Mackey the next day. Bosch nodded.

'I have to be able to sell it,' he said. 'Besides, I can wear long sleeves for a while. It isn't summer yet.'

'But what if it's not necessary? What if he sees the story in the paper and gets on the phone and starts talking a blue streak?'

'Something tells me that isn't going to happen. Anyway, it isn't permanent. Vicki Landreth told me it lasts a couple weeks at the most, depending on how often you shower. It's not like those henna tattoos kids get on the Santa Monica pier. They last longer.'

She nodded her agreement.

'Okay, Harry. I'll catch you in the a.m., then.'

'See ya, Kiz. Have a good one.'

She started walking out of the alcove.

'Hey, Kiz?' Bosch called after her.

'What?' she said, stopping and looking back at him.

'What do you think? You happy to be back on it?'

She knew what he was talking about. Being back in homicide.

'Oh yeah, Harry, I'm happy. I'll be downright giddy once we take this pale rider down and solve the mystery.'

'Yeah,' Bosch said.

After she left, Bosch thought for a few moments about what she meant by calling Mackey a pale rider. He thought it might be some sort of biblical reference but he couldn't place it. Maybe in the south end it was what some people called racists. He decided to ask her about it the next day. He started to look through the probation file again but soon gave up. He knew it was time to focus on the here and now. Not the past. Not the choices made and the paths not taken. He got up and stacked the file and the murder book under his arm. If things were slow on the surveillance the next day, they might make for good reading. He stuck his head in Abel Pratt's office to say good-bye.

'Good luck, Harry,' Pratt said. 'Close it out.'

'We're going to.'

26

Bosch parked in the rear lot and walked in through the back doors of Hollywood Division. It had been a long time since he had been in the place and he immediately found it different. The earthquake renovation that Edgar had spoken of had seemingly touched every space in the building. He found the watch office in the place where a holding tank had been located. He found a report writing room for patrol officers, whereas before they'd had to steal space in the detective bureau.

Before going upstairs to the vice unit he had to go by the detective bureau to see if he could pull a file. He went down the rear hallway, passing a patrol sergeant named McDonald whose first name he couldn't remember.

'Hey, Harry, you back? Long time no see, man.'

'I'm back, Six.'

'Good deal.'

Six was the radio designation for Hollywood Division. Calling the patrol sergeant Six was like calling a homicide detective Roy. It worked and it got Bosch past his awkward memory loss. By the time he got to the end of the hallway he remembered that the sergeant's name was Bob.

The homicide unit was at the back end of the vast detective squad room. Edgar had been right. It didn't look like any detective bureau Bosch had ever seen. It was gray and sterile. It looked like a warehouse where yaks made cold calls and ripped off businesses and old ladies for overpriced pens or time-share units. He recognized the top of Edgar's head just cresting above one of the sound partitions between the cubicles. It looked like he was the only one left in the whole bureau. It was late in the day but not that late.

He walked over and looked over the partition and down on Edgar. He had his head down and was working on the *Times* crossword puzzle. It had always been a ritual with Edgar. He'd work the puzzle throughout each day, taking it with him to the restroom and to lunch and out on surveillances. He never liked to go home without finishing it.

Edgar hadn't noticed Bosch's presence. Bosch quietly stepped back and ducked into the cubicle next to Edgar's. He carefully lifted the steel trash can out of the desk's foot well and duck-walked out of the cubicle to a position right behind Edgar. He stood up and let the trash can fall to the new gray linoleum from about four feet. The resulting sound was loud and sharp, almost like a shot. Edgar leaped out of his seat, his crossword pencil flying toward the ceiling. He was about to yell something when he saw it was Bosch.

'Goddamn it, Bosch!'

'How you doin', Jerry?' Bosch said, barely getting it out while laughing.

'Goddamn it, Bosch!'

'Yeah, you said that. I take it things are pretty slow in Hollywood tonight.'

'What the fuck you doing here? I mean, besides scaring the shit out of me.'

'I'm working, man. I've got an appointment with the vice artist upstairs. What are you doing?'

'I'm finishing up. I was about to get out of here.'

Bosch leaned forward and saw that the grid of the crossword was almost entirely filled out with words. There were several erasure marks. Edgar never worked a crossword in ink. Bosch noticed his old red dictionary was off the shelf and on the desk.

'Cheating again, Jerry? You know you aren't supposed to be using the dictionary like that.'

Edgar dropped back into his seat. He looked exasperated by the scare and now the questions.

'Bullshit. I can do whatever I want. There aren't any rules, Harry. Why don't you get on upstairs and leave me alone? Have her put some eyeliner on you and put you out on the stroll.'

'Yeah, you wish. You'd be my first customer.'

'All right, all right. Is there something you need here or did you just drop by to bust my chops?'

Edgar finally smiled and Bosch knew everything was all right between them.

'A little of both,' Bosch said. 'I need to pull an old file. Where do they keep them now in this palace?'

'How old is it? They started shipping stuff downtown to be microfilmed.'

'Would've been in two thousand. You remember Michael Allen Smith?'

Edgar nodded.

'Of course I do. Someone like me isn't going to forget Smith. What do you want with him?'

'I just want his picture. That file still here?'

'Yeah, anything that fresh is still around. Follow me.'

He led Bosch to a locked door. Edgar had a key and soon they were in a small room lined with shelves crowded with blue binders. Edgar located the

Michael Allen Smith murder book and pulled it off a shelf. He dropped it into Bosch's hands. It was heavy. It had been a tough case.

Bosch took the murder book to the cubicle next to Edgar's and started flipping through it until he came to a section of photographs that showed Smith's upper torso and several close-ups of his tattoos. His markings had been used to identify and charge him with the murders of three prostitutes five years earlier. Bosch, Edgar and Rider had worked the case. Smith was an avowed white supremacist who secretly hired black transvestite prostitutes he picked up on Santa Monica Boulevard. Then out of guilt for crossing both racial and sexual lines, he would kill them. It somehow made him feel better about his transgressions. The key break in the case came when Rider found a prostitute who had seen one of the victims get into a van with a customer. He was able to describe a distinctive tattoo on the john's hand. That eventually led them to Smith, who had collected a variety of tattoos while in various prisons around the country. He was tried, convicted and sent to death row, where he was still dodging the needle with a barrage of legal appeals.

Bosch removed the photos that showed Smith's neck, hands and upper left arm, all of which were festooned with prison ink.

'I need these while I'm upstairs. If you're leaving and need to lock the file room I can just leave these on your desk.'

Edgar nodded.

'That'll be fine. So what are you getting into, man? You're going to put that shit on yourself?'

'That's right. I want to be like Mike.'

Edgar narrowed his eyes.

'This connected to that Chatsworth Eights stuff we were talking about yesterday?'

Bosch smiled.

'You know, Jerry, you ought to be a detective. You're good at it.'

Edgar nodded like he was merely putting up with another sarcastic assault.

'You going to get the haircut, too?' he asked.

'Nah, I wasn't planning on going that far,' Bosch said. 'I'm going to be sort of a reformed skinhead, I think.'

'I get it.'

'So, listen, are you busy tonight? This shouldn't take too long up there. If you want to wait and finish your puzzle, we could go grab a steak over at Musso's.'

Just saying it made Bosch hungry for it. That and a vodka martini.

'Nah, Harry, I gotta go over the hill to the Sportsmen's Lodge for Sheree Riley's retirement gig. That's why I was killing time here. I was just waiting out the traffic.'

Sheree Riley was a sex crimes investigator. Bosch had worked with her on occasion but they had never been close. When sex and murder entwined, the cases were usually so brutal and difficult there wasn't much room for anything but the work. Bosch didn't know she was retiring.

'Maybe we can get that steak some other time,' Edgar said. 'That cool?'

'Everything's cool, Jerry. Have a good time up there and tell her I said hello and good luck. And thanks for the pictures. They'll be on your desk.'

Bosch headed back toward the hallway but heard Edgar curse. He turned around and saw his old partner standing and looking into his cubicle with his arms wide.

'Where'd my damn pencil go?'

Bosch scanned the floor and didn't see it. Eventually his eyes rose and he saw the pencil stuck into the sound-absorption tiles in the ceiling above Edgar's head.

'Jerry, sometimes what goes up doesn't come down.'

Edgar looked up and saw his pencil. It took him two jumps to grab it.

The door to the vice unit on the second floor was locked but this was not unusual. Bosch knocked and it was quickly answered by an undercover officer Bosch didn't recognize.

'Is Vicki here? She's expecting me.'

'Then come on in.'

The officer stepped back and let Bosch enter. He saw that this room had not been changed dramatically during the retrofitting. It was a long room with work counters running down both sides. Above each vice officer's space was a framed movie poster. In Hollywood Division, only posters from movies actually filmed in the division were allowed to grace the walls. He found Vicki Landreth at a workspace under a poster from *Blue Neon Night,* a film Bosch had not seen. She and the other officer were the only ones in the office. Bosch guessed everybody else was already out on the streets for the night shift.

'Hey, Bosch,' Landreth said.

'Hey, Vic. You still have time to do this?'

'For you, honey, I will always make time.'

Landreth was a former Hollywood makeup artist. One day twenty years earlier she was talked into taking a ride-along with one of the off-duty officers working security on the set. The guy was just trying to make time with her, hoping maybe she'd catch a thrill on the ride-along and it would lead to something else. What it led to was Landreth's enrollment in the police academy and her becoming a reserve officer, working two shifts a month on patrol, filling in where needed. Then someone in vice found out about her daytime job and asked her to work her two shifts in vice, where she could be used to make undercover officers look more like prostitutes and pimps and drug users and street people. Soon Vicki found the cop work more interesting than the movie work. She quit the industry and became a full-time cop. Her makeup skills were highly coveted and her niche in Hollywood Division was secure.

Bosch showed her the photos of Michael Allen Smith's tattoos and she studied them for a few moments.

'Nice guy, huh?' she finally said.

'One of the best.'

'And you want all of this done tonight?'

'No. I was thinking about the lightning bolts on the neck. And maybe the bicep, if you could do it.'

'It's all jailhouse. No real art to it. One color. I can do it. Sit down over here and take off your shirt.'

She led him to a makeup station, where he sat on a stool next to a rack of various body paints and powders. On an upper shelf there were mannequin heads with wigs and beards on them. Below these someone had taped the names of various supervisors in the division.

Bosch took off his shirt and tie. He was wearing a T-shirt underneath.

'I want these to be seen but I don't want to be too obvious about it,' he said. 'I was thinking that you could work it so if I had on a T-shirt like this you would sort of see parts of the tats sticking out. Enough to know what they are and what they mean.'

'Not a problem. Hold still.'

She used a piece of chalk to mark the lines on his skin where the shirt's sleeve and neck reached.

'These will be the visibility lines,' she explained. 'You just tell me how much you want to go above and below them.'

'Got it.'

'Now take it all off, Harry.'

She said it with undisguised sensuality in her voice. Bosch pulled his shirt over his head and tossed it over a chair with his other shirt and the tie. He turned back to her and Landreth was studying his chest and shoulders. She reached over and touched the scar on his left shoulder.

'That's new,' she said.

'That's old.'

'Well, it has been a long time since I saw you naked, Harry.'

'Yeah, I guess so.'

'Back when you were a boy in blue and could talk me into anything, even joining the cops.'

'I talked you into my car, not the department. Blame yourself for that.'

Bosch felt embarrassed and felt his skin blush. Their liaison twenty years earlier had flickered out for no reason other than that neither was looking for any sort of commitment to or from anybody. They went their separate ways but always remained easy friends, especially when Bosch was transferred to the Hollywood Division homicide squad and they were working out of the same building.

'Look at you blushing,' Landreth said. 'After all these years.'

'Well, you know . . . '

He said nothing further. Landreth rolled her stool closer to Bosch. She reached up and rubbed her thumb over the tunnel rat tattoo at the top of his right arm.

'I do remember this one,' she said. 'It's not holding up so well, is it?'

She was right. That tattoo he had gotten in Vietnam had lost its lines over time and the colors had blurred. The character of the rat with a gun emerging from a tunnel was not recognizable. That tattoo looked like a painful bruise.

'I'm not holding up so well myself, Vicki,' Bosch said.

She ignored his complaint and got down to work. She first used an eye-liner pencil to sketch out the tattoos on his body. Michael Allen Smith had what he had called a Gestapo collar tattooed on his neck. On each side of his neck was the twin lightning bolt insignia of the SS. This symbolized the emblems attached to the collar points of the uniforms worn by Hitler's elite force. Landreth etched these onto Bosch's skin easily and quickly. It tickled and he had a hard time holding still. Then it was time for the bicep piece.

'Which arm?' she asked.

'I think the left.'

He was thinking of the play with Mackey. He thought the chances were better that he would end up sitting on Mackey's right as opposed to his left. That meant his left arm would be in Mackey's line of sight.

Landreth asked him to hold the photo of Smith's arm up next to his own so she could copy it. Tattooed on Smith's bicep was a skull with a swastika inside a circle on the crown. While Smith had never admitted to the murders he was charged with, he had always been quite open about his racist beliefs and the origins of his many body markings. The bicep skull, he said, had been copied from a World War II propaganda poster.

Shifting the sketch work from his neck to his arm allowed Bosch to breathe easier and Landreth to engage him in conversation.

'So what's new with you?' she asked.

'Not a lot.'

'Retirement was boring?'

'You could say that.'

'What did you do with yourself, Harry?'

'I worked a couple old cases, but mostly I spent time in Las Vegas trying to get to know my daughter.'

She leaned back away from her work and looked up at Bosch with surprise in her eyes.

'Yeah, I was surprised too when I found out,' he said.

'How old?'

'Almost six.'

'You still going to be able to see her now that you're on the job?'

'Doesn't matter, she's not there.'

'Well, where is she?'

'Her mother took her to Hong Kong for a year.'

'Hong Kong? What's in Hong Kong?'

'A job. She signed a year contract.'

'She didn't consult you about it?'

'I don't know if "consulted" is the right word. She told me she was going. I talked to a lawyer about it and there wasn't much I could do.'

'That's not fair, Harry.'

'I'm all right. I talk to her once a week. As soon as I earn up some vacation I'll go over there.'

'I'm not talking about it being unfair to you. I'm talking about her. A girl should be close to her father.'

Bosch nodded because that was all he could do. A few minutes later Landreth finished the sketch work, opened a case and took out a jar of Hollywood tattoo ink along with a penlike applicator.

'This is Bic blue,' she said. 'It's what most of them use in the jails. I won't be perforating the skin so it should come off in a couple weeks.'

'Should?'

'Most times. There was one actor I worked with, though. I put an ace of spades on his arm. And the funny thing was that it wouldn't come off. Not all the way. So he just ended up having a real tattoo put over my piece. He wasn't too happy about it.'

'Just like I'm not going to be happy if I have lightning bolts on my neck for the rest of my life. Before you start putting that stuff on me, Vicki, is there—'

He stopped when he realized she was laughing at him.

'Just kidding, Bosch. It's Hollywood magic. It comes off with a couple of good scrubs, okay?'

'Okay, then.'

'Then hold still and let's get this done.'

She went to work applying the dark blue ink to the pencil drawing on his skin. She blotted it regularly with a cloth and repeatedly told him to stop breathing, which he told her he couldn't do. She was finished in under a half hour. She gave him a hand mirror and he studied his neck. It looked good in that it looked real to him. It also looked strange to see such displays of hate on his own skin.

'Can I put my shirt on now?'

'Give it a few more minutes.'

She touched the scar on his shoulder once again.

'Is that from when you got shot in that tunnel downtown?'

'Yes.'

'Poor Harry.'

'More like Lucky Harry.'

She started packing up her equipment while he sat there with his shirt off and feeling awkward about it.

'So what's the assignment tonight?' he asked, just to be saying something.

'For me? Nothing. I'm out of here.'

'You're done?'

'Yeah, we worked a day shift today. Working girls invading the hotel by the Kodak Center. Can't have that in the new Hollywood, can we? So we bagged four of them.'

'I'm sorry, Vicki. I didn't know I was holding you up. I would've come in sooner. Hell, I was downstairs shooting the shit with Edgar before coming up. You should've told me you'd be waiting on me.'

'It's all right. It was good to see you. And I wanted to tell you I'm glad you're back on the job.'

Bosch suddenly thought of something.

'Hey, you want to hit Musso's for dinner or are you going up to the Sportsmen's Lodge?'

'Forget the Sportsmen's Lodge. Those things remind me too much of wrap parties. I didn't like them either.'

'Then what do you think?'

'I don't know if I want to be seen in that place with such an obvious racist pig.'

This time Bosch knew she was kidding. He smiled and she smiled and she said dinner was a go.

'I'll go on one condition,' she said.

'What's that?'

'You put your shirt back on.'

27

Without need of an alarm, Bosch awoke at five-thirty the next morning. This was not unusual for him. He knew that this was what happened when you surfed into the tube on a case. Waking hours overpowered the sleeping hours. You did all you could to stay up on that board and in the pipeline. Though not scheduled to begin work for more than twelve hours, he knew this would be the pivotal day in the case. He could not sleep anymore.

In darkness and unfamiliar surroundings he got dressed and made his way to the kitchen, where he found a pad for writing down needed grocery items. He wrote a note and left it in front of the automatic coffeemaker, which he had watched Vicki Landreth set the night before to begin brewing at 7 a.m. The note said very little other than thank you for the evening and good-bye. There were no promises or see-you-laters. Bosch knew she would not be expecting any. They both knew that little had changed in the twenty years between their liaisons. They liked each other fine but that wasn't enough to build a house on.

The streets between Vicki Landreth's Los Feliz home and the Cahuenga Pass were misted and gray. People drove with their lights on, either because they had been driving through the night or because they thought it might help wake up the world. Bosch knew the dawn had nothing on the dusk. Dawn always came up ugly, as if the sun was clumsy and in a hurry. The dusk was smoother, the moon more graceful. Maybe it was because the moon was more patient. In life and nature, Bosch thought, darkness always waits.

He tried to push thoughts of the night before out of his mind so that he could focus only on the case. He knew the others would be moving into position now on Mariano Street in Woodland Hills and in the ListenTech sound room in the City of Industry. While Roland Mackey slept, the forces of justice were quietly closing in on him. That's how Bosch looked at it. That was what put the wire in his blood. He still believed it was unlikely that Mackey had been the one to pull the trigger on Rebecca Verloren. But Bosch felt no doubt that Mackey provided the gun and would lead them on this day to the triggerman, whether it would be William Burkhart or someone else.

Bosch pulled into the parking lot in front of the Poquito Mas at the bottom of the hill from his house. He left the Mercedes running and got out and went to the row of newspaper boxes. He saw the face of Rebecca Verloren staring out at him through the smeared plastic window of the box. He felt a little catch in his rhythm. It didn't matter what the story said, they were now in play.

He dropped the coins into the box and took a paper out. He repeated the process, taking a second paper. One for the files and one for Mackey. He didn't bother reading the story until he had driven up the hill to his house. He put a pot of coffee on and read the story while standing in the kitchen. The window photo was a shot of Muriel Verloren sitting on her daughter's bed. The room was neat and the bed perfectly made, right down to the ruffle skirting the floor. There was an inset photograph of Rebecca in the top corner. It turned out that the *Daily News* archives had held the same shot as the yearbook. A headline above the photo said a mother's long vigil.

The bedroom photograph was credited to Emerson Ward, the photographer apparently using her given name. Below it was a caption that read: 'Muriel Verloren sits in her daughter's bedroom. The room, like Mrs. Verloren's grief, has been untouched by time.'

Beneath the photo and above the body of the story was what a reporter had once told Bosch was a deck headline – a fuller description of the story. It read: 'HAUNTED: Muriel Verloren has waited 17 years to learn who took her daughter's life. In a renewed effort the LAPD may be close to finding out.'

Bosch thought the deck was perfect. If and when Mackey saw it, he would feel the cold finger of fear poke him in the chest. Bosch anxiously read the story.

By McKenzie Ward, Staff Writer

Seventeen years ago this summer, a young and beautiful high-school girl named Rebecca Verloren was stolen away from her Chatsworth home and brutally murdered on Oat Mountain. The case was never solved, leaving in its wake a splintered family, haunted police officers and a community with no sense of closure from the crime.

But in a measure of hope for the victim's mother, the Los Angeles Police Department has launched a new investigation of the case that may see results and closure for Muriel Verloren. This time out the detectives have something they didn't in 1988: the killer's DNA.

The LAPD's Open-Unsolved Unit began the intense refocus on the Verloren case after one of the original detectives – now a Valley area commander – urged that it be reopened two years ago when the squad was formed to investigate cold cases.

'As soon as I heard we were going to start looking at cold cases I was on the phone to them,' Cmdr. Arturo Garcia said yesterday from his office in the Valley Bureau command center. 'This was the case that always stuck with me. That beautiful young girl taken from her home like that. No murder in our society is acceptable, but this one hurt more than most. It haunted me all these years.'

So, too, Muriel Verloren. Rebecca's mother has continued to live in the house on Red Mesa Way from which her 16-year-old daughter was taken. Rebecca's bedroom remains unaltered from the night she was carried out a back door, never to return.

'I don't want to change anything,' the tearful mother said yesterday while smoothing the spread on her daughter's bed. 'It's my way of remaining close to her. I will never change this room and I will never leave this house.'

Det. Harry Bosch, who is assigned to the renewed investigation, told the News that there are several promising leads in the case now. The greatest aid in the case has been the technological advances made since 1988. Blood that did not belong to Rebecca Verloren was actually found inside the murder weapon. Bosch explained that the pistol's hammer 'bit' the shooter on the hand, taking a sample of blood and tissue. In 1988 it could only be analyzed, typed and preserved. Now it can be directly matched to a suspect. The challenge is finding that suspect.

'The case was thoroughly investigated previously,' Bosch said. 'Hundreds of people were questioned and hundreds of leads were followed. We are backtracking on all of that but our real hope lies in the DNA. It will be the case breaker, I think.'

The detective explained that while the victim was not sexually assaulted, there were elements to the crime of a psychosexual nature. Ten years ago the state Department of Justice started a database containing DNA samples from every person convicted of a sexually related crime. The DNA from the Verloren case is in the process of being compared to those samples. Bosch believes it is likely that Rebecca Verloren's killing was not an isolated crime.

'I think it is unlikely that this killer only committed this one crime and then led a law-abiding existence. The nature of this offense indicates to us that this person likely committed other crimes. If he was ever caught and his DNA put into a data bank, then it's only a matter of time before we identify him.'

Rebecca was carried from her home in the dead of night on July 5, 1988. For three days police and community members searched for her. A woman riding a horse on Oat Mountain found the body secreted by a fallen tree. While the investigation revealed many things, including that Rebecca had terminated a pregnancy about six weeks before her death, the police were unable to determine who her killer was and how he got into the house.

In the years since, the crime has echoed through many lives. The victim's parents have split up and Muriel Verloren could not say where her husband, Robert Verloren, a former Malibu restaurateur, is now located. She said the disintegration of their marriage was directly attributed to the strain and grief brought on by their daughter's murder.

One of the original investigators on the case, Ronald Green, retired early from the department and later committed suicide. Garcia said he believes the unsolved Verloren case played a part in his former partner's decision to end his life.

'Ronnie took things to heart, and I think this one always bothered him,' Garcia said.

And at Hillside Preparatory School, where Rebecca Verloren was a popular student, there is a daily reminder of her life and death. A plaque erected by her classmates remains affixed to the wall in the exclusive school's main hallway.

'We don't ever want to forget someone like Rebecca,' said Principal Gordon Stoddard, who was a teacher when Verloren was a student at the school.

One of Rebecca's friends and classmates is now a teacher at Hillside. Bailey Koster Sable spent an evening with Rebecca just two days before she was murdered. The loss has haunted her, and she says she thinks about her friend all the time.

'I think about it because it feels like it could have happened to anybody,' Sable said after classes yesterday. 'So it leads me to always ask the same thing: why her?'

That is a question the Los Angeles police hope to finally answer soon.

Bosch looked at the photo on the inside page where the story jumped to. It showed Bailey Sable and Gordon Stoddard standing on either side of the plaque on the wall at Hillside Prep. Emerson Ward was credited with this photo as well. The caption read: 'FRIEND AND TEACHER: Bailey Sable went to school with Rebecca Verloren, and Gordon Stoddard taught her science class. Now school principal, Stoddard said, "Becky was a good kid. This shouldn't have happened."'

Bosch poured coffee into a mug and then read the story again while sipping his breakfast. He then excitedly grabbed the phone off the counter and called Kizmin Rider's home number. She answered with a blurry voice.

'Kiz, the story is perfect. She put in everything we wanted.'

'Harry? What time is it, Harry?'

'Almost seven. We're in business.'

'Harry, we have to work all night. What are you doing awake? What are you doing calling me at seven o'clock?'

Bosch realized his mistake.

'I'm sorry. I'm just excited about it.'

'Call me back in two hours.'

She hung up. There had not been a pleasant tone in her voice.

Undaunted, Bosch pulled a folded sheet of paper from his jacket pocket. It was the sheet of numbers Pratt had passed out during the staff meeting. He called Tim Marcia's cell number.

'It's Bosch,' he said. 'You guys in position?'

'Yeah, we're here.'

'Anything shaking?'

'It's a sleepy hollow right now. We figure if this guy worked till midnight last night, then he's going to be sleeping late.'

'His car is there? The Camaro?'

'Yes, Harry, it's here.'

'Okay. Did you read the story in the paper?'

'Not yet. But we've got two teams sitting on this house for Mackey and Burkhart. We're about to break off to get coffee and pick up the paper.'

'It's good. It's going to work.'

'Let's hope so.'

After Bosch hung up he realized that until Mackey or Burkhart left the house on Mariano there would be double surveillance on the place. It was a waste of time and money but he didn't see any way around it. There was no telling when one of the surveillance subjects might take off from the house. They knew very little about Burkhart. They didn't even know if he had a job.

He next called Renner in the sound room at Listen-Tech. He was the oldest detective on the squad and had used seniority to get him and his partner the day shift in the sound room.

'Anything yet?' Bosch asked him.

'Not yet, but you'll be the first to know.'

Bosch thanked him and hung up. He checked his watch. It wasn't even seven-thirty and he knew it was going to be a long day waiting for his surveillance shift to begin. He refilled his coffee mug and looked at the paper again. The photo of the dead girl's bedroom bothered him in a way he could not pinpoint. There was something there but he could not pull it out. He closed his eyes for a five count and then brought them open, hoping the trick would jar something loose. But the photo did not reveal the secret. A sense of frustration started to rise in him but then the phone rang.

It was Rider.

'Great, now I can't go back to sleep. You better be bright-eyed tonight, Harry, because I won't be.'

'Sorry, Kiz. I will.'

'Read me the story.'

He did, and when he was finished she seemed to have caught some of his excitement. They both knew that the story would play perfectly into provoking a response from Mackey. The key would be to make sure that he saw it and read it, and they thought they had that covered.

'Okay, Harry, I'm going to get going. I have some things to do today.'

'All right, Kiz, see you up there. How 'bout we meet at quarter to six on Tampa about a block south of the service station?'

'I'll be there unless something happens before.'

'Yeah, me too.'

After hanging up, Bosch went into his bedroom and changed into fresh clothes that would be comfortable during an all-night surveillance and useful as well for the play he intended for Mackey. He chose a white T-shirt that had been washed many times and had shrunk so that its sleeves were tight and short on his biceps. Before putting on a shirt over it he checked his look in the mirror. A full half of the skull was exposed and the SS bolts pointed up above the cotton on his neck.

The tattoos looked more authentic than they had the night before. He had taken a shower at Vicki Landreth's and she told him that the water would slightly blur the ink on his skin as was the case with most prison-applied tattoos. She warned him that the ink would start to wash away after two or three showers and, if needed, she could maintain his look with further applications. He told her he wasn't planning on needing the tattoos more than one day. They would work or not work when he made his play.

He put on a long-sleeved button-down shirt over the T-shirt. He checked this in the mirror and thought he could see details of the skull tattoo showing through the cotton. The thick black swastika on the crown was coming through.

Ready to go but with hours before he was needed, Bosch paced nervously around his living room for a few moments, wondering what to do. He decided to call his daughter, hoping that her sweet voice and cheerfulness would give him an added charge for the day.

He got the number for the Intercontinental Hotel in Kowloon off the Post-it on his refrigerator and punched it into his phone. It would be almost 8 p.m. there. His daughter should still be awake. But when his call was connected to Eleanor Wish's room there was no answer. He wondered if he had the time change wrong. Maybe he was calling too early or too late.

After six rings an answering service picked up, giving Bosch instructions in English and Cantonese in how to leave a message. He left a short message for both Eleanor and his daughter and hung up the phone.

Now not wanting to dwell on his daughter or thoughts about where she was, Bosch opened the murder book and began reviewing its contents again, always looking for details of the case he had possibly missed. Despite everything he had learned about the case and how it was pushed off track by the powers that be, he still believed in the book. He believed the answers to the mysteries were always found in the details.

He finished a read-through and was going to take up the copy of Mackey's probation file when he thought of something and called Muriel Verloren. She was at home.

'Did you see the story in the paper?' he asked.

'Yes, it makes me feel so sad to see that.'

'Why is that?'

'Because it makes it all real to me. I had pushed it away.'

'I'm sorry but it is going to help us. I promise. I'm glad you did it. Thank you.'

'Whatever will help I want to do.'

'Thank you, Muriel. Listen, I wanted to tell you that I located your husband. I spoke to him yesterday morning.'

There was a long silence before she spoke.

'Really? Where is he?'

'Down on Fifth Street. He runs a soup kitchen for the homeless. He serves breakfast to them. It's called the Metro Shelter. I thought you might want to know.'

Again a silence. Bosch guessed she wanted to ask him questions and he was willing to wait.

'You mean he works there?'

'Yes. He's sober now. He said it's been three years. I guess he first went there for a meal and he's sort of worked his way up. He runs the kitchen now. And it's good food. I ate there yesterday.'

'I see.'

'Um, I have a number that he gave me. It's not a direct line. He doesn't have a phone in his room. But it's in the kitchen and he's there in the mornings. He said it slows down after about nine.'

'Okay.'

'Do you want the number, Muriel?'

This question was followed by the longest silence of all. Bosch finally answered the question himself.

'I'll tell you what, Muriel. I've got the number, and if you ever want it you can just call me. Is that okay?'

'That would be fine, Detective. Thank you.'

'No problem. I'm going to go now. We're hoping something breaks on the case today.'

'Please call me.'

'It will be the first call I make.'

After hanging up, Bosch realized that talking about breakfast had made him hungry. It was now almost noon and he hadn't eaten anything since the steak at Musso's the night before. He decided that he would go into the bedroom and rest for a while and then have a late lunch before reporting for the surveillance. He would go over to Dupar's in Studio City. It was on the way out to Northridge. Pancakes were the perfect surveillance food.

He would order a full stack of buttered pancakes and they would sit in his stomach like clay and keep him full all night if necessary.

In the bedroom he lay on his back and shut his eyes. He tried to think of the case but his mind wandered to the drunken time he got the tattoo put on his arm in a dirty studio in Saigon. As he drifted off to sleep he remembered the man with the needle and his smile and his body odor. He remembered the man had said, 'Are you sure? Remember, you'll be marked forever with this.'

Bosch had smiled back and said, 'I already am.'

Then in his dream the man's smiling face turned into Vicki Landreth's face. She had red lipstick smeared across her mouth. She held up a buzzing tattoo needle.

She said, 'Are you ready, Michael?'

He said, 'I'm not Michael.'

She said, 'It's all right. It doesn't matter who you are. Everybody's dodging the needle. But nobody gets away.'

28

Kiz Rider was already at the meeting spot when Bosch got there. He got out of his car and brought the murder book and the other files to her car, a nondescript white Taurus.

'You have any room in your trunk?' he asked before getting in.

'It's empty. Why?'

'Pop it. I forgot to leave my spare tire at home.'

He went back to his car, a Mercedes-Benz SUV, and took the spare tire out of the back and transferred it to Rider's trunk. Using a screwdriver from the tool kit he removed the license plates from his car and put them in the trunk as well. He then got in with her and they drove up Tampa to the plaza shopping center across from the service station where Mackey worked. The day team, Marcia and Jackson, were waiting in their car in the lot.

The space next to them was open and Rider pulled in. Everybody put down their windows so they could talk and transfer the two rovers without having to get out of their cars. Bosch took the radios but knew he and Rider wouldn't use them.

'Well?' Bosch asked.

'Well, nothing,' Jackson said. 'Seems like we're pumping a dry hole here, Harry.'

'Nothing at all?' Rider asked.

'There has been absolutely no indication at all that he's seen the paper or that anybody he knows has seen it. We checked with the sound room twenty minutes ago and this guy hasn't even gotten a phone call, let alone one about this. He hasn't even had a tow call since he came on.'

Bosch nodded. He wasn't concerned yet. Sometimes things needed a little push and that was what he was ready to do.

'I hope you've got a good plan, Harry,' Marcia called over. He was in the driver's side of their car and Bosch was furthest away on the passenger side of Rider's car.

'You want to stick around?' Bosch replied. 'No use waiting on it if there hasn't been any action. I'm ready to go.'

Jackson nodded.

'I don't mind,' he said. 'You going to need backup?'

'I doubt it. I'm just going to plant a seed. But you never know. It couldn't hurt.'

'All right. We'll watch anyway. Just in case, what's your flare going to be?'

Bosch hadn't thought about how he would send up a flare if things went wrong and he had to call in backup.

'I guess I'll hit the horn,' he said. 'Or you'll hear the shots.'

He smiled and everybody nodded and then Rider backed out of the space and they headed back down Tampa to his car. 'You sure about this?' Rider asked as she pulled in next to the Mercedes.

'I'm sure.'

He had noticed on the way over that she had brought an accordion file with her. It was on the armrest between the seats.

'What's this?'

'Since you woke me up early I decided to go to work. I traced down the other five members of the Chatsworth Eights.'

'Great work. Any of them still local?'

'Two of them are still around. But it looks like they have grown out of their so-called youthful indiscretions. No records. They've got pretty decent jobs.'

'What about the others?'

'The only one that still seems like he's a believer in the cause is a guy named Frank Simmons. Moved down here from Oregon when he was in high school. A couple years later he joins the Eights. He now lives in Fresno. But he did a two-year bit in Obispo for selling machine guns.'

'I might be able to use that. When was he there?'

'Hold on a second.'

She opened her file and dug through it until she came up with a slim manila folder with the name Frank Simmons on it. She opened it and showed Bosch a prison mug shot of Simmons.

'Six years ago,' she said. 'He got out six years ago.'

Bosch studied the photo, committing the details of Simmons's look to memory. He had dark short hair and dark eyes. His skin was very pale and his face was tracked with acne scars. He tried to cover these with a goatee that would also make him look tougher.

'Where was the case, here?' he asked.

'No, actually, it was from Fresno. He apparently moved up there after the troubles down here.'

'Who was he selling the machine guns to?'

'I called the FBI office up there, talked to the agent. He didn't want to cooperate with me until he checked me out. I'm still waiting for the call-back.'

'Great.'

'I got the feeling that Mr. Simmons is still of active interest to the bureau up there and the agent wasn't into sharing.'

Bosch nodded.

'Where was Simmons living at the time of the Verloren thing?'

'Can't tell. He was one of the younger ones, so he was probably living with his parents. AutoTrack doesn't trace him back further than 'ninety. By then he was in Fresno.'

'So unless his parents moved out after this thing, he was probably right there in the Valley.'

'It's possible.'

'Okay, this is good, Kiz. I might be able to use some of this. Follow me over to the top of Balboa Park by Woodley. I think that's a good spot. There's a golf course there with a parking lot. There will be a lot of cars. You guys will be able to park there and it will be good cover. Okay?'

'Okay.'

'Tell the other guys.'

He took out his badge wallet, his cuffs and his service pistol and put them all down on the floor of the car.

'Harry, you got a backup?'

'I've got you, right?'

'I mean it.'

'Yes, Kiz, I've got a little popper on my ankle. I'll be all right.'

He got out and got into his own car. On the drive over to the park he rehearsed the play in his mind. He got ready and got excited.

Ten minutes later he pulled over onto the shoulder of the park road, killed the engine and got out. He went to the right front side of the car and let the air out of the tire through the valve. Because he knew some tow trucks come equipped with compressed air, he opened his pocket knife and slashed open the stem of the tire's valve. The tire would have to be repaired, not refilled.

Ready to go, he opened his cell phone and called the service station where Mackey worked. He said he needed a tow and was put on hold. A whole minute went by before another voice came on the line. Roland Mackey.

'What do you need?'

'I need a tow. I got a flat and the valve looks like it's fucked up.'

'What kind of car is it?'

'Black Mercedes SUV.'

'What about the spare?'

'It got stolen by some ni – it was stolen when I was in South-Central last week.'

'That's too bad. Shouldn't go down there.'

'I had no choice. Can you tow me or not?'

'Okay, okay. Where are you?'

Bosch told him. It was close enough that this time Mackey didn't try to talk him into calling someone else.

'All right, ten minutes,' Mackey said. 'Be there with your car when I get there.'

'I've got nowhere else to go.'

Bosch closed the phone and opened the back of the SUV. He pulled his outer shirt out of his pants and then took it off. He put it in the back. His new tattoos were now partially displayed. He sat down on the tailgate and waited. Two minutes later his cell phone chirped. It was Rider.

'Harry, they were able to pipe the call over to me from ListenTech. You sounded legit.'

'Good.'

'I just talked to the guys. Mackey's moving. They're with him.'

'Okay, I'm ready.'

'I kind of wish now we had gotten you a body wire. You never know what this guy is going to say to you.'

'Too risky in just a T-shirt. Besides, the chances of the guy telling a stranger he was the one who killed the girl in the newspaper story are probably longer than me winning the lotto without buying a ticket.'

'I guess.'

'I gotta go, Kiz.'

'Good luck, Harry. Be careful.'

'All the time.'

He closed the phone.

29

The tow truck slowed as it approached the Mercedes. Bosch looked up from the rear hatch, where he was sitting below the shade of the overhead door and reading the Daily News. He waved the paper at the tow truck driver and stood up. The truck drove by and then onto the shoulder in front of the Mercedes. It then backed up to within five feet of it. Its driver got out. It was Roland Mackey.

Mackey was wearing leather gloves that were grease-stained dark in the palms. Rather than acknowledge Bosch, he walked around the front of the Mercedes and looked down at the flattened tire. As Bosch came around, still holding the paper, Mackey squatted down and looked at the tire's valve. He reached out and bent it back and forth, exposing the slice that had been cut into it.

'Almost looks like it was cut,' Mackey said.

'Maybe glass in the road or something,' Bosch offered.

'And no spare. Ain't that a bitch?'

He looked up at Bosch, squinting in the light from the sun that was beginning to go down behind Bosch.

'You're telling me,' Bosch replied.

'Well, I can tow it in and then have my guy put a new valve on the tire. Take about fifteen minutes once we get it into the garage.'

'Fine. Do it.'

'This going to be on Triple A or insurance?'

'No, cash.'

Mackey told him it would be eighty-five dollars for the tow plus three dollars for every mile his car was towed. The charge for the valve replacement would be another twenty-five plus the cost of the valve.

'Fine, do it,' Bosch said again.

Mackey stood up and looked at Bosch. He appeared to glance directly at Bosch's neck and then away. He said nothing about the tattoos.

'You should close the back,' he said instead. 'Unless you want to dump everything out on the way.'

He smiled. A little tow truck humor.

'I'll grab my shirt out of there and close it,' Bosch said. 'All right if I ride with you?'

'Unless you want to call a cab and ride in style.'

'I'd rather ride with somebody who speaks English.'

Mackey laughed loudly while Bosch went to the back of his car. Bosch then stood off to the side while Mackey went through the procedures for hooking the vehicle to the truck. It took him no more than ten minutes before he was standing at the side of his truck, holding down a lever that raised the front end of the SUV into the air. After it was high enough for Mackey, he checked all the chains and harnesses and said he was ready to go.

When Bosch got into the tow truck he had his shirt over his arm and the folded newspaper in his hand. It was folded so the photo of Rebecca Verloren was noticeable.

'Does this thing have air-conditioning?' Bosch said as he pulled the door closed. 'I was sweating my ass off out there.'

'You and me both. You should've stayed in the vehicle with your own AC blowing while you waited. This piece of shit doesn't have air in the summer or heat in the winter. Kind of like my ex-wife.'

More tow truck humor, Bosch guessed. Mackey handed him a clipboard with an information page and a pen attached.

'Fill that out,' he said. 'Then we're set.'

'Okay.'

Bosch started to fill the form in with the false name and address he had come up with earlier. Mackey pulled a microphone off the dashboard and spoke into it.

'Hey, Kenny?'

A few moments later there was a response.

'Go ahead.'

'Tell Spider not to leave yet,' Mackey said. 'I'm bringing in a tire that needs a valve.'

'He's not going to like that. He's already washed up.'

'Just tell him. Out.'

Mackey returned the microphone to its dash holder.

'Think he'll stay?' Bosch asked.

'You better hope so. Or you're going to be waiting till tomorrow for your tire to get done.'

'I can't do that. I have to get back on the road.'

'Yeah? Where to?'

'Barstow.'

Mackey started the tow truck and turned his body to the left so he could look out the side window and make sure it was okay to pull off the shoulder onto the road. He could not see Bosch from this position. Bosch quickly hiked the left sleeve on his T-shirt up so that more than half of the skull tattoo was visible.

The tow truck pulled into the street and they started off. Bosch glanced out his window and saw the cars belonging to both Rider and the other surveillance team in the parking lot of the golf course. Bosch put his elbow on the sill of the open window and his hand on the top frame. Out of Mackey's view, he was able to give the thumbs-up sign to the watchers.

'What's out in Barstow?' Mackey asked.

'Home, that's all. I want to get home tonight.'

'What have you been doing down here?'

'This and that.'

'What about South-Central? What were you doing down there with those people last week?'

Bosch understood the reference to *those people* as meaning the predominant minority population of South L.A. He turned and looked pointedly at Mackey, as if telling him he was asking too many questions.

'This and that,' he said evenly.

'That's cool,' Mackey responded, taking his hands off the wheel in a backing off gesture.

'Tell you what, though, it doesn't matter what I was doing, you can just fucking keep this city, man.'

Mackey smiled.

'I know what you mean,' he said.

Bosch thought they were close to sharing more than small talk. He believed Mackey had gotten a glimpse of the tattoos and was trying to draw from Bosch a signal as to what kind of person he was. He thought the moment was right for another subtle move toward the newspaper article.

Bosch put the newspaper down on the seat between them, making sure the photo of Rebecca Verloren was still noticeable. He then started putting his shirt back on. He leaned forward and extended his arms to do it. He didn't look at Mackey but knew the skull on his left arm would be very noticeable as he did this. He put his right arm into the shirt first and then brought the shirt behind his back and put his left arm into its sleeve. He leaned back and started buttoning the shirt.

'Just a little too third world around here for me,' Bosch said.

'I'm with you on that.'

'Yeah? Is this where you're from?'

'My whole life.'

'Well, pal, you ought to take your family – if you have a family – and the flag with you and leave. Just fucking leave this place.'

Mackey laughed and nodded.

'I got a friend says the same thing. All the time.'

'Yeah, well, it's not an original idea.'

'Got that right.'

Then the radio interrupted the momentum of the conversation.

'Hey, Ro?'

Mackey grabbed the mike.

'Yeah, Ken?'

'I'm gonna run over to KFC while Spider's waiting on you. You want something?'

'Nah, I'll go out later. Out.'

He hung the mike up. They drove in silence for a few moments while Bosch tried to think of a way to naturally get the conversation going again and in the right direction. Mackey had driven down to Burbank Boulevard and gone right. They were coming up on Tampa. He would turn right again and then it would be a straight shot to the station. In less than ten minutes the ride would be over.

But it was Mackey who got it going again.

'So where'd you do your time?' he suddenly asked.

Bosch waited a moment so that his excitement wouldn't show.

'What are you talking about?' he asked.

'I saw your markings, man. It's no big deal. But they're either homemade or prison-made. That's obvious.'

Bosch nodded.

'Obispo. I spent a nickel up there.'

'Yeah? For what?'

Bosch turned and looked at him again.

'This and that.'

Mackey nodded, apparently not put off by his passenger's reluctance to open up.

'That's cool, man. I have a friend that was there for a while. Late nineties. He said it wasn't so bad. It's kind of a white-collar place. Not as many niggers there as other places, at least.'

Bosch was silent for a long moment. He knew Mackey's use of the racial slur was like a password. If Bosch responded in the proper way, then he would be accepted. It was code work.

'Yeah,' Bosch said, nodding his head. 'That made the conditions a little more livable. I probably missed your friend, though. I got out in early 'ninety-eight.'

'Frank Simmons. That's his name. He was only there for like eighteen months or something. He was from Fresno.'

'Frank Simmons from Fresno,' Bosch said as if trying to recall the name. 'I don't think I knew him.'

'He's good people.'

Bosch nodded.

'There was one guy who came in like a few weeks before I walked out of that place,' he said. 'I heard he was from Fresno. But, man, I was on short time and I wasn't into meeting new people, you know what I mean?'

'Yeah, that's cool. I was just wondering, you know.'

'Did your guy have dark hair and his face had a lot a scars like from zits and stuff?'

Mackey started smiling and nodding.

'That's him! That's Frank. We used to call him Crater Face from Crater Lake.'

'And I'm sure he was happy about that.'

The tow truck turned onto Tampa and headed north. Bosch knew he might have more time with Mackey in the service station while the tire was being fixed but he couldn't count on it. There could be another tow call or myriad other distractions. He had to finish the play and plant the seed now, while he was alone with the target. He picked up the newspaper and held it in his lap, glancing down as if he was reading the headlines. He had to figure out a way to naturally steer the conversation directly toward the Verloren article.

Mackey took his right hand off the wheel and pulled off his glove by biting one of the fingers. It reminded Bosch of the way a child would do it. Mackey then extended his hand to Bosch.

'I'm Ro, by the way.'

Bosch shook his hand.

'Ro?'

'Short for Roland. Roland Mackey. Pleased to meet you.'

'George Reichert,' Bosch said, giving the name he had made up after careful thought earlier in the day.

'Reichert?' Mackey said. 'German, right?'

'Means "heart of the Reich."'

'That's cool. And I guess that explains the Mercedes. You know, I deal with cars all fucking day. You can tell a lot about people by the cars they drive and how they take care of them.'

'I suppose.'

Bosch nodded. He now saw the direct way to his goal. Once again Mackey had unwittingly helped.

'German engineering,' Bosch said. 'The best fucking carmakers in the world. What do you drive when you're not in this rig?'

'I'm restoring a 'seventy-two Camaro. It's going to be a sweet ride when I'm finished.'

'Good year,' Bosch offered.

'Yeah, but I wouldn't buy anything out of Detroit nowadays. You know who's making our cars now, don't you? All the fucking mud people. I wouldn't drive one, let alone put my family in one.'

'In Germany,' Bosch responded, 'you go into a factory and everybody's got blue eyes, you know what I mean? I've seen pictures.'

Mackey nodded thoughtfully. Bosch thought it was time to make the direct move. He unfolded the newspaper on his lap. He held it up so that the full front page, and the full Verloren story, could be seen.

'Talk about mud people,' he said. 'Did you read this story?'

'No, what's it say?'

'It's about this mother sittin' on a bed boohooing about her mud child who got killed seventeen years ago. And the police are still on the case. But I mean, who cares, man?'

Mackey glanced over at the paper and saw the photo with the inset shot of Rebecca Verloren's face. But he didn't say anything and his own face did not betray any recognition. Bosch lowered the paper so as not to be too obvious about it. He refolded it and discarded it on the seat between them. He pushed things one more time.

'I mean, you mix the races like that and what are you going to get?' he asked.

'Exactly,' Mackey said.

It wasn't a strong reply. It was almost hesitant, as if Mackey was thinking about something else. Bosch took this as a good sign. Maybe Mackey had just felt that cold finger go down his spine. Maybe it was the first time in seventeen years.

Bosch decided he had given it his best shot. If he tried to do anything more he might cross the line into obviousness and give himself away. He decided to ride the rest of the way silently, and Mackey seemed to make the same choice.

But a few blocks later Mackey swerved the truck into the second lane to get around a slow-moving Pinto.

'You believe there is still one of those on the street?' he said.

As they passed the little car Bosch saw a man of Asian descent huddled behind the wheel. Bosch thought he might be Cambodian.

'Figures,' Mackey said, as he saw the driver. 'Watch this.'

Mackey then steered back into the original lane, squeezing the Pinto between the towed Mercedes and a row of cars parked against the curb. The Pinto driver had no choice but to pull to a screeching stop. Mackey's laughter drowned out the weak horn blast from the Pinto.

'Fuck you!' Mackey yelled. 'Get back on your fucking boat!'

He looked to Bosch for affirmation and Bosch smiled, the hardest thing he'd had to do in a long while.

'Hey, man, that was my car you almost hit that guy with,' he said in mock protest.

'Hey, were you in Vietnam?' Mackey asked.

'Why?'

'Because, man. You were there, weren't you?'

'So?'

'So, man, I had a friend who was there. He said they dusted mooks like that guy back there like it was nothing. A dozen for breakfast and another dozen for lunch. I wish I'd been there, is all I'm saying.'

Bosch looked away from him and out the side window. Mackey's statement had left an opening for him to ask about guns and killing people. But Bosch couldn't bring himself to go there. All at once he just wanted to get away from Mackey.

But Mackey kept talking.

'I tried to sign up for the Gulf – the first one – but they wouldn't take me.'

Bosch recovered some and got back into it.

'Why not?' he asked.

'I don't know. They needed the slot for a nigger, I guess.'

'Or maybe you had a criminal record.'

Bosch had turned to look at him as he said this. He immediately thought he had sounded too accusatory about it. Mackey turned and held his stare for as long as he could before having to return his eyes to the road.

'I've got a record, man, big fucking deal. They still could've used me over there.'

The conversation died there, and in a few blocks they were pulling into the service station.

'I don't think we'll need to put it in the garage,' Mackey said. 'Spider can just take the wheel off while I have it on the hook. We'll do it quick.'

'Whatever you want to do,' Bosch said. 'You're sure he didn't leave yet?'

'No, that's him right there.'

As the tow truck went by the double bays of the garage a man emerged from the shadows and headed toward the back of the truck. He was holding a pneumatic drill with one hand and pulling the air line with the other. Bosch saw the webwork tattooed on his neck. Prison blue. Something about the man's face immediately struck Bosch as familiar. In a rushed moment of dread he thought he knew the man because he'd had dealings with him as a cop. He had arrested him or questioned him before, maybe even sent him to the prison where he had gotten the webwork done.

Bosch suddenly knew he had to stay clear of the man called Spider. He pulled his phone off his belt.

'All right if I sit here and make a call?' he asked Mackey, who was getting out of the truck.

'Yeah, go ahead. This won't take long.'

Mackey closed the door, leaving Bosch alone. As he heard the drill start taking the lugs off the wheel of his SUV, Bosch rolled the window up and called Rider's cell phone.

'How's it going?' she said by way of a greeting.

'It was going good till we got back to the station,' Bosch said in a low voice. 'I think I know the mechanic. If he knows me, this could be a problem.'

'You mean he might know you're a cop?'

'Exactly.'

'Shit.'

'Exactly.'

'What do you want us to do? Tim and Rick are still floating around.'

'Call them and tell them what's happening. Tell them to stay loose until I get clear. I'm going to stay in the truck as long as I can. If I hold the phone up like I am talking I can keep him from seeing my face.'

'Okay.'

'I just hope Mackey doesn't want to introduce me. I think I made an impression on him. He might want to show me off.'

'Okay, Harry, just stay cool and we'll move in if we have—'

'I'm not worried about me. I'm worried about the play with—'

'Hey, he's coming over.'

Just as she said the warning there was a sharp rap on the window. Bosch lowered the phone and turned to see Mackey staring at him. He rolled the window down.

'It's done,' he said.

'Already?'

'Yup. You can come into the office and pay while he puts the wheel back on. You'll make it home in a couple hours.'

'Great.'

Holding the phone up to his right ear, Bosch got out of the truck and walked to the office, never allowing Spider a decent look at his face. He spoke to Rider while he walked.

'It looks like I'm getting out of here,' he said.

'Good,' she said. 'The man in question is putting on your wheel. Watch yourself when you leave.'

'Will do.'

Once he was in the little office Bosch closed the phone. Mackey had gone behind a greasy, cluttered desk. He took several seconds to use a calculator to do the simple arithmetic of the tow and repair charges.

'Comes to one twenty-five even,' he said. 'Four miles towing and the valve was three bucks.'

Bosch sat down in a chair in front of the desk and pulled out his fold of money.

'Can I get a receipt for it?'

As he counted out six twenties and a five he heard the drill outside. The tire was being put back on. He held the money out, but Mackey was preoccupied by looking at a Post-it note he had found on the desk. He held it at an angle that allowed Bosch to read it.

Ro – FYI. Visa called to confirm employment on your app.

Bosch read it in a few seconds, but Mackey looked at it for a long time before finally dropping the note back on the desk and taking the money from Bosch. Mackey put the money in a cash drawer and then started fishing around on the desk for a receipt pad. He was taking a long time.

'Kenny usually writes up the receipts,' he said. 'And he went to get some chicken.'

Bosch was about to say never mind about the receipt when he heard the scrape of a step behind him and knew that someone had entered the office. He didn't turn in case it was Spider.

'All right, Ro, it's done. You just need to let her down.'

Bosch knew this was the tight moment. Mackey would either introduce him or not.

'All right, Spider,' Mackey said.

'Then I'm outta here.'

'Okay, man, thanks for sticking. Catch you tomorrow.'

Spider left the office without Bosch ever turning around. Mackey found what he was looking for in the center drawer and scribbled something on it. He gave it to Bosch. It was a blank receipt. He had written $125 in a childlike scrawl at the bottom.

'You can just fill that out,' Mackey said as he got up. 'I'll go drop your machine and you can get out of here.'

Bosch followed him out, realizing he had left the newspaper on the seat of the truck. He wondered if he should leave it there or come up with an excuse to go back into the truck so he could get it and maybe leave it in the office where he knew Mackey watched television during the slow parts of his shift.

He decided to leave it where it was. He had planted the seed as best he could. It was time now to just step back and see what grew from it.

The Mercedes was off the truck now. Bosch walked around to the driver's side. Mackey was stowing the harness in the back of the tow truck.

'Thanks, Roland,' Bosch said.

'Just Ro, man,' Mackey responded. 'You take care, man. And do yourself a favor and stay out of South-Central.'

'Don't worry about me,' Bosch said. 'I will.'

Mackey smiled and winked as he pulled off his glove again and offered Bosch his hand. Bosch shook it and smiled back. He then looked down at their hands and saw a tiny white scar in the fleshy part between Mackey's right thumb and finger. The tattoo from a Colt .45.

'I'll catch you later,' he said.

30

Bosch drove to the spot where he had met Rider at the start of the surveillance shift and she was there waiting. He parked and got into her Taurus.

'That was close,' she said. 'Turns out you probably did know that guy. Jerry Townsend. Ring a bell? We ran the plate on his pickup when he left work and got the ID.'

'Jerry Townsend? No, not the name. I just recognized his face.'

'He has a manslaughter conviction in 'ninety-six. Served five years. Sounds like it was a domestic abuse case, but that's all they could pull off the computer. I bet if we pulled the file your name would be on it. That's how you recognized him.'

'You think he could be connected to this thing we're working?'

'I doubt it. What's probably going on is that whoever owns that station doesn't mind hiring ex-cons. They come cheap, you know? And if he's scamming on repairs, then who's going to complain?'

'Well, let's get back and see what happens.'

She put the car into gear and pulled out on Tampa to head back up to the intersection where the service station was.

'How did it go with him?' Rider asked.

'Pretty good. I did all but read the story to him. He didn't show anything, no recognition, but the seed is definitely planted.'

'Did he see the tattoos?'

'Yeah, they worked good. He started asking questions right after he saw them. Your file on Simmons paid off, too. He came up in the conversation. And for what it's worth, he had a scar on the webbing by his right thumb. From the bite.'

'Harry, man, you covered everything. I guess all we do now is sit back and see what happens.'

'Did the other guys take off?'

'As soon as we get back on post they're leaving.'

When they got to the intersection of Tampa and Roscoe they saw Mackey's tow truck waiting to pull onto Roscoe to head west.

'He's on the move,' Bosch said. 'Why didn't anybody tell us?'

Just as he said it Rider's cell phone buzzed. She handed it to Bosch so she could concentrate on driving. She cut into the left turn lane so she would be able to follow Mackey onto Roscoe. Bosch opened her phone. It was Tim Marcia. He explained that Mackey went on the move without a call coming into the station for a tow. Jackson had checked with the sound room. There had been no call on the lines they were listening to.

'All right,' Bosch said. 'He said something when I was in the truck about going to grab dinner. Maybe this is it.'

'Maybe.'

'Okay, Tim, we got him now. Thanks for sticking around. Tell Rick the same.'

'Good luck, Harry.'

They followed the tow truck to a plaza shopping center and watched Mackey go into a Subway fast food restaurant. He did not take the newspaper Bosch had left in the truck with him, but after getting his food he sat down at one of the inside tables and started to eat.

'You going to get hungry, Harry?' Rider asked. 'Now might be the time.'

'I did Dupar's on the way in so I'll be fine. Unless we see a Cupid's around. I'd go for that.'

'No way. That's one thing I got over after you left. I don't eat that fast food crap anymore.'

'What do you mean? We ate good. Didn't we go to Musso's every Thursday?'

'If you call chicken pot pie a healthy meal, yeah, we ate good. Besides, I'm talking about stakeouts. Did you hear about Rice and Beans in Hollywood?'

Rice and Beans was the designation given to a pair of robbery detectives in Hollywood Division named Choi and Ortega. They were there when Bosch worked in the division.

'No, what happened?'

'They were on a surveillance gig on these guys that were taking down street prostitutes, and Ortega was sittin' in the car eating a hotdog. He suddenly started choking on it and he couldn't clear himself. He's turning purple and pointing to his throat and Choi's like, what the fuck? So finally Beans jumps out of the car and Choi finally gets what's going on. He comes running around to give him the Heimlich. He popped the hotdog onto the hood of the car. And they blew the surveillance.'

Bosch laughed as he pictured it. He knew it was a story Rice and Beans would never live down in the division. Not with people like Edgar there to tell and retell it to anyone who transferred in.

'Well, see, they don't have a Cupid's down in Hollywood,' he said. 'If he'd been eating a nice soft dog from Cupid's there wouldn't have been a problem like that.'

'I don't care, Harry. No hotdogs on stakeout. No crap. That's my new rule. I don't want people talking about me like that the rest of my—'

Bosch's phone chirped. It was Robinson, who was working the late shift in the sound room with Nord.

'They just had a tow call come into the station. They then turned around and called Mackey. He must not be at the station.'

Bosch explained the situation and apologized for not keeping the sound room in the loop.

'Where's the tow?' he asked.

'It's an accident on Reseda at Parthenia. I guess the car's DOA. He's got to tow it into a dealership.'

'Okay, we're with him.'

A few minutes later Mackey came out of the fast food restaurant carrying a large soda cup with a straw sticking out. They followed him to Reseda Boulevard and Parthenia Street, where a Toyota with the front end caved in had been pushed off the road. Another tow truck was just jacking up the other car, a large SUV that had its back end realigned by the accident. Mackey spoke briefly with the other tow truck driver – a professional courtesy – and went to work on the Toyota. An LAPD patrol car was sitting in the parking lot of the corner plaza and the officer inside was writing up a report. Bosch saw no drivers. He thought this meant that they might have all been transported to an emergency room because of injuries.

Mackey towed the Toyota to a dealership all the way over on Van Nuys Boulevard. While he was there, letting the wreck down in the service drive, Bosch got another call. Robinson told him that Mackey had been summoned again. This time to the Northridge Fashion Center, where an employee of the Borders bookstore needed a battery jump.

'This guy isn't going to have time to read the paper if he stays busy like this,' Rider said after Bosch reported on the phone call.

'I don't know,' Bosch said. 'I'm wondering if he can even read.'

'You mean the dyslexia?'

'Yeah, but not just that. I haven't seen him do any reading or writing. He told me to fill in the forms for the tow. Then he either didn't want to or couldn't fill out a receipt at the end. And then there was this note on the desk for him.'

'What note?'

'He picked it up and stared at it for a long time but I wasn't really sure he knew what it said.'

'Could you read it? What did it say?'

'It was a note from the dayshift people. Visa had called to confirm his employment on an application he had made, I guess.'

Rider wrinkled her brow.

'What?' Bosch asked.

'Just seems weird, him applying for a credit card. That would make him findable, which I thought he was trying to avoid.'

'Maybe he's starting to feel safe.'

Mackey went from the Toyota dealership straight to the shopping mall, where he jump-started a woman's car. He then turned his truck toward the home base. It was almost ten o'clock by the time he pulled back into the station. Bosch's sagging hopes were buoyed when he looked through the binoculars from the plaza across the street and saw Mackey walking from the truck to the office.

'We might still be in play,' he said to Rider. 'He's carrying the paper with him.'

It was hard to keep track of Mackey inside the station. The front office was glass on two sides and that was not a problem. But the garage doors were now closed and oftentimes it seemed that Mackey would disappear into these areas, where Bosch could not see him.

'You want me to be the eyes for a while?' Rider asked.

Bosch lowered the binoculars and looked at her. He could barely read her face in the darkness of the car.

'Nah, I'm okay. You're doing all the driving anyway. Why don't you rest? I woke you up early today.'

He raised the binoculars back up.

'I'm fine,' Rider said. 'But anytime you need a break …'

'Besides,' Bosch said, 'I sort of feel responsible for this guy.'

'What do you mean?'

'You know. This whole thing. I mean, we could've just pulled Mackey in and sweated him in the box, tried to break him. Instead we went this way, and it's my plan. I'm responsible.'

'We can still sweat him. If this doesn't work, then that's probably what we'll need to do.'

Bosch's phone began to chirp.

'Maybe this is what we're waiting for,' he said as he answered.

It was Nord.

'I thought you told us this guy got his general education degree, Harry.'

'He did. What's going on?'

'He just had to call someone to read the story to him out of the paper.'

Bosch sat up a little straighter. They were in play. It didn't matter how the story was communicated to Mackey, the important thing was that he wanted to know what it said.

'Who did he call?'

'A woman named Michelle Murphy. Sounded like an old girlfriend. He asked if she still got the paper every day, like he wasn't sure anymore. She said yeah and he asked her to read the story to him.'

'Did they talk about it after she read it?'

'Yeah. She asked him if he knew the girl the story was about. He said no, but then he said, 'I knew the gun.' Just like that. Then she said she didn't want to know anything else and that was it. They hung up.'

Bosch thought about all of this. The play earlier in the day had worked. It had kicked over a rock that had not been moved in seventeen years. He was excited, and he could feel the charge building in his blood.

'Can you pipe the recording over the line to us here?' he asked. 'I want to hear it.'

'I think we can,' Nord said. 'Let me get one of the techs who are floating around here to – hey, Harry, I gotta call you back. Mackey's making a call.'

'Call me back.'

Bosch quickly closed the phone so Nord could get back to her monitor. He excitedly recounted for Rider the report on Mackey's phone call to Michelle Murphy. He could tell Rider caught the charge as well.

'We might be in business, Harry.'

Bosch was looking through the binoculars at Mackey. He was sitting behind the desk in the office and talking on his cell phone.

'Come on, Mackey,' Bosch whispered. 'Spill it. Tell us the story.'

But then Mackey closed the phone. Bosch knew the call was too short.

Ten seconds later Nord called Bosch back.

'He just called Billy Blitzkrieg.'

'What did he say?'

'He said, "I might be in trouble" and "I might need to make a move," and then Burkhart cut him off and said, "I don't care what it is, don't talk about it on the phone." So they agreed to meet after Mackey gets off work.'

'Where?'

'Sounded like at the house. Mackey said, "You'll be up?" and Burkhart said he would be. Mackey then said, "What about Belinda, she still there?" and Burkhart said she'd be asleep and not to worry about her. They ended it like that.'

Bosch immediately felt a crushing blow to his hopes of breaking the case that night. If Mackey met Burkhart inside the house, they would not hear what transpired inside. They'd be locked out of the confession they had set up the surveillance to get.

'Call me if he makes any other calls,' he said quickly and then hung up.

He looked at Rider, who was waiting expectantly in the dark.

'Not good?' she asked. She had obviously read something in his tone to Nord.

'Not good.'

He told her about the calls and the obstacle they would face if Mackey met with Burkhart to discuss his 'trouble' behind closed doors.

'It's not all bad, Harry,' she said after hearing everything. 'He made a solid admission to the Murphy woman and a lesser admission to Burkhart. But we're getting close so don't get depressed. Let's figure this out. What can we do to make them meet outside of the house? Like at a Starbucks or something.'

'Yeah, right. Mackey ordering a latte.'

'You know what I mean.'

'Even if we roust them out of the house, how are we going to get close? We can't. We need this to be a phone call. It's the blind spot – my blind spot – to this whole thing.'

'We just need to sit tight and see what happens. It's all we can do right now. Look, it would be good to have an ear on this but maybe it's not the end of the world. We already have Mackey on the phone saying he might have to make a move. If he does, if he runs, then that could be seen by a jury as a shading of guilt. And if you take that and what we already have on tape it might be enough to squeeze more out of him when we finally bring him in. So all is not lost here, okay?'

'Okay.'

'You want me to call it in to Abel? He'd want to know.'

'Yeah. Fine, call it in. There's nothing to call in, but go ahead.'

'Just cool down, Harry.'

Bosch shut her out by raising the binoculars and looking at Mackey. He was still behind the desk and appeared deep in thought. The other night man, the one Bosch assumed was Kenny, was sitting on another chair and his face was angled up for viewing the television. He was laughing at something he was watching.

Mackey was not laughing or watching. His face was cast down. He was looking at something in memory.

The wait until midnight was the longest ninety minutes of surveillance Bosch had ever spent. As they waited for the station to close and Mackey to head to his rendezvous with Burkhart, nothing happened. The phones were silent, Mackey did not move from his spot at the desk and Bosch came up with no plan to either avert the rendezvous or infiltrate it in some way. It was as though they were all frozen until the clock struck twelve.

Finally, the exterior lights of the station went off and the two men closed the business for the night. When Mackey walked out, he was carrying the newspaper he could not read. Bosch knew he was going to show it to Burkhart and most likely discuss the murder.

'And we won't be there,' Bosch mumbled as he tracked Mackey through the binoculars.

Mackey got into his Camaro and revved the engine loudly after firing it up. He then pulled out onto Tampa and headed south toward his home, the intended meeting place. Rider waited an appropriate amount of time and then pulled out of the plaza lot, cut across the northbound lanes of Tampa and headed south as well. Bosch called Nord in the sound room and told her Mackey had left the station and they should switch their monitoring to the house line.

The lights of Mackey's car were three blocks ahead. Traffic was sparse and Rider kept a safe distance back. As they passed the lot where Bosch had left his car he checked on the Mercedes just to make sure it was still there.

'Uh oh,' Rider said.

Bosch turned back to the street ahead in time to see Mackey's car complete a fast U-turn. He was now heading back toward Bosch and Rider.

'Harry, what do I do?' Rider asked.

'Nothing. Don't do anything obvious.'

'He's coming right back at us. He must have seen the tail!'

'Sit tight. Maybe he saw my car parked back there.'

The deep-throated engine of the Camaro could be heard long before the car got to them. It sounded menacing and evil, like a monster roaring and coming for them.

31

The old Camaro went screaming by Bosch and Rider without hesitation. It blew the light at Saticoy and kept going. Bosch watched its lights disappearing to the north.

'What was that?' Rider said. 'You think he knows there's a tail?'

'I don't—'

Bosch's cell phone sounded and he quickly answered it. It was Robinson.

'He just got called back by the Triple A answering service. He seemed pretty upset but they have to take it, I guess.'

'What do you mean, he's got a tow?'

'Yeah. It was Triple A dispatch. I guess if he didn't take it they would go to another company and that could mean trouble. Like losing the Triple A business.'

'Where's the tow?'

'It's a breakdown on the Reagan. On the westbound side near the Tampa Avenue overpass. So it's close. He said he was on the way.'

'Okay. We got him.'

Bosch closed the phone and told Rider to turn around, that their cover was still intact, that Mackey was simply hurrying back to get the tow truck.

By the time they were back to the intersection of Tampa and Roscoe, the tow truck was pulling out of the darkened station. Mackey wasn't wasting any time.

Since they knew Mackey's destination Rider could afford to hang back and not risk being noticed in the tow truck's rear-view mirror. They headed north on Tampa toward the freeway. The Reagan was the 118 Freeway, which ran east-west across the northern stretch of the Valley. It was one of the few freeways that was not crowded with traffic twenty-four hours a day. Named after the late governor and president, it led to Simi Valley, where Reagan's presidential library was located. Still, it had been jarring to Bosch to hear Robinson call it the Reagan. To Bosch it was always simply the 118.

The westbound entrance to the 118 ramped down from Tampa Avenue to the ten lanes of freeway. Rider slowed and hung back and they watched the tow truck turn left and head down the ramp out of sight. She then pulled up and made the same turn. As they came on the ramp and started down they immediately realized their problem. The disabled car was not on the freeway as Nord had said but actually on the entrance ramp. They were quickly coming up on the tow truck. It was pulled onto the ramp's shoulder about fifty yards ahead. Its rear spreader lights were on and it was backing toward a small red car that was parked on the shoulder with its emergency lights blinking.

'What do we do, Harry?' Rider said. 'If we pull over it's going to be obvious.'

She was right. They would blow their cover.

'Just go on by,' he replied.

He had to think quickly. He knew that once they were on the freeway they could pull onto the shoulder and wait until Mackey's tow truck came by with the disabled car on its hook. But that was risky. Mackey might recognize Rider's car, or even stop to see if they needed assistance. If he saw Bosch then the surveillance would be blown.

'You got a Thomas Guide?'

'Under the seat.'

Rider drove by the disabled car and the tow truck as Bosch reached under the seat for the map book. Once they were clear of the tow truck he put on the overhead light and quickly flipped through the map pages. A Thomas map book was the driving bible of Los Angeles. Bosch had years of experience with them and quickly found the page depicting the section of the city they were in. He made a quick study of their situation and gave Rider directions.

'The next exit is Porter Ranch Drive,' he said. 'Less than a mile. We get off and go right and then another right on Rinaldi. It takes us back to Tampa. We either wait up on top of the overpass and watch or we just keep circling.'

'I think we wait up on top,' Rider said. 'If we keep going down that ramp in the same car he might notice.'

'Sounds like a plan.'

'I don't like it but I don't know what choice we have.'

They covered the distance to the Porter Ranch exit quickly.

'Did you check out the tow car?' Bosch asked. 'I was looking for the map book.'

'Small foreign job,' Rider responded. 'It looked like one person behind the wheel and that was it. The lights from the truck were too bright to see anything else.'

Rider kept her speed up until they pulled into the exit lane for Porter Ranch Drive. As instructed, she took a right and then another right and they were quickly heading back toward Tampa. They got stopped at the light at Corbin but then Rider drove through it after checking to make sure it was clear. Less than three minutes after passing the tow truck they were back on Tampa. Rider pulled to the side of the road in the middle of the overpass. Bosch cracked his door.

'I'll check it out,' he said.

He stepped out of the car. At this angle he couldn't see the tow truck but the spreader lights on the top of the cab cast a glow above the entrance ramp.

'Harry, take this,' Rider called.

Bosch ducked back into the car and took the rover Rider was holding out to him.

He walked back along the overpass. The freeway wasn't crowded, but it was still loud with the cars passing beneath him. When he got to the top of the ramp and looked down, it took him a few moments to adjust his vision because the lights from the back of the tow truck were still slashing through the darkness.

But soon he realized that the blinking lights of the disabled car were not there. He looked closer and saw that the car was no longer on the shoulder. His eyes traveled down the ramp to the freeway and he saw the red taillights of dozens of cars moving westbound into the distance.

He looked back at the tow truck. Everything was still. There was no sign of Mackey.

Bosch raised the radio to his mouth and keyed the mike.

'Kiz?'

'Yeah, Harry?'

'You better get over here.'

Bosch started walking down the ramp. As he did so he drew his weapon and carried it down by his side. In thirty seconds lights flashed behind him and Rider pulled her car onto the shoulder. She got out with a flashlight and they continued down the ramp.

'What's going on?' she asked.

'I don't know.'

There was still no sign of Mackey in or around the tow truck. Bosch felt his chest tighten. He instinctively knew something was wrong. The closer they got the more he knew it.

'What do we say if he's here and everything's okay?' Rider whispered.

'It isn't,' Bosch said.

The light from the back of the truck was almost blinding and Bosch knew they were in a vulnerable position. He could not see anyone on the front side of the tow truck. He moved to his right so that he and Rider would be spread apart. Rider could not move to the left or she would be walking into the entrance lane.

A semi-truck roared by on the ramp, wafting petroleum-tinged wind and sound over them and making the ground shake like an earthquake.

Bosch was now walking in the weeds that were on the upward slope off the shoulder. He still didn't see anyone up ahead.

Bosch and Rider did not communicate. The noise from passing traffic on the freeway just below was echoing from beneath the overpass. They would have to shout now and that would detract from their concentration.

They came back together when they got to the tow truck. Bosch checked the cab and there was no sign of Mackey. The truck was still running. He stepped back to the rear and looked at the ground illuminated by the spreader lights. There were curving black tire marks leading right up to the truck's rear gate. And on the gravel was one of the leather gloves, grease-stained in the palm, that he had seen Mackey wearing earlier in the day.

'Let me borrow this,' he said, taking the flashlight from Rider. He noticed that it was one of the short rubber models approved by the police chief after an officer was videotaped beating a suspect with one of the heavy steel lights.

Bosch pointed the beam at the truck's rear gate, running it over the underside that had been cast in shadows by the bright glare from the spreader above.

Blood reflected brightly on the dark steel. It could not be mistaken for oil. It was as red and real as life. Bosch squatted down and pointed the light beneath the truck. It had been dark here, too, made all the more impervious to vision by the bright lights above.

He saw Mackey's body crumpled against the rear axle differential. Fully one-half of his face was bathed in blood from a long and deep laceration that cut across the left side of his head. His blue uniform shirt was maroon down the front from blood from other unseen injuries. The crotch of his pants was stained with blood or urine or both. The one arm Bosch could see was bent oddly at the forearm and a jagged, ivory white bone protruded from the flesh. The arm was cradled against Mackey's chest, which heaved with non-rhythmic gasps. He was still alive.

'Oh God!' Rider called out from behind Bosch.

'Get an ambulance!' Bosch ordered as he started to crawl under the truck.

Hearing Rider's feet crunch on the gravel as she ran back to her car and the radio, Bosch moved as close to Mackey as he could get. He knew he might be destroying a crime scene but he had to get close.

'Ro, can you hear me? Ro, who did this? What happened?'

Mackey seemed to stir at the sound of his name. His mouth started moving and that was when Bosch could tell his jaw was broken or dislocated. Its movements were uncoordinated. It was like Mackey was trying it out for the first time.

'Take your time, Ro. Tell me who did this. Did you see him?'

Mackey whispered something but a car speeding by on the entrance ramp drowned it out.

‘Tell me again, Ro. Say it again.’

Bosch pushed forward and leaned his head down by Mackey’s mouth. What he heard was half gasp, half whisper.

‘... sworth ...’

He pulled back and looked at Mackey. He put the light into his face, hoping it might rouse him. He saw that the bone structure around Mackey’s left eye was also crushed and hemorrhaging. He wasn’t going to make it.

‘Ro, if you have something to say, say it now. Did you kill Rebecca Verloren? Were you there that night?’

Bosch leaned forward. If Mackey said anything it was drowned in the noise of another car going by. When Bosch pulled back to look at him again he appeared to be dead. Bosch pushed two fingers into the bloodied side of Mackey’s neck and could not find a pulse.

‘Ro? Roland, are you still with me?’

The one undamaged eye was open but at half-mast. Bosch moved the light in close and saw no pupil movement. He was gone.

Bosch carefully crawled out from beneath the truck. Rider was standing there, her arms folded tightly in front of her.

‘Ambulance on the way,’ she said.

‘Call ’em off.’

He handed her back her flashlight.

‘Harry, if you think he’s dead, the paramedics should confirm it.’

‘Don’t worry, he’s dead. They’ll just get under there and ruin our crime scene. Call them off.’

‘Did he say anything?’

‘It sounded like he said “Chatsworth.” That was it. Anything else, I couldn’t hear.’

She seemed to be pacing now, in a small track, nervously moving back and forth.

‘Oh God,’ she said. ‘I think I’m going to be sick.’

‘Then move back over there, away from the scene.’

She walked off behind her car. Bosch felt sick to his stomach as well, but he knew he could keep it in. It wasn’t seeing Mackey’s torn and broken body that was causing the bile to rise in his throat. Bosch, like Rider, had seen far worse. It was the circumstances that were sickening. Instinctively he knew that this was no accident. This had been an assassination. And it was he who had put it all into motion.

He was sick because he had just gotten Roland Mackey killed. And with the death he might have lost the last, best link to Rebecca Verloren’s killer.

Part Three
Darkness Waits

32

The Tampa Avenue entrance ramp to the Ronald Reagan Freeway was closed and traffic was routed down Rinaldi to the Porter Ranch Drive entrance. The entire freeway ramp was choked with official police vehicles. The LAPD's Scientific Investigation Division, California Highway Patrol and the Medical Examiner's Office were all represented, along with members of the Open-Unsolved Unit. Abel Pratt had made calls and had greased the takeover of the case by the unit. Because the murder of Roland Mackey had taken place on a state freeway entrance, the case technically belonged to the jurisdiction of the CHP. But the agency was more than happy to hand it off, especially since the death was seen as part of an ongoing LAPD investigation. In other words, the LAPD was going to be allowed to clean up its own mess.

The commander of the local CHP barracks did offer the use of his squad's best accident expert, and Pratt took him up on that. Added to this, Pratt had assembled some of the best forensics people the department could muster, all in the middle of the night.

Bosch and Rider spent much of the time during the crime scene investigation sitting in the back of Pratt's car, where they were interviewed at length by Pratt and then by Tim Marcia and Rick Jackson, who were called in from home to head up the investigation into Mackey's death. Since Bosch and Rider were part of some events and witnesses to others, it was determined that they would not investigate the case as leads. This was a technical formality. It was clear that Bosch and Rider would be continuing to pursue the Verloren case, and in doing so they would obviously be pursuing Roland Mackey's killer.

At about 3 a.m. the forensics investigators gathered with the homicide detectives to go over what they knew so far. Mackey's body had just been removed from beneath the truck and the scene had been thoroughly photographed, videoed and sketched. It was now considered an open scene and everyone could walk freely about.

Pratt asked the CHP investigator, a tall man named David Allmand, to go first. Allmand used a laser pointer to delineate the tire marks on the roadway and the gravel that he believed were involved in the incident with

Mackey. He also pointed to the back of the tow truck, where chalk circles had been drawn around several scratches, dents and breaks in the heavy steel gate. He said he concluded the same thing Bosch and Rider had concluded within seconds of finding Mackey. He was murdered.

'The tire markings tell us that the victim pulled the tow truck onto the shoulder about thirty yards west of this point,' Allmand said. 'This was likely to avoid the disabled vehicle already on the shoulder. The tow truck was then backed down the shoulder to this position here. The driver put the transmission in park and set the parking brake before exiting the truck. If he was in a hurry, as some of the ancillary information indicates, he may have gone right to the tail here to lower the towing assembly. This is where he got it.

'The disabled car was obviously not disabled. The driver floored the accelerator and it lurched forward, striking the tow truck driver and pinning him against the back of the truck and the tow assembly. To get ready for the tow the vic would have bent over here to free the hook assembly. He was likely doing this when he was struck, and this would explain the head injuries. He went face first into the assembly. There's blood on the tow arm.'

Allmand ran the red eye of his laser over the tow truck's hook assembly to illustrate.

'The car then backed up,' he continued. 'And that's where you get the striated markings on the asphalt here. He then moved forward for another strike. The victim was probably already fatally injured from the first impact. But he wasn't dead yet. It is likely he fell to the ground after the first impact and with his last strength crawled under the truck to avoid the second impact. Either way, the vehicle did strike the tow truck a second time. And of course, the victim succumbed to his injuries while beneath the truck.'

Allmand paused there for questions but he was met only with grim silence. Bosch could think of nothing to ask. Unchecked, Allmand finished up his report by pointing to two tire lines made in the gravel and asphalt.

'You've got a wheel base on the striking vehicle that is not very wide,' he said. 'That will cut it down some. It's probably going to be a little foreign job. I took measurements, and as soon as I consult my manufacturers' catalogs I will be able to come up with a list of cars those treads could have come from. I'll let you know.'

When no one said anything Allmand used his laser to circle a small oil spot on the asphalt.

'Additionally, the striking vehicle was leaking oil. Not a big deal, but if it becomes important for a prosecutor to be able to say how long the killer sat here and waited for the victim, then we can time the leak once the vehicle is recovered and come up with a rough estimate of how long it would have taken to make this little spot here.'

Pratt nodded.

'Good to know,' he said.

Pratt thanked Allmand and asked the assistant medical examiner, Ravi Patel, to report on his preliminary examination of the body. Patel began by listing the numerous broken bones and injuries that were obvious from external examination of the body. He said the impact had likely fractured Mackey's skull, crushed the orbit of his left eye and dislocated his jaw. His hips were crushed along with the left side of his upper torso. His left arm and left thigh were broken as well.

'It is likely these injuries were sustained in one initial impact,' he said. 'The victim was likely standing and the impact came from the right rear side.'

'Would he have been able to crawl under the truck?' Rick Jackson asked.

'It is possible,' Patel answered. 'We have seen the instinct for survival allow people to do amazing things. I won't know until I open him up, but what we often see in cases like this is that the compression perforates the lungs. The lungs fill with blood. This takes time. He could have crawled to what he thought was safety.'

And then drowned on the side of the freeway, Bosch thought.

Next to report was the lead SID investigator, who happened to be Ravi Patel's brother, Raj. Bosch knew them both from previous cases and knew they were both among the best.

Raj Patel gave the basics of the crime scene investigation and reported that Mackey's efforts to save his life by crawling under the truck could ultimately allow the investigators to catch his killer.

'The second impact on the truck was without the body as a buffer, you see. It was metal on metal. We have both metal and paint transference and we have collected several samples. If you find the vehicle that did this, we can match it with one hundred percent accuracy.'

That was one piece of light in all the darkness, Bosch thought.

After Patel finished his report the crime scene began to break up, with the investigators heading out to follow various assignments Pratt wanted completed before the entire unit was to meet at the Pacific Dining Car at 9 a.m. to discuss the case.

Marcia and Jackson were assigned to search Mackey's home. This would entail rousting a judge from sleep and getting a search warrant signed, because Mackey shared the home with William Burkhart and Burkhart was a possible suspect in the killing. The home – with Burkhart presumed to be in it – was under surveillance at the time Mackey was cut down on the freeway. Nevertheless, Burkhart could have directed someone else to carry out the killing and was viewed as a suspect until cleared of involvement.

One of the first calls Bosch and Rider had made after finding Mackey beneath the tow truck was to Kehoe and Bradshaw, the two RHD detectives watching the home on Mariano Street. They immediately went to the house and took Burkhart and a woman identified as Belinda Messier into custody.

They were now waiting to be interviewed at Parker Center and Bosch and Rider drew that assignment from Pratt.

But as they turned to walk up the slope of the freeway exit to Rider's car, Pratt asked them to hold up. He then huddled with them and spoke so no one else remaining at the scene could hear.

'I guess I don't have to tell you two that we're going to get some heat on this,' he said.

'We know,' Rider said.

'I don't know what form the review will take but I think you can count on a review,' Pratt said.

'We'll be ready,' Rider said.

'You might want to talk about that on the way downtown,' Pratt suggested. 'Make sure everybody's on the same page.'

Bosch knew Pratt was telling them to get their story straight so that it could be presented in unison and in the light that served them best, even if they were interviewed separately.

'We'll be all right,' Rider said.

Pratt glanced at Bosch and then looked away, back at the tow truck.

'I know,' Bosch said. 'I'm a boot. If somebody takes a fall for this it will be me. That's okay. The whole thing was my idea.'

'Harry,' Rider said. 'That's not—'

'It was my plan,' Bosch said, cutting her off. 'I'm the one.'

'Well, you might not have to be the one,' Pratt said. 'The sooner we get this thing put together the better off we'll be. Success makes a lot of bad shit go away. So let's close this fucker by breakfast.'

'You got it, Boss,' Rider said.

As Bosch and Rider headed up the slope they didn't speak.

33

Parker Center was deserted when they arrived. Though several investigative units operated from the headquarters building, it was primarily filled each day with command staff and support services. It didn't come alive until after sunup. In the elevator Bosch and Rider split up, Bosch going directly to the Robbery-Homicide Division on the third floor to relieve Kehoe and Bradshaw, while Rider made a stop by the Open-Unsolved office to pick up the file she had put together earlier on William Burkhart.

'See you in a few,' she said to Bosch as he stepped off. 'I hope Kehoe and Bradshaw made some coffee.'

Bosch turned the corner out of the elevator alcove and headed down the hallway to the double doors of RHD. A voice from behind stopped him.

'What did I tell you about retreads?'

Bosch turned. It was Irving, coming from the opposite hallway. There was nothing down that way but computer services. Bosch guessed that he had been waiting in the hallway. He tried not to show surprise that Irving apparently already knew about what had happened on the freeway.

'What are you doing here?'

'Oh, I wanted to get an early start. It's going to be a big day.'

'Is that right?'

'That's right. And I'll give you fair warning. In the morning the media will be alerted to this middle-of-the-night fuckup of yours. The reporters will be told how you used this man Mackey as bait, only to let him be killed in a most horrible way. They will ask questions about how a retired detective could have been allowed back into the department to do this. But don't worry. These questions will most likely be addressed to the chief of police who set it all in motion.'

Bosch laughed and shook his head, acting as though he didn't feel the threat.

'Is that all?' he asked.

'I will also be urging the commander of the Internal Affairs Division to open an investigation into how you conducted this investigation, Detective Bosch. I wouldn't get too used to being back.'

Bosch took a step toward Irving, hoping to turn some of the threat back at him.

'Good, Chief, you do that. I hope you also prepare the commander for what I will be telling his investigators as well as the reporters about your own culpability in all of this.'

There was a long pause before Irving bit.

'What nonsense are you talking about?'

'This man you're so worried about being used as bait was cut loose by you seventeen years ago, Chief. Cut loose so you could make your deal with Richard Ross. Mackey should've been in jail. Instead he used the gun from one of his little burglaries to kill an innocent sixteen-year-old girl.'

Bosch waited but Irving didn't say anything.

'That's right,' Bosch said. 'I might have Roland Mackey's blood on my hands but you've got Rebecca Verloren's on yours. You want to go to the media and IAD with it? Fine, take your best shot and we'll see how it all comes out.'

A pinched look formed in Irving's eyes. He took a step toward Bosch until their faces were only inches apart.

'You are wrong, Bosch. All of those kids back then, they were cleared of involvement in Verloren.'

'Yeah, how? Who cleared them? Green and Garcia sure didn't. They were pushed away from them by you. Just like the girl's father. You and one of your dogs scared him away from it, too.'

Bosch pointed a finger at his chest.

'You let murderers walk so you could keep your little deal intact.'

An urgency entered Irving's voice when he responded.

'You are completely wrong on this,' he said. 'Do you really think that we would let murderers walk?'

Bosch shook his head, stepped back and almost laughed.

'As a matter of fact, I do.'

'Listen to me, Bosch. We checked alibis on every last one of those boys. They were all clean. For some of them, *we* were the alibi because we were still watching them. But we made sure every member of that group was clean on this, *then* we told Green and Garcia to back off. The father was told, too, but he wouldn't stand down.'

'So you pushed him down, right, Chief? Pushed him into a hole.'

'Things had to be done. The city was very tense back then. We couldn't have her father running around saying things that weren't true.'

'Don't give me that good-of-the-community bullshit, Chief. You had your deal, that's all you cared about. You had Ross and IAD in your pocket and you wanted to keep it that way. Only you were dead wrong. The DNA proves it. Mackey was good for Verloren and your investigation was for shit.'

'No, wait just a minute. It only proves one thing. That he had the gun. I read the story you planted in the paper today, too. The DNA connects him to the gun, not to the murder.'

Bosch waved him off. He knew there was no sense going back and forth with Irving. His only hope was that his own threat to go to the media and IAD would neutralize Irving's threat. He believed they were at a stalemate.

'Who checked the alibis?' he asked calmly.

Irving didn't answer.

'Let me guess. McClellan. He's got his prints all over this.'

Again Irving didn't answer. It was like he had drifted off into the memory of seventeen years before.

'Chief, I want you to call your dog. I know he still works for you. Tell him I want to know about the alibis. I want details. I want reports. I want everything he's got by seven a.m. today or that's it. We do what we have to do and we see where the chips fall.'

Bosch was about to turn away when Irving finally spoke.

'There are no alibi reports,' he said. 'There never would have been any.'

Bosch heard the elevator open and Rider soon rounded the corner, carrying a file. She stopped dead when she saw the confrontation. She said nothing.

'No reports?' Bosch said to Irving. 'Then you better hope he's got a good memory. Good night, Chief.'

Bosch turned and started down the hall. Rider hurried to catch up to him. She looked back over her shoulder to make sure Irving was not following. After they turned in through the double doors to RHD, she spoke.

'Are we in trouble, Harry? Is he going to turn this against the man up on six?'

Bosch looked at her. The mix of dread and fear on her face told him how important his answer was going to be.

'Not if I can help it,' he told her.

34

William Burkhart and Belinda Messier were being held in separate interview rooms. Bosch and Rider decided to take Messier first so that Burkhart would have to sit and wait and wonder. It would also give them time to let Marcia and Jackson get the warrant and get into the house on Mariano. What they found might be helpful during the interview with Burkhart.

Belinda Messier had come up in the investigation before. The number on the cell phone Mackey carried around was registered to her. In the briefing Kehoe and Bradshaw had given Bosch and Rider upon their arrival she was described as Burkhart's girlfriend. She had volunteered as much when the RHD detectives had taken both of them into custody. She told them little else after that.

Belinda Messier was a petite woman with mousy blonde hair that framed her face. Her look belied the hard case she turned out to be. She asked to see an attorney the moment Rider and Bosch entered the room.

'Why do you want to see an attorney?' Bosch asked. 'Do you think you are under arrest?'

'Are you telling me I can leave?'

She stood up.

'Sit down,' Bosch said. 'Roland Mackey was killed tonight and you could be in danger, too. You're in protective custody. That means you're not getting out of here until we get some things straight.'

'I don't know anything about it. I was with Billy all night until you people showed up.'

Over the next forty-five minutes Messier gave up information only grudgingly. She explained that she knew Mackey through Burkhart and that she agreed to apply for cell phone service and turn the phone over to Mackey because he didn't have a viable credit report. She told the detectives that Burkhart did not work and lived off a damages award he had received after a car accident two years before. He bought the house on Mariano Street with the payout and charged Mackey rent. Messier said she didn't live in the house but spent many nights there visiting Burkhart. When asked about Burkhart and Mackey's past ties to white power groups, she feigned surprise. When asked about the tiny swastika tattooed on the webbing between her right thumb and forefinger, she said she thought it was a Navajo good luck symbol.

'Do you know who killed Roland Mackey?' Bosch asked after the long preamble of questions.

'No,' she said. 'He was a real nice guy. That's all I know.'

'What did your boyfriend say after Mackey called him?'

'Nothin'. He just told me he was going to stay up and talk to Ro about something when he came home. He said they might go out for some privacy.'

'That's all?'

'Yeah, that's what he said.'

They went at her several times and from several different angles, with Bosch and Rider trading the lead back and forth, but the interview produced nothing of real value to the investigation.

Burkhart was next, but before going into the interview Bosch called Marcia and Jackson for an update.

'You guys in the house yet?' Bosch asked Marcia.

'Yeah, we're in. We haven't found anything yet.'

'What about a cell phone?'

'No cell phone so far. Do you think Burkhart could have slipped out on Kehoe and Bradshaw?'

'Anything's possible but I doubt it. They weren't sleeping.'

They were silent a moment as they thought about things and then Marcia spoke.

'How long was it between the time Mackey got it and you called Kehoe and Bradshaw and told them to take Burkhart in?'

Bosch reviewed his actions on the freeway before answering.

'It was pretty quick,' he finally said. 'Ten minutes max.'

'Then there you go,' Marcia said. 'Getting from the one eighteen in Porter Ranch all the way to Mariano Street in Woodland Hills in ten minutes max? And without being seen by our guys? No way. It wasn't him. Kehoe and Bradshaw are his alibi.'

'And no cell phone in the house ...'

They all already knew that the landline in the house was not used to make a call because it would have registered on the monitoring equipment at ListenTech.

'Nope,' Marcia said. 'No cell phone and no call on the landline. I don't think this is our guy.'

Bosch wasn't ready to agree yet. He thanked him and hung up, then gave the bad news to Rider.

'So what do we do with him?' she asked.

'Well, he might not be our guy on Mackey, but Mackey called him after the story was read to him. I still like him for Verloren.'

'But that doesn't make sense. Whoever hit Mackey had to have been his partner on Verloren – unless you're saying what happened on the on-ramp is just coincidental to all of this.'

Bosch shook his head.

'No, I'm not saying that. We're just missing something. Burkhart had to have gotten a message out of that house.'

'You mean like dial-a-hitman or something? It's not working for me, Harry.'

Now Bosch nodded. He knew she was right. It wasn't coming together.

'All right, then let's just go in there and see what he has to say for himself.'

Rider agreed and they spent a few minutes working out an interview strategy before going back into the hallway behind the squad room and entering the interview room where Burkhart waited.

The room was stuffy with Burkhart's body odor and Bosch left the door open. Burkhart had his head down on his folded arms. When he didn't rouse from his feigned sleep Bosch kicked the leg of his chair and that brought his head up.

'Rise and shine, Billy Blitzkrieg,' Bosch said.

Burkhart had scraggly dark hair that flopped around a face of pasty white skin. He looked like he didn't go out much except at night.

'I want a lawyer,' Burkhart said.

'We all do. But let's start with first things first. My name is Bosch and this is Rider. You are William Burkhart and you are under arrest for suspicion of murder.'

Rider started to read him his rights but he cut her off.

'Are you crazy? I never left my house. My girlfriend was there the whole time.'

Bosch held a finger to his lips.

'Let her finish, Billy, and then you can lie to us as much as you like.'

Rider finished reading the rights off the back of one of her business cards. Then Bosch took back over.

'Now, you were saying?'

'I'm saying you are fucked. I was home the whole time and I have a witness who can prove it. Besides, Ro was my friend. Why would I kill him? This is just a fucking joke, so why don't you go ahead and get me my lawyer now so he can laugh your asses out of here.'

'You finished, Bill? 'Cause I have some news for you. We're not talking about Roland Mackey. We're taking you back seventeen years to Rebecca Verloren. You remember her? You and Mackey? The girl you took up into the hills? That's who we're talking about here.'

Burkhart showed nothing. Bosch had been hoping for a tell, some sort of sign that he was on the right track.

'I don't know what you're talking about,' Burkhart said, his face a stone.

'We've got you on tape. Mackey called last night. It's over, Burkhart.

Seventeen years is a long run, but it's over.'

'You got shit. If there is a tape then all you'll hear is me tellin' him to shut up. I don't have a cell phone and I don't trust 'em. That's standing operating procedure. If he was going to start telling me his problems I didn't want to do it on a goddamn cell phone. As far as Rebecca whatever-her-name-is, I don't know nothing about that. I guess you should've asked Ro while you had the chance.'

He looked at Bosch and winked and Bosch felt like coming across the table at him. But he didn't.

They verbally sparred for another twenty minutes but neither Bosch nor Rider put a ding in Burkhart's armor. Eventually Burkhart stopped taking part in the back-and-forth, saying once more that he wanted an attorney and not responding in any form to any question that followed.

Rider and Bosch left the room to discuss their options, which they agreed were minimal. They had thrown a bluff at Burkhart. He had called them on it and they either had to book him and get him his lawyer or kick him loose.

'We don't have it, Harry,' Rider said. 'We shouldn't kid ourselves. I say we kick him.'

Bosch nodded. He knew it was true. They didn't have a case now, and for that matter they might never have one. Mackey, the one direct connection to Verloren they had, was gone. Bosch's own doing had lost him. Now they would have to go back in time and run a full field on Burkhart and search for something that was missed or hidden or ignored seventeen years before. The full depression of their case situation was descending on him like a lead blanket.

He opened his phone and called Marcia once more.

'Anything?'

'Nothing, Harry. No phone, no evidence, nothing.'

'Okay. Just so you know, we're going to kick him. He might show up there in a little while.'

'Great. He won't like what he finds here.'

'Good.'

Bosch closed the phone and looked at Rider. Her eyes told the story. Disaster. He knew he had let her down. For the first time he thought maybe Irving had been right – maybe he shouldn't have come back.

'I'll go tell him he's a free man,' he said.

After he walked away Rider called after him.

'Harry, I don't blame you.'

He looked back at her.

'I went along every step of the way. It was a good plan.'

He nodded.

'Thanks, Kiz.'

35

Bosch went home to take a shower, get fresh clothes and maybe close his eyes for a while before heading back downtown for the unit meeting. Once again he drove through a city that was just waking for the day. And once more it came up ugly in his eyes, all sharp edges and harsh glare. Everything seemed ugly to him now.

Bosch didn't look forward to the unit meeting. He knew all eyes would be on him. Everybody in Open-Unsolved understood that their actions would now be analyzed and second-guessed following Mackey's death. They also understood that if they were looking for a reason for the potential threat to their careers, they didn't have to look far.

Bosch threw his keys on the kitchen counter and checked the phone. No messages. He looked at his watch and determined that he had at least a couple hours before he needed to head toward the Pacific Dining Car. Checking the time reminded him of the ultimatum he had given Irving during their confrontation in the hallway outside RHD. But Bosch doubted he would hear from Irving or McClellan now. It seemed as though everybody was calling his bluffs.

He knew sleeping for a couple hours wasn't really an option, not with everything that weighed on him. He had carried the murder book and the accumulated files into the house. He decided he would work on them. He knew that when all else went wrong there was always the murder book. He had to keep his eyes on the prize. The case.

He started the coffee brewer, took a five-minute shower and then went to work rereading the murder book while a remastered release of *Kind of Blue* sounded from the CD player.

The feeling that he was missing something right in front of him was grinding on him. He felt that he would be haunted by the case, that he would carry it around with him forever, unless he cracked through and found that missing thing. And he knew that if it was to be found anywhere, it would be in the book.

He decided that this time he would not read through the documents in the order they had been presented to him by the first investigators of the case. He snapped open the rings and took the documents out. He started reading them in random order, taking his time, making sure that he absorbed every name, every word, every photo.

Fifteen minutes later he was staring once again at the crime scene photos of Rebecca Verloren's bedroom when he heard a car door close in front of his house. Curious about who would be parking out there so early he got up and went to the door. Through the peephole he saw a man approaching by himself. It was hard to clearly see him through the convex lens of the peep. Bosch opened the door anyway, before the man had a chance to knock.

It did not surprise the man that his approach had been watched. Bosch could tell by his demeanor that he was a cop.

'McClellan?'

He nodded.

'Lieutenant McClellan. And I assume you are Detective Bosch.'

'You could have called.'

Bosch stepped back to let him in. Neither man offered to shake hands. Bosch thought it was typical of Irving to send his man to the house. A standard procedure in the old I-know-where-you-live intimidation strategy.

'I thought it better that we talk face to face,' McClellan said.

'You thought? Or Chief Irving thought?'

McClellan was a big man with sandy, almost transparent hair and wide, florid cheeks. Bosch thought he could best be described as well fed. His cheeks turned a darker shade at Bosch's question.

'Look, I'm here to cooperate with you, Detective.'

'Good. Can I get you something? I have water.'

'Water'd be fine.'

'Have a seat.'

Bosch went into the kitchen and chose the dustiest glass from the cabinet and then filled it with tap water. He flicked off the switch on the coffeemaker and warmer. He wasn't going to let McClellan get cozy.

When he returned to the living room McClellan was looking out through the sliding glass door and across the deck. The air was clear in the pass. But it was still early.

'Nice view,' McClellan said.

'I know. I don't see any files in your hand, Lieutenant. I hope this isn't a social call or like one of those visits you made to Robert Verloren seventeen years ago.'

McClellan turned to Bosch and accepted the glass of water and the insult with the same blank expression.

'There are no files. If there were, they disappeared a long time ago.'

'And what? You're here to try to convince me with your memories?'

'As a matter of fact, I have great recall of that time period. You have to understand something. I was a detective first grade assigned to the PDU. If I was given a job, I did it. You don't question command in that situation. You do and you're out.'

'So you were a good soldier just doing your job. I get it. What about the Chatsworth Eights and the Verloren murder? What about the alibis?'

'There were eight principal players in the Eights. I cleared them all. And don't think I wanted to clear them and so I just did. I was told to see if any of these little pissants could have been involved. And I checked it out, but they all came up clean – on the murder at least.'

'Tell me about William Burkhart and Roland Mackey.'

McClellan sat down on a chair by the television. He put his glass of water, which he had yet to drink from, down on the coffee table. Bosch turned off Miles Davis in the middle of 'Freddie Freeloader' and stood with his hands in his pockets near the sliding doors.

'Well, first of all, Burkhart was easy. We were already watching him that night.'

'Explain that.'

'He had just gotten out of Wayside a few days before. We had gotten tipped that while he was up there he was re-upping on the racial religion, so it was thought to be prudent to keep an eye on him to see if he was going to try to start things up again.'

'Who ordered that?'

McClellan just looked at him.

'Irving, of course,' Bosch answered. 'Keeping the deal safe. So PDU was watching Burkhart. Who else?'

'Burkhart got out and hooked up with two guys from the old group. A guy named Withers and another named Simmons. It looked like they might've been planning something, but on the night in question they were in a pool hall on Tampa drinking themselves into oblivion. It was solid. Two undercovers were in there with them the whole time. That's what I'm here to tell you. They were all solid, Detective.'

'Yeah? Well, tell me about Mackey. The PDU wasn't watching him, was it?'

'No, not Mackey.'

'Then how was he so solid?'

'What I remember about Mackey was that on the night the girl was taken he was getting tutored at Chatsworth High. He was going to night school, getting his high school degree.'

'Actually, his general education degree. Not exactly the same thing.'

'That's right. A judge had ordered it as a condition of probation. Only he had to pass and he wasn't doing too good. But he was getting tutored on the off nights – when there was no school. And the night the girl got grabbed, he was with his tutor. I confirmed it.'

Bosch shook his head. McClellan was trying to feed him a line.

'You're telling me Mackey was getting tutored through the middle of the night? Either you're full of shit or you believed a line of bullshit from Mackey and his tutor. Who was the tutor?'

'No, no, they were together earlier in the evening. I don't remember the guy's name now, but they were done by like eleven at the latest and then they went their separate ways. Mackey went home.'

Bosch looked astonished.

'That's no alibi, *Lieutenant!* Time of death on the girl was two in the a.m. Didn't you know that?'

'Of course I did. But time of death wasn't the only alibi point. I was given the summaries put together by the guys on the case. There was no forced entry to that house. And the father had gone around and checked all the doors and locks after he got home at ten that night. That meant the killer had to have been inside the house at that point. He was in there hiding, waiting for everybody to go to sleep.'

Bosch sat down on the couch and leaned forward, elbows on his knees. He suddenly realized that McClellan was right and that everything was now different. He had seen the same report McClellan had seen seventeen years before but its meaning had not registered. The killer had been inside by the time Robert Verloren came home from work.

This changed a lot, Bosch knew. It changed how he looked not only at the first investigation, but also at his own.

Not registering Bosch's inner turmoil, McClellan continued.

'So Mackey couldn't have gotten into that house because he was with his tutor. He checked out. All those little assholes checked out. So I gave my boss a verbal report and then he told the two guys working the case. And that was the end of it until this DNA thing came up.'

Bosch was nodding to what McClellan was saying but he was thinking about other things.

'If Mackey was clean, how do you explain his DNA on the murder weapon?' he asked.

McClellan looked dumbfounded. He shook his head.

'I don't know what to say. I can't explain it. I cleared him of involvement in the actual murder, but he must've . . . '

He didn't finish. Bosch thought that he actually looked wounded by the idea that he might have helped a murderer or at least the person who provided the weapon for a murder to get away with it. He looked as though he knew all at once that he had been corrupted by Irving. He looked crushed.

'Is Irving still planning to tip the media and IAD to all of this?' Bosch asked quietly.

McClellan slowly shook his head.

'No,' he said. 'He told me to give you a message. He said to tell you an agreement is only an agreement if both sides keep their end of it. That's it.'

'One last question,' Bosch said. 'The evidence box on the Verloren case is gone. You know anything about that?'

McClellan stared at him. Bosch could tell he had badly insulted the man.

'I had to ask,' Bosch said.

'All I know is that stuff disappears from the place,' McClellan said through a tight jaw. 'Anybody could have walked off with it in seventeen years. But it wasn't me.'

Bosch nodded. He stood up.

'Well, I have to get back to work on this,' he said.

McClellan took the cue and stood. He seemed to swallow his anger over the last question, maybe accepting Bosch's explanation that it had to be asked.

'All right, Detective,' he said. 'Good luck with this thing. I hope you catch the guy. And I really mean that.'

He held his hand out to Bosch. Bosch didn't know McClellan's story. He didn't know all the circumstances of life in the PDU in 1988. But it looked like McClellan was leaving the house with a greater burden than he had come in with. So Bosch decided he could shake his hand.

After McClellan left, Bosch sat down again, thinking about the idea that Rebecca Verloren's killer had been hiding in the house. He got up and went to the dining room table, where the files from the murder book were spread out. The photos from the dead girl's room were at center in the spread. He looked through the reports until he found the SID report on latent fingerprint analysis.

The report was several pages long and contained the analysis of several fingerprints lifted from surfaces in the Verloren household. The main summary concluded that no print lifted from the house was an unknown, therefore it was likely the suspect or suspects wore gloves or simply avoided touching surfaces likely to retain prints.

The summary said that all latent fingerprints lifted from the house were matched to samples from members of the Verloren family or people who had an appropriate reason to have been in the house and touching the surfaces where the prints were found.

This time Bosch read the report differently and in its entirety. This time he was no longer interested in the analysis. He wanted to know where the SID techs had looked for prints.

The report was dated a day after the discovery of Rebecca's body. It detailed a routine search for fingerprints in the household. All topical surfaces were examined. All doorknobs and locks. All windowsills and frames. Every place it was logical to think that the killer/kidnapper might have touched a surface during the crime. While several prints on windowsills and latches were recovered and matched to Robert Verloren, the report stated that no usable prints at all were recovered from doorknobs in the house. It noted that this was not unusual because of the smudging that routinely occurred when knobs were turned.

It was in what was not included in the report that Bosch saw the crack through which a killer might have escaped. The SID team had gone into the house a day after the victim's body was discovered. This would have been after the case had been misread twice, first as a missing-persons case and second as a suicide. Added to this, when a murder investigation was finally mounted the latents team was sent in blind. There was no understanding of the case at that point. The idea that the killer might have hidden in the garage or somewhere else in the house for several hours had not been formulated yet. The search for fingerprints and other evidence, such as hairs and fibers, never went beyond the obvious, beyond the surface.

Bosch knew it was too late now. Too many years had passed. A cat roamed the house and who knows what objects from yard sales had come in and gone out of the house where a killer had hidden and waited.

Then his eyes fell to the spread of photos on the table and he realized something. Rebecca's bedroom was the one place that had not been contaminated over time. It was like a museum with its artwork encased and almost hermetically sealed.

Bosch spread all the crime scene photos of the bedroom in front of him. There had been something gnawing at him about these photos since the first time he had seen them. He still couldn't get to it but now he felt urgent about it. He studied the shots of the bureau and the bed table and then the open closet. Last he studied the bed.

He thought of the photo that had run in the newspaper and took the second copy of the paper out of the file containing all reports and documents accumulated during the reinvestigation of the case. He unfolded the paper and studied Emmy Ward's photo and then compared it to the photographs of seventeen years before.

The room seemed exactly the same, as if untouched by the grief emanating from it like heat from an oven. Then Bosch noticed a small difference. In the *Daily News* shot the bed had been carefully straightened and smoothed by Muriel before the photograph was taken. In the older SID shots the bed was made, but the ruffle fluffed outward along one side of the bed and inward along the foot.

Bosch's eyes moved back and forth from one photo to the other. He felt something breaking loose inside. He felt a little charge drop into his blood. This was what had bothered him. It was the something that was not right.

'In and out,' he said to himself.

It was possible, he knew, that the ruffle had been pushed inward at the bottom of the bed by someone crawling underneath it. That would make it likely that the outward fluffing of the ruffle at the side of the bed would have occurred when that same person slid or crawled out.

After everyone was asleep.

Bosch got up and started pacing as he worked it through again. In the photo taken after the abduction and murder, the bed clearly showed the possibility of entrance and exit. Rebecca's killer could have been waiting right below her as she fell asleep.

‘In and out,’ Bosch said again.

He worked it further. He knew that no readable fingerprints had been recovered at the house. But only obvious surfaces had been checked. This did not necessarily mean the killer had worn gloves. It only meant he was smart enough not to touch obvious places with his bare hands, or smudged the prints when he needed to. Even if gloves had been worn during the entry to the house, might not the killer have removed them while waiting – possibly for hours – under the bed?

It was worth a shot. Bosch went to the kitchen and called SID and asked for Raj Patel.

‘Raj, what are you doing?’

‘I am cataloging the evidence we gathered last night on the freeway.’

‘I need your best latents man to meet me back up there in Chatsworth.’

‘Now?’

‘Right now, Raj. I might not even have a job later. We have to do this now.’

‘What is it we are to do?’

‘I want to lift a bed and look underneath it. It’s important, Raj. If we find something, it will lead us to the killer.’

There was a short silence and then Patel replied.

‘I am my best latents man, Harry. Give me the address.’

‘Thanks, Raj.’

He gave Patel the address and then hung up the phone. He drummed his fingers on the counter, wondering if he should call Kiz Rider. She had been so distressed and discouraged as they had walked out of Parker Center that she said all she wanted to do was go home to sleep. Should he wake her for the second day in a row? He knew that wasn’t really the question. The question was whether he should wait to see if there was anything beneath the bed before telling her and getting her hopes up.

He decided to hold off on the call until there was something solid to tell her. Instead he picked up the phone and woke up Muriel Verloren. He told her he was on his way.

36

Bosch got to the squad meeting at the Pacific Dining Car late because of traffic coming in from the Valley. Everyone was in a private area in the back of the restaurant. Most of them already had plates of food in front of them.

His excitement must have showed. Pratt interrupted a report from Tim Marcia to look at Bosch and say, 'You either got lucky during the time you had off or you just don't care about the deep shit we're in here.'

'I got lucky,' Bosch said as he took the only empty chair and sat down. 'But not in the way you mean. Raj Patel just pulled a palm print and two fingers off a wood slat that was beneath Rebecca Verloren's bed.'

'That's good,' Pratt said dryly. 'What's it mean?'

'It means that as soon as Raj runs it through the database we might have our killer.'

'How so?' Rider asked.

Bosch had never called her. He could already feel a hostile vibe from her.

'I didn't want to wake you up,' Bosch said to her. Then to the others, he said, 'I was looking through the original latents report in the murder book. I realized that they went in there for prints the day after the girl's body was found. They never went back after it became a strong possibility that the abductor had come into the house earlier in the day when the garage was left open and hid somewhere until everybody was asleep.'

'So why the bed?' Pratt asked.

'The crime scene photos showed the ruffle at the foot of the bed had been pushed in. Like somebody had crawled underneath. They missed it because they weren't looking for it.'

'Good work, Harry,' Pratt said. 'If Raj gets a hit we change directions and move with it. All right, let's get back to our reports. You can check with your partner on what you've missed so far.'

Pratt then turned to Robinson and Nord at the other end of the long table and said, 'What did you come up with on the call for the tow truck?'

'Not a lot that helps,' Nord said. 'Because the call was made after we had switched our monitoring to the line at the Burkhart property, we don't have an audio recording of it. But we do have the pen registers and they show that the call came directly to Tampa Towing before being bounced over to the Triple A answering service. The call came from a pay phone outside the Seven-Eleven on Tampa by the freeway entrance. He probably made the call, then drove down the entrance and waited.'

'Prints on the phone?' Pratt asked.

'We asked Raj to take a look after he cleared the scene,' Robinson said. 'The phone had been wiped.'

'Figures,' Pratt said. 'You talked to Triple A?'

'Yes. No help other than to say the caller was a male.'

He turned to Bosch.

'You have anything to add that your partner didn't already tell us?'

'Probably just more of the same. Burkhart looks like he is clear on last night and he looks like he's clear on Verloren as well. Both nights he happened to be under LAPD surveillance.'

Rider gave him her knotted-brow look. He had even more information she didn't know. He looked away.

'Well, that's just perfect,' Pratt said. 'So who, what and where does that leave us, people?'

'Well, basically, our newspaper plant backfired,' Rider said. 'It may have worked in terms of getting Mackey to want to talk about Verloren, but he never got the chance. Somebody else saw the story.'

'That somebody being the actual killer,' Pratt said.

'Exactly,' Rider said. 'The person Mackey helped and/or gave the gun to seventeen years ago. That person also saw the story and knew it wasn't his blood on the gun, so that meant it had to be Mackey's. He knew Mackey was the link to him, so Mackey had to go.'

'So how did he set it up?' Pratt asked.

'He was either smart enough to figure the story was a plant and we were watching Mackey, or he just figured the best way to get to Mackey was the way he did it. Get him out there alone. Like I said, he was smart. He picked a time and place that would result in Mackey being alone and vulnerable. On that entrance ramp you are up above the freeway. Even with the tow truck's lights on, nobody would see up there.'

'It was also a good spot in case Mackey had a tail,' Nord added. 'The killer knew a tail car would have to just keep moving by, and then he'd have Mackey alone.'

'Aren't we giving this guy a little too much credit?' Pratt asked. 'How would he know the cops were onto this guy? Just from a newspaper article? Come on.'

Neither Bosch nor Rider answered and everyone else silently digested the unspoken suggestion that the killer had a connection to the department or, more specifically, the investigation.

'All right, what's next?' Pratt said. 'I think the containment on this is maybe another twenty-four hours tops. After that it's going to be in the papers and upstairs on six, and there's going to be hair on the walls if we don't wrap it up first. What do we do?'

'We'll take the pen registers,' Bosch said, speaking for himself and Rider. 'And go from there.'

Bosch had been thinking about the note to Mackey he had seen on the desk in the service station the day before. A call to verify employment from Visa. As Rider had pointed out when she first heard about it, Mackey wasn't into leaving trails like credit cards. It was something that didn't fit and therefore he wanted to go after it.

'We have all of the printouts right here,' Robinson said. 'The line that was busiest was the one into the station. All kinds of business calls.'

'Okay, Harry, Kiz, you want the registers?' Pratt asked.

Rider looked at Bosch and then at Pratt.

'If that's what Harry wants. He seems to be on a roll today.'

As if on cue Bosch's phone began to chirp. He looked at the screen. It was Raj Patel.

'We'll see what kind of a roll right now,' he said as he opened the phone.

Patel said he had good and bad news.

'The good news is we still had the exemplar skid from the house in records here. The latents we recovered this morning did not match any of them. You found somebody new, Harry. It could be your killer.'

What this meant was that fingerprint examples from the members of the Verloren family and others who had appropriate access to the house were still on file in the SID print lab. None of those examples matched the fingerprints and palm print recovered that morning from beneath Rebecca Verloren's bed. Of course fingerprints could not be dated, and it was possible that the prints discovered that morning had been left by whoever had installed the bed. But it seemed unlikely. The prints were taken off the underside of the wooden slat. Whoever had left them had most likely been under the bed.

'And the bad news?' Bosch asked.

'I just ran them through the California system. No matches.'

'What about the FBI?'

'That's next but that won't be so fast. They have to process it. I will send it through with an expedite request but you know how that goes.'

'I do, Raj. Let me know when you know, and thanks for the effort.'

Bosch closed the phone. He felt a steep letdown and his face showed it. He could already tell the others knew the score before he delivered the news.

'No match on the DOJ database,' he said. 'He'll try the bureau's base but that will take a while.'

'Shit!' said Renner.

'Speaking of Raj Patel,' Pratt said, 'his brother scheduled the autopsy for two o'clock today. I want one team there. Who wants to take it?'

Renner weakly raised his hand. He and Robleto would take it. It was an easy assignment if you didn't mind the visuals.

The meeting soon broke up after Pratt assigned Robinson and Nord the service station and the interviews of the people Mackey worked with there. Marcia and Jackson would work on pulling reports together and into a murder book. They were still the lead investigators and would coordinate things from room 503.

Pratt looked at the bill, divided it by nine and told everyone to put in ten. This meant Bosch had to throw in a ten even though he hadn't even had a cup of coffee.

He didn't protest. It was the price of being late and being the guy who put them on this path.

As everyone stood Bosch caught Rider's eye.

'Did you come directly here or did you ride with somebody?'

'Abel gave me a lift.'

'Want to ride back together?'

'Sure.'

Outside the restaurant she gave Bosch the silent treatment while they waited for his car from the valet. She stared at the large plastic steer that was atop the restaurant's sign. Under her arm was a file containing the printouts from the pen registers.

Finally the car came and they got in. Before pulling out of the lot Bosch turned and looked at her.

'All right, say it,' he said.

'Say what?'

'Whatever it is you want to say so you can feel better.'

'You should've called me, Harry, that's all.'

'Look, Kiz, I called you yesterday and you chewed me out. I was just working off of recent experience.'

'This was different and you know it. You called me yesterday because you were excited about something. Today you were following a lead. I should have been with you. And then to not find out what you came up with until you went in there and told everybody. That was embarrassing, Harry. Thanks for that.'

Bosch nodded his contrition.

'You're right about that part. I'm sorry. I should've called you when I was coming in. I just forgot. I knew I was late and I had both hands on the wheel and was just trying to get here.'

She didn't say anything, so he finally did.

'Can we get back to solving this case now?'

She shrugged and he finally put the car in drive. On the way to Parker Center he tried to fill her in on all the details he hadn't mentioned during the breakfast meeting. He told her about McClellan's visit to his house and how that led him to the discovery of the prints under the bed.

Twenty minutes later they were in their alcove in room 503. Bosch finally had a cup of coffee in front of him. They sat across from each other and had the pen register printouts spread between them.

Bosch was concentrating on the reports on the service station phones. The listing was at least a couple hundred entries – calls going in or out on the station's two phones – between 6 a.m., when the surveillance started, and 4 p.m., when Mackey reported for work and Renner and Robleto started live-monitoring the line.

Bosch scanned down the list. Nothing looked immediately familiar. Many of the calls were to or from business listings with some automobile connection clearly apparent in the name. Many others came in from the AAA dispatch center and these were likely tow calls.

There were also several calls that came from personal phones. Bosch looked closely at these names but saw nothing that jumped out at him. No one listed was an already established player in the case.

There were four entries on the list that were attributed to Visa, all the same number. Bosch picked up the phone and called it. He never heard it ring. He just got the loud screeching sound of a computer hookup. It was so loud that even Rider heard it.

'What is that?'

Bosch hung up.

'I'm trying to run down that note I saw on the desk in the station about Visa calling to confirm Mackey's employment. Remember you said it didn't fit?'

'I forgot about that. Was that the number?'

'I don't know. There are four listings for Visa but – wait a minute.'

He realized that the Visa calls were outgoing calls.

'Never mind, these were outgoing. It must be the number the machine calls when you use a credit card to pay. That's not it. There is no incoming call listed as Visa.'

Bosch picked up the phone again and called Nord's cell phone.

'Are you at the service station yet?'

She laughed.

'We've barely cleared Hollywood. We'll be there in a half hour.'

'Ask them about a phone message somebody left for Mackey yesterday. Something about Visa calling to confirm employment on a credit application. Ask them what they remember from the call and more importantly, what time it came in. Try to get the exact time if you can. Ask them about this first thing and then call me back.'

'Yes, sir. You want us to pick up your laundry, too?'

Bosch realized it was getting to be a bad morning for stepping on toes.

'Sorry,' he said. 'We're working under the gun here.'

'Aren't we all? I'll call you as soon as we see the guy.'

Nord hung up. Bosch put the phone down and looked at Rider. She was looking at the class picture of Rebecca Verloren in the yearbook they had borrowed.

'What are you thinking?' she asked without looking up at Bosch.

'This thing with Visa bothers me.'

'I know, so what are you thinking?'

'Well, say you're the killer and you got the gun you did it with from Mackey.'

'You're completely giving up on Burkhart? You sure liked him last night.'

'Let's just say the facts are persuading me. For now, okay?'

'Okay, go on.'

'All right, so you're the killer and you got the gun from Mackey. He's the one person in the world who can put the thing on you. But seventeen years go by and nothing ever happens and you feel safe and maybe you even lose track of Mackey.'

'Okay.'

'And then yesterday you pick up the paper and you see the picture of Rebecca and you read the story and it says they've got DNA. You know it wasn't your blood, so it was either a big bluff by the cops or it's got to be Mackey's blood. So that's when you know.'

'Mackey's gotta go.'

'Exactly. The cops are getting close. He's got to go. So how do you find him? Well, Mackey's spent his entire life – when he isn't in jail – driving a tow truck. If you knew that then you'd do exactly what we did. You get out the yellow pages and start calling tow companies.'

Rider stood up and went to the bank of file cabinets along the alcove's back wall. The phone books were stacked haphazardly on top. She had to stand on her toes to reach the yellow pages for the Valley. She came back and opened the book to the pages advertising tow services. She ran her finger down a listing until she reached Tampa Towing, where Mackey had worked. She backed up to the previous listing, a company called Tall Order Towing Services. She picked up her phone and dialed the number. Bosch heard only her side of the conversation.

'Yes, who am I speaking with?'

She waited a moment.

'My name is Detective Kizmin Rider with the Los Angeles Police Department. I am investigating a fraud case and wondered if I could ask you a question.'

Rider nodded as she apparently got a go-ahead.

'The suspect I am documenting has a history of calling businesses and identifying himself as someone working for Visa. He then attempts to verify someone else's employment as part of an application for a credit card. Does any of this ring a bell with you? We have information that leads us to believe that this individual was operating in the Valley yesterday. He likes to target automotive businesses.'

Rider waited while there was a response to her question. She looked at Bosch but gave no indication of anything.

'Yes, could you put her on the line, please?'

Rider went through the whole thing again with another person and asked the same question. Then she leaned forward and seemed to take a stiffer attitude in her posture. She covered the mouthpiece and looked at Bosch.

'Bingo,' she said.

She then went back to the phone call and listened some more.

'Was it a male or female?'

She wrote something down.

'And what time was this?'

She wrote another note and Bosch stood up so he could look across his desk to read it. She had written 'male, 1:30 approx' on a scratch pad. While she continued the conversation Bosch consulted the pen register and saw that a call came in on the Tampa Towing line at 1:40 p.m. It was from a personal number. The name on the register was Amanda Sobek. The number's prefix indicated it was a cell phone. Neither the name nor the number meant anything to Bosch. But that didn't matter. He thought they were getting close to something here.

Rider finished her call by asking if the person she was talking to remembered the name the supposed Visa employee had tried to confirm. After she apparently got a negative reply, she asked, 'What about the name Roland Mackey?'

She waited.

'Are you sure?' she asked. 'Okay, thank you for your time, Karen.'

She hung up and looked at Bosch. The excitement in her eyes wiped out everything about being left out of the morning's fingerprints find.

'You were right,' she said. 'They got a call. Same thing. She even remembered the name Roland Mackey once I gave it to her. Harry, somebody was tracking him down the whole time we were watching him.'

'And now we're going to track them down. If they were going down the line in the phone book they would have called Tampa Towing next. The register shows a one-forty call from somebody named Amanda Sobek. I don't recognize it but this might be the call we're looking for.'

'Amanda Sobek,' Rider said as she opened her laptop. 'Let's see what AutoTrack has on her.'

While she was tracing the name, Bosch got a call from Robinson, who had arrived with Nord at Tampa Towing.

'Harry, the dayshift guy says that call came in between one-thirty and two o'clock. He knows because he had just come back from lunch and he was sent out on a tow at two o'clock. A Triple A run.'

'Was it a male or female caller from Visa?'

'Male.'

'Okay, anything else?'

'Yeah, once this guy confirmed that Mackey worked here, the Visa guy asked what hours he worked.'

'Okay. Can you ask the day man another question?'

'He's right here.'

'Ask if they have a customer named Sobek. Amanda Sobek.'

Bosch waited while the question was asked.

'No customer named Sobek,' Robinson reported back. 'Is that good news, Harry?'

'It'll work.'

After closing the phone Bosch got up and walked around the desks so he could look at Rider's computer screen. He told her what Robinson had just reported.

'Anything on Amanda Sobek?' he asked.

'Yeah, this is it. She lives in the West Valley. Farralone Avenue in Chatsworth. But there is not a lot here. No credit cards or mortgage. I think it means it's all in her husband's name. She might be a housewife. I'm running the address to see if I can pull him up.'

Bosch opened the yearbook to Rebecca Verloren's class. He started flipping through the pages looking for the name Sobek or Amanda.

'Here he is,' Rider said. 'Mark Sobek. Everything's basically in his name and it looks like a lot. Four cars, two houses, lots of credit cards.'

'There was nobody named Sobek in her class,' Bosch said. 'But there were two girls named Amanda. Amanda Reynolds and Amanda Riordan. Think she is one of them?'

Rider shook her head.

'I don't think so. The age is off. This says Amanda Sobek is forty-one. That would make her eight years older than Rebecca. Something doesn't fit. Think we should just call her?'

Bosch closed the yearbook with a bang. Rider jumped in her seat.

'No,' he said. 'Let's just go.'

'Where? To see her?'

'Yeah. Time to get off your ass and knock on doors.'

He looked down at Rider and could tell she wasn't amused.

'I don't mean your ass specifically. It's a figure of speech. Let's just go.'

She started getting up.

'You are awfully flippant for somebody who might not have a job at the end of the day.'

'It's the only way to be, Kiz. Darkness waits. But it comes no matter what you do.'

He led the way out of the office.

37

The Farralone Avenue address AutoTrack led Bosch and Rider to belonged to a Mediterranean-style mansion that had to have been on the upper side of 6,000 square feet. It had a separate garage with four dark-stained wooden doors and windows from a guest suite above. The detectives had to view all of this through a wrought iron gate while waiting for someone to answer the intercom. Finally a voice came from the small square box on a pole next to Bosch's open window.

'Yes, who is it?'

It was a woman. She sounded young.

'Amanda Sobek?' Bosch asked in reply.

'No, this is her assistant. Who are you two?'

Bosch looked again at the box and saw the camera lens. They were being watched as well as listened to. He pulled out his badge and held it a foot from the lens.

'Police,' he said. 'We need to talk to Amanda or Mark Sobek.'

'About what?'

'About police business. Open the gate, please, ma'am.'

They waited and Bosch was just about to punch the call button again when the gate slowly started to automatically open. They drove in and parked in a turnaround circle in front of the two-story portico.

'Looks like the kind of place it might be worth killing a tow truck driver to protect,' Bosch said quietly as he cut the engine.

The door was opened before they got there by a woman in her twenties. She was wearing a skirt and a white blouse. The assistant.

'And you are?' Bosch asked.

'Melody Lane. I work for Mrs. Sobek.'

'Is she here?' Rider asked.

'Yes, she's getting dressed and will be right down. You can wait in the living room.'

They were led into an entrance hallway, where there was a table with several family photos on display. It looked like a husband, wife and two teenaged daughters. They followed Melody into a sumptuous living room with large windows looking out on Santa Susana State Park and Oat Mountain beyond.

Bosch checked his watch. It was almost noon. Melody noticed.

'She wasn't sleeping. She worked out earlier and was taking a shower. She should be down—'

She didn't need to finish. An attractive woman in white slacks and blouse left open over a pink chiffon shirt came hurrying into the room.

'What is it? Is something wrong? Are my girls all right?'

'Are you Amanda Sobek?' Bosch asked.

'Of course I am. What is wrong? Why are you here?'

Bosch pointed to the grouping of couch and chairs in the center of the room.

'Why don't we sit down here, Mrs. Sobek.'

'Just tell me if something is wrong.'

The panic on her face looked real to Bosch. He started to think they may have made a wrong turn somewhere.

'Nothing is wrong,' he said. 'This is not about your daughters. Your daughters are fine.'

'Is it Mark?'

'No, Mrs. Sobek. As far as we know he is fine, too. Let's sit down over here.'

She finally relented and walked quickly to the big chair to the right of the couch. Bosch moved around a glass coffee table and sat on the couch. Rider took one of the remaining chairs. Bosch identified himself and Rider and showed his badge again. He noticed that the glass on the table was spotless.

'We are conducting an investigation that I can't tell you about. I need to ask you some questions about your cell phone.'

'My cell phone? You scared me to death over my cell phone?'

'It's actually a very serious investigation, Mrs. Sobek. Do you have your cell phone with you?'

'It's in my purse. Do you need to see it?'

'No, not yet. Can you tell me when you used it yesterday?'

Sobek shook her head like it was an inane question.

'I don't know. In the morning I called Melody from the gym. I can't remember when else. I went to the store and called my daughters to see if they were on their way home after school. I can't remember anything else. I was home almost all day except for the gym. When I'm home I don't use my cell. I use the regular phone.'

Bosch's misgivings were multiplying. Somewhere they had made a wrong move.

'Could someone else have used the phone?' Rider asked.

'My daughters have their own. So does Melody. I don't understand this.'

Bosch pulled the page from the pen register out of his coat pocket. Out loud he read the number of the phone that had called Tampa Towing.

'Is that your number?' he asked.

'No, it's my daughter's. It's Kaitlyn's.'

Bosch leaned forward. This changed things further.

'Your daughter's? Where was she yesterday?'

'I already told you. She was in school. And she didn't use her phone until after, because it's not allowed at school.'

'What school does she go to?' Rider asked.

'Hillside Prep. It's over in Porter Ranch.'

Bosch leaned back and looked at Rider. Something had just come full circle. He wasn't sure what it was but it felt important.

Amanda Sobek read the looks on their faces.

'What is it?' she asked. 'Is something wrong at the school?'

'Not as far as we know, ma'am,' Bosch answered. 'What grade is your daughter in?'

'She is a sophomore.'

'Does she have a teacher named Bailey Sable?' Rider asked.

Sobek nodded.

'She has her for homeroom and English.'

'Is there any reason why Mrs. Sable might have borrowed your daughter's phone yesterday?' Rider asked.

Sobek shrugged.

'Not that I can think of. You have to understand how strange this is. All these questions. Was her phone used to make a threat or something? Is this some kind of terrorist thing?'

'No, ma'am,' Bosch said. 'But it is a serious matter. We are going to have to go to the school now and talk to your daughter. We would appreciate it if you came with us and were there when we spoke to her.'

'Does she need a lawyer?'

'I don't think so, ma'am.'

Bosch stood up.

'Shall we go?'

'Can Melody come too? I want Melody to go with me.'

'Tell you what. Have Melody meet us there. That way she can drive you back if we need to go somewhere else.'

38

On the drive over to Hillside Prep the car was silent. Bosch wanted to talk to Rider, to dope out this latest twist, but he didn't want to do it in front of Amanda Sobek. So they were silent until their passenger asked if she could call her husband and Bosch said that was fine. But she couldn't reach him and left a message in a near-hysterical voice telling him to call her as soon as he could.

When they got to the school it was lunchtime. As they walked down the main hallway to the office they could hear the near-riotous collision of voices from the cafeteria.

Mrs. Atkins was behind the counter in the office. She looked a little confused when she saw Amanda Sobek in the company of the detectives. Bosch asked to see Principal Stoddard.

'Mr. Stoddard took lunch off-campus today,' Mrs. Atkins said. 'Is there something I can help with?'

'Yes, we'd like to see Kaitlyn Sobek. Mrs. Sobek here will be with us when we talk to her.'

'Right now?'

'Yes, Mrs. Atkins, right now. I would appreciate it if you or another school employee could go and get her. It might be better if the other kids didn't see her being accompanied by the police.'

'I could go get her,' Amanda offered.

'No,' Bosch said quickly. 'We want to see her at the same time as you.'

It was a polite way of saying that he didn't want her to ask her daughter about the cell phone before the police did.

'I'll just go to the cafeteria and find her,' Mrs. Atkins said. 'You can use the principal's meeting room for your . . . uh, talk.'

She came around the counter, averted her eyes from Amanda Sobek and headed toward the door that led to the main hallway.

'Thank you, Mrs. Atkins,' Bosch said.

It took Mrs. Atkins almost five minutes to locate and return with Kaitlyn Sobek. While they were waiting, Melody Lane arrived and Bosch told Amanda that her assistant would have to wait outside the interview. The girl accompanied Bosch, Rider and her mother into a room off the principal's office that had a round table with six chairs around it.

After everyone sat down, Bosch nodded to Rider and she took over. Bosch thought it would be best for a woman to lead the interview of the girl and Rider understood this without discussion. She explained to Kaitlyn that they were investigating a phone call that was made on her cell phone at 1:40 p.m. the day before. The girl immediately interrupted.

'That's impossible,' she said.

'Why is that?' Rider asked. 'We had an electronic trap on the line that was called. It showed the call came from your phone.'

'I was in school yesterday. We're not allowed to use cell phones during school hours.'

The girl appeared nervous. Bosch could tell she was lying but couldn't figure out what the play was. He wondered if she was lying because her mother was in the room.

'Where is your phone right now?' Rider asked.

'In my backpack in my locker. And it's turned off.'

'Is that where it was yesterday at one-forty?'

'Uh-huh.'

She looked away from Rider as she lied. She was easy to read and Bosch knew Rider was getting the same thing he was getting.

'Kaitlyn, this is a very serious investigation,' Rider said in a soothing tone. 'If you are lying to us you could find yourself in a lot of trouble.'

'Kaitlyn, don't lie!' Amanda Sobek said forcefully.

'Mrs. Sobek, let's stay calm about this,' Rider said. 'Kaitlyn, these electronic traps I was telling you about are called pen registers. The registers don't lie. Your cell phone was used to make the call. There is no doubt. So is it possible someone got into your locker and used your phone yesterday?'

She shrugged.

'Anything's possible, I guess.'

'Okay, who would have done that?'

'I don't know. You were the one who said it.'

Bosch cleared his throat, which drew the girl's eyes to his. He stared hard at her and said, 'I think maybe we should take a drive downtown. Maybe this is not the right place for an interview.'

He started to push back his chair and get up.

'Kaitlyn, what is going on here?' Amanda pleaded. 'These people are serious. Who did you call?'

'No one, okay?'

'No, it's not okay.'

'I didn't have the phone, all right? It was confiscated.'

Bosch sat back down and Rider took over again.

'Who confiscated your phone?' she asked.

'Mrs. Sable,' the girl said.

'Why?'

'Because we're not supposed to use them inside school once the homeroom bell rings. Yesterday my best friend Rita didn't come to school. So I tried to text message her during homeroom to see if she was all right and Mrs. Sable caught me.'

'And she took your phone?'

'Yes, she took it.'

Bosch's mind was racing, trying to put Bailey Koster Sable into the mold of murderer of Rebecca Verloren. He knew one thing didn't work. A sixteen-year-old Bailey Koster could not have carried her friend's limp body up the hill behind her house.

'Why did you just lie to us about this?' Rider asked Kaitlyn.

'Because I didn't want her to know I was in trouble,' the girl said, indicating her mother with her chin.

'Kaitlyn, you never lie to the police,' Amanda shot back. 'I don't care what—'

'Mrs. Sobek, you can talk to her about this later,' Bosch said. 'Let us continue.'

'When did you get the phone back, Kaitlyn?' Rider asked.

'At the end of the day.'

'So Mrs. Sable had your phone all day?'

'Yes. I mean, no. Not all day.'

'Well, who had it?'

'I don't know. When they take your phone they tell you that you have to pick it up at the end of the day at the principal's office. That's what I did. Mr. Stoddard gave it back to me.'

Gordon Stoddard. Things all at once started to come together. Bosch had tucked into the water tunnel and the case and all its details were swirling around him. He rode the wave of clarity and grace. Everything was clicking. Stoddard clicked. Mackey's last word clicked. Stoddard was Rebecca's teacher. He was close to her. He was her lover and the late night caller. It all clicked into place.

Mr. X.

Bosch stood up and left the room without a word. He walked past Stoddard's office door. It was open and the desk was empty. He went out to the front counter.

'Mrs. Atkins, where is Mr. Stoddard?'

'He was just here but then he stepped out.'

'To where?'

'I don't know. Maybe the cafeteria. I told him you and the other detective were here talking to Kaitlyn.'

'And then he left?'

'Yes. Oh, I just realized – he might be in the parking lot. He said he got a new car today. Maybe he's showing it to one of the teachers.'

'What kind of car? Did he say?'

'A Lexus. He said it had a model number but I forget which one.'

'Does he have an assigned parking space?'

'Uh, yes, it is in the first row on the right as you come out of the entrance hall.'

Bosch turned from her and went out the door to the hallway. It was crowded with students leaving the cafeteria to start afternoon classes. Bosch started moving through the crowd, dodging students and picking up speed. Soon he was free of them and running. He came into the parking lot and immediately trotted down the parking lane to the right. He found an empty space with Stoddard's name painted on the curb.

He turned to go back in to get Rider. He was pulling his phone off his belt when he saw a silver blur to his right. It was a car coming right at him and it was too late to get out of the way.

39

Bosch was helped up into a sitting position on the asphalt.

'Harry, are you all right?'

He focused and saw that it was Rider. He nodded shakily. He tried to remember what had just happened.

'It was Stoddard,' he said. 'He was coming right at me.'

'In his car?'

Bosch laughed. He had left that part out.

'Yeah, his new car. A silver Lexus.'

Bosch started to get up. Rider put a hand on his shoulder to hold him down.

'Just wait a minute. Are you sure you're all right? Does anything hurt?'

'Just my head.'

It was coming back to him now.

'I banged it when I landed,' he said. 'I jumped out of the way. I saw his eyes, you know? The rage, I mean.'

'Let me see your eyes.'

He looked up at her and she held his chin while she checked his pupils.

'You look all right,' she said.

'Okay, then, I'll sit here for a second while you go back in and get Stoddard's home address from Mrs. Atkins.'

Rider nodded.

'All right. You wait here.'

'Hurry. We have to find him.'

She ran back into the school. Bosch reached up and felt the bump on the back of his head. He replayed the clearing memory. He had seen Stoddard's face behind the windshield. It was angry, contorted.

But then he had yanked the wheel to the left as Bosch jumped the other way.

Bosch reached for his phone so he could call in a wanted bulletin for Stoddard. It wasn't on his belt. He looked around and saw the phone on the asphalt near the rear tire of a BMW. He crawled over and grabbed it, then stood up.

Bosch was hit with mild vertigo and had to lean on the car. Suddenly an electronic voice said, 'Please step away from the car!'

Bosch pulled his hand away and started walking toward the part of the lot where he had parked his own car. On the way he called central dispatch and put out the wanted bulletin for Stoddard and his silver Lexus.

Bosch closed the phone and hooked it on his belt. He got to his car, started it and pulled up to the entrance so they would be ready to go as soon as Rider came out with the address.

After what seemed like an interminable wait Rider finally emerged and trotted to the car. But she came to his side, opened his door and waved him out.

'It's not far,' she announced. 'It's a house on Chase off of Winnetka. But you're not driving. I am.'

Bosch knew that arguing would waste time. He got out and moved as quickly as his balance allowed around the front of the car and got in on the passenger side. Rider hit the gas and they moved out of the parking lot.

As Rider made her way on surface streets toward Stoddard's home Bosch called for backup from Devonshire Division patrol and then called Abel Pratt to quickly fill him in on the morning's revelations.

'Where do you think he's going?' Pratt asked.

'No idea. We're on the way to his house.'

'Is he suicidal?'

'No idea.'

Pratt was silent for a moment as he digested this. He then asked a few more questions about minor details and hung up.

'He sounded happy,' Bosch told Rider. 'Says if we get this guy it'll help turn a lemon into lemonade.'

'Good,' Rider replied. 'We can pull prints from Stoddard's office or home and match them to the print from underneath the bed. Then it's a done deal whether he's in the wind or not.'

'Don't worry, we'll get him.'

'Harry, what are you thinking, Stoddard and Mackey did this together?'

'I don't know. But I remember that photo of Stoddard from the yearbook. He looked pretty lean. He might have been able to carry her up the hill by himself. We'll never know unless we find him and ask him.'

Rider nodded.

'The key question,' she then said, 'is how Stoddard connected with Mackey.'

'The gun.'

'I know that. That's obvious. I mean, how did he know Mackey back then? Where is the intersection and how did he know him well enough to get the gun from him?'

'I think it was right there in front of us all along,' Bosch said. 'And Mackey told me with his last word.'

'Chatsworth?'

'Chatsworth High.'

'How do you mean?'

'That summer he was getting his GED at Chatsworth High. On the night of the murder Mackey's alibi was his tutor. Maybe it was the other way around. Maybe Mackey was the tutor's alibi.'

'Stoddard?'

'He told us that first day that all of the teachers at Hillside had outside jobs. Maybe Stoddard was working as a tutor. Maybe he was Mackey's tutor.'

'That's a lot of maybes, Harry.'

'That's why we've got to find Stoddard before he does anything to himself.'

'You think he's suicidal? You told Abel you didn't know.'

'I don't know anything for sure. But back in that parking lot he turned away from me at the last second. It makes me think that he only wants to hurt one person.'

'Himself? Maybe he just didn't want to dent his new car.'

'Maybe.'

Rider turned onto Winnetka, a four-lane street, and started moving faster. They were almost at Stoddard's home. Bosch rode silently, thinking about what might be waiting for them ahead. Rider finally turned west on Chase and there was a black-and-white patrol car with both of its front doors open in the street up ahead. Rider pulled to a quick stop behind it and they jumped out of the car. Bosch took his gun off his belt and carried it at his side. Rider had a point about Stoddard maybe only thinking about his car when he avoided hitting Bosch.

The front door of the small World War II-era house was open. There was no sign of the patrol officers from the car. Bosch looked at Rider and saw that she was unholstered as well. They were ready to go in. At the door, Bosch shouted, 'Detectives coming in!'

He stepped into the threshold and got a response from inside.

'It's clear! It's clear!'

Bosch didn't relax or lower his weapon as he entered the living room. He scanned the room and didn't see anyone. He looked down at the coffee table and saw the *Daily News* from the previous day unfolded, the story on Rebecca Verloren on display.

'Patrol coming out!' a voice called from a hallway to the right.

Soon two patrol officers stepped out of the hallway into the living room. They carried their weapons at their sides. Now Bosch relaxed and lowered his own.

'All clear,' said the patrolman with the P2 stripes on his uniform. 'We found the door open and came in. There's something you ought to see back here in the bedroom.'

The patrolmen led the way and Bosch and Rider followed. They went down a short hallway that passed the open doors to a bathroom and a small bedroom that was used as a home office. They entered a bedroom and the P2 pointed to an oblong wooden box that was open on the bed. The box had a foam lining with a cutout in the shape of a long-barreled revolver. The cutout was empty and the gun was gone. There was a small rectangular cutout in the foam for a box of bullets. It was empty, too, but the box was nearby on the bed.

'Is there someone he's going after?' the P2 asked.

Bosch didn't look up from the gun box.

'Probably just himself,' he said. 'Either of you guys have gloves? Mine are in the car.'

'Right here,' the P2 said.

He pulled a pair of latex gloves out of a small compartment on his equipment belt. He handed them to Bosch, who snapped them on and then picked up the bullet box. Bosch opened it and slid out a plastic tray in which the bullets were stored. There was only one bullet missing.

Bosch was staring at the space left by the missing bullet and thinking about things when Rider tapped him on the elbow. He looked at her and then followed her gaze to the table on the other side of the bed.

There was a framed photo of Rebecca Verloren. It was a shot of her standing in a green field with the Eiffel Tower behind her. She was wearing a black beret and she was smiling in an unforced way. Bosch thought the look in her eyes was sincere and showed love for the person she was looking at.

'He wasn't in any of the pictures in the yearbook because he was the one behind the camera,' Bosch said.

Rider nodded. She, too, was in the water tunnel.

'That's where it started,' she said. 'That's where she fell in love with him. My true love.'

They stared in somber silence for a few moments until the P2 spoke.

'Detectives, can we clear?'

'No,' Bosch said. 'We need you to stay here and secure the house until SID gets here. And be ready in case he comes back.'

'You're leaving?' the P2 asked.

'We're leaving.'

40

They moved quickly back to Bosch's car and Rider once again got behind the wheel.

'Where to?' she said as she turned the ignition.

'The Verloren house,' Bosch said. 'And let's hurry.'

'What are you thinking?'

'I've been thinking about the picture they ran in the paper, with Muriel sitting on the bed. It showed how the room was still the same, you know?'

Rider thought for a moment and then nodded.

'Yeah.'

Rider understood. The photo showed that Rebecca's room was unchanged since the night she was taken. Seeing it might trigger something in Stoddard. A desire for something lost long ago. The photo was like an oasis, it was a reminder of a perfect place where nothing had gone wrong.

Rider pinned the accelerator and the car lurched forward. Bosch opened his cell, called dispatch and called for another backup unit to meet them at Muriel Verloren's house. He also updated the bulletin on Stoddard, describing him now as armed and dangerous and possibly 5150 – meaning mentally unstable. He knew as he closed the phone that he and Rider were close to the Verloren home and would get there first. His next call was to Muriel Verloren but there was no answer. When the message service picked up he closed his phone.

'No answer.'

They turned the corner onto Red Mesa Way five minutes later and Bosch's eyes immediately locked on the silver car parked at a haphazard angle against the curb in front of the Verloren house. It was the Lexus that had come at him in the school parking lot. Rider stopped next to the car and once again they emerged quickly, with weapons ready.

The front door of the house was ajar. Using hand signals they took stances on either side of it. Bosch then pushed the door open and went in first. Rider followed and they immediately moved into the living room.

Muriel Verloren was on the floor. There was a cardboard box and other packing supplies next to her. Brown packing tape had been wrapped several times around her head and face as a gag, and used to bind her hands and ankles. Rider propped her up against the couch and held a finger up to her lips.

'Muriel, is he in the house?' she whispered.

Muriel nodded, her eyes wide and wild.

'Rebecca's room?'

Muriel nodded again.

'Have you heard a gunshot?'

Muriel shook her head no and emitted a muffled sound that would have been a scream if not for the tape across her mouth.

'You have to be quiet,' Rider whispered. 'If I take off the tape you have to be very quiet.'

Muriel nodded intensely and Rider started working on the tape. Bosch huddled in close.

'I'm going up to the room.'

'Wait, Harry,' Rider ordered, her voice louder than a whisper. 'We go up together. Get her ankles.'

Bosch started working on the tape binding Muriel's feet together. Rider finally worked the tape loose from Muriel's mouth and pulled it down over her chin. She shooshed her soothingly as she did this.

'It's Becky's teacher,' Muriel whispered, her voice intense but not loud. 'He's got a gun.'

Rider started working on her wrists.

'Okay,' she said. 'We're going to deal with it.'

'What is he doing?' Muriel asked. 'Is he the one?'

'Yes, he's the one.'

Muriel Verloren let out a long, loud and anguished sigh. Her hands and feet were now loose and they helped her up to her feet.

'We're going up there,' Rider told her. 'We need you to get out of the house.'

They started ushering her toward the entrance hallway.

'I can't leave. He's in her room. I can't—'

'You have to leave, Muriel,' Bosch whispered harshly. 'It's not safe here. Go to a neighbor's house.'

'I don't know my neighbors.'

'Muriel, you have to get out,' Rider said. 'Go down the street. More police are on the way. Wave them down and tell them we're inside already.'

They pushed her through the open front door and then closed it behind her.

'Don't let him ruin her room!' they heard her plead from the other side. 'It's all I have left!'

Bosch and Rider made their way to the back hallway and went up the stairway as quietly as they could. They took positions on either side of the door to Rebecca's bedroom.

Bosch looked across at Rider. They both knew there was little time.

When backup units arrived the situation would change. It was a classic suicide-by-police setup. This was the one chance they might have of getting to Stoddard before he or a SWAT cop put a bullet into his brain.

Rider pointed to the doorknob and Bosch reached out and tried to silently turn it. He shook his head. The door was locked.

They used hand signals to outline a plan, nodded when they were ready, and then Bosch stepped back into the hallway and prepared to drive his heel into the door next to the knob. He knew he had to do it with one kick. They would lose the advantage of surprise after that.

'Who's out there?'

It was Stoddard, his voice coming through the door. Bosch looked at Rider. So much for the element of surprise. He pointed to her and gave her the silent sign. He would do the talking.

'Mr. Stoddard, it's Detective Bosch. How are you doing?'

'Not too good.'

'Yeah, things have sort of gotten out of hand, haven't they?'

Stoddard didn't answer.

'Tell you what,' Bosch said. 'You really need to think about putting the gun down and coming out. You're lucky I'm here. I just came to check on Mrs. Verloren. But my partner and the SWAT team are going to be here soon. You don't want to tangle with SWAT. Now is the time to come out.'

'I just want you to know I loved her, that's all.'

Bosch hesitated before speaking. He glanced over at Rider and then back at the door. He could go two ways with Stoddard. He could work on getting a confession right now or he could work on talking him out of the house and saving his life. Both things were possible but maybe not likely.

'So what happened?' he asked.

There was a long silence before Stoddard spoke.

'What happened was she wanted to keep the baby and she didn't understand how that would ruin everything. We had to get rid of it, and then afterward she changed her mind.'

'About the baby?'

'About me. About all of it.'

Bosch didn't respond. After a few moments Stoddard spoke again.

'I loved her.'

'But you killed her.'

'I made mistakes.'

'Like that night?'

'I don't want to talk about that night. I want to remember all the times before that night.'

'I guess I don't blame you.'

Bosch looked at Rider and held up three fingers. They were going to go on a three count. Rider nodded. She was ready.

Bosch dropped one finger.

'You know what I don't get, Mr. Stoddard?'

He dropped the second finger.

'What?' Stoddard asked.

Bosch dropped the third finger, then raised his right leg and drove it into the door. It was a hollow-interior door. It gave way easily and swung open with a crash. Bosch's momentum took him into the bedroom right behind it. He raised his gun and turned toward the bed.

Stoddard wasn't there.

Bosch continued his turn, catching a glimpse of Stoddard in the mirror. He was standing in the corner to the other side of the door. He was raising the muzzle of a long-barreled revolver to his mouth.

Bosch heard Rider shout and her body came through the door at full speed as she threw herself into Stoddard.

The crack of a gunshot shook the room as Rider and Stoddard went down to the floor. The revolver fell from Stoddard's hand and clattered onto the floor. Bosch moved quickly to them and dropped his weight onto Stoddard as Rider rolled off him.

'Kiz, you hit?'

There was no answer. Bosch tried to look at her while keeping Stoddard under control. Rider was holding one hand to the left side of her head.

'Kiz?'

'I'm not hit!' she yelled. 'I think I'm just deaf in one ear.'

Stoddard tried to get up, even with Bosch's weight on top of him.

'Please!' he said.

Bosch used his forearm to knock one of Stoddard's arms out from supporting him. Stoddard's chest hit the floor and Bosch quickly pulled the arm back and cuffed it. After a minor struggle he pulled the other arm back and completed the cuffing. He then leaned down and spoke to Stoddard.

'Please what?'

'Please let me die.'

Bosch got up and pulled Stoddard to his feet.

'That would be too easy for you, Stoddard. That would be like letting you get away all over again.'

Bosch looked over at Rider, who had gotten to her feet. He could see that some of her hair had been singed by the gun's discharge. It had been that close.

'You going to be okay?'

'As soon as the ringing stops.'

Bosch looked up and saw the bullet hole in the ceiling. He could hear sirens coming. He grabbed Stoddard by the elbow and pulled him toward the bedroom's door.

'I'm going to go down and put this guy in a car. We'll book him at Devonshire, hold him there until the arraignment.'

Rider nodded but Bosch could tell she was still dealing with what had just happened. The ringing in her ear was a reminder of how close it had been.

Bosch held Stoddard by the arm as he walked him down the steps. When they got to the living room, Stoddard spoke with a desperation in his voice.

'You could do it now.'

'Do what?'

'Shoot me. Say I ran. Take one of the cuffs off and say I got loose. You want to kill me, don't you?'

Bosch stopped and looked at him.

'Yes, I'd want to kill you. But that would be too good for you. You are going to have to pay for what you did to that girl and her family. And just putting you down right here wouldn't even cover the interest on seventeen years.'

Bosch roughly pushed him toward the door. They stepped out onto the front lawn just as a patrol car pulled to a stop and cut its siren. Bosch could tell by the streamlined light bar across the roof that it was one of the new cars he had heard about, with state-of-the-art equipment. The department could afford only a few of them in each budget cycle.

The car gave Bosch an idea. He raised his hand and circled his finger in the air, giving the all-clear sign.

As he walked Stoddard toward the car he saw Muriel Verloren walking down the middle of the street to her house. She was staring at Stoddard. Her mouth was wide open as if in a silent scream of horror. She started running toward them.

41

Bosch rode in the backseat of the patrol car with Stoddard on the way to Devonshire Division. Rider was left behind at the Verloren house to calm Muriel and to be checked out herself by paramedics. When they gave her the okay she would drive Bosch's car to the station.

The trip to the division would only take ten minutes. Bosch knew he had to quickly take a shot at getting Stoddard talking. The first thing he did was read the school principal his rights. Stoddard had made some admissions while holed up in Rebecca Verloren's bedroom, but whether they could be used in court was open to question because they had not been recorded and he had not been forewarned about his rights, which included remaining silent.

After reading the Miranda warning off a business card he had borrowed earlier from Rider, Bosch simply asked, 'Now, do you want to talk to me?'

Stoddard was leaning forward because his hands were still cuffed behind his back. His chin was almost down to his chest.

'What is there to say?' he asked.

'I don't know. I mean, I don't need you to talk. We've got you. Actions and evidence – we've got all we need. I just thought you might want to explain things, that's all. At a point like this a lot of people just want to explain themselves.'

Stoddard didn't respond at first. The car was heading east on Devonshire Boulevard. The station was a couple miles ahead. Earlier, when he had conferred with the two patrolmen outside of the car, Bosch had told the driver to take it slow.

'It's funny,' Stoddard finally said.

'What is?'

'I'm a science teacher, you know? I mean, before I was principal I taught science. I was head of the science department.'

'Uh-huh.'

'And I taught my students about DNA. I always told them that it was the secret of life. Decode DNA and you decode life itself.'

'Uh-huh.'

'And now ... now, well, it's used to decode death. By you people. It's the secret of life. It's the secret of death. I don't know. I guess it's not really funny. It's more ironic in my case.'

'If you say so.'

'A guy who taught DNA gets caught by DNA.'

Stoddard started to laugh.

'Hey, that's a good headline,' he said. 'Make sure you tell them that.'

Bosch reached over and used a key to unlock Stoddard's cuffs. He then relocked his wrists in front of his body so that he could sit up.

'Back there at the house, you said you loved her,' Bosch said.

Stoddard nodded.

'I did. I still do.'

'Funny way of showing it, wasn't it?'

'It wasn't planned. Nothing was planned that night. I had been watching her, that's all. Whenever I could, I watched her. I drove by all the time. I followed her when she got to take the car. I watched her at work, too.'

'And all the time you had a gun.'

'No, the gun was for me, not her. But ...'

'You found out it was easier to kill her instead of yourself.'

'That night ... I saw the garage door was open. I went in. I wasn't sure why. I thought I was going to use the gun on myself. On her bed. It would be my way of showing her my devotion.'

'But you went under the bed instead of on top of it.'

'I had to think.'

'Where was Mackey?'

'Mackey? I don't know where he was.'

'He wasn't with you? He didn't help you?'

'He gave me the gun. We made a deal. The gun for the grade. I was his teacher. And his tutor. It was my summer job.'

'But he wasn't with you that night? You carried her up the hill by yourself?'

Stoddard's eyes were open and staring into the distance even though their focus was only on the back of the front seat.

'I was strong back then,' he said in a whisper.

The patrol car pulled through the opening in the concrete block wall that surrounded the back of Devonshire Division. Stoddard looked out the window. Seeing all of the patrol cars and the back of the station must have brought an awakening to him. He realized his situation.

'I don't want to talk anymore,' he said.

'That's fine,' Bosch said. 'We'll put you in a holding room and get you a lawyer if you want.'

The car stopped in front of a set of double doors and Bosch got out. He came around and got Stoddard out and then walked him in through the doors. The detective bureau was on the second floor. They took an elevator and were met by the lieutenant in charge of Devonshire detectives. Bosch had called him from the Verloren house. An interview room was waiting for Stoddard. Bosch put him in a seat and cuffed one of his wrists to a metal ring bolted to the center of the table.

'Sit tight,' Bosch said. 'I'll be back.'

At the door, he looked back at Stoddard. He decided to make one last play.

'And for what it's worth, I think your story is bullshit,' he said.

Stoddard looked at him, surprise on his face.

'What do you mean? I loved her. I didn't want—'

'You stalked her with one purpose. To kill her. She rejected you and you couldn't take it, so you wanted her dead. And now seventeen years later you're going to try to tell it different, like it's Romeo and Juliet or something. You're a coward, Stoddard. You stalked her and killed her and you should own up to it.'

'No, you're wrong. I had the gun for myself.'

Bosch came back into the room and leaned down on the table.

'Yeah? What about the stun gun, Stoddard? Was that for yourself, too? You left that out of your story, didn't you? Why'd you need a stun gun if you went in there to kill yourself?'

Stoddard was silent. It was almost as if after seventeen years he had been able to erase the Professional 100 from his memory.

'We got first degree and we got lying in wait,' Bosch said. 'You're going down for the whole ride, Stoddard. You were never going to kill yourself. Back then, or even today.'

'I think I want a lawyer now,' Stoddard said.

'Yeah, of course you do.'

Bosch left the room and walked down the hallway to an open door. It was the monitoring room. The lieutenant and one of the patrol officers from the ride in were in the small space. There were two active video screens. On one Bosch saw Stoddard sitting in the interview room. The camera angle was from an upper corner of the room. Stoddard seemed to be staring blankly at the wall.

The image on the other screen was frozen. It showed Bosch and Stoddard in the backseat of the patrol car.

'How's the sound?' Bosch asked.

'Beautiful,' the lieutenant said. 'We got it all. Taking off the cuffs was a nice touch. Brought his face up into the camera.'

The lieutenant hit a switch and the picture started moving. Bosch could hear Stoddard's voice clearly. He nodded. The patrol car had been equipped with a dashboard camera used for filming traffic stops and prisoner transports. For the ride in with Stoddard the car's interior microphone was turned on and the exterior was cut off.

It had worked perfectly. Stoddard's admissions in the backseat would help seal the case. Bosch felt no worries from that direction at all. He thanked the lieutenant and the patrolman and asked if he could borrow a desk to make some calls.

Bosch called Abel Pratt to update him and to assure him that Rider was shaken up but otherwise okay. He told Pratt that he needed to get SID teams to both Stoddard's and Muriel Verloren's homes to process crime scenes. He said a search warrant should be applied for and approved before the SID team entered Stoddard's house. He said that Stoddard was about to be booked and his fingerprints taken. The prints would need to be compared to those found on the slat from beneath Rebecca Verloren's bed. He finished by telling Pratt about the video taken during the ride to the station and the admissions Stoddard had made.

'It's all solid and it's on tape,' Bosch said. 'It all came after Miranda.'

'Good going, Harry,' Pratt said. 'I don't think we'll have anything to worry about on this.'

'Not with the case, at least.'

Meaning that Stoddard was going to go down without a problem, but Bosch wasn't sure how he would fare in the review of his handling of the case.

'It's tough to argue with results,' Pratt said.

'We'll see.'

Bosch started getting a call-waiting signal on his phone. He told Pratt he had to go and clicked over to the new call. It was McKenzie Ward from the *Daily News*.

'My sister was listening to the scanner in the photo shop,' she said urgently. 'She said a backup unit and an ambulance were sent to the Verloren house. She recognized the address.'

'That's right.'

'What's going on, Detective? We had a deal, remember?'

'Yeah, I remember. And I was just about to call you.'

42

The kitchen at the Metro Shelter was dark. Bosch went to the small lobby of the adjoining hotel and spoke to the man behind the glass window. He asked for Robert Verloren's room number.

'He's gone, man.'

Something about the finality in his tone put a hollow into Bosch's chest. It didn't sound like he meant Verloren had gone out for the night.

'What do you mean gone?'

'I mean gone. He did his thing and he's gone. That's it.'

Bosch took a step closer to the glass. The man had a paperback novel open on the counter and had not looked up from its yellowed pages.

'Hey, look at me.'

The man flipped the book over to not lose his page and looked up. Bosch showed him his badge. He then glanced down and saw the book was called *Ask the Dust.*

'Yes, Officer.'

Bosch looked back up at the man's tired eyes.

'What do you mean, *He did his thing,* and what do you mean he's gone?'

The man shrugged.

'He came in drunk and that's the one rule we got around here. No drinking. No drunks.'

'He was fired?'

The man nodded.

'What about his room?'

'Room came with the job. Like I said, he's gone.'

'Where?'

The man shrugged one more time. He pointed to the door that led to the sidewalk on Fifth Street. He was telling Bosch that Verloren was out there somewhere.

'It happens,' the man said.

Bosch looked back at him.

'When did he go?'

'Yesterday. It was you cops who did it to him, you know.'

'What do you mean?'

'I heard some cop came in here, told him some shit. I don't know what it was about, but that was right before – know what I'm saying? He got off work and went out and took the taste again. And that was that. All I know is, we need a new chef now 'cause the guy they got fillin' in can't make eggs for shit.'

Bosch said nothing else to the man. He stepped away from the window and went to the door. Outside the shelter the street was teeming with people. The night people. The damaged and displaced. People hiding from others and hiding from themselves. People running from the past, from the things they did and the things they didn't do.

Bosch knew the story was going to hit the news in the morning. He had wanted to tell it to Robert Verloren himself.

Bosch decided he would look for Robert Verloren out there. He didn't know what the news he would bring would do for him. He didn't know if it would bring Verloren out or push him further into the hole. Maybe nothing could help him now. But he needed to tell him anyway. The world was full of people who could not get over things. There was no closure and there was no peace. The truth did not set you free. But you could get through things. That's what Bosch would tell him. You could head toward the light and climb and dig and fight your way out of the hole.

Bosch pushed open the door and headed out into the night.

43

The Police Academy parade field was nestled like a green blanket against one of the wooded hills of Elysian Park. It was a beautiful and shaded place and spoke well of the tradition the police chief had wanted Bosch to be reminded of.

At 8 a.m. on the morning following his fruitless night search for Robert Verloren, Bosch presented himself at the graduation check-in table and was escorted to an assigned seat on the platform beneath the VIP tent. There were four rows of chairs in formation behind the lectern from which the speeches would be made. Bosch's seat looked out across the parade grounds where the new cadets would march, then form up and be inspected. As an invited guest of the chief he would be one of the inspectors.

Bosch was in full uniform. It was tradition to fly the colors at the graduation of new officers – to welcome them to the uniform in the uniform. And he was early.

He sat by himself and listened to the police band play old standards. As other VIPs were taken to their seats, no one bothered him. They were mostly politicians and dignitaries and a few purple heart winners from Iraq who wore the uniform of the U.S. Marine Corps.

Bosch's skin felt raw under his starched collar and tightly knotted tie. He had spent almost an hour in the shower scrubbing away the ink he'd had put to his skin, hoping that it would take all the ugliness of the case down the drain with it.

He didn't notice the approach of Deputy Chief Irvin Irving until the cadet leading him to the tent said, 'Excuse me, sir.'

Bosch looked up and saw that Irving was being seated right next to him. He straightened up and grabbed his program off the seat intended for Irving.

'Enjoy yourself, sir,' the cadet said before snapping into a turn and heading back for another VIP.

Irving didn't say anything at first. He seemed to be spending a lot of time making himself comfortable and looking around to see who might be watching them. They were in the first row, two of the best seats in the place. Finally he spoke without turning or looking at Bosch.

'What is going on here, Bosch?'

'You tell me, Chief.'

Bosch took a turn looking around to see if anyone was watching them. It obviously wasn't happenstance that they were sitting next to each other. Bosch did not believe in coincidences. Not like that.

'The chief said he wanted me to be here,' he said. 'He invited me on Monday when he gave me back my badge.'

'Good for you.'

Another five minutes went by before Irving spoke again. The tent was almost full, except for the spot reserved for the chief of police and his wife at the end of the first row. Irving whispered now.

'You've had a hell of a week, Detective. You land in shit and come out stinking like a rose. Congratulations.'

Bosch nodded. It was an accurate assessment.

'What about you, Chief? Just another week at the office for you?'

Irving didn't respond. Bosch thought about the places he had looked for Robert Verloren the night before. He thought about Muriel Verloren's face when she had seen her daughter's killer being led to the patrol car. Bosch had had to hurry Stoddard into the backseat to keep her away from him.

'It was all because of you,' Bosch said quietly.

Irving glanced at him for the first time.

'What are you talking about?'

'Seventeen years, that's what I'm talking about. You had your man check the alibis on the Eights. He didn't know that Gordon Stoddard was also the girl's teacher. If it had been Green and Garcia running down the alibis – as it should have been – they would have come across Stoddard and easily put the whole thing together. Seventeen years ago. All of that time, that's on you.'

Irving turned fully in his seat to face Bosch.

'We had an agreement, Detective. You break it and I will find other ways of getting to you. I hope that's understood.'

'Yeah, sure, whatever you say, Chief. But you forget one thing. I'm not the only one who knows about you. What are you going to do, make your little deals with everybody? Every reporter, every cop? Every mother and father who has had to live with a hollowed-out life because of what you did?'

'Keep your voice down,' Irving said through his teeth.

Bosch responded in a quiet, calm voice.

'I've said all I want to say to you.'

'Well, let me tell you something, I'm not finished talking to you. If I find—'

He dropped the sentence as the chief of police was escorted by with his wife. Irving straightened himself in his seat as the music swelled and the show began. Twenty-four cadets with shining new badges on their uniformed chests marched into the parade grounds and took their positions in front of the VIP tent.

There were too many preliminary speeches. Then the inspection of the new officers took too long. But finally the program reached the main event, the traditional remarks of the chief of police. The man who had taken Bosch back into the department was relaxed and poised at the lectern. He spoke of rebuilding the police department from the inside out and starting with the twenty-four new officers standing before him. He said he was talking about rebuilding both the image and the practice of the department. He said many of the things he had said to Bosch on Monday morning. He urged the new officers never to break the law to enforce the law. To do their job constitutionally and compassionately at all times.

But then he surprised Bosch with his wrap-up.

'I would also like to draw your attention to two officers here as my guests today. One coming, one going. Detective Harry Bosch has returned to the department this week after a few years of retirement. I guess he learned during his extended vacation that you can't teach an old dog new tricks.'

There was polite laughter from the crowd on the other side of the parade grounds. This was where the families and friends of the cadets sat. The chief continued.

'So he came back to the LAPD family and already he has performed admirably. He has put himself in harm's way for the good of the community. Yesterday he and his partner cleared a seventeen-year-old murder that had been sticking like a thorn into the side of this community. We welcome Detective Bosch back to the fold.'

There was a smattering of applause from the crowd. Bosch felt his face go hot. He looked down at his hands.

'I would also like to thank Deputy Chief Irvin S. Irving for being here today,' the chief continued. 'Chief Irving has served in this department for nearly forty-five years. There is no current officer who has served longer. His decision to retire today and make this graduation his final action while wearing the badge is a fitting end to his tour of duty. We thank him for such service to this department and this city.'

The applause for Irving was much louder and sustained. People started to stand in honor of the man who had served the department and city so long. Bosch turned slightly to his right so that he could see Irving's face and he knew the moment he saw the deputy chief's eyes that he had not seen it coming. He had been sandbagged.

Soon everyone was standing and clapping and Bosch felt compelled to do the same for a man he despised. He knew exactly who had engineered Irving's fall. If Irving protested or tried in some way to recover his position he would face an internal case built by Kizmin Rider. There would be no doubt who would lose that one. No doubt at all.

What Bosch didn't know was when it had been planned. Bosch thought about Rider sitting on the desk in 503, waiting for him with coffee, black just like he liked it. Had she already known then what case the cold hit had come from and where it would lead? He remembered the date on the DOJ report. It was ten days old by the time he had read it. What happened during those ten days? What was planned for his arrival?

Bosch didn't know and he was not sure he even cared. Department politics were played on the sixth floor. Bosch worked out of 503 and that's where he would make his stand. No question.

After the chief finished his remarks he stepped away from the microphone. He gave each cadet, one by one, a certificate of completion of academy training and posed for a photo shaking hands with the recipient. It was all very fast and clean and choreographed perfectly. Three police helicopters flew over the parade grounds in formation and the cadets ended the ceremony by hurling their hats into the air.

Bosch remembered the time more than thirty years before when he had thrown his hat into the air. He smiled at the memory. No one from his class was left. They were dead or retired or washed out. He knew it was up to him to carry the banner and tradition. To fight the good fight.

As the ceremony ended and the crowds rushed to the field to congratulate the new officers, Bosch watched Irving stand up and start walking directly across the parade grounds to the exit area. He stopped for no one, not even those who extended hands of congratulations and thanks to him.

'Detective, you've had a busy week.'

Bosch turned. It was the chief of police. He nodded. He didn't know what to say.

'Thank you for being here,' the chief said. 'How is Detective Rider?'

'She took the day off. She had a close one yesterday.'

'So I heard. Will either of you be attending the press conference today?'

'Well, she's off and I was thinking of skipping it, if that's all right.'

'We'll handle it. I see you already gave the story to the *Daily News*. Now everyone else is clamoring for it. We have to put on the dog-and-pony show.'

'I owed the reporter from the *News* that one.'

'Yes, I understand.'

'When the dust settles, will I still have a job, Chief?'

'Of course, Detective Bosch. As in any investigation, choices must be made. Tough choices. You made the best decisions you could make. There will be a review but I don't think you will have a problem.'

Bosch nodded. He almost said thank you but decided against it. He just looked at the man.

'Is there something else you wanted to ask me, Detective?'

Bosch nodded again.

'I was just sort of wondering,' he said.

'About what?'

'The case started with a letter from the DOJ and that letter was old by the time it got to me. I'm wondering why it was held for me. I guess what I'm saying is, I'm wondering about what you knew and when you knew it.'

'Does any of that matter now?'

Bosch poked his chin in the direction Irving had taken.

'Maybe,' he said. 'I don't know. But he won't just walk away. He'll go to the media. Or to the lawyers.'

'He knows that if he does it will be a mistake. That there will be consequences for him. He's not a stupid man.'

Bosch just nodded. The chief studied him a moment before speaking again.

'You still seem troubled, Detective. Remember what I told you Monday? I told you I carefully reviewed your case and career before deciding whether to welcome you back.'

Bosch just looked at him.

'I meant that,' the chief said. 'I studied you and I think I know something about you. You are on this earth for one thing, Detective Bosch. And you now have the opportunity to do that, to continue to carry out your mission. After that, does anything else matter?'

Bosch held his eyes for a long time before answering.

'I guess what I really wanted to ask is about what you said the other day. When you said all of that about the ripples and the voices, did you mean it? Or were you just winding me up to go after Irving for you?'

Fire quickly spread across the police chief's cheeks. His eyes dropped from Bosch's as he composed his answer. Then he looked back up at Bosch and it was his eyes that held Bosch's this time.

'I meant every word of it. And don't you forget it. You go back to room five oh three and you close cases, Detective. That's what you are here for. Close them out or I'll find reason to close you out. Do you understand?'

Bosch didn't feel threatened. He liked the chief's answer. It made him feel better. He nodded.

'I understand.'

The chief raised his hand and took Bosch by the upper arm.

'Good. Then let's go over here and get a picture taken with some of these young people who have joined our family today. Maybe they can learn something from us. Maybe we can learn something from them.'

As they moved into the crowd Bosch looked off in the direction Irving had taken. But he was long gone.

44

Bosch looked for Robert Verloren for three of the next seven nights but didn't find him until it was too late.

One week after the academy graduation, Bosch and Rider were sitting across from each other at their desks while putting the finishing touches on the case against Gordon Stoddard. The accused murderer had been arraigned in San Fernando Municipal Court earlier in the week and had pleaded not guilty. Now the legal dance had begun. Bosch and Rider had to put together a comprehensive charging document that outlined the case against Stoddard. It would be given to the prosecutor and used in negotiations with Stoddard's defense attorney. After meeting with Muriel Verloren as well as Bosch and Rider, the prosecutor set a case strategy. If Stoddard elected to go to trial the state would seek the death penalty under the lying-in-wait statute. The alternative was for Stoddard to avoid risking death and plead guilty to first-degree murder in a plea agreement that would send him to prison for life without the possibility of parole.

Either way, the case summary Bosch and Rider were composing would be of key importance because it would show Stoddard and his lawyer just how strong the evidence was. It would force their hand, make Stoddard choose between the grim alternatives of life in a jail cell or gambling his life on the slim possibility of beating the case with a jury.

It had been a good week until that point. Rider bounced back from her near miss from Stoddard's bullet and showed full command of her skills in putting together the case summary. Bosch had spent all of Monday going over the investigation with an Internal Affairs investigator and was cleared the next day. The 'no action taken' verdict from IAD meant he was clear within the department, even though the ongoing stories about the case in the media continued to call into question the department's actions in using Roland Mackey as bait.

Bosch was ready to move on to the next investigation. He had already told Rider he wanted to check into the case of the lady he found tied up and drowned in her bathtub on his first day on the job. They would take it up as soon as they put the paper case on Stoddard to rest.

Abel Pratt came out of his office and stepped into their alcove. He had an ashen look on his face. He nodded toward Rider's computer screen.

'Is that Stoddard you're working on?' he asked.

'Yes,' Rider said. 'What's up?'

'You can spike it. He's dead.'

Nobody said anything for a long moment.

'Dead?' Rider finally asked. 'What do you mean, dead?'

'Dead in his cell in Van Nuys jail. Two puncture wounds to the neck.'

'He did it himself?' Bosch asked. 'I didn't think he had it in him.'

'No, somebody did it for him.'

Bosch sat up straight.

'Wait a minute,' he said. 'He was on the high-power floor and on keep-away status. Nobody could've—'

'Somebody did this morning,' Pratt said. 'And that's the bad part.'

Pratt raised a small notebook in his hand. Notes had been scribbled on it. He read from it.

'On Monday night a man was arrested on Van Nuys Boulevard on a drunk and disorderly. He also assaulted one of the cops who hooked him up. He was routinely fingerprinted and booked into Van Nuys jail. He had no ID and gave the name Robert Light. The next day at arraignment he pleaded guilty to all charges and the judge gave him a week in Van Nuys jail. The prints had still not been run through the computer.'

Bosch felt a deep tug in his gut. He felt dread. He knew where this was going. Pratt continued, using his notes to construct the story.

'The man who called himself Robert Light was assigned to kitchen duty at the jail because he claimed and also demonstrated that he had restaurant experience. This morning he traded jobs with one of the others in the kitchen and was pushing the wagon that was carrying food trays to the custodies on high power. According to two guards who witnessed it, when Stoddard went to the slide window on his cell door to accept the food tray, Robert Light reached through the bars and grabbed him. He then stabbed him repeatedly with a shiv made from a sharpened spoon. He got two punctures into the neck before the guards subdued him. But the guards were too late. Stoddard's carotid artery was slashed and he bled out in his cell before they could get help to him.'

Pratt stopped there but Bosch and Rider asked no questions.

'Coincidentally,' Pratt began again, 'Robert Light's fingerprints were finally entered into the database at about the same time that he was killing Stoddard. The computer kicked out a bogie – a custody who gave a false name. The real name, as I am sure you have already guessed, was Robert Verloren.'

Bosch looked across at Rider but couldn't hold her eyes for long. He looked down at his desk. He felt as though he had been punched. He closed his eyes and rubbed his face with his hands. He felt that it was in some way his fault. Robert Verloren had been his responsibility in the investigation. He should have found him.

'How's that for closure?' Pratt said.

Bosch dropped his hands and stood up. He looked at Pratt.

'Where is he?' he asked.

'Verloren? They still have him there. Van Nuys homicide is handling it.'

'I'm going up there.'

'What are you going to do?' Rider asked.

'I don't know. Whatever I can.'

He walked out of the alcove, leaving Rider and Pratt behind. Out in the hallway he punched the elevator button and waited. The heaviness in his chest wasn't going away. He knew it was the feeling of guilt, the feeling that he had not been ready for this case and that his mistakes had been so costly.

'It's not your fault, Harry. He did what he had waited seventeen years to do.'

Bosch turned. Rider had come up behind him.

'I should have found him first.'

'He didn't want to be found. He had a plan.'

The elevator door opened. It was empty.

'Whatever you're doing,' Rider said, 'I'm going with you.'

He nodded. Being with her would make it easier. He motioned her into the elevator and then followed. On the way down he felt a resolve rise inside him. A resolve to carry on the mission. A resolve never to forget Robert and Muriel and Rebecca Verloren along the way. And a promise always to speak for the dead.

Acknowledgements

The author would like to gratefully acknowledge those who helped with the research and writing of this novel. They include Michael Pietsch, Asya Muchnick, Jane Wood and Peggy Leith Anderson as well as Jane Davis, Linda Connelly, Terrill Lee Lankford, Mary Capps, Judy Couwels, John Houghton, Jerry Hooten and Ken Delavigne. Very special thanks go to detectives Tim Marcia, Rick Jackson and David Lambkin of the Los Angeles Police Department, as well as Sergeant Bob McDonald and Police Chief William Bratton.

Echo Park

This is for Jane Wood – who keeps Harry Bosch
well fed and close to the heart. Many, many thanks.

The High Tower 1993

It was the car they had been looking for. The license plate was gone but Harry Bosch could tell. A 1987 Honda Accord, its maroon paint long faded by the sun. It had been updated in '92 with the green Clinton bumper sticker and now even that was faded. The sticker had been made with cheap ink, not meant to last. Back when the election was a long shot. The car was parked in a single-car garage so narrow it made Bosch wonder how the driver had been able to get out. He knew he would have to tell the Forensics people to be extra diligent while checking for prints on the outside of the car and the garage's inner wall. The Forensics people would bristle at being told this but he would become anxious if he didn't.

The garage had a pull-down door with an aluminum handle. Not good for prints but Bosch would point that out to Forensics as well.

'Who found it?' he asked the patrol officers.

They had just strung the yellow tape across the mouth of the cul-de-sac which was made by the two rows of individual garages on either side of the street and the entrance of the High Tower apartment complex.

'The landlord,' the senior officer replied. 'The garage goes with an apartment he's got vacant, so it's supposed to be empty. A couple days ago he opens it up because he's got to store some furniture and stuff and he sees the car. Thinks maybe it's somebody visiting one of the other tenants so he lets it go a few days, but then the car stays put and so he starts asking his tenants about it. Nobody knows the car. Nobody knows whose it is. So then he calls us because he starts thinking it might be stolen because of the missing plates. Me and my partner have got the Gesto bulletin on the visor. Once we got here we put it together pretty fast.'

Bosch nodded and stepped closer to the garage. He breathed in deeply through his nose. Marie Gesto had been missing ten days now. If she was in the trunk he would smell it. His partner, Jerry Edgar, joined him.

'Anything?' he asked.

'I don't think so.'

'Good.'

'Good?'

'I don't like trunk cases.'

'At least we'd have the victim to work with.'

It was just banter as Bosch's eyes roamed over the car, looking for anything that would help them. Seeing nothing, he took a pair of latex gloves out of his coat pocket, blew them up like balloons to stretch the rubber and then pulled them onto his hands. He held his arms up like a surgeon coming into the operating room and turned sideways so that he could try to slide into the garage and get to the driver's door without touching or disturbing anything.

He slid into darkness as he moved into the garage. He batted spider threads away from his face. He moved back out and asked the patrol officer if he could use the Maglite on his equipment belt. Once he was back in the garage he turned the light on and put its beam through the windows of the Honda. He saw the backseat first. The riding boots and helmet were on the seat. There was a small plastic grocery bag next to the boots with the Mayfair Supermarket insignia on it. He couldn't tell what was in the bag but knew that it opened an angle on the investigation they hadn't thought of before.

He moved forward. On the front passenger seat he noticed a small stack of neatly folded clothing on top of a pair of running shoes. He recognized the blue jeans and the long-sleeved T-shirt, the outfit Marie Gesto was wearing when last seen by witnesses as she was heading to Beachwood Canyon to ride. On top of the shirt were carefully folded socks, panties and bra. Bosch felt the dull thud of dread in his chest. Not because he took the clothing as confirmation that Marie Gesto was dead. In his gut he already knew that. Everybody knew it, even the parents who appeared on TV and pleaded for their daughter's safe return. It was the reason why the case had been taken from Missing Persons and reassigned to Hollywood Homicide.

It was her clothes that got to Bosch. The way they were folded so neatly. Did she do that? Or had it been the one who took her from this world? It was the little questions that always bothered him, filled the hollow inside with dread.

After surveying the rest of the car through the glass, Bosch carefully worked his way out of the garage.

'Anything?' Edgar asked again.

'Her clothes. The riding equipment. Maybe some groceries. There's a Mayfair at the bottom of Beachwood. She could've stopped on her way up to the stables.'

Edgar nodded. A new lead to check out, a place to look for witnesses.

Bosch stepped out from beneath the overhead door and looked up at the High Tower Apartments. It was a place unique to Hollywood. A conglomeration of apartments built into the extruded granite of the hills behind the Hollywood Bowl. They were of Streamline Moderne design and all linked at the center by the slim structure that housed the elevator – the high tower from which the street and complex took its name. Bosch had lived in this neighborhood for a time while growing up. From his home on nearby Camrose he could hear the orchestras practicing in the bowl on summer days. If he stood on the roof he could see the fireworks on the Fourth and at the close of the season.

At night he had seen the windows on the High Tower glowing with light. He'd see the elevator pass in front of them on its way up, delivering another person home. He had thought as a boy that living in a place where you took an elevator home had to be the height of luxury.

'Where's the manager?' he asked the patrol officer with two stripes on his sleeves.

'He went back up. He said take the elevator to the top and his place is the first one across the walkway.'

'Okay, we're going up. You wait here for SID and the OPG. Don't let the tow guys touch the car until Forensics takes a look.'

'You got it.'

The elevator in the tower was a small cube that bounced with their weight as Edgar slid the door open and they stepped in. The door then automatically closed and they had to slide an interior safety door closed as well. There were only two buttons, 1 and 2. Bosch pushed 2 and the car lurched upward. It was a small space, with enough room for four people at the most before everybody would start tasting each other's breath.

'Tell you what,' Edgar said, 'nobody in this place has a piano, that's for sure.'

'Brilliant deduction, Watson,' Bosch said.

On the top level they pulled the doors open and stepped out onto a concrete runway that was suspended between the tower and the separate apartments built into the hillside. Bosch turned and looked past the tower to a view that took in almost all of Hollywood and had the mountain breeze to go with it. He looked up and saw a red-tailed hawk floating above the tower, as if watching them.

'Here we go,' Edgar said.

Bosch turned to see his partner pointing to a short set of stairs that led to one of the apartment doors. There was a sign that said MANAGER below a doorbell. The door was opened before they got to it by a thin man with a white beard. He introduced himself as Milano Kay, the manager of the apartment complex. After they badged him Bosch and Edgar asked if they could see the vacant apartment to which the garage with the Honda in it was assigned. Kay led the way.

They walked back past the tower to another runway that led to an apartment door. Kay started working a key into the door lock.

'I know this place,' Edgar said. 'This complex and the elevator, it's been in the movies, right?'

'That's right,' Kay said. 'Over the years.'

It stood to reason, Bosch thought. A place as unique as this could not escape the eye of the local industry.

Kay opened the door and signaled Bosch and Edgar in first. The apartment was small and empty. There was a living room, kitchen with a small eat-in space and a bedroom with an attached bathroom. No more than four hundred square feet and Bosch knew that with furniture it would look even smaller. But the view was what the place was about. A curving wall of windows looked out on the same view of Hollywood seen from the walkway to the tower. A glass door led to a porch that followed the curve of glass. Bosch stepped out and saw the view was expanded out here. He could see the towers of downtown through the smog. He knew the view would be best at night.

'How long has this apartment been vacant?' he asked.

'Five weeks,' Kay answered.

'I didn't see a FOR RENT sign down there.'

Bosch looked down at the cul-de-sac and saw the two patrol officers waiting for Forensics and the flatbed from the police garage. They were on opposite sides of their cruiser, leaning on the hood with their backs to each other. It didn't look like a thriving partnership.

'I never need to put up signs,' Kay said. 'The word that we have a vacancy usually gets out. A lot of people want to live in this place. It's a Hollywood original. Besides, I've been in the process of getting it ready, repainting and small repairs. I haven't been in any hurry.'

'What's the rent?' Edgar asked.

'A thousand a month.'

Edgar whistled. It seemed high to Bosch, too. But the view told him there would be somebody who would pay it.

'Who would have known that that garage down there was empty?' he asked, getting back on track.

'Quite a few people. The residents here, of course, and in the last five weeks I've shown the place to several interested parties. I usually point out the garage to them. When I go on vacation there's a tenant here who sort of watches things for me. He showed the apartment, too.'

'The garage is left unlocked?'

'It's left unlocked. There's nothing in it to steal. When the new tenant comes in they can choose to put a padlock on it if they want to. I leave it up to them but I always recommend it.'

'Did you keep any kind of records on who you showed the apartment to?'

'Not really. I might have a few call-back numbers but there is no use in keeping anybody's name unless they rent it. And as you can see, I haven't.'

Bosch nodded. It was going to be a tough angle to follow. Many people knew the garage was empty, unlocked and available.

'What about the former tenant?' he asked. 'What happened to him?'

'It was a woman, actually,' Kay said. 'She lived here five years, trying to make it as an actress. She finally gave up and went back home.'

'It's a tough town. Where was home?'

'I sent her deposit back to Austin, Texas.'

Bosch nodded.

'She live here alone?'

'She had a boyfriend who visited and stayed a lot but I think that ended before she moved out.'

'We'll need that address in Texas from you.'

Kay nodded.

'The officers, they said the car belonged to a missing girl,' he said.

'A young woman,' Bosch said.

He reached into an inside pocket of his jacket and pulled out a photograph of Marie Gesto. He showed it to Kay and asked if he recognized her as someone who might have looked at the apartment. He said he didn't recognize her.

'Not even from TV?' Edgar asked. 'She's been missing ten days and it's been in the news.'

'I don't have a TV, Detective,' Kay said.

No television. In this town that qualified him as a free thinker, Bosch thought.

'She was in the newspapers, too,' Edgar tried.

'I read the papers from time to time,' Kay said. 'I get them out of the recycle bins downstairs. They're usually old by the time I see them. But I didn't see any story about her.'

'She went missing ten days ago,' Bosch said. 'That would have been Thursday the ninth. You remember anything from back then? Anything unusual around here?'

Kay shook his head.

'I wasn't here. I was on vacation in Italy.'

Bosch smiled.

'I love Italy. Where'd you go?'

Kay's face brightened.

'I went up to Lake Como and then over to a small hill town called Asolo. It's where Robert Browning lived.'

Bosch nodded like he knew the places and knew who Robert Browning was.

'We've got company,' Edgar said.

Bosch followed his partner's gaze down to the cul-de-sac. A television truck with a satellite dish on top and a big number 9 painted on the side had pulled up to the yellow tape. One of the patrol officers was walking toward it.

Harry looked back at the landlord.

'Mr. Kay, we'll need to talk more later. If you can, see what numbers or names you can find of people who looked at or called about the apartment. We'll also need to talk to the person who handled things while you were in Italy and get the name and forwarding address of the former tenant who moved back to Texas.'

'No problem.'

'And we're going to need to talk to the rest of the tenants to see if anybody saw that car being dropped off in the garage. We will try not to be too intrusive.'

'No problem with any of that. I'll see what I can dig up on the numbers.'

They left the apartment and walked with Kay back to the elevator. They said good-bye to the manager and went down, the steel cube lurching again before smoothing out on the descent.

'Harry, I didn't know you love Italy,' Edgar said.

'I've never been.'

Edgar nodded, realizing it had been a tactic to draw Kay out, to put more alibi information on record.

'You thinking about him?' he asked.

'Not really. Just covering the bases. Besides, if it was him, why put the car in his place's own garage? Why call it in?'

'Yeah. But then, maybe he's smart enough to know we'd think he'd be too smart to do that. See what I mean? Maybe he's outsmarting us, Harry. Maybe the girl came to look at the place and things went wrong. He hides the body but knows he can't move that car because he might get pulled over by the cops. So he waits ten days and calls it in like he thinks it might be stolen.'

'Then maybe you should run his Italian alibi down, Watson.'

'Why am I Watson? Why can't I be Holmes?'

'Because Watson is the one who talks too much. But if you want, I'll start calling you "Homes." Maybe that would be better.'

'What's bothering you, Harry?'

Bosch thought of the clothing neatly folded on the front seat of the Honda. He felt that pressure on his insides again. Like his body was wrapped in wire being tightened from behind.

'What's bothering me is that I've got a bad feeling about this one.'

'What kind of bad feeling?'

'The kind that tells me we're never going to find her. And if we never find her, then we never find him.'

'The killer?'

The elevator jerked to a hard stop, bounced once and came to a rest. Bosch pulled open the doors. At the end of the short tunnel that led to the cul-de-sac and the garages, he saw a woman holding a microphone and a man holding a television camera waiting for them.

'Yeah,' he said. 'The killer.'

Part One
The Killer

1

The call came in while Harry Bosch and his partner, Kiz Rider, were sitting at their desks in the Open-Unsolved Unit, finishing the paperwork on the Matarese filing. The day before, they had spent six hours in a room with Victor Matarese discussing the 1996 murder of a prostitute named Charisse Witherspoon. DNA that had been extracted from semen found in the victim's throat and stored for ten years had been matched to Matarese. It was a cold hit. His DNA profile had been banked by the DOJ in 2002 after a forcible rape conviction. It had taken another four years before Bosch and Rider came along and reopened the Witherspoon case, pulled the DNA and sent it to the state lab on a blind run.

It was a case initially made in the lab. But because Charisse Witherspoon had been an active prostitute the DNA match was not an automatic slam dunk. The DNA could have come from someone who was with her before her killer turned up and hit her repeatedly on the head with a two-by-four.

So the case didn't come down to the science. It came down to the room and what they could get from Matarese. At 8 a.m. they woke him up at the halfway house where he had been placed upon his parole in the rape case and took him to Parker Center. The first five hours in the interview room were grueling. In the sixth he finally broke and gave it all up, admitting to killing Witherspoon and throwing in three more, all prostitutes he had murdered in South Florida before coming to L.A.

When Bosch heard his name called out for line one, he thought it was going to be Miami calling him back. It wasn't.

'Bosch,' he said after grabbing the phone.

'Freddy Olivas. Northeast Division Homicide. I'm over in Archives looking for a file and they say you've already got it signed out.'

Bosch was silent a moment while his mind dropped out of the Matarese case. Bosch didn't know Olivas but the name sounded familiar. He just couldn't place it. As far as signed-out files went, it was his job to review old cases and look for ways to use forensic advances to solve them. At any given time he and Rider could have as many as twenty-five files from Archives.

'I've pulled a lot of files from Archives,' Bosch said. 'Which one are we talking about?'

'Gesto. Marie Gesto. It's a 'ninety-three case.'

Bosch didn't respond right away. He felt his insides tighten. They always did when he thought about Gesto, even thirteen years later. In his mind, he always came up with the image of those clothes folded so neatly on the front seat of her car.

'Yeah, I've got the file. What's happening?'

He noticed Rider look up from her work as she registered the change in his voice. Their desks were in an alcove and pushed up against one another, so Bosch and Rider faced each other while they worked.

'It's kind of a delicate matter,' Olivas said. 'Eyes only. Relates to an ongoing case I've got and the prosecutor just wants to review the file. Could I hop on by there and grab it from you?'

'Do you have a suspect, Olivas?'

Olivas didn't answer at first and Bosch jumped in with another question.

'Who's the prosecutor?'

Again no answer. Bosch decided not to give in.

'Look, the case is active, Olivas. I'm working it and have a suspect. If you want to talk to me, then we'll talk. If you've got something working, then I am part of it. Otherwise, I'm busy and you can have a nice day. Okay?'

Bosch was about to hang up when Olivas finally spoke. The friendly tone was gone from his voice.

'Tell you what, let me make a phone call, Hotshot. I'll call you right back.'

He hung up without a good-bye. Bosch looked at Rider.

'Marie Gesto,' he said. 'The DA wants the file.'

'That's your own case. Who was calling?'

'A guy from Northeast. Freddy Olivas. Know him?'

Rider nodded.

'I don't know him but I've heard of him. He's lead on the Raynard Waits case. You know the one.'

Now Bosch placed the name. The Waits case was high profile. Olivas probably viewed it as his ticket to the show. The LAPD was broken into nineteen geographic divisions, each with a police station and its own detective bureau. Divisional Homicide units worked the less complicated cases and the positions were viewed as stepping stones to the elite Robbery-Homicide Division squads working out of the police headquarters at Parker Center. That was the show. And one of those squads was the Open-Unsolved Unit. Bosch knew that if Olivas's interest in the Gesto file was even remotely tied to the Waits case, then he would jealously guard his position from RHD encroachment.

'He didn't say what he has going?' Rider asked.

'Not yet. But it must be something. He wouldn't even tell me which prosecutor he's working with.'

'Ricochet.'

'What?'

She said it slower.

'Rick O'Shea. He's on the Waits case. I doubt Olivas has anything else going. They just finished the prelim on that and are heading to trial.'

Bosch didn't say anything as he considered the possibilities. Richard 'Ricochet' O'Shea ran the Special Prosecutions Section of the DA's office. He was a hotshot and he was in the process of getting hotter. Following the announcement in the spring that the sitting district attorney had decided against seeking re-election, O'Shea was one of a handful of prosecutors and outside attorneys who filed as candidates for the job. He had come through the primary with the most votes but not quite a majority. The runoff was shaping up as a tighter race but O'Shea still held the inside track. He had the backing of the outgoing DA, knew the office inside and out, and had an enviable track record as a prosecutor who won big cases – a seemingly rare attribute in the DA's office in the last decade. His opponent was named Gabriel Williams. He was an outsider who had credentials as a former prosecutor but he had spent the last two decades in private practice, primarily focusing on civil rights cases. He was black, while O'Shea was white. He was running on the promise of watchdogging and reforming the county's law enforcement practices. While members of the O'Shea camp did their very best to ridicule Williams's platform and qualifications for the position of top prosecutor, it was clear that his outsider stance and platform of reform were taking hold in the polls. The gap was closing.

Bosch knew what was happening in the Williams–O'Shea campaigns because this year he had been following local elections with an interest he had never exhibited before. In a hotly contested race for a city council seat, he was backing a candidate named Martin Maizel. Maizel was a three-term incumbent who represented a west-side district far from where Bosch lived. He was generally viewed as a consummate politician who made backroom promises and was beholden to big-money interests to the detriment of his own district. Nevertheless, Bosch had contributed generously to his campaign and hoped to see his re-election. His opponent was a former deputy police chief named Irvin S. Irving, and Bosch would do whatever was within his power to see Irving defeated. Like Gabriel Williams, Irving was promising reform and the target of his campaign speeches was always the LAPD. Bosch had clashed numerous times with Irving while he served in the department. He didn't want to see the man sitting on the city council.

The election stories and wrap-ups that ran almost daily in the *Times* had kept Bosch up to date on other contests as well as the Maizel–Irving contest. He knew all about the fight O'Shea was involved in. The prosecutor was in the process of bolstering his candidacy with high-profile advertisements and prosecutions designed to show the value of his experience. A month earlier he had parlayed the preliminary hearing in the Raynard Waits case into daily headlines and top-of-the-broadcast reports. The accused double murderer had been pulled over in Echo Park on a late-night traffic stop. Officers spied trash bags on the floor of the man's van with blood leaking from them. A subsequent search found body parts from two women in the bags. If ever there was a safe, slam-bang case for a prosecutor-candidate to use to grab media attention, the Echo Park Bagman case appeared to be it.

The catch was that the headlines were now on hold. Waits was bound over for trial at the end of the preliminary hearing and, since it was a death penalty case, that trial and the attendant renewal of headlines were still months off and well after the election. O'Shea needed something new to grab headlines and keep momentum going. Now Bosch had to wonder what the candidate was up to with the Gesto case.

'Do you think Gesto could be related to Waits?' Rider asked.

'That name never came up in 'ninety-three,' Bosch said. 'Neither did Echo Park.'

The phone rang and he quickly picked it up.

'Open-Unsolved. This is Detective Bosch. How can I help you?'

'Olivas. Bring the file over to the sixteenth floor at eleven o'clock. You'll meet with Richard O'Shea. You're in, Hotshot.'

'We'll be there.'

'Wait a minute. What's this *we* shit? I said *you*, you be there with the file.'

'I have a partner, Olivas. I'll be with her.'

Bosch hung up without a good-bye. He looked across at Rider.

'We're in at eleven.'

'What about Matarese?'

'We'll figure it out.'

He thought about things for a few moments, then got up and went to the locked filing cabinet behind his desk. He pulled the Gesto file and brought it back to his spot. Since returning to the job from retirement the year before, he had checked the file out of Archives three different times. Each time, he read through it, made some calls and visits and talked to a few of the individuals who had come up in the investigation thirteen years before. Rider knew about the case and what it meant to him. She gave him the space to work it when they had nothing else pressing.

But nothing came of the effort. There was no DNA, no fingerprints, no lead on Gesto's whereabouts – though to him there still was no doubt that she was dead – and no solid lead to her abductor. Bosch had leaned repeatedly on the one man who came closest to being a suspect and got nowhere. He was able to trace Marie Gesto from her apartment to the supermarket but no further. He had her car in the garage at the High Tower Apartments but he couldn't get to the person who had parked it there.

Bosch had plenty of unsolved cases in his history. You can't clear them all and any Homicide man would admit it. But the Gesto case was one that stuck with him. Each time he would work the case for a week or so, hit the wall and then return the file to Archives, thinking he had done all that could be done. But the absolution only lasted a few months and then there he was at the counter filling out the file request form again. He would not give up.

'Bosch,' one of the other detectives called out. 'Miami on two.'

Bosch hadn't even heard the phone ring in the squad room.

'I'll take it,' Rider said. 'Your head's somewhere else.'

She picked up the phone and once more Bosch opened the Gesto file.

2

Bosch and Rider were ten minutes late because of the backup of people waiting for elevators. He hated coming to the Criminal Courts Building because of the elevators. The wait and the jostling for position just to get on one of them put a layer of anxiety on him that he could live without.

In reception in the DA's office on the sixteenth floor they were told to wait for an escort back to O'Shea's office. After a couple minutes a man stepped through the doorway and pointed to the briefcase Bosch was holding.

'You got it?' he asked.

Bosch didn't recognize him. He was a dark-complected Latino in a gray suit.

'Olivas?'

'Yeah. You brought the file?'

'I brought the file.'

'Then come on back, Hotshot.'

Olivas headed back toward the door he had come through. Rider made a move to follow but Bosch put his hand on her arm. When Olivas looked back and saw they were not following him, he stopped.

'You coming or not?'

Bosch took a step toward him.

'Olivas, let's get something clear before we go anywhere. You call me "Hotshot" again and I'm going to shove the file up your ass without taking it out of my briefcase.'

Olivas raised his hands in surrender.

'Whatever you say.'

He held the door and they followed him into the internal hallway. They went down a long corridor and took two rights before coming to O'Shea's office. It was a large space, particularly by district attorney's office standards. Most of the time prosecutors shared offices, two or four to a room, and held their meetings in strictly scheduled interview rooms at the end of each hallway. But O'Shea's office was double-sized with room for a piano-crate desk and a separate seating area. Being the head of Special Prosecutions obviously had its perks. Being the heir apparent to the top job did as well.

O'Shea welcomed them from behind his desk, standing up to shake hands. He was about forty and handsome with jet-black hair. He was short, as Bosch already knew, even though he had never met him before. He had noticed while catching some of the TV coverage of the Waits prelim that most of the reporters who gathered around O'Shea in the hallway outside the courtroom were taller than the man they pointed their microphones at. Personally, Bosch liked short prosecutors. They were always trying to make up for something and usually it was the defendant who ended up paying the price.

Everybody took seats, O'Shea behind his desk, Bosch and Rider in chairs facing him, and Olivas to the right side of the desk in a chair positioned in front of a stack of RICK O'SHEA ALL THE WAY posters leaning against the wall.

'Thank you for coming in, Detectives,' O'Shea said. 'Let's start by clearing the air a little bit. Freddy tells me you two got off to a rough start.'

He was looking at Bosch as he spoke.

'I don't have any problem with Freddy,' Bosch said. 'I don't even know Freddy enough to call him Freddy.'

'I should tell you that any reluctance on his part to fill you in on what we have here came directly from me because of the sensitive nature of what we are doing. So if you are angry, be angry with me.'

'I'm not angry,' Bosch said. 'I'm happy. Ask my partner – this is me when I'm happy.'

Rider nodded.

'He's happy,' she said. 'Definitely happy.'

'Okay, then,' O'Shea said. 'Everybody's happy. So let's get down to business.'

O'Shea reached over and put his hand above a thick accordion file placed on the right side of his desk. It was open and Bosch saw that it contained several individual files with blue tabs on them. Bosch was too far away to read them – especially without putting on the glasses he had recently begun carrying with him.

'Are you familiar with the Raynard Waits prosecution?' O'Shea asked.

Bosch and Rider nodded.

'It would have been kind of hard to miss,' Bosch said.

O'Shea nodded and offered a slight smile.

'Yes, we have pushed it out in front of the cameras. The guy's a butcher. A very evil man. We've said from the start that we are going for the death penalty on it.'

'From what I've heard and seen, he's a poster boy for it,' Rider said encouragingly.

O'Shea nodded somberly.

'That's one reason why you are here. Before I explain what we have going, let me ask you to tell me about your investigation of the Marie Gesto case.

Freddy said you've had the file out of Archives three times in the past year. Is there something active?'

Bosch cleared his throat after deciding to give first and then receive.

'You could say I've had the case for thirteen years. I caught it back in 'ninety-three, when she went missing.'

'But nothing ever came of it?'

Bosch shook his head.

'We had no body. All we ever found was her car and that was not enough. We never made anybody for it.'

'Not even a suspect?'

'We looked at a lot of people, one in particular. But we couldn't make the connections and so nobody rose to the level of active suspect. Then I retired in 'oh-two and it went into Archives. A couple years go by and things don't work out the way I thought they would in retirement and I come back on the job. That was last year.'

Bosch didn't think it was necessary to tell O'Shea that he had copied the Gesto file and taken it with him, along with several other open cases, when he left his badge behind and walked out the door in 2002. Copying the files had been an infraction of department regs, and the fewer people who knew that the better.

'In the last year I pulled the Gesto file every time I had a little time to work it,' he continued. 'But there's no DNA, no latents. There's only leg-work. I've talked to all the principals again – everybody I could find. There's still the one guy out there who I always felt could be the guy, but I never could make anything out of it. I talked to him twice this year, leaned pretty hard.'

'And?'

'Nothing.'

'Who is it?'

'His name's Anthony Garland. He comes from Hancock Park money. You ever heard of Thomas Rex Garland, the oilman?'

O'Shea nodded.

'Well, T. Rex, as he is known, is Anthony's father.'

'What's Anthony's connection to Gesto?'

'"Connection" might be too strong a word. Marie Gesto's car was found in a single garage attached to a Hollywood apartment building. The apartment it corresponded to was empty. Our sense of things at the time was that it wasn't just coincidence that the car ended up in there. We thought whoever hid the car there knew the apartment was vacant and that he'd get a decent ride out of hiding it there.'

'Okay. Anthony Garland knew about the garage or he knew Marie?'

'He knew about the garage. His former girlfriend had lived in the apartment. She had broken up with him and then moved back to Texas. So he knew the apartment and the garage were empty.'

'That's pretty thin. That's all you had?'

'Pretty much. We thought it was thin, too, but then we pulled the ex-girlfriend's DMV mug and it turned out she and Marie looked a lot alike. We started to think that maybe Marie had been some sort of replacement victim. He couldn't get to his ex-girlfriend because she had left, so he got to Marie instead.'

'Did you go to Texas?'

'Twice. We talked to the ex and she told us that the main reason she split with Anthony was because of his temper.'

'Was he violent with her?'

'She said no. She said she left before it got to that point.'

O'Shea leaned forward.

'So, did Anthony Garland know Marie?' he asked.

'We don't know. We are not sure he did. Until his father brought his lawyer into it and he stopped talking to us, he denied ever knowing her.'

'When was this? – the lawyer, I mean.'

'Back then, and now. I came at him again a couple times this year. I pressed him and he lawyered up again. Different lawyers this time. They were able to get a restraining order reissued against me. They convinced a judge to order me to stay away from Anthony unless he had a lawyer with him. My guess is that they convinced the judge with money. It's the way T. Rex Garland gets things done.'

O'Shea leaned back, nodding thoughtfully.

'Does this Anthony Garland have any kind of criminal record before or after Gesto?'

'No, not a criminal record. He hasn't been a very productive member of society – he lives off his old man's handouts, as near as I can tell. He runs security for his father and his various enterprises. But there's never been anything criminal that I could find.'

'Wouldn't it stand to reason that someone who had kidnapped and killed a young woman would have other criminal activity on his record? These things usually aren't aberrations, are they?'

'If you went with the percentages, yeah. But there are always exceptions to the rule. Plus, there's the old man's money. Money smooths a lot of things over, makes a lot of things go away.'

O'Shea nodded again like he was learning about criminals and crime for the first time. It was a bad act.

'What was your next move going to be?' he asked.

Bosch shook his head.

'I didn't have one. I sent the file back to Archives and thought that was it. Then a couple weeks ago I went down and pulled it again. I don't know what I was going to do. Maybe talk to some of Garland's more recent friends, see if he ever mentioned Marie Gesto or anything about her. All I knew for sure was that I wasn't going to give up.'

O'Shea cleared his throat and Bosch knew he would now get down to the reason they were there.

'Did the name Ray or Raynard Waits ever come up in all these years of investigating Gesto's disappearance?'

Bosch looked at him for a moment, his stomach twisting.

'No, it didn't. Should it have come up?'

O'Shea pulled one of the folders out of the accordion file and opened it on the desk. He lifted a document that looked like a letter off the top.

'As I said, we've made it public that we're going for the death penalty on Waits,' he said. 'After the prelim I think he realized the writing was on the wall. He's got an appeal on the probable cause for the traffic stop. But it will go nowhere and he and his lawyer know it. An insanity defense is a non-starter as well. This guy's as calculating and organized as any killer I've ever prosecuted. So they responded last week with this. Before I show it to you I have to know that you understand that this is a letter from an attorney. It is a proffer. No matter what happens, whether we move forward with this or not, the information contained in this letter is off the record. If we choose to ignore this offer, no investigation can come of the information in this letter. Do you understand that?'

Rider nodded. Bosch didn't.

'Detective Bosch?' O'Shea prompted.

'Maybe I shouldn't see it, then,' Bosch said. 'Maybe I shouldn't be here.'

'You were the one who wouldn't give Freddy the file. If the case means that much to you, then I think you should be here.'

Bosch finally nodded.

'Okay,' he said.

O'Shea slid the paper across the desk and Bosch and Rider leaned forward to read it together. Bosch first unfolded his glasses and put them on.

Sept. 12, 2006

Richard O'Shea, Assistant District Attorney
Los Angeles County District Attorney's Office
Office 16-11
210 West Temple Street
Los Angeles, CA 90012-3210

Re: *California* v. *Raynard Waits*

Dear Mr. O'Shea:

This letter is intended to open discussions regarding a disposition in the above-referenced case. All statements made herein and hereafter in connection with these discussions are made with the understanding that they are inadmissible under California Evidence Code §1153,

California Penal Code §1192.4 and *People* v. *Tanner,* 45 Cal. App.3d 345, 350, 119 Cal. Rptr. 407 (1975).

I suggest to you that Mr. Waits would be willing, on terms and conditions outlined below, to share with you and investigators of your choice information regarding nine homicides, excluding the two in the above-referenced case, and to plead guilty to the charges in the above-referenced case, in exchange for the People's agreement not to seek the death penalty on the instant homicide charges or to file charges in regard to the homicides about which he would provide information.

Furthermore, in return for the cooperation and information Mr. Waits would provide, you must agree that any and all statements by Mr. Waits and any information derived therefrom, will not be used against him in any criminal case; no information provided pursuant to this agreement may be divulged to any other state or federal law enforcement agencies unless and until those agencies, through their representatives, agree to be bound by the terms and conditions of this agreement; no statements made or other information provided by Mr. Waits during any 'off-the-record' proffer or discussion may be used against him in the prosecution's case-in-chief; nor may you make derivative use of or pursue any investigative leads suggested by any statements made or information provided by the defendant.

In the event the above-referenced case goes to trial, if Mr. Waits offers testimony materially different from any statements made or other information provided during any proffers or discussion, then you may, of course, impeach him concerning such prior inconsistent statements or information.

I suggest that the families of eight young women and one male victim will attain some form of closure with the knowledge of what transpired in regard to their loved ones and, in eight of these instances, be able to conduct proper religious ceremonies and burials after Mr. Waits leads your investigators to the places where these victims now rest. Additionally, these families will find, perhaps, some comfort in knowing that Mr. Waits is serving a prison sentence of life without the possibility of parole.

Mr. Waits offers to provide information in regard to nine known and unknown homicides between 1992 and 2003. As an initial offer of credibility and good faith, he suggests that investigators review the investigation into the death of Daniel Fitzpatrick, 63, who was burned to death in his Hollywood Boulevard pawnshop on April 30, 1992. Investigative files will reveal that Mr. Fitzpatrick was armed and standing behind the roll-down security fence at the front of his store when he was set afire by an assailant using lighter fluid and a butane lighter. The can of EasyLight lighter fluid was left behind, standing upright in front of the security fence. This information was never made public.

Further, Mr. Waits suggests that police investigative files in regard to the September 1993 disappearance of Marie Gesto be reviewed as an additional showing of his credibility and good faith. The records will reveal that while the whereabouts of Ms. Gesto were never determined, her car was located by police in a garage at a Hollywood apartment complex known as the High Tower. The car contained Ms. Gesto's clothing and equestrian equipment plus a grocery bag containing a one-pound package of carrots. Ms. Gesto intended to use the carrots to feed the horses she groomed in exchange for riding time at the Sunset Ranch stables in Beachwood Canyon. Again, this information was never made public.

I would suggest that if an agreement of disposition could be achieved, such an agreement would fall within the exceptions to California's prohibition against plea bargaining serious felonies inasmuch as, absent Mr. Waits's cooperation, there are insufficient evidence and material witnesses to prove the People's case in regard to these nine homicides. Moreover, the People's forbearance regarding the death penalty is entirely discretionary and does not represent a substantial change in sentence. (California Penal Code §1192.7a.)

Please contact me at your earliest convenience if the foregoing is acceptable.

Sincerely,
Maurice Swann, PA
101 Broadway
Suite 2
Los Angeles, CA 90013

Bosch realized he had read almost the entire letter without taking a breath. He now gulped down some air but it did not displace the cold tightness that was forming in his chest.

'You're not going to agree to this, are you?' he asked.

O'Shea held his gaze for a moment before responding.

'As a matter of fact, I am negotiating with Swann right now. That was the initial proffer. I've improved the State's take substantially since that arrived.'

'In what way?'

'He'll have to plead to all the cases. We'll get eleven murder convictions.'

And you'll get more headlines in time for the election, Bosch thought but didn't say.

'But he still walks?' he asked.

'No, Detective, he doesn't walk. He never sees the light of day again.

Have you ever been up to Pelican Bay, the place they send sex offenders? It only sounds like a nice place.'

'But no death penalty. You're giving him that.'

Olivas smirked as if Bosch didn't see the light.

'Yes, that is what we are giving,' O'Shea said. 'That's all we're giving. No death penalty and he goes away forever and a day.'

Bosch shook his head, looked at Rider and then back at O'Shea. He said nothing because he knew it wasn't his decision to make.

'But before we agree to such a deal,' O'Shea said, 'we need to make damn sure he is good for those nine. Waits is no dummy. This could all be a trick to avoid the needle or it could be the real thing. I want to bring you two into this to work with Freddy in finding out which it is. I'll make the calls and you will be cut loose. That will be the assignment.'

Neither Bosch nor Rider responded. O'Shea pressed on.

'It is obvious he knows things about the two bait cases cited in the letter. Freddy confirmed the Fitzpatrick thing. He was killed during the riots after the Rodney King verdict came in, burned to death behind the roll-down fence in his pawnshop. He was heavily armed at the time and what is not clear is how his killer got close enough to set him on fire. The can of EasyLight was found just like Waits said, standing upright in front of the security fence.

'The mention of the Gesto case we could not confirm because you've got the file, Detective Bosch. You've already confirmed the part about the garage. Did he get that right about the clothes and the carrots?'

Bosch reluctantly nodded.

'The car was public information,' he said. 'The media was all over it. But the bag of carrots was our ace in the hole. Nobody knew about that except me, my partner at the time and the evidence tech who opened the bag. We held it back because that's where we ended up thinking she crossed his path. The carrots came from a Mayfair Supermarket on Franklin at the bottom of Beachwood Canyon. Turned out it was her routine to stop there before going up to the stables. The day she disappeared she followed the routine. She came out with the carrots and probably her killer as a trailer. We found witnesses who put her in the store. Nothing else after that. Until we found her car.'

O'Shea nodded. He pointed to the letter, which was still on the desk in front of Bosch and Rider.

'Then this is looking good.'

'No, it's not,' Bosch said. 'Don't do this.'

'Don't do what?'

'Don't make the deal.'

'Why shouldn't we?'

'Because if he is the one who took Marie Gesto and killed her and he killed those eight other people, maybe even chopped them up like the two they caught him with, then he isn't someone who should be allowed to live, whether in a prison cell or not. They ought to strap him down, put the juice in him and send him on down the hole to where he belongs.'

O'Shea nodded as if it were a valid consideration.

'What about all of those open cases?' he countered. 'Look, I don't like the idea of this guy living out his life in a private room at Pelican Bay any more than you do. But we have a responsibility to clear those cases and provide answers to the families of those people. Also, you have to remember, we have announced that we are *seeking* the death penalty. That doesn't mean it's automatic. We have to go to trial and win and *then* we have to do it all over again to get the jury to recommend death. I'm sure you know that there are any number of things that could go wrong. It only takes one juror to hang a case. And it only takes one to stop the death penalty. It only takes one soft judge to ignore the jury's recommendation, anyway.'

Bosch didn't respond. He knew how the system worked, how it could be manipulated and how nothing was a sure thing. Still, it bothered him. He also knew that a life sentence didn't always mean a life sentence. Every year people like Charlie Manson and Sirhan Sirhan got their shot. Nothing lasts forever, not even a life sentence.

'Plus, there is the cost factor,' O'Shea continued. 'Waits doesn't have money but Maury Swann took the case for publicity value. If we take this to trial he will be ready for battle. Maury's a damn good lawyer. We can expect experts to cancel out our experts, scientific analysis to cancel out our analysis – the trial will last months and cost the county a fortune. I know you don't want to hear that money is a consideration here but that is the reality. I have the budget management office already on my back about this one. This proffer could be the safest and best way to make sure this man harms no one else in the future.'

'The best way?' Bosch asked. 'Not the right way, if you ask me.'

O'Shea picked up a pen and drummed it lightly on his desk before responding.

'Detective Bosch, why did you sign out the Gesto file so many times?'

Bosch felt Rider turn and look at him. She had asked him the same thing on more than one occasion.

'I told you,' he said. 'I pulled it because it had been my case. It bothered me that we never made anybody for it.'

'In other words, it has haunted you.'

Bosch nodded hesitantly.

'Did she have family?'

Bosch nodded again.

'She had parents up in Bakersfield. They had a lot of dreams for her.'

'Think about them. And think about the families of the others. We can't tell them that Waits was the one unless we know for sure. My guess is that they will want to know and that they are willing to trade that knowledge for his life. It's better that he plead guilty to all of them than that we get him for only two.'

Bosch said nothing. He had registered his objection. He now knew it was time to go to work. Rider was on the same vibe.

'What is the time frame on this?' she asked.

'I want to move quickly,' O'Shea said. 'If this is legit, I want to clean it up and get it done.'

'Gotta get it in before the election, right?' Bosch asked.

He then immediately regretted it. O'Shea's lips formed a tight line. Blood seemed to collect beneath the skin around his eyes.

'Detective,' he said. 'I will give you that. I'm running for election and clearing eleven murders with convictions would be helpful to my cause. But do not suggest the election is my only motivation here. Every night that those parents who carried dreams for their daughter go to bed not knowing where she is or what happened to her is a night of terrible pain as far as I am concerned. Even after thirteen years. So I want to move quickly and assuredly and you can keep your speculations about anything else to yourself.'

'Fine,' Bosch said. 'When do we talk to this guy?'

O'Shea looked at Olivas and then back at Bosch.

'Well, I think we should have an exchange of files first. You should come up to speed on Waits and I'd like Freddy to familiarize himself with the Gesto file. Once that is done we'll set something up with Maury Swann. What about tomorrow?'

'Tomorrow's fine,' Bosch said. 'Swann will be there during the interview?'

O'Shea nodded.

'Maury's riding this one all the way. He'll milk every angle, probably end up with a book and a movie deal before this thing's over. Maybe even a guest anchor slot on Court TV.'

'Yeah, well,' Bosch said, 'at least then he'd be out of the courtroom.'

'Never thought of it that way,' O'Shea said. 'Did you bring the Gesto records?'

Bosch opened his briefcase on his lap and took out the investigation file, which was contained in a three-inch-thick binder generally known as a murder book. He handed it to O'Shea, who turned and gave it to Olivas.

'And I will give you this in return,' O'Shea said.

He slid the file back into the accordion folder and handed it all across the desk.

'Happy reading,' he said. 'Are you sure about tomorrow?'

Bosch looked at Rider to see if she had an objection. They had another day before they needed to walk the Matarese filing to the DA. But the work was mostly finished and he knew Rider could handle the rest. When Rider said nothing Bosch looked back at O'Shea.

'We'll be ready,' he said.
'Then I will call Maury and set it up.'
'Where is Waits?'
'Right here in the building,' O'Shea said. 'We've got him in high-power on keep-away status.'
'Good,' Rider said.
'What about the other seven?' Bosch asked.
'What about them?'
'Are there no files?'
'The proffer, as well as Maury Swann, indicates that these were women who were never found and possibly never reported missing in the first place,' O'Shea said. 'Waits is willing to lead us to them but there is no prep work we can do for them.'
Bosch nodded.
'Any other questions?' O'Shea asked, signaling that the meeting was over.
'We'll let you know,' Bosch said.
'I know I am repeating myself but I feel I need to,' O'Shea said. 'This investigation is all off the record. That file is a proffer that is part of a plea negotiation. Nothing in that file or anything that he tells you can ever be used to make a case against him. If this falls apart, then you will not be able to use the information to pursue him. Is that clearly understood?'
Bosch didn't answer.
'It's clear,' Rider said.
'There is one exception that I have negotiated. If he lies, if you catch him at any time in a lie or if any piece of information he gives you during this process proves to be knowingly false, all bets are off and we can go after him for all of it. He has been made quite aware of this, too.'
Bosch nodded. He stood up. Rider did, too.
'Do you need me to call someone to free you two up?' O'Shea asked. 'I can flex a muscle if needed.'
Rider shook her head.
'I don't think so,' she said. 'Harry was already working the Gesto case. The seven women might be unknown victims but there's got to be a file in Archives on the man in the pawnshop. It all cuts Open-Unsolved in. We can handle our supervisor.'
'Okay, then. As soon as I have the interview set up I will call. Meantime, all of my numbers are in the file. Freddy's, too.'
Bosch nodded to O'Shea and threw a glance at Olivas before turning to the door.
'Detectives?' O'Shea said.
Bosch and Rider turned back to him. He was standing now. He wanted to shake their hands.
'I am hoping you are on my side on this,' O'Shea said.

Bosch shook his hand, unsure whether O'Shea was talking about the case or the election.

He said, 'If Waits can help me bring Marie Gesto home to her parents, then I'm on your side.'

It wasn't a completely accurate summation of his feelings, but it got him out of the office.

3

Back at Open-Unsolved they sat in their supervisor's office and brought him up to date on the day's developments. Abel Pratt was four weeks away from retirement after twenty-five years on the job. He was attentive to them but not overly so. On the side of his desk was a stack of Fodor's guidebooks for Caribbean islands. His plan was to pull the pin, leave the city and find an island to live on with his family. It was a common retirement dream among law enforcement officers – to pull back from all the darkness witnessed for so long on the job. The reality, however, was that after about six months on the beach the island got pretty boring.

A detective three from RHD named David Lambkin was set to be the squad's top after Pratt split. He was a nationally recognized sex crimes expert chosen for the job because so many of the cold cases they were working in the unit were sexually motivated. Bosch was looking forward to working with him and would have liked to be briefing him instead of Pratt but the timing was off.

They went with who they had, and one of the positive things about Pratt was that he was going to give them free rein until he was out the door. He just didn't want any waves, no blowback in his face. He wanted a quiet, uneventful last month on the job.

Like most cops with twenty-five-plus years in the department, Pratt was a throwback. He was old school. He preferred working on a typewriter over a computer. Rolled halfway up in the IBM Selectric next to his desk was a letter he had been working on when Bosch and Rider stepped in. Bosch had grabbed a quick glance at it while he was sitting down and saw it was a letter to a casino in the Bahamas. Pratt was trying to line up a security gig in paradise, and that about said it all when it came to where his mind was at these days.

After hearing their briefing, Pratt gave his approval for them to work with O'Shea and only became animated when he issued a warning about Raynard Waits's attorney, Maury Swann.

'Let me tell you about Maury,' Pratt said. 'Whatever you do when you meet him do not shake his hand.'

'Why not?' Rider asked.

'I had a case with him once. This is way back. It was a gangbanger on a one-eighty-seven. Every day when we started court, Maury made a big deal of shaking my hand and then the prosecutor's. He probably would have shaken the judge's hand, too, if he'd gotten the chance.'

'So?'

'So after his guy was convicted he tried to get a reduced sentence by snitching out the others involved in the murder. One of the things he told me during the debriefing was that he thought I was dirty. He said that during the trial Maury had told him he could buy all of us. Me, the prosecutor, everybody. So the banger had his homegirl get him the cash and Maury explained to him that every time he was shaking our hands he was paying us off. You know, passing the cash palm to palm. He always did those two-handed shakes, too. He was really selling it to his guy while all along he was keeping the cash.'

'Holy shit!' Rider exclaimed. 'Didn't you guys work up a case on him?'

Pratt dismissed the idea with a wave.

'It was after the fact and besides it was a bullshit he-said-he-said case. It wouldn't have gone anywhere – not with Maury being a member of the bar in good standing and all. But ever since then I heard that Maury likes shaking hands a lot. So when you get in that room with him and Waits, don't shake his hand.'

They left Pratt's office, smiling at the story, and returned to their own workstation. The division of labor had been worked out on their walk back from the courthouse. Bosch would take Waits, and Rider would take Fitzpatrick. They would know the files inside and out by the time they sat across the table from Waits in the interview room the following day.

Since Rider had less to read in the Fitzpatrick case she also would finish the filing on Matarese. This meant Bosch was cleared to study full-time the world of Raynard Waits. After pulling out the Fitzpatrick file for Rider, he chose to take the accordion folder O'Shea had given them down to the cafeteria. He knew the lunch crowd would be thinning out and he would be able to spread the files out and work without the distractions of the constantly ringing phones and chatter of the Open-Unsolved squad room. He had to use a napkin to clean a table in the corner but then quickly settled into his review of the materials.

There were three files on Waits. They included the LAPD murder book compiled by Olivas and Ted Colbert, his partner in the Northeast Division Homicide squad, a file on a prior arrest and the prosecution file compiled by O'Shea.

Bosch decided to read the murder book first. He quickly became acquainted with Raynard Waits and the details of his arrest. The suspect was thirty-four years old and lived in a ground-floor apartment on Sweetzer Avenue in West Hollywood. He wasn't a large man, standing five foot six and weighing 142 pounds. He was the owner-operator of a one-man business

– a residential window-cleaning company called ClearView Residential Glass Cleaners. According to the police reports, he came to the attention of two patrol officers, a boot named Arnolfo Gonzalez and his training officer, Ted Fennel, at 1:50 a.m. on the night of May 11. The officers were assigned to a Crime Response Team which was watching a hillside neighborhood in Echo Park because of a recent rash of home burglaries that had been occurring on the nights of Dodgers home games. Though in uniform, Gonzalez and Fennel were in an unmarked cruiser near the intersection of Stadium Way and Chavez Ravine Place. Bosch knew the location. It was at the remote edge of the Dodger Stadium complex and above the Echo Park neighborhood that the CRT teams were watching. He also knew that they were following a standard CRT strategy: to stay out on the perimeter of the target neighborhood and follow in any vehicle or persons who looked suspicious or out of place.

According to the report filed by Gonzalez and Fennel, they grew suspicious as to why a van marked on the sides with signs that said ClearView Residential Glass Cleaners was out and about at two in the morning. They followed at a distance and Gonzalez used night-vision binoculars to get the van's plate number. He then entered it into the car's mobile digital terminal – the officers choosing to use the onboard computer rather than the radio in case the burglar working the neighborhood was equipped with a police radio scanner. The computer kicked back a flag. The plate was registered to a Ford Mustang with an address out in Claremont. Believing that the license plate on the van was stolen and that they now had probable cause to stop it, Fennel accelerated, put on the UC car's grille lights and stopped the van on Figueroa Terrace near the intersection of Beaudry Avenue.

'The driver of the vehicle appeared agitated and leaned out of the van's window to talk to Officer Gonzalez, an effort to block the officer from conducting a visual survey of the interior of the vehicle,' the arrest summary read. 'Officer Fennel approached the vehicle's passenger side and beamed his flashlight into the van. Without entering the vehicle, Officer Fennel was able to notice what appeared to be several black plastic trash bags on the floorboard in front of the front passenger seat of the vehicle. A substance appearing to be blood could be seen leaking from the cinched mouth of one of the bags and onto the floor of the van.'

According to the report, 'The driver was asked if that was blood leaking from one of the bags and he stated that he had cut himself earlier in the day when a large plate glass window he was cleaning shattered. He stated that he had used several glass-cleaning rags to clean up the blood. When asked to show where he was cut the driver smiled and then suddenly made a move to restart the vehicle's ignition. Officer Gonzalez reached through the window to restrain him. After a short struggle the driver was removed from the vehicle and placed on the ground and handcuffed. He was then moved to the backseat of the unmarked car. Officer Fennel opened the vehicle and inspected the bags. At this time Officer Fennel found the first bag he opened contained human body parts. Investigative units were immediately summoned to the scene.'

The driver's license of the man taken out of the van identified him as Raynard Waits. He was booked into the holding tank at Northeast Division while an investigation of his van and the plastic trash bags carried on through the night on Figueroa Terrace. Only after Detectives Olivas and Colbert, the on-call team that night, took over the investigation and retraced some of the steps taken by Gonzalez and Fennel was it learned that the rookie officer had typed the wrong license plate number into the MDT, typing an *F* for an *E* and getting the plate registration for the Mustang out in Claremont.

In law enforcement terms it was a 'good faith error,' meaning the probable cause to have stopped the van should still hold because the officers had been acting in good faith when an honest mistake was committed. Bosch assumed that this was the point of the appeal Rick O'Shea had mentioned earlier.

Bosch put aside the murder investigation file and opened the prosecution file. He quickly looked through the documents until he found a copy of the appeal. He scanned it quickly and found what he had expected. Waits was claiming that typing in the wrong plate number was a custom and practice within the LAPD and often employed when officers on specialty squads wanted to pull over and search a vehicle without legitimate probable cause to do so. Though a Superior Court judge found that Gonzalez and Fennel had acted on good faith and upheld the legality of the search, Waits was appealing that decision to the District Court of Appeal.

Bosch went back to the investigative file. No matter the question of the legality of the traffic stop, the investigation of Raynard Waits had moved rapidly. The morning after the arrest Olivas and Colbert obtained a search warrant for the apartment on Sweetzer where Waits lived alone. A four-hour search and forensics examination of the apartment produced several samples of human hair and blood taken from the bathroom's sink and tub traps, as well as a hidden space beneath the floor containing several pieces of women's jewelry and multiple Polaroid photos of nude young women who appeared to be sleeping, unconscious or dead. In a utility room was an upright freezer which was empty, except for the two samples of pubic hair found by an SID tech.

Meantime, the three plastic bags found in the van had been transported to the coroner's office and opened. They were found to contain the body parts of two young women, each of whom had been strangled and dismembered after death in the same way. Of note was the fact that the parts from one of the bodies showed indications of having been thawed after being frozen.

Though no cutting tools were found in Waits's apartment or van, it was clear from the evidence gathered that while officers Gonzalez and Fennel were looking for a burglar, they had stumbled onto what appeared to be a serial killer at work. The belief was that Waits had already discarded or hidden his tools and was in the process of disposing of the bodies of the two victims when he drew the attention of the CRT officers. The indications were that there might be other victims as well. The reports in the file detailed the efforts made in the next several weeks to identify the two bodies as well as the other women in the Polaroids found in the apartment. Waits of course offered no help in this regard, engaging the services of Maury Swann on the morning of his capture and choosing to remain silent as the law enforcement processes continued and Swann mounted an attack on the probable cause of the traffic stop.

Only one of the two known victims was identified. Fingerprints taken from one of the dismembered women drew a hit on the FBI's latent database. She was identified as a seventeen-year-old runaway from Davenport, Iowa. Lindsey Mathers had left home two months before being found in Waits's van and had not been heard from during that time by her parents. With photos supplied by her mother, detectives were able to piece together her trail in Los Angeles. She was recognized by youth counselors at several Hollywood shelters. She had been using a variety of names to avoid being identified and possibly sent home. There were indications she was involved in drug use and street prostitution. Needle marks found on her body during the autopsy were believed to have been the result of a long and ongoing practice of injecting drugs. A blood screen taken during the autopsy found heroin and PCP in her bloodstream.

The shelter counselors who helped identify Lindsey Mathers were also shown the Polaroid photographs found in Waits's apartment and were able to provide a variety of different names for at least three of the women. Their stories were similar to Mathers's journey. They were runaways possibly engaged in prostitution as a means of earning money for drugs.

It was clear to Bosch from the gathered evidence and information that Waits was a predator who targeted young women who would not be immediately missed, fringe dwellers who were unaccounted for by society in the first place and therefore not missed when they disappeared.

The Polaroids from the hidden space in Waits's apartment were in the file, encased in plastic sheets, four to a page. There were eight pages with multiple shots of each woman. An accompanying analysis report stated that the photo collection contained shots of nine different women – the two women whose remains were found in Waits's van and seven unknowns. Bosch knew that the unknowns were likely to be the seven women Waits was offering to tell authorities about in addition to Marie Gesto and the pawnshop man, but he studied the photos anyway for the face of Marie Gesto.

She wasn't there. The faces in the photos belonged to women who had not caused the same sort of stir that Marie Gesto had. Bosch sat back and took off his reading glasses to rest his eyes for a few moments. He remembered one of his early teachers in Homicide. Detective Ray Vaughn had a special sympathy for the ones he called 'murder's nobodies,' the victims who didn't count. He taught Bosch early on that in society all victims are not created equal, but to the true detective they must be.

'Every one of them was somebody's daughter,' Ray Vaughn had told him. 'Every one of them counted.'

Bosch rubbed his eyes. He thought about Waits's offer to clear up nine murders, including Marie Gesto's and Daniel Fitzpatrick's and those of seven women who never caused a blip on anybody's radar. Something seemed not right about that. Fitzpatrick was an anomaly because he was a male and the killing didn't appear to be sexually motivated. He had always assumed that Marie Gesto was a sex killing. But she was not a throwaway victim. She had hit the radar big time. Had Waits learned from her? Had he honed his craft after her killing to make sure he never drew such police and media heat again? Bosch thought that maybe the heat he had applied on the Gesto case was what caused Waits to change, to become a more skilled and cunning killer. If that was so, then he would have to deal with that guilt at a later time. For now he had to focus on what was in front of him.

He put his glasses on again and went back to the files. The evidence against Waits was solid. Nothing like being caught in possession of body parts. A defense attorney's nightmare; a prosecutor's dream. The case sailed through a preliminary hearing in four days, and then the DA's office upped the ante with O'Shea announcing he would go for the death penalty.

Bosch had a legal pad to the side of the open file so that he could write down questions for O'Shea, Waits or others. It was blank when he came to the end of his review of the investigation and prosecution files. He now wrote the only questions that came to mind.

If Waits killed Gesto, why was there no photo of her in his apartment?
Waits lived in West Hollywood. What was he doing in Echo Park?

The first question could be easily explained. Bosch knew killers evolved. Waits could have learned from the Gesto killing that he needed reminders of his work. The photos could have started after Gesto.

The second question was more troubling to him. There was no report in the file that dealt with this question. It was thought simply that Waits had been on his way to get rid of the bodies, possibly to bury them in the parklands that surrounded Dodger Stadium. No further investigation of this was contemplated or called for. But to Bosch it was something to consider. Echo Park would have been at least a half hour away by car from Waits's apartment in West Hollywood. That was a long time to be driving with body parts in bags. Additionally, Griffith Park, which was larger and had more pockets of isolated and difficult terrain than the area around the stadium, was far closer to the West Hollywood apartment and would have been the better choice for a body dump.

To Bosch it meant that Waits had a specific destination in mind in Echo Park. This had been missed or dismissed as unimportant in the original investigation.

He next wrote two words.

psych profile?

No psychological study of the defendant had been conducted and Bosch was mildly surprised by this. Perhaps, he thought, it had been a strategic decision by the prosecution. O'Shea might have chosen not to take this route because he didn't know exactly where it would lead. He wanted to try Waits on the facts and send him to the death chamber. He didn't want to be responsible for opening a door to a possible insanity defense.

Still, Bosch thought, a psychological study could have been useful for understanding the defendant and his crimes. It should have been done. Whether the subject was cooperative or not, a profile could have been drawn from the crimes themselves as well as from what was known about Waits through his history, appearance, the findings in his apartment and interviews conducted with those he knew and worked for. Such a profile might have also been useful to O'Shea as an edge against a move by the defense to claim insanity.

Now it was too late. The department had a small psych staff and there would be no way for Bosch to get anything done before the interview with Waits the next day. And farming a request out to the FBI would result in a two-month wait at best.

Bosch suddenly had an idea about that but decided to grind it over for a little while before acting on anything. He put the questions aside for the moment and got up to refill his coffee mug. He was using a real coffee mug he had brought down from the Open-Unsolved Unit because he preferred it over Styrofoam. His mug had come from a famous writer and television producer named Stephen Cannell who had spent time with the OU unit while researching a project. Printed on the side of the mug was Cannell's favorite piece of writing advice. It said *'What's the bad guy up to?'* Bosch liked it because he thought it was a good question for a real detective to always be considering as well.

He came back to the cafeteria table and looked at the last file. It was thin and the oldest of the three. He put aside thoughts of Echo Park and psychological profiles, sat down and opened the file. It involved the reports and investigation related to Waits's arrest in February 1993 for prowling. It was the only blip on the radar involving Waits until his arrest in the van with the body parts thirteen years later.

The reports said Waits was arrested in the backyard of a home in the

Fairfax District after a neighbor with insomnia happened to look out her window while walking through her dark house. She saw a man looking in the rear windows of the house next door. The woman woke her sleeping husband and he promptly snuck out of the house, jumped the man and held him until police arrived. The man was found in possession of a screw-driver and charged with prowling. He carried no identification and gave the name Robert Saxon to the arresting officers. He said he was only seventeen. But his ruse crumbled and he was identified as Raynard Waits, twenty-one, a short time later when a thumbprint taken during the booking process scored a match in DMV records to a driver's license issued nine months earlier to Raynard Waits. That license carried the same day and month of birth with one change. It said Raynard Waits was four years older than he had claimed to be as Robert Saxon.

Once identified, Waits admitted to police during questioning that he had been looking for a home to burglarize. However, it was noted in the report that the window he had been seen looking through corresponded to the bedroom of a fifteen-year-old girl who lived in the house. Still, Waits avoided any sort of sex offender jacket in a plea agreement negotiated by his attorney, Mickey Haller. He was sentenced to eighteen months' probation, which, according to the reports, he completed with high marks and no violations.

Bosch realized that the incident was an early warning of what was to come. But the system was too overburdened and inefficient to recognize the danger that was in Waits. He worked the dates and realized that while Waits was successfully completing probation in the eyes of the justice system, he was also graduating from prowler to murderer. Marie Gesto was taken before he cleared his tail.

'Howzit going?'

Bosch looked up and quickly took off his glasses so he could focus on distance. Rider had come down to get coffee. She was holding an empty *'What's the bad guy up to?'* mug. The writer had given one to everybody in the squad.

'Almost done,' he said. 'How about you?'

'I'm done with what O'Shea gave us. I called Evidence Archives for the box on Fitzpatrick.'

'What's in there?'

'I don't know for sure but the inventory in the book just lists the contents as pawn records. That's why I'm having it pulled. And while I'm waiting I'm going to finish up on Matarese and have it ready to walk over tomorrow. Depending on when we get to talk to Waits, I'll walk Matarese in either first thing or last thing. Did you eat lunch?'

'Forgot. What did you see in the Fitzpatrick file?'

She pulled out the chair opposite Bosch and sat down.

'The case was handled by the short-lived Riot Crimes Task Force, remember them?'

Bosch nodded.

'They had a clearance rate of like ten percent,' she said. 'Basically, anybody who did anything during those three days got away with it unless they were caught on camera, like that kid who bricked the truck driver while a news chopper was right on top of him.'

Bosch remembered that there were more than fifty deaths during the three days of riots in 1992 and very few were ever solved or explained. It had been a free-for-all, a lawless time in the city. He remembered walking down the middle of Hollywood Boulevard and seeing flaming buildings on both sides of the street. One of those buildings probably contained Fitzpatrick's pawnshop.

'It was an impossible task,' he said.

'I know,' Rider said. 'Putting together cases out of that chaos. I can tell from the file on Fitzpatrick that they didn't spend a lot of time with it. They worked the crime scene with a SWAT line guarding the place. The whole thing was pretty quickly written off as random violence, even when there was some stuff they should have routinely looked at.'

'Like what?'

'Well, for starters, Fitzpatrick looks like he was a straight arrow. He took thumbprints off of everybody who brought in stuff to pawn.'

'His edge against taking in stolen property.'

'Exactly. And what pawnbroker do you know of back then who voluntarily did that? He also kept an eighty-six list – customers who were persona non grata for various reasons and customers who complained or threatened him. Apparently it isn't uncommon for people to come back in to buy back the property they've pawned, only to find they are past the holding period and it's been sold. They get mad, sometimes they threaten the pawnbroker, and so on. Most of this came from a guy who worked for him in the store. He wasn't there the night of the fire.'

'So, was the eighty-six list checked out?'

'It looks like they were going down the list when something happened. They stopped and wrote the case off as random violence associated with the riot. Fitzpatrick was set on fire with lighter fluid. Half the stores on the Boulevard that were burned down were started the same way. So they stopped spinning their wheels on it and went on to the next one. There were two guys on it. One's retired and the other works Pacific. He's a patrol sergeant now, p.m. watch. I left a message.'

Bosch knew he didn't have to ask if Raynard Waits was a name on the eighty-six list. That would have been the first thing Rider said.

'You might have an easier time getting to the retired guy,' Bosch suggested. 'Retired guys always want to talk.'

Rider nodded.

‘That’s an idea,’ she said.

‘The other thing is Waits used an alias when he got popped in ninety-three on a prowling charge. Robert Saxon. I know you checked for Waits on the eighty-six list. You might want to check Saxon as well.’

‘Got it.’

‘Look, I know you have all of that going, but do you have time to do an AutoTrack run on Waits today?’

The division of labor in their partnership had her doing most of the computer work. AutoTrack was a computer database that could provide an individual’s address history through utility and cable hookups, DMV records and other sources. It was tremendously useful in tracing people back through time.

‘I think I can swing it.’

‘I just want to see where he’s lived. I can’t figure out why he was in Echo Park and it looks like nobody else has given it much thought.’

‘To dump the bags, I thought.’

‘Right, yeah, we know that. But why Echo Park? He lived closer to Griffith Park and that would’ve probably been a better place for burying or dumping bodies. I don’t know, something is missing or doesn’t fit right. I think he was going somewhere he knew.’

‘He could have wanted the distance. You know, he thought the farther away from him the better.’

Bosch nodded but he wasn’t convinced.

‘I think I’m going to ride over there.’

‘And what? You think you’ll find where he was going to bury those bags? You turning psychic on me now, Harry?’

‘Not yet. I just want to see if I can get a feel for Waits before we actually talk to the guy.’

Saying the name made Bosch grimace and shake his head.

‘What?’ Rider asked.

‘You know what we’re doing here? We’re helping to keep this guy alive. A guy who cuts women up and keeps them in the freezer until he runs out of room and has to take them out like trash. That’s our job, find the way to let him live.’

Rider frowned.

‘I know how you feel, Harry, but I have to tell you, I kind of come down on O’Shea’s side on this. I think it’s better that all the families know and we clear all the cases. It’s like with my sister. We wanted to know.’

When Rider was a teenager her older sister was murdered in a drive-by shooting. The case was cleared and three bangers went away for it. It was the main reason she became a cop.

‘It’s probably like you with your mother, too,’ she added.

Bosch looked up at her. His mother had been murdered when he was a boy. More than three decades later he solved the crime himself because he wanted to know.

'You're right,' he said. 'But it just doesn't sit right with me at the moment, that's all.'

'Why don't you take that ride and clear your head a little bit. I'll call you if anything comes up on the AutoTrack.'

'I guess I will.'

He started closing the files and putting them away.

4

In the shadows of downtown's spires and under the glow of lights from Dodger Stadium, Echo Park was one of L.A.'s oldest and ever-changing neighborhoods. Over the decades it had been the destination of the city's immigrant underclass – the Italians coming first and then the Mexicans, the Chinese, the Cubans, Ukrainians and all of the others. By day a walk down the main drag of Sunset Boulevard might require skills in five or more languages to read all of the storefronts. By night it was the only place in the city where the air could be split by the sound of gang gunfire, the cheers for a homerun ball, and the baying of the hillside coyotes – all in the same hour.

These days Echo Park was also a favored destination of another class of newcomer – the young and hip. The cool. Artists, musicians and writers were moving in. Cafés and vintage clothing shops were squeezing in next to the bodegas and *mariscos* stands. A wave of gentrification was washing across the flats and up the hillsides below the baseball stadium. It meant the character of the place was changing. It meant real-estate prices were going up, pushing out the working class and the gangs.

Bosch had lived for a short time in Echo Park when he was a boy. And many years back, there had been a police bar on Sunset called the Short Stop. But cops were no longer welcome there. The place offered valet parking and catered to the Hollywood crowd – two things sure to keep the off-duty officer away. For Bosch the neighborhood of Echo Park had dropped off the radar. To him it wasn't a destination. It was a drive-through neighborhood, a shortcut on his way to the Medical Examiner's Office for work or to a Dodgers game for fun.

From downtown he took a quick jog on the 101 Freeway north to Echo Park Road and then took that north again toward the hillside neighborhood where Raynard Waits had been arrested. As he passed Echo Lake he saw the statue known as the *Lady of the Lake* watching over the water lilies, her hands palm up like the victim of a hold-up. As a boy he had lived for almost a year with his mother in the Sir Palmer Apartments across from the lake, but it had been a bad time for her and him and the memory was all but erased. He vaguely remembered that statue but almost nothing else.

At Sunset he turned right and took it down to Beaudry. From there he drove up the hillside to Figueroa Terrace. He pulled to the curb near the intersection where Waits had been pulled over. A few old bungalow homes built in the thirties and forties were still there, but for the most part the houses were postwar concrete-block construction. They were modest with gated yards and barred windows. The cars in the driveways were not new or flashy. It was a working-class neighborhood that Bosch knew would be largely Latino and Asian now. From the back of the homes on the west side there would be nice views of the downtown towers with the DWP Building front and center. The homes on the east side would have backyards that stretched up into the rugged terrain of the hills. And at the top of those hills would be the far parking lots of the baseball stadium complex.

He thought about Waits's window-washing van and wondered again why he had been on this street in this neighborhood. It wasn't the kind of neighborhood where he would have customers. It wasn't the kind of street where a commercial van would be expected at two in the morning, anyway. The two CRT officers had been correct in taking notice.

Bosch pulled over and put the car in park. He stepped out and looked around and then leaned against the car as he contemplated the questions. He still didn't get it. Why had Waits chosen this place? After a few moments he opened his cell phone and called his partner.

'You run that AutoTrack yet?' he asked.

'Just did. Where are you?'

'Echo Park. Anything come up near here?'

'Uh-uh, I was just looking. The farthest east it puts him is the Montecito Apartments on Franklin.'

Bosch knew that the Montecito wasn't near Echo Park but it was not far from the High Tower Apartments, where Marie Gesto's car had been found.

'When was he at the Montecito?' he asked.

'After Gesto. He moved in, let's see, in 'ninety-nine, and out the next year. A one-year stay.'

'Anything else worth mentioning?'

'No, Harry. Just the usual. The guy moved house every one or two years. Didn't like staying put, I guess.'

'Okay, Kiz. Thanks.'

'You coming back to the office?'

'In a little while.'

He closed the phone and got back in the car. He took Figueroa Lane to Chavez Ravine Place and hit another stop sign. At one time the whole area up here was known only as Chavez Ravine. But that was before the city moved all the people out and bulldozed the bungalows and shacks they had called home. A grand housing project was supposed to rise in the ravine, with playgrounds and schools and shopping plazas that would invite back those who had been displaced. But once they cleared it all out the housing project was scratched from the city's plans and it was a baseball stadium that went in instead. To Bosch it seemed that as far back as he could remember in L.A., the fix was always in.

Bosch had been listening lately to the Ry Cooder CD called *Chavez Ravine*. It wasn't jazz but that was okay. It was its own kind of jazz. He liked the song 'It's Just Work for Me,' a dirge about a bulldozer driver who came to the ravine to knock down the poor people's shacks and refused to feel guilty about it.

You got to go where they send you
When you're a dozer-drivin' man ...

He took a left on Chavez Ravine and in a few moments he came to Stadium Way and the spot where Waits had first drawn the attention of the CRT patrol as he passed on his way down into Echo Park.

At the stop sign he surveyed the intersection. Stadium Way was the feeder line to the stadium's huge parking lots. For Waits to have come into the neighborhood this way, as the arrest report stated, he would have to have come in from downtown, the stadium, or the Pasadena Freeway. This would not have been the way in from his home in West Hollywood. Bosch puzzled with this for a few moments but determined there was not enough information to draw any conclusion. Waits could have driven through Echo Park, making sure he was not followed, and then drawn the CRT tail after turning around to go back.

He realized that there was much about Waits he didn't know and it bothered him that he would come face-to-face with the killer the next day. Bosch felt unprepared. He once again considered the idea he'd had earlier, but this time he didn't hesitate. He opened his phone and called the FBI field office in Westwood.

'I'm looking for an agent named Rachel Walling,' he told the operator. 'I'm not sure what squad she's with.'

'Hold one.'

By 'one' she had apparently meant a minute. As he waited he was honked at by a car that had come up from behind. Bosch moved through the intersection, made a U-turn and then pulled off the road into the shade of a eucalyptus tree. Finally near the two-minute mark his call was transferred and picked up and a male voice said, 'Tactical.'

'Agent Walling, please.'

'Hold one.'

'Right,' Bosch said after he heard the click.

But this time the transfer was made quickly and Bosch heard Rachel Walling's voice for the first time in a year. He hesitated and she almost hung up on him.

'Rachel, it's Harry Bosch.'

Now she hesitated before responding.

'Harry ...'

'So what's "Tactical" mean?'

'It's just the squad designation.'

He understood. She didn't answer because it was eyes-only stuff and the line was probably on tape somewhere.

'Why are you calling, Harry?'

'Because I need a favor. I could use your help, actually.'

'With what? I'm sort of in the middle of something here.'

'Then don't worry about it. I thought maybe you'd ... well, never mind, Rachel. It's no big deal. I can handle it.'

'You sure?'

'Yeah, I'm sure. I'll let you get back to Tactical, whatever that is. You take care.'

He closed the phone and tried not to let her voice and the memory it conjured distract him from the task at hand. He looked back across the intersection and realized he was probably in the same position the CRT car had been in when Gonzalez and Fennel spotted Waits's van. The eucalyptus tree and night shadows had provided them cover.

Bosch was hungry now, having missed lunch. He decided he would cross over the freeway into Chinatown and grab takeout to bring back to the squad room. He pulled back onto the street and was debating whether to call the office to see if anybody wanted anything from Chinese Friends when his cell rang. He checked the screen but saw the ID was blocked. He answered anyway.

'It's me.'

'Rachel.'

'I wanted to switch to my cell.'

There was a pause. Bosch knew he had been right about the phones at Tactical.

'How have you been, Harry?'

'I've been fine.'

'So you did like you said you were going to do. You went back to the cops. I read about you last year with that case up in the Valley.'

'Yeah, my first case back. Everything's been below the radar since then. Until this thing I've got working now.'

'And that's why you called me?'

Bosch noted the tone in her voice. It had been more than eighteen months since they had spoken. And that was at the end of an intense week when they had crossed paths on a case, Bosch working on a private ticket before coming back to the department and Walling working on resuscitating her career with the bureau. The case led Bosch back to the blue fold and Walling to the L.A. field office. Whether Tactical, whatever that was, constituted an improvement over her previous posting in South Dakota was something Bosch didn't know. What he did know was that before she had fallen from grace and been cast out to the reservation beat in the Dakotas, she had been a profiler in the Behavioral Science Unit at Quantico.

'I called because I thought maybe you'd be interested in putting some of your old skills to work again,' he said.

'You mean a profile?'

'Sort of. Tomorrow I have to go head to head in a room with an admitted serial killer and I don't know the first thing about what makes him tick. This guy wants to confess to nine murders in a deal to avoid the needle. I have to make sure he's not playing us. I have to figure out if he's telling the truth before we turn around and tell all the families – what families we know of – that we've got the right guy.'

He waited a moment for her to react. When she didn't he pressed on.

'I've got crimes, a couple crime scenes and forensics. I've got his apartment inventory and photos. But I don't have a handle on him. I was calling because I was wondering if I could show you some of this stuff and, you know, maybe get some ideas from you on how to handle him.'

There was another long silence before she answered.

'Where are you, Harry?' she finally asked.

'Right now? Right now I'm heading into Chinatown to pick up some shrimp fried rice. I missed lunch.'

'I'm in downtown. I could meet you. I missed lunch, too.'

'You know where Chinese Friends is?'

'Of course. How about a half hour?'

'I'll order before you get there.'

Bosch closed the phone and felt a thrill that he knew came from something other than the idea that Rachel Walling might be able to help him with the Waits case. Their last encounter had ended badly but the sting of it had eroded over time. What was left in his memory was the night they had made love in a Las Vegas motel room and he had believed he had connected with a kindred soul.

He looked at his watch. He had time to kill even if he was going to order food before she got there. In Chinatown he pulled to the curb outside the restaurant and opened up his phone again. Before he had turned the Gesto murder book over to Olivas he had written down names and numbers he might need. He now called Bakersfield and the home of Marie Gesto's parents. The call would not be a complete shock to them. His habit had always been to call them every time he pulled the file to take another look at the case. He thought it was some measure of comfort for them to know he had not given up.

The missing woman's mother answered the phone.

'Irene, it's Harry Bosch.'

'Oh!'

There was always that initial note of hope and excitement when one of them answered.

'Nothing yet, Irene,' he responded quickly. 'I just have a question for you and Dan, if you don't mind.'

'Of course, of course. It's just good to hear from you.'

'It's nice to hear your voice, too.'

It had been more than ten years since he had actually seen Irene and Dan Gesto. After two years they had stopped coming to L.A. in hopes of finding their daughter, had given up her apartment and gone home. After that, Bosch always called.

'What is your question, Harry?'

'It's a name, actually. Do you remember Marie ever mentioning someone named Ray Waits? Maybe Raynard Waits? Raynard is an unusual name. You might remember it.'

He heard her breath catch and he immediately knew he had made a mistake. The recent arrest and court hearings involving Waits had made it into the media in Bakersfield. He should have known that Irene would have a keen eye on such things in L.A. She would know what Waits was accused of. She would know they were calling him the Echo Park Bagman.

'Irene?'

He guessed that her imagination had taken terrible flight.

' – Irene, it's not what you think. I'm just running some checks on this guy. It sounds like you've heard of him from the news.'

'Of course. Those poor young girls. Ending up like that. I . . .'

He knew what she was thinking, maybe not what she was feeling.

'Can you think back before you saw him on the news. The name. Do you remember if your daughter ever mentioned it?'

'No, I don't remember it, thank God.'

'Is your husband there? Can you check with him?'

'He's not here. He's still at work.'

Dan Gesto had given everything of himself to the search for his missing daughter. After two years, when he had nothing left spiritually, physically or financially, he went home to Bakersfield and went back to work at a John Deere franchise. Selling farmers their tractors and tools kept him alive now.

'Can you ask him when he comes home and then call me back if he remembers the name?'

'I will, Harry.'

'One other thing, Irene. Marie's apartment had that tall window in the living room. You remember that?'

'Of course. That first year we came down for Christmas instead of her coming up. We wanted her to feel like it was a two-way road. Dan put up the tree in that window and you could see its lights from up and down the block.'

'Yes. Do you know if she ever hired a window washer to keep that window clean?'

There was a long silence while Bosch waited. It was a hole in the investigation, an angle he should have followed thirteen years before but hadn't even thought of.

'I don't remember, Harry. I'm sorry.'

'It's okay, Irene. It's okay. Do you remember when you and Dan went back to Bakersfield and you took everything from the apartment?'

'Yes.'

She said it in a strangled voice. He knew that she was crying now and that the couple had felt that in some way they were abandoning their daughter as well as their hope when they had gone home after two years of searching and waiting.

'Did you keep it all? All the records and bills and all of the stuff we gave you when we were finished with it?'

He knew that if there had been a receipt for a window washer, it would have been a lead that was checked out. But he had to ask her anyway to confirm the negative, to make sure it hadn't slipped through the cracks.

'Yes, we have it. It's in her room. We have a room with her things in it. In case she ...'

Ever came home. Bosch knew their hope would not be fully extinguished until Marie was found, one way or the other.

'I understand,' he said. 'I need you to look through that box, Irene. If you can. I want you to look for a receipt from a window washer. Go through her check books and see if she paid a window washer. Look for a company called ClearView Residential Glass Cleaners, or maybe an abbreviation of that. Call me if you find anything. Okay, Irene? Do you have a pen there? I think I got a new cell number since the last time I gave it to you.'

'Okay, Harry,' Irene said. 'I have a pen.'

'The number is three-two-three, two-four-four, five-six-three-one. Thank you, Irene. I'm going to go now. Please give your husband my best.'

'I will. How's your daughter, Harry?'

He paused. Over the years it seemed like he had told them everything about himself. It was a way of keeping solid the bond and his promise to find their daughter.

'She's fine. She's great.'

'What grade now?'

'Third, but I don't get to see her that much. She's living in Hong Kong with her mother at the moment. I went over last month for a week. They've got a Disneyland over there now.'

He didn't know why he threw in that last line.

'It must be very special when you are with her.'

'Yes. She is also sending me e-mail now. She's better at it than me.'

It was awkward speaking about one's daughter to a woman who had lost her own and didn't know where or why.

'I hope she comes back soon,' Irene Gesto said.

'Me, too. Good-bye, Irene. Call me on the cell whenever you want.'

'Good-bye, Harry. Good luck.'

She always said good luck at the end of every conversation. Bosch sat in the car and thought about the contradiction in his desire for his daughter to live here in Los Angeles with him. He feared for her safety in the far-off place where she lived now. He wanted to be close so that he could protect her. But would bringing her to a city where young girls disappeared without a trace or ended up in pieces in trash bags be a move toward safety? He knew deep down that he was being selfish and that he couldn't really protect her no matter where she lived. Everybody had to make their own way in this world. It was Darwin's rules out there and all he could do was hope that her path didn't cut across the path of someone like Raynard Waits.

He gathered up the files and got out of the car.

5

Bosch didn't see the closed sign until he got to the door of Chinese Friends. It was only then that he realized the restaurant closed in the late afternoon before the dinner rush started. He opened his phone to call Rachel Walling but remembered she blocked her number when she had called him back. With nothing to do but wait he bought a copy of the *Times* out of a box at the curb and paged through it while leaning against his car.

He scanned the headlines quickly, feeling that he was somehow wasting time or losing momentum by reading the paper. The only story he read with any interest was a brief item reporting that district attorney candidate Gabriel Williams had picked up the endorsement of the South County Fellowship of Christian Churches. It wasn't much of a surprise but it was significant because it was an early indication that the minority vote was going with Williams, the civil rights attorney. The story also mentioned that Williams and Rick O'Shea would be appearing the next night at a candidate forum being sponsored by another coalition representing the south side, the Citizens for Sensitive Leadership. The candidates would not debate each other but would give speeches and take questions from the audience. The CSL would announce its endorsement afterward. Also appearing at the forum would be city council candidates Irvin Irving and Martin Maizel.

Bosch lowered the paper and daydreamed for a moment about showing up at the forum and sandbagging Irving from the audience, asking him how his skills as a police department fixer qualified him for elected office.

He came out of the reverie when an unmarked federal cruiser pulled to the curb in front of his car. He watched Rachel Walling step out. She was dressed casually in black slacks and blazer with a cream-colored blouse. Her dark brown hair was down to her shoulders now and that was probably what was most casual of all. She looked good and Bosch jumped back to that night in Vegas.

'Rachel,' he said, smiling.

'Harry.'

He walked toward her. It was an awkward moment. He didn't know whether to hug her or kiss her or just shake her hand. There was that night in Vegas but it had been followed by that day in L.A., on the back deck of his house, when everything had come apart and things had ended before they really started.

She saved him from making a choice by reaching out and touching him lightly on the arm.

'I thought you were going to go in and order food.'

'For some reason they're closed. They don't open up for dinner until five. You want to wait or go somewhere else?'

'Where?'

'I don't know. There's Philippe's.'

She shook her head emphatically.

'I'm tired of Philippe's. We eat there all the time. In fact, I didn't eat lunch today because everybody in the squad was going there.'

'Tactical, huh?'

If she was tired of a downtown place, then Bosch knew she wasn't working out of the main field office in Westwood.

'I know a place. I'll drive and you can look at the files.'

He walked back over and opened the door of his car. He had to grab the files off the passenger seat so she could get in. He then handed her the files and went around to the driver's side. He tossed his newspaper onto the backseat.

'Wow, this is so Steve McQueen,' she said of the Mustang. 'What happened to the SUV?'

Bosch shrugged.

'Just needed a change.'

He revved the engine to humor her and then pulled away from the curb. He went down to Sunset and turned toward Silver Lake. The route would take them through Echo Park on the way.

'So what exactly do you want from me, Harry?'

She opened the top file that was on her lap and started reading.

'I want you to take a look and then tell me your impressions of this guy. I'm talking to him tomorrow and I want to have any edge I can get. I want to make sure that if anybody is manipulated, it's him and not me.'

'I've heard about this guy. He's the Echo Park Butcher, right?'

'Actually, they call him the Bagman.'

'Got it.'

'I have a previous connection to the case.'

'Which is?'

'Back in 'ninety-three I was working out of Hollywood Division. I caught a case involving a missing girl. Her name was Marie Gesto and she was never found. It was big at the time, a lot of media. This guy I'm going into the room with, Raynard Waits – he says that's one of the cases he'll trade us.'

She looked over at him and then back down at the file.

'Knowing how I have seen you take a case straight to heart, Harry, I wonder, then, if it is wise for you to be dealing with this man now.'

'I'm fine. It's still my case. And taking it straight to heart is the way of the true detective. The only way.'

He glanced over at her in time to see her roll her eyes.

'Spoken like the Zen master of Homicide. Where are we going?'

'A place called Duffy's in Silver Lake. We'll be there in five minutes and you'll love it. Just don't start taking your bureau buddies there. That'll ruin it.'

'I promise.'

'You still have the time?'

'I told you, I didn't take lunch. But I do need to go back to check out at some point.'

'So are you working out of the federal courthouse?'

She answered while continuing to scan and turn pages in the file.

'No, we're off campus.'

'One of those secret federal locations, huh?'

'You know the story. If I told you I'd have to kill you.'

Bosch nodded at the joke.

'That mean you can't tell me what Tactical is?'

'It's nothing. Short for Tactical Intelligence. We're gatherers. We analyze raw data we pull off the Internet, cell transmissions, satellite feeds. It's actually quite boring.'

'But is it legal?'

'For now.'

'Sounds like a terrorism gig.'

'Except more often than not we end up feeding leads to the DEA. And last year we came up with more than thirty different Internet scams involving hurricane relief. Like I said, it's raw data. It can lead anywhere.'

'And you traded the wide open spaces of South Dakota for downtown L.A.'

'As far as the career choice goes, it was the right move. I don't regret it. But I do miss some things about the Dakotas. Anyway, let me concentrate on this. You do want my take on it, right?'

'Yes, sorry. Have at it.'

He drove silently for the last few minutes and then pulled to a stop in front of the small storefront restaurant. He brought the newspaper in with him. She told him to order her what he was having. But when the waiter came and Bosch ordered an omelet she changed her mind and started scanning the menu.

'I thought you said we were having lunch, not breakfast.'

'I missed breakfast, too. And the omelets are good.'

She ordered a turkey sandwich and handed back the menu.

'My warning is that my take is going to be very superficial,' she said when they were left alone. 'There is obviously not going to be enough time for me to do a full psychological. I'll only be scratching the surface.'

Bosch nodded.

'I know that,' he said. 'But I don't have the time to give you, so I will take whatever you can give me.'

She said nothing else and went back to the files. Bosch glanced at the sports pages but wasn't that interested in the rundown on the Dodgers game the night before. His appreciation for the game had dropped markedly in recent years. He used the newspaper section mostly as a blind so that he could hold it up and appear to be reading while he was actually looking at Rachel. Other than the longer hair, she had changed little since he had last been with her. Still vibrantly attractive with an intangible sense of damage about her. It was in the eyes. They weren't the hardened cop's eyes he had seen in so many other faces, including his own when he looked in the mirror. They were eyes that were hurt from the inside out. She had a victim's eyes and that drew him to her.

'Why are you staring at me?' she suddenly said.

'What?'

'You're so obvious.'

'I was just—'

He was saved by the waiter, who appeared and put down plates of food. Walling moved the files aside and he detected a small smile on her face. They continued their silence as they began to eat.

'This is good,' she finally said. 'I'm starving.'

'Yeah, me, too.'

'So what were you looking for?'

'When?'

'When you were acting like you were reading the newspaper but you really weren't.'

'Um, I ... I guess I was trying to see if you were really interested in looking at this. You know, it sounds like you have a lot going. Maybe you don't want to get into this sort of stuff again.'

She held up half her sandwich but stopped herself from taking a bite.

'I hate my job, okay? Or rather, I hate what I am doing right now. But it will get better. Another year and it will be better.'

'Fine. And this? This is okay?'

He pointed to the files on the table next to her plate.

'Yes, but there is too much. I can't even begin to help you. It's information overload.'

'I only have today.'

'Why can't you delay the interview?'

'Because it's not my interview to delay. And because it's got politics on it. The prosecutor is running for DA. He needs headlines. He's not going to wait for me to get up to speed.'

She nodded.

'All the way with Rick O'Shea.'

'I had to push my way into the case because of Gesto. They're not going to slow down to let me catch up.'

She put her hand on top of the stack of files as if taking some sort of measure from them that would help her make a decision.

'Let me keep the files when you drive me back. I'll finish my work, clock out and continue with this. I'll come see you tonight at your place and give you what I've got. Everything.'

He stared at her, looking for the hidden meaning.

'When?'

'I don't know, as soon as I get through it. Nine o'clock at the latest. I have an early start tomorrow. Will that work?'

He nodded. He wasn't expecting this.

'Do you still live in that house up on the hill?' she asked.

'Yeah. I'm there. Woodrow Wilson.'

'Good. My place is down off Beverly, not too far. I'll come up to your place. I remember the view.'

Bosch didn't respond. He wasn't sure what he had just invited into his life.

'Can I give you something to think about until then?' she asked. 'Maybe do some checking?'

'Sure, what?'

'The name. Is that his real name?'

Bosch frowned. He had never considered the name. He assumed it was real. Waits was incarcerated. His fingerprints would have been run through the system to confirm identity.

'I assume so. His fingerprints matched a previous arrest. That previous time he tried to give a false name but a DMV thumbprint made him as Waits. Why?'

'Do you know what a reynard is? *Reynard* spelled *R-E-Y* instead of *R-A-Y*.'

Bosch shook his head. This was coming from left field. He hadn't even been thinking about the name.

'No, what is it?'

'It's a name for a young male fox. A young female is a vixen and the male is a reynard. I studied European folklore in college – back when I thought I wanted to be a diplomat. In medieval French folklore there is a character that is a fox named Reynard. He is a trickster. There are stories and epics about the scheming fox named Reynard. The character has appeared repeatedly through the centuries in books – children's books mostly. You can Google it when you get back to the office and I am sure you will get many hits.'

Bosch nodded. He wasn't going to tell her he didn't know how to Google. He barely knew how to e-mail his eight-year-old daughter. She tapped a finger on the stack of files.

'A young fox would be a small fox,' she said. 'In the description Mr. Waits is small in stature. You take it all in context of the full name and—'

'The little fox waits,' Bosch said. 'The young fox waits. The trickster waits.'

'For the vixen. Maybe that's how he saw it with his victims.'

Bosch nodded. He was impressed.

'We missed that. I can do some checking on the ID as soon as I get back.'

'And hopefully I will have more for you tonight.'

She went back to eating and Bosch went back to watching her.

6

As soon as Bosch dropped Rachel Walling at her car he opened his phone and called his partner. Rider reported that she was finishing up the paperwork on the Matarese case and that they would soon be good to go on it and able to file charges at the DA's office the following day.

'Good. Anything else?'

'I got the box on Fitzpatrick from Evidence Archives and it turned out to be two boxes.'

'Containing what?'

'Mostly old pawn records that I can tell were never even looked at. They were sopping wet back then from when the fire was put out. The guys from Riot Crimes put them in plastic tubs and they've been moldering in them ever since. And, man, do they stink.'

Bosch nodded as he computed this. It was a dead end and it didn't matter. Raynard Waits was about to confess to the killing of Daniel Fitzpatrick anyway. He could tell that Rider was looking at it the same way. An uncoerced confession is a royal flush. It beats everything.

'Have you heard from Olivas or O'Shea?' Rider asked.

'Not yet. I was going to call Olivas but wanted to talk to you first. Do you know anybody in city licensing?'

'No, but if you want me to call over there I can in the morning. They're closed now. What are you looking for?'

Bosch checked his watch. He didn't realize how late it had gotten. He guessed that the omelet at Duffy's was going to count as breakfast, lunch and dinner.

'I was thinking we should run Waits's business and see how long he's had it, whether there were ever any complaints, that sort of thing. Olivas and his partner should have done it but there is nothing in the files about it.'

She was silent for a while before speaking.

'You think that could have been the connection to the High Tower?'

'Maybe. Or maybe to Marie. She had a nice big picture window in her apartment. It isn't something I remember coming up back then. But maybe we missed it.'

'Harry, you never miss a thing, but I'll get on it first thing.'

‘The other thing is the guy’s name. It could be phony.’

‘How so?’

He told her about contacting Rachel Walling and asking her to look at the files. This was initially met with resounding silence because Bosch had crossed one of those invisible LAPD lines by inviting the FBI into the case without command approval, even if the invitation to Walling was unofficial. But when Bosch told Rider about Reynard the Fox she dropped her silence and became skeptical.

‘You think our window-washing serial killer was schooled in medieval folklore?’

‘I don’t know,’ he answered. ‘Walling says he could have picked it up from a children’s book. Doesn’t matter. There is enough there that I think we’ve got to look at birth certificates, make sure there is someone named Raynard Waits. In the first file, when he was popped for prowling in ’ninety-three, he was booked under the name Robert Saxon – the name he gave – but then they got Raynard Waits when his thumbprint hit the DMV computer.’

‘What are you seeing there, Harry? If they had his thumb on file back then, I’m thinking maybe the name isn’t phony after all.’

‘Maybe. But you know it isn’t impossible to get a DL with a false name on it in this state. What if Saxon actually was his real name but the computer spit out his alias and he just went with it? We’ve seen it happen before.’

‘Then why keep the name after? He had a record under Waits. Why not go back to Saxon or whatever his real name is?’

‘Good questions. I don’t know. But we’ve got to check it out.’

‘Well, we’ve got him no matter what his name is. I’ll Google *Raynard the Fox* right now.’

‘Spell it with an *E*.’

He waited and could hear her fingers on the computer keyboard.

‘Got it,’ she finally said. ‘There’s a lot of stuff about Reynard the Fox.’

‘That’s what Walling said.’

There was silence for a long moment while Rider read. Then she spoke.

‘Says here that part of the legend is that Reynard the Fox had a secret castle that nobody could find. He used all kinds of trickery to draw his victims close. Then he would take them back to the castle and eat them.’

That hung out there untouched for a while. Finally Bosch spoke.

‘Do you have time to run another AutoTrack and see if you can get anything on Robert Saxon?’

‘Sure.’

There was not a lot of conviction in her tone. But Bosch wasn’t going to let her off the hook. He wanted to keep things in motion.

‘Read me his DOB off the arrest report,’ Rider said.

‘I can’t. I don’t have it here.’

‘Where is it? I don’t see it on your desk.’

'I gave the files to Agent Walling. I'll get them back later tonight. You'll have to go on the computer to pull the arrest report.'

A lengthy silence went by before Rider responded.

'Harry, those are official investigative files. You know you shouldn't have parted with them. And we're going to need them tomorrow for the interview.'

'I told you, I'll have them back tonight.'

'Let's hope so. But I've gotta tell you, partner, you're doing the cowboy thing again and I don't like it very much.'

'Kiz, I'm just trying to keep things moving. And I want to be ready for this guy in that room tomorrow. What Walling is giving me will give us an edge.'

'Fine. I trust you. Maybe at some point you will trust me enough to ask my opinion before you go off and make decisions that affect both of us.'

Bosch felt his cheeks flare hot, mostly because he knew she was right. He didn't say anything because he knew that apologizing for leaving her out of the loop wasn't going to cut it.

'Call me back if Olivas gives us a time for tomorrow,' she said.

'You got it.'

After closing the phone Bosch thought about things for a moment. He tried to move on from his embarrassment over Rider's indignation. He focused on the case and what he had left out of the investigation so far. After a few minutes he reopened the phone, called Olivas and asked if a time and place had been set for the Waits interview.

'Tomorrow morning, ten o'clock,' Olivas said. 'Don't be late.'

'Were you going to tell me, Olivas, or was I supposed to pick it up telepathically?'

'I just found out myself. You called me before I could call you.'

Bosch ignored his excuse.

'Where?'

'The DA's office. We'll have him brought down from high-power and set him up in an interview room here.'

'You're at the DA's now?'

'I had some things to go over with Rick.'

Bosch let that float out there without a response.

'Anything else?' Olivas asked.

'Yeah, I have a question,' Bosch said. 'Where's your partner in all of this, Olivas? What happened to Colbert?'

'He's in Hawaii. He'll be back next week. If this thing carries over till then he'll be part of it.'

Bosch wondered if Colbert even knew what was happening or that he was missing out on a potentially career-making case while he was off on vacation. From everything Bosch knew about Olivas, there would be no surprise if he was scheming to ace out his own partner on a glory case.

'Ten o'clock, then?' Bosch asked.

'Ten.'

'Anything else I should know, Olivas?'

He was curious about why Olivas was at the DA's office but didn't want to directly ask why.

'Matter of fact, there is one more thing. Sort of a delicate thing, you could say. I've been talking to Rick about it.'

'What's that?'

'Well, take a guess at what I'm looking at here.'

Bosch blew out his breath. Olivas was going to string it out. Bosch had known him less than one day and already knew without a doubt that he didn't like the man and never would.

'I have no idea, Olivas. What?'

'Your fifty-ones from Gesto.'

He was referring to the Investigative Chronology, a master listing kept by date and time of all aspects of a case, ranging from an accounting of detectives' time and movements to notations on routine phone calls and messages to media inquiries and tips from citizens. Usually, these were handwritten with all manner of shorthand and abbreviations employed as they were updated throughout each day, sometimes hourly. Then, when a page became full, it was typed up on a form called a 51, which would be complete and legible when and if the case ever moved into the courts, and lawyers, judges and juries needed to review the investigative files. The original handwritten pages were then discarded.

'What about them?' Bosch asked.

'I'm looking at the last line on page fourteen. The listing is for September twenty-ninth, nineteen ninety-three at six-forty p.m. Must've been quitting time. The initials on the entry are JE.'

Bosch felt the bile rising in his throat. Whatever it was Olivas was getting at, he was enjoying milking it.

'Obviously,' he said impatiently, 'that would've been my partner at the time, Jerry Edgar. What's the entry say, Olivas?'

'It says … I'll just read it. It says, "Robert Saxon DOB eleven/three/'seventy-one. Saw *Times* story. Was at Mayfair and saw MG alone. Nobody following." It gives Saxon's phone number and that's all it says. But that's enough, Hotshot. You know what it means?'

Bosch did. He had just given the name Robert Saxon to Kiz Rider to background. It was either an alias or perhaps the real name of the man known currently as Raynard Waits. That name on the fifty-ones now connected Waits to the Gesto case. It also meant that thirteen years ago Bosch and Edgar had at least a shot at Waits/Saxon. But for reasons he didn't recall or didn't know about they never took it. He did not recall the specific entry in the fifty-ones. There were dozens of pages in the Investigative Chronology filled with one- and two-line entries. Remembering them all

– even with his frequent returns to the investigation over the years – would have been impossible.

It took him a long moment to find his voice.

'That's the only mention in the murder book?' he asked.

'That I've seen,' Olivas said. 'I've been through everything twice. I even missed it the first time through. Then the second time I said, "Hey, I know that name." It's an alias Waits used back in the early nineties. It should be in the files you have.'

'I know. I saw it.'

'It meant he called you guys, Bosch. The killer called you and you and your partner blew it. Looks like nobody ever followed up with him or ran his name through the box. You had the killer's alias and a phone number and didn't do anything. 'Course, you didn't know he was the killer. Just some citizen calling in about what he saw. He must've been trying to play you guys in some way, trying to find out about the case. Only Edgar didn't play. It was late in the day and he probably wanted to get to that first martini.'

Bosch said nothing and Olivas was only too happy to continue to fill the void.

'Too bad, you know? Maybe this whole thing could've ended right then. I guess we'll ask Waits about it in the morning.'

Olivas and his petty world no longer mattered to Bosch. The barbs couldn't penetrate the thick, dark cloud that was already coming down on him. For he knew that if the name Robert Saxon had come up in the Gesto investigation, then it should have been routinely run through the computer. It would have scored a match in the alias database and taken them to Raynard Waits and his prior arrest for prowling. That would have made him a suspect. Not just a person of interest like Anthony Garland. A strong suspect. And that would have undoubtedly taken the investigation in a whole new direction.

But that never happened. Apparently neither Edgar nor Bosch had run the name through the box. It was an oversight that Bosch now knew had probably cost the lives of the two women who ended up in trash bags and the seven others Waits was going to tell them about the next day.

'Olivas?' Bosch said.

'What, Bosch?'

'Make sure you bring the book with you tomorrow. I want to see the fifty-ones.'

'Oh, I will. We'll need it to do the interview.'

Bosch closed his phone without another word. He felt the pace of his breathing increase. Soon he was close to hyperventilating. His back felt hot against the car seat and he was starting to sweat. He opened the windows and tried to slow the measure of each breath. He was close to Parker Center but pulled to a stop at the curb.

It was every detective's nightmare. The worst-case scenario. A lead ignored or bungled, allowing something awful to be loose in the world. Something dark and evil, destroying life after life as it moved through the shadows. It was true that all detectives made mistakes and had to live with the regrets. But Bosch instinctively knew that this one was malignant. It would grow and grow inside until it darkened everything and he became the last victim, the last life destroyed.

He pulled out from the curb and into traffic to get air moving through the windows. He made a screeching U-turn and headed home.

7

From the rear deck of his house Bosch watched the sky start to dim. He lived up on Woodrow Wilson Drive in a cantilevered house that clung to the side of the hill like a cartoon character hanging on to the edge of a cliff. Sometimes Bosch felt like that character. Like on this night. He was drinking vodka sprinkled liberally over ice, the first time he'd gone with hard liquor since coming back on the job the year before. The vodka made his throat feel as though he had swallowed a torch, but that was okay. He was trying to burn away his thoughts and cauterize his nerve endings.

Bosch considered himself a true detective, one who took it all inside and cared. Everybody counts or nobody counts. That's what he always said. It made him good at the job but it also made him vulnerable. The mistakes could get to him and this one was the worst of all mistakes.

He shook the ice and vodka and took another deep drink until he finished the glass. How could anything so cold burn so intensely hot on the way down? He walked back inside the house to put more vodka on the ice. He wished he had some lemon or lime to squeeze in the drink but he had made no stops on his way home. In the kitchen, with fresh drink in hand, he picked up the phone and called Jerry Edgar's cell phone. He still knew the number by heart. A partner's number was something you never forgot.

Edgar answered and Bosch could hear TV noise in the background. He was at home.

'Jerry, it's me. I gotta ask you something.'

'Harry? Where are you?'

'Home, man. But I'm working on one of our old ones.'

'Oh, well let me go down the list of Harry Bosch obsessions. Let's see, Fernandez?'

'No.'

'That kid, Spike whatever-her-name-was?'

'Nope.'

'I give up, man. You've got too many ghosts for me to keep track of.'

'Gesto.'

'Shit, I should've gone with her first. I know you've been working it on and off since you've been back. What's the question?'

'There's an entry in the fifty-ones. It's got your initials on it. Says a guy named Robert Saxon called and said he saw her in the Mayfair.'

Edgar waited a moment before replying.

'That's it? That's the entry?'

'That's it. You remember talking to the guy?'

'Shit, Harry, I don't remember entries in cases I worked last month. That's why we have the fifty-ones. Who is Saxon?'

Bosch shook his glass and took a drink before answering. The ice tumbled against his mouth, and vodka spilled down his cheek. He wiped it with the sleeve of his jacket and then brought the phone back to his mouth.

'He's the guy ... I think.'

'You've got the killer, Harry?'

'Pretty sure. But ... we could've had him back then. Maybe.'

'I don't remember anybody named Saxon calling me. He must've been trying to get his rocks off, calling us. Harry, are you drunk, man?'

'Gettin' there.'

'What's wrong, man? If you got the guy it's better late than never. You should be happy. I'm happy. Did you call her parents yet?'

Bosch was leaning against the kitchen counter and felt the need to sit down. But the phone was on a cord and he couldn't go out to the living room or the deck. Being careful not to spill his drink, he slid down to the floor, his back against the cabinets.

'No, I haven't called them.'

'What am I missing here, Harry? You're fucked up and that means something's wrong.'

Bosch waited a moment.

'What's wrong is that Marie Gesto wasn't the first and she wasn't the last.'

Edgar was silent as it registered. The background sound of television went quiet and he then spoke in the weak voice of a child asking what his punishment will be.

'How many came after?'

'Looks like nine,' Bosch said in an equally quiet voice. 'I'll probably know more tomorrow.'

'Jesus,' Edgar whispered.

Bosch nodded. Part of him was angry with Edgar and wanted to blame him for everything. But the other part said they were partners and they shared the good and the bad. Those fifty-ones were in the murder book for both of them to read and react to.

'So you don't remember the call?'

'No, nothing. It's too far back. All I can say is that if there was no follow-up, then the call didn't sound legit or I got all there was to get from the caller. If he was the killer, he was probably just fucking with us anyway.'

'Yeah, but we didn't put the name in the box. It would have drawn a match in the alias files. Maybe that's what he wanted.'

They were both silent as their minds sifted the sands of disaster. Finally, Edgar spoke.

'Harry, did you come up with this? Who knows about it?'

'A homicide guy from Northeast came up with it. He has the Gesto file. He knows and a DA working the suspect knows. It doesn't matter. We fucked up.'

And people are dead, he thought but didn't say.

'Who is the DA?' Edgar asked. 'Can this be contained?'

Bosch knew that Edgar had already moved on to thinking about how to limit the career damage something like this could cause. Bosch wondered whether Edgar's guilt over the nine victims that came after Marie Gesto had simply vanished or just been conveniently compartmentalized. Edgar was not a true detective. He kept his heart out of it.

'I doubt it,' Bosch said. 'And I don't really care. We should have been onto this guy in 'ninety-three but we missed it and he's been out there cutting up women ever since.'

'What are you talking about, cutting up? Is this the Echo Park Bagman you're talking about? What's his name, Waits? *He* was our guy?'

Bosch nodded and held the cold glass against his left temple.

'That's right. He's going to confess tomorrow. Eventually it will get out because Rick O'Shea is going to run with it. There will be no way to hide it because some smart reporter is going to ask whether Waits ever came up way back when in the Gesto case.'

'So we say no, because that's the truth. Waits's name never came up. It was an alias and we don't need to tell them about that. You have to make O'Shea see that, Harry.'

His voice had an urgent tone to it. Bosch now regretted making the call. He wanted Edgar to share the burden of guilt with him, not figure out a way to avoid blame.

'Whatever, Jerry.'

'Harry, that's easy for you to say. You're downtown on your second ride. I'm up for one of the D-two slots in RHD and this thing will fuck up any chance I have if it gets out.'

Bosch now wanted to get off the line.

'Like I said, whatever. I'll do what I can, Jerry. But you know, sometimes when you fuck up you have to take the consequences.'

'Not this time, partner. Not now.'

It angered Bosch that Edgar had pulled the old 'partner act,' calling on Bosch to protect him out of loyalty and the unwritten rule that the bond of partnership lasts forever and is stronger than even a marriage.

'I said I'd do what I can,' he told Edgar. 'I have to go now, *partner*.'

He got up off the floor and hung the phone on the wall.

Before returning to the back deck he educated the ice in his glass once more with vodka. Outside, he went to the rail and leaned his elbows down on it. The traffic noise from the freeway far down the hill was a steady hiss that he was used to. He looked up at the sky and saw that the sunset was a dirty pink. He saw a red-tailed hawk floating on an upper current. It reminded him of the one he had seen way back on the day they had found Marie Gesto's car.

His cell phone started to chime and he struggled to pull it out of his jacket pocket. Finally, he got it out and opened it before he lost the call. He hadn't had time to look at the caller ID on the screen. It was Kiz Rider.

'Harry, did you hear?'

'Yeah, I heard. I just talked to Edgar about it. All he cares about is protecting his career and his chances at RHD.'

'Harry, what are you talking about?'

Bosch paused. He was confused.

'Didn't that asshole Olivas tell you? I thought by now he would have told the whole world.'

'Told me what? I was calling to see if you heard whether the interview's been set for tomorrow.'

Bosch realized his mistake. He walked to the edge of the deck and dumped his drink over the side.

'Ten o'clock tomorrow at the DA's office. They'll put him in a room there. I'm sorry, Kiz, I guess I forgot to call you.'

'Are you all right? It sounds like you've been drinking.'

'I'm home, Kiz. I'm entitled.'

'What did you think I was calling about?'

Bosch held his breath and composed his thoughts, then spoke.

'Edgar and I, we should have had Waits or Saxon or whatever his name is back in 'ninety-three. Edgar spoke to him on the phone and he used the name Saxon. But neither of us ran the name on the computer. We screwed up bad, Kiz.'

Now she was silent as she tracked what he had said. It didn't take her long to realize the connection the alias would have given them to Waits.

'I'm sorry, Harry.'

'Tell it to the nine victims that followed.'

He was staring down at the brush beneath the deck.

'You going to be all right?'

'I'm all right. I just have to figure out how to get past this so I'm ready for tomorrow.'

'Do you think you should stick with it at this point? Maybe one of the other OU teams should take over for us.'

Bosch responded immediately. He wasn't sure how he was going to deal with the fatal mistake of thirteen years ago but he wasn't going to walk away now.

'No, Kiz, I'm not leaving the case. I might have missed him in 'ninety-three but I'm not going to miss him now.'

'Okay, Harry.'

She didn't hang up but she didn't say anything after that. Bosch could hear a siren from far down in the pass below.

'Harry, can I make a suggestion?'

He knew what was coming.

'Sure.'

'I think you should put away the booze and start thinking about tomorrow. When we get into that room it's not going to matter what mistakes were made in the past. It will be all about the moment with this man. We'll need to be frosty.'

Bosch smiled. He didn't think he'd heard that term since he'd been on a patrol in Vietnam.

'Stay frosty,' he said.

'That's right. You want to meet in the squad and walk over from there?'

'Yeah. I'll be there early. I want to go by the Hall of Records first.'

Bosch heard a knock at his front door and started into the house.

'Me, too, then,' Rider said. 'I'll meet you in the squad. Are you going to be all right tonight?'

Bosch opened the front door and Rachel Walling was standing there holding the files with both hands.

'Yes, Kiz,' he said into the phone. 'I'll be fine. Good night.'

He closed the phone and invited Rachel in.

8

Since Rachel had been in his home before, she didn't bother looking around. She put the files down on the small table in the dining area and looked at Bosch.

'What's wrong? Are you all right?'

'I'm fine. I sort of forgot you were coming by.'

'I can leave if—'

'No, I'm glad you're here. Did you find more time to look at the stuff?'

'A little bit. I have some notes and some thoughts that might help you tomorrow. And if you want me to be there, I can make arrangements to be there – unofficially.'

Bosch shook his head.

'Officially, unofficially doesn't matter. This is Rick O'Shea's ticket and if I bring an FBI agent into it, then that will be my ticket out.'

She smiled and shook her head.

'Everybody thinks that all the bureau wants are the headlines. It's not always like that.'

'I know but I can't turn this into the test case for O'Shea. Do you want something to drink?'

He gestured to the table so that she could sit down.

'What are you having?'

'I was having vodka. I think I'm going to switch to coffee now.'

'Can you make a vodka tonic?'

He nodded.

'I can make one without tonic,' he said.

'Tomato juice?'

'Nope.'

'Cranberry juice?'

'Just vodka.'

'Hard-core Harry. I think I'll have coffee.'

He went into the kitchen to get a pot brewing. He heard her pull out a chair at the table and sit down. When he came back he saw that she had spread the files out and had a page of notes in front of her.

'Did you do anything about the name yet?' she asked.

'In motion. We'll start early tomorrow and hopefully we'll know something before we get into the room with this guy at ten.'

She nodded and waited for him to sit down across from her.

'Ready?' she asked.

'Ready.'

She leaned forward and looked at her notes, talking at first without looking up from them.

'Whoever he is, whatever his name is, he's obviously smart and manipulative,' she said. 'Look at his size. Short and slightly built. This means he had a good act. He somehow was able to get these victims to go with him. That's the key thing. It is unlikely he used physical force – at least not at the start. He is too small for that. Instead, he employed charm and cunning and he was practiced and polished at it. Even if a girl is just off the bus on Hollywood Boulevard she is going to be wary and have some measure of street smarts. He was smarter.'

Bosch nodded.

'The trickster,' he said.

She nodded and referred to a short stack of documents.

'I did a little Internet work on that,' she said. 'In the Reynard epic he is often depicted as a member of the clergy and he is able to woo his audience closer to him that way so that he can grab them. The clergy at the time – we're talking about the twelfth century – was the ultimate authority. Today it would be different. The ultimate authority would be the government, notably represented by the police.'

'You're saying he might have posed as a cop?'

'Just a thought, but it's possible. He had to have had something that worked.'

'What about a weapon? Or money? He could have just flashed the green. These women … these girls would have gone for money.'

'I think it was more than a weapon and more than money. To use either of them you still need to get close. Money doesn't lower the safety threshold. It had to be something else. His style or patter, something more than or in addition to money. When he got them close, then he would use the weapon.'

Bosch nodded and wrote a few notes on a page of a notebook he grabbed off a shelf behind where he sat.

'What else?' he asked.

'Do you know how long he's had his business?'

'No, but we'll know tomorrow morning. Why?'

'Well, because it shows another dimension of his skills. But my interest in it is not just because he ran his own business. I'm also curious about the choice of business. It allowed him to be mobile and to travel throughout the city. If you saw his van in your neighborhood, there would be no cause for concern – except late at night, which obviously led to his downfall. And the job also allowed him inside people's homes. I'm curious as to whether he started the job to help him fulfill his fantasies – the killings – or already had the business before he began acting on these impulses.'

Bosch made a few more notes. Rachel had a good point with her questions about the job. He had questions that ran along the same lines. Could Waits have had his business thirteen years before? Had he cleaned windows at the High Tower and known about the vacant apartment? Maybe it was another mistake, a connection they had missed.

'I know I don't need to tell you this, Harry, but you are going to have to be careful and cautious with him.'

He looked up from his notes.

'Why?'

'Something about what I see here – and obviously this is a very rushed response to a lot of material – but something doesn't fit right about this.'

'What?'

She composed her thoughts before answering.

'You have to remember that it was a fluke that he was even caught. Officers looking for a burglar stumbled onto a killer. Up until the moment those officers found the bags in his van, Waits was completely unknown to law enforcement. He had been flying below the radar for years. As I said, it shows he had a certain level of cunning and skill. And it says something about the pathology as well. He wasn't sending notes to the police like the Zodiac or BTK. He wasn't displaying his victims as an affront to society or a taunt to police. He was quiet. He moved below the surface. And he chose victims, with the exception of the first two killings, who could be pulled under without so much as leaving a ripple behind. You understand what I mean?'

Bosch hesitated for a moment, not sure he wanted to tell her about the mistake he and Edgar had made so many years ago.

She read him.

'What?'

He didn't answer.

'Harry, I don't want to be spinning my wheels here. If there is something you know that I need to know, then tell me or I might as well get up and go.'

'Just hold on until I get the coffee. I hope you like it black.'

He got up and went into the kitchen and poured coffee into two mugs. He found some packets of sugar and sweetener in a basket where he threw condiments that came with to-go orders and brought them out for Rachel. She put sweetener in her mug.

'Okay,' she said after the first sip. 'What aren't you telling me?'

'My partner and I made a mistake back when we worked this in 'ninety-three. I don't know if it contradicts what you just said about Waits staying beneath the radar but it looks like he called us back then. About three weeks into the case. He talked to my partner on the phone and he used an alias. At least we think it was an alias. With this Reynard the Fox thing you've brought up, maybe he used his real name. Anyway, we blew it. We never checked him out.'

'What do you mean?'

He slowly, reluctantly, told her in detail about the call from Olivas and his finding of Waits's alias in the fifty-ones. She cast her eyes down at the table and nodded as he told it. She worked the pen she was holding in a circle on the page of notes in front of her.

'And the rest is history,' he said. 'He kept right on going … and killing people.'

'When did you find this out?' she asked.

'Right after I left you today.'

She nodded.

'Which explains why you were hitting the vodka so hard.'

'I guess so.'

'I thought … never mind what I thought.'

'No, it wasn't because of seeing you, Rachel. Seeing you was – I mean, is – actually very nice.'

She took up her mug and drank from it, then looked down at her work and seemed to steel herself to move on.

'Well, I don't see how his calling you back then changes my conclusions,' she said. 'Yes, it does seem out of character for him to have made contact under any name. But you have to remember the Gesto case took place in the early stages of his formation. There are a number of aspects involving Gesto that don't fit with the rest. So for it to be the only case where he made contact would not be all that unusual.'

'Okay.'

She referred to her notes again, continuing to avoid his eyes since he had told her of the mistake.

'So where was I before you brought that up?'

'You said that after the first two killings he chose victims he could pull beneath the surface without notice.'

'Exactly. What I'm saying is that he was getting his satisfaction in the work. He didn't need anybody else to know he was doing it. He wasn't getting off on the attention. He wanted no attention. His fulfillment was self-contained. It needed no outside or public component.'

'So then, what bothers you?'

She looked up at him.

'What do you mean?'

'I don't know. But you look like something about your own profile of the guy bothers you. Something you don't believe.'

She nodded, acknowledging that he had read her correctly.

'It's just that his profile doesn't support someone who would cooperate at this stage of the game, who would tell you about the other crimes. What I see here is someone who would never admit to it. Any of it. He would deny it, or at the very least keep quiet about it, until they put the needle in his arm.'

'All right, so that's a contradiction. Don't all of these guys have contradictions? They're all messed up in some way. No profile is ever a hundred percent, right?'

She nodded.

'That's true. But it still doesn't fit and so I guess what I am trying to say is that from his point of view, there is something else. A higher goal, if you will. A plan. This whole confession thing is indicative of manipulation.'

Bosch nodded like what she had said was obvious.

'Of course it is. He's manipulating O'Shea and the system. He's using this to avoid the needle.'

'Maybe so, but there may be other motives as well. Be careful.'

She said the last two words sternly, as if she were correcting a subordinate or even a child.

'Don't worry, I will,' Bosch said.

He decided not to dwell on it.

'What do you think about the dismemberment?' he asked. 'What's it say?'

'I actually spent most of my time studying the autopsies. I have always believed that you learn the most about a killer from his victims. Cause of death in each case was determined to be strangulation. There were no stab wounds on the bodies. There was just the dismemberment. These are two different things. I think the dismemberment was simply part of the cleanup. It was a way for him to easily dispose of the bodies. Again, it shows his skills, planning and organization. The more I read, the more I realized how lucky we were to get him that night.'

She ran a finger down the sheet of notes she had written and then continued.

'I find the bags very intriguing. Three bags for two women. One bag held both heads and all four hands. It was as if he possibly had a separate destination or plan for the bag containing the identifiers; the heads and the hands. Have they been able to determine where he was going when they pulled him over?'

Bosch shrugged.

'Not really. The assumption was that he was going to bury the bags somewhere around the stadium, but that doesn't really work because they saw him drive off of Stadium Way and into a neighborhood. He was driving away from the stadium and the woods and the places he could bury the bags. There were some open lots down in the neighborhood and access to the hillsides below the stadium, but it seems to me that if he was going to bury them he would not have gone into a neighborhood. He would go deep into the park, where there was less chance of being noticed.'

'Exactly.'

She glanced at some of her other documents.

'What?' Bosch asked.

'Well, this Reynard the Fox thing might have nothing to do with all of this. It may all be coincidence.'

'But in the epic Reynard had a castle that was his secret hideaway.'

She raised her eyebrows.

'I didn't think you had a computer, let alone knew how to research online.'

'I don't. My partner did the search. But I gotta tell you, I was over in the neighborhood right before I called you today. I didn't see any castle.'

She shook her head.

'Don't take everything so literally,' she said.

'Well, there's still a big question about the Reynard stuff,' he said.

'Which is?'

'Did you look at the booking sheet in the file? He wouldn't talk to Olivas and his partner but he did answer the protocol questions at the jail when he was booked. He listed his education level as high school. No higher education. I mean, look, the guy's a window washer. How would he even know about this medieval fox?'

'I don't know. But as I said, the character has popped up repeatedly in all cultures. Children's books, television shows, there are any number of ways the character could have made an impact on this man. And don't underestimate this man's intelligence because he washed windows for a living. He owned and operated a business. That is significant in terms of showing some of his capabilities. The fact that he operated as a killer with impunity for so long is another strong indicator of intelligence.'

Bosch wasn't completely convinced. He fired off another question that would take her in a new direction.

'How do the first two fit in? He went from public spectacle with the riots and then a big media splash with Marie Gesto to, as you say, diving completely beneath the surface.'

'Every serial killer's MO changes. The simple answer is that he was on a learning curve. I think the first killing – with the male victim – was an opportunity killing. Like a spree killing. He had thought about killing for a long time but wasn't sure he could do it. He found himself in a situation – the chaos of the riots – where he could test himself. It was an opportunity to see if he could actually kill someone and then get away with it. The sex of the victim was not important. The identity of the victim was not important. At that moment he just wanted to find out if he could do it and almost any victim would do.'

Bosch could see that. He nodded.

'So he did,' he said. 'And then we come to Marie Gesto. He picks a victim who draws the police and the media's attention.'

'He was still learning, forming,' she said. 'He knew he could kill and now he wanted to go out and hunt. She was his first victim. She crossed his path, something about her fit his fantasy program and she simply became prey. At that time his focus was on victim acquisition and self-protection. In that case he chose badly. He chose a woman who would be sorely missed and whose disappearance would draw an immediate response. He probably didn't know this going into it. But he learned from it, from the heat he brought upon himself.'

Bosch nodded.

'Anyway, after Gesto he learned to add a third element to his focus: victim backgrounding. He made sure that he chose victims who not only met the needs of his program but who would also come from a societal fringe, where their comings and goings would not be cause for notice, let alone alarm.'

'And he went beneath the surface.'

'Exactly. He went under and he stayed there. Until we got lucky in Echo Park.'

Bosch nodded. All of this was helpful.

'It makes you wonder, doesn't it?' he asked. 'About how many of these guys are out there. The under-the-surface killers.'

Walling nodded.

'Yes. Sometimes it scares me to death. Makes me wonder how long this guy would have gone on killing if we hadn't gotten so lucky.'

She checked her notes and said nothing further.

'Is that all you've got?' Bosch asked.

Walling looked up at him sharply and he realized he had chosen his words poorly.

'I didn't mean it like that,' he said quickly. 'This is all great and it's going to help me a lot. I just meant is there anything else you wanted to talk about?'

She held his eyes for a moment before replying.

'Yes, there is something else. It's not about this, though.'

'Then, what is it?'

'You've got to give yourself a break on that phone call, Harry. You can't let that bring you down. The work ahead is too important.'

Bosch nodded insincerely. It was easy for her to say that. She wouldn't have to live with the ghosts of all the women Raynard Waits would begin to tell them about the next morning.

'Don't just nod it off like that,' Rachel said. 'Do you know how many cases I worked in Behavioral where the guy kept killing? How many times we got calls and notes from these creeps but still couldn't get to them before the next victim was dead?'

'I know, I know.'

'We all have ghosts. It's part of the job. With some jobs it's a bigger part than with others. I had a boss once, he used to say, if you can't stand the ghosts, get out of the haunted house.'

He nodded again, this time while looking directly at her. He meant it this time.

'How many murders have you solved, Harry? How many killers have you put away?'

'I don't know. I don't keep track.'

'Maybe you should.'

'What's the point?'

'The point is, how many of those killers would have done it again if you hadn't taken them down? More than a few, I bet.'

'Probably.'

'There you go. You're way ahead in the long run. Think about that.'

'Okay.'

His mind flashed on one of those killers. Bosch had arrested Roger Boylan many years before. He drove a pickup with a camper shell on the back. He had used marijuana to entice a couple young girls into the back while parked up at Hansen Dam. He raped and killed them, injecting them with an overdose of a horse tranquilizer. He then threw their bodies into the dry bed of the nearby slough. When Bosch put the cuffs on him Boylan had only one thing to say.

'Too bad. I was just getting started.'

Bosch wondered how many victims there would have been if he hadn't stopped him. He wondered if he could trade Roger Boylan for Raynard Waits and call it even. On the one hand, he thought he could. On the other hand, he knew it wasn't a zero-sum game. The true detective knew that coming out even in homicide work was not good enough. Not by a long shot.

'I hope I've helped,' Rachel said.

He looked up from the memory of Boylan to Rachel's eyes.

'I think you did. I think I'll know better who and what I am dealing with when I go into the room with him tomorrow.'

She stood up from the table.

'I meant about the other thing.'

Bosch stood.

'That, too. You've helped a lot.'

He came around the table so he could walk her to the door.

'Be careful, Harry.'

'I know. You said that. But you don't have to worry. It will be a full-security situation.'

'I don't mean the physical danger as much as I mean the psychological. Guard yourself, Harry. Please.'

'I will,' he said.

It was time to go to the door but she was hesitating. She looked down at the contents of the file spread across the table and then at Bosch.

'I was hoping you would call me sometime,' she said. 'But not about a case.'

Bosch had to take a few moments before coming back.

'I thought because of what I said – what we said – that …'

He wasn't sure how to finish. He wasn't sure what he was trying to say. She reached up and put her hand lightly on his chest. He took a step closer, coming into her space. He then put his arms around her and pulled her close.

9

Later, after they had made love, Bosch and Rachel remained in bed, talking about anything they could think of except what they had just done. Eventually they came back around to the case and the next morning's interview with Raynard Waits.

'I can't believe that after all this time I'm going to sit down face-to-face with her killer,' Bosch said. 'It's kind of like a dream. I actually have dreamed of catching the guy. I mean, it was never Waits in the dream but I dreamed about closing out the case.'

'Who was it in the dream?' she asked.

Her head was resting on his chest. He couldn't see her face but he could smell her hair. Under the sheets she had one leg over one of his.

'It was this guy I always thought could be good for it. But I never had anything on him. I guess because he was always an asshole, I wanted it to be him.'

'Well, did he have any connection to Gesto?'

Bosch tried to shrug but it was difficult with their bodies so entwined.

'He knew about the garage where we found the car and had an ex-girlfriend who was a ringer for Gesto. And he had anger-management issues. No real evidence. I just thought it was him. I followed him once way back during the first year of the investigation. He was working as a security guard up in the oil fields behind Baldwin Hills. You know where that is?'

'You mean where you see the oil pumps when you're coming in on La Cienega from the airport?'

'Yeah, right. That's the place. Well, this kid's family owned a chunk of those fields, and his old man was trying to straighten him out, I guess. You know, make him work for a living even though they had all the money in the world. So he was working security up there and I was watching him one day. He came across these kids who were fooling around up in there, just trespassing and messing around. They were just kids, maybe thirteen or fourteen. Two boys from the nearby neighborhood.'

'What did he do to them?'

'He drew down on them, then handcuffed them to one of the pumps. Their backs were to each other and they were cuffed around this pole that was sort of like an anchor for the pump. And then he got back in his pickup and drove away.'

'He just left them there?'

'That's what I thought he was doing but he was coming back. I was watching with binoculars from a ridge all the way across La Cienega and could see the whole oil field from up there. He had another guy with him and they drove over to this shack where I guess they kept samples of the oil they were pumping out of the ground. They went in there and came out with two buckets of this stuff, put 'em in the back of the pickup and drove back. They then dumped that shit all over the two kids.'

Rachel got up on one elbow and looked at him.

'And you just watched this happen?'

'I told you, I was clear across La Cienega on the next ridge. Before they built houses up there. If he went any further I was going to try to intervene somehow, but then he let them go. Besides, I didn't want him to know I was watching him. At that point he didn't know I was thinking of him for Gesto.'

She nodded like she understood and no longer questioned his lack of action.

'He just let them go?' she asked.

'He uncuffed them, kicked one of them in the butt and let them go. I could tell they were crying and scared.'

Rachel shook her head in disgust.

'What's this guy's name?'

'Anthony Garland. His father is Thomas Rex Garland. You might have heard of him.'

Rachel shook her head, not recognizing the name.

'Well, Anthony might not have been Gesto's killer but he sounds like a complete asshole.'

Bosch nodded.

'He is. You want to see him?'

'What do you mean?'

'I've got a "greatest hits" video. I've had him in an interview room three times in thirteen years. Each interview was on tape.'

'You have the tape here?'

Bosch nodded, knowing that she might find it strange or off-putting that he studied interrogation tapes at home.

'I had them copied onto one tape. I brought it home to watch the last time I worked the case.'

Rachel seemed to consider his answer before she responded.

'Then pop it in. Let's take a look at this guy.'

Bosch got out of bed, slipped on his boxer shorts and turned on the lamp. He went out to the living room and looked in the cabinet beneath the television. He had several crime scene tapes from old cases, as well as various other tapes and DVDs. He finally located a VHS tape marked GARLAND on the box and took it back to the bedroom.

He had a television with a built-in VCR on the bureau. He turned it on, slid in the tape and sat on the edge of the bed with the remote. He kept his boxers on now that he and Rachel were working. Rachel stayed under the covers and as the tape was cuing up she reached a foot toward him and tapped her toes on his back.

'Is this what you do with all the girls you bring here? Show them your interrogation techniques?'

Bosch glanced back at her and was almost serious with his response.

'Rachel, I think you're the only person in the world I could do this with.'

She smiled.

'I think I get you, Bosch.'

He looked back at the screen. The tape was playing. He hit the mute with the remote.

'This first one is March eleventh of 'ninety-four. It's about six months after Gesto disappeared and we were grasping for anything. We didn't have enough to arrest him – it wasn't even close – but I was able to convince him to come into the station to give a statement. He didn't know I had the bead on him. He thought he was just going to talk about the apartment where his ex-girlfriend had lived.'

On the screen was a grainy color picture of a small room with a table at which two men sat. One was a much younger-looking Harry Bosch and the other was a man in his early twenties with wavy surfer-white hair. Anthony Garland. He was wearing a T-shirt that said *Lakers* across the chest. The sleeves were tight on his arms, and tattoo ink was visible on his left biceps. Black barbed wire wrapped the muscles of the arm.

'He came in voluntarily. He came in looking like he was headed to a day at the beach. Anyway ...'

He brought up the sound. On the screen, Garland was looking all around the room with a slight smile on his face.

'So this is where it happens, huh?' he asked.

'Where what happens?' Bosch asked.

'You know, you break the bad guys down and they confess to all the crimes.'

He smiled coyly.

'Sometimes,' Bosch said. 'But let's talk about Marie Gesto. Did you know her?'

'No, I told you I didn't know her. Never saw her before in my life.'

'Before what?'

'Before you showed me her picture.'

'So if somebody told me you knew her, then they'd be lying.'

'Fucking-A right. Who told you that shit?'

'But you knew about the empty garage at the High Tower, right?'

'Yeah, well, my girlfriend had just moved out and so, yeah, I knew the place was empty. That doesn't mean I stashed the car in there. Look, you asked me all of this stuff at the house. I thought there was something new going on here. Am I under arrest or something?'

'No, Anthony, you are not under arrest. I just wanted you to come down so we could go over some of this stuff.'

'I've already gone over it with you.'

'But that was before we knew some other things about you and about her. Now it's important to go over the same ground again. Make a formal record of it.'

Garland's face seemed to momentarily contort in anger. He leaned across the table.

'What things? What the fuck are you talking about? I had nothing to do with this. I've told you that at least twice now. Why aren't you out there looking for the person who did it?'

Bosch waited until Garland calmed a bit before answering.

'Because maybe I think I'm with the person who did it.'

'Fuck you, man. You've got nothing on me because there's nothing to get. I've told you this from day one. I'm not the guy!'

Now Bosch leaned across the table. Their faces were a foot apart.

'I know what you told me, Anthony. But that was before I went to Austin and talked to your girlfriend. She told me some things about you that, frankly, Anthony, require me to pay a little more attention.'

'Fuck her. She's a whore!'

'Yeah? If she's all of that, then why'd you get angry with her when she left you? Why did she have to run from you? Why didn't you just let her go?'

'Because nobody leaves me. I leave them. Okay?'

Bosch leaned back and nodded.

'Okay. So in as much detail as you can remember, tell me what you did on September ninth of last year. Tell me where you went and who you saw.'

Using the remote, Bosch started fast-forwarding the tape.

'He didn't have an alibi for the time we believed Marie was grabbed outside the supermarket. But we can skip ahead here because that part of the interview took forever.'

Rachel was now sitting up in the bed behind him with the sheet wrapped around her. Bosch looked back at her.

'What do you think of this guy so far?'

She shrugged her bare shoulders.

'He seems like a typical rich asshole. But that doesn't make him a murderer.'

Bosch nodded.

'This now is two years later. The lawyers from his daddy's firm slapped a TRO on me and I could only interview the kid if he had counsel present. So there's nothing much here but there's one thing I want you to see. His lawyer in this is Dennis Franks, an associate of Cecil Dobbs, a big-shot Century City guy who handles things for T. Rex.'

'T. Rex?'

'The father. Thomas Rex Garland. Likes to be called T. Rex.'

'Figures.'

Bosch slowed the fast-forward down a notch so he could better see where the action on the tape was. On the screen was Garland sitting at a table with a man right next to him. As the image moved in fast motion the lawyer and his client conferred many times in mouth-to-ear communications. Bosch finally slowed it to normal speed and the audio came back up. It was Franks, the lawyer, doing the talking.

'My client has fully cooperated with you but you continue to harass him at work and home with these suspicions and questions that have not one ounce of evidentiary support.'

'I'm working on that part of it, Counselor,' Bosch said. 'And when I get it, there won't be a lawyer in the world who can help him.'

'Fuck you, Bosch!' Garland said. 'You better hope you never come for me alone, man. I'll put you down in the dirt.'

Franks put a calming hand on Garland's arm. Bosch was silent for a few moments before responding.

'You want to threaten me now, Anthony? You think I'm like one of those teenagers you cuff out in the oil fields and dump crude on? You think I'm going to go away with my tail between my legs?'

Garland's face pinched together and turned dark. His eyes looked like frozen black marbles.

Bosch hit the pause button on the VCR remote.

'There,' he said to Rachel, pointing at the screen with the remote. 'That's what I wanted you to see. Look at his face. Pure, perfect rage. That's why I thought it was him.'

Walling didn't respond. Bosch glanced at her and she looked as though she had seen the face of pure, perfect rage before. She looked to be almost intimidated by it. Bosch wondered if she had seen it in one of the killers she had faced, or in someone else.

Bosch turned back to the television and hit the fast-forward button again.

'Now we jump almost ten years, to when I brought him in last April. Frank was gone and a new guy had the case in Dobbs's office. He dropped the ball and they never went back to the judge when the first restraining order expired. So I took another shot at him. He was surprised to see me. I grabbed him when he came out of Kate Mantilini's at lunch one day. He probably thought I was long gone from his life.'

He stopped the fast-forward and played the tape. On the screen Garland looked older and wider. His face had spread and he wore his now-thinning hair cropped short. He wore a white shirt with a tie. The taped interviews had followed him from the end of boyhood to well into manhood.

This time he sat in a different interview room. This one was at Parker Center.

'If I'm not under arrest, then I should be free to go,' he said. 'Am I free to go?'

'I was hoping you'd answer a few questions first,' Bosch replied.

'I answered all your questions years ago. This is a vendetta, Bosch. You will not give up. You will not leave me alone. Am I free to go or not?'

'Where did you hide her body?'

Garland shook his head.

'My God, this is unbelievable. When will this end?'

'It will never end, Garland. Not until I find her and not until I lock you up.'

'This is fucking crazy! *You're* crazy, Bosch. What can I say to make you believe me? What can—'

'You can tell me where she is and then I'll believe you.'

'Well, that's the one thing I can't tell you, because I don't—'

Bosch suddenly killed the TV with the remote. For the first time, he realized how case-blind he had been, going after Garland as relentlessly as a dog chasing a car. He was unaware of the traffic, unaware that right in front of him in the murder book was the clue to the real killer. Watching the tape with Walling had heaped humiliation upon humiliation. He had thought by showing her the tape she would see why he had focused on Garland. She would understand and absolve him of the mistake. But now seeing it through the prism of Waits's impending confession he couldn't even absolve himself.

Rachel leaned toward him and touched his back, her soft fingers tracing down his spine.

'It happens to all of us,' she said.

Bosch nodded. Not to me, he thought.

'I guess when this is all over I'm going to have to find him and apologize,' he said.

'Fuck him. He's still an asshole. I wouldn't bother.'

Bosch smiled. She was trying to make it easy for him.

'You think?'

She pulled back the elastic waistband on his boxers and then snapped them against his back.

'I think I have at least another hour before I should be thinking about getting home.'

Bosch turned to look at her and she smiled.

10

The next morning Bosch and Rider walked from the Hall of Records to the CCB and despite the wait for an elevator, still got to the DA's office twenty minutes early. O'Shea and Olivas were ready for them. Everyone took the same seats as before. Bosch noticed that the posters that had been leaning against the wall were gone. They had probably been put to good use somewhere, maybe sent to the public hall where the candidates' forum was scheduled for that night.

As he sat down Bosch saw the Gesto murder book on O'Shea's desk. He took it without asking and immediately opened it to the chronological record. He combed through the fifty-ones until he found the page for September 29, 1993. He looked at the entry Olivas had told him about the evening before. It was, as it had been read to Bosch, the last entry of the day. Bosch felt the deep sense of regret tug at him all over again.

'Detective Bosch, we all make mistakes,' O'Shea said. 'Let's just move on from it and do the best we can today.'

Bosch looked up at him and eventually nodded. He closed the book and put it back on the desk. O'Shea continued.

'I am told that Maury Swann is in the interview room with Mr. Waits and is ready to go. I have been thinking about this and I want to take the cases one at a time and in order. We start with Fitzpatrick and when we are satisfied by the confession, we move on to the Gesto case, and when we are satisfied there, we move on to the next one and so on.'

Everybody nodded except for Bosch.

'I am not going to be satisfied until we have her remains,' he said.

Now O'Shea nodded. He lifted a document off his desk.

'I understand that. If you can locate the victim based on the statements from Waits, then fine. If it is a matter of him leading us to the body, I have a release order ready to go to the judge. I would say that if we reach a point where we are taking this man out of lockup, then the security should be extraordinary. There will be a lot riding on this and we cannot have any mistakes.'

O'Shea took the time to look from detective to detective to make sure they understood the gravity of the situation. He would be gambling his campaign and political life on the security of Raynard Waits.

'We'll be ready for anything,' Olivas said.

The look of concern on O'Shea's face didn't change.

'You're going to have a uniformed presence, right?' he asked.

'I don't think it is necessary – uniforms draw attention,' Olivas said. 'We can handle him. But if you want it we'll have it.'

'I think it would be good to have, yes.'

'No problem, then. We'll either get a car from Metro to go with us or a couple deputies from the jail.'

O'Shea nodded his approval.

'Then, are we ready to start?'

'There's one thing,' Bosch said. 'We're not sure who that is in the interview room waiting for us, but we're pretty sure his name isn't Raynard Waits.'

A look of surprise played off O'Shea's face and immediately became contagious. Olivas dropped his mouth open an inch and leaned forward.

'We made him on fingerprints,' Olivas protested. 'On the prior.'

Bosch nodded.

'Yes, the prior. As you know, when he was popped thirteen years ago for prowling, he first gave the name Robert Saxon along with the birth date of eleven/three/'seventy-five. This is the same name he used later that year when he called about Gesto, only then he gave the birth date of eleven/three/'seventy-one. But when he was pulled in on the prowling and they ran his prints through the computer, they matched the thumb to the DL of Raynard Waits, with a birth date of eleven/three/'seventy-one. So we keep getting the same month and day but different years. Anyway, when confronted with the thumbprint he copped to being Raynard Waits, saying he had given the false name and year because he was hoping to be handled as a juvenile. This is all in the file.'

'But where does all of it go?' O'Shea said impatiently.

'Just let me finish. He got probation for the prowling because it was a first offense. In the probation report bio he said he was born and raised in L.A., okay? We just came from the Hall of Records. There is no record of Raynard Waits being born in L.A. on that date or any other. There have been a lot of Robert Saxons born in L.A. but none on November third of either of the years mentioned in the files.'

'The bottom line,' Rider said, 'is we don't know who the man we are about to talk to is.'

O'Shea pushed back from his desk and stood up. He paced around the spacious office as he thought and spoke about this latest information.

'Okay, so what are you saying, that the DMV had the wrong prints on file or there was some sort of a mix-up?'

Bosch turned in his seat so he could look at O'Shea while he answered.

'I'm saying that this guy, whoever he really is, could have gone to the DMV thirteen, fourteen, years ago to set up a false ID. What do you need to get a driver's license? Proof of age. Back then, you could buy phony IDs and birth certificates on Hollywood Boulevard, no problem. Or he could have bribed a DMV employee, could have done a lot of things. The point is, there is no record of him being born here in L.A., as he said he was. That puts all the rest in doubt.'

'Maybe that's the lie,' Olivas said. 'Maybe he *is* Waits and he lied about being born here. It's like when you're born out in Riverside, you tell everybody you're from L.A.'

Bosch shook his head. He didn't accept the logic Olivas was slinging.

'The name is false,' Bosch insisted. 'Raynard is a take on a character from medieval folklore known as Reynard the Fox. It's spelled with an *E* but it's pronounced the same. Put that with the last name and you have "the little fox waits." Get it? You can't convince me somebody gave him that name at birth.'

That brought a momentary silence to the room.

'I don't know,' O'Shea said, thinking out loud. 'Seems a little far-fetched, this medieval connection.'

'It's only far-fetched because we can't nail it down,' Bosch countered. 'You ask me, it's more far-fetched that this would be his given name.'

'So what are you saying?' Olivas asked. 'That he changed his name and continued to use it, even after he had an arrest tail on it? That doesn't make sense to me.'

'Doesn't make a lot of sense to me, either. But we don't know the story behind it yet.'

'Okay, so what are you suggesting we do?' O'Shea asked.

'Not much,' Bosch said. 'I'm just bringing it up. But I do think we ought to go on the record with it up there. You know, ask him to state his name, DOB, and place of birth. As if it is the routine way to start one of these interviews. If he gives us Waits, then we might be able to catch him in the lie down the road and prosecute him for everything. You said that was the deal; if he lies, he fries. We can turn it all against him.'

O'Shea was standing by the coffee table behind where Bosch and Rider sat. Bosch turned again, to watch him take in the suggestion. The prosecutor was grinding it over and nodding.

'I don't see where it could hurt,' he finally said. 'Just get it on the record but let it go at that. Real subtle and routine. We can come back to him on it later – if we find out more about this.'

Bosch looked at Rider.

'You'll be the one starting out with him, asking about the first case. Your first question can be about his name.'

'Fine,' she said.

O'Shea came back around the desk.

'Okay, then,' he said. 'Are we ready? It's time to go. I will try to stay with it as long as my schedule allows. Don't be offended if I jump in from time to time with a question.'

Bosch answered by standing up. Rider followed suit and then Olivas.

'One last thing,' Bosch said. 'We picked up a Maury Swann story yesterday that maybe you guys ought to know.'

Both Bosch and Rider took turns telling the story Abel Pratt had told them. By the end, Olivas was laughing and shaking his head and Bosch could tell by O'Shea's face that he was trying to count how many times he had shaken Maury Swann's hand in court. Maybe he was worrying about potential political fallout.

Bosch headed to the door of the office. He felt a mixture of excitement and dread rising. He was excited because he knew he was finally about to find out what had happened to Marie Gesto so long ago. At the same time, he dreaded finding out. And he dreaded the fact that the details he would soon learn would place a heavy burden on him. A burden he would have to transfer to a waiting mother and father up in Bakersfield.

11

Two uniformed sheriff's deputies stood at the door to the interview room in which sat the man who called himself Raynard Waits. They stepped aside and allowed the prosecutorial entourage to enter. The room contained one long table. Waits and his defense attorney, Maury Swann, were sitting on one side of it. Waits was directly in the middle and Swann was to his left. When the investigators and the prosecutor entered, only Maury Swann stood. Waits was held to the arms of his chair with plastic snap cuffs. Swann, a thin man with black-framed glasses and a luxurious mane of silver hair, offered his hand but no one shook it.

Rider took the chair directly across the table from Waits, and Bosch and O'Shea sat on either side of her. Since Olivas would not be up in the interview rotation for some time, he took the last remaining chair, which was next to the door.

O'Shea handled the introductions but again nobody bothered shaking anybody else's hand. Waits was in an orange jumpsuit that had black letters stenciled across the chest.

L.A. COUNTY JAIL
KEEP AWAY

The second line was not intended as a warning but it was just as good as one. It meant that Waits was on keep-away status within the jail, indicating he was housed by himself and not allowed into the general inmate population. This status was taken as a protective measure for both Waits and the other inmates.

As Bosch studied the man he had been hunting for thirteen years he realized that the most frightening thing about Waits was how ordinary he looked. Slightly built, he had an everyman's face. Pleasant, with soft features and short dark hair, he was the epitome of normality. The only hint of the evil that lay within was found in the eyes. Dark brown and deeply set, they carried an emptiness that Bosch recognized from other killers he had sat face-to-face with over the years. Nothing there. Just a hollowness that could never be filled, no matter how many other lives he stole.

Rider turned on the tape recorder that was on the table and started the interview perfectly, giving Waits no reason to suspect he was stepping into a trap with the very first question of the session.

'As was probably explained to you already by Mr. Swann, we are going to record each session with you and then turn the tapes over to your attorney, who will hold them until we have a completed agreement. Is that understood and approved by you?'

'Yes, it is,' Waits said.

'Good,' Rider said. 'Then let's begin with an easy one. Can you state your name, birth date and place of birth for the record?'

Waits leaned forward and made a face like he was stating the obvious to schoolchildren.

'Raynard Waits,' he said impatiently. 'Born November third, nineteen seventy-one in the city of angles – oh, I mean angels. The city of angels.'

'If you mean Los Angeles, could you please say it?'

'Yes, Los Angeles.'

'Thank you. Your first name is unusual. Could you spell it for the tape?'

Waits complied. Again, it was a good move by Rider. It would make it even more difficult for the man in front of them to argue later that he had not knowingly lied during the interview.

'Do you know where the name came from?'

'My father pulled it out of his ass, I guess. I don't know. I thought we were here to talk about dead people, not the piddly basic shit.'

'We are, Mr. Waits. We are.'

Bosch felt an enormous sense of relief inside. He knew that they were about to sit through a retelling of horrors but he felt they already had Waits caught in a lie that might spring a fatal trap on him. There was now a chance that he was not going to walk away from this to a private cell and a life of public maintenance and celebrity.

'We want to take these in order,' Rider said. 'Your attorney's proffer suggests that the first homicide you were ever involved in was the death of Daniel Fitzpatrick in Hollywood on April thirtieth, nineteen ninety-two. Is that correct?'

Waits answered with the sort of matter-of-fact demeanor one would expect from someone giving directions to the nearest gas station. His voice was cold and calm.

'Yes, I burned him alive behind his security cage. It turned out that he wasn't so secure back there. Not even with all of his guns.'

'Why did you do that?'

'Because I wanted to see if I could. I had been thinking about it for a long time and I just wanted to prove myself.'

Bosch thought about what Rachel Walling had said to him the night before. She had called it a 'spree killing.' It looked like she had been right.

'What do you mean by "prove yourself," Mr. Waits?' Rider asked.

'I mean there is a line out there that everybody thinks about but not many have the guts to cross. I wanted to see if I could cross it.'

'When you say you had been thinking about it for a long time, had you been thinking about Mr. Fitzpatrick in particular?'

Annoyance flared in Waits's eyes. It was as if he were putting up with her.

'No, you stupid cunt,' he replied calmly. 'I had been thinking about killing someone. You understand? All my life I had wanted to do it.'

Rider shook off the insult without a flinch and kept moving.

'Why did you choose Daniel Fitzpatrick? Why did you choose that night?'

'Well, because I was watching TV and I saw the whole city coming apart. It was chaos out there and I knew the police couldn't do anything about it. It was a time when people were doing just what they wanted. I saw a guy on the tube talking about Hollywood Boulevard and how places were burning and I decided to go out to see it. I didn't want the TV showing it to me. I wanted to see it for myself.'

'Did you drive there?'

'No, I could walk. Back then I lived on Fountain near LaBrea. I just walked up.'

Rider had the Fitzpatrick file open in front of her. She glanced down at it for a moment while collecting her thoughts and formulating the next set of questions. That gave O'Shea the opportunity to jump in.

'Where did the lighter fluid come from?' he asked. 'Did you take it with you from your apartment?'

Waits shifted his focus to O'Shea.

'I thought the dyke was asking the questions,' he said.

'We're all asking the questions,' O'Shea said. 'And could you please keep the personal attacks out of your responses?'

'Not you, Mr. District Attorney. I don't want to talk to you. Only her. And them.'

He pointed to Bosch and Olivas.

'Let me just back up a little bit before we get to the lighter fluid,' Rider said, smoothly pushing O'Shea to the side. 'You said you walked up to Hollywood Boulevard from Fountain. Where did you go and what did you see?'

Waits smiled and nodded at Rider.

'I got that right, didn't I?' he said. 'I can always tell. I can always smell it on a woman, when she likes pussy.'

'Mr. Swann,' Rider said, 'can you please tell your client that this is about him answering our questions, not the other way around?'

Swann put his hand on Waits's left forearm, which was bound to the arm of his chair.

'Ray,' he said. 'Don't play games. Just answer the questions. Remember, we want this. We brought it to them. It's our show.'

Bosch saw a slow burn move across Waits's face as he turned and looked at his lawyer. But then it quickly disappeared and he looked back at Rider.

'I saw the city burning, that's what I saw.'

He smiled after giving the answer.

'It was like a Hieronymus Bosch painting.'

He turned to Bosch as he said this. It froze Bosch for a moment. How did he know?

Waits nodded toward Bosch's chest.

'It's on your ID card.'

Bosch had forgotten that they'd had to clip their IDs on once they entered the DA's office. Rider moved in quickly with the next question.

'Okay, which way did you walk once you got to Hollywood Boulevard?'

'I took a right and headed east. The bigger fires were down that way.'

'What was in your pockets?'

The question seemed to give him pause.

'I don't know. I don't remember. My keys, I guess. Cigarettes and a lighter, that was all.'

'Did you have your wallet?'

'No, I didn't want to have ID with me. In case the police stopped me.'

'Did you already have the lighter fluid with you?'

'That's right, I did. I thought I might join in the fun, help burn the city to the ground. Then I walked by that pawnshop and got a better idea.'

'You saw Mr. Fitzpatrick?'

'Yeah, I saw him. He was standing inside his security fence holding a shotgun. He also was wearing a holster like he was Wyatt Earp or something.'

'Describe the pawnshop.'

Waits shrugged.

'A small place. It was called Irish Pawn. It had this neon sign out front that flashed a green three-leaf clover and then the three balls, you know, that are like the symbol for a pawnshop, I guess. Fitzpatrick was standing there, watching me when I passed by.'

'And you kept walking?'

'At first I did. I passed by and then I thought about the challenge, you know? How could I get to him without getting shot by that big fucking bazooka he was holding.'

'What did you do?'

'I took the can of EasyLight out of my jacket pocket and filled my mouth with it. Squirted it right in, like those flame breathers do on the Venice boardwalk. I then put the can away and got out a cigarette and my lighter. I don't smoke anymore. It's a terrible habit.'

He looked at Bosch as he said this.

'Then what?' Rider asked.

'I went back to the asshole's shop and walked into the alcove in front of the security fence. I acted like I was just looking for a blind to try to light my smoke. It was windy that night, you understand?'

'Yes.'

'So he started yelling at me to get the fuck away. He came right up to the fence to yell at me. And I was counting on that.'

He smiled, proud of how well his plan worked.

'The guy hit the stock of his shotty against the steel fence to get my attention. You see, he saw my hands, so he didn't realize the danger. And when he was about two feet away I got a flame on the lighter and looked him right in the eyes. I took the cigarette out of my mouth and spit all of that lighter fluid into his face. Of course, it hit the lighter on the way and I was a fucking flame thrower. He had a face full a' flames before he knew what hit him. He dropped the shotty pretty fast so he could try to slap at the flames. But his clothes went up and pretty soon he was one crispy critter. It was like being hit by napalm, man.'

Waits tried to raise his left arm but couldn't. It was bound to the armrest at the wrist. He turned and raised his hand instead.

'Unfortunately, I burned my hand a little bit. Blisters, the whole thing. It really hurt, too. I can't imagine what that asshole Wyatt Earp felt. Not a good way to go, if you ask me.'

Bosch looked at the upraised hand. He saw a discoloration in the skin tone, but not a scar. The burn had not gone deep.

After a long measure of silence, Rider asked another question.

'Did you seek medical attention for your hand?'

'No, I didn't think that would be too smart, considering the situation. And from what I heard, the hospitals were overflowing. So I went on home and took care of it myself.'

'When did you place the can of lighter fluid in front of the store?'

'Oh, that was when I was walking away. I just took it out, wiped it off and put it down.'

'Did Mr. Fitzpatrick call out for help at any time?'

Waits paused as if to ponder the question.

'Well, that's hard to say. He was yelling something, but I am not sure it was for help. He just kind of sounded like an animal to me. I closed the door on my dog's tail once when I was a kid. It sort of reminded me of that.'

'What were you thinking as you were walking home?'

'I was thinking, Far fucking out! I finally did it! And I knew I was going to get away with it, too. I felt like I was pretty goddamn invincible, if you want to know the truth.'

'How old were you?'

'I was … I was twenty, man, and I fuckin' did it!'

'Did you ever think about the man you killed, who you burned to death?'

'No, not really. He was just there. There for the taking. Like the rest of them that came after. It was like they were there for me.'

Rider spent another forty minutes questioning him, eliciting smaller details that nonetheless matched those contained in the investigative reports. Finally, at 11:15 she seemed to relax her posture and pull back from her place at the table. She turned to look at Bosch and then at O'Shea.

'I think I have enough for the moment,' she said. 'Maybe we could take a short break at this point.'

She turned off the tape recorder, and the three investigators and O'Shea stepped out into the hallway to confer. Swann stayed in the interview room with his client.

'What do you think?' O'Shea said to Rider.

She nodded.

'I'm satisfied. I don't think there is any doubt that he did it. He solved the mystery of how he got to him. I don't think he's telling us everything but he knows enough of the details. He either did it or he was right there.'

O'Shea looked at Bosch.

'Should we move on?'

Bosch thought about this for a moment. He was ready. As he had watched Rider interview Waits his anger and disgust had grown. The man in the interview room showed such a callous disregard for his victim that Bosch recognized it as the classic profile of a psychopath. As before, he dreaded what he would next hear from the man but he was ready to hear it.

'Let's do it,' he said.

They all moved back into the interview room and Swann immediately suggested that they break for lunch.

'My client is hungry.'

'Gotta feed the dog,' Waits added with a smile.

Bosch shook his head, taking charge of the room.

'Not yet,' he said. 'He'll eat when we all eat.'

He took the seat directly across from Waits and turned the recorder back on. Rider and O'Shea took the wing positions and Olivas sat once again in the chair by the door. Bosch had taken the Gesto file back from Olivas but had it closed in front of him on the table.

'We're going to move on now to the Marie Gesto case,' he said.

'Ah, sweet Marie,' Waits said.

He looked at Bosch with a brightness in his eyes.

'Your attorney's proffer suggests that you know what happened to Marie Gesto when she disappeared in nineteen ninety-three. Is that true?'

Waits frowned and nodded.

'Yes, I'm afraid so,' he said with mock sincerity.

'Do you know the current whereabouts of Marie Gesto or the location of her remains?'

'Yes, I do.'

Here it was, the moment Bosch had waited on for thirteen years.

'She's dead, isn't she?'

Waits looked at him and nodded.

'Is that a yes?' Bosch asked for the tape.

'That is a yes. She's dead.'

'Where is she?'

Waits broke into a broad smile, the smile of a man who had not an atom of regret or guilt in his DNA.

'She's right here, Detective,' he said. 'She's right here with me. Just like all the others. Right here with me.'

His smile turned into a laugh and Bosch almost went across the table at him. But Rider moved her hand under the table and put it on his leg. It immediately calmed him.

'Hold on a second,' O'Shea said. 'Let's step out again, and this time I would like you to join us, Maury.'

12

O'Shea charged into the hallway first and managed to pace back and forth twice before all the others were out of the interview room. He then instructed the two deputies to go into the room and keep an eye on Waits. The door was then closed.

'What the fuck, Maury?' O'Shea barked. 'We're not going to spend our time in there laying the groundwork for an insanity defense for you. This is a confession, not a defense maneuver.'

Swann turned his palms up in a what-can-I-do gesture.

'The guy obviously has issues,' he said.

'Bullshit. He's a stone-cold killer and he's in there vamping like Hannibal Lecter. This isn't a movie, Maury. This is real. You hear what he said about Fitzpatrick? He was more worried about a little burn on his hand than he was about the guy whose face he spit flames into. So I'll tell you what, you go back in there and take five minutes with your client. Set him straight or we walk away from this and everybody takes their chances.'

Bosch was unconsciously nodding. He liked the anger in O'Shea's voice. He also liked the way this was going.

'I'll see what I can do,' Swann said.

He went back into the interview room and the deputies came back out to give the attorney and his client privacy. O'Shea continued to pace while he cooled down.

'Sorry about that,' he said to no one in particular. 'But I'm not going to let them control this thing.'

'They already are,' Bosch said. 'Waits is, at least.'

O'Shea looked at him, ready for a fight.

'What are you saying?'

'I mean we're all here because of him. The bottom line is, we are engaged in an effort to save his life – at his own request.'

O'Shea emphatically shook his head.

'I'm not going to go back and forth on that issue with you again, Bosch. The decision has been made. At this point, if you're not on board, the elevator's right down the hall to the left. I'll handle your part of the interview. Or Freddy will.'

Bosch waited a beat before answering.

'I didn't say I wasn't on board. Gesto is my case and I will see it through.'

'Nice to hear it,' O'Shea said with full sarcasm. 'Too bad you weren't so attentive back in 'ninety-three.'

He reached over and knocked harshly on the interview room door. Bosch stared at his back with anger welling up from some place deep inside. Swann opened the door almost immediately.

'We're ready to continue,' he said as he stepped back to let them in.

After everyone retook their seats, and the recorder was turned back on, Bosch shook off his anger at O'Shea and locked eyes with Waits again. He asked the same question again.

'Where is she?'

Waits smiled slightly, like he was tempted to set things off again, but then the smile turned into a smirk and he answered.

'Up in the hills.'

'Where in the hills?'

'Up near the stables. That's where I got her. Right when she was getting out of her car.'

'Is she buried?'

'Yes, she is buried.'

'Exactly where is she buried?'

'I would have to show you. It's a place I know but I can't describe … I would just have to show you.'

'Try to describe it.'

'It's just a place in the woods near where she parked. You go in and there's a path and then I went off the path. Way off the path. You could go look and either find it right away or maybe never find it. There's a lot of territory up there. You remember, they searched up there but they never found her.'

'And after thirteen years you believe you could lead us to this spot?'

'It hasn't been thirteen years.'

A sudden rush of horror came over Bosch. The idea that he had held her captive was too abhorrent to think about.

'It's not what you think, Detective,' Waits said.

'How do you know what I am thinking?'

'I just do. But it's not what you think. Marie has been buried for thirteen years. But it has not been thirteen years since I was there. That's what I'm saying. I visited her, Detective. I visited her there quite often. So I can certainly lead you there.'

Bosch paused, took out a pen and wrote a note on the inside flap of the Gesto file. It wasn't a note of any importance. It just gave him a moment to disengage from the emotions that were coming up.

'Let's go back to the beginning,' he said. 'Did you know Marie Gesto before September nineteen ninety-three?'

'No, I didn't.'

'Had you ever seen her before the day you abducted her?'

'Not that I remember.'

'Where did you first cross paths with her?'

'At the Mayfair. I saw her in there shopping and she was just my type. I followed her.'

'Where?'

'She got in her car and drove up Beachwood Canyon. She parked in the gravel lot below the stables. I believe it is called Sunset Ranch. There was no one around when she was getting out, so I decided to take her.'

'It wasn't planned before you saw her in the store?'

'No, I went there to buy some Gatorade. It was a hot day. I saw her and decided right then that I had to have her. You know, it was an impulse. I couldn't do anything about it, Detective.'

'You approached her in the lot below the stables?'

He nodded.

'I pulled in right next to her in my van. She didn't think a thing about it. The parking area is down the hill from the ranch, from the stables. There was no one around, no one who could see. It was perfect. It was like God said I could have her.'

'What did you do?'

'I went into the back of the van and I opened the sliding door on the side where she was. I had a knife and I just stepped out and told her to get in. She did. It was a simple operation really. She was no trouble at all.'

He spoke as if he were a babysitter reporting on a child's behavior when the parents have returned home.

'Then what?' Bosch asked.

'I asked her to remove her clothes and she complied. She told me she would do whatever I wanted as long as I didn't hurt her. I agreed to that deal. She folded her clothes very nicely. As if she thought she would get the chance to put them back on again.'

Bosch rubbed a hand over his mouth. The most difficult part of his job were the times he was face-to-face with a killer, when he saw firsthand the intersection of their warped and terrifying world with reality.

'Go on,' he said to Waits.

'Well, you know the rest. We had sex but she was no good at it. She couldn't relax. So I did what I had to do.'

'Which was what?'

Waits locked eyes with Bosch.

'I killed her, Detective. I put my hands around her neck and I squeezed and then I squeezed harder and I watched her eyes go still. Then I finished up.'

Bosch stared at him but couldn't bring himself to open his mouth. It was moments like these that made him feel inadequate as a detective, moments when he was cowed by the depravity that was possible in the human form. They stared at each other for a long moment until O'Shea spoke.

'You had sex with her body?' he asked.

'That's right. While she was still warm. I always say a woman is at her best when she is dead but still warm.'

Waits glanced at Rider to see if he had gotten a reaction. She showed nothing.

'Waits,' Bosch said. 'You are a worthless piece of trash.'

Waits looked back at Bosch and put the smirk back on his face.

'If that is your best shot, Detective Bosch, then you'll have to do much better. Because it will only get worse for you from here. Sex is nothing. Alive or dead, it is transitory. But I took her soul and no one will ever get that back from me.'

Bosch looked down at the open file in front of him but did not see the words printed on the documents.

'Let's move on,' he finally said. 'What did you do next?'

'I tidied up the van. I always had plastic drop sheets in the back. I wrapped her up and prepared her for burial. I then got out and locked the van. I took her things back to her car. I had her keys, too. I got in her car and drove it away. I thought that would be the best way to throw the police off.'

'Where did you go?'

'You know where I went, Detective. The High Tower. I knew there was an empty garage that I could use there. A week or so before, I had gone to look for work there and the manager happened to mention there was an open apartment. He showed it to me because I acted like I was interested.'

'He showed you the garage, too?'

'No, just pointed it out. On my way out I noticed that there was no lock on the latch.'

'So you drove Marie Gesto's car there and stashed it in the garage.'

'That's right.'

'Did anyone see you? Did you see anyone?'

'No and no. I was very careful. Remember, I had just killed someone.'

'What about your van? When did you go back up Beachwood to get it?'

'I waited until that night. I thought that would be better because I had some digging to do. You understand, I'm sure.'

'Was this van painted with the name of your business?'

'No, not then. I had just started and was not trying to draw attention yet. I worked mostly off referrals. I didn't have a city license yet. All of that came later. In fact, that was another van altogether. That was thirteen years ago. I've gotten a new van since then.'

'How did you get back up to the stables to get your van?'

'Took a cab.'

'You remember which cab company?'

'I don't remember because I didn't call for it. After dropping off the car at the High Tower I walked over to a restaurant I used to enjoy when I lived on Franklin. Bird's – have you ever been there? Good roasted chicken. Anyway, it was a long walk. I had dinner and when it was late enough I had them call me a cab. I went up to my van, only I had him drop me up at the stables so it wouldn't look like the van was mine. When I was sure there was no one around I went to the van and I found a nice private spot to plant my little flower.'

'And this is a spot you will still be able to find?'

'Absolutely.'

'You dug a hole.'

'I did.'

'How deep?'

'I don't know, not too deep.'

'What did you use to dig it?'

'I had a shovel.'

'You always carried a shovel in your window-washing van?'

'No, actually. I found it leaning against the barn up at the stables. I think it was for cleaning out the stalls, that sort of thing.'

'You put it back when you were finished?'

'Of course, Detective. I steal souls, not shovels.'

Bosch looked at the files in front of him.

'When was the last time you were at the place where you buried Marie Gesto?'

'Mmmm, a little over a year ago. I usually made the trip every September ninth. You know, to celebrate our anniversary. This year I was a bit tied up, as you know.'

He smiled good-naturedly.

Bosch knew he had covered everything in general terms. It would all come down to whether Waits could lead them to the body and if forensics would then match his story.

'There came a time after the murder when the media paid a lot of attention to Marie Gesto's disappearance,' Bosch said. 'Do you remember that?'

'Of course. That taught me a good lesson. I never acted so impulsively again. I was more careful about the flowers I picked after that.'

'You called the investigators on the case, didn't you?'

'As a matter of fact I did. I remember that. I called and told them that I had seen her in the Mayfair store and that she hadn't been with anybody.'

'Why did you call?'

Waits shrugged.

'I don't know. I just thought it would be fun. You know, to actually talk to one of the men who was hunting me. Was it you?'

'My partner.'

'Yes, I thought I might be able to shift the focus away from the Mayfair. After all, I had been in there and I thought, who knows, maybe someone could describe me.'

Bosch nodded.

'You gave the name Robert Saxon when you called. Why?'

Waits shrugged again.

'It was just a name I used from time to time.'

'It's not your real name?'

'No, Detective, you know my real name.'

'What if I told you I don't believe a fucking word you've said here today? What would you say to that?'

'I would say, take me to Beachwood Canyon and I will prove every word of what I have said here.'

'Yeah, well, we'll see about that.'

Bosch pushed back his chair and told the others he would like to confer with them in the hallway. Leaving Waits and Swann behind, they stepped out of the room into the cooler air of the hallway.

'Can you guys give us some space?' O'Shea said to the two deputies.

When everybody else was in the hallway and the interview room door was closed, O'Shea continued.

'Getting stuffy in there,' he said.

'Yeah, with all of his bullshit,' Bosch said.

'What now, Bosch?' the prosecutor asked.

'"What now" is that I don't believe him.'

'Why not?'

'Because he knows every answer. And some of them don't work. We spent a week with the cab companies going over records for every pickup and drop. We knew that if the guy moved her car to the High Tower, then he needed some kind of ride back to his own car. The stables were one of the points we checked. Every cab company in the city. Nobody made a pickup or a drop-off up there that day or night.'

Olivas injected himself into the conversation by stepping up next to O'Shea.

'That's not a hundred percent and you know it, Bosch,' he said. 'A cabby could've given him a ride off the books. They do it all the time. There's also gypsy cabs. They hang outside restaurants all over the city.'

'I still don't buy his bullshit stories. He's got an answer for everything. The shovel just happens to be leaning against the barn. How was he going to bury her if he didn't happen to see it?'

O'Shea spread his arms wide.

'There's one way to test him,' he said. 'We take him out on a field trip and if he leads us to that girl's body, then the little details that bother you aren't going to matter. On the other hand, if there is no body, then there is no deal.'

'When do we go?' Bosch asked.

'I'll go see the judge today. We'll go tomorrow morning if you want.'

'Wait a minute,' Olivas said. 'What about the other seven? We still have a lot to talk to this bastard about.'

O'Shea held one hand up in a calming motion.

'Let's make Gesto the test case. He either puts up or shuts up with this one. Then we'll go from there.'

O'Shea turned and looked directly at Bosch.

'You going to be ready for this?' he asked.

Bosch nodded.

'I've been ready for thirteen years.'

13

That night, Rachel brought dinner up to the house after calling first to see if Bosch was home. Bosch put some music on the stereo, and Rachel laid the dinner out on the dining room table on plates from the kitchen. The dinner was pot roast with a side of creamed corn. She'd brought a bottle of Merlot, too, and it took Bosch five minutes of hunting through kitchen drawers to find a corkscrew. They didn't talk about the case until they were sitting across from each other at the table.

'So,' she said, 'how did it go today?'

Bosch shrugged before answering.

'It went okay. Your take on everything was very helpful. Tomorrow's the field trip, and in Rick O'Shea's words, it will be put-up or shut-up time.'

'Field trip? Where to?'

'The top of Beachwood Canyon. He says that's where he buried her. I drove up there today after the interview and looked around – couldn't find anything, even using his description. Back in 'ninety-three we had the cadets looking in the canyon for three days and they found nothing. The woods are thick up there but he says he can find the spot.'

'Do you believe he's the guy?'

'It looks like it. He's convinced everybody else and there's that call he made to us back then. That's pretty convincing.'

'But what?'

'I don't know. Maybe it's my ego not being ready to accept I was so wrong, that for thirteen years I was looking at one guy and I was wrong about him. Nobody wants to face that, I guess.'

Bosch concentrated on eating for a few moments. He then chased a mouthful of pot roast with some wine and wiped his mouth with a napkin.

'Man, this stuff is great. Where'd you get it?'

She smiled.

'Just another restaurant.'

'No, this is the best pot roast I think I've ever had.'

'It's a place called Jar. They say it stands for Just Another Restaurant.'

'Oh, I get it.'

'It's off Beverly near my place. They've got a long bar where you can eat.

After moving out here I ate there a lot at first. Alone. Suzanne and Preech always take care of me. They let me take food to go and it's not that kind of place.'

'They're the cooks?'

'Chefs. Suzanne's also the owner. I love sitting there at the bar and watching the people come in, watching their eyes scanning the place to see who's who. A lot of celebrities go there. You also get the foodies and you get the regular people. They're the most interesting.'

'Somebody once said that if you circle around a murder long enough you get to know a city. Maybe it's the same with sitting at the counter in a restaurant.'

'And easier to do. Harry, are you changing the subject or are you going to tell me about Raynard Waits's confession?'

'I'm getting to it. I thought we'd finish eating first.'

'That bad, huh?'

'It's not that. I think I just need a break from it. I don't know.'

She nodded like she understood. She poured more wine into their glasses.

'I like the music. Who is this?'

Bosch nodded, his mouth full once again.

'I call this "miracle in a box." It's John Coltrane and Thelonious Monk at Carnegie Hall. The concert was recorded in 1957, and the tape sat in an unmarked box in archives for almost fifty years. Just sat there, forgotten. Then some Library of Congress guy was going through all the boxes and performance tapes and recognized what they had there. They finally put this out last year.'

'It's nice.'

'It's more than nice. It's a miracle to think it was there all that time. It took the right person to find it. To recognize it.'

He looked at her eyes for a moment. He then looked down at his plate and saw he was down to his last bite.

'What would you have done for dinner if I hadn't called?' Rachel asked.

Bosch looked back at her and shrugged. He finished eating and started telling her about Raynard Waits's confession.

'He's lying,' she said when he was finished.

'About the name? We've got that covered.'

'No, about the plan. Rather, the lack of a plan. He tells you he just saw her in the Mayfair, followed her and grabbed her. Uh-uh, no way. I don't buy that. The whole thing doesn't feel like a spur-of-the-moment thing. There was a plan to this, whether he's telling you or not.'

Bosch nodded. He had the same misgivings about the confession.

'We'll know more tomorrow, I guess,' he said.

'I wish I could be there.'

Bosch shook his head.

'I can't make a federal case out of this. Besides, it's not what you do anymore. Your own people wouldn't let you go, even if you were invited.'

'I know. I can still wish.'

Bosch got up and started clearing the plates. They worked side by side at the sink and after everything was cleaned and put away they took the bottle out on the deck. There was enough left for them each to have a half glass.

The evening chill drew them close to one another as they stood at the railing and looked down at the lights in the Cahuenga Pass.

'Are you staying tonight?' Bosch asked.

'Yes.'

'You don't have to call, you know. I'll give you a key. Just come up.'

She turned and looked at him. He put his arm around her waist.

'That fast? Are you saying all is forgiven?'

'There's nothing to forgive. The past is past and life's too short. You know, all of those clichés.'

She smiled and they sealed it with a kiss. They finished their wine and went inside to the bedroom. They made love slowly and quietly. At one point Bosch opened his eyes and looked at her and lost his rhythm. She noticed.

'What?' she whispered.

'Nothing. It's just that you keep your eyes open.'

'I'm looking at you.'

'No, you're not.'

She smiled and turned her face away from him.

'This is sort of an awkward time for a discussion,' she said.

He smiled and used his hand to turn her face to his. He kissed her and they both kept their eyes open now. Halfway through the kiss they started laughing.

Bosch craved the intimacy and reveled in the escape it brought. He knew she knew this, too. Her gift to him was in taking him away from the world. And that was why the past no longer mattered. He closed his eyes but didn't stop smiling.

Part Two
The Field Trip

14

It seemed to Bosch to take forever to amass the motorcade, but by 10:30 Wednesday morning the entourage was finally pulling out of the basement garage of the Criminal Courts Building.

The first car in line was unmarked. It was driven by Olivas. A sheriff's deputy from the jail division was riding shotgun, while in the back, Bosch and Rider were positioned on either side of Raynard Waits. The prisoner was in a bright orange jumpsuit and was bound by shackles on his ankles and wrists. The manacles on his wrists were secured in front to a chain that went around his waist.

Another unmarked car, driven by Rick O'Shea and carrying Maury Swann and a DA's office evidence videographer, was second in the motorcade. It was followed by two vans, one from the LAPD's Scientific Investigation Division and the other from the coroner's office. The group was prepared to locate and disinter the body of Marie Gesto.

It was a perfect day for a field trip. A brief overnight rain shower had cleared the sky and it was a brilliant blue with just the last wisps of upper-level clouds in view. The streets were still wet and shiny. The precipitation had also kept the temperature from climbing with the sun's ascent. Though there can never be a good day to dig up the body of a twenty-two-year-old woman, the glory of the weather would offer a counterbalance to the grim duty at hand.

The vehicles stayed in a tight formation as they made their way onto the North 101 Freeway off the Broadway ramp. Traffic was heavy in downtown and moving at a slower than usual pace because of the wet streets. Bosch asked Olivas to crack a window to let in some fresh air and hopefully wash out the funk of Waits's body odor. It had become apparent that the admitted killer had not been allowed a shower or issued a laundered jumpsuit that morning.

'Why don't you just go ahead and light up, Detective?' Waits said.

Since they were sitting shoulder to shoulder Bosch had to turn awkwardly to look at Waits.

'I want the window open because of you, Waits. You stink. I haven't had a smoke in five years.'

'I'm sure.'

'Why do you think you know me? We've never met. What makes you think you know me, Waits?'

'I don't know you. I know your type. You have an addictive personality, Detective. Murder cases, cigarettes, maybe even the alcohol I smell coming out of your pores. You're not that hard to read.'

Waits smiled and Bosch looked away. He thought about things for a moment before speaking again.

'Who are you?' he asked.

'Are you talking to me?' Waits asked.

'Yes, I'm talking to you. I want to know. Who are you?'

'Bosch,' Olivas quickly interjected from the front. 'The deal is, we don't question him without Maury Swann being present. So leave him alone.'

'This isn't an interrogation. I'm just making conversation back here.'

'Yeah, well, I don't care what you want to call it. Don't.'

Bosch could see Olivas looking at him in the rearview mirror. They held each other's stare until Olivas had to put his eyes back on the road.

Bosch leaned forward so that he could turn and look past Waits and over at Rider. She rolled her eyes at him. It was her don't-make-trouble look.

'Maury Swann,' Bosch said. 'Yeah, he's a good goddamn lawyer, all right. Got this man the deal of a lifetime.'

'Bosch!' Olivas said.

'I'm not talking to him. I'm talking to my partner.'

Bosch leaned back, deciding to drop it. Next to him the manacles clinked as Waits tried to adjust his position.

'You didn't have to take the deal, Detective Bosch,' he said quietly.

'It wasn't my choice,' Bosch said without looking at him. 'If it had been, we wouldn't be doing this.'

Waits nodded.

'An eye for an eye, man,' he said. 'I could have guessed. You're the kind of man who would—'

'Waits,' Olivas said sharply. 'Just keep your mouth shut.'

Olivas reached toward the dash and turned on the radio. Loud mariachi music blared from the speakers. He immediately slapped the button to kill the sound.

'Who the fuck was driving this last?' he asked of no one in particular.

Bosch knew Olivas was covering up. He was embarrassed that he had not changed the channel or lowered the volume when he brought the car back last time.

The car remained silent. They were cutting through Hollywood now, and Olivas put on his turn signal and moved into the exit lane for Gower Avenue. Bosch turned around to look out the back window and see if they still had the other three vehicles with them. The group remained intact. But Bosch could now see a helicopter trailing above the motorcade. It had a large number 4 on its white underbelly. Bosch jerked back around and looked at Olivas in the rearview.

'Who called out the media, Olivas? Was that you or your boss?'

'My boss? I don't know what you're talking about.'

Olivas glanced at him in the mirror but then quickly back at the road. It was too furtive a move. Bosch knew he was lying.

'Yeah, right. What's in this for you? Ricochet's going to make you chief of investigations after he wins? Is that it?'

Now Olivas held his eyes in the mirror.

'I'm not getting anywhere in the department. I might as well go where I'm respected and my skills are valued.'

'What, is that the line you say to yourself in the mirror each morning?'

'Fuck you, Bosch.'

'Gentlemen, gentlemen,' Waits said. 'Can't we all just get along here?'

'Shut up, Waits,' Bosch said. 'You might not care that this is being turned into a commercial for Candidate O'Shea, but I do. Olivas, pull over. I want to talk to O'Shea.'

Olivas shook his head.

'No way. Not with a custody in the car.'

They were coming down the exit ramp to Gower. Olivas took a quick right and they came to the light at Franklin. It turned green as they got there and they crossed Franklin and started up Beachwood Drive.

Olivas would not have to stop until they got to the top. Bosch pulled out his cell phone and called the number O'Shea had given everyone in the CCB garage that morning before heading off.

'O'Shea.'

'It's Bosch. I don't think it was a smart thing to call the media out on this.'

O'Shea held for a moment before answering.

'They're a safe distance. They're in the air.'

'And who's going to be waiting for us at the top of Beachwood?'

'No one, Bosch. I was very specific with them. They could track us from the air but anyone on the ground would compromise the operation. You don't have to worry. They are working with me. They know they have to establish the relationship.'

'Whatever.'

Bosch closed his phone and jammed it back into his pocket.

'You need to calm down, Detective,' Waits said.

'And, Waits, you need to keep quiet.'

'Just trying to be helpful.'

'Then shut the fuck up.'

The car turned silent again. Bosch decided that his anger over the trailing media chopper and everything else was a distraction he didn't need. He tried to put it out of his mind and think about what was ahead.

Beachwood Canyon was a quiet neighborhood on the slope of the Santa Monica Mountains between Hollywood and Los Feliz. It didn't have the rustic, wooded charm of Laurel Canyon to the west but it was preferred by its inhabitants because it was quieter, safer, and self-contained. Unlike most of the canyon passes to the west, Beachwood reached a dead-end at the top. It was not a route for going over the mountains, and consequently, the traffic in Beachwood did not consist of people just passing through. It consisted of people who belonged. That made it feel like a real neighborhood.

As they ascended, the Hollywood sign atop Mount Lee was directly in view through the windshield. It had been put up on the next ridge more than eighty years ago to advertise the Hollywoodland real-estate development at the top of Beachwood. The sign was eventually shortened and now advertised a state of mind more than anything else. The only official indication left of Hollywoodland was the fortresslike stone gateway halfway up Beachwood.

The gateway, with its historical plaque commemorating the development, led to a small village circle with shops, a neighborhood market and the enduring Hollywoodland real-estate office. Further up, at the dead-end at the top, was the Sunset Ranch, the starting point of more than fifty miles of horse trails that stretched over the mountains into and throughout Griffith Park. This was where Marie Gesto traded menial work in the stables for time on horseback. This was where the grim motorcade of investigators, body recovery experts and a manacled killer finally came to a stop.

The Sunset Ranch parking lot was merely a level clearing located on the slope below the ranch itself. Gravel had been dumped and spread. Visitors to the ranch had to park here and then leg it up to the stables at the top. The parking lot was isolated and surrounded by dense woods. It could not be seen from the ranch and that was what Waits had counted on when he had stalked and abducted Marie Gesto.

Bosch waited impatiently in the car until Olivas disabled the rear door locks. He then got out and looked up at the helicopter circling above. He had to work hard to keep his anger in check. He closed the car door and made sure it was locked. The plan was to leave Waits locked inside until everyone was sure the area was secure. Bosch walked directly to O'Shea as he was getting out of his car.

'Call your contact at Channel Four and ask them to take the chopper up another five hundred feet. The noise is a distraction we don't—'

'I already did, Bosch. Okay? Look, I know you don't like the media presence but it is an open society we live in and the public has a right to know what is going on here.'

'Especially when it can help with your election, right?'

O'Shea spoke to him impatiently.

'Educating voters is what a campaign is all about. Excuse me, we have a body to find.'

O'Shea abruptly walked away from him and over to Olivas, who was maintaining a vigil next to the car containing Waits. Bosch noticed that the sheriff's deputy was also standing guard at the rear of the car. He was holding a shotgun at ready position.

Rider came up to Bosch.

'Harry, are you all right?'

'Never better. Just watch your back with these people.'

He was watching O'Shea and Olivas. They were now conferring about something. The sound of the helicopter's rotor blades prevented Bosch from hearing their exchange.

Rider put her hand on his arm in a calming gesture.

'Let's just forget about the politics and get this over with,' Rider said. 'There's something more important than all of that. Let's find Marie and bring her home. That's what is important.'

Bosch looked down at her hand on his arm, realized she was right and nodded.

'Okay.'

A few minutes later O'Shea and Olivas convened everyone except Waits in a circle in the gravel parking lot. In addition to the lawyers, investigators, and the sheriff's deputy, there were two body recovery experts from the coroner's office, along with a forensic archaeologist named Kathy Kohl, an LAPD forensic tech, as well as the videographer from the DA's office. Bosch had worked with almost all of them before.

O'Shea waited until the videographer had his camera going before he addressed the troops.

'Okay, people, we are here on a grim duty, to find and collect the remains of Marie Gesto,' he said somberly. 'Raynard Waits, the man in the car, is going to lead us to the place where he has told us he buried her. Our primary concern here is the security of the suspect and the safety of all of you people at all times. Be careful and be alert. Four of us are armed. Mr. Waits will be manacled and under the watchful eyes of the detectives and Deputy Doolan, with the shotgun. Mr. Waits will lead the way and we all will be watching his every move. I would like the video and the gas probe to go along with us while the rest of you wait here. When we find the location and confirm the body we will back away until we can secure Mr. Waits and then all of you will come to the location, which will, of course, be handled as the crime scene it is. Any questions so far?'

Maury Swann raised his hand.

'I am not staying here,' he said. 'I am going to be with my client at all times.'

'That's fine, Mr. Swann,' O'Shea said. 'But I don't think you are dressed for it.'

It was true. Inexplicably, Swann had worn a suit to a body excavation. Everyone else was dressed for the job. Bosch wore blue jeans, hiking boots, and an old academy sweatshirt with cut-off sleeves. Rider wore similar attire. Olivas was in jeans, a T-shirt, and nylon windbreaker that said LAPD across the back. The others in the troop were dressed the same way.

'I don't care,' Swann said. 'If I ruin my shoes I'll write them off as a business expense. But I stay with my client. Not negotiable.'

'Fine,' O'Shea said. 'Just don't get too close or get in the way.'

'Not a problem.'

'Okay, then, people, let's do this.'

Olivas and the deputy went to the car to retrieve Waits. Bosch heard the noise of the circling helicopter getting louder as the news crew came down for a better angle and a closer look with their camera.

After Waits was helped up out of the car, his manacles were checked by Olivas and he was led into the clearing. The deputy stayed six feet behind him at all times with the shotgun up and ready. Olivas kept a grip on Waits's upper left arm. They stopped when they reached the others in the group.

'Mr. Waits, fair warning,' O'Shea said. 'If you make an attempt to run, these officers will shoot you down. Do you understand that?'

'Of course,' Waits said. 'And they would do it gladly, I'm sure.'

'Then we understand each other. Lead the way.'

15

Waits led them toward a dirt path that fed off the lower end of the gravel parking lot. It disappeared beneath a canopy created by a grove of acacia trees, white oaks and heavy brush. He walked without hesitation, like he knew just where he was going. Soon the troop was in shadow and Bosch figured the cameraman in the helicopter wasn't getting much usable video from above the canopy. The only one who spoke was Waits.

'Not too much farther,' he said, as though he were a nature guide leading them to a secluded waterfall.

The path became narrower as the trees and brush encroached and the trail evolved from the well-trodden to the seldom used. They were in a stretch where few hikers ventured. Olivas had to change position from holding Waits by the arm and walking next to him to following the killer, with a hand grasping the waist chain from behind. It was clear that Olivas was not going to let go of his suspect and this was comforting to Bosch. What wasn't comforting was that the new position blocked everybody else's shot at Waits should he try to run.

Bosch had traversed numerous jungles in his life. Most often they were the kind where you kept your eyes and ears on the distance, alert and waiting for ambush, and at the same time watched each step you took, wary of the booby trap. This time he kept his eyes focused on the two men moving in front of him, Waits and Olivas, without waver.

The terrain grew more difficult as the path followed the downslope of the mountain. The soil was soft and moist from the overnight precipitation as well as all the rain in the past year. In some places Bosch felt his hiking boots sink and catch. And at one point, there was the sound of breaking branches behind him and then the thud of a body hitting the mud. Though Olivas and Deputy Doolan stopped and turned to see what the commotion was about, Bosch never moved his eyes from Waits. From behind him he heard Swann curse and the others ask if he was okay as they helped him up.

After Swann stopped swearing and the troop regrouped, they moved farther down the slope. Progress was slow, as Swann's mishap caused everyone to step even more carefully than before. In another five minutes they stopped at the precipice of a steep drop-off. It was a place where the weight of water that pooled in the ground had caused a small mudslide in recent months. The ground had sheared away next to an oak tree, exposing half of its root system. The drop was almost ten feet down.

'Well, this wasn't here last time I came,' Waits said in a tone that indicated he was put out by the inconvenience.

'Is that the way?' Olivas asked, pointing to the bottom of the drop-off.

'Yes,' Waits confirmed. 'We go down there.'

'All right, wait a minute.'

Olivas turned and looked at Bosch.

'Bosch, why don't you go down first and then I'll send him down to you.'

Bosch nodded and moved past them. He grabbed one of the lower branches of the oak for balance as he tested the stability of the soil on the steep slope. It was loose and slippery.

'No good,' he said. 'This is going to be like a sliding board going down. And once we get down, how do we get back up?'

Olivas blew out his breath in frustration.

'Then what do—'

'There was a ladder on top of one of the vans,' Waits suggested.

They all looked at him for a long moment.

'He's right. Forensics has a ladder on top of the truck,' Rider said. 'We get it, put it down on the incline and go up and down on it like stairs. Simple.'

Swann broke into the huddle.

'Simple, except my client is not going up and down that slope or up and down a ladder with his hands chained to his waist,' he said.

After a momentary pause everyone looked at O'Shea.

'I think we can work something out,' he said.

'Wait a minute,' Olivas said. 'We're not taking the—'

'Then he's not going down there,' Swann said. 'It's that simple. I'm not allowing you to endanger him. He's my client and my responsibility to him is not only in the arena of the law but in all—'

O'Shea held his hands up in a calming manner.

'One of *our* responsibilities is the safety of the accused,' he said. 'Maury makes a point. If Mr. Waits falls going down the ladder without being able to use his hands, then we're responsible. And then we've got a problem. I am sure that with all of you people holding guns and shotguns, we can control this situation for the ten seconds it takes him to go down a ladder.'

'I'll go get the ladder,' said the forensic tech. 'Can you hold this?'

Her name was Carolyn Cafarelli and Bosch knew most people called her Cal. She handed the gas probe, a yellow T-shaped device, to Bosch and started back through the woods.

'I'll help her with it,' Rider said.

'No,' Bosch said. 'Everybody carrying a weapon stays with Waits.'

Rider nodded, realizing he was right.

'I can handle it,' Cafarelli called out. 'It's lightweight aluminum.'

'I just hope she can find her way back,' O'Shea said after she was gone.

For the first few minutes they waited in silence, then Waits spoke to Bosch.

'Anxious, Detective?' he asked. 'Now that we're so close.'

Bosch didn't respond. He wasn't going to let Waits get inside his head.

Waits tried again.

'I think about all the cases you have worked. How many are like this one? How many are like Marie? I bet she—'

'Waits, shut the fuck up,' Olivas commanded.

'Ray, please,' Swann said in a soothing voice.

'Just making conversation with the detective.'

'Well, make it with yourself,' Olivas said.

The silence returned until a few minutes later, when they all heard the sound of Cafarelli carrying the ladder through the woods. She banged it a few times on low-level limbs but finally got it to their position. Bosch helped her slide it down the slope and they made sure it was steady on the steep incline. When he stood up and turned back to the group Bosch saw that Olivas was uncuffing one of Waits's hands from the chain running around the prisoner's waist. He left the other hand secured.

'The other hand, Detective,' Swann said.

'He can climb with one hand free,' Olivas insisted.

'I am sorry, Detective, but I am not going to allow that. He has to be able to hold on and break a fall if he happens to slip. He needs both hands free.'

'He can do it with one.'

While the posturing and debate continued Bosch swung himself onto the ladder and went down the slope backwards. The ladder was steady. At the bottom he looked around and realized that there was no discernible path. From this point the trail to Marie Gesto's body was not as obvious as it had been above. He looked back up at the others and waited.

'Freddy, just do it,' O'Shea instructed in an annoyed tone. 'Deputy, you go down first and be ready with that shotgun in case Mr. Waits gets any ideas. Detective Rider, you have my permission to unholster your weapon. You stay up here with Freddy and be ready as well.'

Bosch climbed back up a few steps on the ladder so the deputy could carefully hand him the shotgun. He then stepped back down and the uniformed man came down the ladder. Bosch gave him back the weapon and returned to the ladder.

'Toss me the cuffs,' Bosch called up to Olivas.

Bosch caught the cuffs and then took a position two rungs up on the ladder. Waits began to go down while the videographer stood at the edge and recorded his descent. When Waits was three rungs from the bottom Bosch reached up and grabbed the waist chain to guide him the rest of the way to the lower ground.

'This is it, Ray,' he whispered in his ear from behind. 'Your only chance. You sure you don't want to make a run for it?'

Safely at the bottom, Waits stepped off the ladder and turned to Bosch, holding his hands up for the cuffs. His eyes held on Bosch's.

'No, Detective, I think I like living too much.'

'I thought so.'

Bosch cuffed his hands to the waist chain and looked back up the slope at the others.

'Okay, we're secure.'

One by one the others came down the ladder. Once they had regrouped at the bottom O'Shea looked around and saw that there was no longer a path. They could go in any direction.

'Okay, which way?' he said to Waits.

Waits turned in a half circle as if seeing the area for the first time.

'Ummmm ...'

Olivas almost lost it.

'You better not be pulling—'

'That way,' Waits said coyly as he nodded to the right of the slope. 'Lost my bearings there for a second.'

'No bullshit, Waits,' Olivas said. 'You take us to the body right now or we go back, go to trial and you get the hot shot of Jesus juice you've got coming. You got that?'

'I got it. And like I said, this way.'

The group moved off through the brush with Waits leading the way, Olivas clinging to the chain at the small of his back and the shotgun never more than five feet behind.

The ground on this level was softer and more muddy. Bosch knew that runoff from last spring's rains had likely gone down the slope and collected here. He felt his thigh muscles begin to tighten as every step was a labor to pull his work boots from the sucking mud.

In five minutes they came to a small clearing shaded by a tall, fully mature oak. Bosch saw Waits looking up and followed his eyes. A yellowish-white hair band hung limply from an overhead branch.

'It's funny,' Waits said. 'It used to be blue.'

Bosch knew that at the time of Marie Gesto's disappearance she was believed to have had her hair tied back with a blue hairband known as a scrunchy. A friend who had seen her earlier on that last day had provided a description of what she was wearing. The scrunchy was not with the clothing found neatly folded in her car at the High Tower Apartments.

Bosch looked up at the hair band. Thirteen years of rain and exposure had taken its color.

Bosch lowered his eyes to Waits, and the killer was waiting for him with a smile.

'We're here, Detective. You've finally found Marie.'

'Where?'

Waits's smile broadened.

'You're standing on her.'

Bosch abruptly stepped back a pace and Waits laughed.

'Don't worry, Detective Bosch, I don't think she minds. What was it the great man wrote about sleeping the big sleep? About not caring about the nastiness of how you died or where you fell?'

Bosch looked at him for a long moment, wondering once again about the literary airs of the window washer. Waits seemed to read him.

'I've been in jail since May, Detective. I've done a lot of reading.'

'Step back,' Bosch said.

Waits opened his cuffed hands in a surrender move and stepped toward the trunk of the oak. Bosch looked at Olivas.

'You got him?'

'I got him.'

Bosch looked down at the ground. He had left footprints in the muddy earth but it also looked like there was another, recent disturbance in the soil. It looked as though an animal had made a small dig in the ground, either foraging or burying its own dead. Bosch signaled the forensics tech over to the center of the clearing. Cafarelli stepped forward with the gas probe and Bosch pointed to the spot directly below the colorless hair band. The tech pushed the point of the probe into the soft soil and easily sank it a foot into the earth. She clicked on the reader and began studying the electronic display. Bosch stepped toward her to look over her shoulder. He knew that the probe measured the level of methane in the soil. A buried body releases methane gas as it decomposes. Even a body wrapped in plastic.

'We're getting a read,' Cafarelli said. 'We're above normal levels.'

Bosch nodded. He felt strange inside. Out of sorts. He had been with the case for more than a decade and a part of him liked holding on to the mystery of Marie Gesto. But, while he didn't believe in something called closure, he did believe in the need to know the truth. He felt that the truth was about to reveal itself, and yet it was disconcerting. He felt the – He needed to know the truth to move on, but how could he move on once he no longer needed to find and avenge Marie Gesto?

He looked at Waits.

'How far down is she?'

'Not too far,' Waits replied matter-of-factly. 'Back in 'ninety-three we were in drought, remember? The ground was hard and, man, I wore my ass out digging a hole for her. I was lucky she was just a little thing. But, anyway, that's why I changed it up. No more digging big holes for me after that.'

Bosch looked away from him and back at Cafarelli. She was taking another probe reading. She would be able to delineate the grave site by charting the highest methane readings.

They all watched the grim work silently. After taking several readings in a grid pattern Cafarelli finally moved her hand in a north-south sweep to indicate how the body was likely positioned. She then marked the limits of the grave site by dragging the point of the probe in the dirt. When she was finished she had marked out a rectangle about six feet by two feet. It was a small grave for a small victim.

'Okay,' O'Shea said. 'Let's get Mr. Waits back and secured in the car and then bring in the excavation group.'

The prosecutor told Cafarelli that she should stay at the site so there would be no crime scene integrity issues. The rest of the group headed back toward the ladder. Bosch was last in the single-file line, his mind deep in thought about the ground they were traversing. There was something sacred about it. It was hallowed ground. He hoped that Waits had not lied to them. He hoped that Marie Gesto had not been forced to make the walk to her grave while alive.

At the ladder Rider and Olivas went up first. Bosch then walked Waits to the ladder, uncuffed him and started him up.

As the killer climbed, the deputy trained the shotgun, finger on the trigger, on his back. In that moment, Bosch realized he could slip on the muddy soil, fall into the deputy and possibly cause the shotgun to discharge and hit Waits with the deadly fusillade. He looked away from the temptation and up at the top of the sheer facing. His partner was looking down at him with eyes that told him she had just read his thoughts. Bosch tried to put an innocent look on his face. He spread his hands while mouthing the word *What?*

Rider shook her head with disapproval and moved back from the edge. Bosch noticed that she was holding her weapon at her side. As Waits got to the top of the ladder, he was welcomed by Olivas with opened arms.

'Hands,' Olivas said.

'Certainly, Detective.'

From Bosch's angle below he could only see Waits's back. He could tell by his posture that he had brought his hands together at his front for recuffing to the waist chain.

But then there was a sudden movement. A quick twist in the prisoner's posture as he leaned too far into Olivas. Bosch instinctively knew something was wrong. Waits was going for the gun holstered on Olivas's hip under the windbreaker.

'Hey!' Olivas shouted in panic. 'Hey!'

But before Bosch or anyone else could react, Waits used his hold and leverage on Olivas to spin their bodies so that the detective's back was now at the top of the ladder. The deputy had no angle for a shot. Neither did

Bosch. With a pistonlike move, Waits raised his knee and drove it twice into Olivas's crotch. Olivas started to collapse, and there were two quick gunshots, muffled by his body. Waits pushed the detective off the edge and Olivas came crashing down the ladder onto Bosch.

Waits then disappeared from view.

Olivas's weight took Bosch down hard into the mud. As he struggled to pull his weapon Bosch heard two more shots from above and shouts of panic from those on the lower ground. Behind him he heard the sound of running. With Olivas still on top of him, he looked up but could not see Waits or Rider. Then the prisoner appeared at the edge of the precipice, calmly holding a gun. He fired down at them and Bosch felt two impacts on Olivas's body. He had become Bosch's shield.

The blast of the deputy's shotgun split the air but the slug thwacked into the trunk of an oak tree to the left of Waits. Waits returned fire at the same moment and Bosch heard the deputy go down like a dropped suitcase.

'Run, you coward!' Waits yelled. 'How's your bullshit deal looking now?'

He fired twice more indiscriminately into the woods below. Bosch managed to free his gun and fire up the ladder at Waits.

Waits ducked back out of sight as he used his free hand to grab the ladder by the top rung and yank it up to the top of the embankment. Bosch pushed Olivas's body off and got up, his gun aimed and ready for Waits to show again.

But then he heard the sound of running from above and he knew Waits was gone.

'Kiz!' Bosch yelled.

There was no reply. Bosch quickly checked both Olivas and the deputy but saw they were both dead. He holstered his weapon and scrambled up the incline, using exposed roots as handholds. The ground gave way as he dug his feet into it. A root snapped in his hand and he slid back down.

'Kiz, talk to me!'

Again no response. He tried again, this time going at an angle across the steep incline instead of by a straight-up assault. Grabbing roots and kicking his feet into the soft facing, he finally made it to the top and crawled over the edge. As he pulled himself up, he saw Waits moving off through the trees in the direction of the clearing, where the others waited. He pulled his gun again and fired five more shots but Waits never slowed.

Bosch got up, ready to give chase. But then he saw his partner's body lying crumpled and bloody in the nearby brush.

16

Kiz Rider was faceup, clutching her neck with one hand while the other lay limp at her side. Her eyes were wide and searching but not focusing. It was as if she were blind. Her limp arm was so bloody it took a moment for Bosch to spot the bullet entrance in the palm of her hand, just below the thumb. It was a through and through shot and he knew it wasn't as serious as the neck wound. Blood was steadily seeping from between her fingers. The bullet must have hit the carotid artery, and Bosch knew that blood loss or depletion of oxygen in the brain could kill his partner in minutes, if not seconds.

'Okay, Kiz,' he said as he knelt next to her. 'I'm here.'

He could see that her left hand, holding the wound on the right side of her neck, was creating insufficient pressure to stop the bleeding. She was losing the strength to hold on.

'Let me take over here,' he said.

He moved his hand under hers and pressed against what he now realized were two wounds, bullet entry and exit. He could feel the blood pulsing against his palm.

'O'Shea!' he shouted.

'Bosch?' O'Shea called back from below the drop-off. 'Where is he? Did you kill him?'

'He's gone. I need you to get on Doolan's rover and get us a medevac up here. Now!'

It took a moment before O'Shea responded, in a panicked voice.

'Doolan's shot! So is Freddy!'

'They're dead, O'Shea. You need to get on the radio. Rider is alive and we need to get her—'

In the distance there were two gunshots, followed by a shout. It was a female voice and Bosch thought about Kathy Kohl and the people up at the parking lot. There were two more shots and Bosch heard a change in the overhead sound of the helicopter. It was banking away. Waits was shooting at it.

'Come on, O'Shea!' he shouted. 'We're running out of time.'

When he heard nothing in response he brought Rider's hand back up and pressed in against the neck wounds again.

'Hold it there, Kiz. Press as hard as you can and I'll be right back.'

Bosch jumped up and grabbed the ladder Waits had pulled up. He lowered it back into place between the bodies of Olivas and Doolan and quickly climbed down. O'Shea was on his knees next to Olivas's body. The prosecutor's eyes were as wide and as blank as those of the dead cop next to him. Swann was standing in the lower clearing with a dazed look on his face. Cafarelli had come from the grave site and was on her knees next to Doolan, trying to turn him over to get to the radio. The deputy had fallen chest down after being shot by Waits.

'Cal, let me do it,' Bosch ordered. 'You go up and help Kiz. We've got to stop the bleeding from her neck.'

Without a word the forensics tech scurried up the ladder and out of sight. Bosch turned Doolan over and saw that he had been hit in the forehead. His eyes were open and looked surprised. Bosch grabbed the radio off Doolan's equipment belt and made the 'officer down' call and requested a medical airship and paramedics to the lower parking lot at Sunset Ranch. Once he was assured that medical help was on the way, he reported that an armed murder suspect had escaped custody. He gave a detailed description of Raynard Waits, then shoved the radio into his belt. He went to the ladder and as he climbed back up he called down to O'Shea, Swann and the videographer, who was still holding the camera up and recording the scene.

'All of you get up here. We need to carry her out to the parking lot for the evac.'

O'Shea continued to look down in shock at Olivas.

'They're dead!' Bosch shouted from the top. 'There's nothing we can do for them. I need you up here.'

He turned back to Rider. Cafarelli was holding her neck but Bosch could see that time was growing short. The life was leaving his partner's eyes. Bosch bent down and grabbed and held her unhurt hand. He rubbed it between his two hands. He noticed that Cafarelli had used a hair band to wrap the wound on Rider's other hand.

'Come on, Kiz, hang in there. We've got an airship coming and we're going to get you out of here.'

He looked around to see what was available to them and got an idea as he saw Maury Swann come up the ladder. He quickly moved to the edge and helped the defense attorney off the last rung. O'Shea was coming up behind him and the videographer was waiting his turn.

'Leave the camera,' Bosch ordered.

'I can't. I'm respons—'

'You bring it up here and I'm going to take it and throw it as far as I can.'

The cameraman reluctantly put his equipment on the ground, popped out the digital tape and put it in one of the big equipment pockets on his cargo pants. He then climbed up the ladder. Once everyone was on top

Bosch pulled the ladder up and carried it over to Rider. He put it down next to her.

'Okay, we're going to use the ladder as a stretcher. Two men on each side and, Cal, I need you to walk beside us and keep that pressure on her neck.'

'Got it,' she said.

'Okay, let's put her on the ladder.'

Bosch moved by Rider's right shoulder while the other three men took positions at her legs and other shoulder. They carefully lifted her onto the ladder. Cafarelli kept her hands in place on Rider's neck.

'We have to be careful,' Bosch urged. 'We tip the thing and she'll fall. Cal, keep her on the ladder.'

'Got it. Let's go.'

They raised the ladder and started moving back up the trail. Rider's weight, distributed among the four carriers, was not a problem. But the mud was. Two times Swann, in his courthouse shoes, slipped, and the makeshift stretcher almost went over. Each time Cafarelli literally hugged Rider to the ladder and kept her in place.

It took less than ten minutes to get to the clearing. Bosch immediately saw that the coroner's van was now missing, but Kathy Kohl and her two assistants were still there, standing unharmed by the SID van.

Bosch scanned the sky for a helicopter but saw none. He told the others to put Rider down next to the SID van. Carrying it the last distance with one hand hooked under the ladder, he used his free hand to operate the radio.

'Where's my airship?' he yelled at the dispatcher.

The response was that it was on the way with a one-minute ETA. They softly lowered the ladder to the ground and looked around to make sure there was enough open space in the lot to set a helicopter down. Behind him he heard O'Shea interrogating Kohl.

'What happened? Where did Waits go?'

'He came out of the woods and shot at the news helicopter. Then he took our van at gunpoint and headed down the hill.'

'Did the chopper follow him?'

'We don't know. I don't think so. It flew away when he started shooting.'

Bosch heard the sound of an approaching helicopter and hoped it wasn't the Channel 4 chopper coming back. He walked to the middle of the most open area of the parking lot and waited. In a few moments a silver-skinned medevac airship crested the mountaintop and he started waving it down.

Two paramedics jumped from the aircraft the moment it landed. One carried an equipment case, while the other brought a folding stretcher. They knelt on either side of Rider and went to work. Bosch stood and watched with his arms folded tightly across his chest. He saw them put a breathing mask over her face and then begin to examine her wounds. To himself

Bosch repeated the mantra, *Come on, Kiz, come on, Kiz, come on, Kiz . . .*

It was more like a prayer.

One of the paramedics turned toward the chopper and made a hand signal to the pilot, spinning an upraised finger in the air. Bosch knew it meant that they had to get going. Time would be of the essence on this run. The helicopter's engine started to rev higher. The pilot was ready.

The stretcher was unfolded and Bosch helped the paramedics move Rider onto it. He then took one of the handles and helped them carry it to the waiting airship.

'Can I go?' Bosch yelled loudly as they moved toward the open door of the helicopter.

'What?' yelled one of the paramedics.

'CAN I GO?'

The paramedic shook his head.

'No, sir. We need room to work on her. It's going to be close.'

Bosch nodded.

'Where are you taking her?'

'St. Joe's.'

Bosch nodded again. St. Joseph's was in Burbank. By air it was just on the other side of the mountain, five minutes' flying time at most. By car it would be a lengthy drive around the mountain and through the Cahuenga Pass.

Rider was carefully loaded into the airship and Bosch stepped back. As the door was being closed he wanted to yell something to his partner but he couldn't come up with any words. The door snapped closed and it was too late. He decided that if Kiz was conscious and even cared about such things, she would know what he had wanted to say.

The helicopter took off as Bosch was moving backwards, wondering if he would ever again see Kiz Rider alive.

Just as the airship banked away a patrol car came roaring up the hill to the parking lot, its blue lights flashing. Two uniforms out of Hollywood Division jumped out. One of them had his gun out and he pointed it at Bosch. Covered with mud and blood, Bosch understood why.

'I'm a police officer! My shield's in my back pocket.'

'Then, let's see it,' said the man with the gun. 'Slowly!'

Bosch pulled out his badge case and flipped it open. It passed inspection and the gun was lowered.

'Get back in the car,' he ordered. 'We have to go!'

Bosch ran to the rear door of the car. The two officers piled in and Bosch told them to head back down Beachwood.

'Then where?' the driver said.

'You have to take me around the mountain to St. Joe's. My partner was in that airship.'

'You got it. Code three, baby.'

The driver hit the switch that would add the siren to the already flashing emergency lights and pinned the accelerator. The car U-turned in a screech of tires and a spray of gravel, then headed downhill. The suspension was shot, as with most of the cars the LAPD put out on the street. The car swerved dangerously around the curves on the way down but Bosch didn't care. He had to get to Kiz. At one point they almost collided with another patrol car that was moving with the same speed up to the crime scene.

Finally, halfway down the hill the driver slowed when they were passing through the pedestrian-crowded shopping area of the Hollywoodland village.

'Stop!' Bosch yelled.

The driver complied with screeching efficiency on the brakes.

'Back it up. I just saw the van.'

'What van?'

'Just back it up!'

The patrol car reversed and moved back past the neighborhood market. There in the side lot Bosch saw the pale blue coroner's van parked in the back row.

'Our custody got loose and got a gun. He took that van.'

Bosch gave them a description of Waits and the warning that he was unhesitant about using the weapon. He told them about the two dead cops back up the hill in the woods.

They decided to sweep the parking lot first and then enter the market. They called for backup but decided not to wait for it. They got out with their weapons drawn.

They searched and cleared the parking lot quickly, coming to the coroner's van last. It was unlocked and empty. But in the back Bosch found an orange jail-issue jumpsuit on the floor. Waits had either been wearing another set of clothes beneath the jumpsuit, or he had found clothes to change into in the back of the van.

'Be careful,' Bosch announced to the others. 'He could be wearing anything. Stay close to me. I know what he looks like.'

In a tight formation they moved into the store through the automatic doors at the front. Once inside Bosch quickly realized that they were too late. A man with a manager's tag on his shirt was consoling a woman who was crying hysterically and holding the side of her face. The manager saw the two uniforms and signaled them over. He didn't even seem to notice all the mud and blood on Bosch's clothes.

'We're the ones who called,' the manager said. 'Mrs. Shelton here just got carjacked.'

Mrs. Shelton nodded tearfully.

'Can you give us a description of your car and what the man who did this was wearing?' Bosch asked.

'I think so,' she whined.

'Okay, listen,' Bosch said to the two officers. 'One of you stays here, gets the description of what he's wearing and the car and puts it out on the air. The other leaves now and gets me to St. Joe's. Let's go.'

The driver took Bosch, and the other patrolman stayed behind. In another three minutes they came screeching out of Beachwood Canyon and were moving toward the Cahuenga Pass. On the radio they heard a BOLO broadcast for a silver BMW 540 wanted in connection with a 187 LEO – murder of a law enforcement officer. The suspect was described as wearing a baggy white jumpsuit, and Bosch knew he had found the change of clothes in the back of the forensics van.

The siren was clearing a path for them but Bosch estimated that they were still fifteen minutes away from the hospital. He had a bad feeling about it. He had a bad feeling about everything. He didn't think that they were going to get there in time. He tried to push that thought out of his mind. He tried to think about Kiz Rider alive and well and smiling at him, scolding him the way she always did. And when they got to the freeway, he concentrated on scanning all eight lanes of northbound traffic, looking for a carjacked silver BMW with a killer at the wheel.

17

Bosch strode through the emergency room entrance with his badge out. An intake receptionist sat behind a counter, taking information from a man huddled over on a chair in front of her. When Bosch came close he saw that the man was cradling his left arm like a baby. The wrist was bent at an unnatural angle.

'The police officer who was brought in on a medevac?' he said, not caring about interrupting.

'I have no information, sir,' the desk woman said. 'If you'll take—'

'Where can I get information? Where's the doctor?'

'The doctor is with the patient, sir. If I asked him to come out to speak to you, then he wouldn't be taking care of the officer, would he?'

'Then, she's still alive?'

'Sir, I can't give out any information at this time. If you'll—'

Bosch walked away from the counter and over to a set of double doors. He pushed a button on the wall that automatically swung them open. Behind him he heard the desk woman yelling to him. He didn't stop. He stepped through the doors into the emergency treatment area. There were eight curtained patient bays, four on each side of the room, and the nurses' and physicians' stations were in the middle. The place was abuzz. Outside a patient bay on the right Bosch saw one of the paramedics from the helicopter. He went to him.

'How is she?'

'She's holding on. She lost a lot of blood and—'

He stopped when he turned and saw that it was Bosch next to him.

'I'm not sure you're supposed to be in here, Officer. I think you better step out to the waiting room and—'

'She's my partner and I want to know what is happening.'

'She's got one of the best ER attendants in the city trying to keep her alive. My bet is that he will do just that. But you can't stand here and watch.'

'Sir?'

Bosch turned. A man in a private security uniform was approaching with the desk woman. Bosch held his hands up.

'I just want to be told what is happening.'

'Sir, you will have to come with me, please,' the guard said.

He put his hand on Bosch's arm. Bosch shrugged it off.

'I'm a police detective. You don't need to touch me. I just want to know what is happening with my partner.'

'Sir, you will be told all you need to know in good time. If you will please come—'

The guard made the mistake of attempting to take Bosch by the arm again. This time Bosch didn't shrug it off. He slapped the man's hand away.

'I said, don't—'

'Hold on, hold on,' said the paramedic. 'Tell you what, Detective, let's go to the machines and get a coffee or something and I'll tell you everything that's happening with your partner, okay?'

Bosch didn't answer. The paramedic sweetened the offer.

'I'll even get you some clean scrubs so you can get out of those muddy and bloody clothes. Sound good?'

Bosch relented, the security man nodded his approval and the paramedic led the way, first to a supply closet where he looked at Bosch and guessed that he would need mediums. He pulled pale blue scrubs and booties off the shelves and handed them over. They then went down a hallway to the nurses' break room, where there were coin-operated machines serving coffee, sodas and snacks. Bosch took a black coffee. He had no change but the paramedic did.

'You want to clean up and change first? You can use the lav right over there.'

'Just tell me what you know first.'

'Have a seat.'

They sat at a round table across from each other. The paramedic reached his hand across the table.

'Dale Dillon.'

Bosch quickly shook his hand.

'Harry Bosch.'

'Good to meet you, Detective Bosch. The first thing I need to do is thank you for your efforts out there in the mud. You and the others there probably saved your partner's life. She lost a lot of blood but she's a fighter. They're putting her back together and hopefully she'll be all right.'

'How bad is it?'

'It's bad but it's one of those cases where they won't know until she stabilizes. The bullet hit one of her carotid arteries. That's what they are working on now – repairing the artery. Meantime, since she lost a lot of blood, the risk right now is stroke. So she's not out of the woods yet, but if she avoids going into stroke she should come out of this okay. "Okay" meaning alive and functioning with a lot of rehab ahead of her.'

Bosch nodded.

'That's the unofficial version. I'm not a doctor and I shouldn't have told you any of that.'

Bosch felt his cell phone vibrating in his pocket but he ignored it.

'I appreciate that you did,' he said. 'When will I be able to see her?'

'I have no idea, man. I just bring 'em in here. I told you all I know and that was probably too much. If you're going to wait around I suggest you wash your face and change out of those clothes. You're probably scaring people with the way you look.'

Bosch nodded and Dillon stood up. He had defused a potentially explosive ER situation and his work was done.

'Thanks, Dale.'

'No problemo. Take her easy and if you see the security guard, you might want to . . .'

He left it at that.

'I will,' Bosch said.

After the paramedic left, Bosch went into the lavatory and stripped off his sweatshirt. Because there were no pockets in the surgical clothes and no place for him to carry his weapon, phone, badge and other things, he decided to leave his dirty jeans on. He looked at himself in the mirror and saw that he had blood and dirt smeared on his face. He spent the next five minutes washing up, running the soap and water over his hands until he finally saw the water running clear into the drain.

When he stepped out of the lavatory he noticed that someone had come into the break room and either taken or thrown out his coffee. He checked his pockets again for change but still didn't find any.

Bosch walked back to the ER reception area and now found it crowded with police, both uniformed and not. His supervisor, Abel Pratt, was there among the suits. He looked as though the blood had completely drained from his face. He saw Bosch and immediately came over.

'Harry, how is she? What happened?'

'They're not giving me anything official. The paramedic who brought her in said it looks like she'll be okay, unless something new happens.'

'Thank Christ! What happened up there?'

'I'm not sure. Waits got a gun and started shooting. Anything on whether they've got a bead on him?'

'He dumped the car he jacked by the Red Line station on Hollywood Boulevard. They don't know where the fuck he is.'

Bosch thought about that. He knew that if Waits had gone underground on the Red Line, he could have gone anywhere from North Hollywood to downtown. The downtown line had a stop near Echo Park.

'Are they looking in Echo Park?'

'They're looking everywhere, man. OIS is sending a team here to talk to you. I didn't think you'd be willing to leave to go to Parker.'

'Right.'

'Well, you know how to handle it. Just tell it like it was.'

'Right.'

The Officer Involved Shooting squad would not be a problem. As far as Bosch could see he had not personally done anything wrong in the handling of Waits. OIS was a rubber-stamp squad, anyway.

'They'll be a while,' Pratt said. 'They're up at Sunset Ranch right now interviewing the others. How the fuck did he get a gun?'

Bosch shook his head.

'Olivas got too close to him while he was coming up a ladder. He grabbed it then and started shooting. Olivas and Kiz were up top. It happened so fast and I was down below them.'

'Jesus Christ!'

Pratt shook his head and Bosch knew he wanted to ask more questions about what had happened and how it could have happened. He was probably worried about his own situation as much as he was worried about Rider pulling through. Bosch decided he needed to tell him about the thing that could be a containment problem.

'He wasn't cuffed,' he said in a low voice. 'We had to take off the cuffs so he could go up a ladder. The cuffs were going to be off for thirty seconds at the max, and that's when he made his move. Olivas let him get too close. That's how it started.'

Pratt looked stunned. He spoke slowly, as if not understanding.

'You took the cuffs off?'

'O'Shea told us to.'

'Good. They can blame him. I don't want any blowback on Open-Unsolved. I don't want any on me. It's not my idea of the way to go out after thirty fucking years.'

'What about Kiz? You're not going to cut her loose, are you?'

'No, I'm not going to cut her loose. I'll stand behind Kiz but I'm not standing behind O'Shea. Fuck him.'

Bosch's phone vibrated again and this time he took it out of his pocket to check the screen. It said 'unknown number.' He answered it anyway to get away from Pratt's questions, judgments, and ass-covering strategies. It was Rachel.

'Harry, we just got the BOLO on Waits. What happened?'

Bosch realized he was going to be telling the story over and over for the rest of the day and possibly the rest of his life. He excused himself and stepped into an alcove where there were pay phones and a water fountain so he could speak privately. As concisely as possible he told her what had happened at the top of Beachwood Canyon and what the situation was with Rider. As he told the story he replayed the visual memories of the moment he saw Waits go for the gun. He replayed their efforts to stop the bleeding and save his partner.

Rachel offered to come to the ER but Bosch talked her out of it, saying he wasn't sure how long he would be there and reminding her he would likely be taken into a private interview with OIS investigators.

'Will I see you tonight?' she asked.

'If I get done with everything and Kiz is stable. Otherwise, I might stay here.'

'I'm going to go to your place. Call me and let me know what you know.'

'I will.'

Bosch stepped out of the alcove and saw that the ER waiting room was beginning to fill with media now as well as cops. Bosch guessed this probably meant the word had gone out that the chief of police was on his way. Bosch didn't mind. Maybe the leverage of having the chief in the ER would get the hospital to open up with some information about his partner's condition.

He walked up to Pratt, who was standing with his boss, Captain Norona, the head of the Robbery-Homicide Division.

'What's going to happen with the excavation?' he asked both of them.

'I've got Rick Jackson and Tim Marcia headed up there,' Pratt said. 'They'll handle it.'

'It's my case,' Bosch said, a mild protest in his voice.

'Not anymore,' Norona said. 'You're with OIS until they finish this thing up. You're the only one with a badge who was up there and is still able to talk about it. That's front burner. The Gesto dig is back burner and Marcia and Jackson will handle it.'

Bosch knew there would be no use arguing. The captain was right. Though there were four others present at the shooting who were unharmed, it would be Bosch's description and memory that would count the most.

There was a commotion at the ER entrance as several men with TV cameras on their shoulders jostled one another for position on either side of the double doors. When the doors came open, an entourage entered with the chief of police at the center. The chief strode to the reception desk, where he was met by Norona. They spoke to the same woman who had rejected Bosch earlier. This time she was the picture of cooperation, immediately picking up a phone and making a call. She obviously knew who counted and who didn't.

Inside of three minutes the hospital's chief surgeon came through the ER doors and invited the chief back for a private consultation. As they moved through the doors Bosch hitched a ride, joining the group of sixth-floor commanders and assistants in the chief's wake.

'Excuse me, Dr. Kim,' a voice from behind the group called.

They all stopped and turned. It was the desk woman. She pointed at Bosch and said, 'He's not with that group.'

The chief noticed Bosch for the first time and corrected her.

'He most certainly is,' he said in a tone that invited no disagreement.

The desk woman looked chastened. The group moved forward and Dr.

Kim ushered them into an unused ER patient bay. They gathered around an empty bed.

'Chief, your officer is being—'

'Detective. She's a detective.'

'I'm sorry. Your detective is being cared for in ICU by Drs. Patel and Worthing. I cannot interrupt their care to have them update you, so I am prepared to answer what questions you might have.'

'Fine. Is she going to make it?' the chief said bluntly.

'We think so, yes. That is really not the question. The question is about permanent damage and we won't know that for some time. One of the bullets damaged one of the carotid arteries. The carotid delivers blood and oxygen to the brain. We don't know at this point what the interruption of the flow was or is, and what damage might have occurred.'

'Aren't there tests that can be conducted?'

'Yes, sir, there are and, preliminarily, we are seeing routine brain activity at this time. That is very good news so far.'

'Is she able to talk?'

'Not at this time. She was anesthetized during surgery and it is going to be several hours before she might be able to talk. Accent on "might." We won't know what we have until late tonight or tomorrow, when she comes out of it.'

The chief nodded.

'Thank you, Doctor Kim.'

The chief started to make a move toward the opening in the curtain and everyone else turned to leave as well. Then he turned back to the head surgeon.

'Doctor Kim,' he said in a low voice. 'At one time this woman worked directly for me. I don't want to lose her.'

'We are doing our very best, Chief. We won't lose her.'

The police chief nodded. As the group then shuffled toward the doors to the waiting room Bosch felt a hand grasp his shoulder. He turned to see that it was the chief. He pulled Bosch aside and into a private discussion.

'Detective Bosch, how are you doing?'

'I'm okay, Chief.'

'Thank you for getting her here so quickly.'

'It didn't seem that quick at the time, and it wasn't just me. There were a few of us. We worked together.'

'Right, yes, I know. O'Shea's already on the news talking about carrying her out of the jungle. Making hay out of his part.'

It didn't surprise Bosch to hear that.

'Walk with me for a moment, Detective,' the chief said.

They walked through the waiting area and out to the ambulance drive-up area. The police chief didn't speak until they were out of the building and out of earshot of all others.

'We're going to take a big hit for this,' he finally said. 'We've got a goddamn admitted serial killer running around loose in the city. I want to know what happened up on that mountain, Detective. How did things go so awfully wrong?'

Bosch nodded his contrition. He knew that what had happened in Beachwood Canyon would be like a bomb detonating and sending a shock wave through the city and the department.

'That's a good question, Chief,' he replied. 'I was there but I'm not sure what happened.'

Once again, Bosch began to tell the story.

18

Little by little the media and the police left the ER waiting room. In a way, Kiz Rider was a disappointment because she didn't die. If she had died, everything would have been an immediate sound bite. Get in, go live and then move on to the next spot and the next press conference. But she hung on and people couldn't wait around. As the hours went by, the number of people in the waiting room got smaller until only Bosch was left. Rider was not currently in a relationship and her parents had left Los Angeles after the death of her sister, so there was no one but Bosch to wait for the chance to see her.

Shortly before 5 p.m. Dr. Kim came through the double doors looking for the chief of police or at least someone in uniform or above the rank of detective. He had to settle for Bosch, who stood up to receive the news.

'She's doing well. She's conscious, and nonverbal communication skills are good. She is not talking because of the trauma to the neck and we have her intubated, but the initial indications are all positive. No stroke, no infection, everything looks good. The other wound is stabilized and we'll deal further with that tomorrow. She's had enough surgery for one day.'

Bosch nodded. He felt a tremendous relief begin to flood through him. Kiz was going to make it.

'Can I see her?'

'For a few minutes, but as I said, she's not talking at this time. Come with me.'

Bosch followed the chief surgeon once more through the double doors. They walked through the ER to the intensive care unit. Kiz was in the second room on the right. Her body seemed small in the bed, surrounded with all the equipment and monitors and tubes. Her eyes were at half-mast and showed no change when he entered her focal range. He could tell she was conscious but just barely.

'Kiz,' Bosch said. 'How are ya, partner?'

He reached down and grabbed her good hand.

'Don't try to answer. I shouldn't have asked anything. I just wanted to see you. The chief surgeon just told me that you are going to be okay. You'll have some rehab but then you'll be as good as new.'

A high-pitched sigh came from her mouth. Bosch couldn't read it as relief or anguish or anything in between. He felt her squeeze his hand, though, and he took that as something good.

He pulled a chair over from the wall and sat down so he could keep her hand in his. Over the next half hour he said very little to her. He just held her hand and she squeezed it from time to time.

At 5:30 a nurse entered the room and told Bosch that two men had asked for him in the ER waiting room. Bosch gave Rider's hand a final squeeze and told her he would be back in the morning.

The two men waiting for him were OIS investigators. Their names were Randolph and Osani. Randolph was the lieutenant in charge of the unit. He had been investigating cop shootings so long that he had supervised the investigations the last four times Bosch had fired his weapon.

They took him out to their car so they could speak privately. With a tape recorder on the seat next to him, he told his story, beginning with the start of his part of the investigation. Randolph and Osani asked no questions until Bosch began recounting that morning's field trip with Waits. At that point they asked many questions obviously designed to elicit answers that went with the department's preconceived plan for dealing with the day's disaster. It was clear that they wanted to establish that the important decisions, if not *all* the decisions, came through the DA's office and Rick O'Shea. This was not to say that the department planned to announce that the disaster should be placed at the door of O'Shea's office. But the department was getting ready to defend itself against attack.

So when Bosch recounted the momentary disagreement over whether Waits should be uncuffed to descend the ladder, Randolph pressed him for exact quotes of what was said and by whom. Bosch knew that he was their last interview. They presumably had already talked to Cal Cafarelli, Maury Swann and O'Shea and his videographer.

'Have you looked at the video?' Bosch asked when he was finished telling his view of things.

'Not yet. We will.'

'Well, it should have everything on it. I think the guy was rolling video when the shooting started. In fact, I'd like to see that tape myself.'

'Well, to be honest, we are having a bit of a problem with that,' Randolph said. 'Corvin says he must have lost the tape in the woods.'

'Corvin's the camera guy?'

'Right. Says it must've come out of his pocket when you people were carrying Rider on the ladder. We haven't found it.'

Bosch nodded and did the political math. Corvin worked for O'Shea. The tape would show O'Shea instructing Olivas to take the handcuffs off Waits.

'Corvin's lying,' Bosch said. 'He was wearing the kind of pants with all the pockets, right? For carrying equipment. Cargo pants. I definitely saw him pop the tape out of the camera and put it in one of those pockets with the flap on the side of his leg. It was when he was the last one left at the bottom. Only I saw it. But it wouldn't have fallen out. He closed the flap. He's got the tape.'

Randolph just nodded as though he'd assumed all along that what Bosch had said was the situation, as though being lied to was simply par for the course in the OIS Unit.

'The tape's got O'Shea telling Olivas to take off the cuffs,' Bosch said. 'That's not the kind of video O'Shea would want on the news or in the LAPD's hands during an election year or any year. So it's a question of whether Corvin's keeping the tape to run his own play on O'Shea or O'Shea has told him to hang on to the tape. My bet would be on O'Shea.'

Randolph didn't even bother nodding to any of that.

'Okay, let's go over it all once more from the top and then we can get you out of here,' he said instead.

'Sure,' Bosch said, understanding that he was being told that the tape was not his concern. 'Whatever you need.'

Bosch finished the second run-through of the story before seven o'clock and asked Randolph and Osani if he could ride with them back to Parker Center so he could retrieve his car. On the ride back, the OIS men did not discuss the investigation. Randolph turned on KFWB at the top of the hour and they listened to the media version of the events in Beachwood Canyon and the latest update on the search for Raynard Waits.

A third report was on the growing political fallout from the escape. If the elections needed an issue, Bosch and company had certainly provided it. Everyone from city council candidates to Rick O'Shea's opponent weighed in with criticism of the way the LAPD and district attorney's office had handled the fatal field trip. O'Shea sought to distance himself from the potentially election-killing catastrophe by releasing a statement that characterized him as merely an observer on the trip, an observer who made no decisions concerning the security and transport of the prisoner. He said he relied on the LAPD for all of that. The report concluded with a mention of O'Shea's bravery in helping to save a wounded police detective, carrying her to safety while the armed fugitive was at large in the wooded canyon.

Having heard enough, Randolph turned the radio off.

'That guy O'Shea?' Bosch said. 'He's got it down. He's going to make a great DA.'

'No doubt,' Randolph said.

Bosch said good night to the OIS men in the garage behind Parker Center and then walked to a nearby pay lot where he kept a parking space reserved to retrieve his car. He was drained from the day but there was almost an hour of daylight left. He headed back up the freeway toward Beachwood Canyon. Along the way he plugged his dead cell phone into its charger and called Rachel Walling. She was already at his house.

'It will be a while,' he said. 'I'm going back up to Beachwood.'
'Why?'
'Because it's my case and they're up there working it.'
'Right. You should be there.'
He didn't respond. He just listened to the silence after that. It was comforting.
'I'll get home as soon as I can,' he finally said.
Bosch closed the phone as he was exiting the freeway at Gower, and a few minutes later he was heading up Beachwood Drive. Near the top he rounded a curve just as a pair of vans were passing on their way down. He recognized them as a body wagon followed by the SID van with the ladder on top. He felt a space open up in his chest. He knew they had come from the excavation. Marie Gesto was in that front van.
When he got to the parking lot he saw Marcia and Jackson, the two detectives who had been assigned to take over the excavation, peeling off the jumpsuits they had worn over their clothes and throwing them into the open trunk of their car. They were finished for the day. Bosch parked next to them and got out.
'Harry, how's Kiz?' Marcia asked immediately.
'They say she's going to be okay.'
'Thank goodness.'
'What a mess, huh?' Jackson said.
Bosch just nodded.
'What did you find?'
'We found her,' Marcia said. 'Or, I should say, we found a body. It's going to be a dental identification. You've got dental records, right?'
'In the file on the top of my desk.'
'We'll get it and take it over to Mission.'
The coroner's office was on Mission Road. A medical examiner with dental expertise would compare Marie Gesto's dental X-rays with those taken from the body reclaimed at the spot Waits had led them to that morning.
Marcia closed the trunk of the car and he and his partner looked at Bosch.
'You doing all right?' Jackson asked.
'Long day,' Bosch said.
'And from what I hear, they might get longer,' Marcia said. 'Until they catch this guy.'
Bosch nodded. He knew they wanted to know how it could have happened. Two cops dead and another in ICU. But he was tired of telling the story.
'Listen,' he said, 'I don't know how long I'm going to be hung up on this. I'm going to try to get clear tomorrow but obviously it's not going to be up to me. Either way, if you get the ID I'd appreciate it if you'd let me make the

call to the parents. I've been talking to them for thirteen years. They'll want it to come from me. I want it to come from me.'

'You got it, Harry,' Marcia said.

'I've never complained about not having to make a notification,' Jackson added.

They spoke for another few moments and then Bosch looked up and appraised the dying light of the day. In the woods the path would already be in deep shadows. He asked if they had a flashlight in the car that he could borrow.

'I'll bring it back tomorrow,' he promised, though they all knew he might not be back the following day.

'Harry, there's no ladder in the woods,' Marcia said. 'SID took it with them.'

Bosch shrugged and looked down at his mud-caked boots and pants.

'I might get a little dirty,' he said.

Marcia smiled as he popped the trunk and reached in for a Maglite.

'You want us to stick around?' he asked as he gave Bosch the heavy light. 'You slip in there and break an ankle, it'll be just you and the coyotes all night.'

'No, I'll be fine. I've got my cell, anyway. And, besides, I like coyotes.'

'Be careful in there.'

Bosch stood by while they got into their car and drove off. He checked the sky again and headed down the path Waits had taken them on that morning. It took him five minutes to get to the drop-off where the shooting had occurred. He turned on the flashlight and for a few moments played the beam over the area. The place had been trampled by the coroner's people, OIS investigators and forensics techs. There was nothing left to see. Eventually, he slid down the incline using the same tree root he had used to climb up that morning. In another two minutes he came to the final clearing, now delineated by yellow police-line tape tied from tree to tree at the edges. In the center was a rectangular excavation hole no more than four feet deep.

Bosch ducked under the tape and entered the hallowed ground of the hidden dead.

Part Three
Hallowed Ground

19

In the morning Bosch was making coffee for Rachel and himself when he got the call. It was his boss, Abel Pratt.

'Harry, you're not coming in. I just got the word.'

Bosch had half expected it.

'From who?'

'The sixth floor. OIS hasn't wrapped it up and because the thing is so hot with the media, they want you to cool it on the sidelines for a few days until they see how it's going to go.'

Bosch didn't say anything. The sixth floor was where the department administration was located. The 'they' Pratt had referred to was a collective of groupthink commanders who became frozen whenever a case hit big on TV or in politics, and this one had hit both. Bosch wasn't surprised by the call, just disappointed. The more things changed, the more they stayed the same.

'Did you watch the news last night?' Pratt asked.

'No. I don't watch the news.'

'Maybe you should start. We've now got Irvin Irving all over the box weighing in on this mess and he's zeroed in on you specifically. Gave a speech last night on the south side, saying that hiring you back was an example of the chief's ineptitude and the department's moral corruption. I don't know what you did to the guy but he's got a real hard-on for you, man. "Moral corruption," that's taking the gloves off.'

'Yeah, soon he'll be blaming me for his hemorrhoids. Is the sixth floor sidelining me in reaction to him or to OIS?'

'Come on, Harry, you think I'd be privy to that conversation? I just got the call where I was told to make the call, know what I mean?'

'Yeah.'

'But look at it this way – with Irving punking you like that, the last thing the chief would do is cut you loose, because it would look like Irving was right. So the way I would read this thing is that they want to go by the numbers and nail it down tight before they close it down. So enjoy home duty and stay in touch.'

'Yeah, and what do you hear about Kiz?'

‘Well, they don’t have to worry about home duty with her. She’s not going anywhere.’

‘That’s not what I mean.’

‘I know what you mean.’

‘And?’

It was like peeling a label off a beer bottle. It never came all at once.

‘And I think Kiz could be in some trouble. She was up on top with Olivas when Waits made his move. The question is, why didn’t she take *his* ass out when she had the chance. It looks like she froze, Harry, and that means she could get hurt in this thing.’

Bosch nodded. Pratt’s political take on the situation seemed on target. It made Bosch feel bad. Right now Rider had to fight to stay alive. Later she’d have to fight to keep her job. He knew that no matter what the fight was he would stand beside her the whole way.

‘Okay,’ he said. ‘Anything new on Waits?’

‘Nothing, man. He’s in the wind. Probably down in Mexico by now. If that guy knows what’s best for him, he’ll never raise his head above sea level again.’

Bosch wasn’t so sure about that but didn’t express his disagreement. Something, some instinct, told him that Waits was lying low, yes, but that he had not gone very far. He thought about the Red Line subway Waits had apparently disappeared into and its many stops between Hollywood and downtown. He remembered the legend of Reynard the fox and the secret castle.

‘Harry, I gotta go,’ Pratt said. ‘You cool?’

‘Yeah, right, cool. Thanks for running it down for me, Top.’

‘All right, man. Technically, you are supposed to check in with me every day until we get the word you’re back on active.’

‘You got it.’

Bosch hung the phone up. A few minutes later when Rachel came into the kitchen, he poured coffee into an insulated cup that came with the Lexus she had leased when she transferred to L.A. She had brought the cup in with her the night before.

She was dressed and ready for work.

‘I don’t have anything here for breakfast,’ he said. ‘We could go down the hill to Du-par’s if you have time.’

‘No, that’s okay. I need to get going.’

She tore open a pink packet of sugar substitute and dumped it into the coffee. She opened the refrigerator and took out a quart of milk she had brought with her the night before as well. She whitened the coffee and put the top on the cup.

‘What was the call you just got?’ she asked.

‘My boss. I just got sidelined while all of this is going on.’

‘Oh, baby …’

She came over and hugged him.

'In a way it's routine. The media and politics of the case make it a necessity. I'm on home duty until the OIS wraps things up and clears me of any wrongdoing.'

'You going to be okay?'

'I already am.'

'What are you going to do?'

'I don't know. Home duty doesn't mean I have to stay home. So I'm going to the hospital to see if they'll let me hang with my partner for a while. Take it from there, I guess.'

'Want to have lunch?'

'Yeah, sure, that sounds good.'

They had quickly slipped into a domestic comfort that Bosch liked. It was almost as though they didn't have to talk.

'Look, I'm fine,' he said. 'You go to work and I'll try to come down around lunchtime. I'll call you.'

'Okay, I'll talk to you.'

She kissed him on the cheek before leaving through the kitchen door to the carport. He had told her to use the space in the carport on the days she came to stay with him.

Bosch drank a cup of coffee on the back deck while looking over the Cahuenga Pass. The skies were still clear from the rain two days earlier. It would be another beautiful day in paradise. He decided to go to Du-par's on his own to eat breakfast before heading to the hospital to check on Kiz. He could pick up the papers, see what was reported about the events of the day before and then bring them to Kiz, maybe read them to her if she wanted.

He walked back inside and decided to leave on the suit and tie he had dressed in that morning before getting the call from Pratt. Home duty or not, he was going to act and look like a detective. He did, however, go into the closet in the bedroom and from the shelf above pull down the box containing the case file copies he had made four years earlier, when he had retired. He looked through the stacks until he found the copy of the Marie Gesto murder book. Jackson and Marcia would have the original, since they were running with the investigation now. He decided to take the copy with him in case he needed something to read while visiting with Rider or if Jackson or Marcia called with any questions.

He drove down the hill and up to Ventura Boulevard and followed it west into Studio City. At Du-par's he bought copies of the *Los Angeles Times* and the *Daily News* out of racks in front of the restaurant, then went in and ordered French toast and coffee at the counter.

The Beachwood Canyon story was on the front page of both papers. Both displayed color booking photos of Raynard Waits, and the articles played up the hunt for the mad killer, the formation of an LAPD task force, and a toll-free telephone tip line just for finding Waits. The editors of the newspapers apparently considered that angle more important to the readers and a better selling point than the killing of two cops in the line of duty and the wounding of a third.

The stories contained information released during the numerous press conferences held the day before but very few details about what had actually happened in the woods at the top of Beachwood Canyon. According to the stories it was all under continuing investigation and information was being jealously guarded by those in charge. The short bios of the officers involved in the shooting and Deputy Doolan were sketchy at best. Both of the victims killed by Waits had been family men. The wounded detective, Kizmin Rider, had recently separated from a 'life partner' – code for reporting that she was gay. Bosch didn't recognize the names of the reporters on the stories and thought maybe they were new to the police beat and without sources close enough to the investigation to reveal the inside details.

On the jump pages of both papers he found sidebar stories that focused on the political response to the shooting and escape. Both papers quoted a variety of local pundits who for the most part said it was too early to tell whether the Beachwood incident would help or hinder Rick O'Shea's candidacy for district attorney. While it was his case that went horribly awry, the reports of his selfless efforts to help save the wounded law officer while an armed killer was loose in the very same woods could be a balancing positive.

Said one pundit: 'In this city, politics are like the movie business; nobody knows anything. This could be the best thing that happens to O'Shea. It could be the worst.'

Of course, O'Shea's opponent, Gabriel Williams, was quoted liberally in both papers, calling the incident an unpardonable disgrace and laying all blame at O'Shea's feet. Bosch thought about the missing videotape and wondered how much it would be worth to the Williams camp. Perhaps, he thought, Corwin the videographer had already found out.

In both papers Irvin Irving got his licks in and in doing so took a specific swipe at Bosch for being the epitome of what was wrong in the police department, something Irving as a city councilman would right. He said Bosch should never have been hired back into the department the year before and that Irving, as a deputy chief at the time, had lobbied hard against it. The papers said Bosch was under investigation by the department's OIS squad and could not be reached for comment. Neither noted that the OIS routinely conducted an investigation of every shooting that involved a police officer, so what was presented to the public seemed unusual and therefore suspicious.

Bosch noticed that the sidebar in the *Times* had been written by Keisha Russell, who had worked the cop beat for a number of years before finally reaching a level of burnout that led her to ask for a new beat. She had landed in politics – a beat with its own high burnout rate. She had called and left a message for Bosch the night before but he had been in no mood to talk to a reporter, even one he trusted.

He still had her numbers programmed in his cell. When she worked cops he had been her source on a number of occasions, and she had provided him with help several times in return. He put the papers aside and took his first bites of French toast. His breakfast had both powdered sugar and maple syrup on it and he knew the sugar high would help charge him into the day.

After getting through about half of the meal he pulled out his cell and called the reporter's number. She answered right away.

'Keisha,' he said. 'It's Harry Bosch.'

'Harry Bosch,' she said. 'Well, long time no see.'

'Well, with you being a big shot on the political scene now . . .'

'Ah, but now it is politics *and* police coming together in a violent collision, isn't it? How come you didn't call me back yesterday?'

'Because you know I can't comment on an ongoing investigation, especially an investigation involving myself. Besides that, you called after my phone died. I didn't get your message until I got home, and it was probably after your deadline.'

'How is your partner?' she said, putting the banter aside for a serious tone.

'Hanging in.'

'And you came away unscathed as reported?'

'In the physical sense.'

'But not the political.'

'That's right.'

'Well, the story is already in the paper. Calling to comment and defend yourself now doesn't exactly work.'

'I'm not calling to comment or defend myself. I don't like my name in the paper.'

'Oh, then I get it. You want to go off the record and be my Deep Throat on this.'

'Not quite.'

He heard her blowing out her breath in frustration.

'Then why are you calling, Harry?'

'First of all, I always like hearing your voice, Keisha. You know that. And second, on the political beat, you probably have direct lines to all of the candidates. You know, so you can get them to give a quick comment on any issue that comes up in the course of a day. Right? Just like yesterday?'

She hesitated before answering, trying to get a read on where this was going.

'Yes, we're known to be able to get hold of people when we have to. Except cantankerous police detectives. Sometimes they can be a problem.'

Bosch smiled.

'There you go,' he said.

'Which brings us to the reason you are calling.'

'Right. I want the number that will get me directly to Irvin Irving.'

This time the pause was longer.

'Harry, I can't give you that number. It was entrusted to me and if he knows I gave—'

'Come on. Entrusted to you and every other reporter covering the campaign and you know it. He wouldn't know who gave it to me unless I told him, and I'm not going to tell him. You know you can trust me when I say that.'

'Still, I just don't feel comfortable giving it out without his permission. If you want me to call him and ask if I can—'

'He won't want to talk to me, Keisha. That's the point. If he wanted to talk to me I could leave a message at campaign headquarters – which is where, by the way?'

'On Broxton in Westwood. I still don't feel comfortable just giving you the number.'

Bosch quickly grabbed the *Daily News,* which was folded to the page with the political fallout story. He read the byline.

'Okay, well maybe Sarah Weinman or Duane Swierczynski will feel comfortable giving it to me. They might want to have an IOU from somebody who's in the middle of this thing.'

'All right, Bosch, all right, you don't have to go to them, okay? I can't believe you.'

'I want to talk to Irving.'

'All right, but you don't say where you got the number.'

'Obviously.'

She gave him the number and he committed it to memory. He promised to call her back when there was something relating to the Beachwood Canyon incident that he could give her.

'Look, it doesn't have to be political,' she urged. 'Anything to do with the case, okay? I can still write a cop story if I'm the one who gets the story.'

'Got it, Keisha. Thanks.'

He closed his phone and left money for the bill and tip on the counter. As he stepped out of the restaurant he reopened the phone and punched in the number the reporter had just given him. Irving answered after six rings without identifying himself.

'Irvin Irving?'

'Yes, who is this?'

'I just wanted to thank you for confirming everything I always thought about you. You are nothing but a political opportunist and hack. That's what you were in the department and that's what you are out of it.'

'Is this Bosch? Is this Harry Bosch? Who gave you this number?'

'One of your own people. I guess somebody in your own camp doesn't like the message you're putting out.'

'Don't worry about it, Bosch. Don't worry about a thing. When I get in, you can start counting the days until you—'

Message delivered, Bosch closed his phone. It felt good to have said what he said, and to not worry that Irving was a superior officer who could say and do whatever he wanted without redress from those he slighted.

Happy with his response to the newspaper stories, Bosch got in his car and drove to the hospital.

20

On the way down the hallway in ICU Bosch passed a woman who had just left Kiz Rider's room. He recognized her as Rider's former lover. They had met briefly a few years earlier when Bosch happened to see Rider at the Playboy Jazz Festival at the Hollywood Bowl.

He nodded to the woman as she passed but she didn't stop to talk. He knocked once on Rider's door and went in. His partner looked much better than she had the day before but still not even close to a hundred percent. She was conscious and alert when Bosch entered her room and her eyes tracked him to the side of her bed. There was no longer a tube in her mouth but the right side of her face drooped and Bosch immediately feared that she had suffered a stroke during the night.

'Don't worry,' she said in slow, slurred words. 'They've made my neck numb and it's working on half of my face, too.'

He squeezed her hand.

'Okay,' he said. 'Other than that how do you feel?'

'Not so good. It hurts, Harry. It really hurts.'

He nodded.

'Yeah.'

'I have surgery on my hand in the afternoon. That's going to hurt, too.'

'But then you'll be on the road to recovery. Rehab and all of that good stuff.'

'I hope so.'

She sounded depressed and Bosch didn't know what to say. Fourteen years earlier, when he had been about her age, Bosch had woken up in the hospital after taking a bullet in his left shoulder. He still remembered the screaming pain that had set in every time the morphine started to wear off.

'I brought the papers,' he said. 'You want me to read 'em to you?'

'Yeah. Nothing good, I suppose.'

'No, nothing good.'

He held the *Times* front page up so she could see the mug shot of Waits. He then read the lead story and then the sidebar. When he was finished he looked over at her. She looked distressed.

'You okay?'

'You should've left me, Harry, and gone after him.'

'What are you talking about?'

'In the woods. You could've gotten him. Instead you saved me. Now look at the shit you're in.'

'It comes with the territory, Kiz. The only thing I could think about out there was getting you to the hospital. I feel really guilty about everything.'

'What exactly do you have to feel guilty about?'

'A lot. When I came out of retirement last year I made you leave the chief's office and partner with me again. You wouldn't have been there yesterday if I—'

'Oh, please! Would you shut your fucking mouth!'

He didn't remember ever hearing her use such language. He did what she told him.

'Just shut up,' she said. 'No more of that. What else did you bring me?'

Bosch held up the copy of the Gesto murder book.

'Oh, nothing. I brought this for me. To read if you were asleep or something. It's the copy of the Gesto file I made back when I retired the first time.'

'So what are you going to do with that?'

'Like I said, I was just going to read it. I keep thinking there's something we missed.'

'"We"?'

'Me. Something I missed. I've been listening a lot lately to a recording of Coltrane and Monk playing together at Carnegie Hall. It was right there in the Carnegie archives for like fifty years until somebody found it. The thing is, the guy who found it had to know their sound to know what they had in that box in the archives.'

'And that relates to the file how?'

Bosch smiled. She was in a hospital bed with two bullet wounds and she was still giving him shit.

'I don't know. I keep thinking there's something in here and I'm the only one who can find it.'

'Good luck. Why don't you sit on that chair and read your file. I think I'm going to go to sleep for a while.'

'Okay, Kiz. I'll be quiet.'

He pulled the chair away from the wall and brought it closer to the bed. As he sat down she spoke again.

'I'm not coming back, Harry.'

He looked at her. It was not what he wanted to hear but he wouldn't object. Not now, at least.

'Whatever you want, Kiz.'

'Sheila, my old girl, was just visiting. She saw the news and came in. She says she'll take care of me until I get better. But she doesn't want me going back to the cops.'

Which explained why she hadn't wanted to talk to Bosch out in the hallway.

'That was always a point of contention with us, you know?'

'I remember you told me. Look, you don't have to tell me any of this stuff now.'

'It's not just Sheila, though. It's me. I shouldn't be a cop. I proved that yesterday.'

'What are you talking about? You are one of the best cops I know.'

He saw a tear roll down her cheek.

'I froze out there, Harry. I fucking froze and I let him … just shoot me.'

'Don't do this to yourself, Kiz.'

'Those men are dead because of me. When he grabbed Olivas, I couldn't move. I just watched. I should have put him down, but I just stood there. I just stood there and I let him shoot me next. Instead of raising my gun I raised my hand.'

'No, Kiz. You didn't have an angle on him. If you had fired you might have hit Olivas. After that it was too late.'

He hoped she understood that he was telling her what to say when the OIS came around.

'No, I have to own up to it. I—'

'Kiz, you want to quit, that's fine. I'll back you one hundred percent. But I won't back you on this other shit. You understand?'

She tried to turn her face away from him but the bandages on her neck prevented her from turning.

'Okay,' she said.

More tears came down and Bosch knew that she had wounds that were far deeper than those in her neck and hand.

'You know, you should have gone up top,' she said.

'What are you talking about?'

'Out there with the ladder. If you had been up top instead of me none of this would've happened. Because you wouldn't have hesitated, Harry. You would've blown his shit away.'

Bosch shook his head.

'Nobody knows how they're going to react in a situation until they're in that situation.'

'I froze.'

'Look, go to sleep, Kiz. Get better and then make your decision. If you don't come back I will understand. But I'm always going to be your backup, Kiz. No matter what happens and where you go.'

She used her left hand to wipe her face.

'Thanks, Harry.'

She closed her eyes and he watched as she finally gave it up. She mumbled something he couldn't understand and then was asleep. Bosch watched her for a while and thought about not having her as a partner anymore. They had worked well together, like family. He would miss it.

He didn't want to think about the future right now. He opened the murder book and decided to start reading about the past. He started from page one, the initial crime report.

A few minutes later he had it covered and was about to turn to the witness reports when his phone began vibrating in his pocket. He walked out of the room to answer the call in the hallway. It was Lt. Randolph from the Officer Involved Shooting Unit.

'Sorry we're holding you off active while we take our time with this thing,' he said.

'It's all right. I know why.'

'Yeah, a lot of pressure.'

'What can I do for you, Lieutenant?'

'I was hoping maybe you'd take a ride down here to Parker Center and look at this videotape we've got.'

'You have the tape from O'Shea's cameraman?'

There was a pause before Randolph answered.

'We have *a* tape from him, yes. I'm not sure it's a complete tape and that's what I want you to look at. You know, tell us what might be missing. Can you come down?'

'I'll be there in forty-five minutes.'

'Good. I'll be waiting. How's your partner?'

Bosch wondered if Randolph knew where he was.

'She's still hanging in. I'm at the hospital now but she's still out of it.'

He hoped to delay Rider's OIS interview as long as possible. In a few days, once she was off the painkillers and clear of mind, maybe she'd think better of volunteering that she had frozen when Waits made his move.

'We're waiting to hear when we can interview her,' Randolph said.

'Probably be a few days, I would think.'

'Probably. Anyway, see you soon. Thanks for coming down.'

Bosch closed the phone and went back into the room. He picked the murder book up off the chair where he had left it and checked on his partner. She was asleep. He quietly left the room.

He made good time on the drive in and called Rachel to tell her that lunch looked good, since he was already going to be downtown. They agreed to go fancy and she said she would make a reservation at the Water Grill for noon. He said he would see her there.

The OIS squad was on the third floor at Parker Center. It was at the opposite end of the building from the Robbery-Homicide Division. Randolph had a private office with video equipment set up on a stand. He was sitting behind the desk, while Osani was working with the equipment and getting ready to play the tape. Randolph motioned Bosch to the only other seat.

'When did you get the tape?' Bosch asked.

'It was delivered this morning. Corvin said it took him twenty-four hours to remember he had put it in one of those cargo pockets you mentioned. This, of course, came after I had reminded him I had a witness who saw the tape go in the pocket.'

'And you think it's been doctored?'

'We'll know for sure after I give it to SID but, yeah, it's been edited. We found his camera at the crime scene, and Osani here was bright enough to write down the number on the counter. When you roll this tape the counter on the tape doesn't match. About two minutes of tape are missing. Why don't you roll it, Reggie.'

Osani started the tape and Bosch watched as it began with the huddle of investigators and techs in the Sunset Ranch parking lot. Corvin had stayed close to O'Shea at all times and there was an uninterrupted flow of raw video footage which seemed to always keep the candidate for district attorney at center. This continued as the group followed Waits into the woods and until they all stopped at the top of the steep drop-off. Then it was clear there was a cut where it was to be presumed that Corvin had turned the camera off and then back on again. There was no discussion on the tape of whether the handcuffs should be removed from Waits's wrists. The video cut from Kiz Rider saying they could use the SID ladder to Cafarelli returning to the spot with the ladder.

Osani stopped the tape so they could discuss it. 'It's likely that he did stop the camera while we were waiting for the ladder,' Bosch said. 'That probably took ten minutes max. But he probably didn't stop it until after the back and forth about the cuffs on Waits.'

'Are you sure?'

'No, I'm just assuming. But I wasn't watching Corvin. I was watching Waits.'

'Right.'

'Sorry.'

'Don't be. I don't want you to give me anything that wasn't there.'

'Did any of the other witnesses back me on this? Did they say they heard the discussion about uncuffing him?'

'Cafarelli, the SID tech, heard it. Corvin said he didn't and O'Shea said it never happened. So you got two from the LAPD saying yes and two from the DA's office saying no. And no tape to back it up either way. Classic pissing match.'

'What about Maury Swann?'

'He'd be the tiebreaker except he's not talking to us. Says it is in his client's best interest to remain mute.'

That didn't surprise Bosch, coming from a defense lawyer.

'Is there another edit you wanted to show me?'

'Possibly. Go ahead, Reggie.'

Osani started the video again and it took them through the descent on the ladder and then to the clearing where Cafarelli methodically used the probe to mark the location of the body. The shot was uninterrupted. Corvin simply turned the camera on and shot everything, probably with the idea that he would edit it later if the tape was ever needed in a court hearing. Or possibly a campaign documentary.

The tape continued and documented the group's return to the ladder. Rider and Olivas went up to the top and Waits was uncuffed by Bosch. But as the prisoner started his climb up the ladder, the tape cut off just as he reached the upper rungs and Olivas was leaning down to grab him.

'That's it?' Bosch asked.

'That's it,' Randolph said.

'I remember after the shooting, when I told Corvin to leave the camera and come up the ladder to help with Kiz, he had it on his shoulder. He was rolling.'

'Yeah, well, we asked about why the tape ended and he claimed that he thought he was going to run short on tape. He wanted to keep some for when the diggers came in and excavated the body. So he turned the camera off when Waits was going up the ladder.'

'That make sense to you?'

'I don't know. You?'

'Nope. I think that's bullshit. He had the whole thing on tape.'

'That's just an opinion.'

'Whatever,' Bosch said. 'The question is why cut the tape at this point? What was on it?'

'You tell me. You were there.'

'I told you everything I could remember.'

'Well, you better remember more. You're not in such good shape here.'

'What are you talking about?'

'There's no discussion on the tape of whether the man should or shouldn't be cuffed. What is on the tape is Olivas uncuffing him for the climb down and you uncuffing him for the climb back up.'

Bosch realized that Randolph was right and that the tape made him look like he had uncuffed Waits without even discussing it with the others.

'O'Shea's setting me up.'

'I don't know if anyone is setting anyone up. Let me ask you something. When the shit hit the fan out there and Waits grabbed the gun and started shooting, do you remember seeing O'Shea at that point?'

Bosch shook his head.

'I ended up on the ground with Olivas on top of me. I was worried about where Waits was, not O'Shea. I don't know where O'Shea was. All I can tell you is that he wasn't in my picture. He was behind me somewhere.'

'Maybe that's what Corvin had on the tape. O'Shea running away like a coward.'

Randolph's use of the word *coward* sparked something in Bosch.

He now remembered. From on top of the embankment Waits had called someone, presumably O'Shea, a coward. Bosch remembered hearing the sound of running behind him. O'Shea had run.

Bosch thought about this. First of all, O'Shea had no weapon with which to protect himself from the man he was going to put in prison for life. By all rights, running from the gun would not be unexpected or unreasonable. It would have been an act of self-preservation, not cowardice. But since O'Shea was a candidate for top prosecutor in the county, running away under any circumstances would probably not look so good – especially if it was on video on the six o'clock news.

'I remember now,' Bosch said. 'Waits called somebody a coward for running. It must've been O'Shea.'

'Mystery solved,' Randolph said.

Bosch turned back to the monitor.

'Can we back it up and look at that last part again?' he asked. 'Just before it cuts off, I mean.'

Osani worked the video and they watched it silently from the moment Waits was uncuffed for the second time.

'Can you stop it right before the cut?' Bosch asked.

Osani froze the image on the screen. It showed Waits past the halfway point on the ladder and Olivas reaching down to grab him. The angle of Olivas's body had caused his windbreaker to fall open. Bosch could see his pistol in a pancake holster on his left hip, grips out so that he could take the gun with an across-the-body pull.

Bosch stood up and walked to the monitor. He took out a pen and tapped it on the screen.

'You notice that?' he said. 'It looks like he's got the snap on his holster open.'

Randolph and Osani studied the screen. The safety snap was something they obviously hadn't noticed before.

'Could've been that he wanted to be ready if the prisoner made a move,' Osani said. 'It's within regs.'

Neither Bosch nor Randolph responded. Whether it fell within department regulations or not, it was a curiosity that could not be explained, since Olivas was dead.

'You can turn it off, Reg,' Randolph finally said.

'No, can you show it one more time?' Bosch asked. 'Just this part at the ladder.'

Randolph nodded to Osani and the tape was backed up and replayed. Bosch tried to use the images on the monitor to build momentum and carry him into his own memory of what happened when Waits got to the top. He remembered looking up and watching Olivas being swung around so that his back was to those below and there was no clear shot at Waits. He now remembered wondering where Kiz was and why she wasn't reacting.

Then there were shots and Olivas was falling backwards down the ladder toward him. Bosch raised his hands to try to lessen the impact. On the ground with Olivas on top of him he heard more shots and then the yelling.

The yelling. Forgotten in all the adrenaline rush and panic. Waits had come to the precipice and fired down at them. And he had yelled. He called O'Shea a coward for running. But he had said more than just that.

'Run, you coward! How's your bullshit deal looking now?'

Bosch had forgotten the taunt in the commotion and confusion of the shooting, escape and effort to save Kiz Rider. In the charge of fear that came with those moments.

What did that mean? What was Waits saying by calling the agreement a 'bullshit deal'?

'What is it?' Randolph asked.

Bosch looked at him, coming out of his thoughts.

'Nothing. I was just trying to concentrate on what happened during the moments where there's no tape.'

'It looked like you remembered something.'

'I just remembered how close I came to getting killed like Olivas and Doolan. Olivas landed on me. He ended up shielding me.'

Randolph nodded.

Bosch wanted to get out of there. He wanted to take his discovery – *'How's your bullshit deal looking now?'* – and work it. He wanted to grind it down to a powder and analyze it under the microscope.

'Lieutenant, you have anything else for me right now?'

'Not right now.'

'Then I'm going to go. Call me if you need me.'

'You call me when you remember what you can't remember.'

He gave Bosch a knowing look. Bosch looked away.

'Right.'

Bosch left the OIS office and went out to the elevator lobby. He should have left the building then. But instead he pushed the button to go up.

21

Remembering what Waits had yelled changed things. To Bosch it meant something had been going on up there in Beachwood Canyon and it was something he'd had no clue about. His first thought now was to retreat and consider everything before making a move. But the appointment at OIS had given him a reason to be in Parker Center and he planned to make the most of it before leaving.

He entered room 503, the offices of the Open-Unsolved Unit, and headed toward the alcove where his desk was located. The squad room was almost vacant. He checked the work station shared by Marcia and Jackson and saw that they were out. Bosch had to walk by the open door of Abel Pratt's office to get to his own work station, so he decided to be up-front. He stuck his head in the door and saw his boss ensconced at his desk. He was eating raisins out of a little red box that looked like it was meant for a child. He looked surprised to see Bosch.

'Harry, what are you doing here?' he asked.

'OIS called me down to look at the video O'Shea's guy took of the Beachwood field trip.'

'He's got the shooting on it?'

'Not quite. He claimed the camera was off.'

Pratt's eyebrows arched.

'Randolph doesn't believe him?'

'Hard to tell. The guy sat on the tape until this morning and it looks like it might have been altered. Randolph's going to have SID check it. Anyway, listen, I thought that while I was here I would take a bunch of files and stuff back to Archives so it's not all lying around. Kiz had some files out, too, and it will be a while before she gets back to them.'

'That's probably a good idea.'

Bosch nodded.

'Hey,' Pratt said, his mouth full of raisins. 'I just heard from Tim and Rick. They're leaving Mission right now. The autopsy was this morning and they got the ID. Marie Gesto, confirmed. They got it on the dental.'

Bosch nodded again as he considered the finality of this news. The search for Marie Gesto was over.

'I guess that's it, then.'

'They said you were going to make the next-of-kin call on it. You wanted to do it.'

'Yeah. But I'll probably wait until tonight, when Dan Gesto comes home from work. It'll be better if both parents are together.'

'However you want to handle it. We'll keep the lid on it from this end. I'll call the ME and tell them not to put it out until tomorrow.'

'Thanks. Did Tim or Rick tell you if they got a cause of death?'

'Looks like manual strangulation. Hyoid was fractured.'

He touched the front of his neck in case Bosch didn't remember where the fragile hyoid bone was located. Bosch had only worked about a hundred strangulation cases in his time but he didn't bother saying anything.

'Sorry, Harry. I know you're close to this one. When you started pulling the file every couple of months, I knew it meant something to you.'

Bosch nodded more to himself than to Pratt. He went to his desk, thinking about the confirmation of the body's identification and remembering how thirteen years earlier he had been all but convinced that Marie Gesto would never be found. It was always strange how things turned out. He started gathering all the files associated with the Waits investigation. Marcia and Jackson had the Gesto murder book but this didn't bother Bosch, because he had his own copy in his car.

He walked around to his partner's desk to gather the files she had on Daniel Fitzpatrick, the Hollywood pawnbroker Waits said he murdered during the 1992 riots, and saw two plastic cartons on the floor. He opened one and found it contained the pawn records salvaged from the burned-out pawnshop. Bosch remembered Rider mentioning these. The musty smell of the once-wet documents hit him and he quickly snapped the top back on the carton. He decided he would take these as well, but it would mean two trips past Pratt's open door to get everything down to his car, and that would give his boss two opportunities to become curious about what Bosch was really up to.

Bosch was considering leaving the cartons behind when he got lucky. Pratt stepped out of his office and looked over at him.

'I don't know who decided raisins are a good snack food,' he said. 'I'm still hungry. You want anything from downstairs, Harry? A doughnut or something?'

'No thanks, I'm fine. I'm going to take this stuff over and then get out of here.'

Bosch noticed that Pratt was holding one of the guidebooks usually stacked on his desk. It said West Indies on the cover.

'Doing some research?' he asked.

'Yeah, checking things out. You ever heard of a place called Nevis?'

'Uh-uh.'

Bosch had heard of few of the places Pratt asked about during his researches.

'Says here you can buy an old sugar mill on eight acres for less than four hundred. Shit, I'll clear more than that on my house alone.'

It was probably true. Bosch had never been to Pratt's home but knew that he owned a property up in Sun Valley that was big enough to keep a couple horses on. He'd lived there nearly twenty years and was sitting on a gold mine in real-estate value. There was only one problem, though. A few weeks earlier Rider had been at her desk and had overheard Pratt on the phone in his office asking questions about child custody and communal property. She told Bosch about the call and they both assumed that Pratt had been talking to a divorce lawyer.

'You want to make sugar?' Bosch asked.

'No, man, it's just what the property was used for at one time. Now you'd probably buy it, fix it up, and make it a bed-and-breakfast or something.'

Bosch just nodded. Pratt was moving into a world he knew and cared nothing about.

'Anyway,' Pratt said, sensing he didn't have an audience, 'I'll see you. And by the way, it's nice that you got dressed up for the OIS. Most guys on home duty would've slogged in here in jeans and a T-shirt, looking more like a suspect than a cop.'

'Yeah, no problem.'

Pratt left the office and Bosch waited thirty seconds for him to get the elevator. He then put a stack of files on one of the evidence cartons and carried it all out the door. He was able to take it down and out to his car and get back before Pratt returned from the cafeteria. He then took the second carton and left. No one questioned what he was doing or where he was going with the materials.

After pulling out of the pay lot Bosch checked his watch and saw that he had less than an hour to kill before he was supposed to meet Rachel for lunch. It wasn't enough time to drive home, drop the documents and come back – besides, that would be a waste of time and gas. He thought about canceling the lunch so he could go home right away and get going on the review of the records, but he decided against it because he knew Rachel would be a good sounding board and might even have some ideas about what Waits had meant when he yelled during the shooting.

He could also get to the restaurant early and start his review while waiting at the table for Rachel. But he knew that might cause a problem if a customer or waiter happened to catch a glimpse of some of the photos in the murder books.

The city's main library was located in the same block as the restaurant, and he decided he would go there. He could do some file work in one of the private cubicles and then meet Rachel on time at the restaurant.

After parking in the garage beneath the library he carried the murder books from the Gesto and Fitzpatrick cases with him onto the elevator. Once inside the confines of the sprawling library, he found an open cubicle in a reference room and set to work reviewing the documents he had brought. Since he had begun rereading the Gesto files in Rider's hospital room, he decided to stick with them and finish his review.

Moving through the book in the order the documents and reports were filed, he didn't reach the Investigative Chronology – usually filed at the back of a murder book – until the end. He casually read through the fifty-one forms, and nothing about the investigative moves made, the subjects interviewed or the calls received struck him as any more important than when they had been originally added to the chrono.

Then suddenly he was struck by what he had not seen in the chronology. He quickly flipped pages backwards until he came to the fifty-one for September 29, 1993, and looked for the entry on the call Jerry Edgar had taken from Robert Saxon.

It wasn't there.

Bosch leaned forward to read the document more clearly. This made no sense. In the official murder book the entry was there. Raynard Waits's alias, Robert Saxon. The entry date was September 29, 1993, and the time of the call was 6:40 p.m. Olivas had found it during his review of the case and the next day in O'Shea's office Bosch had seen it clear as day. He had studied it, knowing that it was confirmation of an error that allowed Waits another thirteen years of freedom to kill.

But the entry was not in Bosch's copy of the murder book.

What the hell?

At first Bosch couldn't put it together. The copy of the chronology in front of him was made four years earlier, when Bosch had decided to retire. He had secretly copied murder books from a handful of open cases that still gnawed at his insides. They were his retirement cases. His plan had been to work them on his own and at his leisure, to solve them before he could finally let the mission go and sit on a beach in Mexico with a fishing pole in one hand and a Corona in the other.

But it didn't work out that way. Bosch learned that the mission was best served with a badge and he came back to the job. After he was assigned with Rider to the Open-Unsolved Unit, one of the first murder books he pulled out of Archives was the Gesto case. The book he pulled was the live record, the investigative file that was updated each time he or anybody else worked it. What he had in front of him was a copy that had sat on a shelf in his closet and had not been updated in four years. Even so, how could one have a notation entered on a fifty-one form in 1993, while the other one didn't?

The logic of it dictated only one answer.

The official record of the investigation had been tampered with. The notation entering the name Robert Saxon into the murder book was added after Bosch had made his copy of the book. That of course left a four-year window during which the false notation could have been added, but common sense told Bosch he was dealing with days not years.

Just a few days earlier Freddy Olivas had called him, looking for the murder book. Olivas took possession of the book and then became the one who discovered the Robert Saxon entry. It was Olivas who had brought it to light.

Bosch flipped through the chronology. Almost all of the pages corresponding with the dates of the initial investigation were filled in completely with time-marked notations. Only the page marked September 29 had space at the bottom. This would have allowed Olivas to remove the page from the binder, type in the Saxon entry and then return it to its place, setting the stage for his supposed discovery of this link between Waits and Gesto. Back in 1993 Bosch and Edgar did the fifty-ones on a typewriter in the Hollywood squad room. It was all done on computer now but there were still plenty of typewriters around most squad rooms for the old-school cops – like Bosch – who couldn't quite grasp the idea of working on a computer.

Bosch felt a heavy mixture of relief and anger start to overtake him. The burden of guilt over the mistake he and Edgar had supposedly made was lifting. They were in the clear and he needed to tell Edgar as soon as he could. But Bosch couldn't embrace the feeling – not yet – because of the growing rage he felt at being victimized by Olivas. He stood up and walked away from the cubicle. He stepped out of the reference room and into the library's main rotunda, where a circular mosaic high up on the walls told the story of the city's founding.

Bosch felt like yelling something, exorcizing the demon, but he kept quiet. A security guard walked quickly across the floor of the cavernous structure, maybe on his way to put the collar on a book thief or a flasher in the stacks. Bosch watched him go and then went back to his own work.

Back in the cubicle he tried to think through what had happened. Olivas had tampered with the murder book, typing a two-line entry into the chronology that would make Bosch believe he had made a profound mistake in the early stages of the investigation. The entry said that Robert Saxon had called to report seeing Marie Gesto at the Mayfair Supermarket on the afternoon she had disappeared.

That was all. It wasn't the content of the call that was important to Olivas. It was the caller. Olivas had wanted to somehow get Raynard Waits into the murder book. Why? To put Bosch on some sort of a guilt trip that would allow Olivas the upper hand and control of the current investigation?

Bosch dismissed this. Olivas already had the upper hand and control. He was lead investigator in the Waits case and Bosch's proprietary hold on the Gesto case would not change that. Bosch was along for the ride, yes, but he wasn't steering the car. Olivas was steering, and therefore the Robert Saxon name plant was not necessary.

There had to be another reason.

Bosch worked it over for a while but only came to the weak conclusion that Olivas needed to connect Waits to Gesto. By putting the killer's alias into the book, he was going back thirteen years in time and firmly tying Raynard Waits to Marie Gesto.

But Waits was about to admit he murdered Gesto. There could be no stronger tie than an uncoerced confession. He was even going to lead authorities to the body. The notation in the chronology would be a minor connection compared with these two. So then, why put it in?

Ultimately, Bosch was confounded by the risk Olivas had taken. He had tampered with the official record of the murder investigation for seemingly little reason or gain. He had run the risk that Bosch would discover the deceit and call him on it. He had run the risk of the deceit possibly being revealed by a smart lawyer like Maury Swann in court one day. And he did all of this knowing that he didn't have to, knowing that Waits would be tied solidly into the case with a confession.

Now Olivas was dead and could not be confronted. There was no one to answer why.

Except maybe Raynard Waits.

'*How's your bullshit deal looking now?*'

And maybe Rick O'Shea.

Bosch thought about everything and all in a moment it came together. Bosch suddenly knew why Olivas had taken the risk and put the specter of Raynard Waits into the Marie Gesto murder book. He saw it with a clarity that left him no room for doubt.

Raynard Waits didn't kill Marie Gesto.

He jumped up and started gathering the files together. Clutching them with both hands, he hurried through the rotunda toward the exit. His footfalls echoed behind him in the great room like a crowd of people chasing him. He looked back but there was nobody there.

22

Bosch had lost track of time while in the library. He was late. Rachel was already seated and waiting for him. She was holding a large one-sheet menu that obscured the look of annoyance on her face as Bosch was led to the table by a waiter.

'Sorry,' Bosch said as he sat down.

'It's okay,' she replied. 'But I already ordered for myself. I didn't know if you were going to show or not.'

She handed the menu across to him. He immediately handed it to the waiter.

'I'll have what she's having,' he said. 'And just the water is fine.'

He drank from the glass already poured for him while the waiter hurried away. Rachel smiled at him, but not in a nice way.

'You're not going to like it. You'd better call him back.'

'Why? I like seafood.'

'Because I ordered the sashimi. You told me the other night that you like your seafood cooked.'

The news gave him momentary pause but he decided he deserved to pay for his mistake of arriving late.

'It all goes to the same place,' he said, dismissing the issue. 'But why do they call this place the Water *Grill* if they're not grilling the food?'

'Good question.'

'Forget about it. We need to talk. I need your help, Rachel.'

'With what? What's wrong?'

'I don't think Raynard Waits killed Marie Gesto.'

'What do you mean? He led you to her body. Are you saying that wasn't Marie Gesto?'

'No, ID was confirmed today at the autopsy. It was definitely Marie Gesto in that grave.'

'And Waits was the one who led you to it, right?'

'Right.'

'And Waits was the one who confessed to killing her, right?'

'Right.'

'At autopsy, was the cause of death in agreement with that confession?'

'Yeah, from what I hear, it was.'

'Then, Harry, you're not making sense. With all of that, how can he not be the killer?'

'Because something is going on that we don't know about, that I don't know about. Olivas and O'Shea had some sort of play going with him. I'm not sure what it was but it all went to shit in Beachwood Canyon.'

She held up her hands in a hold-it-right-there gesture.

'Why don't you start at the beginning. Only tell me facts. No theory, no conjecture. Just give me what you've got.'

He told her everything, starting with the tampering with the murder book by Olivas and concluding with the detail-by-detail accounting of what had happened when Waits started to climb up the ladder in Beachwood Can-yon. He told her what Waits had yelled at O'Shea and what had been edited out of the field trip video.

It took him fifteen minutes and during that time their lunch was served. Of course it came fast, Bosch thought. It didn't have to be cooked! He felt lucky to be the one doing all the talking. It gave him a ready excuse not to eat the raw fish put down in front of him.

By the time he was finished recounting the story he could see that Rachel's mind had gone to work on everything. She was grinding it down.

'Putting Waits in the murder book doesn't make sense,' she said. 'It connects him to the case, yes, but he is already connected through his confession and his leading you to the body. So why bother with the murder book?'

Bosch leaned across the table to respond.

'Two things. One, Olivas thought he might need to sell the confession. He had no idea if I'd be able to punch holes in it, so he wanted some insurance. He put Waits in the file. And it put me in a position of being preconditioned to believe the confession.'

'Okay, and two?'

'This is where it gets tricky,' he said. 'Putting Waits in the book was a way of preconditioning me but it was also about knocking me off my game.'

She looked at him, but what he was saying didn't register.

'You'd better explain that.'

'This is where we go off the known facts and talk about what the facts might mean. Theory, conjecture, whatever you want to call it. Olivas put that line in the chronology and then threw it in my face. He knew that if I saw it and believed it, then I would believe that my partner and I had horribly messed up back in 'ninety-three, that I would believe people were dead because of our mistake. The weight of all those women Waits killed since then would be on me.'

'Okay.'

'And it would connect me with Waits on an emotional level of pure hate. Yes, I've wanted the guy who killed Marie Gesto for thirteen years. But adding in all those other women and putting their deaths on me would bring things to a raw edge when I finally came face-to-face with the guy. It would distract me.'

'From what?'

'From the fact that Waits didn't kill her. He was confessing to killing Marie Gesto but he didn't kill her. He made some sort of deal with Olivas and probably O'Shea to take the fall for it because he was already going down for all the others. I was so overcome with my hatred that I didn't have my eyes on the prize. I wasn't paying attention to the details, Rachel. All I wanted to do was jump across the table and choke the guy out.'

'You are forgetting something.'

'What?'

Now she leaned across the table, keeping her voice down so as not to disturb the other diners.

'He *led* you to her body. If he didn't kill her, how did he know where to go in the woods? How did he lead you right to her?'

Bosch nodded. It was a good point but one he had already thought about.

'It could have been done. He could have been schooled in his cell by Olivas. It could've been a Hansel and Gretel trick, a trail marked in such a way that only he would notice the markers. I'm going back up to Beachwood this afternoon. My guess is that when I go through there this time, I'll find the markers.'

Bosch reached over and took her empty plate and exchanged it with his untouched plate. She didn't object.

'So you're saying that the whole field trip was a setup to convince you,' she said. 'That Waits was fed the basic information about the Marie Gesto murder and he just regurgitated it all in the confession, then happily led you like Little Red Riding Hood through the woods to the spot where she was buried.'

He nodded.

'Yeah, that's what I am saying. When you boil it all down to that, it sounds a little far-fetched, I know, but—'

'More than a little.'

'What?'

'More than a little far-fetched. First of all, how did Olivas know the details to give Waits? How did he know where she was buried so he could mark a trail for Waits to follow? Are you saying Olivas killed Marie Gesto?'

Bosch shook his head emphatically. He thought she was going over the top with her devil's advocate logic and he was getting annoyed.

'No, I'm not saying that Olivas was the killer. I am saying he was gotten to by the killer. He and O'Shea. The real killer came to them and made some sort of a deal.'

'Harry, this just sounds so ...'

She didn't finish. She pushed the sashimi on her plate around with her chop sticks but ate very little of it. The waiter used the moment to approach the table.

'You didn't like your sashimi?' he said to her in a trembling voice.

'No, I—'

She stopped when she realized she had almost a full portion on the plate in front of her.

'I guess I wasn't very hungry.'

'She doesn't know what she's missing,' Bosch said, smiling. 'I thought it was great.'

The waiter took the plates off the table and said he would be back with dessert menus.

'"I thought it was great,"' Walling said in a mocking voice. 'You jerk.'

'Sorry.'

The waiter brought the dessert menus and they both handed them back and ordered coffee. Walling remained quiet after that and Bosch decided to wait her out.

'Why now?' she finally asked.

Bosch shook his head.

'I don't know exactly.'

'When was the last time you pulled the case and actively worked it?'

'About five months ago. The last video I showed you last night – that was the last time I worked it. I was just about to make another run at it.'

'What did you do besides pull Garland in again?'

'Everything. I talked to everybody. I knocked on all the same doors again. I only brought Garland in at the end.'

'You think it was Garland who got to Olivas?'

'For Olivas and maybe O'Shea to make a deal, it would have had to be somebody with juice. Lots of money and power. The Garlands have both.'

The waiter came with their coffee and the check. Bosch put a credit card on it but the waiter had already left.

'You want to at least split it?' Rachel asked. 'You didn't even eat.'

'It's okay. Hearing what you have to say makes it worth it.'

'I bet you say that to all the girls.'

'Only the ones who are federal agents.'

She shook her head. He saw the doubt creep back into her eyes.

'What?'

'I don't know, it's just . . .'

'Just what?'

'What if you look at it from Waits's view of things?'

'And?'

'It's such a long shot, Harry. It's like one of those mumbo-jumbo conspiracies. You take all the facts after it's over and move them around to fit some far-fetched theory. Marilyn Monroe didn't overdose, the Kennedys used the mob to kill her. Like that.'

'So what about Waits's point of view?'

'I'm just saying, why would he do it? Why would he confess to a murder he didn't commit?'

Bosch made a dismissive gesture with his hands, as if he were easily pushing something away.

'That's an easy one, Rachel. He would do it because he had nothing to lose. He was already going down as the Echo Park Bagman. If he went to trial, he was no doubt going to get the Jesus juice, just like Olivas reminded him out there yesterday. So his only shot at living was to confess to his crimes, and if, say, the investigator and the prosecutor wanted him to add another killing in for good measure, what was Waits going to say about that? No deal? Don't kid yourself, they had the leverage and if they told Waits to jump, he would've nodded his head and said, "On who?"'

She nodded.

'And there was something else,' Bosch added. 'He knew there would be a field trip and I'll bet that gave him hope. He knew he might get a shot at an escape. Once they told him that he'd be leading us through the woods, that shot got a little bigger and no doubt his cooperation got a little better. His whole motivation was probably getting to the field trip.'

She nodded again. He couldn't tell whether he had convinced her of anything. They were silent for a long moment. The waiter came and took his credit card. Lunch was over.

'So what are you going to do?' she asked.

'Like I told you, next stop Beachwood Canyon. After that, I'm going to find the man who can explain everything to me.'

'O'Shea? He'll never talk to you.'

'I know. That's why I'm not going to talk to him. Not yet, at least.'

'You're going to find Waits?'

He could hear the doubt in her voice.

'That's right.'

'He's long gone, Harry. You think he would stay around here? He killed two cops. His life expectancy in L.A. is zero. You think he'd stick around with every person with a gun and badge in this county looking for him with a license to kill?'

He nodded slowly.

'He's still here,' he said with conviction. 'Everything you said is right, except you forgot one thing. He's got the leverage now. When he escaped, the leverage shifted to Waits. And if he is smart, and it appears he is, he'll use it. He'll stick around and he'll use O'Shea to maximum potential.'

'You mean blackmail?'

'Whatever. Waits carries the truth. He knows what went down. If he can make it believable that he's a danger to O'Shea and his whole election machine, and if he can contact O'Shea, he can now make the candidate do the jumping.'

She nodded.

'You raise a good point about leverage,' she said. 'What if this grand conspiracy of yours had gone down as planned? You know, Waits takes the fall for Gesto and all the others and heads off to Pelican Bay or San Quentin to do his life without. Then the conspirators have this guy sitting in a cell and he has all the answers – and the leverage. He's still a danger to O'Shea and his whole political machine. Why would the future district attorney of Los Angeles County put himself in that position?'

The waiter brought back the credit card and the final bill. Bosch added a tip and signed it. It had to be the most expensive lunch he had never eaten.

He looked up at Rachel when he was finished scribbling his name.

'Good question, Rachel. I don't know the exact answer to it but I assume O'Shea or Olivas or somebody had a plan for an endgame. And maybe that's why Waits decided to run.'

She frowned.

'You can't be talked out of this, can you?'

'Not yet.'

'Well, good luck. I think you are going to need it.'

'Thanks, Rachel.'

He stood up and so did she.

'Did you valet?' she asked.

'No, I'm over in the library garage.'

It meant they would leave the restaurant by different doors.

'Will I see you tonight?' he asked.

'If I'm not held up. There's word of a case coming our way from Washington headquarters. How about if I call you?'

He said that was fine and walked with her to the door that led to the garage where the valets waited. He hugged her there and said good-bye.

23

On the way out of downtown Bosch took Hill Street up to Caesar Chavez and turned left. It soon became Sunset Boulevard and he drove it through Echo Park. He wasn't expecting to see Raynard Waits crossing at the light or coming out of a *medicina* clinic or one of the *migra* offices that lined the street. But Bosch was running way out on his instincts on this case and they told him Echo Park was still in play. The more he drove through, the more he would get a feel for the neighborhood and the better he would be at his search. Instincts or not, he was sure of one thing. Waits had originally been arrested while on his way to a specific destination in Echo Park. Bosch was going to find it.

He pulled into a no-parking zone near Quintero Street and walked up to the Pescado Mojado grill. He ordered *camarones a la diabla* and showed the booking photo of Waits to the man who took his order and to the patrons waiting in line. He got the usual shake of the head from each customer, and the Spanish conversation among them died off. Bosch took his shrimp plate to a table and finished his food quickly.

From Echo Park he drove home to change from his suit into jeans and a pullover shirt. Then he drove over to Beachwood Canyon and made his way to the top of the hill. The parking clearing below Sunset Ranch was empty and Bosch wondered if all the activity and media attention from the day before had kept riders away. He got out of his car and went to its trunk. He pulled out a coiled thirty-foot length of rope and headed into the brush on the same path he had taken behind Waits the day before.

He was only a few steps down the path when his cell phone started vibrating. He stopped, dug the phone out of his blue jeans and saw on the screen that it was Jerry Edgar calling. Bosch had left him a message earlier while driving home.

'How's Kiz?'

'Doing better. You ought to go visit her, man. Get over whatever it is you two need to get over and visit her. You didn't even call yesterday.'

'Don't worry, I will. In fact, I was thinking about cutting out of here early and dropping by. You going to be there?'

'I might. Give me a call when you're going and I'll try to meet you.

Anyway, that's not really why I called. There's a couple things I wanted to tell you. First, they got a confirmation on the ID at the autopsy today. It was Marie Gesto.'

Edgar was silent a moment before responding.

'Have you talked to her parents?'

'No, not yet. Dan's got that job selling tractors. I was going to call up there tonight when he's home and they're together.'

'That's what I'd do. What else you got, Harry? I got a guy in a room here and I'm about to go in and break his ass down on a murder-rape we're working.'

'Sorry to interrupt. I thought you called me.'

'I did, man, but I was calling you back real quick in case it was important.'

'It is important. I thought you'd want to know, I think that line that was found in the fifty-ones on this case was phonied. I think when it all shakes out we'll be clear on it.'

This time there was no hesitation in his old partner's response.

'What are you saying, Waits never called us back then?'

'That's right.'

'Then how'd that entry get in the chrono?'

'Somebody added it. Recently. Somebody trying to fuck with me.'

'Goddamn it!' Bosch could hear the anger and relief in Edgar's voice. 'I haven't slept since you called me up and told me that shit, Harry. They didn't only fuck with you, man.'

'That's what I figured. That's why I called. I haven't figured it all out, but that's the way it's looking. When I get the whole story I'll let you know. Now go back to your interview and nail that guy.'

'Harry, my man, you just made my day. I'm going to go into the room and crunch this asshole's bones.'

'I'm glad to hear that. Call me if you're going to see Kiz.'

'You got it.'

But Bosch knew Edgar was just paying lip service to the idea. He wouldn't be visiting Kiz, not if he was in the middle of a breaking case like he said. After closing and pocketing the phone, Bosch looked around and took in his surroundings. He looked high and low, from the ground to the overhead canopy, and didn't see any obvious markings. He guessed that there would've been no need for a Hansel and Gretel trail while Waits had been on the clearly defined path. If there were markers, they would be at the bottom of the mudslide embankment. He headed that way.

At the top of the precipice he looped the rope around the trunk of the white oak at the top and was able to rappel down the sheer surface to the lower level. He left the rope in place and once again assessed the area from floor to canopy. He saw nothing that readily marked the way to the grave site where Marie Gesto had been found. He started walking toward the grave site, looking for carvings in the trunks of the trees, ribbons in the branches, anything that Waits might have used to lead the way.

Bosch got to the grave site without seeing a single indication of a marked trail. He was disappointed. His lack of findings went against the theory he had outlined for Rachel Walling. But Bosch was sure he was right in his thinking and he refused to believe there was no trail. He thought it was possible that whatever markings had been there had been trampled over and obliterated by the army of investigators and technicians who had descended on the woods the day before.

Refusing to give up, he made his way back to the embankment and then turned and looked toward the grave site. He tried to put his mind into the position Waits was in. He had never been to the spot before, yet he had to readily choose a direction to go in while everyone else watched.

How did he do it?

Bosch stood motionless, thinking and looking off into the woods in the direction of the grave site. He did not move for five minutes. After that he had the answer.

In the middle distance on the sight line to the grave site was a tall eucalyptus tree. It was split at ground level and two fully mature trunks rose at least fifty feet through the canopy of other trees. In the split, about ten feet off the ground, was a branch that had fallen and become lodged horizontally between the trunks. The formation of split trunk and branch created an inverted *A* that was clearly recognizable and could have been noticed quickly by someone scanning the woods and looking specifically for it.

Bosch headed toward the eucalyptus, certain that he had the first marker that Waits had followed. When he reached the position, he looked again in the direction of the grave site. He slowly scanned until he again picked up on an anomaly that was obvious and unique in terms of the immediate vicinity. He walked toward it.

It was a young California oak. What made it noticeable to Bosch from a distance was that its natural balance was off. It had lost the symmetrical spread of its branches because one of the lower limbs was missing. Bosch walked to it and looked up at a broken outcropping on the trunk where a four-inch-thick limb had been attached about eight feet up. By grabbing a lower branch and pulling himself up into the tree he was able to examine the break more closely and found that it was not a natural break. The outcropping showed a smooth cut through the top half of the branch. Someone had sawed across the top of the branch and then pulled down on it to break it. Bosch was no tree surgeon but he thought the cut and break looked recent. The exposed inner wood was light in color and there was no indication of regrowth or natural repair.

Bosch dropped to the ground and looked around in the brush. The fallen limb was nowhere to be found. It had been dragged away so as not to be noticed and cause suspicion. To him it was further proof that a Hansel and Gretel trail had been left for Waits to follow.

He turned and looked in the direction of the final clearing. He was less than twenty yards from the grave site and he was easily able to pick out what he believed to be the last marker. High up in the oak tree that shaded the grave site was a nest that looked like the home of a large bird, an owl or a hawk.

He walked to the clearing and looked up. The hair scrunchy Waits had said marked the spot had been removed by the forensics team. Looking further up into the tree, Bosch could not see the nest from directly beneath. Olivas had planned it well. He had used three markers recognizable only from a distance. Nothing that would draw a second glance from those following Waits, yet three markers that could easily lead him to the grave site.

As his eyes dropped to the open grave at his feet he remembered that he had noticed a disturbance in the soil the day before. He had credited it to animals foraging in the dirt. Now he believed the disturbance had been left by the first digging into the soil to confirm the grave site. Olivas had been out here before any of them. He had come out to mark the trail and confirm the grave. He had either been told where to find it or had been led to it by the real killer.

Bosch had been staring at the grave and putting the scenario together for several seconds before he realized he was hearing voices. At least two men in conversation, their voices approaching. Bosch could hear them moving through the brush, their footfalls heavy in the mud and on the bed of fallen leaves. They were coming from the same direction Bosch had come from.

He moved quickly across the small clearing and got behind the massive trunk of the oak tree. He waited and soon he could tell that the men had reached the clearing.

'Right here,' said the first voice. 'She was right here for thirteen years.'

'No shit! This is spooky.'

Bosch didn't dare look around the tree and risk exposing himself. No matter who it was – media, cops or even tourists – he didn't want to be seen here.

The two men stayed in the clearing and batted meaningless conversation back and forth for a few moments. Luckily, neither approached the trunk of the oak and Bosch's position. Then finally Bosch heard the first voice say, 'Well, let's go get this done and get out of here.'

The men trod off in the direction from which they had come. Bosch looked around the tree and caught a glimpse of them just before they disappeared back into the brush. He saw Osani and another man he assumed was also from the OIS Unit. After giving them a head start Bosch moved from around the tree and crossed the clearing. He took a position behind an old eucalyptus and watched as the OIS men walked back to the sheer facing left by the mudslide.

Osani and his partner made so much noise walking through the brush that it was quite easy for Bosch to pick and move his way toward the embankment as well. Under cover of their noise he got to the eucalyptus that was Waits's first marker and watched the two men as they set up to take measurements from the bottom of the embankment to the top. There was a ladder on the facing now, positioned much like the ladder had been the day before. Bosch realized that the two men were cleaning up the official report. They were taking distance measurements that had either been forgotten or deemed unnecessary the day before. Today, in light of the political fallout involved, everything was necessary.

Osani climbed the ladder to the top while his partner remained below. He then took a tape measure off his belt and pulled out several lengths, passing the end down to his partner. They took measurements with Osani calling out the lengths and his partner writing them down in a notebook. It looked to Bosch as though they were measuring various lengths from the spot on the ground where he had been the day before to the positions where Waits, Olivas and Rider had been. Bosch had no idea what the importance of such measurements would be to the investigation.

Bosch's phone started to vibrate in his pocket and he quickly pulled it out and shut it off. As the screen died he saw that the incoming number had a 485 prefix, which he knew meant Parker Center.

A few seconds later Bosch heard the ringing of a cell phone in the clearing where Osani and the other man were working. Bosch peeked around the tree and saw Osani take a phone off his belt. He listened to the caller and then took a sweeping look around the woods, doing a 360-degree turn. Bosch ducked back.

'No, Lieutenant,' Osani said. 'We don't see him. The car's in the lot but we don't see him. We don't see anybody out here.'

Osani listened some more and said yes several times before closing the phone and returning it to his belt. He went back to work with the tape measure and within another minute or so the two OIS men had what they needed.

Osani climbed the ladder and then both men pulled it up the embankment. It was at that moment that Osani noticed the rope looped around the trunk of the white oak at the edge of the embankment. He put the ladder down on the ground and went to the tree. He pulled the rope from around the trunk and started coiling it. He looked out into the woods as he did this and Bosch moved back behind one of the eucalyptus's two trunks.

A few minutes later they were gone, loudly trudging back through the woods to the parking clearing, the ladder carried between them. Bosch went to the embankment but waited until he could no longer hear the OIS men before using the roots as handholds to climb up.

When he got to the parking clearing, there was no sign of Osani and his partner. Bosch turned his phone back on and waited for it to boot up. He wanted to see if the caller from Parker Center had left a message. Before he could listen, the phone started vibrating in his hand. He recognized the number as one of the lines from the Open-Unsolved Unit. He took the call.

'This is Bosch.'

'Harry, where are you?'

It was Abel Pratt. There was an urgency in his voice.

'Nowhere. Why?'

'Where *are* you?'

Something told Bosch that Pratt knew exactly where he was.

'I'm in Beachwood Canyon. What's going on?'

There was a moment of silence before Pratt responded, the urgent tone replaced with one of annoyance.

'What's going on is that I just got a call from Lieutenant Randolph at OIS. He says there's a Mustang registered to you sitting in the lot up there. I tell him that's really strange, because Harry Bosch is on home duty and is supposed to be staying a million miles away from the investigation in Beachwood Canyon.'

Thinking quickly, Bosch came up with what he thought was a way out.

'Look, I'm not investigating anything. I'm looking for something. I lost my challenge coin out here yesterday. I'm just looking for it.'

'What?'

'My RHD chip. It must've come out of my pocket when I was sliding down the embankment or something. I got home last night and it wasn't in my pocket.'

As he spoke Bosch reached into his pocket and pulled out the coin he was claiming to have lost. It was a heavy metal coin about the size and width of a casino chip. One side showed a gold detective's badge and the other side showed the caricature of a detective – suit, hat, gun and exaggerated chin – set against an American flag background. It was known as a challenge coin or chip and was a carryover from the practice of elite and specialized military units. Upon acceptance into the unit a soldier is given a challenge coin and is expected to carry it always. At any time or place a fellow unit member can ask to see the coin. This most often takes place in a bar or canteen. If the soldier fails to be carrying the coin, then he picks up the tab. The tradition had been observed for several years in the RHD. Bosch had been given his coin upon returning from retirement.

'Fuck the coin, Harry,' Pratt said angrily. 'You can replace it for ten bucks. *Stay away* from the investigation. Go home and stay home until you hear from me. Am I clear?'

'You're clear.'

'Besides, what the fuck? If you lost your coin out there the forensics people would have found it already. They went over that scene with a metal detector looking for cartridges.'

Bosch nodded.

'Yeah, I sort of forgot about that.'

'Yeah, Harry, you forgot? Are you bullshitting with me?'

'No, Top, I'm not. I forgot. I was bored and decided to come look for it. I saw Randolph's people and decided to keep my head down. I just didn't think they'd call in my plate.'

'Well, they did. And then I got the call. I don't like blowback like this, Harry. You know that.'

'I'm going home right now.'

'Good. Stay there.'

Pratt didn't wait for Bosch's response. He clicked off and Bosch closed his phone. He flipped the heavy coin into the air, caught it in his palm, badge side up, and pocketed it. He then walked to his car.

24

Something about being told to go home made Bosch not go home. After leaving Beachwood Canyon he made a stop at St. Joe's to check in on Kiz Rider. She had changed locations again. She was now out of ICU and on a regular patient floor. She didn't have a private room but the other bed in the room was empty. They often did that for cops.

Speaking was still difficult for her and the malaise of depression she exhibited that morning had not lifted. Bosch didn't stay long. He passed on a get-well from Jerry Edgar and then left, finally going home as instructed and hauling in the two cartons and files he had collected earlier from the Open-Unsolved Unit.

He put the cartons on the floor in the dining room and spread the files out on the table. There was a lot and he knew he could probably occupy himself for at least a couple days with what he had taken from the office. He went over to the stereo and turned it on. He knew that he already had the Coltrane-Monk collaboration from Carnegie Hall in the machine. The player was on shuffle and the first song out was called 'Evidence.' Bosch took that as a good sign as he went back to the table.

To begin he had to take an inventory of exactly what he had so he could decide how to approach his review of the material. First and foremost was the copy of the investigative record in the current case Raynard Waits was being prosecuted for. This had been turned over by Olivas but not studied closely by Bosch and Rider because their assignments and priorities were the Fitzpatrick and Gesto cases. On the table Bosch also had the Fitzpatrick murder book Rider had pulled out of archives as well as his secret copy of the Gesto murder book, of which he had already completed a review.

Finally, on the floor were the two plastic cartons containing whatever pawn records had been salvaged after Fitzpatrick's business was torched and then soaked by fire hoses during the 1992 riots.

There was a small drawer in the side of the dining room table. Bosch figured that it had been designed for silverware but since he used the table more often to work on than to eat at, the drawer contained an assortment of pens and legal pads. He withdrew one of each, deciding that he needed to write down the important aspects of the current investigation. After twenty minutes and three torn-off and crumpled pages, his free-form thoughts had filled less than half a page.

/ arrest
Echo Park
\ escape (Red Line)
Who is Waits? Where is the castle? (destination: Echo Park)
Beachwood Canyon – set up, false confession
Who benefits? Why now?

Bosch studied the notes for a few moments. He knew that the last two questions he had written were actually the starting point. If things had gone according to plan, who would have benefited from Waits's false confession? Waits, for one, by avoiding a death sentence. But the real winner was the real killer. The case would have been closed, all investigations halted. The real killer would escape justice.

Bosch looked at the two questions again. *Who benefits? Why now?* He considered them carefully and then reversed their order and considered them again. He came to a single conclusion. His continued investigations of the Marie Gesto case had created a need for something to be done now. He had to believe that he had knocked too hard on someone's door and that the entire Beachwood Canyon plan had come about because of pressure he was continuing to exert on the case.

This conclusion led to the answer to the other question at the bottom of the sheet. *Who benefits?* Bosch wrote:

Anthony Garland – Hancock Park

For thirteen years Bosch's instinct had told him Garland was the one. But beyond his instincts there was no evidence directly connecting Garland to the murder. Bosch had not yet been made privy to the evidence, if any, that was developed during the excavation of the body and the autopsy, but he doubted that after thirteen years there would be anything usable – no DNA or forensics that could tie the killer to the body.

Garland was a suspect under the 'replacement victim' theory. That is, his rage toward the woman who had dropped him led him to kill a woman who reminded him of her. The shrinks would call it a long-shot theory but Bosch now moved it front and center. Do the math, he thought. Garland was the son of Thomas Rex Garland, wealthy oil baron from Hancock Park. O'Shea was in a highly contested election battle, and money was the gasoline that kept a campaign engine running. It was not inconceivable that a quiet approach had been made to T. Rex, a deal struck and a plan enacted. O'Shea gets the money he needs to win the election, Olivas gets the head investigator nod in O'Shea's office and Waits takes the fall for Gesto while Garland takes a ride on it.

It was said that L.A. was a sunny place for shady people. Bosch knew that better than most. He had no hesitation in believing Olivas had been part of such a scheme. And the thought of O'Shea, a career prosecutor, selling his soul for a shot at the top slot didn't give him pause for very long either.

'Run, you coward! How's your bullshit deal looking now?'

He opened his phone and called Keisha Russell at the *Times.* After several rings he checked his watch and saw it was a few minutes after five. He realized she was probably on deadline and ignoring her calls. He left a message at the prompt, asking her to call back.

Since it was so late in the day Bosch decided he had earned a beer. He went to the kitchen and got an Anchor Steam out of the box. He was happy he had gone high end the last time he bought beer. He took the bottle out on the deck and watched as the heart of rush hour gripped the freeway below. The traffic slowed to a crawl and the incessant sound of car horns of every variety began. It was just far enough away to be less than intrusive. Bosch was glad he was not down there in the fight.

His phone buzzed and he pulled it out of his pocket. It was Keisha Russell calling back.

'Sorry, I was going over tomorrow's story with the copyeditor.'

'I hope you spelled my name right.'

'Actually, you're not in this one, Harry. Surprise.'

'Glad to hear it.'

'What can you do for me?'

'Uh, I was actually going to ask you to do something for me.'

'Of course you were. What could it be?'

'You're a political reporter now, right? Does that mean you look at campaign contributions?'

'I do. I review every filing by every one of my candidates. Why?'

He walked back inside and muted the stereo.

'This is off the record, Keisha. I'd like to know who has been supporting Rick O'Shea's campaign.'

'O'Shea? Why?'

'I'll tell you when I can tell you. I just need the information right now.'

'Why do you always do this to me, Harry?'

It was true. They had danced like this many times in the past. But their history was that Bosch was always true to his word when he said he would tell her when he could tell her. He hadn't double-crossed her once. And so her protests were banter, a mere prequel to her doing what Bosch wanted her to do. That was part of the dance as well.

'You know why,' he said, playing his part. 'Just help me out and there will be something for you when the time is right.'

'Someday I want to decide when the time is right. Hold on.'

She clicked off and was gone for almost a minute. As he waited Bosch stood over the spread of documents on the dining room table. He knew that he was spinning his wheels with this angle on O'Shea and Garland. They could not be touched at the moment. They were guarded by money and the law and the rules of evidence. Bosch knew the correct angle of investigation was to go at Raynard Waits. His job was to find him and break open the case.

'Okay,' Russell said after getting back on the line. 'I have the most up-to-date filing. What do you want to know?'

'How up-to-date is up-to-date?'

'This was filed last week. Friday.'

'Who are his main contributors?'

'There's nobody who is really big, if that is what you mean. He's mostly running a grassroots campaign. Most of his contributors are fellow lawyers. Almost all of them.'

Bosch thought of the Century City law firm that handled things for the Garland family and had gotten the court orders preventing Bosch from questioning Anthony Garland about Marie Gesto without an attorney present. The head of the firm was Cecil Dobbs.

'Is one of those lawyers Cecil Dobbs?'

'Um … yes, C. C. Dobbs, Century City address. He gave a thousand.'

Bosch remembered the lawyer in his collection of videotaped interviews with Anthony Garland.

'What about Dennis Franks?'

'Franks, yes. A lot of people from that firm contributed.'

'What do you mean?'

'Well, according to election law, you give your home and work address when you make a contribution. Dobbs and Franks have a Century City work address and, let's see, nine, ten, eleven other people gave the same address. They each gave a thousand, too. It's probably all the lawyers in the same firm.'

'So thirteen thousand dollars from there. Is that it?'

'That's it from there, yes.'

Bosch thought about whether to specifically ask if the name Garland was on the contributors list. He didn't want her making phone calls or snooping around in his investigation.

'No big corporate contributors?'

'Nothing of major consequence. Why don't you tell me what you are looking for, Harry? You can trust me.'

He decided to go for it.

'You have to hold on to it until you hear from me. No phone calls, no inquiries. You just sit on this, right?'

'Right, until I hear from you.'

'Garland. Thomas Rex Garland, Anthony Garland, anybody like that on there?'

'Mmmm, no. Isn't Anthony Garland the kid you were looking at once for Marie Gesto?'

Bosch almost cursed out loud. He was hoping she wouldn't make the connection. A decade earlier, when she was a hellion on the cop beat, she had come across a search warrant application he had filed in an effort to search Anthony Garland's home. The application had been rejected for lack of probable cause but the filing was public record, and at the time, Russell, the ever industrious reporter, routinely combed through the search warrants at the court house. Bosch had talked her out of writing a story identifying the scion of the local oil family as a suspect in the Gesto murder but here it was a decade later and she remembered the name.

'You can't do anything with this, Keisha,' he responded.

'What are you doing? Raynard Waits confessed to Gesto. Are you saying that was bullshit?'

'I'm not saying anything. I was simply curious about something, that's all. Now, you cannot do anything with this. We have a deal. You sit on this until you hear from me.'

'You're not my boss, Harry. How come you are talking to me like you're my boss?'

'I'm sorry. I just don't want you running off and going crazy on this. It could hurt what I've got going. We have a deal, right? You just said I can trust you.'

It was a long time before she answered.

'Yes, we have a deal. And, yes, you can trust me. But if this is going where I think you are going with it, I want updates and reports. I'm not just going to sit around waiting to hear from you after you get the full package put together. If I don't hear from you, Harry, I'm going to get nervous. When I get nervous I do some crazy things, make some crazy phone calls.'

Bosch shook his head. He should never have made the call to her.

'I understand, Keisha,' he said. 'You'll be hearing from me.'

He closed the phone, wondering what fresh hell he might have just unleashed on earth and when it would come back to bite him. He trusted Russell but only to the limit he could trust any reporter. He finished his beer and went to the kitchen for another. As soon as he popped the top his phone buzzed.

It was Keisha Russell again.

'Harry, have you ever heard of GO! Industries?'

He had. GO! Industries was the current corporate titling of a company started eighty years earlier as Garland Oil Industries. The company had a logo in which the word GO! had wheels and was slanted forward to look as if it were a speeding car.

'What about it?' he responded.

'Headquartered downtown in the ARCO plaza. I count twelve employees of GO! making one-thousand-dollar contributions to O'Shea. How's that?'

'That's fine, Keisha. Thanks for calling back.'

'Did O'Shea take a payoff to put Gesto on Waits? Is that it?'

Bosch groaned into the phone.

'No, Keisha, that's not what happened and that's not what I am looking at. If you make any calls in this regard you will compromise what I am doing and could be putting yourself, me, and others in danger. Now would you please drop it until I can tell you exactly what is going on and when you can run with it?'

Once again she hesitated before answering, and it was in that space of silence that Bosch began to wonder if he could still trust her. Maybe her move from police to politics had changed something in her. Maybe, as with most who worked in the realm of politics, her sense of integrity had been sanded down by exposure to the world's oldest profession: political whoring.

'Okay, Harry, I got it. I was just trying to help. But you remember what I said. I want to hear from you. Soon!'

'You will, Keisha. Good night.'

He closed the phone and tried to shake off his concerns about the reporter. He thought about the information he had gotten from her. Between GO! and the law firm of Cecil Dobbs, O'Shea had received at least twenty-five thousand in campaign contributions from people who could be directly tied to the Garlands. It was spread out and legal, but nevertheless, it was a strong indication that Bosch was on the right track.

He felt a satisfying tug in his guts. He had something to work with now. He just had to find the right angle from which to work it. He went to the table in the dining room and looked at the array of police reports and records spread out in front of him. He picked up the file marked WAITS – BACKGROUND and started to read.

25

From the standpoint of law enforcement, Raynard Waits was a rarity as a murder suspect. When his van was pulled over in Echo Park, the LAPD in effect had captured a killer the department wasn't even looking for. In fact, Waits was a killer no department or agency was looking for. There was no file on him in any drawer or computer anywhere. No FBI profile or background briefing existed to refer to. They had a killer and they had to start from scratch with him.

This presented a whole new angle of investigation for Detective Freddy Olivas and his partner, Ted Colbert. The case came to them with a momentum that simply dragged them with it. Everything was about moving forward, toward prosecution. There was little time or inclination to go backwards. Waits was arrested in possession of bags containing the parts of two murdered women. It was a slam dunk, and that precluded the need to know exactly who they had in custody and what had brought him to be in that van on that street at that time.

Consequently, little in the file on the present case helped Bosch. The file contained records of the investigative work related to attempts to identify the victims and drawing the physical evidence together for the impending prosecution.

The background information in the file was simply basic data on Waits either provided by the suspect himself or culled by Olivas and Colbert during routine computer searches. The bottom line was that they knew little about the man they were prosecuting, but what they knew was enough.

Bosch completed his read-through of the file in twenty minutes. When he was finished, once again he had less than a half page of notes on his pad. He had constructed a short timeline that charted the suspect's arrests, admissions, and use of the names Raynard Waits and Robert Saxon.

4/30/92 – Daniel Fitzpatrick murdered, Hollywood
5/18/92 – Raynard Waits, dob 11/3/71, DL issued, Hollywood
2/01/93 – Robert Saxon, dob 11/3/75 – arrested, prowling
– IDed as Raynard Waits, dob 11/3/71, through DL thumbprint

9/09/93 – Marie Gesto abducted, Hollywood
5/11/05 – Raynard Waits, dob 11/3/71, arrested 187 Echo Park

Bosch studied the timeline. He found two things worth noting. Waits supposedly didn't get a driver's license until he was twenty, and no matter which name he used, he always gave the same month and day of birth. While he once offered 1975 as his year of birth in an attempt to be considered a juvenile, he uniformly gave 1971 at other times. Bosch knew that the latter was a practice often employed by people switching identities. Change the name but keep some of the other details the same to avoid getting confused or forgetting basic information – an obvious giveaway, especially if it's a cop asking for it.

Bosch knew from the record searches earlier in the week that there was no birth record of Raynard Waits or Robert Saxon with the corresponding 11/03 birth date in Los Angeles County. The conclusion he and Kiz Rider had reached from this was that both names were false. But now Bosch considered that maybe the birth date of 11/03/71 was not false. Maybe Waits, or whoever he was, kept his real date of birth as he changed his name.

Bosch now looked at the close proximity between the date of the Fitzpatrick murder and the date of issue of Waits's driver's license. It was less than a month. He added to this the fact that according to the records Waits did not apply for a driver's license until he was twenty. He thought it was unlikely that a boy growing up in the autotopia of L.A. would wait until he was twenty to get his driver's license. It was yet one more indication that Raynard Waits was not his name.

Bosch started to feel it. Like a surfer waiting for the right swell before starting to paddle, he felt his wave coming in. He thought that what he was looking at was the birth of a new identity. Eighteen days after he murdered Daniel Fitzpatrick under cover of the riots, the man who killed him walked into a DMV office in Hollywood and applied for a driver's license. He gave November 3, 1971, as a date of birth and the name Raynard Waits. He would have had to provide a birth certificate, but that would not have been too hard to come up with if he knew the right people. Not in Hollywood. Not in L.A. Getting a phony birth certificate would have been an easy, almost risk-free task.

Bosch believed that the Fitzpatrick murder and the change of ID were connected. It was a cause-and-effect. Something about the murder caused the killer to change his identity. This belied the confession given two days earlier by Raynard Waits. He had characterized the murder of Daniel Fitzpatrick as a thrill kill, an opportunity to indulge a long-held fantasy. He went out of his way to depict Fitzpatrick as a victim chosen at random, chosen simply because he was there.

But if that was truly the case and if the killer had no previous connection to the victim, then why did the killer act almost immediately to reinvent himself with a new identity? Within eighteen days the killer procured a false birth certificate and got a new driver's license. Raynard Waits was born.

Bosch knew there was a contradiction in what he was considering. If the killing of Fitzpatrick had taken place as Waits had confessed, then there would have been no reason for him to quickly create a new identity. But the facts – the timeline of the murder and the issuance of the driver's license – contradicted this. The conclusion to Bosch was obvious. There *was* a connection. Fitzpatrick was not a random victim. He could, in fact, be linked in some way to his killer. And that was why his killer changed his name.

Bosch got up and took his empty bottle to the kitchen. He decided that two beers was enough. He needed to stay sharp and up on the wave. He went back out to the stereo and put in the masterpiece. *Kind of Blue.* It never failed to give him the charge. 'All Blues' was the first song out of the shuffle, and it was like being dealt blackjack at a twenty-five-dollar table. It was his favorite and he let it ride.

Back at the table he opened the Fitzpatrick murder book and started to read. Kiz Rider had handled it earlier but she had simply been engaged in a review to prepare for taking Waits's confession. She wasn't looking for the hidden connection Bosch was now seeking.

The investigation of Fitzpatrick's death had been carried out by two detectives temporarily assigned to the Riot Crimes Task Force. Their work was cursory at best. Few leads were followed, because there weren't many to follow in the first place and because of the overriding pallor of futility that fell over all the cases associated with the riots. Almost all acts of violence associated with the three days of widespread unrest were random. People robbed, raped and murdered indiscriminately and at will – simply because they could.

No witnesses to the attack on Fitzpatrick were located. No forensic evidence was found other than the can of lighter fluid – and it had been wiped clean. Most of the shop's records had been destroyed by fire or water. What was left was put in two cartons and ignored. The case was treated as a dead-end from the moment it was born. It was orphaned and archived.

The murder book was so thin that Bosch finished his front-to-back read-through in less than twenty minutes. He had taken no notes, gotten no ideas, seen no connections. He felt the tide ebbing. His ride on the wave was coming to an end.

He thought about getting another beer out of the box and attacking the case all over again the next day. Then the front door opened and Rachel Walling walked in, carrying takeout cartons from Chinese Friends. Bosch stacked the reports on the dining room table so there would be room to eat. Rachel brought plates from the kitchen and opened the cartons. Bosch got the last two Anchors out of the refrigerator.

They small-talked for a while and then he told her what he had been doing since lunch and what he had learned. He could tell by her reserved comments that she was not convinced by his description of the trail he had found in Beachwood Canyon. But when he showed her the timeline he had worked up, she readily agreed with his conclusions about the killer's changing of ID after the Fitzpatrick murder. She also agreed that, while they didn't have the killer's real name, they might have his real birth date.

Bosch looked down at the two plastic cartons on the floor.

'Then I guess it's worth the shot,' he said.

She leaned to the side so she could see what he was looking at.

'What are those?'

'Pawn slips mostly. All the records salvaged after the fire. Back in 'ninety-two they were all wet. They dropped them in these boxes and forgot about them. Nobody's ever looked through them all.'

'Is that what we're doing tonight, Harry?'

He looked up at her and smiled. He nodded.

After they were finished eating they decided that they would take a carton each. Bosch suggested that they take them out onto the back deck because of the musty smell that would come from the cartons once they were opened. Rachel readily agreed. Bosch lugged the cartons out and then got two empty cardboard boxes from the carport. They sat down in deck chairs and began the work.

Taped to the top of the carton Bosch chose was a 3 × 5 card that said MAIN FILE CABINET. Bosch took the top off and used it to try to wave away the fumes that came out. The carton contained mostly pink pawn slips and 3 × 5 cards that had been haphazardly put in the container as if with a shovel. There was nothing ordered or neat about the records.

Water damage was high. Many of the slips had stuck together while wet and the ink on others was smeared and unreadable. Bosch looked over at Rachel and saw her dealing with the same issues.

'This is bad, Harry,' she said.

'I know. Just do the best you can. It might be our last hope.'

There was no way to begin but simply to dig in. Bosch pulled out a wad of slips, brought them up to his lap and started going through them, attempting to make out the name, address and birth date of each customer who had pawned something through Fitzpatrick. Each time he looked at a slip, he checked the top corner with a red pencil from the dining room table drawer and dropped it into the cardboard box on the other side of his chair.

They were at it a solid half hour, working without conversation, when Bosch heard the phone in the kitchen ring. He thought about letting it go but knew it might be a call from Hong Kong. He got up.

'I didn't even know you had a landline,' Walling said.

'Not many people do.'

He grabbed the phone on the eighth ring. It wasn't his daughter. It was Abel Pratt.

'Just checking on you,' he said. 'I figure if I get you on the house line and you say you are home, then you're really home.'

'What, am I under house arrest now?'

'No, Harry, I'm just worried about you, that's all.'

'Look, there will be no blowback from me, okay? But home duty does not mean I have to be at home twenty-four-seven. I checked with the union.'

'I know, I know. But it does mean you do not take part in any job-related investigation.'

'Fine.'

'What are you doing, then?'

'I'm sitting on the back deck with a friend. We're having a beer and enjoying the night air. Is that okay with you, Top?'

'Anybody I know?'

'I doubt it. She doesn't like cops.'

Pratt laughed and it seemed that Bosch had finally put him at ease about what he was doing.

'Then, I'll let you get back to it. Have a good one, Harry.'

'I will if I can stay off the phone. I'll call in tomorrow.'

'I'll be there.'

'And I'll be here. Good night.'

He hung up, checked the refrigerator for hidden or lost beers and returned to the deck empty-handed. Rachel was waiting for him with a smile on her face and a water-stained 3 × 5 card in her hand. Attached to it with a paperclip was a pink pawn slip.

'Got it,' she said.

She handed it to him and Bosch stepped back inside the house, where the lighting was better. He read the card first. It was written on with blue ink that was partially smeared by water but still legible.

> Unsatisfied Customer – 02/12/92
> Customer complained that property was sold before 90-day pawn period expired. Shown pawn slip and corrected. Customer complained that 90 days should not have included weekends and holidays. Cursed/slammed door.
> DGF

The pink pawn slip attached to the complaint card carried the name Robert Foxworth, the DOB 11/03/71 and an address on Fountain in Hollywood. The item pawned on October 8, 1991, was listed as an 'heirloom medallion.' Foxworth had been given eighty dollars for it. There was a fingerprint square at the bottom right corner of the slip. Bosch could see the ridges of a fingerprint but the ink had either worn away or leached out of the paper because of the moisture contained in the storage carton.

'The DOB is a match,' Rachel said. 'Plus the name connects on two levels.'

'What do you mean?'

'Well, he took Robert forward when he used the name Robert Saxon and he took the Fox in Foxworth forward when he used Raynard. Maybe that's where this whole Raynard thing came from. If his real name is Foxworth, maybe when he was a kid, his parents told him stories about a fox named Reynard.'

'If his real name is Foxworth,' Bosch repeated. 'Maybe we just found another alias.'

'Maybe. But at least it's something you didn't have before.'

Bosch nodded. He could feel his excitement building. She was right. Finally they had a new angle to pursue. Bosch pulled out his phone.

'I'm going to run the name and see what happens.'

He called central dispatch and asked a service operator to run the name and birth date they had found on the pawn slip. It came back clean and with no record of a current driver's license. He thanked the operator and hung up.

'Nothing,' he said. 'Not even a driver's license.'

'But that's good,' Rachel said. 'Don't you see? Robert Foxworth would be about to turn thirty-five right now. If there's no history or current license, then that is further confirmation that he is no more, that he's either dead or he became someone else.'

'Raynard Waits.'

She nodded.

'I guess I was hoping for a DL with an Echo Park address,' Bosch said. 'I guess that's too much to ask for.'

'Maybe not. Is there a way in this state to check defunct driver's licenses? Robert Foxworth, if that's his real name, probably got a license when he turned sixteen in nineteen eighty-seven. When he switched identities it would have expired.'

Bosch considered this. He knew that the state did not start requiring a thumbprint from licensed drivers until the early nineties. It meant Foxworth could have gotten a driver's license in the late eighties and there would be no way to connect him to his new identity as Raynard Waits.

'I could check with DMV in the morning. It's not something I can get through communications dispatch tonight.'

'There is something else you can check tomorrow,' she said. 'Remember the quick and dirty profile I did the other night? I said these early crimes weren't aberrations. He built up to them.'

Bosch understood.

'A juvy jacket.'

She nodded.

'You might find a juvenile record on Robert Foxworth – again, if that's his real name. It wouldn't have been accessible through dispatch either.'

She was right. State law kept juvenile records from trailing an offender into adulthood. The name may have come up clean when Bosch called dispatch to run it but that didn't mean it was squeaky clean. As with the driver's license information, Bosch would have to wait until morning, when he could get into the juvenile records at the Department of Probation.

But as soon as his hopes were lifted he knocked them down again.

'Wait a minute, that doesn't work,' he said. 'His prints would have drawn a match. When they ran his prints as Raynard Waits, they would have hit the prints taken from Robert Foxworth as a juvenile. His record might not be available but the prints stay in the system.'

'Maybe, maybe not. Two separate systems. Two separate bureaucracies. The crossover doesn't always work.'

That was true, but it was more wishful thinking than anything else. Bosch now reduced the juvenile angle to a long shot. It was more likely that Robert Foxworth had never been in the juvenile system. Bosch was beginning to think the name was just another false identity in a string of them.

Rachel tried to change the subject.

'What do you think about this heirloom medallion he pawned?' she asked.

'I have no idea.'

'The fact that he wanted to get it back is interesting. Makes me think maybe it wasn't stolen. Like maybe it belonged to someone in his family and he needed to get it back.'

'It would explain him cursing and slamming doors, I guess.'

She nodded.

Bosch yawned and all at once he realized how tired he was. He had been running all day just to get to this name and the uncertainties that accompanied it. The case was crowding his brain. Rachel seemed to read him.

'Harry, I say we quit while we're ahead and have another beer.'

'I don't know how far ahead we are but I could use another beer,' Bosch said. 'There's only one problem with that.'

'What?'

'No more beer.'

'Harry, you invited a girl over to do your dirty work and help you crack the case and all you give her is one beer? What's wrong with you? What about wine? You have some wine?'

Bosch shook his head sadly.

'But I'm on my way to the store.'

'That's good. I'm on my way to the bedroom. I'll be waiting for you there.'

'Then, I won't delay.'

'Make mine a red wine, will you?'

'I'm on it.'

Bosch hurried from the house. He had parked earlier at the front curb so that Rachel could use the carport if she came over. As he walked out the front door he noticed a vehicle sitting at the opposite curb two houses down. The vehicle, a silver SUV, caught his eye because it was parked in a red zone. There was no parking allowed along that curb, since it was too close to the next curve in the road. A car could come around the bend and easily collide with any car parked there.

As Bosch looked up the street the SUV suddenly took off without its lights on. It sped north around the bend and disappeared.

Bosch ran to his car, jumped in and headed north after the SUV. He drove as fast as he could safely go. Within two minutes he had followed the curving street around to the four-way stop at Mulholland Drive. There was no sign of the SUV and it could have gone in any of three directions from the stop.

'Shit!'

Bosch sat at the intersection for a long moment, thinking about what he had just seen and what it might mean. He decided that it either meant nothing or it meant someone was watching his house and therefore watching him. But at the moment there was nothing he could do. He let it go. He turned left and drove down Mulholland at a safe speed all the way down to Cahuenga. He knew there was a liquor store near Lankershim. He headed there, checking the rearview mirror for a trailer the whole way.

26

Home duty or not, Bosch dressed in a suit the next morning before heading out. He knew it would give him an aura of authority and confidence while dealing with government bureaucrats. And by twenty minutes after nine it had paid off. He had a solid lead. The Department of Motor Vehicles' archives had produced a driver's license issued to a Robert Foxworth on November 3, 1987, the day he turned sixteen and was eligible to drive. The license was never renewed in California but there was no DMV record of the holder being deceased. This meant Foxworth had either moved to another state and was licensed there, decided he no longer wanted to drive or changed identities. Bosch was betting on the third option.

The address on the license was the lead. It listed Foxworth's residence as the Los Angeles County Department of Children and Family Services, 3075 Wilshire Blvd., Los Angeles. In 1987 he had been a juvenile ward of the county. He either had no parents or they had been declared unfit to raise him and he was removed from them. The designation of DCFS as his address meant that he was either housed in one of the department's youth halls or had been placed in its foster care program. Bosch knew all of this because he, too, had had such a designation on his first driver's license. He, too, had been a ward of the county.

As Bosch stepped out of the DMV offices on Spring Street he felt a renewed surge of energy. He had broken through what had seemed to be a dead-end the night before and had turned it into a solid lead. As he headed to his car his cell phone vibrated and he answered it without breaking stride or looking at the screen, hoping that it would be Rachel and that he'd be able to share the good news.

'Harry, where are you? No one answered the home line.'

It was Abel Pratt. Bosch was getting tired of his constant checking up on him.

'I'm on my way in to visit Kiz. Is that all right with you?'

'Sure, Harry, except you're supposed to check in with me.'

'Once a day. It's not even ten o'clock!'

'I want to hear from you every morning.'

'Whatever. Tomorrow's Saturday, should I call you? What about Sunday?'

'Don't go overboard. I'm just trying to look out for you, you know.'

'Sure, Top. Whatever you say.'

'You heard the latest, I take it.'

Bosch stopped in his tracks.

'They caught Waits?'

'No, I wish.'

'Then, what?'

'It's all over the news. Everybody's worked up about it down here. Some girl got snatched off the street in Hollywood last night. Pulled into a van on Hollywood Boulevard. The division had those new street cameras installed last year and one of the cameras caught part of the abduction. I haven't seen it but they say it's Waits. He's changed his look – shaved his head, I think – but they're saying it was him. There's a press conference at eleven and they're going to show the tape to the world.'

Bosch felt a dull thud pound in his chest. He had been right about Waits not leaving town. He wished now he had been wrong. As he had these thoughts he realized that he still thought of the killer as Raynard Waits. It didn't matter if he was truly Robert Foxworth, Bosch knew he would always think of him as Waits.

'Did they get a plate off the van?' he asked.

'No, it was covered. All they put out was that it was a plain white Econoline van. Like the other one he used but older. Look, I've gotta go. I just wanted to check in. Hopefully, this is the last day. OIS will finish up and you'll be back in the unit.'

'Yeah, that would be good. But listen, during his confession, Waits said he had a different van in the nineties. Maybe the task force should get somebody to look through old DMV registrations under his name. They might come up with a plate to go with the van.'

'It's worth a shot. I'll tell them.'

'Okay.'

'Stay close to home, Harry. And give my regards to Kiz.'

'Right.'

Bosch closed the phone, happy that he'd been able to come up with the Kiz line on the spot like that. But he also knew that he was becoming a good liar with Pratt, and that didn't make him very happy.

Bosch got into his car and headed toward Wilshire Boulevard. The call from Pratt had increased his sense of urgency. Waits had abducted another woman, but there had been nothing in the files to indicate that he killed his victims immediately. That meant the latest victim might still be alive. Bosch knew that if he could get to Waits he could save her.

The DCFS offices were crowded and loud. He waited at a records counter for fifteen minutes before he got the attention of a clerk. After taking

Bosch's information and typing it into a computer, she told him that there was indeed a juvenile file relating to Robert Foxworth, DOB 11/03/71, but that to see it he would need a court order authorizing his search of the records.

Bosch just smiled. He was too excited by the fact that a file was actually still in existence to be upset by one more frustration. He thanked her and told her he would be back with the court order.

Bosch stepped back out into the sunlight. He knew he was at a crossroads now. Dancing around the truth of where he was during phone calls with Abel Pratt was one thing. But if he was to apply for a search warrant seeking the DCFS records without departmental approval – coming in the form of a supervisor's okay – then he would be completely going off the reservation: He would be conducting a rogue investigation and committing a firing offense.

He figured he could take what he had into Randolph at OIS or the Fugitive Task Force and let them run with it, or he could go the rogue route and accept the possible consequences. Since coming back from retirement Bosch had felt less constricted by the rules and regulations of the department. He had already walked out the door once and knew that if push came to shove he would be able to do it again. The second time would be easier. He didn't want it to come to that but he could do it if he had to.

He pulled out his phone and made the one call he knew might save him from making a choice between two bad options. Rachel Walling answered her cell on the second ring.

'So what's happening over there in Tactical?' he asked.

'Oh, we always have something happening here. How did it go downtown? Did you hear that Waits abducted another woman last night?'

She had a habit of asking more than one question at a time, especially when she was excited. Bosch told her that he had heard about the abduction and then related the tale of his morning's activities.

'So what are you going to do?'

'Well, I'm thinking about seeing if the FBI might be interested in joining the case.'

'And what about the case would carry it across the federal threshold?'

'You know, corruption of public officials, campaign finance violations, kidnapping, cats and dogs living together – the usual stuff.'

She stayed serious.

'I don't know, Harry. You open that door and there's no telling where it will go.'

'But I've got an insider. Somebody who will watch out for me and safeguard the case.'

'Wrong. They probably wouldn't let me anywhere near this. It's not my group and there's the conflict of interest.'

'What conflict? We've worked together before.'

'I'm just telling you how this will likely be received.'

'Look, I need a search warrant. If I go off the reservation to get one I probably won't be able to come back on again. I know it will be the last straw with Pratt, that's for sure. But if I can say that I was brought into a federal investigation, then that would give me a valid explanation. It would give me an out. All I want is to look at Foxworth's DCFS file. I think it will lead us to whatever's in Echo Park.'

She was quiet for a long moment before responding.

'Where are you right now?'

'I'm still at DCFS.'

'Go get a doughnut or something. I'll be there as soon as I can.'

'You sure?'

'No, but that's what we're going to do.'

She hung up the phone. Bosch closed his and looked around. Instead of a doughnut he went over to a newspaper box and got the morning edition of the *Times*. He took a seat on the planter that ran along the front length of the DCFS building and looked through the paper for stories on the Raynard Waits and Beachwood Canyon investigations.

There was no story on the abduction on Hollywood Boulevard because that had occurred during the night and long after the paper's deadline. The coverage of the Waits story had moved off the front page to the state and local section but it was still extensive. There were three stories in all. The most prominent report was on the so-far unsuccessful nationwide search for the escaped serial killer. Most of the information had already been rendered obsolete by the events of the night. There was no nationwide search anymore. Waits was still here in the city.

This story jumped inside the section and was framed by two sidebars. One was an update on the investigation that filled in some of the details of what had happened during the shoot-out and escape, and the other story was a political update. This latter story was written by Keisha Russell and Bosch quickly scanned it to see if anything they had discussed about Rick O'Shea's campaign financing had gotten into the paper. Luckily there was nothing, and he felt his trust in her rising.

Bosch finished reading the stories and there was still no sign of Rachel. He moved into other sections of the paper, studying the box scores of sporting events he cared nothing about and reading reviews of movies he would never see. When there was nothing left for him to read he put the paper aside and started pacing in front of the building. He became anxious, worried that he'd lose the edge the morning's discoveries had given him.

He got out his phone to call her but decided instead to call St. Joseph's Hospital and check on Kiz Rider's condition. He was transferred to the third-floor nursing station and was then put on hold. While he was waiting to be connected he saw Rachel finally pull up in a federal cruiser. He closed the phone, crossed the sidewalk and met her as she was getting out.

'What's the plan?' he said by way of greeting.

'What, no "how are you doing" or "thanks for coming"?'

'Thanks for coming. What's the plan?'

They started walking into the building.

'The plan is the federal plan. I go in and draw down on the man in charge the full force and weight of the government of this great country. I raise the specter of terrorism and he gives us the file.'

Bosch stopped.

'You call that a plan?'

'It's worked pretty well for us for more than fifty years.'

She didn't stop. He now had to hurry to catch up.

'How do you know it's a man in charge?'

'Because it always is. Which way?'

He pointed straight ahead in the main hallway. Rachel didn't break stride.

'I didn't wait around for forty minutes for this, Rachel.'

'You have a better idea?'

'I *had* a better idea. A federal search warrant, remember?'

'That was a nonstarter, Bosch. I told you, I open that door and you get trampled. This is better. In and out. If I get you the file, I get you the file. Doesn't matter how.'

She was two paces in front of him now, moving with federal momentum. Bosch secretly started to believe. She moved through the double doors beneath the sign that said records with an authority and command presence that could not be questioned.

The clerk Bosch had dealt with was at the counter speaking with another citizen. Walling stepped right up and didn't wait for an invitation to speak. She drew her credentials from her suit jacket pocket in one smooth move.

'FBI. I need to see your office manager in regard to a matter of urgency.'

The clerk looked at her with an unimpressed face.

'I will be with you as soon as I fin—'

'You're with me now, honey. Go get your boss or I'll go get him. This is life-or-death urgent.'

The woman made a face that seemed to indicate she had never encountered such rudeness before. Without a word to the citizen in front of her or anyone else she stepped away from the counter and walked to a door behind a row of cubicles.

They waited less than a minute. The clerk stepped back out through the door, followed by a man wearing a white, short-sleeved shirt and a maroon tie. He came directly to Rachel Walling.

'I'm Mr. Osborne. How can I help you?'

'We need to step into your office, sir. This is a highly confidential matter.'

'Over this way, please.'

He pointed to a swing door at the far end of the counter. Bosch and Walling walked down to it and its lock was buzzed open. They followed Osborne back through the rear door to his office. Rachel let him get a look at her credentials once he was seated behind a desk festooned with dusty Dodgers memorabilia. There was a wrapped sandwich from Subway front and center on his desk.

'What's this all—'

'Mr. Osborne, I work for the Tactical Intelligence Unit here in Los Angeles. I'm sure you understand what that means. And this is Detective Harry Bosch of the LAPD. We're working a joint investigation of high importance and urgency. We've learned from your clerk that there exists a file pertaining to an individual named Robert Foxworth, date of birth eleven/three/'seventy-one. It is vitally important that we be allowed to review that file immediately.'

Osborne nodded, but what he said didn't go with a nod.

'I understand. But here at DCFS we work under very precise laws. State laws that protect the children. The records of our juvenile wards are not open to the public without court order. My hands are—'

'Sir, Robert Foxworth is no longer a juvenile. He is thirty-four years old. The file might contain information that will lead us to the containment of a very grave threat to this city. It will undoubtedly save lives.'

'I know, but you have to understand that we are not—'

'I do understand. I understand perfectly that if we don't see that file now, we could be talking about a loss of human life. You don't want that on your conscience, Mr. Osborne, and neither do we. That's why we are on the same team. I'll make a deal with you, sir. We will review the file right here in your office with you watching. In the meantime, I will get on the phone and instruct a member of my team at Tactical to draw up a search warrant. I will see to it that it is signed by a judge and furnished to you before the end of business today.'

'Well … I'd have to call it up from Archives.'

'Are the archives here in the building?'

'Yes, down below.'

'Then, please call Archives and get that file up here. We don't have a lot of time, sir.'

'Just wait here. I will handle it personally.'

'Thank you, Mr. Osborne.'

The man left the office and Rachel looked at Bosch with a slight smile.

'Now let's hope he doesn't change his mind,' she said.

'You're good,' he responded. 'I tell my daughter that she could talk a zebra out of its stripes. I think you could talk a tiger out of its.'

'If I get this, you owe me another lunch at Water Grill.'

'Fine. Just no sashimi.'

They waited for Osborne's return for nearly fifteen minutes. When he came back to the office he was carrying a file folder that was nearly an inch thick. He presented it to Walling, who took the file as she was standing up. Bosch took the cue and stood as well.

'We'll get this back to you as soon as possible,' she said. 'Thank you, Mr. Osborne.'

'Wait a minute! You said you were going to look at it here.'

Rachel was heading toward the office door, gathering that momentum again.

'There's no longer time, Mr. Osborne. We have to move. You'll have the file back by tomorrow morning.'

She was already through the door. Bosch followed, closing it behind him on Osborne's final words.

'What about the court ord—'

As they passed behind the clerk, Walling asked her to buzz them out. Rachel kept a two-pace lead on Bosch as they headed out into the hallway. He liked walking behind her and admiring how she handled herself. Command presence in spades.

'Is there a Starbucks around here where we could sit and look at this thing? I'd like to look before heading back.'

'There's always a Starbucks around.'

Out on the sidewalk they walked east until they came to a tiny luncheonette that had a small inside counter with stools. It beat looking for a Starbucks, so they went in. While Bosch ordered two coffees from the man behind the counter Rachel opened the file.

By the time the coffees were put down on the counter and paid for she had a one-page lead on him. They sat side by side and she passed each page to him after she was finished her review of it. They worked silently and neither one drank their coffee. Buying the coffee had merely bought them the work space at the counter.

The first document in the file was a copy of Foxworth's birth certificate. He was born at Queen of Angels Hospital. The mother was listed as Rosemary Foxworth, DOB 6/21/54, Philadelphia, Pa., and the father was listed as unknown. The mother's address was an apartment on Orchid Avenue in Hollywood. Bosch placed the address in the middle of what was now called the Kodak Center, part of the Hollywood renovation and rebirth plan. It was all glitz and glass and red carpets now, but back in 1971 it would have been a neighborhood patrolled by streetwalkers and hypes.

The birth certificate also listed the doctor who delivered the child and a hospital social worker involved in the case.

Bosch did the math. Rosemary Foxworth was seventeen years old when she gave birth to her son. No father listed or in attendance. No father known. The listing of a social worker meant the county was picking up the tab on the delivery, and the home address did not bode well for a happy start for baby Robert.

All of this led to a picture developing like a Polaroid in Bosch's mind. He guessed that Rosemary Foxworth had been a runaway from Philadelphia, that she hit Hollywood and shared a flop apartment with others like her. She probably worked the nearby streets as a prostitute. She probably used drugs. She gave birth to the boy and then the county eventually stepped in and took him away.

As Rachel passed him more documents, the sad story was borne out. Robert Foxworth was removed from his mother's custody at age two and taken into the DCFS system. For the next sixteen years of his life he was in and out of foster homes and youth halls. Bosch noted that among the facilities where he had spent time was the McLaren Youth Hall in El Monte, a place where Bosch himself had spent a number of years as a child.

The file was replete with psychiatric evaluations conducted annually or upon Foxworth's frequent returns from foster care homes. In total the file charted the journey of a broken life. Sad, yes. Unique, no. It was the story of a child taken from his one parent and then equally mistreated by the flawed institution that had taken him. Foxworth floated from place to place. He had no real home or family. He probably never knew what it was like to be wanted or loved.

Reading through the pages brought up memories in Bosch. Two decades before Foxworth's journey through the system Bosch had charted his own path. He had survived with his own set of scars, but the damage was nothing compared with the extent of Foxworth's injuries.

The next document Rachel handed him was a copy of a death certificate for Rosemary Foxworth. She died March 5, 1986, of complications stemming from drug use and Hepatitis C. She had died in the jail ward at County-USC Medical Center. Robert Foxworth would have been fourteen.

'Here we go, here we go,' Rachel suddenly said.

'What?'

'His longest stay in any foster home was in Echo Park. And the people he stayed with? Harlan and Janet Saxon.'

'What's the address?'

'Seven-ten Figueroa Lane. He was there from 'eighty-three to 'eighty-seven. Almost four years total. He must have liked them and I guess they liked him back.'

Bosch leaned over to look at the document in front of her.

'He was on Figueroa Terrace, only a couple blocks from there, when he got pulled over with the bodies,' he said. 'If they had followed him for just one more minute they would've had the place!'

'If that's where he was going.'

'It's got to be where he was going.'

She handed him the page and moved on to the next. But Bosch stood up and walked away from the counter. He had read enough for the time being. He had been looking for the connection to Echo Park and now he knew he had it. He was ready to put the book work aside. He was ready to make a move.

'Harry, these shrink reports from when he was a teenager – he was talking about some sick shit here.'

'Like what?'

'A lot of anger toward women. Young promiscuous women. Prostitutes, drug users. You know what the psychology is here? You know what I think he ended up doing?'

'No and no. What?'

'He was killing his mother over and over again. All those missing women and girls they've hung on him? The one last night? To him they were like his mother. And he wanted to kill her for abandoning him. And maybe kill them before they did the same thing – brought a child into the world.'

Bosch nodded.

'That's a nice shake-and-bake shrink job. If we had the time, you could probably find his Rosebud memory, too. But she didn't abandon him. They took him away from her.'

She shook her head.

'Doesn't matter,' she said. 'Abandonment through lifestyle. The state had no choice but to step in and take him away from her. Drugs, prostitution, the whole thing. By being an unfit mother she abandoned him to this deeply flawed institution where he was trapped until he was old enough to walk away on his own. In his brain chart, that constituted abandonment.'

Bosch nodded slowly. He guessed that she was right but the whole situation made him uncomfortable. It felt too personal to Bosch, too close to his own path. Except for a turn here or there, Bosch and Foxworth had made similar journeys. Foxworth was doomed to kill his own mother over and over again. A police shrink had once told Bosch that he was doomed to solve his own mother's murder over and over again.

'Harry, what is it?'

Bosch looked at her. He had not yet told Rachel his own sordid history. He didn't want her profiling skills turned on him.

'Nothing,' he said. 'I'm just thinking.'

'You look like you've seen a ghost.'

Bosch shrugged. Walling closed the file on the counter and finally raised her coffee cup to sip from it.

'So what now?' she asked.

Bosch looked at her for a long moment before answering.

'Echo Park,' he said.

'What about backup?'

'I'm going to check it out first, then call backup.'

She nodded.

'I'm going with you.'

Part Four
The Dog You Feed

27

Bosch and Walling used Bosch's Mustang, since it would give them at least a small degree of cover compared with her federal cruiser, which screamed law enforcement. They drove to Echo Park but did not approach the Saxon house at 710 Figueroa Lane. There was a problem. Figueroa Lane was a short turnaround street that extended for a block off the end of Figueroa Terrace and curved up along the ridge below Chavez Ravine. There was no cruising by it without being obvious about it. Even in a Mustang. If Waits was there and watching for law enforcement, he would have the advantage of seeing them first.

Bosch stopped the car at the intersection of Beaudry and Figueroa Terrace and drummed his fingers on the steering wheel.

'He picked a good place for the secret castle,' he said. 'There's no getting close to it without being picked up on radar. Especially in daylight.'

Rachel nodded.

'Medieval castles were built on hilltops for the same reason.'

Bosch looked to his left, toward downtown, and saw the tall buildings rising over the roofs of the homes on Figueroa Terrace. One of the closest and tallest buildings was the Department of Water and Power headquarters. It was directly across the freeway.

'I've got an idea,' he said.

They drove out of the neighborhood and back into downtown. Bosch entered the DWP garage and parked in one of the visitor slots. He popped the trunk and went to the surveillance kit he always kept in the car. He got out a pair of high-powered binoculars, a surveillance camera and a rolled-up sleeping bag.

'What are you going to take pictures of?' Walling asked.

'Nothing. But it's got a long lens and you might want to look through it while I use the binocs.'

'And the sleeping bag?'

'We might be lying on the roof. I don't want your fancy federal suit to get dirty.'

'Don't worry about me. Worry about yourself.'

'I'm worried about that girl Waits grabbed. Let's go.'

They headed across the garage floor toward the elevators.

'Did you notice that you still call him Waits, even though we are now sure his name is Foxworth?' she asked when they were going up.

'Yeah, I have noticed. I think it's because when we were face-to-face he was Waits. When he started shooting, he was Waits. And it just sort of stuck.'

She nodded and didn't say anything else about it, though he guessed that she probably had a psychological angle on it.

When they reached the lobby Bosch went to an information desk, showed his badge and credentials and asked to see a security supervisor. He told the desk man that it was urgent.

In less than two minutes a tall black man in gray pants and a navy blazer over his white shirt and tie came through a door and directly toward them. This time Bosch and Walling both showed their creds and the man appeared properly impressed by the federal-local tandem.

'Hieronymus,' he said, reading Bosch's police ID. 'Do you go by Harry?'

'That's right.'

The man put out his hand and smiled.

'Jason Edgar. I believe you and my cousin were partners once.'

Bosch smiled, not just because of the coincidence but because he knew it meant that he would have this man's cooperation. He put the sleeping bag under his other arm and shook his hand.

'That's right. He told me he had a cousin with DWP. You used to get him billing info when we needed it. Nice to meet you.'

'Likewise, man. What do we have here? If the FBI's involved, are we talking about a terrorism situation?'

Rachel raised a hand to calm the situation.

'Not quite,' she said.

'Jason, we're just looking for a place where we can look down on a neighborhood across the freeway in Echo Park. There's a house we're interested in and we can't get close to it without being obvious about it, know what I mean? We were thinking that maybe from one of the offices here or from the roof we could get an angle and just see what's happening over there.'

'I've got just the spot,' Edgar said without hesitation. 'Follow me.'

He led them back to the elevators and had to use a key to get the fifteenth-floor button to light. On the way up he explained that the building was going through a floor-by-floor renovation. At the moment the work had moved to the fifteenth floor. The floor had been gutted and was empty, waiting for the contractor to come in to rebuild according to the renovation plan.

'You can have the whole floor to yourselves,' he said. 'Pick any angle you want for an OP.'

Bosch nodded. OP, as in observation point. That told him something about Jason Edgar.

'Where'd you serve?' he asked.

'Marines, Desert Storm, the whole shebang. That's why I didn't join the PD. Had my fill of war zones. This gig is pretty much nine to five, low stress and just interesting enough, if you know what I mean.'

Bosch didn't but nodded anyway. The elevator doors opened and they stepped out onto a floor that was wide open from glass exterior to glass exterior. Edgar led them toward the glass wall that would look down on Echo Park.

'What's the case about, anyway?' Edgar asked as they approached.

Bosch knew it would come to this. He was ready with an answer.

'There's a place down there we think is being used as a safe house for fugitives. We just want to see if there is anything there to be seen. You know what I mean?'

'Sure do.'

'There's something else you can do to help us,' Walling said.

Bosch turned to her along with Edgar. He was just as curious.

'What do you need?' Edgar said.

'Could you run the address through your computers and tell us who is paying for utilities?'

'Not a problem. Let me just get you situated here first.'

Bosch nodded to Rachel. It was a good move. It would not only get the inquisitive Edgar out of the way for a while, but it could also provide them with some valuable information about the house on Figueroa Lane.

At the floor-to-ceiling glass wall on the north side of the building, Bosch and Walling looked down and across the 101 Freeway at Echo Park. They were farther from the hillside neighborhood than Bosch had thought they would be, but they still had a good vantage point. He pointed out the geographic markers to Rachel.

'There's Fig Terrace,' he said. 'Those three houses up above it on the curve are on Fig Lane.'

She nodded. Figueroa Lane had only the three houses on it. From this height and distance it looked like an afterthought, a developer's discovery that he could jam three more houses onto the hillside after the main street grid had already been laid out.

'Which one is seven-ten?' she asked.

'Good question.'

Bosch dropped the sleeping bag and raised the binoculars. He studied the three houses, looking for an address. He finally zeroed in on a black trash can sitting out front of the house in the middle. In large white numerals someone had painted 712 on the can in an effort to safeguard it from theft. Bosch knew the address numbers would rise as the street extended away from downtown.

'The one on the right is seven-ten,' he said.

'Got it,' she said.

'So that's the address?' Edgar asked. 'Seven-ten Fig Lane?'

'Figueroa Lane,' Bosch said.

'Got it. Let me go see what I can find. If anybody comes up here and asks what you are doing, just tell them to call me on three-three-eight. That's my page.'

'Thanks, Jason.'

'You got it.'

Edgar started walking back to the elevators. Bosch thought of something and called after him.

'Jason, this glass has got film on it, right? Nobody can see us looking out, right?'

'Yeah, no problem. You could stand there naked and nobody would see you from the outside. But don't try that at night, 'cause it's a different story. Internal light changes things and you can look right in.'

Bosch nodded.

'Thanks.'

'When I come back, I'll bring a couple chairs.'

'That would be good.'

After Edgar disappeared into the elevator, Walling said, 'Good, at least we'll be able to *sit* naked at the window.'

Bosch smiled.

'Sounded like he knew all that from experience,' he said.

'Let's hope not.'

Bosch raised the binoculars and looked down at the house at 710 Figueroa Lane. It was of similar design to the other two on the street; built high on the hillside with steps leading down to a street-front garage cut into the embankment below the house. It had a red barrel-tile roof and a Spanish motif. But while the other houses on the street were neatly painted and cared for, 710 appeared run-down. Its pink paint had faded. The embankment between the garage and the house was overrun with weeds. The flagpole that stood at the corner of the front porch flew no flag.

Bosch fine-tuned the focus of the field glasses and moved them from window to window, looking for indications of occupancy, hoping to get lucky and see Waits himself looking back out.

Next to him he heard Walling click off a few photos. She was using the camera.

'I don't think there's any film in that. It's not digital.'

'It's all right. Just force of habit. And I wouldn't expect a dinosaur like you to have a digital camera.'

Beneath the binoculars, Bosch smiled. He tried to think of a rejoinder but let it go. He focused his attention back on the house. It was of a style commonly seen in the city's older hillside neighborhoods. While with newer construction the contour of the land dictated design, the houses on the inclined side of Figueroa Lane were of a more conquering design. At street level the embankment was excavated for a garage. Then, above this, the hillside was terraced and a small single-level home had been constructed. The mountains and hillsides all over the city were molded this way in the forties and fifties as the city sprawled through the flats and grew up the hillsides like a rising tide.

Bosch noticed that at the top of the stairs that ran from the side of the garage up to the front porch there was a small metal platform. He checked the stairs again and saw the metal guide rails.

'There's a lift on the stairs,' he said. 'Whoever's living there now is in a wheelchair.'

He saw no movement behind any window viewable from the angle they had. He dropped his focus down to the garage. It had a pedestrian entrance door and double garage doors that had been painted pink a long time before. The paint, what was left of it, was gray now and the wood was splintering in many places from direct exposure to the afternoon sun. One garage door looked as though it had closed at an uneven angle to the pavement. It didn't look operational anymore. The pedestrian entrance door had a window, but a shade was pulled down behind it. Across the top panel of each of the garage doors was a row of small square windows, but they were being hit with direct sunlight and the dazzling reflection prevented Bosch from seeing in.

Bosch heard the elevator ding and put the binoculars down for the first time. He checked behind him and saw Jason Edgar carrying two chairs toward them.

'Perfect,' Bosch said.

He took one of the chairs and positioned it near the glass so he could sit on it backwards and prop his elbows on the seat back – classic surveillance form. Rachel positioned her chair so she could sit normally in it.

'Did you get a chance to check with records, Jason?' she asked.

'I did,' Edgar said. 'Services to that address are billed to a Janet Saxon and have been for twenty-one years.'

'Thank you.'

'No problem. I take it that's all you need from me right now?'

Bosch looked up at Edgar.

'Jerry, you – I mean, Jason – you've been a great help. We appreciate it. We'll probably stick around a little bit and then split. You want us to let you know or drop these chairs off somewhere?'

'Uh, just tell the guy in the lobby on your way out. He'll get a message to me. And leave the chairs. I can take care of that.'

'Will do. Thanks.'

'Good luck. Hope you get your man.'

Everybody shook hands and Edgar returned to the elevator. Bosch and Walling returned to watching the house on Figueroa Lane. Bosch asked Rachel if she would prefer taking shifts and she said no. He asked if she would rather use the binoculars and she said she would stick with the camera. Its long lens actually allowed her a closer focus than the binoculars did.

Twenty minutes went by and no movement at the house was seen. Bosch had spent the time moving back and forth between the house and the garage but was now training his focus on the heavy brush on the ridgeline up above, looking for another possible observation position that would put them closer. Walling spoke excitedly.

'Harry, the garage.'

Bosch lowered his glasses and picked up the garage. The sun had moved behind a cloud and the glare had dropped off the line of windows across the top panel of each garage door. Bosch saw Rachel's discovery. Through the windows of the garage door that appeared to still be functional he could see the back of a white van.

'I heard that a white van was used in the abduction last night,' Walling said.

'That's what I heard, too. It's part of the BOLO.'

He was excited. A white van in a house where Raynard Waits had lived.

'That's it!' he called out. 'He has to be in there with the girl. Rachel, we gotta go!'

They got up and hurried to the elevator.

28

They debated backup as they sped out of the DWP garage. Walling was for it. Bosch was against.

'Look, all we have is a white van,' he said. 'She might be in that house, but he might not be. If we storm in there with the troops, we could lose him. So all I want to do is check it out up close. We can call for backup when we get there. *If* we need it.'

He believed his view was certainly reasonable, but so was hers.

'And what if he is in there?' she asked. 'The two of us could be walking into an ambush. We need at least one team of backup, Harry, to do this correctly and safely.'

'We'll call them when we get there.'

'That will be too late. I know what you're doing. You want this guy for yourself and you're willing to risk that girl – and us – to get it.'

'You want me to drop you off, Rachel?'

'No, I don't want you to drop me off, Harry.'

'Good. I want you to be there.'

Decision made, they ended the discussion. Figueroa Street ran behind the DWP building. Bosch took it east under the 101 Freeway, crossed Sunset and then followed it as it jogged north and under the 110 Freeway. Figueroa Street became Figueroa Terrace, and they drove to where it ended and Figueroa Lane curved up to the crest of the hillside. Bosch pulled the car to the curb before driving up it.

'We walk up and then we stay close to the line of garages until we get to seven-ten,' he said. 'If we stay in close, he won't have an angle on us from the house.'

'What if he isn't in the house? What if he's in the garage waiting for us?'

'Then we deal with it. We clear the garage first and then go up the stairs to the house.'

'The houses are on the hillside. We still need to cross the street.'

He looked at her across the top of the car as they got out.

'Rachel, are you with me or not?'

'I told you, I'm with you.'

'Then, let's go.'

Bosch got out and started trotting up the sidewalk leading up the hill. He pulled out his phone and turned it off so it wouldn't possibly vibrate while they were sneaking the house.

He was huffing by the time he got to the top. Rachel was right behind him and didn't show the same level of oxygen depletion. Bosch hadn't smoked in years but the damage of twenty-five years before that had been done.

Their only visual exposure to the pink house at the end of the street came when they got to the top and had to cross over to the garages that lined the east side of the street. They walked it, Bosch casually holding Walling by the arm and whispering in her ear.

'I'm using you to block my face,' he said. 'He's seen me but he's never seen you.'

'It doesn't matter,' she said when they got across. 'If he saw us, you can expect he knows what's happening.'

He ignored the warning and started moving in front of the garages, which were built right along the sidewalk line. They got to 710 quickly and Bosch went to the panel of windows over one of the doors. Cupping his hands against the dirty glass, he looked in and saw that the interior was crowded by the van and stacks of boxes, barrels and other junk. He saw no movement and heard no sound. A door at the back wall of the garage was closed.

He stepped over to the garage's pedestrian door and checked the knob.

'Locked,' he whispered.

He stepped back and looked at the two pull-up doors. Rachel was now standing by the far door and leaning in close to it to listen for sounds from inside. She looked at Bosch and shook her head. Nothing. He looked down and saw that there was a handle at the bottom of each pull-up door but no exterior locking mechanism. He went to the first one, bent down and tried to pull the door open. It came about an inch and then stopped. It was locked from the inside. He tried the second door and encountered the same response. The door gave for a few inches but then stopped. Because of the minimal movement each door allowed, Bosch guessed that they were secured inside by padlocks.

Bosch stood up and looked at Rachel. He shook his head and pointed upward, meaning it was time to go up to the house.

They moved to the concrete stairs and quietly started up. Bosch led the way and stopped four steps from the top. He crouched and tried to catch his breath. He looked at Rachel. He knew they were winging it. *He* was winging it. There was no way to approach the house but to go directly to the front door.

He turned from her and studied the windows one by one. He saw no movement, but he thought he could hear the sound of a television or radio coming from inside. He pulled his gun – it was a backup he had gotten out of the hallway closet that morning – and went up the final steps, holding the weapon down at his side as he quietly crossed the porch to the front door.

Bosch knew that a search warrant was not at issue here. Waits had abducted a woman, and the life-and-death nature of the situation assuredly pushed them into no-warrant, no-knock territory. He put his hand on the knob and turned. The door was unlocked.

Bosch slowly pushed the door open, noticing that a two-inch ramp had been placed over the threshold to accommodate a wheelchair. As the door came open the sound of the radio became louder. An evangelical station, a man talking about the impending rapture.

They stepped into the house's entry area. To the right it opened into a living room with a dining area to the back. Directly ahead through an arched opening was the kitchen. A hallway to the left led to the rest of the house. Without looking back at Rachel he pointed to the right, meaning she would go that way while he moved forward and cleared the kitchen before taking the hallway to the left.

As he reached the archway Bosch glanced at Rachel and saw her moving through the living room, weapon up in a two-handed grip. He stepped into the kitchen and saw that it was clean and neat, without a dish in the sink. The radio was on the counter. The speaker was telling his listeners that those who did not believe would be left behind.

There was another archway leading from the kitchen to the dining room. Rachel came through it, pointed her gun up when she saw Bosch and shook her head.

Nothing.

That left the hallway leading to the bedrooms and the rest of the house. Bosch turned and went back through the archway to the entry area. When he turned toward the hallway he was startled to see an old woman sitting in a wheelchair in the threshold to the hallway. On her lap she was holding a long-barrel revolver. It looked like it was too heavy for her frail arm to hold up.

'Who's there?' she said forcefully.

Her head was turned at an angle. Though her eyes were open they were focused on the floor instead of Bosch. It was her ear that was trained toward him and he knew she was blind.

He raised his gun and pointed it at her.

'Mrs. Saxon? Take it easy. My name is Harry Bosch. I'm just looking for Robert.'

A look of puzzlement played on her features.

'Who?'

'Robert Foxworth. Is he here?'

'You've got the wrong place, and how dare you come in here without knocking.'

'I—'

'Bobby uses the garage. I don't let him use the house. All those chemicals, it smells awful.'

Bosch started edging toward her, his eyes on the gun the whole time.

'I'm sorry, Mrs. Saxon. I thought he was up here. Has he been here lately?'

'He comes and goes. He comes up here to give me the rent, that's all.'

'For the garage?'

He was getting closer.

'That's what I said. What do you want him for? Are you his friend?'

'I just want to talk to him.'

Bosch reached down and took the gun out of her hand.

'Hey! That's my protection.'

'It's all right, Mrs. Saxon. I'll give it back. I just think it needs to be cleaned up a little. And oiled. This way it will be sure to work in case you ever really need to use it.'

'I need it.'

'I'm going to take it down to the garage and get Bobby to clean it. Then I'll bring it back.'

'You better.'

Bosch checked the gun. It was loaded and appeared operational. He put it into the waistband at the back of his pants and looked at Rachel. She was standing three feet behind him in the entryway. She made a movement with her hand, pantomiming turning a key. Bosch understood.

'Do you have a key to the garage door, Mrs. Saxon?' he asked.

'No. Bobby came and got the extra key.'

'Okay, Mrs. Saxon. I'll check with him.'

He moved toward the front door. Rachel joined him and they went out. Halfway down the steps to the garage, Rachel grabbed his arm and whispered.

'We have to call backup. Now!'

'Go ahead and call but I'm going into the garage. If he's in there with the girl, we can't wait.'

He shook off her grip and continued down. When he got to the garage he looked once again through the windows on the top panels and saw no movement inside. His eyes focused on the door on the rear wall. It was still closed.

He moved over to the pedestrian door and opened the blade of a small folding knife that was attached to his key ring.

Bosch went to work on the door's lock and got the blade across the tongue. He nodded to Rachel to be ready and pulled the door open. But it didn't come. He tried it again and pulled hard. Again the door would not come open.

'There's an inside lock,' he whispered. 'It means he's in there.'

'No, it doesn't. He could've come out through one of the garage doors.'

He shook his head.

'They're locked from the inside,' he whispered. 'All the doors are locked from the inside.'

Rachel understood and nodded.

'What do we do?' she whispered back.

Bosch thought about things for a moment and then handed her his keys.

'Go back and get the car. When you get up here, park it with the rear end right here. Then pop the trunk.'

'What are you—'

'Just do it. Go!'

She ran down the sidewalk in front of the garages and then crossed the street and dropped from sight down the hill. Bosch moved toward the pull-up door that looked like it had closed awkwardly. It was out of alignment and he knew it would be the better of the two doors to try to breach.

Bosch heard the Mustang's big engine before he saw his car come over the hill. Rachel drove toward him fast. He stepped back against the garage to give her maximum room to maneuver. She made almost a complete turn in the street and then backed toward the garage. The trunk was popped and Bosch immediately reached in for the rope he kept in the back. It was gone. He then remembered that Osani had taken it after discovering it on the tree in Beachwood Canyon.

'Shit!'

He quickly looked through the trunk and found a shorter length of clothesline he had used once to tie down the trunk lid when he was moving a piece of furniture to the Salvation Army. He quickly tied one end of the cord to a steel towing loop underneath the car's bumper and then the other end to the handle at the bottom of the garage door. He knew that something would have to give. The door, the handle or the rope. They had a one-in-three shot at getting the door open.

Rachel had gotten out of the car.

'What are you doing?' she asked.

Bosch quietly closed the car's trunk.

'We're going to pull it open. Get back in the car and go forward. Go slow. A sudden jerk will snap the line. Go ahead, Rachel. Hurry.'

Without a word she got back in the car, dropped it in drive and started moving forward. She watched in the rearview and he rolled a finger to keep her moving. The cord pulled taut and then Bosch could hear the sound of the garage door groaning as the pressure mounted. He stepped back and at the same time drew his gun again.

The garage door gave way all at once and popped up and out three feet.

'Stop!' Bosch yelled, knowing there was no longer any need for whispers.

Rachel stopped pulling but the line remained taut and the garage door was held open. Bosch moved forward quickly and used his momentum to duck and roll beneath it. He came up inside the garage with his gun up and ready. He swept the space but saw no one. Keeping his eyes on the door at the rear wall, he sidestepped over to the van. He jerked one of the side doors open and quickly checked the interior. It was empty.

Bosch moved toward the back wall, making his way around an obstacle course of upright barrels, rolls of plastic, bales of towels, squeegee blades and other window-washing equipment. There was a strong smell of ammonia and other chemicals. Bosch's eyes were beginning to water.

The hinges on the door at the rear wall were visible and Bosch knew it would swing toward him when he opened it.

'FBI!' Walling yelled from outside. 'Coming in!'

'Clear!' Bosch yelled back.

He heard her scrabble under the garage door but kept his attention on the door in the back wall. He moved toward it, listening all the time for any sound.

Taking a position to the side of the door Bosch put his hand on the doorknob and turned it. It was unlocked. He looked back for the first time at Rachel. She was in a combat stance at an angle from the door. She nodded and in one quick move he flung the door open and moved across the threshold.

The room was dark and windowless and he saw no one. He knew he was a target standing in the light in the doorway and quickly sidestepped into the room. He saw a string from an overhead light and reached out and yanked on it. The string snapped in his hand but the light came on, the hanging bulb jumping and swinging in response. He was in a crowded work and storage room that was about ten feet deep. There was no one in the room.

'Clear!'

Rachel entered and they stood there scanning the room. A bench cluttered with old paint cans, household tools and flashlights was on the right. Four old and rusting bikes were stacked against the left wall, along with folding chairs and a pile of collapsed cardboard boxes. The back wall was concrete block. Hung on it was the dusty old flag for the pole up on the front terrace of the house. On the floor in front of it was a stand-up electric fan, its blades caked with dust and crud. It looked like at one time somebody had tried to blow the fetid, damp smell out of the room.

'Shit!' Bosch said.

He lowered his gun, turned and walked past Rachel back into the garage. She followed him.

Bosch shook his head and tried to rub some of the chemical sting out of his eyes. He didn't understand. Were they too late? Were they following the wrong lead altogether?

'Check the van,' he said. 'See if there is any sign of the girl.'

Rachel crossed behind him to the van, and Bosch went to the pedestrian door to check for the flows in his belief that someone had to be in the garage.

He had to be right. There was a deadbolt on the door, meaning it could have only been locked from the inside. He moved over to the garage doors and stooped down to look at their locking mechanisms. He was right again. Both had padlocks on interior slide locks.

He tried to puzzle it out. All three doors had been locked from the inside. It meant that either someone was inside the garage or there was an exit point he hadn't identified yet. But this seemed impossible. The garage was dug directly into the hillside embankment. There was no possibility of a rear exit.

He was checking the ceiling, wondering if it was possible that there was a passageway up to the house when Rachel called from inside the van.

'I've got a roll of duct tape,' she said. 'I've got used strips on the floor with hair.'

It boosted Bosch's belief that they had the right place. He stepped over to the open side door of the van. He looked in at Rachel while he pulled out his phone. He noticed the wheelchair lift in the van.

'I'll call for backup and forensics,' he said. 'We missed him.'

He had to turn the phone back on, and while he waited for it to boot up he realized something. The stand-up fan in the back room wasn't pointed toward the garage doors. If you were going to air the room out, you would point the fan toward the door.

His phone buzzed in his hand and it distracted him. He looked down at the screen. It told him he had a message waiting. He clicked a button to check the call record and saw that he had just missed a call from Jerry Edgar. He'd get to it later. He punched in a number for Communications and told the dispatcher to connect him with the Raynard Waits Fugitive Task Force. An officer identifying himself as Freeman picked up.

'This is Detective Harry Bosch. I have—'

'Harry! Gun!'

It was Rachel who had yelled. Time slowed down. All in a second Bosch looked at her in the van's doorway, her eyes focused over his shoulder at the back of the garage. Without thinking, he jumped forward and into her, pulling his arms around her and taking her to the floor of the van in a crushing tackle. Four shots came from behind him followed by the instantaneous sound of bullets striking metal and glass breaking. Bosch rolled off Rachel and came up with his gun in hand. He caught a glimpse of a figure ducking into the rear storage room. He fired six shots through the doorway and raking across the wall to its right.

'Rachel, okay?'

'I'm okay. Are you hit?'

'I don't think so!'

'It was him! Waits!'

They paused and watched the door to the rear room. No one came back through.

'Did you hit him?' Rachel whispered.

'I don't think so.'

'I thought we cleared that room.'

'I thought we did, too.'

Bosch stood up, keeping his aim on the doorway. He noticed that the light from within was now off.

'I dropped my phone,' he said. 'Call for backup.'

He started moving toward the door.

'Harry, wait. He could—'

'Call for backup! And remember to tell them I'm in there.'

He cut to his left and approached the door from an angle that would give him the widest vision of the interior space. But without the overhead light the room was cast in shadows and he could see no movement. He started taking small steps using his right foot first and maintaining a firing position. Behind him he heard Rachel on her phone identifying herself and asking for a transfer to LAPD dispatch.

Bosch got to the threshold and swung the gun across his body to cover the part of the room he had not had an angle on. He stepped in and side-stepped to the right. There was no movement, no sign of Waits. The room was empty.

He looked at the fan and confirmed his mistake. It was pointed toward the flag hanging on the back wall. It had not been used to blow damp air out. The fan had been used to blow air in.

Bosch took two steps toward the flag. He reached forward, grabbed it by the edge and ripped it down.

In the wall, three feet off the ground, was a tunnel entrance. About a dozen concrete blocks had been removed to create an opening four feet square and the excavation into the hillside continued from there.

Bosch crouched to look into the opening from the safety of the right side. The tunnel was deep and dark, but he saw a glimmer of light thirty feet in. He realized that the tunnel made a turn and that there was a source of light around the bend.

Bosch leaned closer and realized he could hear a sound from the tunnel. It was a low whimpering sound. It was a terrible sound but it was beautiful just the same. It meant that no matter what horrors she had experienced through the night, the woman Waits had abducted was still alive.

Bosch reached back over to the workbench and picked up the shiniest flashlight he saw. He turned it on. It was dead. He tried another and got a weak beam of light. It would have to do.

He flashed the beam into the tunnel and confirmed that the first leg was clear. He took a step toward the tunnel.

'Harry, wait!'

He turned and saw Rachel in the doorway.

'Backup's on the way!' she whispered.

Bosch shook his head.

'She's in there. She's alive.'

He turned back to the tunnel and flashed the light in once more. It was still clear up to the turn. He turned the light off to conserve it. He glanced back at Rachel and then stepped into the darkness.

29

Bosch hesitated a moment in the mouth of the tunnel to let his eyes adjust. He then started moving. He didn't have to crawl. The tunnel was large enough for him to move through in a crouch. Flashlight in his right hand and gun up in his left, he kept his eyes on the dim light ahead. The sound of the woman crying grew louder as he moved forward.

Ten feet into the tunnel the musty smell that he had noticed outside turned into the deeper stench of decay. As rancid as it was, it was not something new to him. Almost forty years before he had been a tunnel rat with the U.S. Army, taking part in more than a hundred missions in the tunnels of Vietnam. The enemy sometimes buried their dead in the clay walls of their tunnels. That hid them from sight but the odor of decay was impossible to hide. Once it got into your nose it was equally impossible to forget.

Bosch knew that he was headed toward something horrific, that the missing victims of Raynard Waits were ahead somewhere in the tunnel. This had been the destination on the night Waits was pulled over in his work van. But Bosch couldn't help but think that maybe it was his own destination as well. He had come many years and many miles but it seemed to him that he had never really left the tunnels behind, that his life had always been a slow movement through darkness and tight spaces on the way to a flickering light. He knew he was then, now, and forever a tunnel rat.

His thigh muscles burned from the strain of moving in a crouched position. Sweat began to sting his eyes. And as he got closer to the turn in the tunnel Bosch saw the light changing and rechanging and knew that this was caused by the undulation of a flame. Candlelight.

Five feet from the turn Bosch slowed to a stop and rested on his heels as he listened. Behind him, he thought he could hear sirens. Backup on the way. He tried to concentrate on what could be heard from the tunnel ahead but there was only the intermittent sound of the woman crying.

He raised himself up and started forward again. Almost immediately the light ahead went out and the whimpering took on a new energy and urgency.

Bosch froze. He then heard nervous laughter from ahead, followed by the familiar voice of Raynard Waits.

'Is that you, Detective Bosch? Welcome to my foxhole.'

There was more laughter and then it stopped. Bosch let ten seconds go by. Waits said nothing else.

'Waits? Let her go. Send her out to me.'

'No, Bosch. She's with me now. Anybody comes in here, I'll kill her on the spot. I'll save the last bullet for myself.'

'Waits, no. Listen. Just let her come out and I will come in. We'll trade.'

'No, Bosch. I like the situation the way it is.'

'Then what are we doing? We need to talk and you need to save yourself. There's not a lot of time. Send the girl out.'

A few seconds went by and then the voice came out of the darkness.

'Save myself from what? For what?'

Bosch's muscles were on the verge of cramping. He carefully lowered himself to a seated position against the right side of the tunnel. He was sure that the candlelight had been coming ahead from the left. The tunnel turned to the left. He kept his gun up but was now employing a cross-wrists bracing with the flashlight up and ready as well.

'There's no way out,' he said. 'Give it up and come out. Your deal is still in play. You don't have to die. Neither does the girl.'

'I don't care about dying, Bosch. That's why I'm here. Because I don't fucking care. I just want it to be on my own terms. Not the state's or anybody else's. Just mine.'

Bosch noticed that the woman had gone silent. He wondered what had happened. Had Waits silenced her? Had he just ...?

'Waits, what's wrong? Is she all right?'

'She passed out. Too much excitement, I guess.'

He laughed and then was silent. Bosch decided that he needed to keep Waits talking. If he was engaged by Bosch he would be distracted from the woman and what was assuredly being planned outside the tunnel.

'I know who you are,' he said quietly.

Waits didn't take the bait. Bosch tried again.

'Robert Foxworth. Son of Rosemary Foxworth. Raised by the county. Foster homes, youth halls. You lived here with the Saxons. For a time you lived at the McLaren Youth Hall out in El Monte. So did I, Robert.'

Bosch was met with a long silence. But then the voice came quietly out of the darkness.

'I'm not Robert Foxworth anymore.'

'I understand.'

'I hated that place. McLaren. I hated them all.'

'They closed it down a couple years ago. After some kid died in there.'

'Fuck them and fuck that place. How did you find Robert Foxworth?'

Bosch felt a rhythm building in the conversation. He understood the cue

Waits was giving by speaking of Robert Foxworth as someone other than himself. He was Raynard Waits now.

'It wasn't that hard,' Bosch answered. 'We figured it out through the Fitzpatrick case. We found the pawn slip in the records and matched birth dates. What was the heirloom medallion that had been pawned?'

There was a long silence before an answer.

'It was Rosemary's. It was all he had from her. He had to pawn it and when he went back to get it, that pig Fitzpatrick had already sold it.'

Bosch nodded. He had Waits answering questions but there wasn't a lot of time. He decided to jump to the present.

'Raynard. Tell me about the setup. Tell me about Olivas and O'Shea.'

There was only silence. Bosch tried again.

'They used you. O'Shea used you and he's going to just walk away from it. Is that what you want? You die here in this hole and he just walks away?'

Bosch put the flashlight down so he could wipe the sweat out of his eyes. He then had to feel around on the floor of the tunnel to find it again.

'I can't give you O'Shea or Olivas,' Waits said in the darkness.

Bosch didn't get it. Was he wrong? He doubled back in his head and started at the beginning.

'Did you kill Marie Gesto?'

There was a long silence.

'No, I didn't,' Waits finally said.

'Then how was this set up? How could you know where—'

'Think about it, Bosch. They're not stupid. They would not directly communicate with me.'

Bosch nodded. He understood.

'Maury Swann,' he said. 'He brokered the deal. Tell me about it.'

'What's to tell? It was a setup, man. He said the whole thing was to make you a believer. He said you were bothering the wrong people and had to be convinced.'

'What people?'

'He didn't tell me that.'

'This is Maury Swann saying this?'

'Yes, but it doesn't matter. You can't get to him either. This is communication between a lawyer and his client. You can't touch it. It's privileged. Besides, it would be my word against his. That won't go anywhere and you know it.'

Bosch did know it. Maury Swann was a tough lawyer and a respected member of the bar. He was also a media darling. There was no way to go after him with just the words of a criminal client – and a serial killer at that. It had been a masterstroke by O'Shea and Olivas to use him as the go-between.

'I don't care,' Bosch said. 'I want to know how it all went down. Tell me.'

A long silence went by before Waits responded.

'Swann went to them with the idea of making a deal. My clearing the books in exchange for my life. He did this without my knowledge. If he had asked me I would have said, don't bother. I'd rather take the needle than forty years in a cell. You understand that, Bosch. You're an eye-for-an-eye guy. I like that about you, believe it or not.'

He ended it there and Bosch had to prompt him again.

'So then what happened?'

'One night in the jail, I was taken to the attorney room and there was Maury. He told me there was a deal on the table. But he said it would only work if I threw in a freebie. Admit to one I didn't do. He told me that there would be a field trip and I would have to lead a certain detective to the body. This detective had to be convinced, and leading him to the body would be the only way to do it. That detective was you, Bosch.'

'And you said yes.'

'When he said there would be a field trip, I said yes. That was the only reason. It meant daylight. I saw a chance at daylight.'

'And you were led to believe that this offer, this deal – that it came directly from Olivas and O'Shea?'

'Who else would it come from?'

'Did Maury Swann ever use their names in connection with the deal?'

'He said this is what they wanted me to do. He said it came directly from them. They would not make a deal if I didn't throw in the freebie. I had to throw in Gesto and take you to her or there was no fucking deal. You get it?'

Bosch nodded.

'Yeah, I got it.'

He felt his face getting hot with anger. He tried to channel it, put it aside so that it was ready to be used, but not at this moment.

'How did you get the details you gave me during the confession?'

'Swann. He got them from them. He said they had the records from the original investigation.'

'And he told you how to find the body up there in the woods?'

'Swann told me there were markers in the woods. He showed me pictures and told me how to lead everybody there. It was easy. The night before my confession I studied up on everything.'

Bosch was silent as he thought about how easily he had been led down the path. He had wanted something so badly and for so long that it had made him blind.

'And what were you supposed to get out of all of this, Raynard?'

'You mean, what was in it for me from their point of view? My life, man. They were offering me my life. Take it or leave it. But the truth is, I didn't care about that. I told you, man, when Maury said there'd be a field trip, I knew that I might have a chance to get away … and to visit my … my foxhole one last time. That was enough for me. I didn't care about anything else. I didn't care if I died trying, either.'

Bosch tried to think of what he should do or ask next. He thought about using his cell to call the district attorney or a judge and have Waits confess over the phone. He put the flashlight down again and reached into his pocket but then he remembered he had dropped his phone when he had jumped onto Rachel as the shooting broke out in the garage.

'Are you still there, Detective?'

'I'm here. What about Marie Gesto? Did Swann tell you why you had to confess to the Marie Gesto killing?'

Waits laughed.

'He didn't have to. It was pretty obvious that the fix was in. Whoever did Gesto was trying to get you off his back.'

'No name was mentioned?'

'No, no name.'

Bosch shook his head. He had nothing. Nothing on O'Shea or Anthony Garland or anybody else. He looked down the tunnel in the direction of the garage. He could see nothing but he knew that there would be people there. They had blacked out that end to prevent backlighting. He knew they would be coming at any moment.

'What about your escape?' he asked in order to keep the dialogue going. 'Was that planned or were you just improvising?'

'A little of both. I met with Swann the night before the field trip. He told me how I would lead you to the body. He showed me the photos and told me about the markings in the trees and how they would begin after we came to where there had been a mudslide and we would have to climb down. That's when I knew. I knew I might have a chance then. So I told him to make them uncuff me if I had to do any climbing. I told him that I wouldn't follow through on the deal if I had to do any climbing with my hands cuffed to my sides.'

Bosch remembered O'Shea overruling Olivas and telling him to take the cuffs off. Olivas's reluctance had all been a play for Bosch's benefit. Everything had been a play for his benefit. Everything was phony and he had been played perfectly.

Bosch heard the sound of men crawling behind him in the tunnel. He turned the flashlight on and saw them. It was the SWAT team. Black Kevlar, automatic rifles, night-vision goggles. They were coming. Any moment they would launch a flash-bang grenade into the tunnel and start coming. He turned the light out. He thought about the woman. He knew Waits would kill her the moment they made the move.

'Were you really at McLaren?' Waits asked.

'I was there. It was before your time but I was there. I was in B dorm. It was closest to the baseball fields so we always got there first at rec time and got the best equipment.'

It was a you-had-to-be-there story, the best Bosch could think of in the moment. He had spent most of his life trying to forget about McLaren.

'Maybe you were there, Bosch.'

'I was.'

'And look at us now. You went your way and I went mine. I guess I fed the wrong dog.'

'What do you mean? What dog?'

'You don't remember. At McLaren they used to pass around that saying about every man having two dogs inside. One good and one bad. They fight all the time because only one can be the alpha dog, the one in charge.'

'And?'

'And the one that wins is always the dog you chose to feed. I fed the wrong one. You fed the right one.'

Bosch didn't know what to say. He heard a click from behind him in the tunnel. They were going to launch the grenade. He quickly stood up, hopeful that they would not shoot him in the back.

'Waits, I'm coming in.'

'No, Bosch.'

'I'll give you my gun. Watch the light. I'll give you my gun.'

He switched on the flashlight and played its beam on the turn in the tunnel ahead. He moved forward and when he got to the turn extended his left hand into the cone of light. He held his gun by the barrel so Waits could see it was no threat.

'I'm coming in now.'

Bosch took the turn and entered the final chamber of the tunnel. The space was at least twelve feet wide but still not tall enough for him to stand in. He dropped to his knees and swept the chamber with his light. The dim amber beam revealed a ghastly sight of bones and skulls and decaying flesh and hair. The stench was overpowering and Bosch had to hold himself from gagging.

The beam came to the face of the man Bosch had known as Raynard Waits. He was propped against the far wall of his foxhole, sitting on what looked like a throne carved into the rock and clay. To his left the woman he had abducted lay naked and unconscious on a blanket. Waits held the barrel of Freddy Olivas's gun to her temple.

'Easy now,' Bosch said. 'I'll give you my gun. Just don't hurt her anymore.'

Waits smiled, knowing he was in complete control of the situation.

'Bosch, you are a fool to the end.'

Bosch lowered his arm and tossed the gun to the right side of the throne. As Waits reached down to grab it he lifted the muzzle of the other gun off the woman. Bosch dropped the flashlight and reached behind him at the same time, his hand finding the grip of the revolver he had taken from the blind woman.

The long barrel made his aim true. He fired twice, hitting Waits in the center of the chest with both rounds.

Waits was knocked back against the wall. Bosch saw his eyes go wide, then they lost that light that separates life from death. His chin dropped and his head tilted forward.

Bosch crawled to the woman and checked her for a pulse. She was still alive. He covered her with the blanket she was lying on. He then called out to the others in the tunnel.

'This is Bosch – RHD! It's clear! We are clear! Raynard Waits is dead!'

A bright light flashed on around the corner in the entrance tunnel. It was a blinding light and he knew the men with guns would be waiting on the other side of it.

No matter, he felt safe now. He slowly moved toward the light.

30

After emerging from the tunnel Bosch was led out of the garage by two SWAT officers wearing gas masks. He was delivered into the hands of the waiting members of the Fugitive Task Force and others associated with the case. Randolph and Osani from OIS were on hand as well as Abel Pratt from the Open-Unsolved Unit. Bosch looked around for Rachel Walling but didn't see her anywhere on the scene.

Next out of the tunnel was Waits's last victim. The young woman was carried to a waiting ambulance and immediately transported to County-USC Medical Center for assessment and treatment. Bosch was pretty sure his own imagination couldn't top the real horrors she had lived through. But he knew the important thing was that she was alive.

The task force leader wanted Bosch to sit in a van and tell his story but Bosch said he didn't want to be in a closed space. Even out in the open air on Figueroa Lane he couldn't get the smell of the tunnel out of his nose and he noticed that the task force members who had crowded around him at first had now all taken a step or two back. He saw a garden hose attached to a faucet alongside the stairway of the house next to 710. He went over, turned it on and then bent over as he ran the water through his hair, on his face and down his neck. It pretty much soaked his clothes but he didn't care. It washed away a good deal of the dirt and sweat and stench and he knew the clothes were trash now anyway.

The task force top was a sergeant named Bob McDonald who had been pulled in from Hollywood Division. Luckily, Bosch knew him from past days in the division and that set the stage for a cordial debriefing. Bosch realized it was just a warmup. He would have to submit to a formal interview with Randolph and the OIS before the end of the day.

'Where's the FBI agent?' Bosch asked. 'Where's Rachel Walling?'

'She's being interviewed,' McDonald said. 'We're using a neighbor's house for her.'

'And the old lady upstairs in the house?'

McDonald nodded.

'She's fine,' McDonald said. 'She's blind and in a wheelchair. They're still talking to her but it turns out Waits lived here when he was a kid. It was a foster home and his real name is Robert Foxworth. She can't get around by herself anymore, so she pretty much stays up there. County assistance brings in her food. Foxworth helped her out financially by renting the garage. He kept supplies for window washing in there. And an old van. It's got a wheelchair lift in it.'

Bosch nodded. He guessed that Janet Saxon had no idea what else her former foster son used her garage for.

McDonald told Bosch it was time to tell his story, and so he did, giving the step-by-step playback of the moves he had made after discovering the connection between Waits and the pawnbroker Fitzpatrick.

There were no questions. Not yet. Nobody asked why he never called the Task Force or Randolph or Pratt or anybody else. They listened and simply locked in his story. Bosch was not too concerned. He and Rachel had saved the girl and he had killed the bad guy. He was sure that these two accomplishments would allow him to rise above all transgressions upon protocol and regulations and save his job.

It took him twenty minutes to tell the story, and then McDonald said they should take a break. As the group around him splintered, Bosch saw his boss waiting to get to him. Bosch knew this conversation would not be easy.

Pratt finally saw an opening and walked up. He looked anxious.

'Well, Harry, what did he tell you in there?'

Bosch was surprised Pratt wasn't jumping all over him for acting on his own, without authority. But he wasn't going to complain about it. In abbreviated form he outlined what he had learned from Waits about the setup in Beachwood Canyon.

'He told me it was all orchestrated through Swann,' he said. 'Swann was the go-between. He took the deal from Olivas and O'Shea to Waits. Waits didn't kill Gesto but agreed to take the fall for her. It was part of the deal for avoiding the death penalty.'

'That's it?'

'That's enough, isn't it?'

'Why would Olivas and O'Shea do this?'

'The oldest reasons in the book. Money and power. And the Garland family has plenty of both.'

'Anthony Garland was the person of interest on Gesto, right? The guy who got the court orders keeping you away.'

'Yeah, until Olivas and O'Shea used Waits to convince me otherwise.'

'You got anything besides what Waits said in there?'

Bosch shook his head.

'Not much. I traced twenty-five thousand in contributions to O'Shea's campaign back to T. Rex Garland's lawyers and oil company. But it was all done legally. It proves a connection, nothing else.'

'Twenty-five seems cheap to me.'

'It is. But the twenty-five is all we know about. We do some digging and there'll probably be more.'

'You tell all of this to McDonald and his crew?'

'Only what Waits told me in there. I didn't tell them about the contributions. Only what Waits said.'

'You think they'll go after Maury Swann for this?'

Bosch thought a moment before answering.

'Not a chance. Whatever was said between them was privileged information. Besides that, nobody would go after him based on the word of a dead madman like Waits.'

Pratt kicked the ground. He had nothing else to say or ask.

'Look, Top, I'm sorry about this,' Bosch said. 'About not being up-front with you on what I was doing, the home duty and everything.'

Pratt waved it off.

'It's okay, man. You got lucky. You ended up doing some good and taking out the bad guy. What am I going to say to that?'

Bosch nodded his thanks.

'Besides, I'm coasting,' Pratt continued. 'Another three weeks and you'll be someone else's problem. He can decide what to do with you.'

Whether Kiz Rider came back or not, Bosch didn't want to leave the unit. He'd heard that David Lambkin, the new top coming up from RHD, was a good man to work for. Bosch hoped when all of this shook out, he'd still be part of the Open-Unsolved Unit.

'Holy shit!' Pratt whispered.

Bosch followed his eyes to a car that had just parked on the perimeter near where the media trucks were and the reporters were setting up for standups and sound bites. Rick O'Shea was getting out of the passenger side. Bosch felt the bile immediately rise in his throat. He made a move to walk toward the prosecutor but Pratt caught his arm.

'Harry, take it easy.'

'What the fuck is he doing here?'

'It's his case, man. He can come if he wants. And you better play it cool. Don't show your hand with him or you might never be able to get to him.'

'And what, meantime he does his dance in front of the cameras and turns this into another campaign commercial? Bullshit. What I ought to do is go over there and kick his ass right in front of the cameras.'

'Yeah, that would be real smart, Harry. Very subtle. That will help the situation a lot.'

Bosch broke free of Pratt's grasp but simply stepped over and leaned against one of the police cars. He folded his arms and kept his head down until he was calmer. He knew Pratt was right.

'Just keep him away from me.'

'That will be kind of hard because he's coming right to you.'

Bosch looked up just as O'Shea and the two men that made up his entourage got to him.

'Detective Bosch, are you okay?'

'Never better.'

Bosch kept his arms folded across his chest. He didn't want one of his hands getting loose and involuntarily taking a swing at O'Shea.

'Thank you for what you have done here today. Thank you for saving the young woman.'

Bosch just nodded while looking down at the ground.

O'Shea turned to the men with him and to Pratt, who had remained nearby in case he had to pull Bosch off the prosecutor.

'Could I speak to Detective Bosch alone?'

O'Shea's minions walked off. Pratt hesitated until Bosch nodded to him, telling him everything was cool. Bosch and O'Shea were left to themselves.

'Detective, I've been briefed on what Waits – or, I should say, Foxworth – revealed to you in the tunnel.'

'Good.'

'I hope you do not give any credence to what an admitted and confirmed serial killer would say about the men who were prosecuting him, especially one who cannot even be here to defend himself?'

Bosch stepped away from the patrol car's fender and finally dropped his arms to his sides. His hands were balled into fists.

'You're talking about your pal Olivas?'

'Yes, I am. And I can tell by your posture that you actually believe what Foxworth allegedly told you.'

'Allegedly? What, now I'm the one making it up?'

'Someone is.'

Bosch leaned a few inches toward him and spoke in a low voice.

'O'Shea, get away from me. I might hit you.'

The prosecutor took a step backwards as if he had already been punched.

'You're wrong, Bosch. He was lying.'

'He was confirming what I already knew before I even went into that tunnel. Olivas was dirty. He put the entry in the murder book that falsely tied Raynard Waits to Gesto. He went out there and marked a trail for Waits to follow and lead us to the body. And he wouldn't have done any of it without somebody telling him to do it. He wasn't that kind of guy. He wasn't smart enough.'

O'Shea stared at him for a long moment. The implication in Bosch's words was clear.

'I can't dissuade you from this bullshit, can I?'

Bosch looked at him and then looked away.

'Dissuade? Not a chance. And I don't care what it does or doesn't do for the campaign, Mr. Prosecutor. Those are the undisputed facts and I don't need Foxworth or what he said to prove them.'

'Then, I guess I'll have to appeal to a higher authority than you.'

Bosch took half a step closer to him. This time he really got into his space.

'You smell that? You smell that on me? That's the fucking putrid smell of death. I've got it all over me, O'Shea. But at least I can wash it off.'

'What is that supposed to mean?'

'Whatever you want it to mean. Who's your higher authority? You going to call T. Rex Garland up in his shiny office?'

O'Shea took a deep breath and shook his head in confusion.

'Detective, I don't know what happened to you in that tunnel but you aren't making much sense.'

Bosch nodded.

'Yeah, well, it will make sense soon enough. Before the election, that's for sure.'

'Help me out, Bosch. What exactly am I missing here?'

'I don't think you're missing anything. You know it all, O'Shea, and before it's all over, so will the whole wide world. Somehow, some way, I'm going to take down you and the Garlands and everybody else who had a part in this. Count on it.'

Now O'Shea took a step toward Bosch.

'Are you saying that I did this, that I set all of this up, for T. Rex Garland?'

Bosch started laughing. O'Shea was the consummate actor to the end.

'You're good,' he said. 'I'll give you that. You're good.'

'T. Rex Garland is a valid contributor to my campaign. Up-front and legal. How you can tie that into—'

'Then, why the fuck didn't you mention he was a valid and legal contributor when I brought up his son the other day and told you he was my suspect on Gesto?'

'Because it would have complicated things. I have never met or even spoken to either of the Garlands. T. Rex contributed to my campaign. So what? The guy spreads money through every election in the county. For me to bring it up at that point would have been to invite your suspicion. I didn't want that. Now I see I have it anyway.'

'You are so full of shit. You—'

'Fuck you, Bosch. There is no connection.'

'Then, we've got nothing else to say.'

'Yes, we do. I've got something to say. Take your best shot with this bullshit and we'll see who comes out at the end still standing.'

He turned and walked away, barking an order to his men. He wanted a telephone with a secured line. Bosch wondered who the first call would go to, T. Rex Garland or the chief of police.

Bosch made a snap decision. He would call Keisha Russell and turn her loose. He would tell her she was clear to look into those campaign contributions Garland had funneled to O'Shea. He put his hand into his pocket and then remembered that his phone was still somewhere in the garage. He walked that way and stopped at the yellow tape that was strung across the now fully opened door behind the white van.

Cal Cafarelli was in the garage, directing the forensic analysis of the scene. She had a breathing filter mask down around her neck. Bosch could tell by her face that she had been to the macabre scene at the end of the tunnel. And she would never be the same again. He waved her over.

'How's it going, Cal?'

'It's going about as well as you'd expect after seeing something like that.'

'Yeah. I know.'

'We're going to be here long into the night. What can I do for you, Harry?'

'Have you found a cell phone somewhere in here? I lost my phone when things started happening.'

She pointed to the floor near the front tire of the van.

'Is that it over there?'

Bosch looked over and saw his phone lying on the concrete. The red message light was blinking. He noticed that someone had circled it on the concrete with chalk. That was not good. Bosch didn't want his phone inventoried as evidence. He might never get it back.

'Can I get it back? I need it.'

'I'm sorry, Harry. Not yet. This place hasn't been photographed. We're starting with the tunnel and moving out from there. It will be a while.'

'Then how about if you give it to me and I use it right here and then I give it back when it's time to take photos. It looks like I've got messages waiting.'

'Harry, come on.'

He knew that his suggestion would break about four rules of evidence.

'Okay, just let me know when I can get it back. Hopefully before the battery's dead.'

'You got it, Harry.'

He turned away from the garage and saw Rachel Walling walking toward the yellow tape that delineated the outside perimeter of the crime scene. There was a federal cruiser there and a man in a suit and sunglasses was waiting for her. She had apparently called for a ride.

Bosch trotted toward the tape, calling her name. She stopped and waited for him.

'Harry,' she said. 'Are you all right?'

'I am now. How about you, Rachel?'

'I'm fine. What happened to you?'

She indicated his wet clothes with her hand.

'I had to hose off. It was bad. I need about a two-hour shower. Are you leaving?'

'Yes. They're done with me for the time being.'

Bosch nodded toward the man in the sunglasses ten feet behind her.

'Are you in trouble?' he asked quietly.

'I don't know yet. I should be all right. You got the bad guy and saved the girl. How can that be a bad thing?'

'*We* got the bad guy and saved the girl,' Bosch corrected. 'But there are people in every institution and bureaucracy who can find a way to turn something good into shit.'

She looked him in the eyes and nodded.

'I know,' she said.

Her look froze him and he knew they were now different.

'Are you mad at me, Rachel?'

'Mad? No.'

'Then, what?'

'Then, nothing. I have to go.'

'Will you call me, then?'

'When I can. Good-bye, Harry.'

She took two steps toward the waiting car but then stopped and turned back to him.

'That was O'Shea you were talking to out by the car, wasn't it?'

'Yeah.'

'Be careful, Harry. If you let your emotions run you the way they did out here today, O'Shea could put you in a world of pain.'

Bosch smiled slightly.

'You know what they say about pain, don't you?'

'No, what?'

'They say pain is weakness leaving the body.'

She shook her head.

'Well "they" are full of shit. Don't put it to the test unless you have to. Good-bye, Harry.'

'I'll see you, Rachel.'

He watched as the man in sunglasses held the tape up for her to duck under. She got into the front passenger seat and Sunglasses drove them off. Bosch knew that something had changed in the way she saw him. His actions in the garage and going into the tunnel had made her change her mind about him. He accepted it and guessed that he might never see her again. He decided that it would be one more thing that he would blame on Rick O'Shea.

He turned back to the scene, where Randolph and Osani were standing waiting for him. Randolph was putting away his cell phone.

'You two again,' Bosch said.

'Gettin' to be like déjà vu all over again, isn't it?' Randolph said.

'Something like that.'

'Detective, we are going to need to take you over to Parker Center and conduct a more formal interview this time around.'

Bosch nodded. He knew the drill. This time it wasn't about shooting into the trees or the woods. He had killed somebody, so this time it would be different. They would need to nail down every detail.

'I'm ready to go,' he said.

31

Bosch was seated in an interview room in the Officer Involved Shooting Unit at Parker Center. Randolph had allowed him to shower in the basement locker room and he'd changed into blue jeans and a black West Coast Choppers sweatshirt, clothing he kept in a locker for the times he was downtown and unexpectedly needed to fly below the radar that a suit would bring. On the way out of the locker room he had dumped his contaminated suit into a trash can. He would now be down to two.

The tape recorder on the table was turned on, and from separate sheets of paper, Osani read to him his constitutional rights as well as the police officer's bill of rights. The double insulation of protections was designed to safeguard the individual and police office from the unfair assault of the government, but Bosch knew that when push came to shove, in one of these little rooms neither piece of paper would do much to protect him. He had to fend for himself. He said he understood his rights and agreed to be interviewed.

Randolph took over from there. At his request Bosch once more told the story of the shooting of Robert Foxworth, aka Raynard Waits, beginning with the discovery made during the review of records from the Fitzpatrick case and ending with the two bullets he fired into Foxworth's chest. Randolph asked few questions until Bosch was finished going through the story. Then he asked many detailed questions about the moves Bosch had made in the garage and then the tunnel. More than once he asked Bosch why he didn't listen to the cautioning words of FBI agent Rachel Walling.

This question told Bosch not only that Rachel had been interviewed by the OIS but also that she had not said things particularly favorable to his case. This disappointed Bosch greatly but he tried to keep his thoughts and feelings about Rachel out of the interview room. To Randolph he repeated as a mantra a sentence that he believed would ultimately win the day for him, no matter what Randolph or Rachel or anyone else thought of his actions and procedures.

'It was a life-or-death situation. A woman was in jeopardy and we had been fired upon. I felt that I could not wait around for backup or anybody else. I did what I had to do. I used as much caution as I could and used deadly force only when necessary.'

Randolph moved on and focused many of the next questions on the actual shooting of Robert Foxworth. He asked Bosch what he was thinking when Foxworth revealed that Bosch had been set up to believe that the Gesto case was solved. He asked Bosch what he was thinking when he saw the remains of Foxworth's victims positioned in the chamber at the end of the tunnel. He asked Bosch what he was thinking when he pulled the trigger and killed the defiler and murderer of those victims.

Bosch patiently answered each question but finally hit his limit. Something was off-kilter about the interview. It was almost as if Randolph were working from a script.

'What's going on here?' Bosch asked. 'I'm sitting here telling you people everything. What aren't you telling me?'

Randolph looked at Osani and then back at Bosch. He leaned forward, arms on the table. He had a habit of turning a gold ring on his left hand. Bosch had noticed him doing it last time. He knew it was a USC ring. Big deal. A lot of the department's ruling class had gone through night school at USC.

Randolph looked back at Osani and reached over to turn the tape recorder off but held his fingers on the buttons.

'Detective Osani, could you go get us a couple bottles of water? All this talking and my voice is about to go. Probably the same with Detective Bosch, too. We'll hold up until you get back.'

Osani got up to leave and Randolph turned off the recorder. He didn't speak until the interview room door was closed.

'The thing is, Detective Bosch, we only have your word on what happened in that tunnel. The female was unconscious. There were only you and Foxworth, and he didn't make it out alive.'

'That's right. Are you saying my word is not acceptable?'

'I'm saying that your description of events might be perfectly acceptable. But the forensics might come in with an interpretation that varies from your statement. You see? It can get messy very quickly. Things can be left open to interpretation and misinterpretation. Public and political interpretation as well.'

Bosch shook his head. He didn't understand what was happening.

'So what?' he said. 'I don't care what the public or politicians think. Waits pushed the action in that tunnel. It was clearly a kill-or-be-killed situation and I did what I had to do.'

'But there is no witness to your description of events.'

'What about Agent Walling?'

'She didn't go into the tunnel. She warned you not to go in.'

'You know, there's a woman over at County-USC who probably wouldn't be alive right now if I hadn't gone in. What is going on here, Lieutenant?'

Randolph started playing with his ring again. He looked like a man with a distaste for what his duty called on him to do.

'That's probably enough for today. You've been through a lot. What we're going to do is keep things open for a few days while we wait for the forensics to come in. You'll continue on home duty. Once we have everything in order I'll bring you in to read and sign your statement.'

'I asked what's going on, Lieutenant.'

'And I told you what's going on.'

'You didn't tell me enough.'

Randolph took his hand away from his ring. It had the effect of underlining with importance what he would say next.

'You rescued the hostage and brought a resolution to the case. That's good. But you were reckless in your actions and got lucky. If we believe your story, then you shot a man who was threatening the lives of you and others. The facts and forensics, however, might just as easily lead to another interpretation, perhaps one that indicates the man you shot was attempting to surrender. So what we're going to do is take our time with it. In a few days we'll get it right. And then we'll let you know.'

Bosch studied him, knowing that he was delivering a message that was not so hidden in his words.

'This is about Olivas, isn't it? The funeral's set for tomorrow, the chief is going to be there and you want to keep Olivas a hero killed in the line of duty.'

Randolph went back to turning his ring.

'No, Detective Bosch, you have that wrong. If Olivas was dirty, then nobody is going to bend over backwards to worry about his reputation.'

Bosch nodded. He now had it.

'Then it's about O'Shea. He reached out to a higher authority. He told me he would. That authority then reached out to you.'

Randolph leaned back in his chair and seemed to search the ceiling for a proper reply.

'There are a great number of people in this department as well as the community who believe Rick O'Shea would make a fine district attorney,' he said. 'They also believe he would be a good friend to have on the side of the LAPD.'

Bosch closed his eyes and slowly shook his head. He couldn't believe what he was hearing. Randolph continued.

'His opponent, Gabriel Williams, has allied himself with an anti-law enforcement constituency. It would not be a good day for the LAPD if he were to be elected.'

Bosch opened his eyes and stared at Randolph.

'You're actually going to do this?' he asked. 'You're going to let this guy skate because you think he could be a friend to the department?'

Randolph shook his head sadly.

'I don't know what you are talking about, Detective. I'm simply making a political observation. But I do know this. There is no evidence real or imagined of this conspiracy you speak of. If you think that Robert Foxworth's attorney will do anything other than deny the conversation you have outlined here, then you would be a fool. So don't be a fool. Be wise. Keep it to yourself.'

Bosch took a moment to compose himself.

'Who made the call on this?'

'Excuse me?'

'How high up did O'Shea reach? It couldn't have been directly to you. He would have gone higher. Who told you to knock me down?'

Randolph spread his hands and shook his head.

'Detective, I have no idea what you are talking about.'

'Right. Of course not.'

Bosch stood up.

'Then, I guess you'll write it up the way you've been told and I'll either sign it or I won't. Simple as that.'

Randolph nodded but said nothing. Bosch leaned down and put both hands on the table so he could get close to his face.

'You going to Deputy Doolan's funeral, Lieutenant? It's right after they put Olivas in the ground. Remember him, the one Waits shot in the face out there? I thought maybe you'd be going to the funeral to explain to his family about how choices had to be made and how the man directly behind that bullet could be a friend to the department and therefore doesn't need to face the consequences of his actions.'

Randolph stared straight ahead at the wall across the table. He said nothing. Bosch straightened up and pulled open the door, startling Osani, who had been standing just outside. He wasn't holding any water bottles. Bosch pushed past him and left the squad room.

At the elevator Bosch pushed the up button. He waited and paced and thought about taking his grievance up to the sixth floor. He envisioned himself charging into the chief of police's suite and demanding to know if he was aware of what was being done in his name and under his command.

But as the elevator opened he dismissed the idea and pushed the 5 button. He knew that the Byzantine levels of bureaucracy and politics in the department were impossible to fully understand. If he didn't watch himself he could end up complaining about all the bullshit to the very person who created it.

The Open-Unsolved Unit was deserted when he got there. It was just after four and most detectives worked seven-to-four shifts that put them on the road home before rush hour. If something wasn't breaking, they left at four on the dot. Even a fifteen-minute delay could cost them an hour on the freeways. The only one still around was Abel Pratt, and that was because as a supervisor he had to work eight to five. Company rules. Bosch waved as he walked by the open door of Pratt's office on the way to his desk.

Bosch dropped into his chair, exhausted by the day's events and the weight of the departmental fix. He looked down and saw that his desk was littered with pink phone message slips. He started looking through them. Most were from colleagues in different divisions and stations. They were all call-backs. Bosch knew they wanted to say nice shooting or words to that effect. Anytime anybody got a clean kill the phones lit up.

There were several messages from reporters, including Keisha Russell. Bosch knew he owed her a call but would wait until he got home. There was also a message from Irene Gesto, and Bosch guessed that she and her husband wanted to know if there was any update on the investigation. He had called them the night before to tell them that their daughter had been found and the ID confirmed. He put that slip in his pocket. Home duty or not, he would make the call back to them. With the autopsy completed the body would be released and at the very least they could finally, after thirteen years, claim their daughter and take her home. He could not tell them that their daughter's killer had been brought to justice, but at least he could help them get her home.

There was also a message from Jerry Edgar, and Bosch remembered that his old partner had called his cell right before the shooting had gone down in Echo Park. Whoever had taken the message had written *Says it's important* on the slip and underlined it. Bosch checked the time on the slip and noted that this call had come in before the shooting as well. Edgar had not been calling to congratulate him on taking out a bad guy. He assumed that Edgar had heard that Harry had met his cousin and that he wanted to chew the fat about it. At the moment Bosch didn't feel up for that.

Bosch wasn't interested in any of the other messages, so he stacked them and put them in a desk drawer. Nothing else to do, he then started straightening the papers and files on his desk. He thought about whether he should call Forensics and see about getting his phone and car back from the Echo Park crime scene.

'I just got the word.'

Bosch looked up. Pratt was standing in the doorway of his office. He was in shirtsleeves, his tie loose at his neck.

'What word?'

'From OIS. You haven't cleared home duty, Harry. I gotta send you home.'

Bosch looked back down at his desk.

'So what's new? I'm leaving.'

Pratt paused as he tried to interpret Bosch's tone of voice.

'Everything okay, Harry?' he asked tentatively.

'Nope, everything's not okay. The fix is in and when the fix is in, then everything's not okay. Not by a long shot.'

'What are you talking about? They're going to cover up Olivas and O'Shea?'

Bosch looked up at him.

'I don't think I should talk to you about it, Top. It could put you in a spot. You wouldn't want the blowback.'

'They're that serious about it, huh?'

Bosch hesitated but then answered.

'Yeah, they're serious. They're willing to jam me up if I don't play the game.'

He stopped there. He didn't want to be having this conversation with his supervisor. In Pratt's position loyalties went both up and down the ladder. It didn't matter if he was only a few weeks from retirement. Pratt had to play the game until the buzzer sounded.

'My cell is back there, part of the crime scene,' he said, reaching for the phone. 'I just came in to make a phone call and then I'm out of here.'

'I was wondering about your phone,' Pratt said. 'Some of the guys have been trying to call you and they said you weren't answering.'

'Forensics wouldn't let me take it from the scene. The phone or my car. What did they want?'

'I think they wanted to take you out for a drink at Nat's. They might still be heading over there.'

Nat's was a dive off Hollywood Boulevard. It wasn't a cop bar but a fair number of off-duty cops passed through there on any given night. Enough for the management to keep The Clash's hard-edged version of 'I Fought the Law' on the jukebox for going on twenty years now. Bosch knew that if he showed up at Nat's the punk anthem would be in heavy if not inappropriate rotation in salute to the recently dispatched Robert Foxworth, aka Raynard Waits. *I fought the law but the law won* ... Bosch could almost hear them all singing the chorus.

'You going?' he asked Pratt.

'Maybe later. I've got something to do first.'

Bosch nodded.

'I don't think I feel like it,' he said. 'I'm going to pass.'

'Suit yourself. They'll understand.'

Pratt didn't move from the doorway so Bosch picked up his phone. He called Jerry Edgar's number just so he could follow through on the lie he had told about having to make a call. But Pratt remained in the doorway, his arm leaning against the jamb as he surveyed the empty squad room. He was really trying to get Bosch out of there. Maybe he had gotten the word from higher up the ladder than Lieutenant Randolph.

Edgar answered the call.

'It's Bosch, you called?'

'Yeah, man, I called.'

'I've been a little busy.'

'I know. I heard. Nice shooting today, partner. You okay?'

'Yeah, fine. What were you calling about?'

'Just something I thought you might want to know. I don't know if it matters anymore.'

'What was it?' Bosch said impatiently.

'My cousin Jason called me from DWP. He said you saw him today.'

'Yeah, nice guy. He helped a lot.'

'Yeah, well, I wasn't checking on how he treated you. I'm trying to tell you that he called me and said there was something you might want to know but you didn't give him a business card or a number or anything. He said that about five minutes after you and the FBI agent you were with left, another cop came and asked for him. Asked at the lobby desk for the guy who was just helping the cops.'

Bosch leaned forward at his desk. He was suddenly very interested in what Edgar was telling him.

'He said this guy showed a badge and said he was monitoring your investigation and he asked Jason what you and the agent had wanted. My cousin took him up to the floor you people had gone to and walked this guy out to the window. They were standing there looking down on the house in Echo Park when you and the lady agent showed up down there. They watched you go into the garage.'

'Then what happened?'

'The guy ran out of there. Grabbed an elevator and went down.'

'Did your cousin get a name off this guy?'

'Yeah, the guy said his name was Detective Smith. When he held up his ID he sort of had his fingers over the part with his name.'

It was an old ploy, Bosch knew, used mostly when detectives were going off the reservation and didn't want their real name out in circulation. Bosch had used it himself on occasion.

'What about a description?' he asked.

'Yeah, he gave me all that. He said white guy, about six feet and one-eighty. The guy had silver-gray hair he kept cut short. Let's see, midfifties and he was wearing a blue suit, white shirt and a striped tie. He had an American flag on the lapel.'

The description matched about fifty thousand men in the immediate vicinity of downtown. And Bosch was looking at one of them. Abel Pratt was still standing in his office doorway. He was staring at Bosch with eyebrows raised in question. He wasn't wearing his suit jacket but Bosch could see it on a hook on the door behind him. There was an American flag pinned to the lapel.

Bosch looked back down at his desk.

'How late does he work to?' he asked quietly.

'Normally, I think he stays till five. But there's a bunch of people hanging up there, watching the scene in Echo Park.'

'Okay, thanks for the tip. I'll call you later.'

Bosch hung up before Edgar could say anything else. He looked up and Pratt was still staring at him.

'What was that?' he asked.

'Oh, just something on the Matarese case. The one we filed this week. It looks like we might have a witness after all. It will help at trial.'

Bosch said it as nonchalantly as he could. He stood up and looked at his boss.

'But don't worry. It will hold until I get back from home duty.'

'Good. Glad to hear it.'

32

Bosch walked toward Pratt. He came too close to him, invading his personal space, which caused Pratt to back into his office and move back to his desk. This was what Bosch wanted. He said good-bye and have a good weekend. He then headed toward the door of the squad room.

The Open-Unsolved Unit had three cars assigned to its eight detectives and one supervisor. The cars were used on a first-come first-served basis and the keys hung on hooks next to the squad room door. The procedure was for a detective taking a car to write his or her name and the estimated time of return on an erasable white board that hung below the keys. When Bosch got to the door he opened it wide to block the view from Pratt's office of the key hooks. There were two sets of keys on the hooks. Bosch grabbed one and left.

A few minutes later he pulled out of the garage behind Parker Center and headed toward the DWP building. The mad rush to empty downtown by sunset was only just beginning and he made the seven blocks in quick time. He parked illegally in front of the fountain at the entrance to the building and jumped out of his car. He checked his watch as he approached the front door. It was twenty minutes to five.

A uniformed security guard came through the doors, waving at him.

'You can't park—'

'I know.'

Bosch showed him his badge and pointed to the radio on the man's belt.

'Can you get Jason Edgar on that thing?'

'Edgar? Yeah. What's this—'

'Get him on there and tell him Detective Bosch is waiting out front. I need to see him as soon as possible. Do it now, please.'

Bosch turned and headed back to his car. He got in and waited five minutes before he saw Jason Edgar come through the glass doors. When he got to the car he opened the passenger door to look in, not get in.

'What's up, Harry?'

'I got your message. Get in.'

Edgar reluctantly got in the car. Bosch pulled away from the curb as he was closing his door.

'Wait a minute. Where are we going? I can't just leave.'
'This should only take a few minutes.'
'Where are we going?'
'Parker Center. We won't even get out of the car.'
'I have to let them know.'
Edgar took a small two-way off his belt. He called in at the DWP security center and said he would be off-location on a police matter for a half hour. He received a 10-4 and put the radio back on his belt.
'You should've asked me first,' he said to Bosch. 'My cousin said you had a habit of acting first and asking questions later.'
'He said that, huh?'
'Yeah, he did. What are we doing at Parker Center?'
'Making an ID of the cop who talked to you after I left today.'
Traffic had already gotten worse. A lot of nine-to-fivers getting an early jump on the commute home. Friday afternoons were particularly brutal. Bosch finally pulled back into the police garage at ten to five and hoped they wouldn't be too late. He found a parking space in the first row. The garage was an open-air structure and the space afforded them a view of San Pedro Street, which ran between Parker Center and the garage.
'You have a cell phone?' Bosch asked.
'Yeah.'
Bosch gave him the general number for Parker Center and told him to call it and ask for the Open-Unsolved Unit. Calls transferred from the main number did not carry forward caller ID. Edgar's name and number would not show up on the OU lines.
'I just want to see if somebody answers,' Bosch said. 'If somebody does, just ask for Rick Jackson. When you're told that he's not there, don't leave a message. Just say you'll get him on his cell and hang up.'
Edgar's call was answered and he went through the routine Bosch had outlined. When he was finished he looked over at Bosch.
'Somebody named Pratt answered.'
'Good. He's still there.'
'So what's that mean?'
'I wanted to make sure he hadn't left. He'll leave at five, and when he does he'll cross the street right over there. I want to see if he's the guy who told you he was monitoring my investigation.'
'Is he IAD?'
'No. He's my boss.'
Bosch slapped the visor down as a precaution against being seen. They were parked a good thirty yards from the crosswalk Pratt would use to get to the garage but he didn't know which way Pratt would go once he was inside the structure. As a squad supervisor he had the perk of being able to park a personal car in the police garage, and most of those assigned spaces were on the second level. There were two sets of stairs and the ramp up. If

Pratt walked up the ramp he would come right by Bosch's position.

Edgar asked questions about the Echo Park shooting and Bosch answered them in short sentences. He didn't want to talk about it but he had just yanked the guy off post and had to respond in some way. It was only being courteous. Finally, at 5:01 he saw Pratt come through the back doors of Parker Center and down the ramp by the jail's intake doors. He walked out to San Pedro and started to cross with a group of four other detective supervisors who were heading home as well.

'Okay,' Bosch said, cutting Edgar off in the middle of a question. 'See those guys crossing the street. Which one came to DWP today?'

Edgar studied the pack crossing the street. He had an unobstructed view of Pratt, who was walking next to another man at the back of the group.

'Yeah, the last guy,' Edgar said without hesitation. 'The one puttin' on the shades.'

Bosch looked over. Pratt had just put on his Ray-Bans. Bosch felt a deep pressure in his chest, like the worst case of heartburn he'd ever had. He kept his eyes on Pratt and watched him turn away from their position once he crossed the street. He was heading toward the far stairwell.

'Now what? You going to follow him?'

Bosch remembered Pratt saying he had something to do after work.

'I want to but I can't. I've got to shoot you back to DWP.'

'Don't worry about it, man. I can walk it. Probably be faster with this traffic, anyway.'

Edgar cracked his door and turned to get out. He looked back at Bosch.

'I don't know what's going on but good luck, Harry. I hope you get who you're looking for.'

'Thanks, Jason. Hope to see you again.'

After Edgar was clear Bosch backed out and left the garage. He took San Pedro over to Temple because he assumed that Pratt would take that route on his way to the freeway. Whether he was going home or not, the freeway was the likely choice.

Bosch crossed Temple and pulled to the curb in a red zone. It gave him a good angle on the exit to the police garage.

In two minutes a silver SUV came out of the garage and headed toward Temple. It was a Jeep Commander with a retro boxy design. Bosch identified Pratt behind the wheel. He immediately fit the dimensions and color of the Commander to those of the mystery SUV he had seen take off from the street near his house the night before.

Bosch leaned down across the seat as the Commander approached Temple. He heard it make the turn and after a few seconds he got back up behind the wheel. Pratt was on Temple up at the light at Los Angeles Street and he was turning right. Bosch waited until he completed the turn and then took off to follow.

Pratt entered the crowded northbound lanes of the 101 Freeway and joined the crawl of rush-hour traffic. Bosch came down the ramp and pushed into the line of cars about six vehicles behind the Jeep. He got lucky in that Pratt's vehicle had a white ball with a face on it atop the radio antenna. It was a giveaway promotion from a fast-food chain. It allowed Bosch to track the Jeep without having to get too close. He was in an unmarked Crown Vic which might as well have had a neon sign on its roof that flashed police!

Slowly but surely Pratt made his way north with Bosch following at a distance. When the freeway cut past Echo Park he looked up to the ridgeline and saw that the crime scene and media soirée on Figueroa Lane was still in full swing. He counted two media choppers still circling overhead. He wondered if his car would be towed from the scene or if he would be able to go back and retrieve it later.

As he drove, Bosch tried to piece together what he had on Pratt. There was little doubt that Pratt had been following him while he was on home duty. His SUV matched the SUV that had been on his street the night before, and Pratt had been IDed by Jason Edgar as the cop who had followed him into the DWP building. It was not feasible to think that he had been following Bosch simply to see if he was abiding by the rules of home duty. There had to be another reason and Bosch could think of only one thing.

The case.

Once he'd made this assumption, other things quickly came together and they served to only stoke the fire that was burning in Bosch's chest. Pratt had told the story about Maury Swann earlier in the week, and that made it clear they knew each other. While he had relayed a negative story about the defense attorney, that could have been a cover or an attempt to distance himself from someone he was actually close to and possibly working with.

Also obvious to Bosch was the fact that Pratt was intimately aware that Bosch had regarded Anthony Garland as a person of interest in the Gesto case. Bosch had routinely informed Pratt of his activities in reopening the case. Pratt was also notified when Garland's lawyers successfully reacquired a court order restraining Bosch from talking to Garland without one of his lawyers present.

Last, and perhaps most important, Pratt had access to the Gesto murder book. It sat most of the time on Bosch's desk. It could have been Pratt who put in the phony connection to Robert Saxon, aka Raynard Waits. He could have planted the connection long before the book was given to Olivas. He could have planted it so Olivas would discover it.

Bosch realized that the whole plan for Raynard Waits to confess to the murder of Marie Gesto and to lead investigators to the body could have completely originated with Abel Pratt. He was in a perfect position as a go-between who could monitor Bosch as well as all the other parties involved.

And he realized that with Swann part of the plan, Pratt wouldn't need Olivas or O'Shea. The more people in a conspiracy, the more likely it is that it will fail or fall apart. All Swann had to do was tell Waits that the prosecutor and investigator were behind it and he would have planted a false trail for someone like Bosch to follow.

Bosch felt the hot flash of guilt start to burn at the back of his neck. He realized that he could be wrong about everything he had been thinking until a half hour before. Totally wrong. Olivas might not be dirty after all. Maybe he had been used as skillfully as Bosch had been used himself, and maybe O'Shea was guilty of nothing more than political maneuvering – taking credit where it was not due him, redirecting blame away from where it was due. O'Shea could have called for the department fix simply to contain Bosch's accusations because they would be politically damaging, not because they were true.

Bosch thought this new theory through again and it held up. He found no air in the brake lines, no sand in the gas tank. It was a car that could drive. The only thing missing was motive. Why would a guy who banked twenty-five years with the department and was looking at retiring at fifty risk it all on a scheme like this? How could a guy who had spent twenty-five years chasing bad guys let a killer go free?

Bosch knew from working a thousand murders that motive was often the most elusive component of crime. Obviously, money could motivate, and the disintegration of a marriage could play a part. But those were unfortunate common denominators in many people's lives. They could not readily explain why Abel Pratt had broken across the line.

Bosch banged the palm of his hand hard on the steering wheel. The question of motive aside, he was embarrassed and angry with himself. Pratt had played him perfectly and the betrayal was deep and painful. Pratt was his boss. They had eaten together, worked cases together, told jokes and talked about their kids together. Pratt was heading toward a retirement that no one in the department believed was anything other than well-earned and well-deserved. It was time to double-dip, collect a department pension and grab a lucrative security job in the islands where the pay was high and the hours low. Everybody was shooting for that and no one would begrudge it. It was blue heaven, the policeman's dream.

But now Bosch saw through all of that.

'It's all bullshit,' he said out loud in the car.

33

Thirty minutes into the drive Pratt exited the freeway in the Cahuenga Pass. He took Barham Boulevard northeast into Burbank. The traffic was still thick and Bosch had no trouble following and maintaining his distance and cover. Pratt drove past the back entrance to Universal and the front entrance to Warner Bros. He then made a few quick turns and pulled to the curb in front of a row of town houses on Catalina near Verdugo. Bosch drove on by quickly, took his first right and then another and then another. He killed his lights before taking one more right and coming up on the town houses again. He pulled to the curb a half block behind Pratt's SUV and slid down in his seat.

Almost immediately Bosch saw Pratt standing in the street, looking both ways before crossing. But he was taking too long to do it. The street was clear but Pratt kept looking back and forth. He was looking for someone or checking to see if he had been followed. Bosch knew that the hardest thing in the world to do was to follow a cop who was looking for it. He slouched down lower in the car.

Finally, Pratt started across the street, still looking back and forth continuously, and when he got to the other curb he turned and stepped up onto it backwards. He took a few steps back, surveying the area in both directions. When his scan came to Bosch's car his eyes held on it for a long moment.

Bosch froze. He didn't think Pratt had seen him – he was slouched too far down – but he might have recognized the car as either an unmarked police cruiser or one of the cars specifically assigned to the Open-Unsolved Unit. If he walked down the street to check it out Bosch knew he would be caught without much of an explanation. And without a gun. Randolph had routinely confiscated his backup weapon for a ballistics analysis in regard to the shooting of Robert Foxworth.

Pratt started walking toward Bosch's car. Bosch grabbed the door handle. If he needed to, he would bail out of the car and run toward Verdugo, where there would be traffic and people.

But suddenly Pratt stopped, his attention drawn to something behind him. He turned around and looked up the steps of the town house he had been standing in front of. Bosch tracked his eyes and saw the front door of the town house was partially open and a woman was looking out and calling to Pratt while smiling. She was hiding behind the door but one of her bare shoulders was exposed. Her expression changed as Pratt said something and signaled her back inside. She put a pout on her face and stuck her tongue out at him. She disappeared from the door, leaving it open six inches.

Bosch wished he had his camera but it was back in his car in Echo Park. However, he didn't need photographic evidence to know that he recognized the woman in the doorway and that she was not Pratt's wife – Bosch had met his wife at the recent squad room party when he had announced his retirement.

Pratt looked toward Bosch's car again, hesitated but then turned back to the town house. He strode up the stairs, went through the open door and shut it behind him. Bosch waited and, as he expected, saw Pratt pull back a curtain and look out at the street. Bosch stayed down as Pratt's eyes lingered on the Crown Vic. There was no doubt that the car had drawn Pratt's suspicion but Bosch guessed that the lure of illicit sex had overpowered his instinct to check the car out.

There was a commotion as Pratt was grabbed from behind and he turned away from the window, and the curtain fell back into place.

Bosch immediately sat up, started the car and made a U-turn away from the curb. He took a right on Verdugo and headed toward Hollywood Way. No doubt the Crown Vic had been blown. Pratt would be actively looking for it when he came back out of the town house. But the Burbank Airport was close. Bosch figured he could dump the Crown Vic at the airport, pick up a rental car and be back to the town house in less than a half hour.

As he drove he tried to place the woman he had seen looking out the door of the town house. He used a few mind-relaxation drills he had employed back when hypnotizing witnesses was accepted by the courts. Soon he was keying in on the woman's nose and mouth, the parts of her that had triggered his recognition center. And soon after that he had it. She was an attractive, young civilian employee of the department who worked in the office down the hall from Open-Unsolved. It was a personnel office, known by the rank and file as Hiring & Firing because it was the place where both things happened.

Pratt was fishing off the company dock, waiting out the rush hour in a Burbank shack-up spot. Not bad work if you could get it and get away with it. Bosch wondered if Mrs. Pratt knew of her husband's extracurricular activities.

He pulled into the airport and entered the valet parking lanes, thinking that that would be fastest. The man in the red coat who took the Crown Vic from him asked when he would be returning.

'I don't know,' Bosch said, not having considered it.

'I need to write something on the ticket,' the man said.

'Tomorrow,' Bosch said. 'If I'm lucky.'

34

Bosch got back to Catalina Street in thirty-five minutes. He drove his rented Taurus past the row of town houses and spotted Pratt's Jeep still at the curb. This time he found a spot on the north side of the town house and parked there. While he slouched down in the car and watched for activity, he turned on the cell phone he had rented with the car. He called Rachel Walling's cell number but got her voice mail. He ended the call without leaving a message.

Pratt didn't come out until it was full-on dark outside. He stood in front of the complex beneath a streetlight and Bosch noticed he was wearing different clothes now. He had on blue jeans and a dark, long-sleeved pullover shirt. The change of attire told Bosch that the liaison with the woman from Hiring & Firing was probably more than a casual shack-up. Pratt kept clothes at her place.

Pratt once again looked up and down the street, his eyes lingering longest on the south side where earlier the Crown Vic had drawn his attention. Apparently satisfied that the car was gone and he wasn't being watched, Pratt went to his Commander and soon pulled away from the curb. He made a U-turn and headed south to Verdugo. He then turned right.

Bosch knew that if Pratt was looking for a tail he would slow on Verdugo and watch his rearview mirror for any vehicle turning off Catalina in his direction. So he U-turned from the curb and went north a block to Clark Avenue. He turned left and gunned the car's weak engine. He drove five blocks to California Street and took a quick left. At the end of the block he would come to Verdugo. It was a risky move. Pratt could be long gone but Bosch was playing a hunch. Seeing the Crown Vic had spooked his boss. He would be on full alert.

Bosch had called it right. Just as he got to Verdugo he saw Pratt's silver Commander go by in front of him. He had obviously delayed on Verdugo, watching for a follower. Bosch let him get some distance and then turned right to follow.

Pratt made no evasive moves after that first effort to smoke out a tail. He stayed on Verdugo into North Hollywood and then turned south on Cahuenga. Bosch almost lost him at the turn but he went through the light on red. It was clear to him now that Pratt was not going home – Bosch knew that he lived in the opposite direction in the northern valley.

Pratt was heading toward Hollywood, and Bosch guessed that he was simply planning to join the other members of the squad at Nat's. But halfway through the Cahuenga Pass he turned right onto Woodrow Wilson Drive and Bosch felt his pulse kick up a notch. Pratt was now heading toward Bosch's own house.

Woodrow Wilson wound up the side of the Santa Monica Mountains, one deep curve after another. It was a lonely street and the only way to follow a vehicle was to do it without headlights and to keep at least one curve behind the brake lights of the lead car.

Bosch knew the curves intimately. He had lived on Woodrow Wilson for more than fifteen years and could make the drive half asleep – which he had done on occasion. But following Pratt, a police officer wary of a tail, was a unique difficulty. Bosch tried to stay two curves back. This meant he lost sight of the lights on Pratt's car from time to time but never for very long.

When he was two curves away from his house, Bosch started to coast and the rental car eventually came to a stop before the final bend. Bosch got out, quietly closed the door and trotted up the curve. He stayed close to the hedge that guarded the home and studio of a famous painter who lived on the block. He edged around it until he could see Pratt's SUV up ahead. He had pulled to the curb two houses before Bosch's house. Pratt's lights were now off and he seemed to be just sitting there and watching the house.

Bosch looked up at his house and saw lights on behind the kitchen and dining room windows. He could see the tail end of a car protruding from his carport. He recognized the Lexus and knew that Rachel Walling was in his home. Even as he was buoyed by the prospect of her being there waiting for him, Bosch was concerned about what Pratt was up to.

It appeared that he was doing exactly what he had been doing the night before, just watching and possibly trying to determine if Bosch was home.

Bosch heard a car coming behind him. He turned and started walking back toward his car as if he were on an evening walk. The car drove by slowly and Bosch then turned and headed back to the hedge. As the car came up behind Pratt's Jeep, rather than pull to the side, Pratt took off again, the lights of his SUV coming on as he sped away.

Bosch turned and ran back toward his rental car. He jumped in and pulled away from the curb. As he drove he hit redial on the rental phone and soon Rachel's line was ringing. This time she answered.

'Yes?'

'Rachel, it's Harry. Are you in my house?'

'Yes, I've been wait—'

'Come outside. I'm going to pick you up. Hurry.'

'Harry, what is—'

'Just come out and bring your gun. Right now.'

He clicked off and pulled to a stop in front of his house. He could see the glow of brake lights disappearing around the curve ahead. But he knew those belonged to the car that had spooked Pratt. Pratt was farther ahead.

Bosch turned and looked at his front door, ready to hit the horn, but Rachel was coming out.

'Close the door,' Bosch yelled through the open passenger window.

Rachel pulled the door closed and hurried out to the car.

'Get in. Hurry!'

She jumped into the car and Bosch took off before she had the door closed.

'What is going on?'

He gave her the shorthand as he sped through the curves on the way up to Mulholland. He told her that his boss, Abel Pratt, was the setup man, that what had happened in Beachwood Canyon had been his plan. He told her that for the second night in a row he had been outside Bosch's home.

'How do you know all of this?'

'I just know. I'll be able to prove it all later. For now, it's a fact.'

'What was he doing outside?'

'I don't know. Trying to see if I was home, I think.'

'Your phone rang.'

'When?'

'Right before you called my cell. I didn't answer it.'

'It was probably him. Something's going on.'

They came around the last bend, and the four-way stop at Mulholland was ahead. Bosch saw the taillights of a large vehicle just as they disappeared to the right. Another car moved up to the stop. It was the car that had made Pratt move on. It went straight through the intersection.

'The first one must have been Pratt. He turned right.'

Bosch got to the stop and also turned right. Mulholland was the winding snake that followed the crest line of the mountains across the city. Its curves were smoother and not as deep as Woodrow Wilson's. It was also a busier street, with plenty of night cruisers. He would be able to follow Pratt without causing much suspicion.

They quickly caught up to the vehicle that had turned and confirmed that it was Pratt's Commander. Bosch then dropped back and for the next ten minutes tailed Pratt along the crest line. The sparkling lights of the Valley sprawled below on the north side. It was a clear night and they could see all the way to the shadowy mountains on the far side of the sprawl. They stayed on Mulholland through the intersection with Laurel Canyon Boulevard and continued west.

'I was waiting at your house to say good-bye,' Rachel suddenly said.

After a moment of silence, Bosch responded.

'I know. I understand.'

'I don't think you do.'

'You didn't like the way I was today, the way I went after Waits. I'm not the man you thought I was. I've heard it before, Rachel.'

'It's not that, Harry. Nobody is ever the man you think they are. I can live with that. But a woman has to feel safe with a man. And that includes when they are not together. How can I feel safe when I've seen firsthand how you work? It doesn't matter whether it is the way I would do it or not. I'm not talking about us cop to cop. What I'm talking about is that I could never feel comfortable and safe. I'd wonder every night if it's the night you won't be coming home. I can't do that.'

Bosch realized he was giving the car too much gas. Her words had made him unconsciously press the pedal down harder. He was getting too close to Pratt. He slowed down and pulled back from the taillights a hundred yards.

'It's a dangerous job,' he said. 'I thought you more than anybody would know that.'

'I do. I do. But what I saw out there today with you was recklessness. I don't want to have to worry about someone who is reckless. There's enough to worry about out there without that.'

Bosch blew out his breath. He gestured toward the red lights moving in front of them.

'Okay,' he said. 'Let's talk about it later. Let's just concentrate on this for tonight.'

As if on cue, Pratt hooked a hard left onto Coldwater Canyon Drive and started dropping down toward Beverly Hills. Bosch delayed as long as he believed he could and made the same turn.

'Well, I'm still glad I've got you with me,' he said.

'Why?'

'Because if he ends up in Beverly Hills I won't need to call the locals because I'm with a fed.'

'Glad I could do something.'

'You have your gun with you?'

'Always. You don't have yours?'

'It was part of the crime scene. I don't know when I'll get it back. And that's the second gun they've taken from me this week. It's gotta be a record of some kind. Most guns lost during reckless gunplay.'

He looked over to see if he was getting under her skin. She showed nothing.

'He's turning,' she said.

Bosch snapped his attention back to the road and saw the left-turn signal on the Commander blinking. Pratt made the turn and Bosch went on by. Rachel bent down so she could see out the window and up at the street sign.

'Gloaming Drive,' she said. 'Are we still in the city?'

'Yeah. Gloaming goes way back in there but there's no way out. I've been in there before.'

The next street down was Stuart Lane. Bosch used it to turn around in and headed back up to Gloaming.

'Do you know where he could be going?' Rachel asked.

'No idea. Another girlfriend's place, for all I know.'

Gloaming was another curving mountain road. But that's where the similarity to Woodrow Wilson Drive ended. The homes here ran a minimum seven figures, easy, and all had nicely manicured lawns and hedges with not so much as a leaf out of place. Bosch drove it slowly, looking for the silver Jeep Commander.

'There,' Rachel said.

She pointed out her window at a Jeep parked in the turnaround of a mansion with a French provincial design. Bosch drove by and parked two houses away. They got out and walked back.

'West Coast Choppers?'

She hadn't been able to see the front of his shirt while he was driving.

'It helped me blend in on a case once.'

'Nice.'

'My daughter saw me in this one time. I told her it was from my dentist.'

The gate to the driveway was open. The cast-iron mailbox had no name on it. Bosch opened it and looked inside. They were in luck. There was mail, a small stack held together with a rubber band. He pulled it out and angled the top envelope toward a nearby streetlight in order to read it.

'"Maurice" – it's Maury Swann's place,' he said.

'Nice,' Rachel said. 'I guess I should've been a defense attorney.'

'You'd've been good working with criminals.'

'Fuck you, Bosch.'

The banter ended with a loud voice coming from behind a tall hedge that ran along the far side of the turnaround and on the left side of the house.

'I said get in there!'

There was a splash and Bosch and Walling headed toward the sound.

35

Bosch searched the hedge with his eyes, looking for an opening. There didn't appear to be one from the front. When they got close he wordlessly signaled Rachel to follow the hedge to the right while he went left. He noticed that she was carrying her weapon down at her side.

The hedge was at least ten feet high and so thick that Bosch could see no light from the pool or house through it. But as he moved along it he heard the sound of splashing and voices, one of which he recognized as belonging to Abel Pratt. The voices were close.

'Please, I can't swim. I can't touch the bottom!'

'Then what d'you have a swimming pool for? Keep paddling.'

'Please! I'm not going to – why would I tell a soul about—'

'You're a lawyer, and lawyers like to play the angles.'

'Please.'

'I'm telling you, if I get even a hint that you're playing an angle on me, then next time it won't be a pool. It will be the fucking Pacific Ocean. You understand that?'

Bosch came to an alcove where the pool's filter pump and heater were located on a concrete pad. There was also a small opening in the hedge for a pool maintenance man to squeeze through. He slipped into the opening and stepped onto the tile surrounding a large oval pool. He was twenty feet behind Pratt, who was standing at the edge, looking down at a man in the water. Pratt held a long blue pole with a curved extension. It was for pulling people in trouble to the side but Pratt was holding it just out of reach of the man. He grabbed at it desperately but each time Pratt jerked it away.

It was hard to identify the man in the water as Maury Swann. The pool was dark with the lights off. Swann's glasses were gone and his hair looked like it had slipped off his scalp to the back of his head like a mud slide. On his gleaming bald dome was a strip of tape for holding his hairpiece in place.

The sound of the pool filter gave Bosch cover. He was able to walk unnoticed to within six feet of Pratt before speaking.

'What's happening, Top?'

Pratt quickly lowered the pole so that Swann could grab the hook.

'Hang on, Maury!' Pratt yelled. 'You're all right.'

Swann grabbed on and Pratt started pulling him toward the side of the pool.

'I gotcha, Maury,' Pratt said. 'Don't worry.'

'You don't have to bother with the lifeguard act,' Bosch said. 'I heard it all.'

Pratt paused and looked down at Swann in the water. He was three feet from the side.

'In that case,' Pratt said.

He let go of the pole and whipped his right hand behind his back to the belt line.

'Don't!'

It was Walling. She had found her own way through the hedge. She was on the other side of the pool, pointing her weapon at Pratt.

Pratt froze and seemed to be making a decision about whether to draw or not. Bosch moved in behind him and yanked the gun out of his pants.

'Harry!' Rachel called. 'I've got him. Get the lawyer.'

Swann was sinking. The blue pole was going down with him. Bosch quickly went to the pool's edge and grabbed it. He pulled Swann to the surface. The lawyer started coughing and spitting water. He held tight to the pole and Bosch walked him down to the shallow end. Rachel came around to Pratt and ordered him to put his wrists behind his head.

Maury Swann was naked. He came up the steps in the shallow end cupping his shriveled balls with one hand and trying to pull his toupee back on with the other. Giving up on the hairpiece, he tore it all the way off and threw it down on the tile, where it landed with a splat. He went directly to a pile of clothes by a bench and started getting dressed while still soaking wet.

'So what was going on here, Maury?' Bosch asked.

'Nothing that concerns you.'

Bosch nodded.

'I get it. A guy comes here to put you in the pool and watch you drown, maybe make it look like suicide or an accident, and you don't want anybody concerned about it.'

'It was a disagreement, that's all. He was scaring me, not drowning me.'

'Does that mean you and he had an agreement before you then had this disagreement?'

'I'm not answering that.'

'Why was he scaring you?'

'I don't have to answer any of your questions.'

'Then maybe we should back on out of here and leave you two to finish your disagreement. Maybe that would be the best thing to do here.'

'Do what you want.'

'You know what I think? I think that with your client Raynard Waits dead, there's only one person who can link Detective Pratt to the Garlands. I think your partner over there was getting rid of that link because he was getting scared. You'd be at the bottom of that pool if we hadn't happened by here.'

'You can do *and* think what you want. But what I am telling you is that we had a disagreement. He happened by while I was taking my nightly swim and we disagreed about something.'

'I thought you didn't know how to swim, Maury. Isn't that what you said?'

'I'm finished talking to you, Detective. You can leave my property now.'

'Not yet, Maury. Why don't you finish getting dressed and join us at the deep end.'

Bosch left him there as he struggled to get his wet legs into a pair of silk pants. At the other end of the pool Pratt was now handcuffed and sitting on a concrete bench.

'I'm not saying anything until I talk to a lawyer,' he said.

'Well, there's one over there putting his clothes on,' Bosch said. 'Maybe you can hire him.'

'I'm not talking, Bosch,' he repeated.

'Good decision,' Swann called from the far end. 'Rule number one: Never talk to the cops.'

Bosch looked at Rachel and almost laughed.

'Can you believe this? Two minutes ago he was trying to drown the guy, and now the guy's giving him free legal advice.'

'*Sound* legal advice,' Swann said.

Swann walked over to where the others were waiting. Bosch noticed that his clothes were sticking to his wet body.

'I wasn't trying to drown him,' Pratt said. 'I was trying to help him. But that's all I'm going to say.'

Bosch looked at Swann.

'Pull your zipper up, Maury, and sit down over here.'

Bosch pointed to a spot on the bench next to Pratt.

'No, I don't think I will,' Swann replied.

He took a step toward the house but Bosch took two steps and cut him off. He redirected him to the bench.

'Sit down,' he said. 'You're under arrest.'

'For *what*?' Swann said indignantly.

'Double murder. Both of you are under arrest.'

Swann laughed as though he were dealing with a child. Now that he had his clothes on he was recovering some of his swagger.

'And what murders would these be?'

'Detective Fred Olivas and Deputy Derek Doolan.'

Now Swann shook his head, the smile intact on his face.

'I'm assuming these charges fall under the felony-homicide rule, since there is ample evidence that we did not actually pull the trigger that fired the bullets that killed Olivas and Doolan.'

'It's always good to deal with a lawyer. I hate having to explain the law all the time.'

'It's a pity you need the law explained to *you,* Detective Bosch. The felony-homicide rule comes into play only when someone is killed during the commission of a serious crime. If that threshold is satisfied, then co-conspirators in the criminal enterprise may be charged with murder.'

Bosch nodded.

'I got that,' he said. 'And I've got you.'

'Then be so kind as to tell me what the threshold crime is that I have conspired to commit.'

Bosch thought for a moment before answering.

'How about suborning perjury and obstruction of justice? We could start there and move up to corruption of a public official, maybe aiding and abetting an escape from lawful custody.'

'And we could end there as well,' Swann said. 'I was representing my client. I committed none of those crimes and you have not a shred of evidence that I did. If you arrest me, it will simply prove your own undoing and embarrassment.'

He stood up.

'Good evening to you all.'

Bosch stepped over and put his hand on Swann's shoulder. He drove him back down onto the bench.

'Sit the fuck down. You are under arrest. I'll leave it to the prosecutors to decide about threshold crimes. I don't give a shit about that. As far as I'm concerned, two cops are dead and my partner is going to end her career because of you, Maury. So fuck you.'

Bosch looked over at Pratt, who sat with a slight smile on his face.

'It's good to have a lawyer in the house, Harry,' he said. 'I think Maury makes a good point. Maybe you should think about this before doing anything rash.'

Bosch shook his head.

'You aren't walking away from this,' he said. 'Not by a long shot.'

He waited a moment but Pratt said nothing.

'I know you're the setup man,' Bosch said. 'The whole thing up in Beachwood Canyon was yours. It was you who made the deal with the Garlands, then you went to Maury here, who took it to Waits. You doctored the murder book after Waits gave you an alias to stick in it. Maury might have a point about the felony-murder rap but there's more than enough there for obstruction, and if I get that then I've got you. That means no island and no pension, Top. That means you go down in flames.'

Pratt's eyes dropped from Bosch to the dark waters of the pool.

'I want the Garlands, and you can give them to me,' Bosch said.

Pratt shook his head without turning his eyes from the water.

'Then, have it your way,' Bosch said. 'Let's go.'

He signaled Pratt and Swann to stand up. They complied. Bosch turned Swann around so he could cuff him. As he did so he looked over the lawyer's shoulder at Pratt.

'After we book you, who're you going to call about bail, your wife or the girl from Hiring and Firing?'

Pratt immediately sat back down as if hit by a sucker punch. Bosch had been saving it for his last shot. He kept the pressure on.

'Which one was going to go with you to the island? To your sugar plantation? My guess is it was what's-her-name.'

'Her name is Jessie Templeton, okay. And I made you on the tail at her place tonight.'

'Yeah, and I made you making me. But tell me, how much does Jessie Templeton know, and is she going to be as strong as you when I go see her after I book you?'

'Bosch, she doesn't know anything. Leave her out of it. Leave my wife and kids out of it, too.'

Bosch shook his head.

'Doesn't work that way. You know that. We're going to turn everything upside down and shake it to see what falls out. I'm going to find the money the Garlands paid you and I'll tie it back to you, to Maury Swann, everybody. I just hope you didn't use your girlfriend to hide it. Because if you did, she goes down, too.'

Pratt leaned forward on the bench. Bosch got the impression that if his hands hadn't been cuffed behind his back, he'd have been using them at that moment to hold his head and hide his face from the world. Bosch had kept at him like a man with an axe chopping at a tree. It was barely standing now. It needed one little push and it would go down.

Bosch walked Swann over to Rachel, who took him by one of his arms. Bosch then turned back to Pratt.

'You fed the wrong dog,' Bosch said.

'What's that supposed to mean?'

'Everybody's got choices and you made the wrong one. Problem is, we don't pay for our mistakes alone. We take people down with us.'

Bosch walked to the edge of the pool and looked down into the water. It shimmered on top but was impenetrably dark beneath the surface. He waited but it didn't take long for the tree to fall.

'Jessie doesn't need to be part of this and my wife doesn't need to know about her,' Pratt said.

It was an opening offer. Pratt was going to talk. Bosch kicked his foot on the tile edging and turned back to face him.

'I'm not a prosecutor but I'll bet something could be worked out.'

'Pratt, you are making a big mistake!' Swann said urgently.

Bosch reached down to Pratt and patted his pockets until he located the keys to the Commander and pulled them out.

'Rachel, take Mr. Swann to Detective Pratt's car. It will be better for transporting him. We'll be right there.'

He threw her the keys and she started walking Swann to the opening in the hedge she had come through. Swann had to be pushed. He looked over his shoulder as he went and called back to Pratt.

'Do not talk to that man,' he yelled. 'Do you hear me? Do not talk to anyone! You will talk us all into prison!'

Swann kept yelling legal advice through the hedge. Bosch waited until he heard the car door close on his voice. He then stood in front of Pratt and noticed that sweat was dripping from his hairline and down his face.

'I don't want Jessie or my family involved,' Pratt said. 'And I want a deal. No jail time, I'm allowed to retire *and* I get to keep my pension.'

'You want a lot for somebody who got two people killed.'

Bosch started to pace, trying to figure out a way of making it all work for both of them. Rachel came back through the hedge. Bosch looked at her and was about to ask why she had left Swann unattended.

'Child-proof locks,' she said. 'He can't get out.'

Bosch nodded and gave his attention back to Pratt.

'Like I said, you want a lot,' he said. 'What are you giving back?'

'I can give you the Garlands, easy,' Pratt said desperately. 'Anthony took me up there two weeks ago and led me to the girl's body. And Maury Swann, I can give you him on a platter. The guy's as dirty as ...'

He didn't finish.

'You?'

Pratt lowered his eyes and slowly nodded his head.

Bosch tried to put everything aside so that he could think clearly about Pratt's offer. The blood of Freddy Olivas and Deputy Doolan was on Pratt's hands. Bosch didn't know whether he'd be able to sell the deal to a prosecutor. He didn't know if he could even sell it to himself. But in that moment, he was willing to try if it meant he would finally get to the man who killed Marie Gesto.

'No promises,' he said. 'We'll go see a prosecutor.'

Bosch moved to the last important question.

'What about O'Shea and Olivas?'

Pratt shook his head once.

'They were clean on this.'

'Garland funneled at least twenty-five grand to O'Shea's campaign. That's documented.'

'He was just covering his bets. If O'Shea got suspicious, T. Rex could keep him in line because it would look like a payoff.'

Bosch nodded. He felt the burn of humiliation over what he had thought about O'Shea and said to him.

'That wasn't the only thing you got wrong,' Pratt said.

'Yeah, what else?'

'You said I went to the Garlands with this thing. I didn't. They came to me, Harry.'

Bosch shook his head. He didn't believe Pratt for the simple reason that if the Garlands had had the idea to buy off a cop, their first overture would have been to the source of their problem: Bosch. That never happened and that made Bosch feel confident that the scheme had been hatched by Pratt as he tried to juggle retirement, a possible divorce, a mistress and whatever other secrets his life held. He had gone to the Garlands with it. He had gone to Maury Swann, too.

'Tell it to the prosecutor,' Bosch said. 'Maybe he'll care.'

He looked at Rachel and she nodded.

'Rachel, you take the Jeep with Swann. I'll take Detective Pratt in my car. I want to keep them separated.'

'Good idea.'

Bosch signaled Pratt up.

'Let's go.'

Pratt stood up again and came face-to-face with Bosch.

'Harry, you've got to know something first.'

'What's that?'

'Nobody was supposed to get hurt. It was a perfect plan with nobody getting hurt. It was Waits – he turned it all to shit out there in the woods. If he had just done what he'd been told, everybody would still be alive and everybody'd be happy. Even you. You would've solved the Gesto case. End of story. That's how it was supposed to be.'

Bosch had to work to hold back his anger.

'Nice fairy tale,' he said. 'Except for the part of the story where the princess never wakes up and the real killer walks, everybody lives happily ever after. Keep telling yourself that one. You might actually be able to live with it someday.'

Bosch roughly took him by the arm and led him toward the opening in the hedge.

Part Five
Echo Park

36

At 10 a.m. on Monday morning Abel Pratt walked from his car across the green lawn of Echo Park to a bench where an old man was sitting beneath the protective arms of the *Lady of the Lake.* There were five pigeons resting on her shoulders and upturned hands and one on her head but she showed no sign of annoyance or fatigue.

Pratt shoved the folded newspaper he carried into the overly full trash can by the statue and then sat on the bench next to the old man. He looked out at the smooth waters of Lake Echo in front of them. The old man, who held a cane down by his knee and wore a tan business suit with a maroon handkerchief in the breast pocket, spoke first.

'I remember when you could take your family here on a Sunday and not have to worry about being shot up by gangbangers.'

Pratt cleared his throat.

'Is that what you're worried about, Mr. Garland? The gangbangers? Well, I'll give you a little tip. Right now is one of the safest hours in any neighborhood in the city. Most of your gangbangers don't roll out of bed until the afternoon. That's why whenever we go out with warrants we go in the morning. We always catch them in bed.'

Garland nodded approvingly.

'That's good to know. But that's not what I am worried about. I'm worried about you, Detective Pratt. Our business was concluded. I was not expecting to hear from you ever again.'

Pratt leaned forward and scanned the park. He studied the rows of tables on the other side of the lake, where the old men played dominoes. His eyes then moved along the cars parked at the curb that edged the park.

'Where's Anthony?' he asked.

'He'll be along. He's taking precautions.'

Pratt nodded.

'Precautions are good,' he said.

'I don't like this place,' Garland said. 'It's full of ugly people, and that includes you. Why are we here?'

'Wait a minute,' a voice said from behind them. 'Don't say another word, Dad.'

Anthony Garland had approached from their blind side. He came around the statue to the bench at the water's edge. He stood in front of Pratt and signaled him to stand up.

'Up,' he said.

'What is this?' Pratt protested mildly.

'Just stand up.'

Pratt did as he was asked and Anthony Garland produced a small electronic wand from the pocket of his blazer. He began moving it up and down in front of Pratt from head to toe.

'If you're transmitting an RF signal this will tell me.'

'Good. I always wondered if I had RF. You never know with those women down in Tijuana.'

Nobody laughed. Anthony Garland seemed satisfied with the scan and started putting his magic wand away. Pratt started to sit down.

'Wait,' Garland said.

Pratt remained standing and Garland started running his hands over Pratt's body, a second precaution.

'Can't be too sure with a slimeball like you, *Detective*.'

He moved his hands to Pratt's waist.

'That's my gun,' Pratt said.

Garland kept searching.

'That's my cell phone.'

The hands went lower.

'And those are my balls.'

Garland then went down both legs and when he was satisfied, he told Pratt he could sit down. The detective returned to his seat next to the old man.

Anthony Garland remained standing in front of the bench, his back to the lake, his arms folded across his chest.

'He's clean,' he said.

'Okay, then,' T. Rex Garland said. 'We can talk. What's this about, Detective Pratt? I thought it was made clear to you: You don't call us. You don't threaten us. You don't tell us where to be and when.'

'If I hadn't threatened you, would you have come?'

Neither of the Garlands answered and Pratt smiled smugly and nodded.

'I rest my case.'

'Why are we here?' the old man asked. 'I made it quite clear before. I don't want my son touched by any of this. Why did he have to be here?'

'Well, because I sort of missed him since our little walk in the woods. We've got a bond, don't we, Anthony?'

Anthony said nothing. Pratt pressed on.

'I mean, a guy leads you to a body in the woods, I'd say normally they'd stay pretty tight. But I haven't heard from Anthony since we were up at the top of Beachwood together.'

'I don't want you talking to my son,' T. Rex Garland said. 'You don't talk to my son. You're bought and paid for, Detective, you get that? This is the only time you will ever call a meeting with me. I call you. You don't call me.'

The old man never looked at Pratt as he spoke. His eyes were cast toward the lake. The message was clear. Pratt wasn't worth his attention.

'Yeah, all that was fine, but things have changed,' Pratt said. 'In case you haven't been reading the papers or watching the news, things have gone to shit out there.'

The old man remained seated but stretched his arms forward and put both palms on the polished gold dragon's head at the top of his cane. He spoke calmly.

'And whose fault is that? You told us you and the lawyer could keep Raynard Waits in line. You told us no one would get hurt. You called it a clean operation. Now look at what you've involved us in.'

Pratt took a few moments to respond.

'You involved yourself. You wanted something and I was the provider. No matter whose fault it is, the bottom line is I now need more money.'

T. Rex Garland shook his head slowly.

'You were paid one million dollars,' he said.

'I had to cut it up with Maury Swann,' Pratt responded.

'Your subcontractor costs were not and are not my concern.'

'The fee was based on everything working smoothly. Waits taking the fall for Gesto, case closed. Now there are complications, ongoing investigations to contend with.'

'Again, not my concern. Our deal is done.'

Pratt leaned forward on the bench and put his elbows on his knees.

'It's not quite done yet, T. Rex,' he said. 'And maybe you *should* be concerned. Because you know who paid me a visit on Friday night? Harry Bosch and he had an FBI agent with him. They took me to a little meeting with Mr. Rick O'Shea. Turns out that before Bosch capped Waits the little bastard told him that he didn't kill Marie Gesto. So that puts Bosch back on your ass, Junior. And it puts all of them on mine. They've damn near worked the whole story out – connecting me and Maury Swann. They just need somebody to fill in the blanks and since they can't get to Swann, they want that somebody to be me. They're starting to apply the pressure.'

Anthony Garland groaned and kicked at the ground with his expensive loafers.

'Goddamn it! I knew this weasel would—'

His father put a hand up for quiet.

'Bosch and the FBI don't matter,' the old man said. 'It's all about what O'Shea will do, and O'Shea is taken care of. He's bought and paid for. Only he doesn't know it yet. Once I apprise him of his situation, he will do what I tell him to do. If he wants to be district attorney.'

Pratt shook his head.

'Bosch isn't going to let go of this. He hasn't for thirteen years. He's not going to now.'

'Then you take care of it. That's your end of the deal. I took care of O'Shea. You take care of Bosch. Let's go, son.'

The old man started to get up, using the cane to push up on. His son stepped over to help him.

'Wait a minute,' Pratt said. 'You aren't going anywhere. I said I want more money and I'm serious. I'll take care of Bosch, but then I need to check out and disappear. I need more money to do that.'

Anthony Garland angrily pointed down at Pratt on the bench.

'You goddamn piece of shit,' he said. 'You were the one who came to us. This whole goddamn thing is your plan from start to finish. You go out there and get two people killed, and then you have the balls to come back to us for more money?'

Pratt shrugged and spread his hands.

'I'm looking at a choice here, same as you. I could sit tight with the way things are and see how close they come to me. Or I could disappear right now. The thing you should know is that they always make deals with the little fish to get to the bigger fish. I'm little fish, Anthony. The big fish? That would be you.'

He turned to look at the old man.

'And the biggest fish? That would be you.'

T. Rex Garland nodded. He was a pragmatic businessman. He seemed to now understand the gravity of the situation.

'How much?' he asked. 'How much to disappear?'

Pratt didn't hesitate.

'I want another million dollars and it will be well worth it to you to give it to me. They can't get to either of you without me. If I'm gone, the case is gone. So it's a million and the price is non-negotiable. Anything less and it is not worth it for me to run. I'll make a deal and take my chances.'

'What about Bosch?' the old man asked. 'You already said he won't give up. Now that he knows Raynard Waits didn't—'

'I'll take care of him before I split,' Pratt said, cutting him off. 'I'll throw that in for free.'

He reached into his pocket and took out a piece of paper with numbers printed on it. He slid it across the bench to the old man.

'There's the bank account and wiring code. Same as before.'

Pratt stood up.

'Tell you what, talk amongst yourselves. I'm going over to the boathouse to take a leak. When I come back I'll need an answer.'

Pratt walked past Anthony, coming close, each man holding the other's eyes in a hard stare of hatred.

37

Harry Bosch studied the monitors in the surveillance van. The FBI had worked through the night setting cameras in eight locations at the park. One whole side of the interior of the van was covered with an array of digital screens that showed a multitude of visual angles on the bench where T. Rex Garland sat and his son stood waiting for Abel Pratt to return. The cameras were located on four of the park's path lights, in two of its flower beds, in the mock lighthouse atop the boathouse and in the fake pigeon perched on top of the *Lady of the Lake*'s head.

Added to this, the bureau techs had set up microwave sound receivers triangulated on the bench. The sound sweep was aided by directional mikes located in the fake pigeon, a flower bed and the folded newspaper Pratt had placed in the nearby trash can. A bureau sound tech named Jerry Hooten sat in the van, wearing a huge set of earphones and manipulating the audio feeds in order to produce the cleanest sound. Bosch and the others had been able to watch Pratt and the Garlands and hear their conversation word for word.

The others were Rachel Walling and Rick O'Shea. The prosecutor was sitting front and center, the video screens spread before him. This was his show. Walling and Bosch sat on either side of him.

O'Shea pulled off his earphones.

'What do we think?' he asked. 'He's going to call. What do I tell him?'

Three of the screens showed Pratt about to enter the park's restroom. According to the plan, he would wait until the room was clear and then call the surveillance van's number on his cell phone.

Rachel pulled her earphones down around her neck and so did Bosch.

'I don't know,' she said. 'It's your call but we don't have much of an admission from the son in regard to Gesto.'

'That's what I was thinking,' O'Shea responded.

'I don't know,' Bosch said. 'When Pratt talked about him leading him through the woods to the body, Anthony didn't deny it.'

'But he didn't admit it either,' Rachel said.

'But if a guy was sitting there talking to you about finding a body you buried and you didn't know what he was talking about, I think you'd say something.'

'Well, that can be an argument for the jury,' O'Shea said. 'I'm just saying that he hasn't yet made anything I would call a statement of admission. We need more.'

Bosch nodded, conceding the point. It had been decided on Saturday morning that Pratt's word was not going to be good enough. His testimony that Anthony Garland had led him to Marie Gesto's body and that he had taken a payoff from T. Rex Garland would not be sufficient to build a solid prosecution on. Pratt was a crooked cop and building a case on his testimony was too risky in an age when juries were highly suspicious of police integrity and behavior. They needed to get admissions from both of the Garlands for the case to move onto solid ground.

'Look, all I'm saying is, I think it's good but we're not quite there yet,' O'Shea said. 'We need to get a direct—'

'What about the old man?' Bosch asked. 'I think Pratt got him to shit all over himself.'

'I agree,' Rachel said. 'He's toast. If you send him back, tell him to work on Anthony.'

As if on cue there was a low-level buzzing sound that indicated an incoming call. O'Shea, unfamiliar with the equipment, raised a finger over the console and looked for the right button to push.

'Here,' Hooten said.

He punched a button that opened the cell line.

'This is the van,' O'Shea said. 'You're on speaker.'

'How'd I do?' Pratt said.

'It's a start,' O'Shea said. 'What took you so long to call?'

'I actually did have to take a leak.'

While O'Shea talked to Pratt about going back to the bench and trying once more for an admission from Anthony Garland, Bosch slipped his earphones back on to hear the conversation taking place at the bench.

From the visuals on the screens it looked like Anthony Garland was arguing with his father. The old man was pointing a finger at him.

Bosch picked it up in the middle.

'It's our only out,' Anthony Garland said.

'I said no!' the old man commanded. 'You cannot do this. You *will* not do this.'

On the screen Anthony stepped away from his father and then stepped right back. It looked like he was on an invisible leash. He bent down close to his father and this time he pointed the finger. What he said was spoken so low that the FBI microphones picked up only a mumble. Bosch pressed his hands over the earphones but couldn't get it.

'Jerry,' he said. 'Can you work on this?'

Bosch pointed to the screens. Hooten pulled on his earphones and went to work on the audio dials. But it was too late. The close conversation between father and son was over. Anthony Garland had just straightened up in front of his father and turned his back to him. He was silently looking out across the lake.

Bosch leaned back so that he could see the screen that showed an angle on the bench from one of the path lights at the water's edge. It was the only screen that showed Anthony's face at the moment. Bosch saw the rage in his eyes. He had seen it before.

Anthony set his jaw tightly and shook his head. He turned back to his father.

'Sorry, Dad.'

With that he started walking toward the boathouse. Bosch watched him take forceful strides toward the door of the restrooms. He saw his hand go inside his blazer.

Bosch slapped off his earphones.

'Anthony's headed to the men's room!' he said. 'I think he's got a gun!'

Bosch jumped up and shoved past Hooten to get to the van's door. Unfamiliar with it, he fumbled with the handle trying to get it open. Behind him he heard O'Shea barking commands into the radio mike.

'Everybody move in! Move in! Suspect is armed. Repeat, suspect is armed!'

Bosch finally got out of the van and started running toward the boathouse. There was no sign of Anthony Garland. He was already inside.

Bosch was on the far side of the park and more than a hundred yards away. Other agents and district attorney's office investigators had been deployed closer and Bosch saw them running with weapons out toward the boathouse as well. Just as the first man, an FBI agent, got to the doorway the sound of gunfire echoed from within the restroom. Four quick shots.

Bosch knew that Pratt's weapon was dry. It was a prop. He had needed to have a gun in case the Garlands checked him. But Pratt was in custody and facing charges. They had taken away his bullets.

As Bosch watched, the agent at the doorway dropped into a combat stance, shouted 'FBI!' and entered. Almost immediately, there were more shots but these were of a different timbre than the first four. Bosch knew these were from the agent's gun.

As Bosch got to the restroom the agent stepped out, gun at his side. He held a radio to his mouth.

'We have two down in the restroom,' he said. 'Scene is secured.'

Winded from his run, Bosch gulped down some air and walked toward the doorway.

'Detective, that's a crime scene in there,' the agent said.

He put his hand up in front of Bosch's chest. Bosch pushed it aside.

'I don't care.'

He entered the restroom and saw the bodies of Pratt and Garland on the dirty concrete floor. Pratt had been shot twice in the face and twice in the chest. Garland had taken three chest shots. The fingers of Pratt's right hand were touching the sleeve of Garland's blazer. Pools of blood on the floor were blossoming from both bodies and soon would mingle.

Bosch watched for a few moments, studying Anthony's open eyes. The rage Bosch had seen moments before was gone, replaced by the empty look of death.

He stepped out of the restroom and looked over at the bench. The old man, T. Rex Garland, sat leaning forward with his face in his hands. The cane with the polished dragon's head had been dropped to the grass.

38

The entirety of Echo Park was closed for the investigation. For the third time in a week Bosch was interviewed about a shooting, only this time it was the feds doing the questioning and his part was peripheral because he had not fired a weapon. When he was finished he walked over to a *mariscos* truck that was parked at the curb and open for business to the crowd of onlookers outside the yellow tape. He ordered a shrimp taco and a Dr Pepper and took them over to one of the nearby federal cruisers. He was leaning on the front fender eating his lunch when Rachel Walling approached.

'Turns out Anthony Garland had a concealed-weapon permit,' she said. 'His security job required it.'

She leaned casually on the fender next to him. Bosch nodded.

'I guess we should've checked,' he said.

He took his last bite, wiped his mouth with a napkin and then balled it up in the aluminum foil the taco came in.

'I remembered your story,' she said.

'What story?' he asked.

'The one you told me about Garland rousting those kids in the oil field.'

'What about it?'

'You said he drew down on them.'

'That's right.'

She didn't say anything. She looked out at the lake. Bosch shook his head like he wasn't sure what was going on. She finally spoke.

'You knew about the permit and you knew Anthony would be carrying, didn't you?'

It was a question but she meant it as a statement.

'Rachel, what are you saying?'

'I'm saying you knew. You knew from way back that Anthony carried a gun. You knew what could happen today.'

Bosch spread his hands wide.

'Look, that thing with the kids was twelve years ago. How would I know that he would have a gun today?'

She got off the fender and turned to face him.

'How many times did you talk to Anthony over the years? How many times did you shake him down?'

Bosch squeezed the ball of aluminum foil tighter in his fist.

'Look, I never—'

'Are you telling me that in all those times you never once came up with a gun? That you didn't check permits? That you didn't know that there was a very high probability that he would bring a gun – and his uncontrolled rage – to a meeting like this? If we had known this guy carried a gun, we would never have set this thing up in the first place.'

Bosch smiled unpleasantly and shook his head in a disbelieving sort of way.

'What was it you said about mumbo-jumbo conspiracies the other day? Marilyn didn't overdose; the Kennedys had her killed. Bosch knew Anthony would bring a gun to the meeting and would start shooting? Rachel, it all sounds like—'

'And what about what *you* said about being a true detective?'

She stared pointedly at him.

'Rachel, listen to me. There was no way anybody could have predicted this. There was no—'

'Predicted, hoped, accidentally set in motion – what's the difference? You remember what you said to Pratt the other night by the pool?'

'I said a lot of things to him.'

Her voice took on a tone of sadness.

'You told him about the choices we all make.'

She pointed across the grass at the boathouse.

'And, well, Harry, I guess this is the dog you chose to feed. I hope you're happy with it. And I hope it fits in perfectly well with the way of the true detective.'

She turned and walked back toward the boathouse and the knot of investigators crowding the crime scene.

Bosch let her go. For a long time he didn't move. Her words had gone through him like the sounds of a roller coaster. Low rumbling and high shrieks. He squeezed the ball of aluminum foil in his hand and shot it toward a trash can sitting next to the *mariscos* truck.

He missed by a mile.

39

Kiz Rider came through the double doors in a wheelchair. She found it embarrassing but that was the hospital rule. Bosch was waiting for her with a smile and a bouquet of flowers he had bought from a vendor at the freeway exit near the hospital. As soon as she was allowed by the nurse, she got up and out of the chair. She tentatively hugged Bosch as though she felt fragile, and thanked him for coming to take her home.

'I'm right out front,' he said.

With his arm across her back he walked her out to the waiting Mustang. He helped her get in, then put a bag of cards and gifts she had received into the trunk and came around to the driver's side.

'You want to go anywhere first?' he asked once he was in the car.

'No, just home. I can't wait to sleep in my own bed.'

'I hear you.'

He started the car and pulled out, heading back to the freeway. They drove silently. When he got back to the 134 the flower vendor was still in the median. Rider looked down at the bouquet in her hand, realized that Bosch had gotten them as an afterthought and started laughing. Bosch joined in.

'Oh, shit, that hurts!' she said, touching her hand to her neck.

'Sorry.'

'It's all right, Harry. I need to laugh.'

Bosch nodded his agreement.

'Is Sheila going to come by today?' he asked.

'Yeah, after work.'

'Good.'

He nodded because there wasn't anything else to do. They lapsed back into silence.

'Harry, I took your advice,' Rider said after a few minutes.

'What was that?'

'I told them I didn't have a shot. I told them I didn't want to hit Olivas.'

'That's good, Kiz.'

He thought about things for a few moments.

'Does that mean you're going to keep your badge?' he asked.

'Yes, Harry, I'm keeping the badge … but not my partner.'

Bosch looked over at her.

'I talked to the chief,' Rider said. 'After I finish rehab I'm going to go back to work in his office, Harry. I hope that will be all right with you.'

'Whatever you want to do is all right with me. You know that. I'm glad you're staying.'

'Me, too.'

A few more minutes went by and when she spoke again it was as if the conversation had never lagged.

'Besides, up there on the sixth floor, I'll be able to watch out for you, Harry. Maybe keep you out of all the politics and bureaucratic scrapping. Lord knows you're still going to need me from time to time.'

Bosch smiled broadly. He couldn't help it. He liked the idea of her being up there one floor above him. Watching out and watching over.

'I like it,' he said. 'I don't think I've ever had a guardian angel before.'

Acknowledgments

The author gratefully acknowledges a number of people who greatly helped in the research and writing of this book. They include Asya Muchnick, Michael Pietsch, Jane Wood, Pamela Marshall, Shannon Byrne, Terrill Lee Lankford, Jan Burke, Pam Wilson, Jerry Hooten and Ken Delavigne. Also of great help to the author were Linda Connelly, Jane Davis, Maryelizabeth Capps, Carolyn Chriss, Dan Daly, Roger Mills and Gerald Chaleff. Also many thanks to Sgt. Bob McDonald and detectives Tim Marcia, Rick Jackson and David Lambkin of the Los Angeles Police Department.